WONDER, HOPE, LOVE, AND LOSS

WONDER, HOPE, LOVE, AND LOSS

THE SELECTED NOVELS OF GENE STRATTON-PORTER

By

GENE STRATTON-PORTER
WITH A FOREWORD BY
SCOTT RUSSELL SANDERS

SKY PONY PRESS
NEW YORK

Sky Pony Press books may be purchased in bulk at special discounts for sales promotion, corporate gifts, fund-raising, or educational purposes. Special editions can also be created to specifications. For details, contact the Special Sales Department, Sky Pony Press, 307 West 36th Street, 11th Floor, New York, NY 10018 or info@skyhorsepublishing.com.

Sky Pony® is a registered trademark of Skyhorse Publishing, Inc.®, a Delaware corporation.

Visit our website at www.skyponypress.com.

10 9 8 7 6 5 4 3 2 1

Library of Congress Cataloging-in-Publication Data is available on file.

Cover design and illustration by Anthony Morais

ISBN: 978-1-63220-320-5
Ebook ISBN: 978-1-63220-942-9

Printed in the United States of America

Contents

Foreword

In the last decade of the nineteenth century, a young woman, recently married, began exploring a vast swamp near her home along the eastern border of Indiana, puzzling and occasionally scandalizing her neighbors. In that age of corsets and voluminous skirts, on her outings she wore breeches like a man, high leather boots to guard against rattlesnakes, and a broad-brimmed hat to shade her bold gray eyes. She carried a box camera, glass photographic plates, a tripod, a butterfly net, and other paraphernalia for capturing images and specimens of the teeming life in that dank place. As a precaution against varmints, including the human sort, and to reassure her husband, she also carried a revolver.

The 13,000-acre wetland was known locally as Limberlost Swamp, a legacy of the glaciers that flattened and watered the northern reaches of the Midwest. The young woman was Gene Stratton-Porter, who would brave the bogs, thickets, mosquitoes, and snakes for two decades, gathering impressions, and would write a series of books that carried the name of the Limberlost to millions of readers worldwide. A few of those books were natural history, chiefly about moths and birds, but most of them were novels, including the three immensely popular tales included in this volume.

Freckles (1904), *A Girl of the Limberlost* (1909), and *The Harvester* (1911), along with half a dozen other Stratton-Porter novels, were made into films, which also attracted large audiences. In fact, these movie adaptations became so profitable that in 1920 she moved to Los Angeles and started her own production company. In December 1924, soon after completing work on a film version of *A Girl of the Limberlost*, she died in Hollywood from injuries sustained when her chauffeur-driven limousine collided with a streetcar. It was an unlikely end to a life that had begun during the Civil War on a farm in the Wabash Valley of Indiana.

Geneva—her given name, later shortened to Gene—was the twelfth and last child of a mother worn out by childbearing and the rigors of pioneer life, and of a father who combined farming with preaching. Gene was two years old when her mother took to bed with typhoid fever, and five when her mother died. That early loss helps account for the frequent appearance of motherless children in Stratton-Porter's novels, and also for the numerous characters who are afflicted by lingering illnesses. Shortly before her ninth birthday, Gene suffered another grievous loss when her teenage brother Leander, whom she knew as Laddie, her favorite among the siblings, drowned in the Wabash River.

Motherless, largely unsupervised as her brothers and sisters left home, young Gene entertained herself, and perhaps consoled herself, by spending most waking hours outdoors. She was especially attracted by birds and wildflowers, but every growing thing interested her, and this passion remained with her lifelong, inform-ing all of her books. Those early experiences prepared her to see nature not as an opponent to be subdued—the prevailing view among pioneers—but as a healing presence, an antidote to loneliness, illness, and loss.

In *Freckles*, *A Girl of the Limberlost*, and *The Harvester*, you will meet virtuous heroines and heroes, dastardly villains, plucky orphans, kindly elders, idealists and scalawags, and young lovers who overcome every obstacle to unite in bliss. Behind all of these characters looms the Limberlost Swamp, a fragment of the wilderness that once spanned the continent. It is a dangerous place—where thieves lurk, a father drowns, a hero is crushed by a falling tree, a scoundrel dies from snakebite. But it is also a comforting place, a tonic for those ailing in body or mind, a refuge of wild beauty in a landscape otherwise tamed.

Acre by acre, the Limberlost was also tamed during the years when Gene Stratton-Porter lived nearby. The old-growth trees were felled for timber, the wetlands were drained for farming, the ground was drilled for oil. Disturbed by this exploitation of the great swamp, which had so entranced her, Stratton-Porter eventually decided to seek out a more natural setting. In 1913, she and her hus-band moved to a lake in northern Indiana, where they settled into a house that she had designed, on an estate she called Wildflower Woods. She had also designed the home they left behind, a 14-room cedar-log house she called Limberlost Cabin. By the time she moved away, the wilderness for which she had named it was all but gone. The subduing of nature to human purposes, yielding profit but also loss, is the larger story told by these three novels, and it also the dominant story of American civilization.

Recently, however, a hopeful new narrative has begun in the place that Gene Stratton-Porter loved, as local people, inspired by her books, have enlisted farmers, scientists, land trusts, and government agencies in a cooperative effort to restore portions of the vanished swamp. Once more, waters gather and wetland plants thrive, nurturing birds, frogs, salamanders, butterflies, and countless other creatures, allowing visitors to sense what drew that bold young woman, more than a century ago, to the Limberlost.

Scott Russell Sanders

Freckles

To all good Irishmen in general
and one Charles Darwin Porter
in particular

Contents

Chapter 1

Wherein Great Risks Are Taken and the Limberlost Guard Is Hired

Freckles came down the corduroy that crosses the lower end of the Limberlost. At a glance he might have been mistaken for a tramp, but he was truly seeking work. He was intensely eager to belong somewhere and to be attached to almost any enterprise that would furnish him food and clothing.

Long before he came in sight of the camp of the Grand Rapids Lumber Company, he could hear the cheery voices of the men, the neighing of the horses, and could scent the tempting odors of cooking food. A feeling of homeless friendlessness swept over him in a sickening wave. Without stopping to think, he turned into the newly made road and followed it to the camp, where the gang was making ready for supper and bed.

The scene was intensely attractive. The thickness of the swamp made a dark, massive background below, while above towered gigantic trees. The men were calling jovially back and forth as they unharnessed tired horses that fell into attitudes of rest and crunched, in deep content, the grain given them. Duncan, the brawny Scotch head-teamster, lovingly wiped the flanks of his big bays with handfuls of pawpaw leaves, as he softly whistled, "O wha will be my dearie, O!" and a cricket beneath the leaves at his feet accompanied him. The green wood fire hissed and crackled merrily. Wreathing tongues of flame wrapped around the big black kettles, and when the cook lifted the lids to plunge in his testing-fork, gusts of savory odors escaped.

Freckles approached him.

"I want to speak with the Boss," he said.

The cook glanced at him and answered carelessly: "He can't use you."

The color flooded Freckles's face, but he said simply: "If you will be having the goodness to point him out, we will give him a chance to do his own talking."

With a shrug of astonishment, the cook led the way to a rough board table where a broad, square-shouldered man was bending over some account-books.

"Mr. McLean, here's another man wanting to be taken on the gang, I suppose," he said.

"All right," came the cheery answer. "I never needed a good man more than I do just now."

The manager turned a page and carefully began a new line.

"No use of your bothering with this fellow," volunteered the cook. "He hasn't but one hand."

The flush on Freckles's face burned deeper. His lips thinned to a mere line. He lifted his shoulders, took a step forward, and thrust out his right arm, from which the sleeve dangled empty at the wrist.

"That will do, Sears," came the voice of the Boss sharply. "I will interview my man when I finish this report."

He turned to his work, while the cook hurried to the fires. Freckles stood one instant as he had braced himself to meet the eyes of the manager; then his arm dropped and a wave of whiteness swept him. The Boss had not even turned his head. He had used the possessive. When he said "my man," the hungry heart of Freckles went reaching toward him.

The boy drew a quivering breath. Then he whipped off his old hat and beat the dust from it carefully. With his left hand he caught the right sleeve, wiped his sweaty face, and tried to straighten his hair with his fingers. He broke a spray of ironwort beside him and used the purple bloom to beat the dust from his shoulders and limbs. The Boss, busy over his report, was, nevertheless, vaguely alive to the toilet being made behind him, and scored one for the man.

McLean was a Scotchman. It was his habit to work slowly and methodically. The men of his camps never had known him to be in a hurry or to lose his temper. Discipline was inflexible, but the Boss was always kind. His habits were simple. He shared camp life with his gangs. The only visible signs of wealth consisted of a big, shimmering diamond stone of ice and fire that glittered and burned on one of his fingers, and the dainty, beautiful thoroughbred mare he rode between camps and across the country on business.

No man of McLean's gangs could honestly say that he ever had been overdriven or underpaid. The Boss never had exacted any deference from his men, yet so intense was his personality that no man of them ever had attempted a familiarity. They all knew him to be a thorough gentleman, and that in the great timber city several millions stood to his credit.

He was the only son of that McLean who had sent out the finest ships ever built in Scotland. That his son should carry on this business after the father's death had been his ambition. He had sent the boy through the universities of Oxford and Edinburgh, and allowed him several years' travel before he should attempt his first commission for the firm.

Then he was ordered to southern Canada and Michigan to purchase a consignment of tall, straight timber for masts, and south to Indiana for oak beams. The young man entered these mighty forests, parts of which lay untouched since the dawn of the morning of time. The clear, cool, pungent atmosphere was intoxicating. The intense silence, like that of a great empty cathedral, fascinated him. He gradually learned that, to the shy wood creatures that darted across his path or peeped inquiringly from leafy ambush, he was brother. He found himself approaching, with a feeling of reverence, those majestic trees that had stood through ages of sun, wind, and snow. Soon it became difficult to fell them. When he had filled his order and returned home, he was amazed to learn that in the swamps and forests he had lost his heart and it was calling—forever calling him.

When he inherited his father's property, he promptly disposed of it, and, with his mother, founded a home in a splendid residence in the outskirts of Grand Rapids. With three partners, he organized a lumber company. His work was to purchase, fell, and ship the timber to the mills. Marshall managed the milling process and passed the lumber to the factory. From the lumber, Barthol made beautiful and useful furniture, which Uptegrove scattered all over the world from a big wholesale house. Of the thousands who saw their faces reflected on the polished surfaces of that furniture and found comfort in its use, few there were to whom it suggested mighty forests and trackless swamps, and the man, big of soul and body, who cut his way through them, and with the eye of experience doomed the proud trees that were now entering the homes of civilization for service.

When McLean turned from his finished report, he faced a young man, yet under twenty, tall, spare, heavily framed, closely freckled, and red-haired, with a homely Irish face, but in the steady gray eyes, straightly meeting his searching ones of blue, there was unswerving candor and the appearance of longing not to be ignored. He was dressed in the roughest of farm clothing, and seemed tired to the point of falling.

"You are looking for work?" questioned McLean.

"Yis," answered Freckles.

"I am very sorry," said the Boss with genuine sympathy in his every tone, "but there is only one man I want at present—a hardy, big fellow with a stout heart and a strong body. I hoped that you would do, but I am afraid you are too young and scarcely strong enough."

Freckles stood, hat in hand, watching McLean.

"And what was it you thought I might be doing?" he asked.

The Boss could scarcely repress a start. Somewhere before accident and poverty there had been an ancestor who used cultivated English, even with an accent. The boy spoke in a mellow Irish voice, sweet and pure. It was scarcely definite enough to be called brogue, yet there was a trick in the turning of the sentence, the wrong sound of a letter here and there, that was almost irresistible to McLean, and presaged a misuse of infinitives and possessives with which he was very familiar and which touched him nearly. He was of foreign birth, and despite years of alienation, in times of strong feeling he committed inherited sins of accent and construction.

"It's no child's job," answered McLean. "I am the field manager of a big lumber company. We have just leased two thousand acres of the Limberlost. Many of these trees are of great value. We can't leave our camp, six miles south, for almost a year yet; so we have blazed a trail and strung barbed wires securely around this lease. Before we return to our work, I must put this property in the hands of a reliable, brave, strong man who will guard it every hour of the day, and sleep with one eye open at night. I shall require the entire length of the trail to be walked at least twice each day, to make sure that our lines are up and that no one has been trespassing."

Freckles was leaning forward, absorbing every word with such intense eagerness that he was beguiling the Boss into explanations he had never intended making.

"But why wouldn't that be the finest job in the world for me?" he pleaded. "I am never sick. I could walk the trail twice, three times every day, and I'd be watching sharp all the while."

"It's because you are scarcely more than a boy, and this will be a trying job for a work-hardened man," answered McLean. "You see, in the first place, you would be afraid. In stretching our lines, we killed six rattlesnakes almost as long as your body and as thick as your arm. It's the price of your life to start through the marshgrass surrounding the swamp unless you are covered with heavy leather above your knees.

"You should be able to swim in case high water undermines the temporary bridge we have built where Sleepy Snake Creek enters the swamp. The fall and winter changes of weather are abrupt and severe, while I would want strict watch kept every day. You would always be alone, and I don't guarantee what is in the Limberlost. It is lying here as it has lain since the beginning of time, and it is alive with forms and voices. I don't pretend to say what all of them come from; but from a few slinking shapes I've seen, and hair-raising yells I've heard, I'd rather not confront their owners myself; and I am neither weak nor fearful.

"Worst of all, any man who will enter the swamp to mark and steal timber is desperate. One of my employees at the south camp, John Carter, compelled me to discharge him for a number of serious reasons. He came here, entered the swamp alone, and succeeded in locating and marking a number of valuable trees that he was endeavoring to sell to a rival company when we secured the lease. He has sworn to have these trees if he has to die or to kill others to get them; and he is a man that the strongest would not care to meet."

"But if he came to steal trees, wouldn't he bring teams and men enough: that all anyone could do would be to watch and be after you?" queried the boy.

"Yes," replied McLean.

"Then why couldn't I be watching just as closely, and coming as fast, as an older, stronger man?" asked Freckles.

"Why, by George, you could!" exclaimed McLean. "I don't know as the size of a man would be half so important as his grit and faithfulness, come to think of it. Sit on that log there and we will talk it over. What is your name?"

Freckles shook his head at the proffer of a seat, and folding his arms, stood straight as the trees around him. He grew a shade whiter, but his eyes never faltered.

"Freckles!" he said.

"Good enough for everyday," laughed McLean, "but I scarcely can put 'Freckles' on the company's books. Tell me your name."

"I haven't any name," replied the boy.

"I don't understand," said McLean.

"I was thinking from the voice and the face of you that you wouldn't," said Freckles slowly. "I've spent more time on it than I ever did on anything else in all me life, and I don't understand. Does it seem to you that anyone would take a newborn baby and row over it, until it was bruised black, cut off its hand, and leave it out in a bitter night on the steps of a charity home, to the care of strangers? That's what somebody did to me."

McLean stared aghast. He had no reply ready, and presently in a low voice he suggested: "And after?"

"The Home people took me in, and I was there the full legal age and several years over. For the most part we were a lot of little Irishmen together. They could always find homes for the other children, but nobody would ever be wanting me on account of me arm."

"Were they kind to you?" McLean regretted the question the minute it was asked.

"I don't know," answered Freckles. The reply sounded so hopeless, even to his own ears, that he hastened to qualify it by adding: "You see, it's like this, sir.

Kindnesses that people are paid to lay off in job lots and that belong equally to several hundred others, ain't going to be soaking into any one fellow so much."

"Go on," said McLean, nodding comprehendingly.

"There's nothing worth the taking of your time to tell," replied Freckles. "The Home was in Chicago, and I was there all me life until three months ago. When I was too old for the training they gave to the little children, they sent me to the closest ward school as long as the law would let them; but I was never like any of the other children, and they all knew it. I'd to go and come like a prisoner, and be working around the Home early and late for me board and clothes. I always wanted to learn mighty bad, but I was glad when that was over.

"Every few days, all me life, I'd to be called up, looked over, and refused a home and love, on account of me hand and ugly face; but it was all the home I'd ever known, and I didn't seem to belong to any place else.

"Then a new superintendent was put in. He wasn't for being like any of the others, and he swore he'd weed me out the first thing he did. He made a plan to send me down the State to a man he said he knew who needed a boy. He wasn't for remembering to tell that man that I was a hand short, and he knocked me down the minute he found I was the boy who had been sent him. Between noon and that evening, he and his son close my age had me in pretty much the same shape in which I was found in the beginning, so I lay awake that night and ran away. I'd like to have squared me account with that boy before I left, but I didn't dare for fear of waking the old man, and I knew I couldn't handle the two of them; but I'm hoping to meet him alone some day before I die."

McLean tugged at his mustache to hide the smile on his lips, but he liked the boy all the better for this confession.

"I didn't even have to steal clothes to get rid of starting in me Home ones," Freckles continued, "for they had already taken all me clean, neat things for the boy and put me into his rags, and that went almost as sore as the beatings, for where I was we were always kept tidy and sweet-smelling, anyway. I hustled clear into this State before I learned that man couldn't have kept me if he'd wanted to. When I thought I was good and away from him, I commenced hunting work, but it is with everybody else just as it is with you, sir. Big, strong, whole men are the only ones for being wanted."

"I have been studying over this matter," answered McLean. "I am not so sure but that a man no older than you and similar in every way could do this work very well, if he were not a coward, and had it in him to be trustworthy and industrious."

Freckles came forward a step.

"If you will give me a job where I can earn me food, clothes, and a place to sleep," he said, "if I can have a Boss to work for like other men, and a place I feel I've a right to, I will do precisely what you tell me or die trying."

He spoke so convincingly that McLean believed, although in his heart he knew that to employ a stranger would be wretched business for a man with the interests he had involved.

"Very well," the Boss found himself answering, "I will enter you on my pay rolls. We'll have supper, and then I will provide you with clean clothing, wading-boots, the wire-mending apparatus, and a revolver. The first thing in the morning, I will take you the length of the trail myself and explain fully what I want done. All I ask of you is to come to me at once at the south camp and tell me as a man if you find this job too hard for you. It will not surprise me. It is work that few men would perform faithfully. What name shall I put down?"

Freckles's gaze never left McLean's face, and the Boss saw the swift spasm of pain that swept his lonely, sensitive features.

"I haven't any name," he said stubbornly, "no more than one somebody clapped on to me when they put me on the Home books, with not the thought or care they'd name a house cat. I've seen how they enter those poor little abandoned devils often enough to know. What they called me is no more my name than it is yours. I don't know what mine is, and I never will; but I am going to be your man and do your work, and I'll be glad to answer to any name you choose to call me. Won't you please be giving me a name, Mr. McLean?"

The Boss wheeled abruptly and began stacking his books. What he was thinking was probably what any other gentleman would have thought in the circumstances. With his eyes still downcast, and in a voice harsh with huskiness, he spoke.

"I will tell you what we will do, my lad," he said. "My father was my ideal man, and I loved him better than any other I have ever known. He went out five years ago, but that he would have been proud to leave you his name I firmly believe. If I give to you the name of my nearest kin and the man I loved best—will that do?"

Freckles's rigid attitude relaxed suddenly. His head dropped, and big tears splashed on the soiled calico shirt. McLean was not surprised at the silence, for he found that talking came none too easily just then.

"All right," he said. "I will write it on the roll—James Ross McLean."

"Thank you mightily," said Freckles. "That makes me feel almost as if I belonged, already."

"You do," said McLean. "Until someone armed with every right comes to claim you, you are mine. Now, come and take a bath, have some supper, and go to bed."

As Freckles followed into the lights and sounds of the camp, his heart and soul were singing for joy.

Chapter 2

Wherein Freckles Proves His Mettle and Finds Friends

Next morning found Freckles in clean, whole clothing, fed, and rested. Then McLean outfitted him and gave him careful instruction in the use of his weapon. The Boss showed him around the timber-line, and engaged him a place to board with the family of his head teamster, Duncan, whom he had brought from Scotland with him, and who lived in a small clearing he was working out between the swamp and the corduroy. When the gang was started for the south camp, Freckles was left to guard a fortune in the Limberlost. That he was under guard himself those first weeks he never knew.

Each hour was torture to the boy. The restricted life of a great city orphanage was the other extreme of the world compared with the Limberlost. He was afraid for his life every minute. The heat was intense. The heavy wading-boots rubbed his feet until they bled. He was sore and stiff from his long tramp and outdoor exposure. The seven miles of trail was agony at every step. He practiced at night, under the direction of Duncan, until he grew sure in the use of his revolver. He cut a stout hickory cudgel, with a knot on the end as big as his fist; this never left his hand. What he thought in those first days he himself could not recall clearly afterward.

His heart stood still every time he saw the beautiful marsh-grass begin a sinuous waving AGAINST the play of the wind, as McLean had told him it would. He bolted half a mile with the first boom of the bittern, and his hat lifted with every yelp of the sheitpoke. Once he saw a lean, shadowy form following him, and fired his revolver. Then he was frightened worse than ever for fear it might have been Duncan's collie.

The first afternoon that he found his wires down, and he was compelled to plunge knee deep into the black swamp-muck to restring them, he became so ill from fear and nervousness that he scarcely could control his shaking hand to do the work. With every step, he felt that he would miss secure footing and be swallowed in that clinging sea of blackness. In dumb agony he plunged forward, clinging to the posts and trees until he had finished restringing and testing the wire. He had consumed much time. Night closed in. The Limberlost stirred gently, then shook herself, growled, and awoke around him.

There seemed to be a great owl hooting from every hollow tree, and a little one screeching from every knothole. The bellowing of big bullfrogs was not sufficiently deafening to shut out the wailing of whip-poor-wills that seemed to come from every bush. Nighthawks swept past him with their shivering cry, and bats struck his face. A prowling wildcat missed its catch and screamed with rage. A straying fox bayed incessantly for its mate.

The hair on the back of Freckles's neck arose as bristles, and his knees wavered beneath him. He could not see whether the dreaded snakes were on the trail, or, in the pandemonium, hear the rattle for which McLean had cautioned him to listen. He stood motionless in an agony of fear. His breath whistled between his teeth. The perspiration ran down his face and body in little streams.

Something big, black, and heavy came crashing through the swamp close to him, and with a yell of utter panic Freckles ran—how far he did not know; but at last he gained control over himself and retraced his steps. His jaws set stiffly and the sweat dried on his body. When he reached the place from which he had started to run, he turned and with measured steps made his way down the line. After a time he realized that he was only walking, so he faced that sea of horrors again. When he came toward the corduroy, the cudgel fell to test the wire at each step.

Sounds that curdled his blood seemed to encompass him, and shapes of terror to draw closer and closer. Fear had so gained the mastery that he did not dare look behind him; and just when he felt that he would fall dead before he ever reached the clearing, came Duncan's rolling call: "Freckles! Freckles!" A shuddering sob burst in the boy's dry throat; but he only told Duncan that finding the wire down had caused the delay.

The next morning he started on time. Day after day, with his heart pounding, he ducked, dodged, ran when he could, and fought when he was brought to bay. If he ever had an idea of giving up, no one knew it; for he clung to his job without the shadow of wavering. All these things, in so far as he guessed them, Duncan, who had been set to watch the first weeks of Freckles's work, carried to the Boss at the south camp; but the innermost, exquisite torture of the thing the big Scotchman never guessed, and McLean, with his finer perceptions, came only a little closer.

After a few weeks, when Freckles learned that he was still living, that he had a home, and the very first money he ever had possessed was safe in his pockets, he began to grow proud. He yet side-stepped, dodged, and hurried to avoid being late again, but he was gradually developing the fearlessness that men ever acquire of dangers to which they are hourly accustomed.

His heart seemed to be leaping when his first rattler disputed the trail with him, but he mustered courage to attack it with his club. After its head had been crushed, he mastered an Irishman's inborn repugnance for snakes sufficiently to cut off its rattles to show Duncan. With this victory, his greatest fear of them was gone.

Then he began to realize that with the abundance of food in the swamp, flesh-hunters would not come on the trail and attack him, and he had his revolver for defence if they did. He soon learned to laugh at the big, floppy birds that made horrible noises. One day, watching behind a tree, he saw a crane solemnly performing a few measures of a belated nuptial song-and-dance with his mate. Realizing that it was intended in tenderness, no matter how it appeared, the lonely, starved heart of the boy sympathized with them.

Before the first month passed, he was fairly easy about his job; by the next he rather liked it. Nature can be trusted to work her own miracle in the heart of any man whose daily task keeps him alone among her sights, sounds, and silences.

When day after day the only thing that relieved his utter loneliness was the companionship of the birds and beasts of the swamp, it was the most natural thing in the world that Freckles should turn to them for friendship. He began by instinctively protecting the weak and helpless. He was astonished at the quickness with which they became accustomed to him and the disregard they showed for his movements, when they learned that he was not a hunter, while the club he carried was used more frequently for their benefit than his own. He scarcely could believe what he saw.

From the effort to protect the birds and animals, it was only a short step to the possessive feeling, and with that sprang the impulse to caress and provide. Through fall, when brooding was finished and the upland birds sought the swamp in swarms to feast on its seeds and berries, Freckles was content with watching them and speculating about them. Outside of half a dozen of the very commonest they were strangers to him. The likeness of their actions to humanity was an hourly surprise.

When black frost began stripping the Limberlost, cutting the ferns, shearing the vines from the trees, mowing the succulent green things of the swale, and setting the leaves swirling down, he watched the departing troops of his friends with dismay. He began to realize that he would be left alone. He made especial efforts toward friendliness with the hope that he could induce some of them to stay. It was then that he conceived the idea of carrying food to the birds; for he saw that they were leaving for lack of it; but he could not stop them. Day after day, flocks gathered and departed: by the time the first snow whitened his trail around the Limberlost, there were left only the little black-and-white juncos, the sapsuckers, yellow-hammers, a few patriarchs among the flaming cardinals, the blue jays, the crows, and the quail.

Then Freckles began his wizard work. He cleared a space of swale, and twice a day he spread a birds' banquet. By the middle of December the strong winds of winter had beaten most of the seed from the grass and bushes. The snow fell, covering the swamp, and food was very scarce and difficult to find. The birds scarcely waited until Freckles's back was turned to attack his provisions. In a few weeks they flew toward the clearing to meet him. During the bitter weather of January they came halfway to the cabin every morning, and fluttered around him as doves all the way to the feeding-ground. Before February they were so accustomed to him, and so hunger-driven, that they would perch on his head and shoulders, and the saucy jays would try to pry into his pockets.

Then Freckles added to wheat and crumbs, every scrap of refuse food he could find at the cabin. He carried to his pets the parings of apples, turnips, potatoes, stray cabbage-leaves, and carrots, and tied to the bushes meat-bones having scraps of fat and gristle. One morning, coming to his feeding-ground unusually early, he found a gorgeous cardinal and a rabbit side by side sociably nibbling a cabbage-leaf, and that instantly gave to him the idea of cracking nuts, from the store he had gathered for Duncan's children, for the squirrels, in the effort to add them to his family. Soon he had them coming—red, gray, and black; then he became filled with a vast impatience that he did not know their names or habits.

So the winter passed. Every week McLean rode to the Limberlost; never on the same day or at the same hour. Always he found Freckles at his work, faithful and brave, no matter how severe the weather.

The boy's earnings constituted his first money; and when the Boss explained to him that he could leave them safe at a bank and carry away a scrap of paper that represented the amount, he went straight on every payday and made his deposit, keeping out barely what was necessary for his board and clothing. What he wanted to do with his money he did not know, but it gave to him a sense of freedom and power to feel that it was there—it was his and he could have it when he chose. In imitation of McLean, he bought a small pocket account-book, in which he carefully set down every dollar he earned and every penny he spent. As his expenses were small and the Boss paid him generously, it was astonishing how his little hoard grew.

That winter held the first hours of real happiness in Freckles's life. He was free. He was doing a man's work faithfully, through every rigor of rain, snow, and blizzard. He was gathering a wonderful strength of body, paying his way, and saving money. Every man of the gang and of that locality knew that he was under the protection of McLean, who was a power; this had the effect of smoothing Freckles's path in many directions.

Mrs. Duncan showed him that individual kindness for which his hungry heart was longing. She had a hot drink ready for him when he came from a freezing day on the trail. She knit him a heavy mitten for his left hand, and devised a way to sew and pad the right sleeve that protected the maimed arm in bitter weather. She patched his clothing—frequently torn by the wire—and saved kitchen scraps for his birds, not because she either knew or cared anything about them, but because she herself was close enough to the swamp to be touched by its utter loneliness. When Duncan laughed at her for this, she retorted: "My God, mannie, if Freckles hadna the birds and the beasts he would be always alone. It was never meant for a human being to be so solitary. He'd get touched in the head if he hadna them to think for and to talk to."

"How much answer do ye think he gets to his talkin', lass?" laughed Duncan.

"He gets the answer that keeps the eye bright, the heart happy, and the feet walking faithful the rough path he's set them in," answered Mrs. Duncan earnestly.

Duncan walked away appearing very thoughtful. The next morning he gave an ear from the corn he was shelling for his chickens to Freckles, and told him to carry it to his wild chickens in the Limberlost. Freckles laughed delightedly.

"Me chickens!" he said. "Why didn't I ever think of that before? Of course they are! They are just little, brightly colored cocks and hens! But 'wild' is no good. What would you say to me 'wild chickens' being a good deal tamer than yours here in your yard?"

"Hoot, lad!" cried Duncan.

"Make yours light on your head and eat out of your hands and pockets," challenged Freckles.

"Go and tell your fairy tales to the wee people! They're juist brash on believin' things," said Duncan. "Ye canna invent any story too big to stop them from callin' for a bigger."

"I dare you to come see!" retorted Freckles.

"Take ye!" said Duncan. "If ye make juist ane bird licht on your heid or eat frae your hand, ye are free to help yoursel' to my corn-crib and wheat bin the rest of the winter."

Freckles sprang in air and howled in glee.

"Oh, Duncan! You're too aisy," he cried. "When will you come?"

"I'll come next Sabbath," said Duncan. "And I'll believe the birds of the Limberlost are tame as barnyard fowl when I see it, and no sooner!"

After that Freckles always spoke of the birds as his chickens, and the Duncans followed his example. The very next Sabbath, Duncan, with his wife and children, followed Freckles to the swamp. They saw a sight so wonderful it will keep them talking all the remainder of their lives, and make them unfailing friends of all the birds.

Freckles's chickens were awaiting him at the edge of the clearing. They cut the frosty air around his head into curves and circles of crimson, blue, and black. They chased each other from Freckles, and swept so closely themselves that they brushed him with their outspread wings.

At their feeding-ground Freckles set down his old pail of scraps and swept the snow from a small level space with a broom improvised of twigs. As soon as his back was turned, the birds clustered over the food, snatching scraps to carry to the nearest bushes. Several of the boldest, a big crow and a couple of jays, settled on the rim and feasted at leisure, while a cardinal, that hesitated to venture, fumed and scolded from a twig overhead.

Then Freckles scattered his store. At once the ground resembled the spread mantle of Montezuma, except that this mass of gaily colored feathers was on the backs of living birds. While they feasted, Duncan gripped his wife's arm and stared in astonishment; for from the bushes and dry grass, with gentle cheeping and queer, throaty chatter, as if to encourage each other, came flocks of quail. Before anyone saw it arrive, a big gray rabbit sat in the midst of the feast, contentedly gnawing a cabbage-leaf.

"Weel, I be drawed on!" came Mrs. Duncan's tense whisper.

"Shu-shu," cautioned Duncan.

Lastly Freckles removed his cap. He began filling it with handfuls of wheat from his pockets. In a swarm the grain-eaters arose around him as a flock of tame pigeons. They perched on his arms and the cap, and in the stress of hunger, forgetting all caution, a brilliant cock cardinal and an equally gaudy jay fought for a perching-place on his head.

"Weel, I'm beat," muttered Duncan, forgetting the silence imposed on his wife. "I'll hae to give in. 'Seein' is believin'.' A man wad hae to see that to believe it. We mauna let the Boss miss that sight, for it's a chance will no likely come twice in a life. Everything is snowed under and thae craturs near starved, but trustin' Freckles that complete they are tamer than our chickens. Look hard, bairns!" he whispered. "Ye winna see the like o' yon again, while God lets ye live. Notice their color against the ice and snow, and the pretty skippin' ways of them! And spunky! Weel, I'm beat fair!"

Freckles emptied his cap, turned his pockets and scattered his last grain. Then he waved his watching friends good-bye and started down the timber-line.

A week later, Duncan and Freckles arose from breakfast to face the bitterest morning of the winter. When Freckles, warmly capped and gloved, stepped to the corner of the kitchen for his scrap-pail, he found a big pan of steaming boiled wheat on the top of it. He wheeled to Mrs. Duncan with a shining face.

"Were you fixing this warm food for me chickens or yours?" he asked.

"It's for yours, Freckles," she said. "I was afeared this cold weather they wadna lay good without a warm bite now and then."

Duncan laughed as he stepped to the other room for his pipe; but Freckles faced Mrs. Duncan with a trace of every pang of starved mother-hunger he ever had suffered written large on his homely, splotched, narrow features.

"Oh, how I wish you were my mother!" he cried.

Mrs. Duncan attempted an echo of her husband's laugh.

"Lord love the lad!" she exclaimed. "Why, Freckles, are ye no bright enough to learn without being taught by a woman that I am your mither? If a great man like yoursel' dinna ken that, learn it now and ne'er forget it. Ance a woman is the wife of any man, she becomes wife to all men for having had the wifely experience she kens! Ance a man-child has beaten his way to life under the heart of a woman, she is mither to all men, for the hearts of mithers are everywhere the same. Bless ye, laddie, I am your mither!"

She tucked the coarse scarf she had knit for him closer over his chest and pulled his cap lower over his ears, but Freckles, whipping it off and holding it under his arm, caught her rough, reddened hand and pressed it to his lips in a long kiss. Then he hurried away to hide the happy, embarrassing tears that were coming straight from his swelling heart.

Mrs. Duncan, sobbing unrestrainedly, swept into the adjoining room and threw herself into Duncan's arms

"Oh, the puir lad!" she wailed. "Oh, the puir mither-hungry lad! He breaks my heart!"

Duncan's arms closed convulsively around his wife. With a big, brown hand he lovingly stroked her rough, sorrel hair.

"Sarah, you're a guid woman!" he said. "You're a michty guid woman! Ye hae a way o' speakin' out at times that's like the inspired prophets of the Lord. If that had been put to me, now, I'd 'a' felt all I kent how to and been keen enough to say the richt thing; but dang it, I'd 'a' stuttered and stammered and got naething out that would ha' done onybody a mite o' good. But ye, Sarah! Did ye see his face, woman? Ye sent him off lookin' leke a white light of holiness had passed ower and settled on him. Ye sent the lad away too happy for mortal words, Sarah. And ye made me that proud o' ye! I wouldna trade ye an' my share o' the Limberlost with ony king ye could mention."

He relaxed his clasp, and setting a heavy hand on each shoulder, he looked straight into her eyes.

"Ye're prime, Sarah! Juist prime!" he said.

Sarah Duncan stood alone in the middle of her two-roomed log cabin and lifted a bony, clawlike pair of hands, reddened by frequent immersion in hot water, cracked and chafed by exposure to cold, black-lined by constant battle with swamp-loam, calloused with burns, and stared at them wonderingly.

"Pretty-lookin' things ye are!" she whispered. "But ye hae juist been kissed. And by such a man! Fine as God ever made at His verra best. Duncan wouldna trade wi' a king! Na! Nor I wadna trade with a queen wi' a palace, an' velvet gowns, an' diamonds big as hazelnuts, an' a hundred visitors a day into the bargain. Ye've been that honored I'm blest if I can bear to souse ye in dish-water. Still, that kiss winna come off! Naething can take it from me, for it's mine till I dee. Lord, if I amna proud! Kisses on these old claws! Weel, I be drawed on!"

Chapter 3

Wherein a Feather Falls and
a Soul Is Born

So Freckles fared through the bitter winter. He was very happy. He had hungered for freedom, love, and appreciation so long! He had been unspeakably lonely at the Home; and the utter loneliness of a great desert or forest is not so difficult to endure as the loneliness of being constantly surrounded by crowds of people who do not care in the least whether one is living or dead.

All through the winter Freckles's entire energy was given to keeping up his lines and his "chickens" from freezing or starving. When the first breath of spring touched the Limberlost, and the snow receded before it; when the catkins began to bloom; when there came a hint of green to the trees, bushes, and swale; when the rushes lifted their heads, and the pulse of the newly resurrected season beat strongly in the heart of nature, something new stirred in the breast of the boy.

Nature always levies her tribute. Now she laid a powerful hand on the soul of Freckles, to which the boy's whole being responded, though he had not the least idea what was troubling him. Duncan accepted his wife's theory that it was a touch of spring fever, but Freckles knew better. He never had been so well. Clean, hot, and steady the blood pulsed in his veins. He was always hungry, and his most difficult work tired him not at all. For long months, without a single intermission, he had tramped those seven miles of trail twice each day, through every conceivable state of weather. With the heavy club he gave his wires a sure test, and between sections, first in play, afterward to keep his circulation going, he had acquired the skill of an expert drum major. In his work there was exercise for every muscle of his body each hour of the day, at night a bath, wholesome food, and sound sleep in a room that never knew fire. He had gained flesh and color, and developed a greater strength and endurance than anyone ever could have guessed.

Nor did the Limberlost contain last year's terrors. He had been with her in her hour of desolation, when stripped bare and deserted, she had stood shivering, as if herself afraid. He had made excursions into the interior until he was familiar with every path and road that ever had been cut. He had sounded the depths of her deepest pools, and had learned why the trees grew so magnificently. He had found that places of swamp and swale were few compared with miles of solid timber-land, concealed by summer's luxuriant undergrowth.

The sounds that at first had struck cold fear into his soul he now knew had left on wing and silent foot at the approach of winter. As flock after flock of the birds returned and he recognized the old echoes reawakening, he found to his surprise that he had been lonely for them and was hailing their return with great joy. All his fears were forgotten. Instead, he was possessed of an overpowering desire to know what they were, to learn where they had been, and whether they would make friends with him as the winter birds had done; and if they did, would they be as fickle? For, with the running sap, creeping worm, and winging bug, most of Freckles's "chickens" had deserted him, entered the swamp, and feasted to such a state of plethora on its store that they cared little for his supply, so that in the strenuous days of mating and nest-building the boy was deserted.

He chafed at the birds' ingratitude, but he found speedy consolation in watching and befriending the newcomers. He surely would have been proud and highly pleased if he had known that many of the former inhabitants of the interior swamp now grouped their nests beside the timber-line solely for the sake of his protection and company.

The yearly resurrection of the Limberlost is a mighty revival. Freckles stood back and watched with awe and envy the gradual reclothing and repopulation of the swamp. Keen-eyed and alert through danger and loneliness, he noted every stage of development, from the first piping frog and unsheathing bud, to full leafage and the return of the last migrant.

The knowledge of his complete loneliness and utter insignificance was hourly thrust upon him. He brooded and fretted until he was in a fever; yet he never guessed the cause. He was filled with a vast impatience, a longing that he scarcely could endure.

It was June by the zodiac, June by the Limberlost, and by every delight of a newly resurrected season it should have been June in the hearts of all men. Yet Freckles scowled darkly as he came down the trail, and the running TAP, TAP that tested the sagging wire and telegraphed word of his coming to his furred and feathered friends of the swamp, this morning carried the story of his discontent a mile ahead of him.

Freckles's special pet, a dainty, yellow-coated, black-sleeved, cock goldfinch, had remained on the wire for several days past the bravest of all; and Freckles, absorbed with the cunning and beauty of the tiny fellow, never guessed that he was being duped. For the goldfinch was skipping, flirting, and swinging for the express purpose of so holding his attention that he would not look up and see a small cradle of thistledown and wool perilously near his head. In the beginning of brooding, the spunky little homesteader had clung heroically to the wire when he was almost paralyzed with fright. When day after day passed and brought only softly whistled repetitions of his call, a handful of crumbs on the top of a locust line-post, and gently worded coaxings, he grew in confidence. Of late he had sung and swung during the passing of Freckles, who, not dreaming of the nest and the solemn-eyed little hen so close above, thought himself unusually gifted in his power to attract the birds. This morning the goldfinch scarcely could believe his ears, and clung to the wire until an unusually vicious rap sent him spinning a foot in air, and his "PTSEET" came with a squall of utter panic.

The wires were ringing with a story the birds could not translate, and Freckles was quite as ignorant of the trouble as they.

A peculiar movement beneath a small walnut tree caught his attention. He stopped to investigate. There was an unusually large Luna cocoon, and the moth was bursting the upper end in its struggles to reach light and air. Freckles stood and stared.

"There's something in there trying to get out," he muttered. "Wonder if I could help it? Guess I best not be trying. If I hadn't happened along, there wouldn't have been anyone to do anything, and maybe I'd only be hurting it. It's—it's—Oh, skaggany! It's just being born!"

Freckles gasped with surprise. The moth cleared the opening, and with many wabblings and contortions climbed up the tree. He stared speechless with amazement as the moth crept around a limb and clung to the under side. There was a big pursy body, almost as large as his thumb, and of the very snowiest white that Freckles ever had seen. There was a band of delicate lavender across its forehead, and its feet were of the same colour; there were antlers, like tiny, straw-colored ferns, on its head, and from its shoulders hung the crumpled wet wings. As Freckles gazed, tense with astonishment, he saw that these were expanding, drooping, taking on color, and small, oval markings were beginning to show.

The minutes passed. Freckles's steady gaze never wavered. Without realizing it, he was trembling with eagerness and anxiety. As he saw what was taking place, "It's going to fly," he breathed in hushed wonder. The morning sun fell on the moth and dried its velvet down, while the warm air made it fluffy. The rapidly growing wings began to show the most delicate green, with lavender fore-ribs, transparent, eye-shaped markings, edged with lines of red, tan, and black, and long, crisp trailers.

Freckles was whispering to himself for fear of disturbing the moth. It began a systematic exercise of raising and lowering its exquisite wings to dry them and to establish circulation. The boy realized that soon it would be able to spread them and sail away. His long-coming soul sent up its first shivering cry.

"I don't know what it is! Oh, I wish I knew! How I wish I knew! It must be something grand! It can't be a butterfly! It's away too big. Oh, I wish there was someone to tell me what it is!"

He climbed on the locust post, and balancing himself with the wire, held a finger in the line of the moth's advance up the twig. It unhesitatingly climbed on, so he stepped to the path, holding it to the light and examining it closely. Then he held it in the shade and turned it, gloating over its markings and beautiful coloring. When he held the moth to the limb, it climbed on, still waving those magnificent wings.

"My, but I'd like to be staying with you!" he said. "But if I was to stand here all day you couldn't grow any prettier than you are right now, and I wouldn't grow smart enough to tell what you are. I suppose there's someone who knows. Of course there is! Mr. McLean said there were people who knew every leaf, bird, and flower in the Limberlost. Oh Lord! How I wish You'd be telling me just this one thing!"

The goldfinch had ventured back to the wire, for there was his mate, only a few inches above the man-creature's head; and indeed, he simply must not be allowed to look up, so the brave little fellow rocked on the wire and piped, as he had done every day for a week: "SEE ME? SEE ME?"

"See you! Of course I see you," growled Freckles. "I see you day after day, and what good is it doing me? I might see you every morning for a year, and then not be able to be telling anyone about it. 'Seen a bird with black silk wings—little, and yellow as any canary.' That's as far as I'd get. What you doing here, anyway? Have you a mate? What's your name? 'See you?' I reckon I see you; but I might as well be blind, for any good it's doing me!"

Freckles impatiently struck the wire. With a screech of fear, the goldfinch fled precipitately. His mate arose from the nest with a whirr—Freckles looked up and saw it.

"O—ho!" he cried. "So THAT'S what you are doing here! You have a wife. And so close my head I have been mighty near wearing a bird on my bonnet, and never knew it!"

Freckles laughed at his own jest, while in better humor he climbed to examine the neat, tiny cradle and its contents. The hen darted at him in a frenzy. "Now, where do you come in?" he demanded, when he saw that she was not similar to the goldfinch.

"You be clearing out of here! This is none of your fry. This is the nest of me little, yellow friend of the wire, and you shan't be touching it. Don't blame you for wanting to see, though. My, but it's a fine nest and beauties of eggs. Will you be keeping away, or will I fire this stick at you?"

Freckles dropped to the trail. The hen darted to the nest and settled on it with a tender, coddling movement. He of the yellow coat flew to the edge to make sure that everything was right. It would have been plain to the veriest novice that they were partners in that cradle.

"Well, I'll be switched!" muttered Freckles. "If that ain't both their nest! And he's yellow and she's green, or she's yellow and he's green. Of course, I don't know, and I haven't any way to find out, but it's plain as the nose on your face that they are both ready to be fighting for that nest, so, of course, they belong. Doesn't that beat you? Say, that's what's been sticking me all of this week on that grass nest in the thorn tree down the line. One day a blue bird is setting, so I think it is hers. The next day a brown bird is on, and I chase it off because the nest is blue's. Next day the brown bird is on again, and I let her be, because I think it must be hers. Next day, be golly, blue's on, and off I send her because it's brown's; and now, I bet my hat, it's both their nest and I've only been bothering them and making a big fool of mesilf. Pretty specimen I am, pretending to be a friend to the birds, and so blamed ignorant I don't know which ones go in pairs, and blue and brown are a pair, of course, if yellow and green are—and there's the red birds! I never thought of them! He's red and she's gray—and now I want to be knowing, are they all different? Why no! Of course, they ain't! There's the jays all blue, and the crows all black."

The tide of Freckles's discontent welled until he almost choked with anger and chagrin. He plodded down the trail, scowling blackly and viciously spanging the wire. At the finches' nest he left the line and peered into the thorn tree. There was no bird brooding. He pressed closer to take a peep at the snowy, spotless little eggs he had found so beautiful, when at the slight noise up raised four tiny baby heads with wide-open mouths, uttering hunger cries. Freckles stepped back. The brown bird alighted on the edge and closed one cavity with a wiggling green worm, while not two minutes later the blue filled another with a white. That settled it. The blue and brown were mates. Once again Freckles repeated his "How I wish I knew!"

Around the bridge spanning Sleepy Snake Creek the swale spread widely, the timber was scattering, and willows, rushes, marsh-grass, and splendid wild flowers grew abundantly. Here lazy, big, black water snakes, for which the creek was named, sunned on the bushes, wild ducks and grebe chattered, cranes and herons fished, and muskrats plowed the bank in queer, rolling furrows. It was always a place full of interest, so Freckles loved to linger on the bridge, watching the marsh and water people. He also transacted affairs of importance with the wild flowers and sweet marsh-grass. He enjoyed splashing through the shallow pools on either side of the bridge.

Then, too, where the creek entered the swamp was a place of unusual beauty. The water spread in darksome, mossy, green pools. Water-plants and lilies grew luxuriantly, throwing up large, rank, green leaves. Nowhere else in the Limberlost could be found frog-music to equal that of the mouth of the creek. The drumming and piping rolled in never-ending orchestral effect, while the full chorus rang to its accompaniment throughout the season.

Freckles slowly followed the path leading from the bridge to the line. It was the one spot at which he might relax his vigilance. The boldest timber thief the swamp ever had known would not have attempted to enter it by the mouth of the creek, on account of the water and because there was no protection from surrounding trees. He was bending the rank grass with his cudgel, and thinking of the shade the denser swamp afforded, when he suddenly dodged sidewise; the cudgel whistled sharply through the air and Freckles sprang back.

From the clear sky above him, first level with his face, then skimming, dipping, tilting, whirling until it struck, quill down, in the path in front of him, came a glossy, iridescent, big black feather. As it touched the ground, Freckles snatched it up with almost a continuous movement facing the sky. There was not a tree of any size in a large open space. There was no wind to carry it. From the clear sky it had fallen, and Freckles, gazing eagerly into the arch of June blue with a few lazy clouds floating high in the sea of ether, had neither mind nor knowledge to dream of a bird hanging as if frozen there. He turned the big quill questioningly, and again his awed eyes swept the sky.

"A feather dropped from Heaven!" he breathed reverently. "Are the holy angels moulting? But no; if they were, it would be white. Maybe all the angels are not for being white. What if the angels of God are white and those of the devil are black? But a black one has no business up there. Maybe some poor black angel is so tired of being punished it's for slipping to the gates, beating its wings trying to make the Master hear!"

Again and again Freckles searched the sky, but there was no answering gleam of golden gates, no form of sailing bird; then he went slowly on his way, turning the feather and wondering about it. It was a wing quill, eighteen inches in length, with a heavy spine, gray at the base, shading to jet black at the tip, and it caught the play of the sun's rays in slanting gleams of green and bronze. Again Freckles's "old man of the sea" sat sullen and heavy on his shoulders and weighted him down until his step lagged and his heart ached.

"Where did it come from? What is it? Oh, how I wish I knew!" he kept repeating as he turned and studied the feather, with almost unseeing eyes, so intently was he thinking.

Before him spread a large, green pool, filled with rotting logs and leaves, bordered with delicate ferns and grasses among which lifted the creamy spikes of the arrow-head, the blue of water-hyacinth, and the delicate yellow of the jewel-flower. As Freckles leaned, handling the feather and staring at it, then into the depths of the pool, he once more gave voice to his old query: "I wonder what it is!"

Straight across from him, couched in the mosses of a soggy old log, a big green bullfrog, with palpitant throat and batting eyes, lifted his head and bellowed in answer. "FIN' DOUT! FIN' DOUT!"

"Wha—what's that?" stammered Freckles, almost too much bewildered to speak. "I—I know you are only a bullfrog, but, be jabbers, that sounded mightily like speech. Wouldn't you please to be saying it over?"

The bullfrog cuddled contentedly in the ooze. Then suddenly he lifted his voice, and, as an imperative drumbeat, rolled it again: "FIN' DOUT! FIN' DOUT! FIN DOUT!"

Freckles had the answer. Something seemed to snap in his brain. There was a wavering flame before his eyes. Then his mind cleared. His head lifted in a new poise, his shoulders squared, while his spine straightened. The agony was over. His soul floated free. Freckles came into his birthright.

"Before God, I will!" He uttered the oath so impressively that the recording angel never winced as he posted it in the prayer column.

Freckles set his hat over the top of one of the locust posts used between trees to hold up the wire while he fastened the feather securely in the band. Then he started down the line, talking to himself as men who have worked long alone always fall into the habit of doing.

"What a fool I have been!" he muttered. "Of course that's what I have to do! There wouldn't likely anybody be doing it for me. Of course I can! What am I a man for? If I was a four-footed thing of the swamp, maybe I couldn't; but a man can do anything if he's the grit to work hard enough and stick at it, Mr. McLean is always saying, and here's the way I am to do it. He said, too, that there were people that knew everything in the swamp. Of course they have written books! The thing for me to be doing is to quit moping and be buying some. Never bought a book in me life, or anything else of much account, for that matter. Oh, ain't I glad I didn't waste me money! I'll surely be having enough to get a few. Let me see."

Freckles sat on a log, took his pencil and account-book, and figured on a back page. He had walked the timber-line ten months. His pay was thirty dollars a month, and his board cost him eight. That left twenty-two dollars a month, and his clothing had cost him very little. At the least he had two hundred dollars in the bank. He drew a deep breath and smiled at the sky with satisfaction.

"I'll be having a book about all the birds, trees, flowers, butterflies, and—Yes, by gummy! I'll be having one about the frogs—if it takes every cent I have," he promised himself.

He put away the account-book, that was his most cherished possession, caught up his stick, and started down the line. The even tap, tap, and the cheery, gladsome whistle carried far ahead of him the message that Freckles was himself again.

He fell into a rapid pace, for he had lost time that morning; when he rounded the last curve he was almost running. There was a chance that the Boss might be there for his weekly report.

Then, wavering, flickering, darting here and there over the sweet marsh-grass, came a large black shadow, sweeping so closely before him that for the second time that morning Freckles dodged and sprang back. He had seen some owls and hawks of the swamp that he thought might be classed as large birds, but never anything like this, for six feet it spread its big, shining wings. Its strong feet could be seen drawn among its feathers. The sun glinted on its sharp, hooked beak. Its eyes glowed, caught the light, and seemed able to pierce the ground at his feet. It cared no more for Freckles than if he had not been there; for it perched on a low tree, while a second later it awkwardly hopped to the trunk of a lightning-riven elm, turned its back, and began searching the blue.

Freckles looked just in time to see a second shadow sweep the grass; and another bird, a trifle smaller and not quite so brilliant in the light, slowly sailed down to perch beside the first. Evidently they were mates, for with a queer, rolling hop the first-comer shivered his bronze wings, sidled to the new arrival, and gave her a silly little peck on her wing. Then he coquettishly drew away and ogled her. He lifted his head, waddled from her a few steps, awkwardly ambled back, and gave her such a simple sort of kiss on her beak that Freckles burst into a laugh, but clapped his hand over his mouth to stifle the sound.

The lover ducked and side-stepped a few feet. He spread his wings and slowly and softly waved them precisely as if he were fanning his charmer, which was indeed the result he accomplished. Then a wave of uncontrollable tenderness moved him so he hobbled to his bombardment once more. He faced her squarely this time, and turned his head from side to side with queer little jerks and indiscriminate peckings at her wings and head, and smirkings that really should have been irresistible. She yawned and shuffled away indifferently. Freckles reached up, pulled the quill from his hat, and looking from it to the birds, nodded in settled conviction.

"So you're me black angels, ye spalpeens! No wonder you didn't get in! But I'll back you to come closer it than any other birds ever did. You fly higher than I can see. Have you picked the Limberlost for a good thing and come to try it? Well, you can be me chickens if you want to, but I'm blest if you ain't cool for new ones. Why don't you take this stick for a gun and go skinning a mile?"

Freckles broke into an unrestrained laugh, for the bird-lover was keen about his courting, while evidently his mate was diffident. When he approached too boisterously, she relieved him of a goodly tuft of feathers and sent him backward in a series of squirmy little jumps that gave the boy an idea of what had happened up-sky to send the falling feather across his pathway.

"Score one for the lady! I'll be umpiring this," volunteered Freckles.

With a ravishing swagger, half-lifted wings, and deep, guttural hissing, the lover approached again. He suddenly lifted his body, but she coolly rocked forward on the limb, glided gracefully beneath him, and slowly sailed into the Limberlost. He recovered himself and gazed after her in astonishment.

Freckles hurried down the trail, shaking with laughter. When he neared the path to the clearing and saw the Boss sitting motionless on the mare that was the pride of his heart, the boy broke into a run.

"Oh, Mr. McLean!" he cried. "I hope I haven't kept you waiting very long! And the sun is getting hot! I have been so slow this morning! I could have gone faster, only there were that many things to keep me, and I didn't know you would be here. I'll hurry after this. I've never had to be giving excuses before. The line wasn't down, and there wasn't a sign of trouble; it was other things that were making me late."

McLean, smiling on the boy, immediately noticed the difference in him. This flushed, panting, talkative lad was not the same creature who had sought him in despair and bitterness. He watched in wonder as Freckles mopped the perspiration from his forehead and began to laugh. Then, forgetting all his customary reserve with the Boss, the pent-up boyishness in the lad broke forth. With an eloquence of which he never dreamed he told his story. He talked with such enthusiasm that McLean never took his eyes from his face or shifted in the saddle until he described the strange bird-lover, and then the Boss suddenly bent over the pommel and laughed with the boy.

Freckles decorated his story with keen appreciation and rare touches of Irish wit and drollery that made it most interesting as well as very funny. It was a first attempt at descriptive narration. With an inborn gift for striking the vital point, a naturalist's dawning enthusiasm for the wonders of the Limberlost, and the welling joy of his newly found happiness, he made McLean see the struggles of the moth and its freshly painted wings, the dainty, brilliant bird-mates of different colors, the feather sliding through the clear air, the palpitant throat and batting eyes of the frog; while his version of the big bird's courtship won for the Boss the best laugh he had enjoyed for years.

"They're in the middle of a swamp now," said Freckles. "Do you suppose there is any chance of them staying with me chickens? If they do, they'll be about the queerest I have; but I tell you, sir, I am finding some plum good ones. There's a new kind over at the mouth of the creek that uses its wings like feet and walks on all fours. It travels like a thrashing machine. There's another, tall as me waist, with a bill a foot long, a neck near two, not the thickness of me wrist and an elegant color. He's some blue and gray, touched up with black, white, and brown. The voice of him is such that if he'd be going up and standing beside a tree and crying at it a few times he could be sawing it square off. I don't know but it would be a good idea to try him on the gang, sir."

McLean laughed. "Those must be blue herons, Freckles," he said. "And it doesn't seem possible, but your description of the big black birds sounds like genuine black vultures. They are common enough in the South. I've seen them numerous around the lumber camps of Georgia, but I never before heard of any this far north. They must be strays. You have described perfectly our nearest equivalent to a branch of these birds called in Europe Pharaoh's Chickens, but if they are coming to the Limberlost they will have to drop Pharaoh and become Freckles's Chickens, like the remainder of the birds; won't they? Or are they too odd and ugly to interest you?"

"Oh, not at all, at all!" cried Freckles, bursting into pure brogue in his haste. "I don't know as I'd be calling them exactly pretty, and they do move like a rocking-horse loping, but they are so big and fearless. They have a fine color for black birds, and their feet and beaks seem so strong. You never saw anything so keen as their eyes! And fly? Why, just think, sir, they must be flying miles straight up, for they were out of sight completely when the feather fell. I don't suppose I've a chicken in the swamp that can go as close heaven as those big, black fellows, and then—"

Freckles's voice dragged and he hesitated.

"Then what?" interestedly urged McLean.

"He was loving her so," answered Freckles in a hushed voice. "I know it looked awful funny, and I laughed and told on him, but if I'd taken time to think I don't believe I'd have done it. You see, I've seen such a little bit of loving in me life. You easily can be understanding that at the Home it was every day the old story of neglect and desertion. Always people that didn't even care enough for their children to keep them, so you see, sir, I had to like him for trying so hard to make her know how he loved her. Of course, they're only birds, but if they are caring for each other like that, why, it's just the same as people, ain't it?"

Freckles lifted his brave, steady eyes to the Boss.

"If anybody loved me like that, Mr. McLean, I wouldn't be spending any time on how they looked or moved. All I'd be thinking of would be how they felt toward me. If they will stay, I'll be caring as much for them as any chickens I have. If I did laugh at them I thought he was just fine!"

The face of McLean was a study; but the honest eyes of the boy were so compelling that he found himself answering: "You are right, Freckles. He's a gentleman, isn't he? And the only real chicken you have. Of course he'll remain! The Limberlost will be paradise for his family. And now, Freckles, what has been the trouble all spring? You have done your work as faithfully as anyone could ask, but I can't help seeing that there is something wrong. Are you tired of your job?"

"I love it," answered Freckles. "It will almost break me heart when the gang comes and begins tearing up the swamp and scaring away me chickens."

"Then what is the trouble?" insisted McLean.

"I think, sir, it's been books," answered Freckles. "You see, I didn't realize it meself until the bullfrog told me this morning. I hadn't ever even heard about a place like this. Anyway, I wasn't understanding how it would be, if I had. Being among these beautiful things every day, I got so anxious like to be knowing and naming them, that it got to eating into me and went and made me near sick, when I was well as I could be. Of course, I learned to read, write, and figure some at school, but there was nothing there, or in any of the city that I ever got to see, that would make a fellow even be dreaming of such interesting things as there are here. I've seen the parks—but good Lord, they ain't even beginning to be in it with the Limberlost! It's all new and strange to me. I don't know a thing about any of it. The bullfrog told me to 'find out,' plain as day, and books are the only way; ain't they?"

"Of course," said McLean, astonished at himself for his heartfelt relief. He had not guessed until that minute what it would have meant to him to have Freckles give up. "You know enough to study out what you want yourself, if you have the books, don't you?"

"I am pretty sure I do," said Freckles. "I learned all I'd the chance at in the Home, and me schooling was good as far as it went. Wouldn't let you go past fourteen, you know. I always did me sums perfect, and loved me history books. I had them almost by heart. I never could get me grammar to suit them. They said it was just born in me to go wrong talking, and if it hadn't been I suppose I would have picked it up from the other children; but I'd the best voice of any of them in the Home or at school. I could knock them all out singing. I was always leader in the Home, and once one of the superintendents gave me carfare and let me go into the city and sing in a boys' choir. The master said I'd the swatest voice of them all until it got rough like, and then he made me quit for awhile, but he said it would be coming back by now, and I'm railly thinking it is, sir, for I've tried on the line a bit of late and it seems to go smooth again and lots stronger. That and me chickens have been all the company I've been having, and it will be all I'll want if I can have some books and learn the real names of things, where they come from, and why they do such interesting things. It's been fretting me more than I knew to be shut up here among all these wonders and not knowing a thing. I wanted to ask you what some books would cost me, and if you'd be having the goodness to get me the right ones. I think I have enough money."

Freckles offered his account-book and the Boss studied it gravely.

"You needn't touch your account, Freckles," he said. "Ten dollars from this month's pay will provide you everything you need to start on. I will write a friend in Grand Rapids today to select you the very best and send them at once."

Freckles's eyes were shining.

"Never owned a book in me life!" he said. "Even me schoolbooks were never mine. Lord! How I used to wish I could have just one of them for me very own! Won't it be fun to see me sawbird and me little yellow fellow looking at me from the pages of a book, and their real names and all about them printed alongside? How long will it be taking, sir?"

"Ten days should do it nicely," said McLean. Then, seeing Freckles's lengthening face, he added: "I'll have Duncan bring you a ten-bushel store-box the next time he goes to town. He can haul it to the west entrance and set it up wherever you want it. You can put in your spare time filling it with the specimens you find until the books come, and then you can study out what you have. I suspect you could collect specimens that I could send to naturalists in the city and sell for you; things like that winged creature, this morning. I don't know much in that line, but it must have been a moth, and it might have been rare. I've seen them by the thousand in museums, and in all nature I don't remember rarer coloring than their wings. I'll order you a butterfly-net and box and show you how scientists pin specimens. Possibly you can make a fine collection of these swamp beauties. It will be all right for you to take a pair of different moths and butterflies, but I don't want to hear of your killing any birds. They are protected by heavy fines."

McLean rode away leaving Freckles staring aghast. Then he saw the point and smiled. Standing on the trail, he twirled the feather and thought over the morning.

"Well, if life ain't getting to be worth living!" he said wonderingly. "Biggest streak of luck I ever had! 'Bout time something was coming my way, but I wouldn't ever thought anybody could strike such magnificent prospects through only a falling feather."

Chapter 4

Wherein Freckles Faces Trouble Bravely and Opens the Way for New Experiences

On Duncan's return from his next trip to town there was a big store-box loaded on the back of his wagon. He drove to the west entrance of the swamp, set the box on a stump that Freckles had selected in a beautiful, sheltered place, and made it secure on its foundations with a tree at its back.

"It seems most a pity to nail into that tree," said Duncan. "I haena the time to examine into the grain of it, but it looks as if it might be a rare ane. Anyhow, the nailin' winna hurt it deep, and havin' the case by it will make it safer if it is a guid ane."

"Isn't it an oak?" asked Freckles.

"Ay," said Duncan. "It looks like it might be ane of thae fine-grained white anes that mak' such grand furniture."

When the body of the case was secure, Duncan made a door from the lid and fastened it with hinges. He drove a staple, screwed on a latch, and gave Freckles a small padlock—so that he might fasten in his treasures safely. He made a shelf at the top for his books, and last of all covered the case with oil-cloth.

It was the first time in Freckles's life that anyone ever had done that much for his pleasure, and it warmed his heart with pure joy. If the interior of the box already had been covered with the rarest treasures of the Limberlost he could have been no happier.

When the big teamster stood back to look at his work he laughingly quoted, "'Neat, but no' gaudy,' as McLean says. All we're, needing now is a coat of paint to make a cupboard that would turn Sarah green with envy. Ye'll find that safe an' dry, lad, an' that's all that's needed."

"Mr. Duncan," said Freckles, "I don't know why you are being so mighty good to me; but if you have any jobs at the cabin that I could do for you or Mrs. Duncan, hours off the line, it would make me mighty happy."

Duncan laughed. "Ye needna feel ye are obliged to me, lad. Ye mauna think I could take a half-day off in the best hauling season and go to town for boxes to rig up, and spend of my little for fixtures."

"I knew Mr. McLean sent you," said Freckles, his eyes wide and bright with happiness. "It's so good of him. How I wish I could do something that would please him as much!"

"Why, Freckles," said Duncan, as he knelt and began collecting his tools, "I canna see that it will hurt ye to be told that ye are doing every day a thing that pleases the Boss as much as anything ye could do. Ye're being uncommon faithful, lad, and honest as old Father Time. McLean is trusting ye as he would his own flesh and blood."

"Oh, Duncan!" cried the happy boy. "Are you sure?"

"Why I know," answered Duncan. "I wadna venture to say so else. In those first days he cautioned me na to tell ye, but now he wadna care. D'ye ken, Freckles, that some of the single trees ye are guarding are worth a thousand dollars?"

Freckles caught his breath and stood speechless.

"Ye see," said Duncan, "that's why they maun be watched so closely. They tak', say, for instance, a burl maple—bird's eye they call it in the factory, because it's full o' wee knots and twists that look like the eye of a bird. They saw it out in sheets no muckle thicker than writin' paper. Then they make up the funiture out of cheaper wood and cover it with the maple—veneer, they call it. When it's all done and polished ye never saw onythin' grander. Gang into a retail shop the next time ye are in town and see some. By sawin' it thin that way they get finish for thousands of dollars' worth of furniture from a single tree. If ye dinna watch faithful, and Black Jack gets out a few he has marked, it means the loss of more money than ye ever dreamed of, lad. The other night, down at camp, some son of Balaam was suggestin' that ye might be sellin' the Boss out to Jack and lettin' him tak' the trees secretly, and nobody wad ever ken till the gang gets here."

A wave of scarlet flooded Freckles's face and he blazed hotly at the insult.

"And the Boss," continued Duncan, coolly ignoring Freckles's anger, "he lays back just as cool as cowcumbers an' says: 'I'll give a thousand dollars to ony man that will show me a fresh stump when we reach the Limberlost,' says he. Some of the men just snapped him up that they'd find some. So you see how the Boss is trustin' ye, lad."

"I am gladder than I can ever expriss," said Freckles. "And now will I be walking double time to keep some of them from cutting a tree to get all that money!"

"Mither o' Moses!" howled Duncan. "Ye can trust the Scotch to bungle things a'thegither. McLean was only meanin' to show ye all confidence and honor. He's gone and set a high price for some dirty whelp to ruin ye. I was just tryin' to show ye how he felt toward ye, and I've gone an' give ye that worry to bear. Damn the Scotch! They're so slow an' so dumb!"

"Exciptin' prisint company?" sweetly inquired Freckles.

"No!" growled Duncan. "Headin' the list! He'd nae business to set a price on ye, lad, for that's about the amount of it, an' I'd nae right to tell ye. We've both done ye ill, an' both meanin' the verra best. Juist what I'm always sayin' to Sarah."

"I am mighty proud of what you have been telling me, Duncan," said Freckles. "I need the warning, sure. For with the books coming I might be timpted to neglect me work when double watching is needed. Thank you more than I can say for putting me on to it. What you've told me may be the saving of me. I won't stop for dinner now. I'll be getting along the east line, and when I come around about three, maybe Mother Duncan will let me have a glass of milk and a bite of something."

"Ye see now!" cried Duncan in disgust. "Ye'll start on that seven-mile tramp with na bite to stay your stomach. What was it I told ye?"

"You told me that the Scotch had the hardest heads and the softest hearts of any people that's living," answered Freckles.

Duncan grunted in gratified disapproval.

Freckles picked up his club and started down the line, whistling cheerily, for he had an unusually long repertoire upon which to draw.

Duncan went straight to the lower camp, and calling McLean aside, repeated the conversation verbatim, ending: "And nae matter what happens now or ever, dinna ye dare let onythin' make ye believe that Freckles hasna guarded faithful as ony man could."

"I don't think anything could shake my faith in the lad," answered McLean.

Freckles was whistling merrily. He kept one eye religiously on the line. The other he divided between the path, his friends of the wire, and a search of the sky for his latest arrivals. Every day since their coming he had seen them, either hanging as small, black clouds above the swamp or bobbing over logs and trees with their queer, tilting walk. Whenever he could spare time, he entered the swamp and tried to make friends with them, for they were the tamest of all his unnumbered subjects. They ducked, dodged, and ambled around him, over logs and bushes, and not even a near approach would drive them to flight.

For two weeks he had found them circling over the Limberlost regularly, but one morning the female was missing and only the big black chicken hung sentinel above the swamp. His mate did not reappear in the following days, and Freckles grew very anxious. He spoke of it to Mrs. Duncan, and she quieted his fears by raising a delightful hope in their stead.

"Why, Freckles, if it's the hen-bird ye are missing, it's ten to one she's safe," she said. "She's laid, and is setting, ye silly! Watch him and mark whaur he lichts. Then follow and find the nest. Some Sabbath we'll all gang see it."

Accepting this theory, Freckles began searching for the nest. Because these "chickens" were large, as the hawks, he looked among the treetops until he almost sprained the back of his neck. He had half the crow and hawk nests in the swamp located. He searched for this nest instead of collecting subjects for his case. He found the pair the middle of one forenoon on the elm where he had watched their love-making. The big black chicken was feeding his mate; so it was proved that they were a pair, they were both alive, and undoubtedly she was brooding. After that Freckles's nest-hunting continued with renewed zeal, but as he had no idea where to look and Duncan could offer no helpful suggestion, the nest was no nearer to being found.

Coming from a long day on the trail, Freckles saw Duncan's children awaiting him much closer the swale than they usually ventured, and from their wild gestures he knew that something had happened. He began to run, but the cry that reached him was: "The books have come!"

How they hurried! Freckles lifted the youngest to his shoulder, the second took his club and dinner pail, and when they reached Mrs. Duncan they found her at work on a big box. She had loosened the lid, and then she laughingly sat on it.

"Ye canna have a peep in here until ye have washed and eaten supper," she said. "It's all ready on the table. Ance ye begin on this, ye'll no be willin' to tak' your nose o' it till bedtime, and I willna get my work done the nicht. We've eaten long ago."

It was difficult work, but Freckles smiled bravely. He made himself neat, swallowed a few bites, then came so eagerly that Mrs. Duncan yielded, although she said she very well knew all the time that his supper would be spoiled.

Lifting the lid, they removed the packing and found in that box books on birds, trees, flowers, moths, and butterflies. There was also one containing Freckles's bullfrog, true to life. Besides these were a butterfly-net, a naturalist's tin specimen-box, a bottle of cyanide, a box of cotton, a paper of long, steel specimen-pins, and a letter telling what all these things were and how to use them.

At the discovery of each new treasure, Freckles shouted: "Will you be looking at this, now?"

Mrs. Duncan cried: "Weel, I be drawed on!"

The eldest boy turned a somersault for every extra, while the baby, trying to follow his example, bunched over in a sidewise sprawl and cut his foot on the axe with which his mother had prized up the box-lid. That sobered them, they carried the books indoors. Mrs. Duncan had a top shelf in her closet cleared for them, far above the reach of meddling little fingers.

When Freckles started for the trail next morning, the shining new specimen-box flashed on his back. The black "chicken," a mere speck in the blue, caught the gleam of it. The folded net hung beside the boy's hatchet, and the bird book was in the box. He walked the line and tested each section scrupulously, watching every foot of the trail, for he was determined not to slight his work; but if ever a boy "made haste slowly" in a hurry, it was Freckles that morning. When at last he reached the space he had cleared and planted around his case, his heart swelled with the pride of possessing even so much that he could call his own, while his quick eyes feasted on the beauty of it.

He had made a large room with the door of the case set even with one side of it. On three sides, fine big bushes of wild rose climbed to the lower branches of the trees. Part of his walls were mallow, part alder, thorn, willow, and dogwood. Below there filled in a solid mass of pale pink sheep-laurel, and yellow St. John's wort, while the amber threads of the dodder interlaced everywhere. At one side the swamp came close, here cattails grew in profusion. In front of them he had planted a row of water-hyacinths without disturbing in the least the state of their azure bloom, and where the ground arose higher for his floor, a row of foxfire, that soon would be open.

To the left he had discovered a queer natural arrangement of the trees, that grew to giant size and were set in a gradually narrowing space so that a long, open vista stretched away until lost in the dim recesses of the swamp. A little trimming of underbush, rolling of dead logs, levelling of floor and carpeting with moss, made it easy to understand why Freckles had named this the "cathedral"; yet he never had been taught that "the groves were God's first temples."

On either side of the trees that constituted the first arch of this dim vista of the swamp he planted ferns that grew waist-high thus early in the season, and so skilfully the work had been done that not a frond drooped because of the change. Opposite, he cleared a space and made a flower bed. He filled one end with every delicate, lacy vine and fern he could transplant successfully. The body of the bed was a riot of color. Here he set growing dainty blue-eyed-Marys and blue-eyed grass side by side. He planted harebells; violets, blue, white, and yellow; wild geranium, cardinal-flower, columbine, pink snake's mouth, buttercups, painted trilliums, and orchis. Here were blood-root, moccasin-flower, hepatica, pitcher-plant, Jack-in-the-pulpit, and every other flower of the Limberlost that was in bloom or bore a bud presaging a flower. Every day saw the addition of new specimens. The place would have driven a botanist wild with envy.

On the line side he left the bushes thick for concealment, entering by a narrow path he and Duncan had cleared in setting up the case. He called this the front door, though he used every precaution to hide it. He built rustic seats between several of the trees, leveled the floor, and thickly carpeted it with rank, heavy, woolly-dog moss. Around the case he planted wild clematis, bittersweet, and wild-grapevines, and trained them over it until it was almost covered. Every day he planted new flowers, cut back rough bushes, and coaxed out graceful ones. His pride in his room was very great, but he had no idea how surprisingly beautiful it would appear to anyone who had not witnessed its growth and construction.

This morning Freckles walked straight to his case, unlocked it, and set his apparatus and dinner inside. He planted a new specimen he had found close the trail, and, bringing his old scrap-bucket from the corner in which it was hidden, from a near-by pool he dipped water to pour over his carpet and flowers.

Then he took out the bird book, settled comfortably on a bench, and with a deep sigh of satisfaction turned to the section headed "V." Past "veery" and "vireo" he went, down the line until his finger, trembling with eagerness, stopped at "vulture."

"'Great black California vulture,'" he read.

"Humph! This side the Rockies will do for us."

"'Common turkey-buzzard.'"

"Well, we ain't hunting common turkeys. McLean said chickens, and what he says goes."

"'Black vulture of the South.'"

"Here we are arrived at once."

Freckles's finger followed the line, and he read scraps aloud.

"'Common in the South. Sometimes called Jim Crow. Nearest equivalent to C-a-t-h-a-r-t-e-s A-t-r-a-t-a.'"

"How the divil am I ever to learn them corkin' big words by mesel'?"

"'—the Pharaoh's Chickens of European species. Sometimes stray north as far as Virginia and Kentucky—'"

"And sometimes farther," interpolated Freckles, "'cos I got them right here in Indiana so like these pictures I can just see me big chicken bobbing up to get his ears boxed. Hey?"

"'Light-blue eggs—'"

"Golly! I got to be seeing them!"

"'—big as a common turkey's, but shaped like a hen's, heavily splotched with chocolate—'"

"Caramels, I suppose. And—"

"'—in hollow logs or stumps.'"

"Oh, hagginy! Wasn't I barking up the wrong tree, though? Ought to been looking close the ground all this time. Now it's all to do over, and I suspect the sooner I start the sooner I'll be likely to find them."

Freckles put away his book, dampened the smudge-fire, without which the mosquitoes made the swamp almost unbearable, took his cudgel and lunch, and went to the line. He sat on a log, ate at dinner-time and drank his last drop of water. The heat of June was growing intense. Even on the west of the swamp, where one had full benefit of the breeze from the upland, it was beginning to be unpleasant in the middle of the day.

He brushed the crumbs from his knees and sat resting awhile and watching the sky to see if his big chicken were hanging up there. But he came to the earth abruptly, for there were steps coming down the trail that were neither McLean's nor Duncan's—and there never had been others. Freckles's heart leaped hotly. He ran a quick hand over his belt to feel if his revolver and hatchet were there, caught up his cudgel and laid it across his knees—then sat quietly, waiting. Was it Black Jack, or someone even worse? Forced to do something to brace his nerves, he puckered his stiffening lips and began whistling a tune he had led in his clear tenor every year of his life at the Home Christmas exercises.

"Who comes this way, so blithe and gay,
Upon a merry Christmas day?"

His quick Irish wit roused to the ridiculousness of it until he broke into a laugh that steadied him amazingly.

Through the bushes he caught a glimpse of the oncoming figure. His heart flooded with joy, for it was a man from the gang. Wessner had been his bunk-mate the night he came down the corduroy. He knew him as well as any of McLean's men. This was no timber-thief. No doubt the Boss had sent him with a message. Freckles sprang up and called cheerily, a warm welcome on his face.

"Well, it's good telling if you're glad to see me," said Wessner, with something very like a breath of relief. "We been hearing down at the camp you were so mighty touchy you didn't allow a man within a rod of the line."

"No more do I," answered Freckles, "if he's a stranger, but you're from McLean, ain't you?"

"Oh, damn McLean!" said Wessner.

Freckles gripped the cudgel until his knuckles slowly turned purple.

"And are you railly saying so?" he inquired with elaborate politeness.

"Yes, I am," said Wessner. "So would every man of the gang if they wasn't too big cowards to say anything, unless maybe that other slobbering old Scotchman, Duncan. Grinding the lives out of us! Working us like dogs, and paying us starvation wages, while he rolls up his millions and lives like a prince!"

Green lights began to play through the gray of Freckles's eyes.

"Wessner," he said impressively, "you'd make a fine pattern for the father of liars! Every man on that gang is strong and hilthy, paid all he earns, and treated with the courtesy of a gentleman! As for the Boss living like a prince, he shares fair with you every day of your lives!"

Wessner was not a born diplomat, but he saw he was on the wrong tack, so he tried another.

"How would you like to make a good big pile of money, without even lifting your hand?" he asked.

"Humph!" said Freckles. "Have you been up to Chicago and cornered wheat, and are you offering me a friendly tip on the invistment of me fortune?"

Wessner came close.

"Freckles, old fellow," he said, "if you let me give you a pointer, I can put you on to making a cool five hundred without stepping out of your tracks."

Freckles drew back.

"You needn't be afraid of speaking up," he said. "There isn't a soul in the Limberlost save the birds and the beasts, unless some of your sort's come along and's crowding the privileges of the legal tinints."

"None of my friends along," said Wessner. "Nobody knew I came but Black, I—I mean a friend of mine. If you want to hear sense and act with reason, he can see you later, but it ain't necessary. We can make all the plans needed. The trick's so dead small and easy."

"Must be if you have the engineering of it," said Freckles. But he heard, with a sigh of relief, that they were alone.

Wessner was impervious. "You just bet it is! Why, only think, Freckles, slavin' away at a measly little thirty dollars a month, and here is a chance to clear five hundred in a day! You surely won't be the fool to miss it!"

"And how was you proposing for me to stale it?" inquired Freckles. "Or am I just to find it laying in me path beside the line?"

"That's it, Freckles," blustered the Dutchman, "you're just to find it. You needn't do a thing. You needn't know a thing. You name a morning when you will walk up the west side of the swamp and then turn round and walk back down the same side again and the money is yours. Couldn't anything be easier than that, could it?"

"Depinds entirely on the man," said Freckles. The lilt of a lark hanging above the swale beside them was not sweeter than the sweetness of his voice. "To some it would seem to come aisy as breathing; and to some, wringin' the last drop of their heart's blood couldn't force thim! I'm not the man that goes into a scheme like that with the blindfold over me eyes, for, you see, it manes to break trust with

41

the Boss; and I've served him faithful as I knew. You'll have to be making the thing very clear to me understanding."

"It's so dead easy," repeated Wessner, "it makes me tired of the simpleness of it. You see there's a few trees in the swamp that's real gold mines. There's three especial. Two are back in, but one's square on the line. Why, your pottering old Scotch fool of a Boss nailed the wire to it with his own hands! He never noticed where the bark had been peeled, or saw what it was. If you will stay on this side of the trail just one day we can have it cut, loaded, and ready to drive out at night. Next morning you can find it, report, and be the busiest man in the search for us. We know where to fix it all safe and easy. Then McLean has a bet up with a couple of the gang that there can't be a raw stump found in the Limberlost. There's plenty of witnesses to swear to it, and I know three that will. There's a cool thousand, and this tree is worth all of that, raw. Say, it's a gold mine, I tell you, and just five hundred of it is yours. There's no danger on earth to you, for you've got McLean that bamboozled you could sell out the whole swamp and he'd never mistrust you. What do you say?"

Freckles's soul was satisfied. "Is that all?" he asked.

"No, it ain't," said Wessner. "If you really want to brace up and be a man and go into the thing for keeps, you can make five times that in a week. My friend knows a dozen others we could get out in a few days, and all you'd have to do would be to keep out of sight. Then you could take your money and skip some night, and begin life like a gentleman somewhere else. What do you think about it?"

Freckles purred like a kitten.

"'Twould be a rare joke on the Boss," he said, "to be stalin' from him the very thing he's trusted me to guard, and be getting me wages all winter throwed in free. And you're making the pay awful high. Me to be getting five hundred for such a simple little thing as that. You're trating me most royal indade! It's away beyond all I'd be expecting. Sivinteen cints would be a big price for that job. It must be looked into thorough. Just you wait here until I do a minute's turn in the swamp, and then I'll be eschorting you out of the clearing and giving you the answer."

Freckles lifted the overhanging bushes and hurried to the case. He unslung the specimen-box and laid it inside with his hatchet and revolver. He slipped the key in his pocket and went back to Wessner.

"Now for the answer," he said. "Stand up!"

There was iron in his voice, and he was commanding as an outraged general. "Anything, you want to be taking off?" he questioned.

Wessner looked the astonishment he felt. "Why, no, Freckles," he said.

"Have the goodness to be calling me Mister McLean," snapped Freckles. "I'm after resarvin' me pet name for the use of me friends! You may stand with your back to the light or be taking any advantage you want."

"Why, what do you mean?" spluttered Wessner.

"I'm manin'," said Freckles tersely, "to lick a quarter-section of hell out of you, and may the Holy Vargin stay me before I leave you here carrion, for your carcass would turn the stummicks of me chickens!"

At the camp that morning, Wessner's conduct had been so palpable an excuse to force a discharge that Duncan moved near McLean and whispered, "Think of the boy, sir?"

McLean was so troubled that, an hour later, he mounted Nellie and followed Wessner to his home in Wildcat Hollow, only to find that he had left there shortly before, heading for the Limberlost. McLean rode at top speed. When Mrs. Duncan told him that a man answering Wessner's description had gone down the west side of the swamp close noon, he left the mare in her charge and followed on foot. When he heard voices he entered the swamp and silently crept close just in time to hear Wessner whine: "But I can't fight you, Freckles. I hain't done nothing to you. I'm away bigger than you, and you've only one hand."

The Boss slid off his coat and crouched among the bushes, ready to spring; but as Freckles's voice reached him he held himself, with a strong effort, to learn what mettle was in the boy.

"Don't you be wasting of me good time in the numbering of me hands," cried Freckles. "The stringth of me cause will make up for the weakness of me mimbers, and the size of a cowardly thief doesn't count. You'll think all the wildcats of the Limberlost are turned loose on you whin I come against you, and as for me cause—I slept with you, Wessner, the night I came down the corduroy like a dirty, friendless tramp, and the Boss was for taking me up, washing, clothing, and feeding me, and giving me a home full of love and tinderness, and a master to look to, and good, well-earned money in the bank. He's trusting me his heartful, and here comes you, you spotted toad of the big road, and insults me, as is an honest Irish gintleman, by hinting that you concaive I'd be willing to shut me eyes and hold fast while you rob him of the thing I was set and paid to guard, and then act the sneak and liar to him, and ruin and eternally blacken the soul of me. You damned rascal," raved Freckles, "be fighting before I forget the laws of a gintlemin's game and split your dirty head with me stick!"

Wessner backed away, mumbling, "But I don't want to hurt you, Freckles!"

"Oh, don't you!" raged the boy, now fairly frothing. "Well, you ain't resembling me none, for I'm itching like death to git me fingers in the face of you."

He danced up, and as Wessner lunged in self-defense, ducked under his arm as a bantam and punched him in the pit of the stomach so that he doubled with a groan. Before Wessner could straighten himself, Freckles was on him, fighting like the wildest fury that ever left the beautiful island. The Dutchman dealt thundering blows that sometimes landed and sent Freckles reeling, and sometimes missed, while he went plunging into the swale with the impetus of them. Freckles could not strike with half Wessner's force, but he could land three blows to the Dutchman's one. It was here that the boy's days of alert watching on the line, the perpetual swinging of the heavy cudgel, and the endurance of all weather stood him in good stead; for he was tough, and agile. He skipped, ducked, and dodged. For the first five minutes he endured fearful punishment. Then Wessner's breath commenced to whistle between his teeth, when Freckles only had begun fighting. He sprang back with shrill laughter.

"Begolly! and will your honor be whistling the hornpipe for me to be dancing of?" he cried.

SPANG! went his fist into Wessner's face, and he was past him into the swale.

"And would you be pleased to tune up a little livelier?" he gasped, and clipped his ear as he sprang back. Wessner lunged at him in blind fury. Freckles, seeing an opening, forgot the laws of a gentleman's game and drove the toe of his heavy wading-boot in Wessner's middle until he doubled and fell heavily. In a flash Freckles was on him. For a time McLean could not see what was happening. "Go! Go to him now!" he commanded himself, but so intense was his desire to see the boy win alone that he did not stir.

At last Freckles sprang up and backed away. "Time!" he yelled as a fury. "Be getting up, Mr. Wessner, and don't be afraid of hurting me. I'll let you throw in an extra hand and lick you to me complate satisfaction all the same. Did you hear me call the limit? Will you get up and be facing me?"

As Wessner struggled to his feet, he resembled a battlefield, for his clothing was in ribbons and his face and hands streaming blood.

"I—I guess I got enough," he mumbled.

"Oh, you do?" roared Freckles. "Well this ain't your say. You come on to me ground, lying about me Boss and intimatin' I'd stale from his very pockets. Now will you be standing up and taking your medicine like a man, or getting it poured down the throat of you like a baby? I ain't got enough! This is only just the beginning with me. Be looking out there!"

He sprang against Wessner and sent him rolling. He attacked the unresisting figure and fought him until he lay limp and quiet and Freckles had no strength left to lift an arm. Then he arose and stepped back, gasping for breath. With his first lungful of air he shouted: "Time!" But the figure of Wessner lay motionless.

Freckles watched him with regardful eye and saw at last that he was completely exhausted. He bent over him, and catching him by the back of the neck, jerked him to his knees. Wessner lifted the face of a whipped cur, and fearing further punishment, burst into shivering sobs, while the tears washed tiny rivulets through the blood and muck. Freckles stepped back, glaring at Wessner, but suddenly the scowl of anger and the ugly disfiguring red faded from the boy's face. He dabbed at a cut on his temple from which issued a tiny crimson stream, and jauntily shook back his hair. His face took on the innocent look of a cherub, and his voice rivaled that of a brooding dove, but into his eyes crept a look of diabolical mischief.

He glanced vaguely around him until he saw his club, seized and twirled it as a drum major, stuck it upright in the muck, and marched on tiptoe to Wessner, mechanically, as a puppet worked by a string. Bending over, Freckles reached an arm around Wessner's waist and helped him to his feet.

"Careful, now," he cautioned, "be careful, Freddy; there's danger of you hurting me."

Drawing a handkerchief from a back pocket, Freckles tenderly wiped Wessner's eyes and nose.

"Come, Freddy, me child," he admonished Wessner, "it's time little boys were going home. I've me work to do, and can't be entertaining you any more today. Come back tomorrow, if you ain't through yet, and we'll repate the perfarmance. Don't be staring at me so wild like! I would eat you, but I can't afford it. Me earnings, being honest, come slow, and I've no money to be squanderin' on the pailful of Dyspeptic's Delight it would be to taking to work you out of my innards!"

Again an awful wrenching seized McLean. Freckles stepped back as Wessner, tottering and reeling, as a thoroughly drunken man, came toward the path, appearing indeed as if wildcats had attacked him.

The cudgel spun high in air, and catching it with an expertness acquired by long practice on the line, the boy twirled it a second, shook back his thick hair bonnily, and stepping into the trail, followed Wessner. Because Freckles was Irish, it was impossible to do it silently, so presently his clear tenor rang out, though there were bad catches where he was hard pressed for breath:

"It was the Dutch. It was the Dutch.
Do you think it was the Irish hollered help?
Not much!
It was the Dutch. It was the Dutch—"

Wessner turned and mumbled: "What you following me for? What are you going to do with me?"

Freckles called the Limberlost to witness: "How's that for the ingratitude of a beast? And me troubling mesilf to show him off me territory with the honors of war!"

Then he changed his tone completely and added: "Belike it's this, Freddy. You see, the Boss might come riding down this trail any minute, and the little mare's so wheedlesome that if she'd come on to you in your prisint state all of a sudden, she'd stop that short she'd send Mr. McLean out over the ears of her. No disparagement intinded to the sinse of the mare!" he added hastily.

Wessner belched a fearful oath, while Freckles laughed merrily.

"That's a sample of the thanks a generous act's always for getting," he continued. "Here's me neglictin' me work to eschort you out proper, and you saying such awful words Freddy," he demanded sternly, "do you want me to soap out your mouth? You don't seem to be realizing it, but if you was to buck into Mr. McLean in your prisint state, without me there to explain matters the chance is he'd cut the liver out of you; and I shouldn't think you'd be wanting such a fine gintleman as him to see that it's white!"

Wessner grew ghastly under his grime and broke into a staggering run.

"And now will you be looking at the manners of him?" questioned Freckles plaintively. "Going without even a 'thank you,' right in the face of all the pains I've taken to make it interesting for him!"

Freckles twirled the club and stood as a soldier at attention until Wessner left the clearing, but it was the last scene of that performance. When the boy turned, there was deathly illness on his face, while his legs wavered beneath his weight. He staggered to the case, and opening it he took out a piece of cloth. He dipped it into the water, and sitting on a bench, he wiped the blood and grime from his face, while his breath sucked between his clenched teeth. He was shivering with pain and excitement in spite of himself. He unbuttoned the band of his right sleeve, and turning it back, exposed the blue-lined, cal-loused whiteness of his maimed arm, now vividly streaked with contusions, while in a series of circular dots the blood oozed slowly. Here Wessner had succeeded in setting his teeth. When Freckles saw what it was he forgave himself the kick in the pit of Wessner's stomach, and cursed fervently and deep.

"Freckles, Freckles," said McLean's voice.

Freckles snatched down his sleeve and arose to his feet.

"Excuse me, sir," he said. "You'll surely be belavin' I thought meself alone."

McLean pushed him carefully to the seat, and bending over him, opened a pocket-case that he carried as regularly as his revolver and watch, for cuts and bruises were of daily occurrence among the gang.

Taking the hurt arm, he turned back the sleeve and bathed and bound the wounds. He examined Freckles's head and body and convinced himself that there was no permanent injury, although the cruelty of the punishment the boy had borne set the Boss shuddering. Then he closed the case, shoved it into his pocket, and sat beside Freckles. All the indescribable beauty of the place was strong around him, but he saw only the bruised face of the suffering boy, who had hedged for the information he wanted as a diplomat, argued as a judge, fought as a sheik, and triumphed as a devil.

When the pain lessened and breath relieved Freckles's pounding heart, he watched the Boss covertly. How had McLean gotten there and how long had he been there? Freckles did not dare ask. At last he arose, and going to the case, took out his revolver and the wire-mending apparatus and locked the door. Then he turned to McLean.

"Have you any orders, sir?" he asked.

"Yes," said McLean, "I have, and you are to follow them to the letter. Turn over that apparatus to me and go straight home. Soak yourself in the hottest bath your skin will bear and go to bed at once. Now hurry."

"Mr. McLean," said Freckles, "it's sorry I am to be telling you, but the afternoon's walking of the line ain't done. You see, I was just for getting to me feet to start, and I was on time, when up came a gintleman, and we got into a little heated argument. It's either settled, or it's just begun, but between us, I'm that late I haven't started for the afternoon yet. I must be going at once, for there's a tree I must find before the day's over."

"You plucky little idiot," growled McLean. "You can't walk the line! I doubt if you can reach Duncan's. Don't you know when you are done up? You go to bed; I'll finish your work."

"Niver!" protested Freckles. "I was just a little done up for the prisint, a minute ago. I'm all right now. Riding-boots are far too low. The day's hot and the walk a good seven miles, sir. Niver!"

As he reached for the outfit he pitched forward and his eyes closed. McLean stretched him on the moss and applied restoratives. When Freckles returned to consciousness, McLean ran to the cabin to tell Mrs. Duncan to have a hot bath ready, and to bring Nellie. That worthy woman promptly filled the wash-boiler, starting a roaring fire under it. She pushed the horse-trough from its base and rolled it to the kitchen.

47

By the time McLean came again, leading Nellie and holding Freckles on her back, Mrs. Duncan was ready for business. She and the Boss laid Freckles in the trough and poured on hot water until he squirmed. They soaked and massaged him. Then they drew off the hot water and closed his pores with cold. Lastly they stretched him on the floor and chafed, rubbed, and kneaded him until he cried out for mercy. As they rolled him into bed, his eyes dropped shut, but a little later they flared open.

"Mr. McLean," he cried, "the tree! Oh, do be looking after the tree!"

McLean bent over him. "Which tree, Freckles?"

"I don't know exact sir; but it's on the east line, and the wire is fastened to it. He bragged that you nailed it yourself, sir. You'll know it by the bark having been laid open to the grain somewhere low down. Five hundred dollars he offered me—to be—selling you out—sir!"

Freckles's head rolled over and his eyes dropped shut. McLean towered above the lad. His bright hair waved on the pillow. His face was swollen, and purple with bruises. His left arm, with the hand battered almost out of shape, stretched beside him, and the right, with no hand at all, lay across a chest that was a mass of purple welts. McLean's mind traveled to the night, almost a year before, when he had engaged Freckles, a stranger.

The Boss bent, covering the hurt arm with one hand and laying the other with a caress on the boy's forehead. Freckles stirred at his touch, and whispered as softly as the swallows under the eaves: "If you're coming this way—tomorrow—be pleased to step over—and we'll repate—the chorus softly!"

"Bless the gritty devil," muttered McLean.

Then he went out and told Mrs. Duncan to keep close watch on Freckles, also to send Duncan to him at the swamp the minute he came home. Following the trail to the line and back to the scent of the fight, the Boss entered Freckles's study quietly, as if his spirit, keeping there, might be roused, and gazed around with astonished eyes.

How had the boy conceived it? What a picture he had wrought in living colors! He had the heart of a painter. He had the soul of a poet. The Boss stepped carefully over the velvet carpet to touch the walls of crisp verdure with gentle fingers. He stood long beside the flower bed, and gazed at the banked wall of bright bloom as if he doubted its reality.

Where had Freckles ever found, and how had he transplanted such ferns? As McLean turned from them he stopped suddenly.

He had reached the door of the cathedral. That which Freckles had attempted would have been patent to anyone. What had been in the heart of the shy, silent boy when he had found that long, dim stretch of forest, decorated its entrance, cleared and smoothed its aisle, and carpeted its altar? What veriest work of God was in these mighty living pillars and the arched dome of green! How similar to stained cathedral windows were the long openings between the trees, filled with rifts of blue, rays of gold, and the shifting emerald of leaves! Where could be found mosaics to match this aisle paved with living color and glowing light? Was Freckles a devout Christian, and did he worship here? Or was he an untaught heathen, and down this vista of entrancing loveliness did Pan come piping, and dryads, nymphs, and fairies dance for him?

Who can fathom the heart of a boy? McLean had been thinking of Freckles as a creature of unswerving honesty, courage, and faithfulness. Here was evidence of a heart aching for beauty, art, companionship, worship. It was writ large all over the floor, walls, and furnishing of that little Limberlost clearing.

When Duncan came, McLean told him the story of the fight, and they laughed until they cried. Then they started around the line in search of the tree.

Said Duncan: "Now the boy is in for sore trouble!"

"I hope not," answered McLean. "You never in all your life saw a cur whipped so completely. He won't come back for the repetition of the chorus. We surely can find the tree. If we can't, Freckles can. I will bring enough of the gang to take it out at once. That will insure peace for a time, at least, and I am hoping that in a month more the whole gang may be moved here. It soon will be fall, and then, if he will go, I intend to send Freckles to my mother to be educated. With his quickness of mind and body and a few years' good help he can do anything. Why, Duncan, I'd give a hundred-dollar bill if you could have been here and seen for yourself."

"Yes, and I'd 'a' done murder," muttered the big teamster. "I hope, sir, ye will make good your plans for Freckles, though I'd as soon see ony born child o' my ain taken from our home. We love the lad, me and Sarah."

Locating the tree was easy, because it was so well identified. When the rumble of the big lumber wagons passing the cabin on the way to the swamp wakened Freckles next morning, he sprang up and was soon following them. He was so sore and stiff that every movement was torture at first, but he grew easier, and shortly did not suffer so much. McLean scolded him for coming, yet in his heart triumphed over every new evidence of fineness in the boy.

The tree was a giant maple, and so precious that they almost dug it out by the roots. When it was down, cut in lengths, and loaded, there was yet an empty wagon. As they were gathering up their tools to go, Duncan said: "There's a big hollow tree somewhere mighty close here that I've been wanting for a watering-trough for my stock; the one I have is so small. The Portland company cut this for elm butts last year, and it's six feet diameter and hollow for forty feet. It was a buster! While the men are here and there is an empty wagon, why mightn't I load it on and tak' it up to the barn as we pass?"

McLean said he was very willing, ordered the driver to break line and load the log, detailing men to assist. He told Freckles to ride on a section of the maple with him, but now the boy asked to enter the swamp with Duncan.

"I don't see why you want to go," said McLean. "I have no business to let you out today at all."

"It's me chickens," whispered Freckles in distress. "You see, I was just after finding yesterday, from me new book, how they do be nesting in hollow trees, and there ain't any too many in the swamp. There's just a chance that they might be in that one."

"Go ahead," said McLean. "That's a different story. If they happen to be there, why tell Duncan he must give up the tree until they have finished with it."

Then he climbed on a wagon and was driven away. Freckles hurried into the swamp. He was a little behind, yet he could see the men. Before he overtook them, they had turned from the west road and had entered the swamp toward the east.

They stopped at the trunk of a monstrous prostrate log. It had been cut three feet from the ground, over three-fourths of the way through, and had fallen toward the east, the body of the log still resting on the stump. The underbrush was almost impenetrable, but Duncan plunged in and with a crowbar began tapping along the trunk to decide how far it was hollow, so that they would know where to cut. As they waited his decision, there came from the mouth of it—on wings—a large black bird that swept over their heads.

Freckles danced wildly. "It's me chickens! Oh, it's me chickens!" he shouted. "Oh, Duncan, come quick! You've found the nest of me precious chickens!"

Duncan hurried to the mouth of the log, but Freckles was before him. He crashed through poison-vines and underbrush regardless of any danger, and climbed on the stump. When Duncan came he was shouting like a wild man.

"It's hatched!" he yelled. "Oh, me big chicken has hatched out me little chicken, and there's another egg. I can see it plain, and oh, the funny little white baby! Oh, Duncan, can you see me little white chicken?"

Duncan could easily see it; so could everyone else. Freckles crept into the log and tenderly carried the hissing, blinking little bird to the light in a leaf-lined hat. The men found it sufficiently wonderful to satisfy even Freckles, who had forgotten he was ever sore or stiff, and coddled over it with every blarneying term of endearment he knew.

Duncan gathered his tools. "Deal's off, boys!" he said cheerfully. "This log mauna be touched until Freckles's chaukies have finished with it. We might as weel gang. Better put it back, Freckles. It's just out, and it may chill. Ye will probably hae twa the morn."

Freckles crept into the log and carefully deposited the baby beside the egg. When he came back, he said: "I made a big mistake not to be bringing the egg out with the baby, but I was fearing to touch it. It's shaped like a hen's egg, and it's big as a turkey's, and the beautifulest blue—just splattered with big brown splotches, like me book said, precise. Bet you never saw such a sight as it made on the yellow of the rotten wood beside that funny leathery-faced little white baby."

"Tell you what, Freckles," said one of the teamsters. "Have you ever heard of this Bird Woman who goes all over the country with a camera and makes pictures? She made some on my brother Jim's place last summer, and Jim's so wild about them he quits plowing and goes after her about every nest he finds. He helps her all he can to take them, and then she gives him a picture. Jim's so proud of what he has he keeps them in the Bible. He shows them to everybody that comes, and brags about how he helped. If you're smart, you'll send for her and she'll come and make a picture just like life. If you help her, she will give you one. It would be uncommon pretty to keep, after your birds are gone. I dunno what they are. I never see their like before. They must be something rare. Any you fellows ever see a bird like that hereabouts?"

No one ever had.

"Well," said the teamster, "failing to get this log lets me off till noon, and I'm going to town. I go right past her place. I've a big notion to stop and tell her. If she drives straight back in the swamp on the west road, and turns east at this big sycamore, she can't miss finding the tree, even if Freckles ain't here to show her. Jim says her work is a credit to the State she lives in, and any man is a measly creature who isn't willing to help her all he can. My old daddy used to say that all there was to religion was doing to the other fellow what you'd want him to do to you, and if I was making a living taking bird pictures, seems to me I'd be mighty glad for a chance to take one like that. So I'll just stop and tell her, and by gummy! maybe she will give me a picture of the little white sucker for my trouble."

Freckles touched his arm.

"Will she be rough with it?" he asked.

"Government land! No!" said the teamster. "She's dead down on anybody that shoots a bird or tears up a nest. Why, she's half killing herself in all kinds of places and weather to teach people to love and protect the birds. She's that plum careful of them that Jim's wife says she has Jim a standin' like a big fool holding an ombrelly over them when they are young and tender until she gets a focus, whatever that is. Jim says there ain't a bird on his place that don't actually seem to like having her around after she has wheedled them a few days, and the pictures she takes nobody would ever believe who didn't stand by and see."

"Will you he sure to tell her to come?" asked Freckles.

Duncan slept at home that night. He heard Freckles slipping out early the next morning, but he was too sleepy to wonder why, until he came to do his morning chores. When he found that none of his stock was at all thirsty, and saw the water-trough brimming, he knew that the boy was trying to make up to him for the loss of the big trough that he had been so anxious to have.

"Bless his fool little hot heart!" said Duncan. "And him so sore it is tearing him to move for anything. Nae wonder he has us all loving him!"

Freckles was moving briskly, and his heart was so happy that he forgot all about the bruises. He hurried around the trail, and on his way down the east side he went to see the chickens. The mother bird was on the nest. He was afraid the other egg might be hatching, so he did not venture to disturb her. He made the round and reached his study early. He ate his lunch, but did not need to start on the second trip until the middle of the afternoon. He would have long hours to work on his flower bed, improve his study, and learn about his chickens. Lovingly he set his room in order and watered the flowers and carpet. He had chosen for his resting-place the coolest spot on the west side, where there was almost always a breeze; but today the heat was so intense that it penetrated even there.

"I'm mighty glad there's nothing calling me inside!" he said. "There's no bit of air stirring, and it will just be steaming. Oh, but it's luck Duncan found the nest before it got so unbearing hot! I might have missed it altogether. Wouldn't it have been a shame to lose that sight? The cunning little divil! When he gets to toddling down that log to meet me, won't he be a circus? Wonder if he'll be as graceful a performer afoot as his father and mother?"

The heat became more insistent. Noon came; Freckles ate his dinner and settled for an hour or two on a bench with a book.

Chapter 5

Wherein an Angel Materializes and a Man Worships

Perhaps there was a breath of sound—Freckles never afterward could remember—but for some reason he lifted his head as the bushes parted and the face of an angel looked between. Saints, nymphs, and fairies had floated down his cathedral aisle for him many times, with forms and voices of exquisite beauty.

Parting the wild roses at the entrance was beauty of which Freckles never had dreamed. Was it real or would it vanish as the other dreams? He dropped his book, and rising to his feet, went a step closer, gazing intently. This was real flesh and blood. It was in every way kin to the Limberlost, for no bird of its branches swung with easier grace than this dainty young thing rocked on the bit of morass on which she stood. A sapling beside her was not straighter or rounder than her slender form. Her soft, waving hair clung around her face from the heat, and curled over her shoulders. It was all of one piece with the gold of the sun that filtered between the branches. Her eyes were the deepest blue of the iris, her lips the reddest red of the foxfire, while her cheeks were exactly of the same satin as the wild rose petals caressing them. She was smiling at Freckles in perfect confidence, and she cried:

"Oh, I'm so delighted that I've found you!"

The wildly leaping heart of Freckles burst from his body and fell in the black swamp-muck at her feet with such a thud that he did not understand how she could avoid hearing. He really felt that if she looked down she would see.

Incredulous, he quavered: "An'—an' was you looking for me?"

"I hoped I might find you," said the Angel. "You see, I didn't do as I was told, and I'm lost. The Bird Woman said I should wait in the carriage until she came back. She's been gone hours. It's a perfect Turkish bath in there, and I'm all lumpy with mosquito bites. Just when I thought that I couldn't bear it another minute, along came the biggest Papilio Ajax you ever saw. I knew how pleased she'd be, so I ran after it. It flew so slow and so low that I thought a dozen times I had it.

Then all at once it went from sight above the trees, and I couldn't find my way back to save me. I think I've walked more than an hour. I have been mired to my knees. A thorn raked my arm until it is bleeding, and I'm so tired and warm."

She parted the bushes farther. Freckles saw that her blue cotton frock clung to her, limp with perspiration. It was torn across the breast. One sleeve hung open from shoulder to elbow. A thorn had torn her arm until it was covered with blood, and the gnats and mosquitoes were clustering around it. Her feet were in lace hose and low shoes. Freckles gasped. In the Limberlost in low shoes! He caught an armful of moss from his carpet and buried it in the ooze in front of her for a footing.

"Come out here so I can see where you are stepping. Quick, for the life of you!" he ordered.

She smiled on him indulgently.

"Why?" she inquired.

"Did anybody let you come here and not be telling you of the snakes?" urged Freckles.

"We met Mr. McLean on the corduroy, and he did say something about snakes, I believe. The Bird Woman put on leather leggings, and a nice, parboiled time she must be having! Worst dose I ever endured, and I'd nothing to do but swelter."

"Will you be coming out of there?" groaned Freckles.

She laughed as if it were a fine joke.

"Maybe if I'd be telling you I killed a rattler curled upon that same place you're standing, as long as me body and the thickness of me arm, you'd be moving where I can see your footing," he urged insistently.

"What a perfectly delightful little brogue you speak," she said. "My father is Irish, and half should be enough to entitle me to that much. 'Maybe—if I'd—be telling you,'" she imitated, rounding and accenting each word carefully.

Freckles was beginning to feel a wildness in his head. He had derided Wessner at that same hour yesterday. Now his own eyes were filling with tears.

"If you were understanding the danger!" he continued desperately.

"Oh, I don't think there is much!"

She tilted on the morass.

"If you killed one snake here, it's probably all there is near; and anyway, the Bird Woman says a rattlesnake is a gentleman and always gives warning before he strikes. I don't hear any rattling. Do you?"

"Would you be knowing it if you did?" asked Freckles, almost impatiently.

How the laugh of the young thing rippled!

"'Would I be knowing it?'" she mocked. "You should see the swamps of Michigan where they dump rattlers from the marl-dredgers three and four at a time!"

Freckles stood astounded. She did know. She was not in the least afraid. She was depending on a rattlesnake to live up to his share of the contract and rattle in time for her to move. The one characteristic an Irishman admires in a woman, above all others, is courage. Freckles worshiped anew. He changed his tactics.

"I'd be pleased to be receiving you at me front door," he said, "but as you have arrived at the back, will you come in and be seated?"

He waved toward a bench. The Angel came instantly.

"Oh, how lovely and cool!" she cried.

As she moved across his room, Freckles had difficult work to keep from falling on his knees; for they were very weak, while he was hard driven by an impulse to worship.

"Did you arrange this?" she asked.

"Yis," said Freckles simply.

"Someone must come with a big canvas and copy each side of it," she said. "I never saw anything so beautiful! How I wish I might remain here with you! I will, some day, if you will let me; but now, if you can spare the time, will you help me find the carriage? If the Bird Woman comes back and I am gone, she will be almost distracted."

"Did you come on the west road?" asked Freckles.

"I think so," she said. "The man who told the Bird Woman said that was the only place the wires were down. We drove away in, and it was dreadful—over stumps and logs, and we mired to the hubs. I suppose you know, though. I should have stayed in the carriage, but I was so tired. I never dreamed of getting lost. I suspect I will be scolded finely. I go with the Bird Woman half the time during the summer vacations. My father says I learn a lot more than I do at school, and get it straight. I never came within a smell of being lost before. I thought, at first, it was going to be horrid; but since I've found you, maybe it will be good fun after all."

Freckles was amazed to hear himself excusing: "It was so hot in there. You couldn't be expected to bear it for hours and not be moving. I can take you around the trail almost to where you were. Then you can sit in the carriage, and I will go find the Bird Woman."

"You'll be killed if you do! When she stays this long, it means that she has a focus on something. You see, when she has a focus, and lies in the weeds and water for hours, and the sun bakes her, and things crawl over her, and then someone comes along and scares her bird away just as she has it coaxed up—why, she kills them. If I melt, you won't go after her. She's probably blistered and half eaten up; but she never will quit until she is satisfied."

"Then it will be safer to be taking care of you," suggested Freckles.

"Now you're talking sense!" said the Angel.

"May I try to help your arm?" he asked.

"Have you any idea how it hurts?" she parried.

"A little," said Freckles.

"Well, Mr. McLean said we'd probably find his son here."

"His son!" cried Freckles.

"That's what he said. And that you would do anything you could for us; and that we could trust you with our lives. But I would have trusted you anyway, if I hadn't known a thing about you. Say, your father is rampaging proud of you, isn't he?"

"I don't know," answered the dazed Freckles.

"Well, call on me if you want reliable information. He's so proud of you he is all swelled up like the toad in Aesop's Fables. If you have ever had an arm hurt like this, and can do anything, why, for pity sake, do it!"

She turned back her sleeve, holding toward Freckles an arm of palest cameo, shaped so exquisitely that no sculptor could have chiseled it.

Freckles unlocked his case, and taking out some cotton cloth, he tore it in strips. Then he brought a bucket of the cleanest water he could find. She yielded herself to his touch as a baby, and he bathed away the blood and bandaged the ugly, ragged wound. He finished his surgery by lapping the torn sleeve over the cloth and binding it down with a piece of twine, with the Angel's help about the knots.

Freckles worked with trembling fingers and a face tense with earnestness.

"Is it feeling any better?" he asked.

"Oh, it's well now!" cried the Angel. "It doesn't hurt at all, any more."

"I'm mighty glad," said Freckles. "But you had best go and be having your doctor fix it right; the minute you get home."

"Oh, bother! A little scratch like that!" jeered the Angel. "My blood is perfectly pure. It will heal in three days."

"It's cut cruel deep. It might be making a scar," faltered Freckles, his eyes on the ground. "'Twould—'twould be an awful pity. A doctor might know something to prevent it."

"Why, I never thought of that!" exclaimed the Angel.

"I noticed you didn't," said Freckles softly. "I don't know much about it, but it seems as if most girls would."

The Angel thought intently, while Freckles still knelt beside her. Suddenly she gave herself an impatient little shake, lifted her glorious eyes full to his, and the smile that swept her sweet, young face was the loveliest thing that Freckles ever had seen.

"Don't let's bother about it," she proposed, with the faintest hint of a confiding gesture toward him. "It won't make a scar. Why, it couldn't, when you have dressed it so nicely."

The velvety touch of her warm arm was tingling in Freckles's fingertips. Dainty lace and fine white ribbon peeped through her torn dress. There were beautiful rings on her fingers. Every article she wore was of the finest material and in excellent taste. There was the trembling Limberlost guard in his coarse clothing, with his cotton rags and his old pail of swamp water. Freckles was sufficiently accustomed to contrasts to notice them, and sufficiently fine to be hurt by them always.

He lifted his eyes with a shadowy pain in them to hers, and found them of serene, unconscious purity. What she had said was straight from a kind, untainted, young heart. She meant every word of it. Freckles's soul sickened. He scarcely knew whether he could muster strength to stand.

"We must go and hunt for the carriage," said the Angel, rising.

In instant alarm for her, Freckles sprang up, grasped the cudgel, and led the way, sharply watching every step. He went as close the log as he felt that he dared, and with a little searching found the carriage. He cleared a path for the Angel, and with a sigh of relief saw her enter it safely. The heat was intense. She pushed the damp hair from her temples.

"This is a shame!" said Freckles. "You'll never be coming here again."

"Oh yes I shall!" said the Angel. "The Bird Woman says that these birds remain over a month in the nest and she would like to make a picture every few days for seven or eight weeks, perhaps."

Freckles barely escaped crying aloud for joy.

"Then don't you ever be torturing yourself and your horse to be coming in here again," he said. "I'll show you a way to drive almost to the nest on the east trail, and then you can come around to my room and stay while the Bird Woman works. It's nearly always cool there, and there's comfortable seats, and water."

"Oh! did you have drinking-water there?" she cried. "I was never so thirsty or so hungry in my life, but I thought I wouldn't mention it."

"And I had not the wit to be seeing!" wailed Freckles. "I can be getting you a good drink in no time."

He turned to the trail.

"Please wait a minute," called the Angel. "What's your name? I want to think about you while you are gone." Freckles lifted his face with the brown rift across it and smiled quizzically.

"Freckles?" she guessed, with a peal of laughter. "And mine is—"

"I'm knowing yours," interrupted Freckles.

"I don't believe you do. What is it?" asked the girl.

"You won't be getting angry?"

"Not until I've had the water, at least."

It was Freckles's turn to laugh. He whipped off his big, floppy straw hat, stood uncovered before her, and said, in the sweetest of all the sweet tones of his voice: "There's nothing you could be but the Swamp Angel."

The girl laughed happily.

Once out of her sight, Freckles ran every step of the way to the cabin. Mrs. Duncan gave him a small bucket of water, cool from the well. He carried it in the crook of his right arm, and a basket filled with bread and butter, cold meat, apple pie, and pickles, in his left hand.

"Pickles are kind o' cooling," said Mrs. Duncan.

Then Freckles ran again.

The Angel was on her knees, reaching for the bucket, as he came up.

"Be drinking slow," he cautioned her.

"Oh!" she cried, with a long breath of satisfaction. "It's so good! You are more than kind to bring it!"

Freckles stood blinking in the dazzling glory of her smile until he scarcely could see to lift the basket.

"Mercy!" she exclaimed. "I think I had better be naming you the 'Angel.' My Guardian Angel."

"Yis," said Freckles. "I look the character every day—but today most emphatic!"

"Angels don't go by looks," laughed the girl. "Your father told us you had been scrapping. But he told us why. I'd gladly wear all your cuts and bruises if I could do anything that would make my father look as peacocky as yours did. He strutted about proper. I never saw anyone look prouder."

"Did he say he was proud of me?" marveled Freckles.

"He didn't need to," answered the Angel. "He was radiating pride from every pore. Now, have you brought me your dinner?"

"I had my dinner two hours ago," answered Freckles.

"Honest Injun?" bantered the Angel.

"Honest! I brought that on purpose for you."

"Well, if you knew how hungry I am, you would know how thankful I am, to the dot," said the Angel.

"Then you be eating," cried the happy Freckles.

The Angel sat on a big camera, spread the lunch on the carriage seat, and divided it in halves. The daintiest parts she could select she carefully put back into the basket. The remainder she ate. Again Freckles found her of the swamp, for though she was almost ravenous, she managed her food as gracefully as his little yellow fellow, and her every movement was easy and charming. As he watched her with famished eyes, Freckles told her of his birds, flowers, and books, and never realized what he was doing.

He led the horse to a deep pool that he knew of, and the tortured creature drank greedily, and lovingly rubbed him with its nose as he wiped down its welted body with grass. Suddenly the Angel cried: "There comes the Bird Woman!"

Freckles had intended leaving before she came, but now he was glad indeed to be there, for a warmer, more worn, and worse bitten creature he never had seen. She was staggering under a load of cameras and paraphernalia. Freckles ran to her aid. He took all he could carry of her load, stowed it in the back of the carriage, and helped her in. The Angel gave her water, knelt and unfastened the leggings, bathed her face, and offered the lunch.

Freckles brought the horse. He was not sure about the harness, but the Angel knew, and soon they left the swamp. Then he showed them how to reach the chicken tree from the outside, indicated a cooler place for the horse, and told them how, the next time they came, the Angel could find his room while she waited.

The Bird Woman finished her lunch, and lay back, almost too tired to speak.

"Were you for getting Little Chicken's picture?" Freckles asked.

"Finely!" she answered. "He posed splendidly. But I couldn't do anything with his mother. She will require coaxing."

"The Lord be praised!" muttered Freckles under his breath.

The Bird Woman began to feel better.

"Why do you call the baby vulture 'Little Chicken'?" she asked, leaning toward Freckles in an interested manner.

"'Twas Duncan began it," said Freckles. "You see, through the fierce cold of winter the birds of the swamp were almost starving. It is mighty lonely here, and they were all the company I was having. I got to carrying scraps and grain down to them. Duncan was that ginerous he was giving me of his wheat and corn from his chickens' feed, and he called the birds me swamp chickens. Then when these big black fellows came, Mr. McLean said they were our nearest kind to some in the old world that they called 'Pharaoh's Chickens,' and he called mine 'Freckles's Chickens.'"

"Good enough!" cried the Bird Woman, her splotched purple face lighting with interest. "You must shoot something for them occasionally, and I'll bring more food when I come. If you will help me keep them until I get my series, I'll give you a copy of each study I make, mounted in a book."

Freckles drew a deep breath.

"I'll be doing me very best," he promised, and from the deeps he meant it.

"I wonder if that other egg is going to hatch?" mused the Bird Woman. "I am afraid not. It should have pipped today. Isn't it a beauty! I never before saw either an egg or the young. They are rare this far north."

"So Mr. McLean said," answered Freckles.

Before they drove away, the Bird Woman thanked him for his kindness to the Angel and to her. She gave him her hand at parting, and Freckles joyfully realized that this was going to be another person for him to love. He could not remember, after they had driven away, that they even had noticed his missing hand, and for the first time in his life he had forgotten it.

When the Bird Woman and the Angel were on the home road, she told of the little corner of paradise into which she had strayed and of her new name. The Bird Woman looked at the girl and guessed its appropriateness.

"Did you know Mr. McLean had a son?" asked the Angel. "Isn't the little accent he has, and the way he twists a sentence, too dear? And isn't it too old-fashioned and funny to hear him call his father 'mister'?"

"It sounds too good to be true," said the Bird Woman, answering the last question first. "I am so tired of these present-day young men who patronizingly call their fathers 'Dad,' 'Governor,' 'Old Man,' and 'Old Chap,' that the boy's attitude of respect and deference appealed to me as being fine as silk. There must be something rare about that young man."

She did not find it necessary to tell the Angel that for several years she had known the man who so proudly proclaimed himself Freckles's father to be a bachelor and a Scotchman. The Bird Woman had a fine way of attending strictly to her own business.

Freckles turned to the trail, but he stopped at every wild brier to study the pink satin of the petals. She was not of his world, and better than any other he knew it; but she might be his Angel, and he was dreaming of naught but blind, silent worship. He finished the happiest day of his life, and that night he returned to the swamp as if drawn by invisible force. That Wessner would try for his revenge, he knew. That he would be abetted by Black Jack was almost certain, but fear had fled the happy heart of Freckles. He had kept his trust. He had won the respect of the Boss. No one ever could wipe from his heart the flood of holy adoration that had welled with the coming of his Angel. He would do his best, and trust for strength to meet the dark day of reckoning that he knew would come sooner or later. He swung round the trail, briskly tapping the wire, and singing in a voice that scarcely could have been surpassed for sweetness.

At the edge of the clearing he came into the bright moonlight and there sat McLean on his mare. Freckles hurried to him.

"Is there trouble?" he inquired anxiously.

"That's what I wanted to ask you," said the Boss. "I stopped at the cabin to see you a minute, before I turned in, and they said you had come down here. You must not do it, Freckles. The swamp is none too healthful at any time, and at night it is rank poison."

Freckles stood combing his fingers through Nellie's mane, while the dainty creature was twisting her head for his caresses. He pushed back his hat and looked into McLean's face. "It's come to the 'sleep with one eye open,' sir. I'm not looking for anything to be happening for a week or two, but it's bound to come, and soon. If I'm to keep me trust as I've promised you and meself, I've to live here mostly until the gang comes. You must be knowing that, sir."

"I'm afraid it's true, Freckles," said McLean. "And I've decided to double the guard until we come. It will be only a few weeks, now; and I'm so anxious for you that you must not be left alone further. If anything should happen to you, Freckles, it would spoil one of the very dearest plans of my life."

Freckles heard with dismay the proposition to place a second guard.

"Oh! no, no, Mr. McLean," he cried. "Not for the world! I wouldn't be having a stranger around, scaring me birds and tramping up me study, and disturbing all me ways, for any money! I am all the guard you need! I will be faithful! I will turn over the lease with no tree missing—on me life, I will! Oh, don't be sending another man to set them saying I turned coward and asked for help. It will just kill the honor of me heart if you do it. The only thing I want is another gun. If it railly comes to trouble, six cartridges ain't many, and you know I am slow-like about reloading." McLean reached into his hip pocket and handed a shining big revolver to Freckles, who slipped it beside the one already in his belt.

Then the Boss sat brooding.

"Freckles," he said at last, "we never know the timber of a man's soul until something cuts into him deeply and brings the grain out strong. You've the making of a mighty fine piece of furniture, my boy, and you shall have your own way these few weeks yet. Then, if you will go, I intend to take you to the city and educate you, and you are to be my son, my lad—my own son!"

Freckles twisted his finger in Nellie's mane to steady himself.

"But why should you be doing that, sir?" he faltered.

McLean slid his arm around the boy's shoulder and gathered him close.

"Because I love you, Freckles," he said simply.

Freckles lifted a white face. "My God, sir!" he whispered. "Oh, my God!"

McLean tightened his clasp a second longer, then he rode down the trail.

Freckles lifted his hat and faced the sky. The harvest moon looked down, sheeting the swamp in silver glory. The Limberlost sang her night song. The swale softly rustled in the wind. Winged things of night brushed his face; and still Freckles gazed upward, trying to fathom these things that had come to him. There was no help from the sky. It seemed far away, cold, and blue. The earth, where flowers blossomed, angels walked, and love could be found, was better. But to One, above, he must make acknowledgment for these miracles. His lips moved and he began talking softly.

"Thank You for each separate good thing that has come to me," he said, "and above all for the falling of the feather. For if it didn't really fall from an angel, its falling brought an Angel, and if it's in the great heart of you to exercise yourself any further about me, oh, do please to be taking good care of her!"

Chapter 6

Wherein a Fight Occurs and
Women Shoot Straight

The following morning Freckles, inexpressibly happy, circled the Limberlost. He kept snatches of song ringing, as well as the wires. His heart was so full that tears of joy glistened in his eyes. He rigorously strove to divide his thought evenly between McLean and the Angel. He realized to the fullest the debt he already owed the Boss and the magnitude of last night's declaration and promises. He was hourly planning to deliver his trust and then enter with equal zeal on whatever task his beloved Boss saw fit to set him next. He wanted to be ready to meet every device that Wessner and Black Jack could think of to outwit him. He recognized their double leverage, for if they succeeded in felling even one tree McLean became liable for his wager.

Freckles's brow wrinkled in his effort to think deeply and strongly, but from every swaying wild rose the Angel beckoned to him. When he crossed Sleepy Snake Creek and the goldfinch, waiting as ever, challenged: "SEE ME?" Freckles saw the dainty swaying grace of the Angel instead. What is a man to do with an Angel who dismembers herself and scatters over a whole swamp, thrusting a vivid reminder upon him at every turn?

Freckles counted the days. This first one he could do little but test his wires, sing broken snatches, and dream; but before the week would bring her again he could do many things. He would carry all his books to the swamp to show to her. He would complete his flower bed, arrange every detail he had planned for his room, and make of it a bower fairies might envy. He must devise a way to keep water cool. He would ask Mrs. Duncan for a double lunch and an especially nice one the day of her next coming, so that if the Bird Woman happened to be late, the Angel might not suffer from thirst and hunger. He would tell her to bring heavy leather leggings, so that he might take her on a trip around the trail. She should make friends with all of his chickens and see their nests.

On the line he talked of her incessantly.

"You needn't be thinking," he said to the goldfinch, "that because I'm coming down this line alone day after day, it's always to be so. Some of these times you'll be swinging on this wire, and you'll see me coming, and you'll swing, skip, and flirt yourself around, and chip up right spunky: 'SEE ME?' I'll be saying 'See you? Oh, Lord! See her!' You'll look, and there she'll stand. The sunshine won't look gold any more, or the roses pink, or the sky blue, because she'll be the pinkest, bluest, goldest thing of all. You'll be yelling yourself hoarse with the jealousy of her. The sawbird will stretch his neck out of joint, and she'll turn the heads of all the flowers. Wherever she goes, I can go back afterward and see the things she's seen, walk the path she's walked, hear the grasses whispering over all she's said; and if there's a place too swampy for her bits of feet; Holy Mother! Maybe—maybe she'd be putting the beautiful arms of her around me neck and letting me carry her over!"

Freckles shivered as with a chill. He sent the cudgel whirling skyward, dexterously caught it, and set it spinning.

"You damned presumptuous fool!" he cried. "The thing for you to be thinking of would be to stretch in the muck for the feet of her to be walking over, and then you could hold yourself holy to be even of that service to her.

"Maybe she'll be wanting the cup me blue-and-brown chickens raised their babies in. Perhaps she'd like to stop at the pool and see me bullfrog that had the goodness to take on human speech to show me the way out of me trouble. If there's any feathers falling that day, why, it's from the wings of me chickens—it's sure to be, for the only Angel outside the gates will be walking this timberline, and every step of the way I'll be holding me breath and praying that she don't unfold wings and sail away before the hungry eyes of me."

So Freckles dreamed his dreams, made his plans, and watched his line. He counted not only the days, but the hours of each day. As he told them off, every one bringing her closer, he grew happier in the prospect of her coming. He managed daily to leave some offering at the big elm log for his black chickens. He slipped under the line at every passing, and went to make sure that nothing was molesting them. Though it was a long trip, he paid them several extra visits a day for fear a snake, hawk, or fox might have found the baby. For now his chickens not only represented all his former interest in them, but they furnished the inducement that was bringing his Angel.

Possibly he could find other subjects that the Bird Woman wanted. The teamster had said that his brother went after her every time he found a nest. He never had counted the nests that he knew of, and it might be that among all the birds of the swamp some would be rare to her.

The feathered folk of the Limberlost were practically undisturbed save by their natural enemies. It was very probable that among his chickens others as odd as the big black ones could be found. If she wanted pictures of half-grown birds, he could pick up fifty in one morning's trip around the line, for he had fed, handled, and made friends with them ever since their eyes opened.

He had gathered bugs and worms all spring as he noticed them on the grass and bushes, and dropped them into the first little open mouth he had found. The babies gladly had accepted this queer tri-parent addition to their natural providers.

When the week had passed, Freckles had his room crisp and glowing with fresh living things that represented every color of the swamp. He carried bark and filled all the muckiest places of the trail.

It was middle July. The heat of the past few days had dried the water around and through the Limberlost, so that it was possible to cross it on foot in almost any direction—if one had an idea of direction and did not become completely lost in its rank tangle of vegetation and bushes. The brighter-hued flowers were opening. The trumpet-creepers were flaunting their gorgeous horns of red and gold sweetness from the tops of lordly oak and elm, and below entire pools were pink-sheeted in mallow bloom.

The heat was doing one other thing that was bound to make Freckles, as a good Irishman, shiver. As the swale dried, its inhabitants were seeking the cooler depths of the swamp. They liked neither the heat nor leaving the field mice, moles, and young rabbits of their chosen location. He saw them crossing the trail every day as the heat grew intense. The rattlers were sadly forgetting their manners, for they struck on no provocation whatever, and did not even remember to rattle afterward. Daily Freckles was compelled to drive big black snakes and blue racers from the nests of his chickens. Often the terrified squalls of the parent birds would reach him far down the line and he would run to rescue the babies.

He saw the Angel when the carriage turned from the corduroy into the clearing. They stopped at the west entrance to the swamp, waiting for him to precede them down the trail, as he had told them it was safest for the horse that he should do. They followed the east line to a point opposite the big chickens' tree, and Freckles carried in the cameras and showed the Bird Woman a path he had cleared to the log. He explained to her the effect the heat was having on the snakes, and creeping back to Little Chicken, brought him to the light. As she worked at setting up her camera, he told her of the birds of the line, while she stared at him, wide-eyed and incredulous.

They arranged that Freckles should drive the carriage into the east entrance in the shade and then take the horse toward the north to a better place he knew.

Then he was to entertain the Angel at his study or on the line until the Bird Woman finished her work and came to them.

"This will take only a little time," she said. "I know where to set the camera now, and Little Chicken is big enough to be good and too small to run away or to act very ugly, so I will be coming soon to see about those nests. I have ten plates along, and I surely won't use more than two on him; so perhaps I can get some nests or young birds this morning."

Freckles almost flew, for his dream had come true so soon. He was walking the timber-line and the Angel was following him. He asked to be excused for going first, because he wanted to be sure the trail was safe for her. She laughed at his fears, telling him that it was the polite thing for him to do, anyway.

"Oh!" said Freckles, "So you was after knowing that? Well, I didn't s'pose you did, and I was afraid you'd think me wanting in respect to be preceding you!"

The astonished Angel looked at him, caught the irrepressible gleam of Irish fun in his eyes, so they stood and laughed together.

Freckles did not realize how he was talking that morning. He showed her many of the beautiful nests and eggs of the line. She could identify a number of them, but of some she was ignorant, so they made notes of the number and color of the eggs, material, and construction of nest, color, size, and shape of the birds, and went to find them in the book.

At his room, when Freckles had lifted the overhanging bushes and stepped back for her to enter, his heart was all out of time and place. The study was vastly more beautiful than a week previous. The Angel drew a deep breath and stood gazing first at one side, then at another, then far down the cathedral aisle. "It's just fairyland!" she cried ecstatically. Then she turned and stared at Freckles as she had at his handiwork.

"What are you planning to be?" she asked wonderingly.

"Whatever Mr. McLean wants me to," he replied.

"What do you do most?" she asked.

"Watch me lines."

"I don't mean work!"

"Oh, in me spare time I keep me room and study in me books."

"Do you work on the room or the books most?"

"On the room only what it takes to keep it up, and the rest of the time on me books."

The Angel studied him closely. "Well, maybe you are going to be a great scholar," she said, "but you don't look it. Your face isn't right for that, but it's got something big in it—something really great. I must find out what it is and then you must work on it. Your father is expecting you to do something. One can tell by the way he talks. You should begin right away. You've wasted too much time already."

Poor Freckles hung his head. He never had wasted an hour in his life. There never had been one that was his to waste.

The Angel, studying him intently, read the thought in his face. "Oh, I don't mean that!" she cried, with the frank dismay of sixteen. "Of course, you're not lazy! No one ever would think that from your appearance. It's this I mean: there is something fine, strong, and full of power in your face. There is something you are to do in this world, and no matter how you work at all these other things, or how successfully you do them, it is all wasted until you find the ONE THING that you can do best. If you hadn't a thing in the world to keep you, and could go anywhere you please and do anything you want, what would you do?" persisted the Angel.

"I'd go to Chicago and sing in the First Episcopal choir," answered Freckles promptly.

The Angel dropped on a seat   the hat she had removed and held in her fingers rolled to her feet. "There!" she exclaimed vehemently. "You can see what I'm going to be. Nothing! Absolutely nothing! You can sing? Of course you can sing! It is written all over you."

"Anyone with half wit could have seen he could sing, without having to be told," she thought. "It's in the slenderness of his fingers and his quick nervous touch. It is in the brightness of his hair, the fire of his eyes, the breadth of his chest, the muscles of his throat and neck; and above all, it's in every tone of his voice, for even as he speak it's the sweetest sound I ever heard from the throat of a mortal."

"Will you do something for me?" she asked.

"I'll do anything in the world you want me to," said Freckles largely, "and if I can't do what you want, I'll go to work at once and I'll try 'til I can."

"Good! That's business!" said the Angel. "You go over there and stand before that hedge and sing something. Just anything you think of first."

Freckles faced the Angel from his banked wall of brown, blue, and crimson, with its background of solid green, and lifting his face to the sky, he sang the first thing that came into his mind. It was a children's song that he had led for the little folks at the Home many times, recalled to his mind by the Angel's exclamation:

> "To fairyland we go,
> With a song of joy, heigh-o.
> In dreams we'll stand upon that shore
> And all the realm behold;
> We'll see the sights so grand

That belong to fairyland,
Its mysteries we will explore,
Its beauties will unfold.

"Oh, tra, la, la, oh, ha, ha, ha!
We're happy now as we can be,
Our welcome song we will prolong,
And greet you with our melody.
O fairyland, sweet fairyland,
We love to sing—"

No song could have given the intense sweetness and rollicking quality of Freckles's voice better scope. He forgot everything but pride in his work. He was singing the chorus, and the Angel was shivering in ecstasy, when clip! clip! came the sharply beating feet of a swiftly ridden horse down the trail from the north. They both sprang toward the entrance.

"Freckles! Freckles!" called the voice of the Bird Woman.

They were at the trail on the instant.

"Both those revolvers loaded?" she asked.

"Yes," said Freckles.

"Is there a way you can cut across the swamp and reach the chicken tree in a few minutes, and with little noise?"

"Yes."

"Then go flying," said the Bird Woman. "Give the Angel a lift behind me, and we will ride the horse back where you left him and wait for you. I finished Little Chicken in no time and put him back. His mother came so close, I felt sure she would enter the log. The light was fine, so I set and focused the camera and covered it with branches, attached the long hose, and went away over a hundred feet and hid in some bushes to wait. A short, stout man and a tall, dark one passed me so closely I almost could have reached out and touched them. They carried a big saw on their shoulders. They said they could work until near noon, and then they must lay off until you passed and then try to load and get out at night. They went on—not entirely from sight—and began cutting a tree. Mr. McLean told me the other day what would probably happen here, and if they fell that tree he loses his wager on you. Keep to the east and north and hustle. We'll meet you at the carriage. I always am armed. Give Angel one of your revolvers, and you keep the other. We will separate and creep toward them from different sides and give them a fusillade that will send them flying. You hurry, now!"

She lifted the reins and started briskly down the trail. The Angel, hatless and with sparkling eyes, was clinging around her waist.

Freckles wheeled and ran. He worked his way with much care, dodging limbs and bushes with noiseless tread, and cutting as closely where he thought the men were as he felt that he dared if he were to remain unseen. As he ran he tried to think. It was Wessner, burning for his revenge, aided by the bully of the locality, that he was going to meet. He was accustomed to that thought but not to the complication of having two women on his hands who undoubtedly would have to be taken care of in spite of the Bird Woman's offer to help him. His heart was jarring as it never had before with running. He must follow the Bird Woman's plan and meet them at the carriage, but if they really did intend to try to help him, he must not allow it. Allow the Angel to try to handle a revolver in his defence? Never! Not for all the trees in the Limberlost! She might shoot herself. She might forget to watch sharply and run across a snake that was not particularly well behaved that morning. Freckles permitted himself a grim smile as he went speeding on.

When he reached the carriage, the Bird Woman and the Angel had the horse hitched, the outfit packed, and were calmly waiting. The Bird Woman held a revolver in her hand. She wore dark clothing. They had pinned a big focusing cloth over the front of the Angel's light dress.

"Give Angel one of your revolvers, quick!" said the Bird Woman. "We will creep up until we are in fair range. The underbrush is so thick and they are so busy that they will never notice us, if we don't make a noise. You fire first, then I will pop in from my direction, and then you, Angel, and shoot quite high, or else very low. We mustn't really hit them. We'll go close enough to the cowards to make it interesting, and keep it up until we have them going."

Freckles protested.

The Bird Woman reached over, and, taking the smaller revolver from his belt, handed it to the Angel. "Keep your nerve steady, dear; watch where you step, and shoot high," she said. "Go straight at them from where you are. Wait until you hear Freckles's first shot, then follow me as closely as you can, to let them know that we outnumber them. If you want to save McLean's wager on you, now you go!" she commanded Freckles, who, with an agonized glance at the Angel, ran toward the east.

The Bird Woman chose the middle distance, and for a last time cautioned the Angel as she moved away to lie down and shoot high.

Through the underbrush the Bird Woman crept even more closely than she had intended, found a clear range, and waited for Freckles's shot. There was one long minute of sickening suspense. The men straightened for breath. Work was difficult with a handsaw in the heat of the swamp. As they rested, the big dark fellow took a bottle from his pocket and began oiling the saw.

"We got to keep mighty quiet," he said, "and wait to fell it until that damned guard has gone to his dinner."

Again they bent to their work. Freckles's revolver spat fire. Lead spanged on steel. The saw-handle flew from Wessner's hand and he reeled from the jar of the shock. Black Jack straightened, uttering a fearful oath. The hat sailed from his head from the far northeast. The Angel had not waited for the Bird Woman, and her shot scarcely could have been called high. At almost the same instant the third shot whistled from the east. Black Jack sprang into the air with a yell of complete panic, for it ripped a heel from his boot. Freckles emptied his second chamber, and the earth spattered over Wessner. Shots poured in rapidly. Without even reaching for a weapon, both men ran toward the east road in great leaping bounds, while leaden slugs sung and hissed around them in deadly earnest.

Freckles was trimming his corners as closely as he dared, but if the Angel did not really intend to hit, she was taking risks in a scandalous manner.

When the men reached the trail, Freckles yelled at the top of his voice: "Head them off on the south, boys! Fire from the south!"

As he had hoped, Jack and Wessner instantly plunged into the swale. A spattering of lead followed them. They crossed the swale, running low, with not even one backward glance, and entered the woods beyond the corduroy.

Then the little party gathered at the tree.

"I'd better fix this saw so they can't be using it if they come back," said Freckles, taking out his hatchet and making saw-teeth fly.

"Now we must leave here without being seen," said the Bird Woman to the Angel. "It won't do for me to make enemies of these men, for I am likely to meet them while at work any day."

"You can do it by driving straight north on this road," said Freckles. "I will go ahead and cut the wires for you. The swale is almost dry. You will only be sinking a little. In a few rods you will strike a cornfield. I will take down the fence and let you into that. Follow the furrows and drive straight across it until you come to the other side. Be following the fence south until you come to a road through the woods east of it. Then take that road and follow east until you reach the pike. You will come out on your way back to town, and two miles north of anywhere they are likely to be. Don't for your lives ever let it out that you did this," he earnestly cautioned, "for it's black enemies you would be making."

Freckles clipped the wires and they drove through. The Angel leaned from the carriage and held out his revolver. Freckles looked at her in surprise.

Her eyes were black, while her face was a deeper rose than usual. He felt that his own was white.

"Did I shoot high enough?" she asked sweetly. "I really forgot about lying down."

Freckles winced. Did the child know how close she had gone? Surely she could not! Or was it possible that she had the nerve and skill to fire like that purposely?

"I will send the first reliable man I meet for McLean," said the Bird Woman, gathering up the lines. "If I don't meet one when we reach town, we will send a messenger. If it wasn't for having the gang see me, I would go myself; but I will promise you that you will have help in a little over two hours. You keep well hidden. They must think some of the gang is with you now. There isn't a chance that they will be back, but don't run any risks. Remain under cover. If they should come, it probably would be for their saw." She laughed as at a fine joke.

Chapter 7

Wherein Freckles Wins Honor and Finds a Footprint on the Trail

Round-eyed, Freckles watched the Bird Woman and the Angel drive away. After they were from sight and he was safely hidden among the branches of a small tree, he remembered that he neither had thanked them nor said good-bye. Considering what they had been through, they never would come again. His heart sank until he had palpitation in his wading-boots.

Stretching the length of the limb, he thought deeply, though he was not thinking of Black Jack or Wessner. Would the Bird Woman and the Angel come again? No other woman whom he ever had known would. But did they resemble any other women he ever had known? He thought of the Bird Woman's unruffled face and the Angel's revolver practice, and presently he was not so sure that they would not return.

What were the people in the big world like? His knowledge was so very limited. There had been people at the Home, who exchanged a stilted, perfunctory kindness for their salaries. The visitors who called on receiving days he had divided into three classes: the psalm-singing kind, who came with a tear in the eye and hypocrisy in every feature of their faces; the kind who dressed in silks and jewels, and handed to those poor little mother-hungry souls worn toys that their children no longer cared for, in exactly the same spirit in which they pitched biscuits to the monkeys at the zoo, and for the same reason—to see how they would take them and be amused by what they would do; and the third class, whom he considered real people. They made him feel they cared that he was there, and that they would have been glad to see him elsewhere.

Now here was another class, that had all they needed of the world's best and were engaged in doing work that counted. They had things worth while to be proud of; and they had met him as a son and brother. With them he could, for the only time in his life, forget the lost hand that every day tortured him with a new pang. What kind of people were they and where did they belong among the classes he knew? He failed to decide, because he never had known others similar to them; but how he loved them!

In the world where he was going soon, were the majority like them, or were they of the hypocrite and bun-throwing classes?

He had forgotten the excitement of the morning and the passing of time when distant voices aroused him, and he gently lifted his head. Nearer and nearer they came, and as the heavy wagons rumbled down the east trail he could hear them plainly. The gang were shouting themselves hoarse for the Limberlost guard. Freckles did not feel that he deserved it. He would have given much to be able to go to the men and explain, but to McLean only could he tell his story.

At the sight of Freckles the men threw up their hats and cheered. McLean shook hands with him warmly, but big Duncan gathered him into his arms and hugged him as a bear and choked over a few words of praise. The gang drove in and finished felling the tree. McLean was angry beyond measure at this attempt on his property, for in their haste to fell the tree the thieves had cut too high and wasted a foot and a half of valuable timber.

When the last wagon rolled away, McLean sat on the stump and Freckles told the story he was aching to tell. The Boss scarcely could believe his senses. Also, he was much disappointed.

"I have been almost praying all the way over, Freckles," he said, "that you would have some evidence by which we could arrest those fellows and get them out of our way, but this will never do. We can't mix up those women in it. They have helped you save me the tree and my wager as well. Going across the country as she does, the Bird Woman never could be expected to testify against them."

"No, indeed; nor the Angel, either, sir," said Freckles.

"The Angel?" queried the astonished McLean.

The Boss listened in silence while Freckles told of the coming and christening of the Angel.

"I know her father well," said McLean at last, "and I have often seen her. You are right, she is a beautiful young girl, and she appears to be utterly free from the least particle of false pride or foolishness. I do not understand why her father risks such a jewel in this place."

"He's daring it because she is a jewel, sir," said Freckles, eagerly. "Why, she's trusting a rattlesnake to rattle before it strikes her, and of course, she thinks she can trust mankind as well. The man isn't made who wouldn't lay down the life of him for her. She doesn't need any care. Her face and the pretty ways of her are all the protection she would need in a band of howling savages."

"Did you say she handled one of the revolvers?" asked McLean.

"She scared all the breath out of me body," admitted Freckles. "Seems that her father has taught her to shoot. The Bird Woman told her distinctly to lie low and blaze away high, just to help scare them. The spunky little thing followed them right out into the west road, spitting lead like hail, and clipping all around the heads and heels of them; and I'm damned, sir, if I believe she'd cared a rap if she'd hit. I never saw much shooting, but if that wasn't the nearest to miss I ever want to see! Scared the life near out of me body with the fear that she'd drop one of them. As long as I'd no one to help me but a couple of women that didn't dare be mixed up in it, all I could do was to let them get away."

"Now, will they come back?" asked McLean.

"Of course!" said Freckles. "They're not going to be taking that. You could stake your life on it, they'll be coming back. At least, Black Jack will. Wessner may not have the pluck, unless he is half drunk. Then he'd be a terror. And the next time—" Freckles hesitated.

"What?"

"It will be a question of who shoots first and straightest."

"Then the only thing for me to do is to double the guard and bring the gang here the first minute possible. As soon as I feel that we have the rarest of the stuff out below, we will come. The fact is, in many cases, until it is felled it's difficult to tell what a tree will prove to be. It won't do to leave you here longer alone. Jack has been shooting twenty years to your one, and it stands to reason that you are no match for him. Who of the gang would you like best to have with you?"

"No one, sir," said Freckles emphatically. "Next time is where I run. I won't try to fight them alone. I'll just be getting wind of them, and then make tracks for you. I'll need to come like lightning, and Duncan has no extra horse, so I'm thinking you'd best get me one—or perhaps a wheel would be better. I used to do extra work for the Home doctor, and he would let me take his bicycle to ride around the place. And at times the head nurse would loan me his for an hour. A wheel would cost less and be faster than a horse, and would take less care. I believe, if you are going to town soon, you had best pick up any kind of an old one at some second-hand store, for if I'm ever called to use it in a hurry there won't be the handlebars left after crossing the corduroy."

"Yes," said McLean; "and if you didn't have a first-class wheel, you never could cross the corduroy on it at all."

As they walked to the cabin, McLean insisted on another guard, but Freckles was stubbornly set on fighting his battle alone. He made one mental condition. If the Bird Woman was going to give up the Little Chicken series, he would yield to the second guard, solely for the sake of her work and the presence of the Angel in the Limberlost. He did not propose to have a second man unless it were absolutely necessary, for he had been alone so long that he loved the solitude, his chickens, and flowers. The thought of having a stranger to all his ways come and meddle with his arrangements, frighten his pets, pull his flowers, and interrupt him when he wanted to study, so annoyed him that he was blinded to his real need for help.

With McLean it was a case of letting his sober, better judgment be overridden by the boy he was growing so to love that he could not endure to oppose him, and to have Freckles keep his trust and win alone meant more than any money the Boss might lose.

The following morning McLean brought the wheel, and Freckles took it to the trail to test it. It was new, chainless, with as little as possible to catch in hurried riding, and in every way the best of its kind. Freckles went skimming around the trail on it on a preliminary trip before he locked it in his case and started his minute examination of his line on foot. He glanced around his room as he left it, and then stood staring.

On the moss before his prettiest seat lay the Angel's hat. In the excitement of yesterday all of them had forgotten it. He went and picked it up, oh! so carefully, gazing at it with hungry eyes, but touching it only to carry it to his case, where he hung it on the shining handlebar of the new wheel and locked it among his treasures. Then he went to the trail, with a new expression on his face and a strange throbbing in his heart. He was not in the least afraid of anything that morning. He felt he was the veriest Daniel, but all his lions seemed weak and harmless.

What Black Jack's next move would be he could not imagine, but that there would be a move of some kind was certain. The big bully was not a man to give up his purpose, or to have the hat swept from his head with a bullet and bear it meekly. Moreover, Wessner would cling to his revenge with a Dutchman's singleness of mind.

Freckles tried to think connectedly, but there were too many places on the trail where the Angel's footprints were yet visible. She had stepped in one mucky spot and left a sharp impression. The afternoon sun had baked it hard, and the horses' hoofs had not obliterated any part of it, as they had in so many places. Freckles stood fascinated, gazing at it. He measured it lovingly with his eye. He would not have ventured a caress on her hat any more than on her person, but this was different. Surely a footprint on a trail might belong to anyone who found and wanted it. He stooped under the wires and entered the swamp. With a little searching, he found a big piece of thick bark loose on a log and carefully peeling it, carried it out and covered the print so that the first rain would not obliterate it.

When he reached his room, he tenderly laid the hat upon his bookshelf, and to wear off his awkwardness, mounted his wheel and went spinning on trail again.

It was like flying, for the path was worn smooth with his feet and baked hard with the sun almost all the way. When he came to the bark, he veered far to one side and smiled at it in passing. Suddenly he was off the wheel, kneeling beside it. He removed his hat, carefully lifted the bark, and gazed lovingly at the imprint.

"I wonder what she was going to say of me voice," he whispered. "She never got it said, but from the face of her, I believe she was liking it fairly well. Perhaps she was going to say that singing was the big thing I was to be doing. That's what they all thought at the Home. Well, if it is, I'll just shut me eyes, think of me little room, the face of her watching, and the heart of her beating, and I'll raise them. Damn them, if singing will do it, I'll raise them from the benches!"

With this dire threat, Freckles knelt, as at a wayside spring, and deliberately laid his lips on the footprint. Then he arose, appearing as if he had been drinking at the fountain of gladness.

Chapter 8

Wherein Freckles Meets a Man of Affairs and Loses Nothing by the Encounter

"Weel, I be drawed on!" exclaimed Mrs. Duncan. Freckles stood before her, holding the Angel's hat. "I've been thinking this long time that ye or Duncan would see that sunbonnets werena braw enough for a woman of my standing, and ye're a guid laddie to bring me this beautiful hat."

She turned it around, examining the weave of the straw and the foliage trimmings, passing her rough fingers over the satin ties delightedly. As she held it up, admiring it, Freckles's astonished eyes saw a new side of Sarah Duncan. She was jesting, but under the jest the fact loomed strong that, though poor, overworked, and with none but God-given refinement, there was something in her soul crying after that bit of feminine finery, and it made his heart ache for her. He resolved that when he reached the city he would send her a hat, if it took fifty dollars to do it.

She lingeringly handed it back to him.

"It's unco guid of ye to think of me," she said lightly, "but I maun question your taste a wee. D'ye no think ye had best return this and get a woman with half her hair gray a little plainer headdress? Seems like that's far ower gay for me. I'm no' saying that it's no' exactly what I'd like to hae, but I mauna mak mysel' ridiculous. Ye'd best give this to somebody young and pretty, say about sixteen. Where did ye come by it, Freckles? If there's anything been dropping lately, ye hae forgotten to mention it."

"Do you see anything heavenly about that hat?" queried Freckles, holding it up.

The morning breeze waved the ribbons gracefully, binding one around Freckles's sleeve and the other across his chest, where they caught and clung as if magnetized.

"Yes," said Sarah Duncan. "It's verra plain and simple, but it juist makes ye feel that it's all of the finest stuff. It's exactly what I'd call a heavenly hat."

"Sure," said Freckles, "for it's belonging to an Angel!"

Then he told her about the hat and asked her what he should do with it.

"Take it to her, of course!" said Sarah Duncan. "Like it's the only ane she has and she may need it badly."

Freckles smiled. He had a clear idea about the hat being the only one the Angel had. However, there was a thing he felt he should do and wanted to do, but he was not sure.

"You think I might be taking it home?" he said.

"Of course ye must," said Mrs. Duncan. "And without another hour's delay. It's been here two days noo, and she may want it, and be too busy or afraid to come."

"But how can I take it?" asked Freckles.

"Gang spinning on your wheel. Ye can do it easy in an hour."

"But in that hour, what if—?"

"Nonsense!" interrupted Sarah Duncan. "Ye've watched that timber-line until ye're grown fast to it, lad. Give me your boots and club and I'll gae walk the south end and watch doon the east and west sides until ye come back."

"Mrs. Duncan! You never would be doing it," cried Freckles.

"Why not?" inquired she.

"But you know you're mortal afraid of snakes and a lot of other things in the swamp."

"I am afraid of snakes," said Mrs. Duncan, "but likely they've gone into the swamp this hot weather. I'll juist stay on the trail and watch, and ye might hurry the least bit. The day's so bright it feels like storm. I can put the bairns on the woodpile to play until I get back. Ye gang awa and take the blessed little angel her beautiful hat."

"Are you sure it will be all right?" urged Freckles. "Do you think if Mr. McLean came he would care?"

"Na," said Mrs. Duncan; "I dinna. If ye and me agree that a thing ought to be done, and I watch in your place, why, it's bound to be all right with McLean. Let me pin the hat in a paper, and ye jump on your wheel and gang flying. Ought ye put on your Sabbath-day clothes?"

Freckles shook his head. He knew what he should do, but there was no use in taking time to try to explain it to Mrs. Duncan while he was so hurried. He exchanged his wading-boots for shoes, gave her his club, and went spinning toward town. He knew very well where the Angel lived. He had seen her home many times, and he passed it again without even raising his eyes from the street, steering straight for her father's place of business.

Carrying the hat, Freckles passed a long line of clerks, and at the door of the private office asked to see the proprietor. When he had waited a moment, a tall, spare, keen-eyed man faced him, and in brisk, nervous tones asked: "How can I serve you, sir?"

Freckles handed him the package and answered, "By delivering to your daughter this hat, which she was after leaving at me place the other day, when she went away in a hurry. And by saying to her and the Bird Woman that I'm more thankful than I'll be having words to express for the brave things they was doing for me. I'm McLean's Limberlost guard, sir."

"Why don't you take it yourself?" questioned the Man of Affairs.

Freckles's clear gray eyes met those of the Angel's father squarely, and he asked: "If you were in my place, would you take it to her yourself?"

"No, I would not," said that gentleman quickly.

"Then why ask why I did not?" came Freckles's lamb-like query.

"Bless me!" said the Angel's father. He stared at the package, then at the lifted chin of the boy, and then at the package again, and muttered, "Excuse me!"

Freckles bowed.

"It would be favoring me greatly if you would deliver the hat and the message. Good morning, sir," and he turned away.

"One minute," said the Angel's father. "Suppose I give you permission to return this hat in person and make your own acknowledgments."

Freckles stood one moment thinking intently, and then he lifted those eyes of unswerving truth and asked: "Why should you, sir? You are kind, indade, to mention it, and it's thanking you I am for your good intintions, but my wanting to go or your being willing to have me ain't proving that your daughter would be wanting me or care to bother with me."

The Angel's father looked keenly into the face of this extraordinary young man, for he found it to his liking.

"There's one other thing I meant to say," said Freckles. "Every day I see some thing, and at times a lot of things, that I think the Bird Woman would be wanting pictures of badly, if she knew. You might be speaking of it to her, and if she'd want me to, I can send her word when I find things she wouldn't likely get elsewhere."

"If that's the case," said the Angel's father, "and you feel under obligations for her assistance the other day, you can discharge them in that way. She is spending all her time in the fields and woods searching for subjects. If you run across things, perhaps rarer than she may find, about your work, it would save her the time she spends searching for subjects, and she could work in security under your protection. By all means let her know if you find subjects you think she could use, and we will do anything we can for you, if you will give her what help you can and see that she is as safe as possible."

"It's hungry for human beings I am," said Freckles, "and it's like Heaven to me to have them come. Of course, I'll be telling or sending her word every time me work can spare me. Anything I can do it would make me uncommon happy, but"—again truth had to be told, because it was Freckles who was speaking—"when it comes to protecting them, I'd risk me life, to be sure, but even that mightn't do any good in some cases. There are many dangers to be reckoned with in the swamp, sir, that call for every person to look sharp. If there wasn't really thieving to guard against, why, McLean wouldn't need be paying out good money for a guard. I'd love them to be coming, and I'll do all I can, but you must be told that there's danger of them running into timber thieves again any day, sir."

"Yes," said the Angel's father, "and I suppose there's danger of the earth opening up and swallowing the town any day, but I'm damned if I quit business for fear it will, and the Bird Woman won't, either. Everyone knows her and her work, and there is no danger in the world of anyone in any way molesting her, even if he were stealing a few of McLean's gold-plated trees. She's as safe in the Limberlost as she is at home, so far as timber thieves are concerned. All I am ever uneasy about are the snakes, poison-vines, and insects; and those are risks she must run anywhere. You need not hesitate a minute about that. I shall be glad to tell them what you wish. Thank you very much, and good day, sir."

There was no way in which Freckles could know it, but by following his best instincts and being what he conceived a gentleman should be, he surprised the Man of Affairs into thinking of him and seeing his face over his books many times that morning; whereas, if he had gone to the Angel as he had longed to do, her father never would have given him a second thought.

On the street he drew a deep breath. How had he acquitted himself? He only knew that he had lived up to his best impulse, and that is all anyone can do. He glanced over his wheel to see that it was all right, and just as he stepped to the curb to mount he heard a voice that thrilled him through and through: "Freckles! Oh Freckles!"

The Angel separated from a group of laughing, sweet-faced girls and came hurrying to him. She was in snowy white—a quaint little frock, with a marvel of soft lace around her throat and wrists. Through the sheer sleeves of it her beautiful, rounded arms showed distinctly, and it was cut just to the base of her perfect neck. On her head was a pure white creation of fancy braid, with folds on folds of tulle, soft and silken as cobwebs, lining the brim; while a mass of white roses clustered against the gold of her hair, crept around the crown, and fell in a riot to her shoulders at the back. There were gleams of gold with settings of blue on her fingers, and altogether she was the daintiest, sweetest sight he ever had seen. Freckles, standing on the curb, forgot himself in his cotton shirt, corduroys, and his belt to which his wire-cutter and pliers were hanging, and gazed as a man gazes when first he sees the woman he adores with all her charms enhanced by appropriate and beautiful clothing.

"Oh Freckles," she cried as she came to him. "I was wondering about you the other day. Do you know I never saw you in town before. You watch that old line so closely! Why did you come? Is there any trouble? Are you just starting to the Limberlost?"

"I came to bring your hat," said Freckles. "You forgot it in the rush the other day. I have left it with your father, and a message trying to ixpriss the gratitude of me for how you and the Bird Woman were for helping me out."

The Angel nodded gravely, then Freckles saw that he had done the proper thing in going to her father. His heart bounded until it jarred his body, for she was saying that she scarcely could wait for the time to come for the next picture of the Little Chicken series. "I want to hear the remainder of that song, and I hadn't even begun seeing your room yet," she complained. "As for singing, if you can sing like that every day, I never can get enough of it. I wonder if I couldn't bring my banjo and some of the songs I like best. I'll play and you sing, and we'll put the birds out of commission."

Freckles stood on the curb with drooped eyes, for he felt that if he lifted them the tumult of tender adoration in them would show and frighten her.

"I was afraid your experience the other day would scare you so that you'd never be coming again," he found himself saying.

The Angel laughed gaily.

"Did I seem scared?" she questioned.

"No," said Freckles, "you did not."

"Oh, I just enjoyed that," she cried. "Those hateful, stealing old things! I had a big notion to pink one of them, but I thought maybe someway it would be best for you that I shouldn't. They needed it. That didn't scare me; and as for the Bird Woman, she's accustomed to finding snakes, tramps, cross dogs, sheep, cattle, and goodness knows what! You can't frighten her when she's after a picture. Did they come back?"

"No," said Freckles. "The gang got there a little after noon and took out the tree, but I must tell you, and you must tell the Bird Woman, that there's no doubt but they will be coming back, and they will have to make it before long now, for it's soon the gang will be there to work on the swamp."

"Oh, what a shame!" cried the Angel. "They'll clear out roads, cut down the beautiful trees, and tear up everything. They'll drive away the birds and spoil the cathedral. When they have done their worst, then all these mills close here will follow in and take out the cheap timber. Then the landowners will dig a few ditches, build some fires, and in two summers more the Limberlost will be in corn and potatoes."

They looked at each other, and groaned despairingly in unison.

"You like it, too," said Freckles.

"Yes," said the Angel, "I love it. Your room is a little piece right out of the heart of fairyland, and the cathedral is God's work, not yours. You only found it and opened the door after He had it completed. The birds, flowers, and vines are all so lovely. The Bird Woman says it is really a fact that the mallows, foxfire, iris, and lilies are larger and of richer coloring there than in the remainder of the country. She says it's because of the rich loam and muck. I hate seeing the swamp torn up, and to you it will be like losing your best friend; won't it?"

"Something like," said Freckles. "Still, I've the Limberlost in me heart so that all of it will be real to me while I live, no matter what they do to it. I'm glad past telling if you will be coming a few more times, at least until the gang arrives. Past that time I don't allow mesilf to be thinking."

"Come, have a cool drink before you start back," said the Angel.

"I couldn't possibly," said Freckles. "I left Mrs. Duncan on the trail, and she's terribly afraid of a lot of things. If she even sees a big snake, I don't know what she'll do."

"It won't take but a minute, and you can ride fast enough to make up for it. Please. I want to think of something fine for you, to make up a little for what you did for me that first day."

Freckles looked in sheer wonderment into the beautiful face of the Angel. Did she truly mean it? Would she walk down that street with him, crippled, homely, in mean clothing, with the tools of his occupation on him, and share with him the treat she was offering? He could not believe it, even of the Angel. Still, in justice to the candor of her pure, sweet face, he would not think that she would make the offer and not mean it. She really did mean just what she said, but when it came to carrying out her offer and he saw the stares of her friends, the sneers of her enemies—if such as she could have enemies—and heard the whispered jeers of the curious, then she would see her mistake and be sorry. It would be only a manly thing for him to think this out, and save her from the results of her own blessed bigness of heart.

"I railly must be off," said Freckles earnestly, "but I'm thanking you more than you'll ever know for your kindness. I'll just be drinking bowls of icy things all me way home in the thoughts of it."

Down came the Angel's foot. Her eyes flashed indignantly. "There's no sense in that," she said. "How do you think you would have felt when you knew I was warm and thirsty and you went and brought me a drink and I wouldn't take it because—because goodness knows why! You can ride faster to make up for the time. I've just thought out what I want to fix for you."

She stepped to his side and deliberately slipped her hand under his arm—that right arm that ended in an empty sleeve.

"You are coming," she said firmly. "I won't have it."

Freckles could not have told how he felt, neither could anyone else. His blood rioted and his head swam, but he kept his wits. He bent over her.

"Please don't, Angel," he said softly. "You don't understand."

How Freckles came to understand was a problem.

"It's this," he persisted. "If your father met me on the street, in my station and dress, with you on me arm, he'd have every right to be caning me before the people, and not a finger would I lift to stay him."

The Angel's eyes snapped. "If you think my father cares about my doing anything that is right and kind, and that makes me happy to do—why, then you completely failed in reading my father, and I'll ask him and just show you."

She dropped Freckles's arm and turned toward the entrance to the building. "Why, look there!" she exclaimed.

Her father stood in a big window fronting the street, a bundle of papers in his hand, interestedly watching the little scene, with eyes that comprehended quite as thoroughly as if he had heard every word. The Angel caught his glance and made a despairing little gesture toward Freckles. The Man of Affairs answered her with a look of infinite tenderness. He nodded his head and waved the papers in the direction she had indicated, and the veriest dolt could have read the words his lips formed: "Take him along!"

A sudden trembling seized Freckles. At sight of the Angel's father he had stepped back as far from her as he could, leaned the wheel against him, and snatched off his hat.

The Angel turned on him with triumphing eyes.

She was highly strung and not accustomed to being thwarted. "Did you see that?" she demanded. "Now are you satisfied? Will you come, or must I call a policeman to bring you?"

Freckles went. There was nothing else to do. Guiding his wheel, he walked down the street beside her. On every hand she was kept busy giving and receiving the cheeriest greetings. She walked into the parlors exactly as if she owned them. A clerk came hurrying to meet her.

"There's a table vacant beside a window where it is cool. I'll save it for you," and he started back.

"Please not," said the Angel. "I've taken this man unawares, when he's in a rush. I'm afraid if we sit down we'll take too much time and afterward he will blame me."

She walked to the fountain, and a long row of people stared with all the varying degrees of insolence and curiosity that Freckles had felt they would. He glanced at the Angel. NOW would she see?

"On my soul!" he muttered under his breath. "They don't aven touch her!"

She laid down her sunshade and gloves. She walked to the end of the counter and turned the full battery of her eyes on the attendant.

"Please," she said.

The white-aproned individual stepped back and gave delighted assent. The Angel stepped beside him, and selecting a tall, flaring glass, of almost paper thinness, she stooped and rolled it in a tray of cracked ice.

"I want to mix a drink for my friend," she said. "He has a long, hot ride before him, and I don't want him started off with one of those old palate-teasing sweet-nesses that you mix just on purpose to drive a man back in ten minutes." There was an appreciative laugh from the line at the counter.

"I want a clear, cool, sparkling drink that has a tang of acid in it. Where's the cherry phosphate? That, not at all sweet, would be good; don't you think?"

The attendant did think. He pointed out the different taps, and the Angel compounded the drink, while Freckles, standing so erect he almost leaned backward, gazed at her and paid no attention to anyone else. When she had the glass brimming, she tilted a little of its contents into a second glass and tasted it.

"That's entirely too sweet for a thirsty man," she said.

She poured out half the mixture, and refilling the glass, tasted it a second time. She submitted that result to the attendant. "Isn't that about the thing?" she asked.

He replied enthusiastically. "I'd get my wages raised ten a month if I could learn that trick."

The Angel carried the brimming, frosty glass to Freckles. He removed his hat, and lifting the icy liquid even with her eyes and looking straight into them, he said in the mellowest of all the mellow tones of his voice: "I'll be drinking it to the Swamp Angel."

As he had said to her that first day, she now cautioned him: "Be drinking slowly."

When the screen-door swung behind them, one of the men at the counter asked of the attendant: "Now, what did that mean?"

"Exactly what you saw," replied he, rather curtly. "We're accustomed to it here. Hardly a day passes, this hot weather, but she's picking up some poor, god-forsaken mortal and bringing him in. Then she comes behind the counter herself and fixes up a drink to suit the occasion. She's all sorts of fancies about what's what for all kinds of times and conditions, and you bet she can just hit the spot! Ain't a clerk here can put up a drink to touch her. She's a sort of knack at it. Every once in a while, when the Boss sees her, he calls out to her to mix him a drink."

"And does she?" asked the man with an interested grin.

"Well, I guess! But first she goes back and sees how long it is since he's had a drink. What he drank last. How warm he is. When he ate last. Then she comes here and mixes a glass of fizz with a little touch of acid, and a bit of cherry, lemon, grape, pineapple, or something sour and cooling, and it hits the spot just as no spot was ever hit before. I honestly believe that the *interest* she takes in it is half the trick, for I watch her closely and I can't come within gunshot of her concoctions. She has a running bill here. Her father settles once a month. She gives nine-tenths of it away. Hardly ever touches it herself, but when she does she makes me mix it. She's just old persimmons. Even the scrub-boy of this establishment would fight for her. It lasts the year round, for in winter it's some poor, frozen cuss that she's warming up on hot coffee or chocolate."

"Mighty queer specimen she had this time," volunteered another. "Irish, hand off, straight as a ramrod, and something worth while in his face. Notice that hat peel off, and the eyes of him? There's a case of 'fight for her!' Wonder who he is?"

"I think," said a third, "that he's McLean's Limberlost guard, and I suspect she's gone to the swamp with the Bird Woman for pictures and knows him that way. I've heard that he is a master hand with the birds, and that would just suit the Bird Woman to a T."

On the street the Angel walked beside Freckles to the first crossing and there she stopped. "Now, will you promise to ride fast enough to make up for the five minutes that took?" she asked. "I am a little uneasy about Mrs. Duncan."

Freckles turned his wheel into the street. It seemed to him he had poured that delicious icy liquid into every vein in his body instead of his stomach. It even went to his brain.

"Did you insist on fixing that drink because you knew how intoxicating 'twould be?" he asked.

There was subtlety in the compliment and it delighted the Angel. She laughed gleefully.

"Next time, maybe you won't take so much coaxing," she teased.

"I wouldn't this, if I had known your father and been understanding you better. Do you really think the Bird Woman will be coming again?"

The Angel jeered. "Wild horses couldn't drag her away," she cried. "She will have hard work to wait the week out. I shouldn't be in the least surprised to see her start any hour."

Freckles could not endure the suspense; it had to come.

"And you?" he questioned, but he dared not lift his eyes.

"Wild horses me, too," she laughed, "couldn't keep me away either! I dearly love to come, and the next time I am going to bring my banjo, and I'll play, and you sing for me some of the songs I like best; won't you?"

"Yis," said Freckles, because it was all he was capable of saying just then.

"It's beginning to act stormy," she said. "If you hurry you will just about make it. Now, good-bye."

Chapter 9

Wherein the Limberlost Falls upon Mrs. Duncan and Freckles Comes to the Rescue

Freckles was halfway to the Limberlost when he dismounted. He could ride no farther, because he could not see the road. He sat under a tree, and, leaning against it, sobs shook, twisted, and rent him. If they would remind him of his position, speak condescendingly, or notice his hand, he could endure it, but this— it surely would kill him! His hot, pulsing Irish blood was stirred deeply. What did they mean? Why did they do it? Were they like that to everyone? Was it pity?

It could not be, for he knew that the Bird Woman and the Angel's father must know that he was not really McLean's son, and it did not matter to them in the least. In spite of accident and poverty, they evidently expected him to do something worth while in the world. That must be his remedy. He must work on his education. He must get away. He must find and do the great thing of which the Angel talked. For the first time, his thoughts turned anxiously toward the city and the beginning of his studies. McLean and the Duncans spoke of him as "the boy," but he was a man. He must face life bravely and act a man's part. The Angel was a mere child. He must not allow her to torture him past endurance with her frank comradeship that meant to him high heaven, earth's richness, and all that lay between, and NOTHING to her.

There was an ominous growl of thunder, and amazed at himself, Freckles snatched up his wheel and raced toward the swamp. He was worried to find his boots lying at the cabin door; the children playing on the woodpile told him that "mither" said they were so heavy she couldn't walk in them, and she had come back and taken them off. Thoroughly frightened, he stopped only long enough to slip them on, and then sped with all his strength for the Limberlost. To the west, the long, black, hard-beaten trail lay clear; but far up the east side, straight across the path, he could see what was certainly a limp, brown figure. Freckles spun with all his might.

Face down, Sarah Duncan lay across the trail. When Freckles turned her over, his blood chilled at the look of horror settled on her face. There was a low humming and something spatted against him. Glancing around, Freckles shivered in terror, for there was a swarm of wild bees settled on a scrub-thorn only a few yards away. The air was filled with excited, unsettled bees making ready to lead farther in search of a suitable location. Then he thought he understood, and with a prayer of thankfulness in his heart that she had escaped, even so narrowly, he caught her up and hurried down the trail until they were well out of danger. He laid her in the shade, and carrying water from the swamp in the crown of his hat, he bathed her face and hands; but she lay in unbroken stillness, without a sign of life.

She had found Freckles's boots so large and heavy that she had gone back and taken them off, although she was mortally afraid to approach the swamp without them. The thought of it made her nervous, and the fact that she never had been there alone added to her fears. She had not followed the trail many rods when her trouble began. She was not Freckles, so not a bird of the line was going to be fooled into thinking she was.

They began jumping from their nests and darting from unexpected places around her head and feet, with quick whirs, that kept her starting and dodging. Before Freckles was halfway to the town, poor Mrs. Duncan was hysterical, and the Limberlost had neither sung nor performed for her.

But there was trouble brewing. It was quiet and intensely hot, with that stifling stillness that precedes a summer storm, and feathers and fur were tense and nervous. The birds were singing only a few broken snatches, and flying around, seeking places of shelter. One moment everything seemed devoid of life, the next there was an unexpected whir, buzz, and sharp cry. Inside, a pandemonium of growling, spatting, snarling, and grunting broke loose.

The swale bent flat before heavy gusts of wind, and the big black chicken swept lower and lower above the swamp. Patches of clouds gathered, shutting out the sun and making it very dark, and the next moment were swept away. The sun poured with fierce, burning brightness, and everything was quiet. It was at the first growl of thunder that Freckles really had noticed the weather, and putting his own troubles aside resolutely, raced for the swamp.

Sarah Duncan paused on the line. "Weel, I wouldna stay in this place for a million a month," she said aloud, and the sound of her voice brought no comfort, for it was so little like she had thought it that she glanced hastily around to see if it had really been she that spoke. She tremblingly wiped the perspiration from her face with the skirt of her sunbonnet.

"Awfu' hot," she panted huskily. "B'lieve there's going to be a big storm. I do hope Freckles will hurry."

Her chin was quivering as a terrified child's. She lifted her bonnet to replace it and brushed against a bush beside her. WHIRR, almost into her face, went a nighthawk stretched along a limb for its daytime nap. Mrs. Duncan cried out and sprang down the trail, alighting on a frog that was hopping across. The horrible croak it gave as she crushed it sickened her. She screamed wildly and jumped to one side. That carried her into the swale, where the grasses reached almost to her waist, and her horror of snakes returning, she made a flying leap for an old log lying beside the line. She alighted squarely, but it was so damp and rotten that she sank straight through it to her knees. She caught at the wire as she went down, and missing, raked her wrist across a barb until she tore a bleeding gash. Her fingers closed convulsively around the second strand. She was too frightened to scream now. Her tongue stiffened. She clung frantically to the sagging wire, and finally managed to grasp it with the other hand. Then she could reach the top wire, and so she drew herself up and found solid footing. She picked up the club that she had dropped in order to extricate herself. Leaning heavily on it, she managed to return to the trail, but she was trembling so that she scarcely could walk. Going a few steps farther, she came to the stump of the first tree that had been taken out.

She sat bolt upright and very still, trying to collect her thoughts and reason away her terror. A squirrel above her dropped a nut, and as it came rattling down, bouncing from branch to branch, every nerve in her tugged wildly. When the disgusted squirrel barked loudly, she sprang to the trail.

The wind arose higher, the changes from light to darkness were more abrupt, while the thunder came closer and louder at every peal. In swarms the blackbirds arose from the swale and came flocking to the interior, with a clamoring cry: "T'CHECK, T'CHECK." Grackles marshaled to the tribal call: "TRALL-A-HEE, TRALL-A-HEE." Red-winged blackbirds swept low, calling to belated mates: "FOL-LOW-ME, FOL-LOW-ME." Big, jetty crows gathered close to her, crying, as if warning her to flee before it was everlastingly too late. A heron, fishing the near-by pool for Freckles's "find-out" frog, fell into trouble with a muskrat and uttered a rasping note that sent Mrs. Duncan a rod down the line without realizing that she had moved. She was too shaken to run far. She stopped and looked around her fearfully.

Several bees struck her and were angrily buzzing before she noticed them. Then the humming swelled on all sides. A convulsive sob shook her, and she ran into the bushes, now into the swale, anywhere to avoid the swarming bees, ducking, dodging, fighting for her very life. Presently the humming seemed to become a little fainter. She found the trail again, and ran with all her might from a few of her angry pursuers.

As she ran, straining every muscle, she suddenly became aware that, crossing the trail before her, was a big, round, black body, with brown markings on its back, like painted geometrical patterns. She tried to stop, but the louder buzzing behind warned her she dared not. Gathering her skirts higher, with hair flying around her face and her eyes almost bursting from their sockets, she ran straight toward it. The sound of her feet and the humming of the bees alarmed the rattler, so it stopped across the trail, lifting its head above the grasses of the swale and rattling inquiringly—rattled until the bees were outdone.

Straight toward it went the panic-stricken woman, running wildly and uncontrollably. She took one leap, clearing its body on the path, then flew ahead with winged feet. The snake, coiled to strike, missed Mrs. Duncan and landed among the bees instead. They settled over and around it, and realizing that it had found trouble, it sank among the grasses and went threshing toward its den in the deep willow-fringed low ground. The swale appeared as if a reaper were cutting a wide swath. The mass of enraged bees darted angrily around, searching for it, and striking the scrub-thorn, began a temporary settling there to discover whether it were a suitable place. Completely exhausted, Mrs. Duncan staggered on a few steps farther, fell facing the path, where Freckles found her, and lay quietly.

Freckles worked over her until she drew a long, quivering breath and opened her eyes.

When she saw him bending above her, she closed them tightly, and gripping him, struggled to her feet. He helped her, and with his arm around and half carrying her, they made their way to the clearing. She clung to him with all her remaining strength, but open her eyes she would not until her children came clustering around her. Then, brawny, big Scotswoman though she was, she quietly keeled over again. The children added their wailing to Freckles's panic.

This time he was so close the cabin that he could carry her into the house and lay her on the bed. He sent the oldest boy scudding down the corduroy for the nearest neighbor, and between them they undressed Mrs. Duncan and discovered that she was not bitten. They bathed and bound the bleeding wrist and coaxed her back to consciousness. She lay sobbing and shuddering. The first intelligent word she said was: "Freckles, look at that jar on the kitchen table and see if my yeast is no running ower."

Several days passed before she could give Duncan and Freckles any detailed account of what had happened to her, even then she could not do it without crying as the least of her babies. Freckles was almost heartbroken, and nursed her as well as any woman could have done; while big Duncan, with a heart full for them both, worked early and late to chink every crack of the cabin and examine every spot that possibly could harbor a snake. The effects of her morning on the trail kept her shivering half the time. She could not rest until she sent for McLean and begged him to save Freckles from further risk, in that place of horrors. The Boss went to the swamp with his mind fully determined to do so.

Freckles stood and laughed at him. "Why, Mr. McLean, don't you let a woman's nervous system set you worrying about me," he said. "I'm not denying how she felt, because I've been through it meself, but that's all over and gone. It's the height of me glory to fight it out with the old swamp, and all that's in it, or will be coming to it, and then to turn it over to you as I promised you and meself I'd do, sir. You couldn't break the heart of me entire quicker than to be taking it from me now, when I'm just on the home-stretch. It won't be over three or four weeks yet, and when I've gone it almost a year, why, what's that to me, sir? You mustn't let a woman get mixed up with business, for I've always heard about how it's bringing trouble."

McLean smiled. "What about that last tree?" he said.

Freckles blushed and grinned appreciatively.

"Angels and Bird Women don't count in the common run, sir," he affirmed shamelessly.

McLean sat in the saddle and laughed.

Chapter 10

Wherein Freckles Strives Mightily and the Swamp Angel Rewards Him

The Bird Woman and the Angel did not seem to count in the common run, for they arrived on time for the third of the series and found McLean on the line talking to Freckles. The Boss was filled with enthusiasm over a marsh article of the Bird Woman's that he just had read. He begged to be allowed to accompany her into the swamp and watch the method by which she secured an illustration in such a location.

The Bird Woman explained to him that it was an easy matter with the subject she then had in hand; and as Little Chicken was too small to be frightened by him, and big enough to be growing troublesome, she was glad for his company. They went to the chicken log together, leaving to the happy Freckles the care of the Angel, who had brought her banjo and a roll of songs that she wanted to hear him sing. The Bird Woman told them that they might practice in Freckles's room until she finished with Little Chicken, and then she and McLean would come to the concert.

It was almost three hours before they finished and came down the west trail for their rest and lunch. McLean walked ahead, keeping sharp watch on the trail and clearing it of fallen limbs from overhanging trees. He sent a big piece of bark flying into the swale, and then stopped short and stared at the trail.

The Bird Woman bent forward. Together they studied that imprint of the Angel's foot. At last their eyes met, the Bird Woman's filled with astonishment, and McLean's humid with pity. Neither said a word, but they knew. McLean entered the swale and hunted up the bark. He replaced it, and the Bird Woman carefully stepped over. As they reached the bushes at the entrance, the voice of the Angel stopped them, for it was commanding and filled with much impatience.

"Freckles James Ross McLean!" she was saying. "You fill me with dark-blue despair! You're singing as if your voice were glass and might break at any minute. Why don't you sing as you did a week ago? Answer me that, please."

Freckles smiled confusedly at the Angel, who sat on one of his fancy seats, playing his accompaniment on her banjo.

"You are a fraud," she said. "Here you went last week and led me to think that there was the making of a great singer in you, and now you are singing—do you know how badly you are singing?"

"Yis," said Freckles meekly. "I'm thinking I'm too happy to be singing well today. The music don't come right only when I'm lonesome and sad. The world's for being all sunshine at prisint, for among you and Mr. McLean and the Bird Woman I'm after being *that* happy that I can't keep me thoughts on me notes. It's more than sorry I am to be disappointing you. Play it over, and I'll be beginning again, and this time I'll hold hard."

"Well," said the Angel disgustedly, "it seems to me that if I had all the things to be proud of that you have, I'd lift up my head and sing!"

"And what is it I've to be proud of, ma'am?" politely inquired Freckles.

"Why, a whole worldful of things," cried the Angel explosively. "For one thing, you can be good and proud over the way you've kept the timber thieves out of this lease, and the trust your father has in you. You can be proud that you've never even once disappointed him or failed in what he believed you could do. You can be proud over the way everyone speaks of you with trust and honor, and about how brave of heart and strong of body you are I heard a big man say a few days ago that the Limberlost was full of disagreeable things—positive dangers, unhealthful as it could be, and that since the memory of the first settlers it has been a rendezvous for runaways, thieves, and murderers. This swamp is named for a man that was lost here and wandered around 'til he starved. That man I was talking with said he wouldn't take your job for a thousand dollars a month—in fact, he said he wouldn't have it for any money, and you've never missed a day or lost a tree. Proud! Why, I should think you would just parade around about proper over that!

"And you can always be proud that you are born an Irishman. My father is Irish, and if you want to see him get up and strut give him a teeny opening to enlarge on his race. He says that if the Irish had decent territory they'd lead the world. He says they've always been handicapped by lack of space and of fertile soil. He says if Ireland had been as big and fertile as Indiana, why, England wouldn't ever have had the upper hand. She'd only be an appendage. Fancy England an appendage! He says Ireland has the finest orators and the keenest statesmen in Europe today, and when England wants to fight, with whom does she fill her trenches? Irishmen, of course! Ireland has the greenest grass and trees, the finest stones and lakes, and they've jaunting-cars. I don't know just exactly what they are, but Ireland has all there are, anyway. They've a lot of great actors, and a few singers, and there never was a sweeter poet than one of theirs. You should hear my father recite 'Dear Harp of My Country.' He does it this way."

The Angel arose, made an elaborate old-time bow, and holding up the banjo, recited in clipping feet and meter, with rhythmic swing and a touch of brogue that was simply irresistible:

"Dear harp of my country" [The Angel ardently clasped the banjo];

"In darkness I found thee" [She held it to the light];

"The cold chain of silence had hung o'er thee long" [She muted the strings with her rosy palm];

"Then proudly, my own Irish harp, I unbound thee" [She threw up her head and swept a ringing harmony];

"And gave all thy chords to light, freedom, and song" [She crashed into the notes of the accompaniment she had been playing for Freckles].

"That's what you want to be thinking of!" she cried. "Not darkness, and lonesomeness, and sadness, but 'light, freedom, and song.' I can't begin to think offhand of all the big, splendid things an Irishman has to be proud of; but whatever they are, they are all yours, and you are a part of them. I just despise that 'saddest-when-I-sing' business. You can sing! Now you go over there and do it! Ireland has had her statesmen, warriors, actors, and poets; now you be her voice! You stand right out there before the cathedral door, and I'm going to come down the aisle playing that accompaniment, and when I stop in front of you—you sing!"

The Angel's face wore an unusual flush. Her eyes were flashing and she was palpitating with earnestness.

She parted the bushes and disappeared. Freckles, straight and tense, stood waiting. Presently, before he saw she was there, she was coming down the aisle toward him, playing compellingly, and rifts of light were touching her with golden glory. Freckles stood as if transfixed.

The cathedral was majestically beautiful, from arched dome of frescoed gold, green, and blue in never-ending shades and harmonies, to the mosaic aisle she trod, richly inlaid in choicest colors, and gigantic pillars that were God's handiwork fashioned and perfected through ages of sunshine and rain. But the fair young face and divinely molded form of the Angel were His most perfect work of all. Never had she appeared so surpassingly beautiful. She was smiling encouragingly now, and as she came toward him, she struck the chords full and strong.

The heart of poor Freckles almost burst with dull pain and his great love for her. In his desire to fulfill her expectations he forgot everything else, and when she reached his initial chord he was ready. He literally burst forth:

"Three little leaves of Irish green,
United on one stem,
Love, truth, and valor do they mean,
They form a magic gem."

The Angel's eyes widened curiously and her lips parted. A deep color swept into her cheeks. She had intended to arouse him. She had more than succeeded. She was too young to know that in the effort to rouse a man, women frequently kindle fires that they neither can quench nor control. Freckles was looking over her head now and singing that song, as it never had been sung before, for her alone; and instead of her helping him, as she had intended, he was carrying her with him on the waves of his voice, away, away into another world. When he struck into the chorus, wide-eyed and panting, she was swaying toward him and playing with all her might.

"Oh, do you love? Oh, say you love
You love the shamrock green!"

At the last note, Freckles's voice ceased and he looked at the Angel. He had given his best and his all. He fell on his knees and folded his arms across his breast. The Angel, as if magnetized, walked straight down the aisle to him, and running her fingers into the crisp masses of his red hair, tilted his head back and laid her lips on his forehead.

Then she stepped back and faced him. "Good boy!" she said, in a voice that wavered from the throbbing of her shaken heart. "Dear boy! I knew you could do it! I knew it was in you! Freckles, when you go into the world, if you can face a big audience and sing like that, just once, you will be immortal, and anything you want will be yours."

"Anything!" gasped Freckles.

"Anything," said the Angel.

Freckles arose, muttered something, and catching up his old bucket, plunged into the swamp blindly on a pretence of bringing water. The Angel walked slowly across the study, sat on the rustic bench, and, through narrowed lids, intently studied the tip of her shoe.

On the trail the Bird Woman wheeled to McLean with a dumbfounded look.

"God!" muttered he.

At last the Bird Woman spoke.

"Do you think the Angel knew she did that?" she asked softly.

"No," said McLean; "I do not. But the poor boy knew it. Heaven help him!"

The Bird Woman stared across the gently waving swale. "I don't see how I am going to blame her," she said at last. "It's so exactly what I would have done myself."

"Say the remainder," demanded McLean hoarsely. "Do him justice."

"He was born a gentleman," conceded the Bird Woman. "He took no advantage. He never even offered to touch her. Whatever that kiss meant to him, he recognized that it was the loving impulse of a child under stress of strong emotion. He was fine and manly as any man ever could have been."

McLean lifted his hat. "Thank you," he said simply, and parted the bushes for her to enter Freckles's room.

It was her first visit. Before she left she sent for her cameras and made studies of each side of it and of the cathedral. She was entranced with the delicate beauty of the place, while her eyes kept following Freckles as if she could not believe that it could be his conception and work.

That was a happy day. The Bird Woman had brought a lunch, and they spread it, with Freckles's dinner, on the study floor and sat, resting and enjoying themselves. But the Angel put her banjo into its case, silently gathered her music, and no one mentioned the concert.

The Bird Woman left McLean and the Angel to clear away the lunch, and with Freckles examined the walls of his room and told him all she knew about his shrubs and flowers. She analyzed a cardinal-flower and showed him what he had wanted to know all summer—why the bees buzzed ineffectually around it while the humming-birds found in it an ever-ready feast. Some of his specimens were so rare that she was unfamiliar with them, and with the flower book between them they knelt, studying the different varieties. She wandered the length of the cathedral aisle with him, and it was at her suggestion that he lighted his altar with a row of flaming foxfire.

As Freckles came to the cabin from his long day at the swamp he saw Mrs. Chicken sweeping to the south and wondered where she was going. He stepped into the bright, cosy little kitchen, and as he reached down the wash-basin he asked Mrs. Duncan a question.

"Mother Duncan, do kisses wash off?"

So warm a wave swept her heart that a half-flush mantled her face. She straightened her shoulders and glanced at her hands tenderly.

"Lord, na! Freckles," she cried. "At least, the anes ye get from people ye love dinna. They dinna stay on the outside. They strike in until they find the center of your heart and make their stopping-place there, and naething can take them from ye—I doubt if even death—Na, lad, ye can be reet sure kisses dinna wash off!"

Freckles set the basin down and muttered as he plunged his hot, tired face into the water, "I needn't be afraid to be washing, then, for that one struck in."

Chapter 11

Wherein the Butterflies Go on a Spree and Freckles Informs the Bird Woman

"I wish," said Freckles at breakfast one morning, "that I had some way to be sending a message to the Bird Woman. I've something at the swamp that I'm believing never happened before, and surely she'll be wanting it."

"What now, Freckles?" asked Mrs. Duncan.

"Why, the oddest thing you ever heard of," said Freckles; "the whole insect tribe gone on a spree. I'm supposing it's my doings, but it all happened by accident, like. You see, on the swale side of the line, right against me trail, there's one of these scrub wild crabtrees. Where the grass grows thick around it, is the finest place you ever conceived of for snakes. Having women about has set me trying to clean out those fellows a bit, and yesterday I noticed that tree in passing. It struck me that it would be a good idea to be taking it out. First I thought I'd take me hatchet and cut it down, for it ain't thicker than me upper arm. Then I remembered how it was blooming in the spring and filling all the air with sweetness. The coloring of the blossoms is beautiful, and I hated to be killing it. I just cut the grass short all around it. Then I started at the ground, trimmed up the trunk near the height of me shoulder, and left the top spreading. That made it look so truly ornamental that, idle like, I chips off the rough places neat, and this morning, on me soul, it's a sight! You see, cutting off the limbs and trimming up the trunk sets the sap running. In this hot sun it ferments in a few hours. There isn't much room for more things to crowd on that tree than there are, and to get drunker isn't noways possible."

"Weel, I be drawed on!" exclaimed Mrs. Duncan. "What kind of things do ye mean, Freckles?"

"Why, just an army of black ants. Some of them are sucking away like old topers. Some of them are setting up on their tails and hind legs, fiddling with their fore-feet and wiping their eyes. Some are rolling around on the ground, contented. There are quantities of big blue-bottle flies over the bark and hanging on the grasses around, too drunk to steer a course flying; so they just buzz away like flying, and all the time sitting still. The snake-feeders are too full to feed anything—even more sap to themselves. There's a lot of hard-backed bugs—beetles, I guess—colored like the brown, blue, and black of a peacock's tail. They hang on until the legs of them are so wake they can't stick a minute longer, and then they break away and fall to the ground. They just lay there on their backs, fably clawing air. When it wears off a bit, up they get, and go crawling back for more, and they so full they bump into each other and roll over. Sometimes they can't climb the tree until they wait to sober up a little. There's a lot of big black-and-gold bumblebees, done for entire, stumbling over the bark and rolling on the ground. They just lay there on their backs, rocking from side to side, singing to themselves like fat, happy babies. The wild bees keep up a steady buzzing with the beating of their wings.

"The butterflies are the worst old topers of them all. They're just a circus! You never saw the like of the beauties! They come every color you could be naming, and every shape you could be thinking up. They drink and drink until, if I'm driving them away, they stagger as they fly and turn somersaults in the air. If I lave them alone, they cling to the grasses, shivering happy like; and I'm blest, Mother Duncan, if the best of them could be unlocking the front door with a lead pencil, even."

"I never heard of anything sae surprising," said Mrs. Duncan.

"It's a rare sight to watch them, and no one ever made a picture of a thing like that before, I'm for thinking," said Freckles earnestly.

"Na," said Mrs. Duncan. "Ye can be pretty sure there didna. The Bird Woman must have word in some way, if ye walk the line and I walk to town and tell her. If ye think ye can wait until after supper, I am most sure ye can gang yoursel', for Duncan is coming home and he'd be glad to watch for ye. If he does na come, and na ane passes that I can send word with today, I really will gang early in the morning and tell her mysel'."

Freckles took his lunch and went to the swamp. He walked and watched eagerly. He could find no trace of anything, yet he felt a tense nervousness, as if trouble might be brooding. He examined every section of the wire, and kept watchful eyes on the grasses of the swale, in an effort to discover if anyone had passed through them; but he could discover no trace of anything to justify his fears.

He tilted his hat brim to shade his face and looked for his chickens. They were hanging almost beyond sight in the sky.

"Gee!" he said. "If I only had your sharp eyes and convenient location now, I wouldn't need be troubling so."

He reached his room and cautiously scanned the entrance before he stepped in. Then he pushed the bushes apart with his right arm and entered, his left hand on the butt of his favorite revolver. Instantly he knew that someone had been there. He stepped to the center of the room, closely scanning each wall and the floor. He could find no trace of a clue to confirm his belief, yet so intimate was he with the spirit of the place that he knew.

How he knew he could not have told, yet he did know that someone had entered his room, sat on his benches, and walked over his floor. He was surest around the case. Nothing was disturbed, yet it seemed to Freckles that he could see where prying fingers had tried the lock. He stepped behind the case, carefully examining the ground all around it, and close beside the tree to which it was nailed he found a deep, fresh footprint in the spongy soil—a long, narrow print, that was never made by the foot of Wessner. His heart tugged in his breast as he mentally measured the print, but he did not linger, for now the feeling arose that he was being watched. It seemed to him that he could feel the eyes of some intruder at his back. He knew he was examining things too closely: if anyone were watching, he did not want him to know that he felt it.

He took the most open way, and carried water for his flowers and moss as usual; but he put himself into no position in which he was fully exposed, and his hand was close his revolver constantly. Growing restive at last under the strain, he plunged boldly into the swamp and searched minutely all around his room, but he could not discover the least thing to give him further cause for alarm. He unlocked his case, took out his wheel, and for the remainder of the day he rode and watched as he never had before. Several times he locked the wheel and crossed the swamp on foot, zigzagging to cover all the space possible. Every rod he traveled he used the caution that sprang from knowledge of danger and the direction from which it probably would come. Several times he thought of sending for McLean, but for his life he could not make up his mind to do it with nothing more tangible than one footprint to justify him.

He waited until he was sure Duncan would be at home, if he were coming for the night, before he went to supper. The first thing he saw as he crossed the swale was the big bays in the yard.

There had been no one passing that day, and Duncan readily agreed to watch until Freckles rode to town. He told Duncan of the footprint, and urged him to guard closely. Duncan said he might rest easy, and filling his pipe and taking a good revolver, the big man went to the Limberlost.

Freckles made himself clean and neat, and raced to town, but it was night and the stars were shining before he reached the home of the Bird Woman. From afar he could see that the house was ablaze with lights. The lawn and veranda were strung with fancy lanterns and alive with people. He thought his errand important, so to turn back never occurred to Freckles. This was all the time or opportunity he would have. He must see the Bird Woman, and see her at once. He leaned his wheel inside the fence and walked up the broad front entrance. As he neared the steps, he saw that the place was swarming with young people, and the Angel, with an excuse to a group that surrounded her, came hurrying to him.

"Oh Freckles!" she cried delightedly. "So you could come? We were so afraid you could not! I'm as glad as I can be!"

"I don't understand," said Freckles. "Were you expecting me?"

"Why of course!" exclaimed the Angel. "Haven't you come to my party? Didn't you get my invitation? I sent you one."

"By mail?" asked Freckles.

"Yes," said the Angel. "I had to help with the preparations, and I couldn't find time to drive out; but I wrote you a letter, and told you that the Bird Woman was giving a party for me, and we wanted you to come, surely. I told them at the office to put it with Mr. Duncan's mail."

"Then that's likely where it is at present," said Freckles. "Duncan comes to town only once a week, and at times not that. He's home tonight for the first in a week. He's watching an hour for me until I come to the Bird Woman with a bit of work I thought she'd be caring to hear about bad. Is she where I can see her?"

The Angel's face clouded.

"What a disappointment!" she cried. "I did so want all my friends to know you. Can't you stay anyway?"

Freckles glanced from his wading-boots to the patent leathers of some of the Angel's friends, and smiled whimsically, but there was no danger of his ever misjudging her again.

"You know I cannot, Angel," he said.

"I am afraid I do," she said ruefully. "It's too bad! But there is a thing I want for you more than to come to my party, and that is to hang on and win with your work. I think of you every day, and I just pray that those thieves are not getting ahead of you. Oh, Freckles, do watch closely!"

She was so lovely a picture as she stood before him, ardent in his cause, that Freckles could not take his eyes from her to notice what her friends were thinking. If she did not mind, why should he? Anyway, if they really were the Angel's friends, probably they were better accustomed to her ways than he.

Her face and bared neck and arms were like the wild rose bloom. Her soft frock of white tulle lifted and stirred around her with the gentle evening air. The beautiful golden hair, that crept around her temples and ears as if it loved to cling there, was caught back and bound with broad blue satin ribbon. There was a sash of blue at her waist, and knots of it catching up her draperies.

"Must I go after the Bird Woman?" she pleaded.

"Indade, you must," answered Freckles firmly.

The Angel went away, but returned to say that the Bird Woman was telling a story to those inside and she could not come for a short time.

"You won't come in?" she pleaded.

"I must not," said Freckles. "I am not dressed to be among your friends, and I might be forgetting meself and stay too long."

"Then," said the Angel, "we mustn't go through the house, because it would disturb the story; but I want you to come the outside way to the conservatory and have some of my birthday lunch and some cake to take to Mrs. Duncan and the babies. Won't that be fun?"

Freckles thought that it would be more than fun, and followed delightedly.

The Angel gave him a big glass, brimming with some icy, sparkling liquid that struck his palate as it never had been touched before, because a combination of frosty fruit juices had not been a frequent beverage with him. The night was warm, and the Angel most beautiful and kind. A triple delirium of spirit, mind, and body seized upon him and developed a boldness all unnatural. He slightly parted the heavy curtains that separated the conservatory from the company and looked between. He almost stopped breathing. He had read of things like that, but he never had seen them.

The open space seemed to stretch through half a dozen rooms, all ablaze with lights, perfumed with flowers, and filled with elegantly dressed people. There were glimpses of polished floors, sparkling glass, and fine furnishings. From somewhere, the voice of his beloved Bird Woman arose and fell.

The Angel crowded beside him and was watching also.

"Doesn't it look pretty?" she whispered.

"Do you suppose Heaven is any finer than that?" asked Freckles.

The Angel began to laugh.

"Do you want to be laughing harder than that?" queried Freckles.

"A laugh is always good," said the Angel. "A little more avoirdupois won't hurt me. Go ahead."

"Well then," said Freckles, "it's only that I feel all over as if I belonged there. I could wear fine clothes, and move over those floors, and hold me own against the best of them."

"But where does my laugh come in?" demanded the Angel, as if she had been defrauded.

"And you ask me where the laugh comes in, looking me in the face after that," marveled Freckles.

"I wouldn't be so foolish as to laugh at such a manifest truth as that," said the Angel. "Anyone who knows you even half as well as I do, knows that you are never guilty of a discourtesy, and you move with twice the grace of any man here. Why shouldn't you feel as if you belonged where people are graceful and courteous?"

"On me soul!" said Freckles, "you are kind to be thinking it. You are doubly kind to be saying it."

The curtains parted and a woman came toward them. Her silks and laces trailed across the polished floors. The lights gleamed on her neck and arms, and flashed from rare jewels. She was smiling brightly; and until she spoke, Freckles had not realized fully that it was his loved Bird Woman.

Noticing his bewilderment, she cried: "Why, Freckles! Don't you know me in my war clothes?"

"I do in the uniform in which you fight the Limberlost," said Freckles.

The Bird Woman laughed. Then he told her why he had come, but she scarcely could believe him. She could not say exactly when she would go, but she would make it as soon as possible, for she was most anxious for the study.

While they talked, the Angel was busy packing a box of sandwiches, cake, fruit, and flowers. She gave him a last frosty glass, thanked him repeatedly for bringing news of new material; then Freckles went into the night. He rode toward the Limberlost with his eyes on the stars. Presently he removed his hat, hung it to his belt, and ruffled his hair to the sweep of the night wind. He filled the air all the way with snatches of oratorios, gospel hymns, and dialect and coon songs, in a startlingly varied programme. The one thing Freckles knew that he could do was to sing. The Duncans heard him coming a mile up the corduroy and could not believe their senses. Freckles unfastened the box from his belt, and gave Mrs. Duncan and the children all the eatables it contained, except one big piece of cake that he carried to the sweet-loving Duncan. He put the flowers back in the box and set it among his books. He did not say anything, but they understood it was not to be touched.

"Thae's Freckles's flow'rs," said a tiny Scotsman, "but," he added cheerfully, "it's oor sweeties!"

Freckles's face slowly flushed as he took Duncan's cake and started toward the swamp. While Duncan ate, Freckles told him something about the evening, as well as he could find words to express himself, and the big man was so amazed he kept forgetting the treat in his hands.

Then Freckles mounted his wheel and began a spin that terminated only when the biggest Plymouth Rock in Duncan's coop saluted a new day, and long lines of light reddened the east. As he rode he sang, while he sang he worshiped, but the god he tried to glorify was a dim and faraway mystery. The Angel was warm flesh and blood.

Every time he passed the little bark-covered imprint on the trail he dismounted, removed his hat, solemnly knelt and laid his lips on the impression. Because he kept no account himself, only the laughing-faced old man of the moon knew how often it happened; and as from the beginning, to the follies of earth that gentleman has ever been kind.

With the near approach of dawn Freckles tuned his last note. Wearied almost to falling, he turned from the trail into the path leading to the cabin for a few hours' rest.

Chapter 12

Wherein Black Jack Captures Freckles and the Angel Captures Jack

As Freckles left the trail, from the swale close the south entrance, four large muscular men arose and swiftly and carefully entered the swamp by the wagon road. Two of them carried a big saw, the third, coils of rope and wire, and all of them were heavily armed. They left one man on guard at the entrance. The other three made their way through the darkness as best they could, and were soon at Freckles's room. He had left the swamp on his wheel from the west trail. They counted on his returning on the wheel and circling the east line before he came there.

A little below the west entrance to Freckles's room, Black Jack stepped into the swale, and binding a wire tightly around a scrub oak, carried it below the waving grasses, stretched it taut across the trail, and fastened it to a tree in the swamp. Then he obliterated all signs of his work, and arranged the grass over the wire until it was so completely covered that only minute examination would reveal it. They entered Freckles's room with coarse oaths and jests. In a few moments, his specimen case with its precious contents was rolled into the swamp, while the saw was eating into one of the finest trees of the Limberlost.

The first report from the man on watch was that Duncan had driven to the South camp; the second, that Freckles was coming. The man watching was sent to see on which side the boy turned into the path; as they had expected, he took the east. He was a little tired and his head was rather stupid, for he had not been able to sleep as he had hoped, but he was very happy. Although he watched until his eyes ached, he could see no sign of anyone having entered the swamp.

He called a cheery greeting to all his chickens. At Sleepy Snake Creek he almost fell from his wheel with surprise: the saw-bird was surrounded by four lanky youngsters clamoring for breakfast. The father was strutting with all the importance of a drum major.

"No use to expect the Bird Woman today," said Freckles; "but now wouldn't she be jumping for a chance at that?"

As soon as Freckles was far down the east line, the watch was posted below the room on the west to report his coming. It was only a few moments before the signal came. Then the saw stopped, and the rope was brought out and uncoiled close to a sapling. Wessner and Black Jack crowded to the very edge of the swamp a little above the wire, and crouched, waiting.

They heard Freckles before they saw him. He came gliding down the line swiftly, and as he rode he was singing softly:

"Oh, do you love,
Oh, say you love—"

He got no farther. The sharply driven wheel struck the tense wire and bounded back. Freckles shot over the handlebar and coasted down the trail on his chest. As he struck, Black Jack and Wessner were upon him. Wessner caught off an old felt hat and clapped it over Freckles's mouth, while Black Jack twisted the boy's arms behind him and they rushed him into his room. Almost before he realized that anything had happened, he was trussed to a tree and securely gagged.

Then three of the men resumed work on the tree. The other followed the path Freckles had worn to Little Chicken's tree, and presently he reported that the wires were down and two teams with the loading apparatus coming to take out the timber. All the time the saw was slowly eating, eating into the big tree.

Wessner went to the trail and removed the wire. He picked up Freckles's wheel, that did not seem to be injured, and leaned it against the bushes so that if anyone did pass on the trail he would not see it doubled in the swamp-grass.

Then he came and stood in front of Freckles and laughed in devilish hate. To his own amazement, Freckles found himself looking fear in the face, and marveled that he was not afraid. Four to one! The tree halfway eaten through, the wagons coming up the inside road—he, bound and gagged! The men with Black Jack and Wessner had belonged to McLean's gang when last he had heard of them, but who those coming with the wagons might be he could not guess.

If they secured that tree, McLean lost its value, lost his wager, and lost his faith in him. The words of the Angel hammered in his ears. "Oh, Freckles, do watch closely!"

The saw worked steadily.

When the tree was down and loaded, what would they do? Pull out, and leave him there to report them? It was not to be hoped for. The place always had been lawless. It could mean but one thing.

A mist swept before his eyes, while his head swam. Was it only last night that he had worshiped the Angel in a delirium of happiness? And now, what? Wessner, released from a turn at the saw, walked to the flower bed, and tearing up a handful of rare ferns by the roots, started toward Freckles. His intention was obvious. Black Jack stopped him, with an oath.

"You see here, Dutchy," he bawled, "mebby you think you'll wash his face with that, but you won't. A contract's a contract. We agreed to take out these trees and leave him for you to dispose of whatever way you please, provided you shut him up eternally on this deal. But I'll not see a tied man tormented by a fellow that he can lick up the ground with, loose, and that's flat. It raises my gorge to think what he'll get when we're gone, but you needn't think you're free to begin before. Don't you lay a hand on him while I'm here! What do you say, boys?"

"I say yes," growled one of McLean's latest deserters. "What's more, we're a pack of fools to risk the dirty work of silencing him. You had him face down and you on his back; why the hell didn't you cover his head and roll him into the bushes until we were gone? When I went into this, I didn't understand that he was to see all of us and that there was murder on the ticket. I'm not up to it. I don't mind lifting trees we came for, but I'm cursed if I want blood on my hands."

"Well, you ain't going to get it," bellowed Jack. "You fellows only contracted to help me get out my marked trees. He belong to Wessner, and it ain't in our deal what happens to him."

"Yes, and if Wessner finishes him safely, we are practically in for murder as well as stealing the trees; and if he don't, all hell's to pay. I think you've made a damnable bungle of this thing; that's what I think!"

"Then keep your thoughts to yourself," cried Jack. "We're doing this, and it's all planned safe and sure. As for killing that buck—come to think of it, killing is what he needs. He's away too good for this world of woe, anyhow. I tell you, it's all safe enough. His dropping out won't be the only secret the old Limberlost has never told. It's too dead easy to make it look like he helped take the timber and then cut. Why, he's played right into our hands. He was here at the swamp all last night, and back again in an hour or so. When we get our plan worked out, even old fool Duncan won't lift a finger to look for his carcass. We couldn't have him going in better shape."

"You just bet," said Wessner. "I owe him all he'll get, and be damned to you, but I'll pay!" he snarled at Freckles.

So it was killing, then. They were not only after this one tree, but many, and with his body it was their plan to kill his honor. To brand him a thief, with them, before the Angel, the Bird Woman, the dear Boss, and the Duncans—Freckles, in sick despair, sagged against the ropes.

Then he gathered his forces and thought swiftly. There was no hope of McLean's coming. They had chosen a day when they knew he had a big contract at the South camp. The Boss could not come before tomorrow by any possibility, and there would be no tomorrow for the boy. Duncan was on his way to the South camp, and the Bird Woman had said she would come as soon as she could. After the fatigue of the party, it was useless to expect her and the Angel today, and God save them from coming! The Angel's father had said they would be as safe in the Limberlost as at home. What would he think of this?

The sweat broke on Freckles's forehead. He tugged at the ropes whenever he felt that he dared, but they were passed around the tree and his body several times, and knotted on his chest. He was helpless. There was no hope, no help. And after they had conspired to make him appear a runaway thief to his loved ones, what was it that Wessner would do to him?

Whatever it was, Freckles lifted his head and resolved that he would bear in mind what he had once heard the Bird Woman say. He would go out bonnily. Never would he let them see, if he grew afraid. After all, what did it matter what they did to his body if by some scheme of the devil they could encompass his disgrace?

Then hope suddenly rose high in Freckles's breast. They could not do that! The Angel would not believe. Neither would McLean. He would keep up his courage. Kill him they could; dishonor him they could not.

Yet, summon all the fortitude he might, that saw eating into the tree rasped his nerves worse and worse. With whirling brain he gazed into the Limberlost, searching for something, he knew not what, and in blank horror found his eyes focusing on the Angel. She was quite a distance away, but he could see her white lips and angry expression.

Last week he had taken her and the Bird Woman across the swamp over the path he followed in going from his room to the chicken tree. He had told them the night before, that the butterfly tree was on the line close to this path. In figuring on their not coming that day, he failed to reckon with the enthusiasm of the Bird Woman. They must be there for the study, and the Angel had risked crossing the swamp in search of him. Or was there something in his room they needed? The blood surged in his ears as the roar of the Limberlost in the wrath of a storm.

He looked again, and it had been a dream. She was not there. Had she been? For his life, Freckles could not tell whether he really had seen the Angel, or whether his strained senses had played him the most cruel trick of all. Or was it not the kindest? Now he could go with the vision of her lovely face fresh with him.

"Thank you for that, oh God!" whispered Freckles. "'Twas more than kind of you and I don't s'pose I ought to be wanting anything else; but if you can, oh, I wish I could know before this ends, if 'twas me mother"—Freckles could not even whisper the words, for he hesitated a second and ended—"IF 'TWAS ME MOTHER DID IT!"

"Freckles! Freckles! Oh, Freckles!" the voice of the Angel came calling. Freckles swayed forward and wrenched at the rope until it cut deeply into his body.

"Hell!" cried Black Jack. "Who is that? Do you know?"

Freckles nodded.

Jack whipped out a revolver and snatched the gag from Freckles's mouth.

"Say quick, or it's up with you right now, and whoever that is with you!"

"It's the girl the Bird Woman takes with her," whispered Freckles through dry, swollen lips.

"They ain't due here for five days yet," said Wessner. "We got on to that last week."

"Yes," said Freckles, "but I found a tree covered with butterflies and things along the east line yesterday that I thought the Bird Woman would want extra, and I went to town to tell her last night. She said she'd come soon, but she didn't say when. They must be here. I take care of the girl while the Bird Woman works. Untie me quick until she is gone. I'll try to send her back, and then you can go on with your dirty work."

"He ain't lying," volunteered Wessner. "I saw that tree covered with butterflies and him watching around it when we were spying on him yesterday."

"No, he leaves lying to your sort," snapped Black Jack, as he undid the rope and pitched it across the room. "Remember that you're covered every move you make, my buck," he cautioned.

"Freckles! Freckles!" came the Angel's impatient voice, closer and closer.

"I must be answering," said Freckles, and Jack nodded. "Right here!" he called, and to the men: "You go on with your work, and remember one thing yourselves. The work of the Bird Woman is known all over the world. This girl's father is a rich man, and she is all he has. If you offer hurt of any kind to either of them, this world has no place far enough away or dark enough for you to be hiding in. Hell will be easy to what any man will get if he touches either of them!"

"Freckles, where are you?" demanded the Angel.

Soulsick with fear for her, Freckles went toward her and parted the bushes that she might enter. She came through without apparently giving him a glance, and the first words she said were: "Why have the gang come so soon? I didn't know you expected them for three weeks yet. Or is this some especial tree that Mr. McLean needs to fill an order right now?"

Freckles hesitated. Would a man dare lie to save himself? No. But to save the Angel—surely that was different. He opened his lips, but the Angel was capable of saving herself. She walked among them, exactly as if she had been reared in a lumber camp, and never waited for an answer.

"Why, your specimen case!" she cried. "Look! Haven't you noticed that it's tipped over? Set it straight, quickly!"

A couple of the men stepped out and carefully righted the case.

"There! That's better," she said. "Freckles, I'm surprised at your being so careless. It would be a shame to break those lovely butterflies for one old tree! Is that a valuable tree? Why didn't you tell us last night you were going to take out a tree this morning? Oh, say, did you put your case there to protect that tree from that stealing old Black Jack and his gang? I bet you did! Well, if that wasn't bright! What kind of a tree is it?"

"It's a white oak," said Freckles.

"Like those they make dining-tables and sideboards from?"

"Yes."

"My! How interesting!" she cried. "I don't know a thing about timber, but my father wants me to learn just everything I can. I am going to ask him to let me come here and watch you until I know enough to boss a gang myself. Do you like to cut trees, gentlemen?" she asked with angelic sweetness of the men.

Some of them appeared foolish and some grim, but one managed to say they did.

Then the Angel's eyes turned full on Black Jack, and she gave the most natural little start of astonishment.

"Oh! I almost thought that you were a ghost!" she cried. "But I see now that you are really and truly. Were you ever in Colorado?"

"No," said Jack.

"I see you aren't the same man," said the Angel. "You know, we were in Colorado last year, and there was a cowboy who was the handsomest man any-where around. He'd come riding into town every night, and all we girls just adored him! Oh, but he was a beauty! I thought at first glance you were really he, but I see now he wasn't nearly so tall nor so broad as you, and only half as handsome."

The men began to laugh while Jack flushed crimson. The Angel joined in the laugh.

"Well, I'll leave it to you! Isn't he handsome?" she challenged. "As for that cowboy's face, it couldn't be compared with yours. The only trouble with you is that your clothes are spoiling you. It's the dress those cowboys wear that makes half their attraction. If you were properly clothed, you could break the heart of the prettiest girl in the country."

With one accord the other men looked at Black Jack, and for the first time realized that he was a superb specimen of manhood, for he stood six feet tall, was broad, well-rounded, and had dark, even skin, big black eyes, and full red lips.

"I'll tell you what!" exclaimed the Angel. "I'd just love to see you on horseback. Nothing sets a handsome man off so splendidly. Do you ride?"

"Yes," said Jack, and his eyes were burning on the Angel as if he would fathom the depths of her soul.

"Well," said the Angel winsomely, "I know what I just wish you'd do. I wish you would let your hair grow a little longer. Then wear a blue flannel shirt a little open at the throat, a red tie, and a broad-brimmed felt hat, and ride past my house of evenings. I'm always at home then, and almost always on the veranda, and, oh! but I would like to see you! Will you do that for me?" It is impossible to describe the art with which the Angel asked the question. She was looking straight into Jack's face, coarse and hardened with sin and careless living, which was now taking on a wholly different expression. The evil lines of it were softening and fading under her clear gaze. A dull red flamed into his bronze cheeks, while his eyes were growing brightly tender.

"Yes," he said, and the glance he gave the men was of such a nature that no one saw fit even to change countenance.

"Oh, goody!" she cried, tilting on her toes. "I'll ask all the girls to come see, but they needn't stick in! We can get along without them, can't we?"

Jack leaned toward her. He was the charmed fluttering bird, while the Angel was the snake.

"Well, I rather guess!" he cried.

The Angel drew a deep breath and surveyed him rapturously.

"My, but you're tall!" she commented. "Do you suppose I ever will grow to reach your shoulders?"

She stood on tiptoe and measured the distance with her eyes. Then she developed timid confusion, while her glance sought the ground.

"I wish I could do something," she half whispered.

Jack seemed to increase an inch in height.

"What?" he asked hoarsely.

"Lariat Bill used always to have a bunch of red flowers in his shirt pocket. The red lit up his dark eyes and olive cheeks and made him splendid. May I put some red flowers on you?"

Freckles stared as he wheezed for breath. He wished the earth would open and swallow him. Was he dead or alive? Since his Angel had seen Black Jack she never had glanced his way. Was she completely bewitched? Would she throw herself at the man's feet before them all? Couldn't she give him even one thought? Hadn't she seen that he was gagged and bound? Did she truly think that these were McLean's men? Why, she could not! It was only a few days ago that she had been close enough to this man and angry enough with him to peel the hat from his head with a shot! Suddenly a thing she had said jestingly to him one day came back with startling force: "You must take Angels on trust." Of course you must! She was his Angel. She must have seen! His life, and what was far more, her own, was in her hands. There was nothing he could do but trust her. Surely she was working out some plan.

The Angel knelt beside his flower bed and recklessly tore up by the roots a big bunch of foxfire.

"These stems are so tough and sticky," she said. "I can't break them. Loan me your knife," she ordered Freckles.

As she reached for the knife, her back was for one second toward the men. She looked into his eyes and deliberately winked.

She severed the stems, tossed the knife to Freckles, and walking to Jack, laid the flowers over his heart.

Freckles broke into a sweat of agony. He had said she would be safe in a herd of howling savages. Would she? If Black Jack even made a motion toward touching her, Freckles knew that from somewhere he would muster the strength to kill him. He mentally measured the distance to where his club lay and set his muscles for a spring. But no—by the splendor of God! The big fellow was baring his head with a hand that was unsteady. The Angel pulled one of the long silver pins from her hat and fastened her flowers securely.

Freckles was quaking. What was to come next? What was she planning, and oh! did she understand the danger of her presence among those men; the real necessity for action?

As the Angel stepped from Jack, she turned her head to one side and peered at him, quite as Freckles had seen the little yellow fellow do on the line a hundred times, and said: "Well, that does the trick! Isn't that fine? See how it sets him off, boys? Don't you forget the tie is to be red, and the first ride soon. I can't wait very long. Now I must go. The Bird Woman will be ready to start, and she will come here hunting me next, for she is busy today. What did I come here for anyway?"

She glanced inquiringly around, and several of the men laughed. Oh, the delight of it! She had forgotten her errand for him! Jack had a second increase in height. The Angel glanced helplessly as if seeking a clue. Then her eyes fell, as if by accident, on Freckles, and she cried, "Oh, I know now! It was those magazines the Bird Woman promised you. I came to tell you that we put them under the box where we hide things, at the entrance to the swamp as we came in. I knew I would need my hands crossing the swamp, so I hid them there. You'll find them at the same old place."

Then Freckles spoke.

"It's mighty risky for you to be crossing the swamp alone," he said. "I'm surprised that the Bird Woman would be letting you try it. I know it's a little farther, but it's begging you I am to be going back by the trail. That's bad enough, but it's far safer than the swamp."

The Angel laughed merrily.

"Oh stop your nonsense!" she cried. "I'm not afraid! Not in the least! The Bird Woman didn't want me to try following a path that I'd been over only once, but I was sure I could do it, and I'm rather proud of the performance. Now, don't go babying! You know I'm not afraid!"

"No," said Freckles gently, "I know you're not; but that has nothing to do with the fact that your friends are afraid for you. On the trail you can see your way a bit ahead, and you've all the world a better chance if you meet a snake."

Then Freckles had an inspiration. He turned to Jack imploringly.

"You tell her!" he pleaded. "Tell her to go by the trail. She will for you."

The implication of this statement was so gratifying to Black Jack that he seemed again to expand and take on increase before their very eyes.

"You bet!" exclaimed Jack. And to the Angel: "You better take Freckles's word for it, miss. He knows the old swamp better than any of us, except me, and if he says 'go by the trail,' you'd best do it."

The Angel hesitated. She wanted to recross the swamp and try to reach the horse. She knew Freckles would brave any danger to save her crossing the swamp alone, but she really was not afraid, while the trail added over a mile to the walk. She knew the path. She intended to run for dear life the instant she felt herself from their sight, and tucked in the folds of her blouse was a fine little 32-caliber revolver that her father had presented her for her share in what he was pleased to call her military exploit. One last glance at Freckles showed her the agony in his eyes, and immediately she imagined he had some other reason. She would follow the trail.

"All right," she said, giving Jack a thrilling glance. "If you say so, I'll return by the trail to please you. Good-bye, everybody."

She lifted the bushes and started toward the entrance.

"You damned fool! Stop her!" growled Wessner. "Keep her till we're loaded, anyhow. You're playing hell! Can't you see that when this thing is found out, there she'll be to ruin all of us. If you let her go, every man of us has got to cut, and some of us will be caught sure."

Jack sprang forward. Freckles's heart muffled in his throat. The Angel seemed to divine Jack's coming. She was humming a little song. She deliberately stopped and began pulling the heads of the curious grasses that grew all around her. When she straightened, she took a step backward and called: "Ho! Freckles, the Bird Woman wants that natural history pamphlet returned. It belongs to a set she is going to have bound. That's one of the reasons we put it under the box. You be sure to get them as you go home tonight, for fear it rains or becomes damp with the heavy dews."

"All right," said Freckles, but it was in a voice that he never had heard before.

Then the Angel turned and sent a parting glance at Jack. She was overpoweringly human and bewitchingly lovely.

"You won't forget that ride and the red tie," she half asserted, half questioned.

Jack succumbed. Freckles was his captive, but he was the Angel's, soul and body. His face wore the holiest look it ever had known as he softly re-echoed Freckles's "All right." With her head held well up, the Angel walked slowly away, and Jack turned to the men.

"Drop your damned staring and saw wood," he shouted. "Don't you know anything at all about how to treat a lady?" It might have been a question which of the cronies that crouched over green wood fires in the cabins of Wildcat Hollow, eternally sucking a corncob pipe and stirring the endless kettles of stewing coon and opossum, had taught him to do even as well as he had by the Angel.

The men muttered and threatened among themselves, but they began working desperately. Someone suggested that a man be sent to follow the Angel and to watch her and the Bird Woman leave the swamp. Freckles's heart sank within him, but Jack was in a delirium and past all caution.

"Yes," he sneered. "Mebby all of you had better give over on the saw and run after the girl. I guess not! Seems to me I got the favors. I didn't see no bouquets on the rest of you! If anybody follows her, I do, and I'm needed here among such a pack of idiots. There's no danger in that baby face. She wouldn't give me away! You double and work like forty, while me and Wessner will take the axes and begin to cut in on the other side."

"What about the noise?" asked Wessner.

"No difference about the noise," answered Jack. "She took us to be from McLean's gang, slick as grease. Make the chips fly!"

So all of them attacked the big tree.

Freckles sat on one of his benches and waited. In their haste to fell the tree and load it, so that the teamsters could start, and leave them free to attack another, they had forgotten to rebind him.

The Angel was on the trail and safely started. The cold perspiration made Freckles's temples clammy and ran in little streams down his chest. It would take her more time to follow the trail, but her safety was Freckles's sole thought in urging her to go that way. He tried to figure on how long it would require to walk to the carriage. He wondered if the Bird Woman had unhitched. He followed the Angel every step of the way. He figured on when she would cross the path of the clearing, pass the deep pool where his "find-out" frog lived, cross Sleepy Snake Creek, and reach the carriage.

He wondered what she would say to the Bird Woman, and how long it would take them to pack and start. He knew now that they would understand, and the Angel would try to get the Boss there in time to save his wager. She could never do it, for the saw was over half through, and Jack and Wessner cutting into the opposite side of the tree. It appeared as if they could fell at least that tree, before McLean could come, and if they did he lost his wager.

When it was down, would they rebind him and leave him for Wessner to wreak his insane vengeance on, or would they take him along to the next tree and dispose of him when they had stolen all the timber they could? Jack had said that he should not be touched until he left. Surely he would not run all that risk for one tree, when he had many others of far greater value marked. Freckles felt that he had some hope to cling to now, but he found himself praying that the Angel would hurry.

Once Jack came to Freckles and asked if he had any water. Freckles arose and showed him where he kept his drinking-water. Jack drank in great gulps, and as he passed back the bucket, he said: "When a man's got a chance of catching a fine girl like that, he ought not be mixed up in any dirty business. I wish to God I was out of this!"

Freckles answered heartily: "I wish I was, too!"

Jack stared at him a minute and then broke into a roar of rough laughter.

"Blest if I blame you," he said. "But you had your chance! We offered you a fair thing and you gave Wessner his answer. I ain't envying you when he gives you his."

"You're six to one," answered Freckles. "It will be easy enough for you to be killing the body of me, but, curse you all, you can't blacken me soul!"

"Well, I'd give anything you could name if I had your honesty," said Jack.

When the mighty tree fell, the Limberlost shivered and screamed with the echo. Freckles groaned in despair, but the gang took heart. That was so much accomplished. They knew where to dispose of it safely, with no questions asked. Before the day was over, they could remove three others, all suitable for veneer and worth far more than this. Then they would leave Freckles to Wessner and scatter for safety, with more money than they had ever hoped for in their possession.

Chapter 13

Wherein the Angel Releases Freckles, and the Curse of Black Jack Falls upon Her

On the line, the Angel gave one backward glance at Black Jack, to see that he had returned to his work. Then she gathered her skirts above her knees and leaped forward on the run. In the first three yards she passed Freckles's wheel. Instantly she imagined that was why he had insisted on her coming by the trail. She seized it and sprang on. The saddle was too high, but she was an expert rider and could catch the pedals as they came up. She stopped at Duncan's cabin long enough to remedy this, telling Mrs. Duncan while working what was happening, and for her to follow the east trail until she found the Bird Woman, and told her that she had gone after McLean and for her to leave the swamp as quickly as possible.

Even with her fear for Freckles to spur her, Sarah Duncan blanched and began shivering at the idea of facing the Limberlost. The Angel looked her in the eyes.

"No matter how afraid you are, you have to go," she said. "If you don't the Bird Woman will go to Freckles's room, hunting me, and they will have trouble with her. If she isn't told to leave at once, they may follow me, and, finding I'm gone, do some terrible thing to Freckles. I can't go that's flat for if they caught me, then there'd be no one to go for help. You don't suppose they are going to take out the trees they're after and then leave Freckles to run and tell? They are going to murder the boy; that's what they are going to do. You run, and run for life! For Freckles's life! You can ride back with the Bird Woman."

The Angel saw Mrs. Duncan started; then began her race.

Those awful miles of corduroy! Would they never end? She did not dare use the wheel too roughly, for if it broke she never could arrive on time afoot. Where her way was impassable for the wheel, she jumped off, and pushing it beside her or carrying it, she ran as fast as she could. The day was fearfully warm. The sun poured with the fierce baking heat of August. The bushes claimed her hat, and she did not stop for it.

Where it was at all possible, the Angel mounted and pounded over the corduroy again. She was panting for breath and almost worn out when she reached the level pike. She had no idea how long she had been—and only two miles covered. She leaned over the bars, almost standing on the pedals, racing with all the strength in her body. The blood surged in her ears while her head swam, but she kept a straight course, and rode and rode. It seemed to her that she was standing still, while the trees and houses were racing past her.

Once a farmer's big dog rushed angrily into the road and she swerved until she almost fell, but she regained her balance, and setting her muscles, pedaled as fast as she could. At last she lifted her head. Surely it could not be over a mile more. She had covered two of corduroy and at least three of gravel, and it was only six in all.

She was reeling in the saddle, but she gripped the bars with new energy, and raced desperately. The sun beat on her bare head and hands. Just when she was choking with dust, and almost prostrate with heat and exhaustion—crash, she ran into a broken bottle. Snap! went the tire; the wheel swerved and pitched over. The Angel rolled into the thick yellow dust of the road and lay quietly.

From afar, Duncan began to notice a strange, dust-covered object in the road, as he headed toward town with the first load of the day's felling.

He chirruped to the bays and hurried them all he could. As he neared the Angel, he saw it was a woman and a broken wheel. He was beside her in an instant. He carried her to a shaded fence-corner, stretched her on the grass, and wiped the dust from the lovely face all dirt-streaked, crimson, and bearing a startling whiteness around the mouth and nose.

Wheels were common enough. Many of the farmers' daughters owned and rode them, but he knew these same farmers' daughters; this face was a stranger's. He glanced at the Angel's tumbled clothing, the silkiness of her hair, with its pale satin ribbon, and noticed that she had lost her hat. Her lips tightened in an ominous quiver. He left her and picked up the wheel: as he had surmised, he knew it. This, then, was Freckles's Swamp Angel. There was trouble in the Limberlost, and she had broken down racing to McLean. Duncan turned the bays into a fence-corner, tied one of them, unharnessed the other, fastened up the trace chains, and hurried to the nearest farmhouse to send help to the Angel. He found a woman, who took a bottle of camphor, a jug of water, and some towels, and started on the run.

Then Duncan put the bay to speed and raced to camp.

The Angel, left alone, lay still for a second, then she shivered and opened her eyes. She saw that she was on the grass and the broken wheel beside her. Instantly she realized that someone had carried her there and gone after help. She sat up and looked around. She noticed the load of logs and the one horse. Someone was riding after help for her!

"Oh, poor Freckles!" she wailed. "They may be killing him by now. Oh, how much time have I wasted?"

She hurried to the other bay, her fingers flying as she set him free. Snatching up a big blacksnake whip that lay on the ground, she caught the hames, stretched along the horse's neck, and, for the first time, the fine, big fellow felt on his back the quality of the lash that Duncan was accustomed to crack over him. He was frightened, and ran at top speed.

The Angel passed a wildly waving, screaming woman on the road, and a little later a man riding as if he, too, were in great haste. The man called to her, but she only lay lower and used the whip. Soon the feet of the man's horse sounded farther and farther away.

At the South camp they were loading a second wagon, when the Angel appeared riding one of Duncan's bays, lathered and dripping, and cried: "Everybody go to Freckles! There are thieves stealing trees, and they had him bound. They're going to kill him!"

She wheeled the horse toward the Limberlost. The alarm sounded through camp. The gang were not unprepared. McLean sprang to Nellie's back and raced after the Angel. As they passed Duncan, he wheeled and followed. Soon the pike was an irregular procession of barebacked riders, wildly driving flying horses toward the swamp.

The Boss rode neck-and-neck with the Angel. He repeatedly commanded her to stop and fall out of line, until he remembered that he would need her to lead him to Freckles. Then he gave up and rode beside her, for she was sending the bay at as sharp a pace as the other horses could keep and hold out. He could see that she was not hearing him. He glanced back and saw that Duncan was close. There was something terrifying in the appearance of the big man, and the manner in which he sat his beast and rode. It would be a sad day for the man on whom Duncan's wrath broke. There were four others close behind him, and the pike filling with the remainder of the gang; so McLean took heart and raced beside the Angel. Over and over he asked her where the trouble was, but she only gripped the hames, leaned along the bay's neck, and slashed away with the blacksnake. The steaming horse, with crimson nostrils and heaving sides, stretched out and ran for home with all the speed there was in him.

When they passed the cabin, the Bird Woman's carriage was there and Mrs. Duncan in the door wringing her hands, but the Bird Woman was nowhere to be seen. The Angel sent the bay along the path and turned into the west trail, while the men bunched and followed her. When she reached the entrance to Freckles's room, there were four men with her, and two more very close behind. She slid from the horse, and snatching the little revolver from her pocket, darted toward the bushes. McLean caught them back, and with drawn weapon, pressed beside her. There they stopped in astonishment.

The Bird Woman blocked the entrance. Over a small limb lay her revolver. It was trained at short range on Black Jack and Wessner, who stood with their hands above their heads.

Freckles, with the blood trickling down his face, from an ugly cut in his temple, was gagged and bound to the tree again; the remainder of the men were gone. Black Jack was raving as a maniac, and when they looked closer it was only the left arm that he raised. His right, with the hand shattered, hung helpless at his side, while his revolver lay at Freckles's feet. Wessner's weapon was in his belt, and beside him Freckles's club.

Freckles's face was white, with colorless lips, but in his eyes was the strength of undying courage. McLean pushed past the Bird Woman crying. "Hold steady on them only one minute more!"

He snatched the revolver from Wessner's belt, and stooped for Jack's.

At that instant the Angel rushed past. She tore the gag from Freckles, and seizing the rope knotted on his chest, she tugged at it desperately. Under her fingers it gave way, and she hurled it to McLean. The men were crowding in, and Duncan seized Wessner. As the Angel saw Freckles stand out, free, she reached her arms to him and pitched forward. A fearful oath burst from the lips of Black Jack. To have saved his life, Freckles could not have avoided the glance of triumph he gave Jack, when folding the Angel in his arms and stretching her on the mosses.

The Bird Woman cried out sharply for water as she ran to them. Someone sprang to bring that, and another to break open the case for brandy. As McLean arose from binding Wessner, there was a cry that Jack was escaping.

He was already far in the swamp, running for its densest part in leaping bounds. Every man who could be spared plunged after him.

Other members of the gang arriving, were sent to follow the tracks of the wagons. The teamsters had driven from the west entrance, and crossing the swale, had taken the same route the Bird Woman and the Angel had before them. There had been ample time for the drivers to reach the road; after that they could take any one of four directions. Traffic was heavy, and lumber wagons were passing almost constantly, so the men turned back and joined the more exciting hunt for a man. The remainder of the gang joined them, also farmers of the region and travelers attracted by the disturbance.

Watchers were set along the trail at short intervals. They patrolled the line and roads through the swamp that night, with lighted torches, and the next day McLean headed as thorough a search as he felt could be made of one side, while Duncan covered the other; but Black Jack could not be found. Spies were set around his home, in Wildcat Hollow, to ascertain if he reached there or aid was being sent in any direction to him; but it was soon clear that his relatives were ignorant of his hiding-place, and were searching for him.

Great is the elasticity of youth. A hot bath and a sound night's sleep renewed Freckles's strength, and it needed but little more to work the same result with the Angel. Freckles was on the trail early the next morning. Besides a crowd of people anxious to witness Jack's capture, he found four stalwart guards, one at each turn. In his heart he was compelled to admit that he was glad to have them there. Close noon, McLean placed his men in charge of Duncan, and taking Freckles, drove to town to see how the Angel fared. McLean visited a greenhouse and bought an armload of its finest products; but Freckles would have none of them. He would carry his message in a glowing mass of the Limberlost's first goldenrod.

The Bird Woman received them, and in answer to their eager inquiries, said that the Angel was in no way seriously injured, only so bruised and shaken that their doctor had ordered her to lie quietly for the day. Though she was sore and stiff, they were having work to keep her in bed. Her callers sent up their flowers with their grateful regards, and the Angel promptly returned word that she wanted to see them.

She reached both hands to McLean. "What if one old tree is gone? You don't care, sir? You feel that Freckles has kept his trust as nobody ever did before, don't you? You won't forget all those long first days of fright that you told us of, the fearful cold of winter, the rain, heat, and lonesomeness, and the brave days, and lately, nights, too, and let him feel that his trust is broken? Oh, Mr. McLean," she begged, "say something to him! Do something to make him feel that it isn't for nothing he has watched and suffered it out with that old Limberlost. Make him see how great and fine it is, and how far, far better he has done than you or any of us expected! What's one old tree, anyway?" she cried passionately.

"I was thinking before you came. Those other men were rank big cowards. They were scared for their lives. If they were the drivers, I wager you gloves against gloves they never took those logs out to the pike. My coming upset them. Before you feel bad any more, you go look and see if they didn't lose courage the minute they left Wessner and Black Jack, dump that timber and run. I don't believe they ever had the grit to drive out with it in daylight. Go see if they didn't figure on leaving the way we did the other morning, and you'll find the logs before you reach the road. They never risked taking them into the open, when they got away and had time to think. Of course they didn't!

"And, then, another thing. You haven't lost your wager! It never will be claimed, because you made it with a stout, dark, red-faced man who drives a bay and a gray. He was right back of you, Mr. McLean, when I came yesterday. He went deathly white and shook on his feet when he saw those men probably would be caught. Some one of them was something to him, and you can just spot him for one of the men at the bottom of your troubles, and urging those younger fellows to steal from you. I suppose he'd promised to divide. You settle with him, and that business will stop."

She turned to Freckles. "And you be the happiest man alive, because you have kept your trust. Go look where I tell you and you'll find the logs. I can see just about where they are. When they go up that steep little hill, into the next woods after the cornfield, why, they could unloose the chains and the logs would roll from the wagons themselves. Now, you go look; and Mr. McLean, you do feel that Freckles has been brave and faithful? You won't love him any the less even if you don't find the logs."

The Angel's nerve gave way and she began to cry. Freckles could not endure it. He almost ran from the room, with the tears in his eyes; but McLean took the Angel from the Bird Woman's arms, and kissed her brave little face, stroked her hair, and petted her into quietness before he left.

As they drove to the swamp, McLean so earnestly seconded all that the Angel had said that he soon had the boy feeling much better.

"Freckles, your Angel has a spice of the devil in her, but she's superb! You needn't spend any time questioning or bewailing anything she does. Just worship blindly, my boy. By heaven! she's sense, courage, and beauty for half a dozen girls," said McLean.

"It's altogether right you are, sir," affirmed Freckles heartily. Presently he added, "There's no question but the series is over now."

"Don't think it!" answered McLean. "The Bird Woman is working for success, and success along any line is not won by being scared out. She will be back on the usual day, and ten to one, the Angel will be with her. They are made of pretty stern stuff, and they don't scare worth a cent. Before I left, I told the Bird Woman it would be safe; and it will. You may do your usual walking, but those four guards are there to remain. They are under your orders absolutely. They are prohibited from firing on any bird or molesting anything that you want to protect, but there they remain, and this time it is useless for you to say one word. I have listened to your pride too long. You are too precious to me, and that voice of yours is too precious to the world to run any more risks."

"I am sorry to have anything spoil the series," said Freckles, "and I'd love them to be coming, the Angel especial, but it can't be. You'll have to tell them so. You see, Jack would have been ready to stake his life she meant what she said and did to him. When the teams pulled out, Wessner seized me; then he and Jack went to quarreling over whether they should finish me then or take me to the next tree they were for felling. Between them they were pulling me around and hurting me bad. Wessner wanted to get at me right then, and Jack said he shouldn't be touching me till the last tree was out and all the rest of them gone. I'm belaying Jack really hated to see me done for in the beginning; and I think, too, he was afraid if Wessner finished me then he'd lose his nerve and cut, and they couldn't be managing the felling without him; anyway, they were hauling me round like I was already past all feeling, and they tied me up again. To keep me courage up, I twits Wessner about having to tie me and needing another man to help handle me. I told him what I'd do to him if I was free, and he grabs up me own club and lays open me head with it. When the blood came streaming, it set Jack raving, and he cursed and damned Wessner for a coward and a softy. Then Wessner turned on Jack and gives it to him for letting the Angel make a fool of him. Tells him she was just playing with him, and beyond all manner of doubt she'd gone after you, and there was nothing to do on account of his foolishness but finish me, get out, and let the rest of the timber go, for likely you was on the way right then. That drove Jack plum crazy.

"I don't think he was for having a doubt of the Angel before, but then he just raved. He grabbed out his gun and turned on Wessner. Spang! It went out of his fist, and the order comes: 'Hands up!' Wessner reached for kingdom come like he was expecting to grab hold and pull himself up. Jack puts up what he has left. Then he leans over to me and tells me what he'll do to me if he ever gets out of there alive. Then, just like a snake hissing, he spits out what he'll do to her for playing him. He did get away, and with his strength, that wound in his hand won't be bothering him long. He'll do to me just what he said, and when he hears it really was she that went after you, why, he'll keep his oath about her.

"He's lived in the swamp all his life, sir, and everybody says it's always been the home of cutthroats, outlaws, and runaways. He knows its most secret places as none of the others. He's alive. He's in there now, sir. Some way he'll keep alive. If you'd seen his face, all scarlet with passion, twisted with pain, and black with hate, and heard him swearing that oath, you'd know it was a sure thing. I ain't done with him yet, and I've brought this awful thing on her."

"And I haven't begun with him yet," said McLean, setting his teeth. "I've been away too slow and too easy, believing there'd be no greater harm than the loss of a tree. I've sent for a couple of first-class detectives. We will put them on his track, and rout him out and rid the country of him. I don't propose for him to stop either our work or our pleasure. As for his being in the swamp now, I don't believe it. He'd find a way out last night, in spite of us. Don't you worry! I am at the helm now, and I'll see to that gentleman in my own way."

"I wish to my soul you had seen and heard him!" said Freckles, unconvinced.

They entered the swamp, taking the route followed by the Bird Woman and the Angel. They really did find the logs, almost where the Angel had predicted they would be. McLean went to the South camp and had an interview with Crowen that completely convinced him that the Angel was correct there also. But he had no proof, so all he could do was to discharge the man, although his guilt was so apparent that he offered to withdraw the wager.

Then McLean sent for a pack of bloodhounds and put them on the trail of Black Jack. They clung to it, on and on, into the depths of the swamp, leading their followers through what had been considered impassable and impenetrable ways, and finally, around near the west entrance and into the swale. Here the dogs bellowed, raved, and fell over each other in their excitement. They raced back and forth from swamp to swale, but follow the scent farther they would not, even though cruelly driven. At last their owner attributed their actions to snakes, and as they were very valuable dogs, abandoned the effort to urge them on. So that all they really established was the fact that Black Jack had eluded their vigilance and crossed the trail some time in the night. He had escaped to the swale; from there he probably crossed the corduroy, and reaching the lower end of the swamp, had found friends. It was a great relief to feel that he was not in the swamp, and it raised the spirits of every man on the line, though many of them expressed regrets that he who was undoubtedly most to blame should escape, while Wessner, who in the beginning was only his tool, should be left to punishment.

But for Freckles, with Jack's fearful oath ringing in his ears, there was neither rest nor peace. He was almost ill when the day for the next study of the series arrived and he saw the Bird Woman and the Angel coming down the corduroy. The guards of the east line he left at their customary places, but those of the west he brought over and placed, one near Little Chicken's tree, and the other at the carriage. He was firm about the Angel's remaining in the carriage, that he did not offer to have unhitched. He went with the Bird Woman to secure the picture, which was the easiest matter it had been at any time yet, for the simple reason that the placing of the guards and the unusual movement around the swamp had made Mr. and Mrs. Chicken timid, and they had not carried Little Chicken the customary amount of food. Freckles, in the anxiety of the past few days, had neglected him, and he had been so hungry, much of the time, that when the Bird Woman held up a sweet-bread, although he had started toward the recesses of the log at her coming, he stopped; with slightly opened beak, he waited anxiously for the treat, and gave a study of great value, showing every point of his head, also his wing and tail development.

When the Bird Woman proposed to look for other subjects close about the line, Freckles went so far as to tell her that Jack had made fearful threats against the Angel. He implored her to take the Angel home and keep her under unceasing guard until Jack was located. He wanted to tell her all about it, but he knew how dear the Angel was to her, and he dreaded to burden her with his fears when they might prove groundless. He allowed her to go, but afterward blamed himself severely for having done so.

Chapter 14

Wherein Freckles Nurses a Heartache and Black Jack Drops Out

"McLean," said Mrs. Duncan, as the Boss paused to greet her in passing the cabin, "do you know that Freckles hasna been in bed the past five nights and all he's eaten in that many days ye could pack into a pint cup?"

"Why, what does the boy mean?" demanded McLean. "There's no necessity for him being on guard, with the watch I've set on the line. I had no idea he was staying down there."

"He's no there," said Mrs. Duncan. "He goes somewhere else. He leaves on his wheel juist after we're abed and rides in close cock-crow or a little earlier, and he's looking like death and nothing short of it."

"But where does he go?" asked McLean in astonishment.

"I'm no given to bearing tales out of school," said Sarah Duncan, "but in this case I'd tell ye if I could. What the trouble is I dinna ken. If it is no' stopped, he's in for dreadful sickness, and I thought ye could find out and help him. He's in sair trouble; that's all I know."

McLean sat brooding as he stroked Nellie's neck.

At last he said: "I suspect I understand. At any rate, I think I can find out. Thank you for telling me."

"Ye'll no need telling, once ye clap your eyes on him," prophesied Mrs. Duncan. "His face is all a glist'ny yellow, and he's peaked as a starving caged bird."

McLean rode to the Limberlost, and stopping in the shade, sat waiting for Freckles, whose hour for passing the foot of the lease had come.

Along the north line came Freckles, fairly staggering. When he turned east and reached Sleepy Snake Creek, sliding through the swale as the long black snake for which it was named, he sat on the bridge and closed his burning eyes, but they would not remain shut. As if pulled by wires, the heavy lids flew open, while the outraged nerves and muscles of his body danced, twitched, and tingled.

He bent forward and idly watched the limpid little stream flowing beneath his feet. Stretching into the swale, it came creeping between an impenetrable wall of magnificent wild flowers, vines, and ferns. Milkweed, goldenrod, ironwort, fringed gentians, cardinal-flowers, and turtle-head stood on the very edge of the creek, and every flower of them had a double in the water. Wild clematis crowned with snow the heads of trees scattered here and there on the bank.

From afar the creek appeared to be murky, dirty water. Really it was clear and sparkling. The tinge of blackness was gained from its bed of muck showing through the transparent current. He could see small and wonderfully marked fish. What became of them when the creek spread into the swamp? For one thing, they would make mighty fine eating for the family of that self-satisfied old blue heron.

Freckles sat so quietly that soon the brim of his hat was covered with snake-feeders, rasping their crisp wings and singing while they rested. Some of them settled on the club, and one on his shoulder. He was so motionless; feathers, fur, and gauze were so accustomed to him, that all through the swale they continued their daily life and forgot he was there.

The heron family were wading the mouth of the creek. Freckles idly wondered whether the nerve-racking rasps they occasionally emitted indicated domestic felicity or a raging quarrel. He could not decide. A sheitpoke, with flaring crest, went stalking across a bare space close to the creek's mouth. A stately brown bittern waded into the clear-flowing water, lifting his feet high at every step, and setting them down carefully, as if he dreaded wetting them, and with slightly parted beak, stood eagerly watching around him for worms. Behind him were some mighty trees of the swamp above, and below the bank glowed a solid wall of goldenrod.

No wonder the ancients had chosen yellow as the color to represent victory, for the fierce, conquering hue of the sun was in it. They had done well, too, in selecting purple as the emblem of royalty. It was a dignified, compelling color, while in its warm tone there was a hint of blood.

It was the Limberlost's hour to proclaim her sovereignty and triumph. Everywhere she flaunted her yellow banner and trailed the purple of her mantle, that was paler in the thistle-heads, took on strength in the first opening asters, and glowed and burned in the ironwort.

He gazed into her damp, mossy recesses where high-piled riven trees decayed under coats of living green, where dainty vines swayed and clambered, and here and there a yellow leaf, fluttering down, presaged the coming of winter. His love of the swamp laid hold of him and shook him with its force.

Compellingly beautiful was the Limberlost, but cruel withal; for inside bleached the uncoffined bones of her victims, while she had missed cradling him, oh! so narrowly.

He shifted restlessly; the movement sent the snake-feeders skimming. The hum of life swelled and roared in his strained ears. Small turtles, that had climbed on a log to sun, splashed clumsily into the water. Somewhere in the timber of the bridge a bloodthirsty little frog cried sharply. "KEEL'IM! KEEL'IM!"

Freckles muttered: "It's worse than that Black Jack swore to do to me, little fellow."

A muskrat waddled down the bank and swam for the swamp, its pointed nose riffling the water into a shining trail in its wake.

Then, below the turtle-log, a dripping silver-gray head, with shining eyes, was cautiously lifted, and Freckles's hand slid to his revolver. Higher and higher came the head, a long, heavy, fur-coated body arose, now half, now three-fourths from the water. Freckles looked at his shaking hand and doubted, but he gathered his forces, the shot rang, and the otter lay quiet. He hurried down and tried to lift it. He scarcely could muster strength to carry it to the bridge. The consciousness that he really could go no farther with it made Freckles realize the fact that he was close the limit of human endurance. He could bear it little, if any, longer. Every hour the dear face of the Angel wavered before him, and behind it the awful distorted image of Black Jack, as he had sworn to the punishment he would mete out to her. He must either see McLean, or else make a trip to town and find her father. Which should he do? He was almost a stranger, so the Angel's father might not be impressed with what he said as he would if McLean went to him. Then he remembered that McLean had said he would come that morning. Freckles never had forgotten before. He hurried on the east trail as fast as his tottering legs would carry him.

He stopped when he came to the first guard, and telling him of his luck, asked him to get the otter and carry it to the cabin, as he was anxious to meet McLean.

Freckles passed the second guard without seeing him, and hurried to the Boss. He took off his hat, wiped his forehead, and stood silent under the eyes of McLean.

The Boss was dumbfounded. Mrs. Duncan had led him to expect that he would find a change in Freckles, but this was almost deathly. The fact was apparent that the boy scarcely knew what he was doing. His eyes had a glazed, far-sighted appearance, that wrung the heart of the man who loved him. Without a thought of preliminaries, McLean leaned in the saddle and drew Freckles to him.

"My poor lad!" he said. "My poor, dear lad! Tell me, and we will try to right it!"

Freckles had twisted his fingers in Nellie's mane. At the kind words his face dropped on McLean's thigh and he shook with a nervous chill. McLean gathered him closer and waited.

When the guard came with the otter, McLean without a word motioned him to lay it down and leave them.

"Freckles," said McLean at last, "will you tell me, or must I set to work in the dark and try to find the trouble?"

"Oh, I want to tell you! I must tell you, sir," shuddered Freckles. "I cannot be bearing it the day out alone. I was coming to you when I remimbered you would be here."

He lifted his face and gazed across the swale, with his jaws set firmly a minute, as if gathering his forces. Then he spoke.

"It's the Angel, sir," he said.

Instinctively McLean's grip on him tightened, and Freckles looked into the Boss's face in wonder.

"I tried, the other day," said Freckles, "and I couldn't seem to make you see. It's only that there hasn't been an hour, waking or sleeping, since the day she parted the bushes and looked into me room, that the face of her hasn't been before me in all the tinderness, beauty, and mischief of it. She talked to me friendly like. She trusted me entirely to take right care of her. She helped me with things about me books. She traited me like I was born a gintleman, and shared with me as if I were of her own blood. She walked the streets of the town with me before her friends with all the pride of a queen. She forgot herself and didn't mind the Bird Woman, and run big risks to help me out that first day, sir. This last time she walked into that gang of murderers, took their leader, and twisted him to the will of her. She outdone him and raced the life almost out of her trying to save me.

"Since I can remimber, whatever the thing was that happened to me in the beginning has been me curse. I've been bitter, hard, and smarting under it hope lessly. She came by, and found me voice, and put hope of life and success like other men into me in spite of it."

Freckles held up his maimed arm.

"Look at it, sir!" he said. "A thousand times I've cursed it, hanging there help-less. She took it on the street, before all the people, just as if she didn't see that it was a thing to hide and shrink from. Again and again I've had the feeling with her, if I didn't entirely forget it, that she didn't see it was gone and I must be pointing it out to her. Her touch on it was so sacred-like, at times since I've caught meself looking at the awful thing near like I was proud of it, sir. If I had been born your son she couldn't be traiting me more as her equal, and she can't help knowing you ain't truly me father. Nobody can know the homeliness or the ignorance of me better than I do, and all me lack of birth, relatives, and money, and what's it all to her?"

Freckles stepped back, squared his shoulders, and with a royal lift of his head looked straight into the Boss's eyes.

"You saw her in the beautiful little room of her, and you can't be forgetting how she begged and plead with you for me. She touched me body, and 'twas sanctified. She laid her lips on my brow, and 'twas sacrament. Nobody knows the height of her better than me. Nobody's studied my depths closer. There's no bridge for the great distance between us, sir, and clearest of all, I'm for realizing it: but she risked terrible things when she came to me among that gang of thieves. She wore herself past bearing to save me from such an easy thing as death! Now, here's me, a man, a big, strong man, and letting her live under that fearful oath, so worse than any death 'twould be for her, and lifting not a finger to save her. I cannot hear it, sir. It's killing me by inches! Black Jack's hand may not have been hurt so bad. Any hour he may be creeping up behind her! Any minute the awful revenge he swore to be taking may in some way fall on her, and I haven't even warned her father. I can't stay here doing nothing another hour. The five nights gone I've watched under her windows, but there's the whole of the day. She's her own horse and little cart, and's free to be driving through the town and country as she pleases. If any evil comes to her through Black Jack, it comes from her angel-like goodness to me. Somewhere he's hiding! Somewhere he is waiting his chance! Somewhere he is reaching out for her! I tell you I cannot, I dare not be bearing it longer!"

"Freckles, be quiet!" said McLean, his eyes humid and his voice quivering with the pity of it all. "Believe me, I did not understand. I know the Angel's father well. I will go to him at once. I have transacted business with him for the past three years. I will make him see! I am only beginning to realize your agony, and the real danger there is for the Angel. Believe me, I will see that she is fully protected every hour of the day and night until Jack is located and disposed of. And I promise you further, that if I fail to move her father or make him understand the danger, I will maintain a guard over her until Jack is caught. Now will you go bathe, drink some milk, go to bed, and sleep for hours, and then be my brave, bright old boy again?"

"Yis," said Freckles simply.

But McLean could see the flesh was twitching on the lad's bones.

"What was it the guard brought there?" McLean asked in an effort to distract Freckles's thoughts.

"Oh!" Freckles said, glancing where the Boss pointed, "I forgot it! 'Tis an otter, and fine past believing, for this warm weather. I shot it at the creek this morning. 'Twas a good shot, considering. I expected to miss."

Freckles picked up the animal and started toward McLean with it, but Nellie pricked up her dainty little ears, danced into the swale, and snorted with fright. Freckles dropped the otter and ran to her head.

"For pity's sake, get her on the trail, sir," he begged. "She's just about where the old king rattler crosses to go into the swamp—the old buster Duncan and I have been telling you of. I haven't a doubt but it was the one Mother Duncan met. 'Twas down the trail there, just a little farther on, that I found her, and it's sure to be close yet."

McLean slid from Nellie's back, led her into the trail farther down the line, and tied her to a bush. Then he went to examine the otter. It was a rare, big specimen, with exquisitely fine, long, silky hair.

"What do you want to do with it, Freckles?" asked McLean, as he stroked the soft fur lingeringly. "Do you know that it is very valuable?"

"I was for almost praying so, sir," said Freckles. "As I saw it coming up the bank I thought this: Once somewhere in a book there was a picture of a young girl, and she was just a breath like the beautifulness of the Angel. Her hands were in a muff as big as her body, and I thought it was so pretty. I think she was some queen, or the like. Do you suppose I could have this skin tanned and made into such a muff as that?—an enormous big one, sir?"

"Of course you can," said McLean. "That's a fine idea and it's easy enough. We must box and express the otter, cold storage, by the first train. You stand guard a minute and I'll tell Hall to carry it to the cabin. I'll put Nellie to Duncan's rig, and we'll drive to town and call on the Angel's father. Then we'll start the otter while it is fresh, and I'll write your instructions later. It would be a mighty fine thing for you to give to the Angel as a little reminder of the Limberlost before it is despoiled, and as a souvenir of her trip for you."

Freckles lifted a face with a glow of happy color creeping into it and eyes lighting with a former brightness. Throwing his arms around McLean, he cried: "Oh, how I love you! Oh, I wish I could make you know how I love you!"

McLean strained him to his breast.

"God bless you, Freckles," he said. "I do know! We're going to have some good old times out of this world together, and we can't begin too soon. Would you rather sleep first, or have a bite of lunch, take the drive with me, and then rest? I don't know but sleep will come sooner and deeper to take the ride and have your mind set at ease before you lie down. Suppose you go."

"Suppose I do," said Freckles, with a glimmer of the old light in his eyes and newly found strength to shoulder the otter. Together they turned into the trail.

McLean noticed and spoke of the big black chickens.

"They've been hanging round out there for several days past," said Freckles. "I'll tell you what I think it means. I think the old rattler has killed something too big for him to swallow, and he's keeping guard and won't let me chickens have it. I'm just sure, from the way the birds have acted out there all summer, that it is the rattler's den. You watch them now. See the way they dip and then rise, frightened like!"

Suddenly McLean turned toward him with blanching face.

"Freckles!" he cried.

"My God, sir!" shuddered Freckles.

He dropped the otter, caught up his club, and plunged into the swale. Reaching for his revolver, McLean followed. The chickens circled higher at their coming, and the big snake lifted his head and rattled angrily. It sank in sinuous coils at the report of McLean's revolver, and together he and Freckles stood beside Black Jack. His fate was evident and most horrible.

"Come," said the Boss at last. "We don't dare touch him. We will get a sheet from Mrs. Duncan and tuck over him, to keep these swarms of insects away, and set Hall on guard, while we find the officers."

Freckles's lips closed resolutely. He deliberately thrust his club under Black Jack's body, and, raising him, rested it on his knee. He pulled a long silver pin from the front of the dead man's shirt and sent it spinning into the swale. Then he gathered up a few crumpled bright flowers and dropped them into the pool far away.

"My soul is sick with the horror of this thing," said McLean, as he and Freckles drove toward town. "I can't understand how Jack dared risk creeping through the swale, even in desperation. No one knew its dangers better than he. And why did he choose the rankest, muckiest place to cross the swamp?"

"Don't you think, sir, it was because it was on a line with the Limberlost south of the corduroy? The grass was tallest there, and he counted on those willows to screen him. Once he got among them, he would have been safe to walk by stooping. If he'd made it past that place, he'd been sure to get out."

"Well, I'm as sorry for Jack as I know how to be," said McLean, "but I can't help feeling relieved that our troubles are over, for now they are. With so dreadful a punishment for Jack, Wessner under arrest, and warrants for the others, we can count on their going away and remaining. As for anyone else, I don't think they will care to attempt stealing my timber after the experience of these men. There is no other man here with Jack's fine ability in woodcraft. He was an expert."

"Did you ever hear of anyone who ever tried to locate any trees excepting him?" asked Freckles.

"No, I never did," said McLean. "I am sure there was no one besides him. You see, it was only with the arrival of our company that the other fellows scented good stuff in the Limberlost, and tried to work in. Jack knew the swamp better than anyone here. When he found there were two companies trying to lease, he wanted to stand in with the one from which he could realize the most. Even then he had trees marked that he was trying to dispose of. I think his sole intention in forcing me to discharge him from my gang was to come here and try to steal timber. We had no idea, when we took the lease, what a gold mine it was."

"That's exactly what Wessner said that first day," said Freckles eagerly. "That 'twas a 'gold mine'! He said he didn't know where the marked trees were, but he knew a man who did, and if I would hold off and let them get the marked ones, there were a dozen they could get out in a few days."

"Freckles!" cried McLean. "You don't mean a dozen!"

"That's what he said, sir—a dozen. He said they couldn't tell how the grain of all of them would work up, of course, but they were all worth taking out, and five or six were real gold mines. This makes three they've tried, so there must be nine more marked, and several of them for being just fine."

"Well, I wish I knew which they are," said McLean, "so I could get them out first."

"I have been thinking," said Freckles. "I believe if you will leave one of the guards on the line—say Hall—that I will begin on the swamp, at the north end, and lay it off in sections, and try to hunt out the marked trees. I suppose they are all marked something like that first maple on the line was. Wessner mentioned another good one not so far from that. He said it was best of all. I'd be having the swelled head if I could find that. Of course, I don't know a thing about the trees, but I could hunt for the marks. Jack was so good at it he could tell some of them by the bark, but all he wanted to take that we've found so far have just had a deep chip cut out, rather low down, and where the bushes were thick over it. I believe I could be finding some of them."

"Good head!" said McLean. "We will do that. You may begin as soon as you are rested. And about things you come across in the swamp, Freckles—the most trifling little thing that you think the Bird Woman would want, take your wheel and go after her at any time. I'll leave two men on the line, so that you will have one on either side, and you can come and go as you please. Have you stopped to think of all we owe her, my boy?"

"Yis; and the Angel—we owe her a lot, too," said Freckles. "I owe her me life and honor. It's lying awake nights I'll have to be trying to think how I'm ever to pay her up."

"Well, begin with the muff," suggested McLean. "That should be fine."

He bent down and ruffled the rich fur of the otter lying at his feet.

"I don't exactly see how it comes to be in such splendid fur in summer. Their coats are always thick in cold weather, but this scarcely could be improved. I'll wire Cooper to be watching for it. They must have it fresh. When it's tanned we won't spare any expense in making it up. It should be a royal thing, and some way I think it will exactly suit the Angel. I can't think of anything that would be more appropriate for her."

"Neither can I," agreed Freckles heartily. "When I reach the city there's one other thing, if I've the money after the muff is finished."

He told McLean of Mrs. Duncan's desire for a hat similar to the Angel's. He hesitated a little in the telling, keeping sharp watch on McLean's face. When he saw the Boss's eyes were full of comprehension and sympathy, he loved him anew, for, as ever, McLean was quick to understand. Instead of laughing, he said: "I think you'll have to let me in on that, too. You mustn't be selfish, you know. I'll tell you what we'll do. Send it for Christmas. I'll be home then, and we can fill a box. You get the hat. I'll add a dress and wrap. You buy Duncan a hat and gloves. I'll send him a big overcoat, and we'll put in a lot of little stuff for the babies. Won't that be fun?"

Freckles fairly shivered with delight.

"That would be away too serious for fun," he said. "That would be heavenly. How long will it be?"

He began counting the time, and McLean deliberately set himself to encourage Freckles and keep his thoughts from the trouble of the past few days, for he had been overwrought and needed quiet and rest.

Chapter 15

Wherein Freckles and the Angel Try Taking a Picture, and Little Chicken Furnishes the Subject

A week later everything at the Limberlost was precisely as it had been before the tragedy, except the case in Freckles's room now rested on the stump of the newly felled tree. Enough of the vines were left to cover it prettily, and every vestige of the havoc of a few days before was gone. New guards were patrolling the trail. Freckles was roughly laying off the swamp in sections and searching for marked trees. In that time he had found one deeply chipped and the chip cunningly replaced and tacked in. It promised to be quite rare, so he was jubilant. He also found so many subjects for the Bird Woman that her coming was of almost daily occurrence, and the hours he spent with her and the Angel were nothing less than golden.

The Limberlost was now arrayed as the Queen of Sheba in all her glory. The first frosts of autumn had bejewelled her crown in flashing topaz, ruby, and emerald. Around her feet trailed the purple of her garments, while in her hand was her golden scepter. Everything was at full tide. It seemed as if nothing could grow lovelier, and it was all standing still a few weeks, waiting coming destruction.

The swamp was palpitant with life. Every pair of birds that had flocked to it in the spring was now multiplied by from two to ten. The young were tame from Freckles's tri-parenthood, and so plump and sleek that they were quite as beautiful as their elders, even if in many cases they lacked their brilliant plumage. It was the same story of increase everywhere. There were chubby little ground-hogs scudding on the trail. There were cunning baby coons and opossums peeping from hollow logs and trees. Young muskrats followed their parents across the lagoons.

If you could come upon a family of foxes that had not yet disbanded, and see the young playing with a wild duck's carcass that their mother had brought, and note the pride and satisfaction in her eyes as she lay at one side guarding them, it would be a picture not to be forgotten. Freckles never tired of studying the devotion of a fox mother to her babies. To him, whose early life had been so embittered by continual proof of neglect and cruelty in human parents toward their children, the love of these furred and feathered folk of the Limberlost was even more of a miracle than to the Bird Woman and the Angel.

The Angel liked the baby rabbits and squirrels. Earlier in the season, when the young were yet very small, it so happened that at times Freckles could give into her hands one of these little ones. Then it was pure joy to stand back and watch her heaving breast, flushed cheek, and shining eyes. Hers were such lovely eyes. Freckles had discovered lately that they were not so dark as he had thought them at first, but that the length and thickness of lash, by which they were shaded, made them appear darker than they really were. They were forever changing. Now sparkling and darkling with wit, now humid with sympathy, now burning with the fire of courage, now taking on strength of color with ambition, now flashing indignantly at the abuse of any creature.

She had carried several of the squirrel and bunny babies home, and had littered the conservatory with them. Her care of them was perfect. She was learning her natural history from nature, and having much healthful exercise. To her, they were the most interesting of all, but the Bird Woman preferred the birds, with a close second in the moths and butterflies.

Brown butterfly time had come. The edge of the swale was filled with milkweed, and other plants beloved of them, and the air was golden with the flashing satin wings of the monarch, viceroy, and argynnis. They outnumbered those of any other color three to one.

Among the birds it really seemed as if the little yellow fellows were in the preponderance. At least, they were until the redwinged blackbirds and bobolinks, that had nested on the upland, suddenly saw in the swamp the garden of the Lord and came swarming by hundreds to feast and adventure upon it these last few weeks before migration. Never was there a finer feast spread for the birds. The grasses were filled with seeds: so, too, were weeds of every variety. Fall berries were ripe. Wild grapes and black haws were ready. Bugs were creeping everywhere. The muck was yeasty with worms. Insects filled the air. Nature made glorious pause for holiday before her next change, and by none of the frequenters of the swamp was this more appreciated than by the big black chickens.

They seemed to feel the new reign of peace and fullness most of all. As for food, they did not even have to hunt for themselves these days, for the feasts now being spread before Little Chicken were more than he could use, and he was glad to have his parents come down and help him.

He was a fine, big, overgrown fellow, and his wings, with quills of jetty black, gleaming with bronze, were so strong they almost lifted his body. He had three inches of tail, and his beak and claws were sharp. His muscles began to clamor for exercise.

He raced the forty feet of his home back and forth many times every hour of the day. After a few days of that, he began lifting and spreading his wings, and flopping them until the down on his back was filled with elm fiber. Then he commenced jumping. The funny little hops, springs, and sidewise bounds he gave set Freckles and the Angel, hidden in the swamp, watching him, into smothered chuckles of delight.

Sometimes he fell to coquetting with himself; and that was the funniest thing of all, for he turned his head up, down, from side to side, and drew in his chin with prinky little jerks and tilts. He would stretch his neck, throw up his head, turn it to one side and smirk—actually smirk, the most complacent and self-satisfied smirk that anyone ever saw on the face of a bird. It was so comical that Freckles and the Angel told the Bird Woman of it one day.

When she finished her work on Little Chicken, she left them the camera ready for use, telling them they might hide in the bushes and watch. If Little Chicken came out and truly smirked, and they could squeeze the bulb at the proper moment to snap him, she would be more than delighted.

Freckles and the Angel quietly curled beside a big log, and with eager eyes and softest breathing they patiently waited; but Little Chicken had feasted before they told of his latest accomplishment. He was tired and sleepy, so he went into the log to bed, and for an hour he never stirred.

They were becoming anxious, for the light soon would be gone, and they had so wanted to try for the picture. At last Little Chicken lifted his head, opened his beak, and gaped widely. He dozed a minute or two more. The Angel said that was his beauty sleep. Then he lazily gaped again and stood up, stretching and yawning. He ambled leisurely toward the gateway, and the Angel said: "Now, we may have a chance, at last."

"I do hope so," shivered Freckles.

With one accord they arose to their knees and trained their eyes on the mouth of the log. The light was full and strong. Little Chicken prospected again with no results. He dressed his plumage, polished his beak, and when he felt fine and in full toilet he began to flirt with himself. Freckles's eyes snapped and his breath sucked between his clenched teeth.

"He's going to do it!" whispered the Angel. "That will come next. You'll best give me that bulb!"

"Yis," assented Freckles, but he was looking at the log and he made no move to relinquish the bulb.

Little Chicken nodded daintily and ruffled his feathers. He gave his head sundry little sidewise jerks and rapidly shifted his point of vision. Once there was the fleeting little ghost of a smirk.

"Now!—No!" snapped the Angel.

Freckles leaned toward the bird. Tensely he waited. Unconsciously the hand of the Angel clasped his. He scarcely knew it was there. Suddenly Little Chicken sprang straight in the air and landed with a thud. The Angel started slightly, but Freckles was immovable. Then, as if in approval of his last performance, the big, overgrown baby wheeled until he was more than three-quarters, almost full side, toward the camera, straightened on his legs, squared his shoulders, stretched his neck full height, drew in his chin and smirked his most pronounced smirk, directly in the face of the lens.

Freckles's fingers closed on the bulb convulsively, and the Angel's closed on his at the instant. Then she heaved a great sigh of relief and lifted her hands to push back the damp, clustering hair from her face.

"How soon do you s'pose it will be finished?" came Freckles's strident whisper.

For the first time the Angel looked at him. He was on his knees, leaning forward, his eyes directed toward the bird, the perspiration running in little streams down his red, mosquito-bitten face. His hat was awry, his bright hair rampant, his breast heaving with excitement, while he yet gripped the bulb with every ounce of strength in his body.

"Do you think we were for getting it?" he asked.

The Angel could only nod. Freckles heaved a deep sigh of relief.

"Well, if that ain't the hardest work I ever did in me life!" he exclaimed. "It's no wonder the Bird Woman's for coming out of the swamp looking as if she's been through a fire, a flood, and a famine, if that's what she goes through day after day. But if you think we got it, why, it's worth all it took, and I'm glad as ever you are, sure!"

They put the holders in the case, carefully closed the camera, set it in also, and carried it to the road.

Then Freckles exulted.

"Now, let's be telling the Bird Woman about it!" he shouted, wildly dancing and swinging his hat.

"We got it! We got it! I bet a farm we got it!"

Hand in hand they ran to the north end of the swamp, yelling "We got it!" like young Comanches, and never gave a thought to what they might do until a big blue-gray bird, with long neck and trailing legs, arose on flapping wings and sailed over the Limberlost.

The Angel became white to the lips and gripped Freckles with both hands. He gulped with mortification and turned his back.

To frighten her subject away carelessly! It was the head crime in the Bird Woman's category. She extended her hands as she arose, baked, blistered, and dripping, and exclaimed: "Bless you, my children! Bless you!" And it truly sounded as if she meant it.

"Why, why—" stammered the bewildered Angel.

Freckles hurried into the breach.

"You must be for blaming it every bit on me. I was thinking we got Little Chicken's picture real good. I was so drunk with the joy of it I lost all me senses and, 'Let's run tell the Bird Woman,' says I. Like a fool I was for running, and I sort of dragged the Angel along."

"Oh Freckles!" expostulated the Angel. "Are you loony? Of course, it was all my fault! I've been with her hundreds of times. I knew perfectly well that I wasn't to let anything—*not anything*—scare her bird away! I was so crazy I forgot. The blame is all mine, and she'll never forgive me."

"She will, too!" cried Freckles. "Wasn't you for telling me that very first day that when people scared her birds away she just killed them! It's all me foolishness, and I'll never forgive meself!"

The Bird Woman plunged into the swale at the mouth of Sleepy Snake Creek, and came wading toward them, with a couple of cameras and dripping tripods.

"If you will permit me a word, my infants," she said, "I will explain to you that I have had three shots at that fellow."

The Angel heaved a deep sigh of relief, and Freckles' face cleared a little.

"Two of them," continued the Bird Woman, "in the rushes—one facing, crest lowered; one light on back, crest flared; and the last on wing, when you came up. I simply had been praying for something to make him arise from that side, so that he would fly toward the camera, for he had waded around until in my position I couldn't do it myself. See? Behold in yourselves the answer to the prayers of the long-suffering!"

Freckles took a step toward her.

"Are you really meaning that?" he asked wonderingly. "Only think, Angel, we did the right thing! She won't lose her picture through the carelessness of us, when she's waited and soaked nearly two hours. She's not angry with us!"

"Never was in a sweeter temper in my life," said the Bird Woman, busily cleaning and packing the cameras.

Freckles removed his hat and solemnly held out his hand. With equal solemnity the Angel grasped it. The Bird Woman laughed alone, for to them the situation had been too serious to develop any of the elements of fun.

Then they loaded the carriage, and the Bird Woman and the Angel started for their homes. It had been a difficult time for all of them, so they were very tired, but they were joyful. Freckles was so happy it seemed to him that life could hold little more. As the Bird Woman was ready to drive away he laid his hand on the lines and looked into her face.

"Do you suppose we got it?" he asked, so eagerly that she would have given much to be able to say yes with conviction.

"Why, my dear, I don't know," she said. "I've no way to judge. If you made the exposure just before you came to me, there was yet a fine light. If you waited until Little Chicken was close the entrance, you should have something good, even if you didn't catch just the fleeting expression for which you hoped. Of course, I can't say surely, but I think there is every reason to believe that you have it all right. I will develop the plate tonight, make you a proof from it early in the morning, and bring it when we come. It's only a question of a day or two now until the gang arrives. I want to work in all the studies I can before that time, for they are bound to disturb the birds. Mr. McLean will need you then, and I scarcely see how we are to do without you."

Moved by an impulse she never afterward regretted, she bent and laid her lips on Freckles's forehead, kissing him gently and thanking him for his many kindnesses to her in her loved work. Freckles started away so happy that he felt inclined to keep watching behind to see if the trail were not curling up and rolling down the line after him.

Chapter 16

Wherein the Angel Locates a Rare Tree and Dines with the Gang

From afar Freckles saw them coming. The Angel was standing, waving her hat. He sprang on his wheel and raced, jolting and pounding, down the corduroy to meet them. The Bird Woman stopped the horse and the Angel gave him the bit of print paper. Freckles leaned the wheel against a tree and took the proof with eager fingers. He never before had seen a study from any of his chickens. He stood staring. When he turned his face toward them it was transfigured with delight.

"You see!" he exclaimed, and began gazing again. "Oh, me Little Chicken!" he cried. "Oh me ilegant Little Chicken! I'd be giving all me money in the bank for you!"

Then he thought of the Angel's muff and Mrs. Duncan's hat, and added, "Or at least, all but what I'm needing bad for something else. Would you mind stopping at the cabin a minute and showing this to Mother Duncan?" he asked.

"Give me that little book in your pocket," said the Bird Woman.

She folded the outer edges of the proof so that it would fit into the book, explaining as she did so its perishable nature in that state. Freckles went hurrying ahead, and they arrived in time to see Mrs. Duncan gazing as if awestruck, and to hear her bewildered "Weel I be drawed on!"

Freckles and the Angel helped the Bird Woman to establish herself for a long day at the mouth of Sleepy Snake Creek. Then she sent them away and waited what luck would bring to her.

"Now, what shall we do?" inquired the Angel, who was a bundle of nerves and energy.

"Would you like to go to me room awhile?" asked Freckles.

"If you don't care to very much, I'd rather not," said the Angel. "I'll tell you. Let's go help Mrs. Duncan with dinner and play with the baby. I love a nice, clean baby."

They started toward the cabin. Every few minutes they stopped to investigate something or to chatter over some natural history wonder. The Angel had quick eyes; she seemed to see everything, but Freckles's were even quicker; for life itself had depended on their sharpness ever since the beginning of his work at the swamp. They saw it at the same time.

"Someone has been making a flagpole," said the Angel, running the toe of her shoe around the stump, evidently made that season. "Freckles, what would anyone cut a tree as small as that for?"

"I don't know," said Freckles.

"Well, but I want to know!" said the Angel. "No one came away here and cut it for fun. They've taken it away. Let's go back and see if we can see it anywhere around there."

She turned, retraced her footsteps, and began eagerly searching. Freckles did the same.

"There it is!" he exclaimed at last, "leaning against the trunk of that big maple."

"Yes, and leaning there has killed a patch of dried bark," said the Angel. "See how dried it appears?"

Freckles stared at her.

"Angel!" he shouted, "I bet you it's a marked tree!"

"Course it is!" cried the Angel. "No one would cut that sapling and carry it away there and lean it up for nothing. I'll tell you! This is one of Jack's marked trees. He's climbed up there above anyone's head, peeled the bark, and cut into the grain enough to be sure. Then he's laid the bark back and fastened it with that pole to mark it. You see, there're a lot of other big maples close around it. Can you climb to that place?"

"Yes," said Freckles, "if I take off my wading-boots I can."

"Then take them off," said the Angel, "and do hurry! Can't you see that I am almost crazy to know if this tree is a marked one?"

When they pushed the sapling over, a piece of bark as big as the crown of Freckles's hat fell away.

"I believe it looks kind of nubby," encouraged the Angel, backing away, with her face all screwed into a twist in an effort to intensify her vision.

Freckles reached the opening, then slid rapidly to the ground. He was almost breathless while his eyes were flashing.

"The bark's been cut clean with a knife, the sap scraped away, and a big chip taken out deep. The trunk is the twistiest thing you ever saw. It's full of eyes as a bird is of feathers!"

The Angel was dancing and shaking his hand.

"Oh, Freckles," she cried, "I'm so delighted that you found it!"

"But I didn't," said the astonished Freckles. "That tree isn't my find; it's yours. I forgot it and was going on; you wouldn't give up, and kept talking about it, and turned back. You found it!"

"You'd best be looking after your reputation for truth and veracity," said the Angel. "You know you saw that sapling first!"

"Yes, after you took me back and set me looking for it," scoffed Freckles.

The clear, ringing echo of strongly swung axes came crashing through the Limberlost.

"'Tis the gang!" shouted Freckles. "They're clearing a place to make the camp. Let's go help!"

"Hadn't we better mark that tree again?" cautioned the Angel. "It's away in here. There's such a lot of them, and all so much alike. We'd feel good and green to find it and then lose it."

Freckles lifted the sapling to replace it, but the Angel motioned him away.

"Use your hatchet," she said. "I predict this is the most valuable tree in the swamp. You found it. I'm going to play that you're my knight. Now, you nail my colors on it."

She reached up, and pulling a blue bow from her hair, untied and doubled it against the tree. Freckles turned his eyes from her and managed the fastening with shaking fingers. The Angel had called him her knight! Dear Lord, how he loved her! She must not see his face, or surely her quick eyes would read what he was fighting to hide. He did not dare lay his lips on that ribbon then, but that night he would return to it. When they had gone a little distance, they both looked back, and the morning breeze set the bit of blue waving them a farewell.

They walked at a rapid pace.

"I am sorry about scaring the birds," said the Angel, "but it's almost time for them to go anyway. I feel dreadfully over having the swamp ruined, but isn't it a delight to hear the good, honest ring of those axes, instead of straining your ears for stealthy sounds? Isn't it fine to go openly and freely, with nothing worse than a snake or a poison-vine to fear?"

"Ah!" said Freckles, with a long breath, "it's better than you can dream, Angel. Nobody will ever be guessing some of the things I've been through trying to keep me promise to the Boss, and to hold out until this day. That it's come with only one fresh stump, and the log from that saved, and this new tree to report, isn't it grand? Maybe Mr. McLean will be forgetting that stump when he sees this tree, Angel!"

"He can't forget it," said the Angel; and in answer to Freckles's startled eyes she added, "because he never had any reason to remember it. He couldn't have done a whit better himself. My father says so. You're all right, Freckles!"

She reached him her hand, and as two children, they broke into a run when they came closer the gang. They left the swamp by the west road and followed the trail until they found the men. To the Angel it seemed complete charm. In the shadiest spot on the west side of the line, at the edge of the swamp and very close Freckles's room, they were cutting bushes and clearing space for a big tent for the men's sleeping-quarters, another for a dining-hall, and a board shack for the cook. The teamsters were unloading, the horses were cropping leaves from the bushes, while each man was doing his part toward the construction of the new Limberlost quarters.

Freckles helped the Angel climb on a wagonload of canvas in the shade. She removed her leggings, wiped her heated face, and glowed with happiness and interest.

The gang had been sifted carefully. McLean now felt that there was not a man in it who was not trustworthy.

They all had heard of the Angel's plucky ride for Freckles's relief; several of them had been in the rescue party. Others, new since that time, had heard the tale rehearsed in its every aspect around the smudge-fires at night. Almost all of them knew the Angel by sight from her trips with the Bird Woman to their leases. They all knew her father, her position, and the luxuries of her home. Whatever course she had chosen with them they scarcely would have resented it, but the Angel never had been known to choose a course. Her spirit of friendliness was inborn and inbred. She loved everyone, so she sympathized with everyone. Her generosity was only limited by what was in her power to give.

She came down the trail, hand in hand with the red-haired, freckled timber guard whom she had worn herself past the limit of endurance to save only a few weeks before, racing in her eagerness to reach them, and laughing her "Good morning, gentlemen," right and left. When she was ensconced on the wagonload of tenting, she sat on a roll of canvas as a queen on her throne. There was not a man of the gang who did not respect her. She was a living exponent of universal brotherhood. There was no man among them who needed her exquisite face or dainty clothing to teach him that the deference due a gentlewoman should be paid her. That the spirit of good fellowship she radiated levied an especial tribute of its own, and it became their delight to honor and please her.

As they raced toward the wagon—"Let me tell about the tree, please?" she begged Freckles.

"Why, sure!" said Freckles.

He probably would have said the same to anything she suggested. When McLean came, he found the Angel flushed and glowing, sitting on the wagon, her hands already filled. One of the men, who was cutting a scrub-oak, had carried to her a handful of crimson leaves. Another had gathered a bunch of delicate marsh-grass heads for her. Someone else, in taking out a bush, had found a daintily built and lined little nest, fresh as when made.

She held up her treasures and greeted McLean, "Good morning, Mr. Boss of the Limberlost!"

The gang shouted, while he bowed profoundly before her.

"Everyone listen!" cried the Angel, climbing a roll of canvas. "I have something to say! Freckles has been guarding here over a year now, and he presents the Limberlost to you, with every tree in it saved; for good measure he has this morning located the rarest one of them all: the one in from the east line, that Wessner spoke of the first day—nearest the one you took out. All together! Everyone! Hurrah for Freckles!"

With flushing cheeks and gleaming eyes, gaily waving the grass above her head, she led in three cheers and a tiger. Freckles slipped into the swamp and hid himself, for fear he could not conceal his pride and his great surging, throbbing love for her.

The Angel subsided on the canvas and explained to McLean about the maple. The Boss was mightily pleased. He took Freckles and set out to re-locate and examine the tree. The Angel was interested in the making of the camp, so she preferred to remain with the men. With her sharp eyes she was watching every detail of construction; but when it came to the stretching of the dining-hall canvas she proceeded to take command. The men were driving the rope-pins, when the Angel arose on the wagon and, leaning forward, spoke to Duncan, who was directing the work.

"I believe if you will swing that around a few feet farther, you will find it better, Mr. Duncan," she said. "That way will let the hot sun in at noon, while the sides will cut off the best breeze."

"That's a fact," said Duncan, studying the conditions.

So, by shifting the pins a little, they obtained comfort for which they blessed the Angel every day. When they came to the sleeping-tent, they consulted her about that. She explained the general direction of the night breeze and indicated the best position for the tent. Before anyone knew how it happened, the Angel was standing on the wagon, directing the location and construction of the cooking-shack, the erection of the crane for the big boiling-pots, and the building of the store-room. She superintended the laying of the floor of the sleeping-tent length-wise, So that it would be easier to sweep, and suggested a new arrangement of the cots that would afford all the men an equal share of night breeze. She left the wagon, and climbing on the newly erected dining-table, advised with the cook in placing his stove, table, and kitchen utensils.

When Freckles returned from the tree to join in the work around the camp, he caught glimpses of her enthroned on a soapbox, cleaning beans. She called to him that they were invited for dinner, and that they had accepted the invitation.

When the beans were steaming in the pot, the Angel advised the cook to soak them overnight the next time, so that they would cook more quickly and not burst. She was sure their cook at home did that way, and the CHEF of the gang thought it would be a good idea. The next Freckles saw of her she was paring potatoes. A little later she arranged the table.

She swept it with a broom, instead of laying a cloth; took the hatchet and ham-mered the deepest dents from the tin plates, and nearly skinned her fingers scouring the tinware with rushes. She set the plates an even distance apart, and laid the forks and spoons beside them. When the cook threw away half a dozen fruit-cans, she gathered them up and melted off the tops, although she almost blistered her face and quite blistered her fingers doing it. Then she neatly covered these improvised vases with the Manila paper from the groceries, tying it with wisps of marshgrass. These she filled with fringed gentians, blazing-star, asters, goldenrod, and ferns, plac-ing them the length of the dining-table. In one of the end cans she arranged her red leaves, and in the other the fancy grass. Two men, watching her, went away proud of themselves and said that she was "a born lady." She laughingly caught up a paper bag and fitted it jauntily to her head in imitation of a cook's cap. Then she ground the coffee, and beat a couple of eggs to put in, "because there is company," she gravely explained to the cook. She asked that delighted individual if he did not like it best that way, and he said he did not know, because he never had a chance to taste it. The Angel said that was her case exactly—she never had, either; she was not allowed anything stronger than milk. Then they laughed together.

She told the cook about camping with her father, and explained that he made his coffee that way. When the steam began to rise from the big boiler, she stuffed the spout tightly with clean marshgrass, to keep the aroma in, placed the boiler where it would only simmer, and explained why. The influence of the Angel's visit lingered with the cook through the remainder of his life, while the men prayed for her frequent return.

She was having a happy time, when McLean came back jubilant, from his trip to the tree. How jubilant he told only the Angel, for he had been obliged to lose faith in some trusted men of late, and had learned discretion by what he suffered. He planned to begin clearing out a road to the tree that same afternoon, and to set two guards every night, for it promised to be a rare treasure, so he was eager to see it on the way to the mills.

"I am coming to see it felled," cried the Angel. "I feel a sort of motherly interest in that tree."

McLean was highly amused. He would have staked his life on the honesty of either the Angel or Freckles; yet their versions of the finding of the tree differed widely.

"Tell me, Angel," the Boss said jestingly. "I think I have a right to know. Who really did locate that tree?"

"Freckles," she answered promptly and emphatically.

"But he says quite as positively that it was you. I don't understand."

The Angel's legal look flashed into her face. Her eyes grew tense with earnestness. She glanced around, and seeing no towel or basin, held out her hand for Sears to pour water over them. Then, using the skirt of her dress to dry them, she climbed on the wagon.

"I'll tell you, word for word, how it happened," she said, "and then you shall decide, and Freckles and I will agree with you."

When she had finished her version, "Tell us, 'oh, most learned judge!'" she laughingly quoted, "Which of us located that tree?"

"Blest if I know who located it!" exclaimed McLean. "But I have a fairly accurate idea as to who put the blue ribbon on it."

The Boss smiled significantly at Freckles, who just had come, for they had planned that they would instruct the company to reserve enough of the veneer from that very tree to make the most beautiful dressing table they could design for the Angel's share of the discovery.

"What will you have for yours?" McLean had asked of Freckles.

"If it's all the same to you, I'll be taking mine out in music lessons—begging your pardon—voice culture," said Freckles with a grimace.

McLean laughed, for Freckles needed to see or hear only once to absorb learning as the thirsty earth sucks up water.

The Angel placed McLean at the head of the table. She took the foot, with Freckles on her right, while the lumber gang, washed, brushed, and straightened until they felt unfamiliar with themselves and each other, filled the sides. That imposed a slight constraint. Then, too, the men were afraid of the flowers, the polished tableware, and above all, of the dainty grace of the Angel. Nowhere do men so display lack of good breeding and culture as in dining. To sprawl on the table, scoop with their knives, chew loudly, gulp coffee, and duck their heads as snapping-turtles for every bite, had not been noticed by them until the Angel, sitting straightly, suddenly made them remember that they, too, were possessed of spines. Instinctively every man at the table straightened.

Chapter 17

Wherein Freckles Offers His Life for His Love and Gets a Broken Body

To reach the tree was a more difficult task than McLean had supposed. The gang could approach nearest on the outside toward the east, but after they reached the end of the east entrance there was yet a mile of most impenetrable thicket, trees big and little, and bushes of every variety and stage of growth. In many places the muck had to be filled to give the horses and wagons a solid foundation over which to haul heavy loads. It was several days before they completed a road to the noble, big tree and were ready to fell it.

When the sawing began, Freckles was watching down the road where it met the trail leading from Little Chicken's tree. He had gone to the tree ahead of the gang to remove the blue ribbon. Carefully folded, it now lay over his heart. He was promising himself much comfort with that ribbon, when he would leave for the city next month to begin his studies and dream the summer over again. It would help to make things tangible. When he was dressed as other men, and at his work, he knew where he meant to home that precious bit of blue. It should be his good-luck token, and he would wear it always to keep bright in memory the day on which the Angel had called him her knight.

How he would study, and oh, how he would sing! If only he could fulfill McLean's expectations, and make the Angel proud of him! If only he could be a real knight!

He could not understand why the Angel had failed to come. She had wanted to see their tree felled. She would be too late if she did not arrive soon. He had told her it would be ready that morning, and she had said she surely would be there. Why, of all mornings, was she late on this?

McLean had ridden to town. If he had been there, Freckles would have asked that they delay the felling, but he scarcely liked to ask the gang. He really had no authority, although he thought the men would wait; but some way he found such embarrassment in framing the request that he waited until the work was practically ended. The saw was out, and the men were cutting into the felling side of the tree when the Boss rode in.

His first word was to inquire for the Angel. When Freckles said she had not yet come, the Boss at once gave orders to stop work on the tree until she arrived; for he felt that she virtually had located it, and if she desired to see it felled, she should. As the men stepped back, a stiff morning breeze caught the top, that towered high above its fellows. There was an ominous grinding at the base, a shiver of the mighty trunk, then directly in line of its fall the bushes swung apart and the laughing face of the Angel looked on them.

A groan of horror burst from the dry throats of the men, and reading the agony in their faces, she stopped short, glanced up, and understood.

"South!" shouted McLean. "Run south!"

The Angel was helpless. It was apparent that she did not know which way south was. There was another slow shiver of the big tree. The remainder of the gang stood motionless, but Freckles sprang past the trunk and went leaping in big bounds. He caught up the Angel and dashed through the thicket for safety. The swaying trunk was half over when, for an instant, a near-by tree stayed its fall. They saw Freckles's foot catch, and with the Angel he plunged headlong.

A terrible cry broke from the men, while McLean covered his face. Instantly Freckles was up, with the Angel in his arms, struggling on. The outer limbs were on them when they saw Freckles hurl the Angel, face down, in the muck, as far from him as he could send her. Springing after, in an attempt to cover her body with his own, he whirled to see if they were yet in danger, and with outstretched arms braced himself for the shock. The branches shut them from sight, and the awful crash rocked the earth.

McLean and Duncan ran with axes and saws. The remainder of the gang followed, and they worked desperately. It seemed a long time before they caught a glimpse of the Angel's blue dress, but it renewed their vigor. Duncan fell on his knees beside her and tore the muck from underneath her with his hands. In a few seconds he dragged her out, choking and stunned, but surely not fatally hurt.

Freckles lay a little farther under the tree, a big limb pinning him down. His eyes were wide open. He was perfectly conscious. Duncan began mining beneath him, but Freckles stopped him.

"You can't be moving me," he said. "You must cut off the limb and lift it. I know."

Two men ran for the big saw. A number of them laid hold of the limb and bore up. In a short time it was removed, and Freckles lay free.

The men bent over to lift him, but he motioned them away.

"Don't be touching me until I rest a bit," he pleaded.

Then he twisted his head until he saw the Angel, who was wiping muck from her eyes and face on the skirt of her dress.

"Try to get up," he begged.

McLean laid hold of the Angel and helped her to her feet.

"Do you think any bones are broken?" gasped Freckles.

The Angel shook her head and wiped muck.

"You see if you can find any, sir," Freckles commanded.

The Angel yielded herself to McLean's touch, and he assured Freckles that she was not seriously injured.

Freckles settled back, a smile of ineffable tenderness on his face.

"Thank the Lord!" he hoarsely whispered.

The Angel leaned toward him.

"Now, Freckles, you!" she cried. "It's your turn. Please get up!"

A pitiful spasm swept Freckles's face. The sight of it washed every vestige of color from the Angel's. She took hold of his hands.

"Freckles, get up!" It was half command, half entreaty.

"Easy, Angel, easy! Let me rest a bit first!" implored Freckles.

She knelt beside him. He reached his arm around her and drew her closely. He looked at McLean in an agony of entreaty that brought the Boss to his knees on the other side.

"Oh, Freckles!" McLean cried. "Not that! Surely we can do something! We must! Let me see!"

He tried to unfasten Freckles's neckband, but his fingers shook so clumsily that the Angel pushed them away and herself laid Freckles's chest bare. With one hasty glance she gathered the clothing together and slipped her arm under his head. Freckles lifted his eyes of agony to hers.

"You see?" he said.

The Angel nodded dumbly.

Freckles turned to McLean.

"Thank you for everything," he panted. "Where are the boys?"

"They are all here," said the Boss, "except a couple who have gone for doctors, Mrs. Duncan and the Bird Woman."

"It's no use trying to do anything," said Freckles. "You won't forget the muff and the Christmas box. The muff especial?"

There was a movement above them so pronounced that it attracted Freckles's attention, even in that extreme hour. He looked up, and a pleased smile flickered on his drawn face.

"Why, if it ain't me Little Chicken!" he cried hoarsely. "He must be making his very first trip from the log. Now Duncan can have his big watering-trough."

"It was Little Chicken that made me late," faltered the Angel. "I was so anxious to get here early I forgot to bring his breakfast from the carriage. He must have been hungry, for when I passed the log he started after me. He was so wabbly, and so slow flying from tree to tree and through the bushes, I just had to wait on him, for I couldn't drive him back."

"Of course you couldn't! Me bird has too amazing good sinse to go back when he could be following you," exulted Freckles, exactly as if he did not realize what the delay had cost him. Then he lay silently thinking, but presently he asked slowly: "And so 'twas me Little Chicken that was making you late, Angel?"

"Yes," said the Angel.

A spasm of fierce pain shook Freckles, and a look of uncertainty crossed his face.

"All summer I've been thanking God for the falling of the feather and all the delights it's brought me," he muttered, "but this looks as if—"

He stopped short and raised questioning eyes to McLean.

"I can't help being Irish, but I can help being superstitious," he said. "I mustn't be laying it to the Almighty, or to me bird, must I?"

"No, dear lad," said McLean, stroking the brilliant hair. "The choice lay with you. You could have stood a rooted dolt like all the remainder of us. It was through your great love and your high courage that you made the sacrifice."

"Don't you be so naming it, sir!" cried Freckles. "It's just the reverse. If I could be giving me body the hundred times over to save hers from this, I'd be doing it and take joy with every pain."

He turned with a smile of adoring tenderness to the Angel. She was ghastly white, and her eyes were dull and glazed. She scarcely seemed to hear or under-stand what was coming, but she bravely tried to answer that smile.

"Is my forehead covered with dirt?" he asked.

She shook her head.

"You did once," he gasped.

Instantly she laid her lips on his forehead, then on each cheek, and then in a long kiss on his lips.

McLean bent over him.

"Freckles," he said brokenly, "you will never know how I love you. You won't go without saying good-bye to me?"

That word stung the Angel to quick comprehension. She started as if arousing from sleep.

"Good-bye?" she cried sharply, her eyes widening and the color rushing into her white face. "Good-bye! Why, what do you mean? Who's saying good-bye? Where could Freckles go, when he is hurt like this, save to the hospital? You needn't say good-bye for that. Of course, we will all go with him! You call up the men. We must start right away."

"It's no use, Angel," said Freckles. "I'm thinking ivry bone in me breast is smashed. You'll have to be letting me go!"

"I will not," said the Angel flatly. "It's no use wasting precious time talking about it. You are alive. You are breathing; and no matter how badly your bones are broken, what are great surgeons for but to fix you up and make you well again? You promise me that you'll just grit your teeth and hang on when we hurt you, for we must start with you as quickly as it can be done. I don't know what has been the matter with me. Here's good time wasted already."

"Oh, Angel!" moaned Freckles, "I can't! You don't know how bad it is. I'll die the minute you are for trying to lift me!"

"Of course you will, if you make up your mind to do it," said the Angel. "But if you are determined you won't, and set yourself to breathing deep and strong, and hang on to me tight, I can get you out. Really you must, Freckles, no matter how it hurts, for you did this for me, and now I must save you, so you might as well promise."

She bent over him, trying to smile encouragement with her fear-stiffened lips.

"You will promise, Freckles?"

Big drops of cold sweat ran together on Freckles's temples.

"Angel, darlin' Angel," he pleaded, taking her hand in his. "You ain't understanding, and I can't for the life of me be telling you, but indade, it's best to be letting me go. This is my chance. Please say good-bye, and let me slip off quick!"

He appealed to McLean.

"Dear Boss, you know! You be telling her that, for me, living is far worse pain than dying. Tell her you know death is the best thing that could ever be happening to me!"

"Merciful Heaven!" burst in the Angel. "I can't endure this delay!"

She caught Freckles's hand to her breast, and bending over him, looked deeply into his stricken eyes.

"'Angel, I give you my word of honor that I will keep right on breathing.' That's what you are going to promise me," she said. "Do you say it?"

Freckles hesitated.

"Freckles!" imploringly commanded the Angel, "YOU DO SAY IT!"

"Yis," gasped Freckles.

The Angel sprang to her feet.

"Then that's all right," she said, with a tinge of her old-time briskness. "You just keep breathing away like a steam engine, and I will do all the remainder."

The eager men gathered around her.

"It's going to be a tough pull to get Freckles out," she said, "but it's our only chance, so listen closely and don't for the lives of you fail me in doing quickly what I tell you. There's no time to spend falling down over each other; we must have some system. You four there get on those wagon horses and ride to the sleeping-tent. Get the stoutest cot, a couple of comforts, and a pillow. Ride back with them some way to save time. If you meet any other men of the gang, send them here to help carry the cot. We won't risk the jolt of driving with him. The others clear a path out to the road; and Mr. McLean, you take Nellie and ride to town. Tell my father how Freckles is hurt and that he risked it to save me. Tell him I'm going to take Freckles to Chicago on the noon train, and I want him to hold it if we are a little late. If he can't, then have a special ready at the station and another on the Pittsburgh at Fort Wayne, so we can go straight through. You needn't mind leaving us. The Bird Woman will be here soon. We will rest awhile."

She dropped into the muck beside Freckles and began stroking his hair and hand. He lay with his face of agony turned to hers, and fought to smother the groans that would tell her what he was suffering.

When they stood ready to lift him, the Angel bent over him in a passion of tenderness.

"Dear old Limberlost guard, we're going to lift you now," she said. "I suspect you will faint from the pain of it, but we will be as easy as ever we can, and don't you dare forget your promise!"

A whimsical half-smile touched Freckles's quivering lips.

"Angel, can a man be remembering a promise when he ain't knowing?" he asked.

"You can," said the Angel stoutly, "because a promise means so much more to you than it does to most men."

A look of strength flashed into Freckles's face at her words.

"I am ready," he said.

With the first touch his eyes closed, a mighty groan was wrenched from him, and he lay senseless. The Angel gave Duncan one panic-stricken look. Then she set her lips and gathered her forces again.

"I guess that's a good thing," she said. "Maybe he won't feel how we are hurting him. Oh boys, are you being quick and gentle?"

She stepped to the side of the cot and bathed Freckles's face. Taking his hand in hers, she gave the word to start. She told the men to ask every able-bodied man they met to join them so that they could change carriers often and make good time.

The Bird Woman insisted upon taking the Angel into the carriage and following the cot, but she refused to leave Freckles, and suggested that the Bird Woman drive ahead, pack them some clothing, and be at the station ready to accompany them to Chicago. All the way the Angel walked beside the cot, shading Freckles's face with a branch, and holding his hand. At every pause to change carriers she moistened his face and lips and watched each breath with heart-breaking anxiety.

She scarcely knew when her father joined them, and taking the branch from her, slipped an arm around her waist and almost carried her. To the city streets and the swarm of curious, staring faces she paid no more attention than she had to the trees of the Limberlost. When the train came and the gang placed Freckles aboard, big Duncan made a place for the Angel beside the cot.

With the best physician to be found, and with the Bird Woman and McLean in attendance, the four-hours' run to Chicago began. The Angel constantly watched over Freckles; bathed his face, stroked his hand, and gently fanned him. Not for an instant would she yield her place, or allow anyone else to do anything for him. The Bird Woman and McLean regarded her in amazement. There seemed to be no end to her resources and courage. The only time she spoke was to ask McLean if he were sure the special would be ready on the Pittsburgh road. He replied that it was made up and waiting.

At five o'clock Freckles lay stretched on the operating-table of Lake View Hospital, while three of the greatest surgeons in Chicago bent over him. At their command, McLean picked up the unwilling Angel and carried her to the nurses to be bathed, have her bruises attended, and to be put to bed.

In a place where it is difficult to surprise people, they were astonished women as they removed the Angel's dainty stained and torn clothing, drew off hose muck-baked to her limbs, soaked the dried loam from her silken hair, and washed the beautiful scratched, bruised, dirt-covered body. The Angel fell fast asleep long before they had finished, and lay deeply unconscious, while the fight for Freckles's life was being waged.

Three days later she was the same Angel as of old, except that Freckles was constantly in her thoughts. The anxiety and responsibility that she felt for his condition had bred in her a touch of womanliness and authority that was new. That morning she arose early and hovered near Freckles's door. She had been allowed to remain with him constantly, for the nurses and surgeons had learned, with his returning consciousness, that for her alone would the active, highly strung, pain-racked sufferer be quiet and obey orders. When she was dropping from loss of sleep, the threat that she would fall ill had to be used to send her to bed. Then by telling Freckles that the Angel was asleep and they would waken her the moment he moved, they were able to control him for a short time.

The surgeon was with Freckles. The Angel had been told that the word he brought that morning would be final, so she curled in a window seat, dropped the curtains behind her, and in dire anxiety, waited the opening of the door.

Just as it unclosed, McLean came hurrying down the hall and to the surgeon, but with one glance at his face he stepped back in dismay; while the Angel, who had arisen, sank to the seat again, too dazed to come forward. The men faced each other. The Angel, with parted lips and frightened eyes, bent forward in tense anxiety.

"I—I thought he was doing nicely?" faltered McLean.

"He bore the operation well," replied the surgeon, "and his wounds are not necessarily fatal. I told you that yesterday, but I did not tell you that something else probably would kill him; and it will. He need not die from the accident, but he will not live the day out."

"But why? What is it?" asked McLean hurriedly. "We all dearly love the boy. We have millions among us to do anything that money can accomplish. Why must he die, if those broken bones are not the cause?"

"That is what I am going to give you the opportunity to tell me," replied the surgeon. "He need not die from the accident, yet he is dying as fast as his splendid physical condition will permit, and it is because he so evidently prefers death to life. If he were full of hope and ambition to live, my work would be easy. If all of you love him as you prove you do, and there is unlimited means to give him anything he wants, why should he desire death?"

"Is he dying?" demanded McLean.

"He is," said the surgeon. "He will not live this day out, unless some strong reaction sets in at once. He is so low, that preferring death to life, nature cannot overcome his inertia. If he is to live, he must be made to desire life. Now he undoubtedly wishes for death, and that it come quickly."

"Then he must die," said McLean.

His broad shoulders shook convulsively. His strong hands opened and closed mechanically.

"Does that mean that you know what he desires and cannot, or will not, supply it?"

McLean groaned in misery.

"It means," he said desperately, "that I know what he wants, but it is as far removed from my power to help him as it would be to give him a star. The thing for which he will die, he can never have."

"Then you must prepare for the end very shortly," said the surgeon, turning abruptly away.

McLean caught his arm roughly.

"You look here!" he cried in desperation. "You say that as if I could do something if I would. I tell you the boy is dear to me past expression. I would do anything—spend any sum. You have noticed and repeatedly commented on the young girl with me. It is that child that he wants! He worships her to adoration, and knowing he can never be anything to her, he prefers death to life. In God's name, what can I do about it?"

"Barring that missing hand, I never examined a finer man," said the surgeon, "and she seemed perfectly devoted to him; why cannot he have her?"

"Why?" echoed McLean. "Why? Well, for many reasons! I told you he was my son. You probably knew that he was not. A little over a year ago I never had seen him. He joined one of my lumber gangs from the road. He is a stray, left at one of your homes for the friendless here in Chicago. When he grew up the superintendent bound him to a brutal man. He ran away and landed in one of my lumber camps. He has no name or knowledge of legal birth. The Angel—we have talked of her. You see what she is, physically and mentally. She has ancestors reaching back to Plymouth Rock, and across the sea for generations before that. She is an idolized, petted only child, and there is great wealth. Life holds everything for her, nothing for him. He sees it more plainly than anyone else could. There is nothing for the boy but death, if it is the Angel that is required to save him."

The Angel stood between them.

"Well, I just guess not!" she cried. "If Freckles wants me, all he has to do is to say so, and he can have me!"

The amazed men stepped back, staring at her.

"That he will never say," said McLean at last, "and you don't understand, Angel. I don't know how you came here. I wouldn't have had you hear that for the world, but since you have, dear girl, you must be told that it isn't your friendship or your kindness Freckles wants; it is your love."

The Angel looked straight into the great surgeon's eyes with her clear, steady orbs of blue, and then into McLean's with unwavering frankness.

"Well, I do love him," she said simply.

McLean's arms dropped helplessly.

"You don't understand," he reiterated patiently. "It isn't the love of a friend, or a comrade, or a sister, that Freckles wants from you; it is the love of a sweetheart. And if to save the life he has offered for you, you are thinking of being generous and impulsive enough to sacrifice your future—in the absence of your father, it will become my plain duty, as the protector in whose hands he has placed you, to prevent such rashness. The very words you speak, and the manner in which you say them, prove that you are a mere child, and have not dreamed what love is."

Then the Angel grew splendid. A rosy flush swept the pallor of fear from her face. Her big eyes widened and dilated with intense lights. She seemed to leap to the height and the dignity of superb womanhood before their wondering gaze.

"I never have had to dream of love," she said proudly. "I never have known anything else, in all my life, but to love everyone and to have everyone love me. And there never has been anyone so dear as Freckles. If you will remember, we have been through a good deal together. I do love Freckles, just as I say I do. I don't know anything about the love of sweethearts, but I love him with all the love in my heart, and I think that will satisfy him."

"Surely it should!" muttered the man of knives and lancets.

McLean reached to take hold of the Angel, but she saw the movement and swiftly stepped back.

"As for my father," she continued, "he at once told me what he learned from you about Freckles. I've known all you know for several weeks. That knowledge didn't change your love for him a particle. I think the Bird Woman loved him more. Why should you two have all the fine perceptions there are? Can't I see how brave, trustworthy, and splendid he is? Can't I see how his soul vibrates with his music, his love of beautiful things and the pangs of loneliness and heart hunger? Must you two love him with all the love there is, and I give him none? My father is never unreasonable. He won't expect me not to love Freckles, or not to tell him so, if the telling will save him."

She darted past McLean into Freckles's room, closed the door, and turned the key.

Chapter 18

Wherein Freckles Refuses Love without Knowledge of Honorable Birth, and the Angel Goes in Quest of it

Freckles lay on a flat pillow, his body immovable in a plaster cast, his maimed arm, as always, hidden. His greedy gaze fastened at once on the Angel's face. She crossed to him with light step and bent over him with infinite tenderness. Her heart ached at the change in his appearance. He seemed so weak, heart hungry, so utterly hopeless, so alone. She could see that the night had been one long terror.

For the first time she tried putting herself in Freckles's place. What would it mean to have no parents, no home, no name? No name! That was the worst of all. That was to be lost—indeed—utterly and hopelessly lost. The Angel lifted her hands to her dazed head and reeled, as she tried to face that proposition. She dropped on her knees beside the bed, slipped her arm under the pillow, and leaning over Freckles, set her lips on his forehead. He smiled faintly, but his wistful face appeared worse for it. It hurt the Angel to the heart.

"Dear Freckles," she said, "there is a story in your eyes this morning, tell me?" Freckles drew a long, wavering breath.

"Angel," he begged, "be generous! Be thinking of me a little. I'm so homesick and worn out, dear Angel, be giving me back me promise. Let me go?"

"Why Freckles!" faltered the Angel. "You don't know what you are asking. 'Let you go!' I cannot! I love you better than anyone, Freckles, I think you are the very finest person I ever knew. I have our lives all planned. I want you to be educated and learn all there is to know about singing, just as soon as you are well enough. By the time you have completed your education I will have finished college, and then I want," she choked a second, "I want you to be my real knight, Freckles, and come to me and tell me that you—like me—a little. I have been counting on you for my sweetheart from the very first, Freckles. I can't give you up, unless you don't like me. But you do like me—just a little—don't you, Freckles?"

Freckles lay whiter than the coverlet, his staring eyes on the ceiling and his breath wheezing between dry lips. The Angel awaited his answer a second, and when none came, she dropped her crimsoning face beside him on the pillow and whispered in his ear:

"Freckles, I—I'm trying to make love to you. Oh, can't you help me only a little bit? It's awful hard all alone! I don't know how, when I really mean it, but Freckles, I love you. I must have you, and now I guess—I guess maybe I'd better kiss you next."

She lifted her shamed face and bravely laid her feverish, quivering lips on his. Her breath, like clover-bloom, was in his nostrils, and her hair touched his face. Then she looked into his eyes with reproach.

"Freckles," she panted, "Freckles! I didn't think it was in you to be mean!"

"Mean, Angel! Mean to you?" gasped Freckles.

"Yes," said the Angel. "Downright mean. When I kiss you, if you had any mercy at all you'd kiss back, just a little bit."

Freckles's sinewy fist knotted into the coverlet. His chin pointed ceilingward while his head rocked on the pillow.

"Oh, Jesus!" burst from him in agony. "You ain't the only one that was crucified!"

The Angel caught Freckles's hand and carried it to her breast.

"Freckles!" she wailed in terror, "Freckles! It is a mistake? Is it that you don't want me?"

Freckles's head rolled on in wordless suffering.

"Wait a bit, Angel?" he panted at last. "Be giving me a little time!"

The Angel arose with controlled features. She bathed his face, straightened his hair, and held water to his lips. It seemed a long time before he reached toward her. Instantly she knelt again, carried his hand to her breast, and leaned her cheek upon it.

"Tell me, Freckles," she whispered softly.

"If I can," said Freckles in agony. "It's just this. Angels are from above. Outcasts are from below. You've a sound body and you're beautifulest of all. You have everything that loving, careful raising and money can give you. I have so much less than nothing that I don't suppose I had any right to be born. It's a sure thing—nobody wanted me afterward, so of course, they didn't before. Some of them should have been telling you long ago."

"If that's all you have to say, Freckles, I've known that quite a while," said the Angel stoutly. "Mr. McLean told my father, and he told me. That only makes me love you more, to pay for all you've missed."

"Then I'm wondering at you," said Freckles in a voice of awe. "Can't you see that if you were willing and your father would come and offer you to me, I couldn't be touching the soles of your feet, in love—me, whose people brawled over me, cut off me hand, and throwed me away to freeze and to die! Me, who has no name just as much because I've no *right* to any, as because I don't know it. When I was little, I planned to find me father and mother when I grew up. Now I know me mother deserted me, and me father was maybe a thief and surely a liar. The pity for me suffering and the watching over me have gone to your head, dear Angel, and it's me must be thinking for you. If you could be forgetting me lost hand, where I was raised, and that I had no name to give you, and if you would be taking me as I am, some day people such as mine must be, might come upon you. I used to pray ivery night and morning and many times the day to see me mother. Now I only pray to die quickly and never risk the sight of her. 'Tain't no ways possible, Angel! It's a wildness of your dear head. Oh, do for mercy sake, kiss me once more and be letting me go!"

"Not for a minute!" cried the Angel. "Not for a minute, if those are all the reasons you have. It's you who are wild in your head, but I can understand just how it happened. Being shut in that Home most of your life, and seeing children every day whose parents did neglect and desert them, makes you sure yours did the same; and yet there are so many other things that could have happened so much more easily than that. There are thousands of young couples who come to this country and start a family with none of their relatives here. Chicago is a big, wicked city, and grown people could disappear in many ways, and who would there ever be to find to whom their little children belonged? The minute my father told me how you felt, I began to study this thing over, and I've made up my mind you are dead wrong. I meant to ask my father or the Bird Woman to talk to you before you went away to school, but as matters are right now I guess I'll just do it myself. It's all so plain to me. Oh, if I could only make you see!"

She buried her face in the pillow and presently lifted it, transfigured.

"Now I have it!" she cried "Oh, dear heart! I can make it so plain! Freckles, can you imagine you see the old Limberlost trail? Well when we followed it, you know there were places where ugly, prickly thistles overgrew the path, and you went ahead with your club and bent them back to keep them from stinging through my clothing. Other places there were big shining pools where lovely, snow-white lilies grew, and you waded in and gathered them for me. Oh dear heart, don't you see? It's this! Everywhere the wind carried that thistledown, other thistles sprang up and grew prickles; and wherever those lily seeds sank to the mire, the pure white of other lilies bloomed. But, Freckles, there was never a place anywhere in the Limberlost, or in the whole world, where the thistledown floated and sprang up and blossomed into white lilies! Thistles grow from thistles, and lilies from other lilies. Dear Freckles, think hard! You must see it! You are a lily, straight through. You never, never could have drifted from the thistle-patch.

"Where did you find the courage to go into the Limberlost and face its terrors? You inherited it from the blood of a brave father, dear heart. Where did you get the pluck to hold for over a year a job that few men would have taken at all? You got it from a plucky mother, you bravest of boys. You attacked single-handed a man almost twice your size, and fought as a demon, merely at the suggestion that you be deceptive and dishonest. Could your mother or your father have been untruthful? Here you are, so hungry and starved that you are dying for love. Where did you get all that capacity for loving? You didn't inherit it from hardened, heartless people, who would disfigure you and purposely leave you to die, that's one sure thing. You once told me of saving your big bullfrog from a rattlesnake. You knew you risked a horrible death when you did it. Yet you will spend miserable years torturing yourself with the idea that your own mother might have cut off that hand. Shame on you, Freckles! Your mother would have done this—"

The Angel deliberately turned back the cover, slipped up the sleeve, and laid her lips on the scars.

"Freckles! Wake up!" she cried, almost shaking him. "Come to your senses! Be a thinking, reasoning man! You have brooded too much, and been all your life too much alone. It's all as plain as plain can be to me. You must see it! Like breeds like in this world! You must be some sort of a reproduction of your parents, and I am not afraid to vouch for them, not for a minute!

"And then, too, if more proof is needed, here it is: Mr. McLean says that you never once have failed in tact and courtesy. He says that you are the most perfect gentleman he ever knew, and he has traveled the world over. How does it happen, Freckles? No one at that Home taught you. Hundreds of men couldn't be taught, even in a school of etiquette; so it must be instinctive with you. If it is, why, that means that it is born in you, and a direct inheritance from a race of men that have been gentlemen for ages, and couldn't be anything else.

"Then there's your singing. I don't believe there ever was a mortal with a sweeter voice than yours, and while that doesn't prove anything, there is a point that does. The little training you had from that choirmaster won't account for the wonderful accent and ease with which you sing. Somewhere in your close blood is a marvelously trained vocalist; we every one of us believe that, Freckles.

"Why does my father refer to you constantly as being of fine perceptions and honor? Because you are, Freckles. Why does the Bird Woman leave her precious work and come here to help look after you? I never heard of her losing any time over anyone else. It's because she loves you. And why does Mr. McLean turn all of his valuable business over to hired men and watch you personally? And why is he hunting excuses every day to spend money on you? My father says McLean is full Scotch-close with a dollar. He is a hard-headed business man, Freckles, and he is doing it because he finds you worthy of it. Worthy of all we all can do and more than we know how to do, dear heart! Freckles, are you listening to me? Oh! Won't you see it? Won't you believe it?"

"Oh, Angel!" chattered the bewildered Freckles, "Are you truly maning it? Could it be?"

"Of course it could," flashed the Angel, "because it just is!"

"But you can't prove it," wailed Freckles. "It ain't giving me a name, or me honor!"

"Freckles," said the Angel sternly, "you are unreasonable! Why, I did prove every word I said! Everything proves it! You look here! If you knew for sure that I could give you a name and your honor, and prove to you that your mother did love you, why, then, would you just go to breathing like perpetual motion and hang on for dear life and get well?"

A bright light shone in Freckles's eyes.

"If I knew that, Angel," he said solemnly, "you couldn't be killing me if you felled the biggest tree in the Limberlost smash on me!"

"Then you go right to work," said the Angel, "and before night I'll prove one thing to you: I can show you easily enough how much your mother loved you. That will be the first step, and then the remainder will all come. If my father and Mr. McLean are so anxious to spend some money, I'll give them a chance. I don't see why we haven't comprehended how you felt and so have been at work weeks ago. We've been awfully selfish. We've all been so comfortable, we never stopped to think what other people were suffering before our eyes. None of us has understood. I'll hire the finest detective in Chicago, and we'll go to work together. This is nothing compared with things people do find out. We'll go at it, beak and claw, and we'll show you a thing or two."

Freckles caught her sleeve.

"Me mother, Angel! Me mother!" he marveled hoarsely. "Did you say you could be finding out today if me mother loved me? How? Oh, Angel! Nothing matters, IF ONLY ME MOTHER DIDN'T DO IT!"

"Then you rest easy," said the Angel, with large confidence. "Your mother didn't do it! Mothers of sons such as you don't do things like that. I'll go to work at once and prove it to you. The first thing to do is to go to that Home where you were and get the clothes you wore the night you were left there. I know that they are required to save those things carefully. We can find out almost all there is to know about your mother from them. Did you ever see them?"

"Yis," he replied.

"Freckles! Were they white?" she cried.

"Maybe they were once. They're all yellow with laying, and brown with blood-stains now," said Freckles, the old note of bitterness creeping in. "You can't be telling anything at all by them, Angel!"

"Well, but I just can!" said the Angel positively. "I can see from the quality what kind of goods your mother could afford to buy. I can see from the cut whether she had good taste. I can see from the care she took in making them how much she loved and wanted you."

"But how? Angel, tell me how!" implored Freckles with trembling eagerness.

"Why, easily enough," said the Angel. "I thought you'd understand. People that can afford anything at all, always buy white for little new babies—linen and lace, and the very finest things to be had. There's a young woman living near us who cut up her wedding clothes to have fine things for her baby. Mothers who love and want their babies don't buy little rough, ready-made things, and they don't run up what they make on an old sewing machine. They make fine seams, and tucks, and put on lace and trimming by hand. They sit and stitch, and stitch—little, even stitches, every one just as careful. Their eyes shine and their faces glow. When they have to quit to do something else, they look sorry, and fold up their work so particularly. There isn't much worth knowing about your mother that those little clothes won't tell. I can see her putting the little stitches into them and smiling with shining eyes over your coming. Freckles, I'll wager you a dollar those little clothes of yours are just alive with the dearest, tiny handmade stitches."

A new light dawned in Freckles's eyes. A tinge of warm color swept into his face. Renewed strength was noticeable in his grip of her hands.

"Oh Angel! Will you go now? Will you be hurrying?" he cried.

"Right away," said the Angel. "I won't stop for a thing, and I'll hurry with all my might."

She smoothed his pillow, straightened the cover, gave him one steady look in the eyes, and went quietly from the room.

Outside the door, McLean and the surgeon anxiously awaited her. McLean caught her shoulders.

"Angel, what have you done?" he demanded.

The Angel smiled defiance into his eyes.

"'What have I done?'" she repeated. "I've tried to save Freckles."

"What will your father say?" groaned McLean.

"It strikes me," said the Angel, "that what Freckles said would be to the point."

"Freckles!" exclaimed McLean. "What could he say?"

"He seemed to be able to say several things," answered the Angel sweetly. "I fancy the one that concerns you most at present was, that if my father should offer me to him he would not have me."

"And no one knows why better than I do," cried McLean. "Every day he must astonish me with some new fineness."

He turned to the surgeon. "Save him!" he commanded. "Save him!" he implored. "He is too fine to be sacrificed."

"His salvation lies here," said the surgeon, stroking the Angel's sunshiny hair, "and I can read in the face of her that she knows how she is going to work it out. Don't trouble for the boy. She will save him!"

The Angel laughingly sped down the hall, and into the street, just as she was.

"I have come," she said to the matron of the Home, "to ask if you will allow me to examine, or, better yet, to take with me, the little clothes that a boy you called Freckles, discharged last fall, wore the night he was left here."

The woman looked at her in greater astonishment than the occasion demanded.

"Well, I'd be glad to let you see them," she said at last, "but the fact is we haven't them. I do hope we haven't made some mistake. I was thoroughly convinced, and so was the superintendent. We let his people take those things away yesterday. Who are you, and what do you want with them?"

The Angel stood dazed and speechless, staring at the matron.

"There couldn't have been a mistake," continued the matron, seeing the Angel's distress. "Freckles was here when I took charge, ten years ago. These people had it all proved that he belonged to them. They had him traced to where he ran away in Illinois last fall, and there they completely lost track of him. I'm sorry you seem so disappointed, but it is all right. The man is his uncle, and as like the boy as he possibly could be. He is almost killed to go back without him. If you know where Freckles is, they'd give big money to find out."

The Angel laid a hand along each cheek to steady her chattering teeth.

"Who are they?" she stammered. "Where are they going?"

"They are Irish folks, miss," said the matron. "They have been in Chicago and over the country for the past three months, hunting him everywhere. They have given up, and are starting home today. They—"

"Did they leave an address? Where could I find them?" interrupted the Angel.

"They left a card, and I notice the morning paper has the man's picture and is full of them. They've advertised a great deal in the city papers. It's a wonder you haven't seen something."

"Trains don't run right. We never get Chicago papers," said the Angel. "Please give me that card quickly. They may escape me. I simply must catch them!"

The matron hurried to the secretary and came back with a card.

"Their addresses are there," she said. "Both in Chicago and at their home. They made them full and plain, and I was to cable at once if I got the least clue of him at any time. If they've left the city, you can stop them in New York. You're sure to catch them before they sail—if you hurry."

The matron caught up a paper and thrust it into the Angel's hand as she ran to the street.

The Angel glanced at the card. The Chicago address was Suite Eleven, Auditorium. She laid her hand on her driver's sleeve and looked into his eyes.

"There is a fast-driving limit?" she asked.

"Yes, miss."

"Will you crowd it all you can without danger of arrest? I will pay well. I must catch some people!"

Then she smiled at him. The hospital, an Orphans' Home, and the Auditorium seemed a queer combination to that driver, but the Angel was always and everywhere the Angel, and her methods were strictly her own.

"I will take you there as quickly as any man could with a team," he said promptly.

The Angel clung to the card and paper, and as best she could in the lurching, swaying cab, read the addresses over.

"O'More, Suite Eleven, Auditorium."

"'O'More,'" she repeated. "Seems to fit Freckles to a dot. Wonder if that could be his name? 'Suite Eleven' means that you are pretty well fixed. Suites in the Auditorium come high."

Then she turned the card and read on its reverse, Lord Maxwell O'More, M. P., Killvany Place, County Clare, Ireland.

The Angel sat on the edge of the seat, bracing her feet against the one opposite, as the cab pitched and swung around corners and past vehicles. She mechanically fingered the pasteboard and stared straight ahead. Then she drew a deep breath and read the card again.

"A Lord-man!" she groaned despairingly. "A Lord-man! Bet my hoecake's scorched! Here I've gone and pledged my word to Freckles I'd find him some decent relatives, that he could be proud of, and now there isn't a chance out of a dozen that he'll have to be ashamed of them after all. It's too mean!"

The tears of vexation rolled down the tired, nerve-racked Angel's cheeks.

"This isn't going to do," she said, resolutely wiping her eyes with the palm of her hand and gulping down the nervous spasm in her throat. "I must read this paper before I meet Lord O'More."

She blinked back the tears and spreading the paper on her knee, read: "After three months' fruitless search, Lord O'More gives up the quest of his lost nephew, and leaves Chicago today for his home in Ireland."

She read on, and realized every word. The likeness settled any doubt. It was Freckles over again, only older and well dressed.

"Well, I must catch you if I can," muttered the Angel. "But when I do, if you are a gentleman in name only, you shan't have Freckles; that's flat. You're not his father and he is twenty. Anyway, if the law will give him to you for one year, you can't spoil him, because nobody could, and," she added, brightening, "he'll probably do you a lot of good. Freckles and I both must study years yet, and you should be something that will save him. I guess it will come out all right. At least, I don't believe you can take him away if I say no."

"Thank you; and wait, no matter how long," she said to her driver.

Catching up the paper, she hurried to the desk and laid down Lord O'More's card.

"Has my uncle started yet?" she asked sweetly.

The surprised clerk stepped back on a bellboy, and covertly kicked him for being in the way.

"His lordship is in his room," he said, with a low bow.

"All right," said the Angel, picking up the card. "I thought he might have started. I'll see him."

The clerk shoved the bellboy toward the Angel.

"Show her ladyship to the elevator and Lord O'More's suite," he said, bowing double.

"Aw, thanks," said the Angel with a slight nod, as she turned away.

"I'm not sure," she muttered to herself as the elevator sped upward, "whether it's the Irish or the English who say: 'Aw, thanks,' but it's probable he isn't either; and anyway, I just had to do something to counteract that 'All right.' How stupid of me!"

At the bellboy's tap, the door swung open and the liveried servant thrust a cardtray before the Angel. The opening of the door created a current that swayed a curtain aside, and in an adjoining room, lounging in a big chair, with a paper in his hand, sat a man who was, beyond question, of Freckles's blood and race.

With perfect control the Angel dropped Lord O'More's card in the tray, stepped past his servant, and stood before his lordship.

"Good morning," she said with tense politeness.

Lord O'More said nothing. He carelessly glanced her over with amused curiosity, until her color began to deepen and her blood to run hotly.

"Well, my dear," he said at last, "how can I serve you?"

Instantly the Angel became indignant. She had been so shielded in the midst of almost entire freedom, owing to the circumstances of her life, that the words and the look appeared to her as almost insulting. She lifted her head with a proud gesture.

"I am not your 'dear,'" she said with slow distinctness. "There isn't a thing in the world you can do for me. I came here to see if I could do something—a very great something—for you; but if I don't like you, I won't do it!"

Then Lord O'More did stare. Suddenly he broke into a ringing laugh. Without a change of attitude or expression, the Angel stood looking steadily at him.

There was a silken rustle, then a beautiful woman with cheeks of satiny pink, dark hair, and eyes of pure Irish blue, moved to Lord O'More's side, and catching his arm, shook him impatiently.

"Terence! Have you lost your senses?" she cried. "Didn't you understand what the child said? Look at her face! See what she has!"

Lord O'More opened his eyes widely and sat up. He did look at the Angel's face intently, and suddenly found it so good that it was difficult to follow the next injunction. He arose instantly.

"I beg your pardon," he said. "The fact is, I am leaving Chicago sorely disappointed. It makes me bitter and reckless. I thought you one more of those queer, useless people who have thrust themselves on me constantly, and I was careless. Forgive me, and tell me why you came."

"I will if I like you," said the Angel stoutly, "and if I don't, I won't!"

"But I began all wrong, and now I don't know how to make you like me," said his lordship, with sincere penitence in his tone.

The Angel found herself yielding to his voice. He spoke in a soft, mellow, smoothly flowing Irish tone, and although his speech was perfectly correct, it was so rounded, and accented, and the sentences so turned, that it was Freckles over again. Still, it was a matter of the very greatest importance, and she must be sure; so she looked into the beautiful woman's face.

"Are you his wife?" she asked.

"Yes," said the woman, "I am his wife."

"Well," said the Angel judicially, "the Bird Woman says no one in the whole world knows all a man's bignesses and all his littlenesses as his wife does. What you think of him should do for me. Do you like him?"

The question was so earnestly asked that it met with equal earnestness. The dark head moved caressingly against Lord O'More's sleeve.

"Better than anyone in the whole world," said Lady O'More promptly.

The Angel mused a second, and then her legal tinge came to the fore again.

"Yes, but have you anyone you could like better, if he wasn't all right?" she persisted.

"I have three of his sons, two little daughters, a father, mother, and several brothers and sisters," came the quick reply.

"And you like him best?" persisted the Angel with finality.

"I love him so much that I would give up every one of them with dry eyes if by so doing I could save him," cried Lord O'More's wife.

"Oh!" cried the Angel. "Oh, my!"

She lifted her clear eyes to Lord O'More's and shook her head.

"She never, never could do that!" she said. "But it's a mighty big thing to your credit that she *thinks* she could. I guess I'll tell you why I came."

She laid down the paper, and touched the portrait.

"When you were only a boy, did people call you Freckles?" she asked.

"Dozens of good fellows all over Ireland and the Continent are doing it today," answered Lord O'More.

The Angel's face wore her most beautiful smile.

"I was sure of it," she said winningly. "That's what we call him, and he is so like you, I doubt if any one of those three boys of yours are more so. But it's been twenty years. Seems to me you've been a long time coming!"

Lord O'More caught the Angel's wrists and his wife slipped her arms around her.

"Steady, my girl!" said the man's voice hoarsely. "Don't make me think you've brought word of the boy at this last hour, unless you know surely."

"It's all right," said the Angel. "We have him, and there's no chance of a mistake. If I hadn't gone to that Home for his little clothes, and heard of you and been hunting you, and had met you on the street, or anywhere, I would have stopped you and asked you who you were, just because you are so like him. It's all right. I can tell you where Freckles is; but whether you deserve to know—that's another matter!"

Lord O'More did not hear her. He dropped in his chair, and covering his face, burst into those terrible sobs that shake and rend a strong man. Lady O'More hovered over him, weeping.

"Umph! Looks pretty fair for Freckles," muttered the Angel. "Lots of things can be explained; now perhaps they can explain this."

They did explain so satisfactorily that in a few minutes the Angel was on her feet, hurrying Lord and Lady O'More to reach the hospital. "You said Freckles's old nurse knew his mother's picture instantly," said the Angel. "I want that picture and the bundle of little clothes."

Lady O'More gave them into her hands.

The likeness was a large miniature, painted on ivory, with a frame of beaten gold. Surrounded by masses of dark hair was a delicately cut face. In the upper part of it there was no trace of Freckles, but the lips curving in a smile were his very own. The Angel gazed at it steadily. Then with a quivering breath she laid the portrait aside and reached both hands to Lord O'More.

"That will save Freckles's life and insure his happiness," she said positively. "Thank you, oh thank you for coming!"

She opened the bundle of yellow and brown linen and gave only a glance at the texture and work. Then she gathered the little clothes and the picture to her heart and led the way to the cab.

Ushering Lord and Lady O'More into the reception room, she said to McLean, "Please go call up my father and ask him to come on the first train."

She closed the door after him.

"These are Freckles's people," she said to the Bird Woman. "You can find out about each other; I'm going to him."

Chapter 19

Wherein Freckles Finds His Birthright and the Angel Loses Her Heart

The nurse left the room quietly, as the Angel entered, carrying the bundle and picture. When they were alone, she turned to Freckles and saw that the crisis was indeed at hand.

That she had good word to give him was his salvation, for despite the heavy plaster jacket that held his body immovable, his head was lifted from the pillow. Both arms reached for her. His lips and cheeks flamed, while his eyes flashed with excitement.

"Angel," he panted. "Oh Angel! Did you find them? Are they white? Are the little stitches there? OH ANGEL! DID ME MOTHER LOVE ME?"

The words seemed to leap from his burning lips. The Angel dropped the bundle on the bed and laid the picture face down across his knees. She gently pushed his head to the pillow and caught his arms in a firm grasp.

"Yes, dear heart," she said with fullest assurance. "No little clothes were ever whiter. I never in all my life saw such dainty, fine, little stitches; and as for loving you, no boy's mother ever loved him more!"

A nervous trembling seized Freckles.

"Sure? Are you sure?" he urged with clicking teeth.

"I know," said the Angel firmly. "And Freckles, while you rest and be glad, I want to tell you a story. When you feel stronger we will look at the clothes together. They are here. They are all right. But while I was at the Home getting them, I heard of some people that were hunting a lost boy. I went to see them, and what they told me was all so exactly like what might have happened to you that I must tell you. Then you'll understand that things could be very different from what you always have tortured yourself with thinking. Are you strong enough to listen? May I tell you?"

"Maybe 'twasn't me mother! Maybe someone else made those little stitches!"

"Now, goosie, don't you begin that," said the Angel, "because I know that it was!"

"Know!" cried Freckles, his head springing from the pillow. "Know! How can you know?"

The Angel gently soothed him back.

"Why, because nobody else would ever sit and do it the way it is done. That's how I know," she said emphatically. "Now you listen while I tell you about this lost boy and his people, who have hunted for months and can't find him."

Freckles lay quietly under her touch, but he did not hear a word that she was saying until his roving eyes rested on her face; he immediately noticed a remarkable thing. For the first time she was talking to him and avoiding his eyes. That was not like the Angel at all. It was the delight of hearing her speak that she looked one squarely in the face and with perfect frankness. There were no side glances and down-drooping eyes when the Angel talked; she was business straight through. Instantly Freckles's wandering thoughts fastened on her words.

"—and he was a sour, grumpy, old man," she was saying. "He always had been spoiled, because he was an only son, so he had a title, and a big estate. He would have just his way, no matter about his sweet little wife, or his boys, or anyone. So when his elder son fell in love with a beautiful girl having a title, the very girl of all the world his father wanted him to, and added a big adjoining estate to his, why, that pleased him mightily.

"Then he went and ordered his younger son to marry a poky kind of a girl, that no one liked, to add another big estate on the other side, and that was different. That was all the world different, because the elder son had been in love all his life with the girl he married, and, oh, Freckles, it's no wonder, for I saw her! She's a beauty and she has the sweetest way.

"But that poor younger son, he had been in love with the village vicar's daughter all his life. That's no wonder either, for she was more beautiful yet. She could sing as the angels, but she hadn't a cent. She loved him to death, too, if he was bony and freckled and red-haired—I don't mean that! They didn't say what color his hair was, but his father's must have been the reddest ever, for when he found out about them, and it wasn't anything so terrible, HE JUST CAVED!

"The old man went to see the girl—the pretty one with no money, of course—and he hurt her feelings until she ran away. She went to London and began studying music. Soon she grew to be a fine singer, so she joined a company and came to this country.

"When the younger son found that she had left London, he followed her. When she got here all alone, and afraid, and saw him coming to her, why, she was so glad she up and married him, just like anybody else would have done. He didn't want her to travel with the troupe, so when they reached Chicago they thought that would be a good place, and they stopped, while he hunted work. It was slow business, because he never had been taught to do a useful thing, and he didn't even know how to hunt work, least of all to do it when he found it; so pretty soon things were going wrong. But if he couldn't find work, she could always sing, so she sang at night, and made little things in the daytime. He didn't like her to sing in public, and he wouldn't allow her when he could *help* himself; but winter came, it was very cold, and fire was expensive. Rents went up, and they had to move farther out to cheaper and cheaper places; and you were coming—I mean, the boy that is lost was coming—and they were almost distracted. Then the man wrote and told his father all about it; and his father sent the letter back unopened with a line telling him never to write again. When the baby came, there was very little left to pawn for food and a doctor, and nothing at all for a nurse; so an old neighbor woman went in and took care of the young mother and the little baby, because she was so sorry for them. By that time they were away in the suburbs on the top floor of a little wooden house, among a lot of big factories, and it kept growing colder, with less to eat. Then the man grew desperate and he went just to find something to eat and the woman was desperate, too. She got up, left the old woman to take care of her baby, and went into the city to sing for some money. The woman became so cold she put the baby in bed and went home. Then a boiler blew up in a big factory beside the little house and set it on fire. A piece of iron was pitched across and broke through the roof. It came down smash, and cut just one little hand off the poor baby. It screamed and screamed; and the fire kept coming closer and closer.

"The old woman ran out with the other people and saw what had happened. She knew there wasn't going to be time to wait for firemen or anything, so she ran into the building. She could hear the baby screaming, and she couldn't stand that; so she worked her way to it. There it was, all hurt and bleeding. Then she was almost scared to death over thinking what its mother would do to her for going away and leaving it, so she ran to a Home for little friendless babies, that was close, and banged on the door. Then she hid across the street until the baby was taken in, and then she ran back to see if her own house was burning. The big factory and the little house and a lot of others were all gone. The people there told her that the beautiful lady came back and ran into the house to find her baby. She had just gone in when her husband came, and he went in after her, and the house fell over both of them."

Freckles lay rigidly, with his eyes on the Angel's face, while she talked rapidly to the ceiling.

"Then the old woman was sick about that poor little baby. She was afraid to tell them at the Home, because she knew she never should have left it, but she wrote a letter and sent it to where the beautiful woman, when she was ill, had said her husband's people lived. She told all about the little baby that she could remember: when it was born, how it was named for the man's elder brother, that its hand had been cut off in the fire, and where she had put it to be doctored and taken care of. She told them that its mother and father were both burned, and she begged and implored them to come after it.

"You'd think that would have melted a heart of ice, but that old man hadn't any heart to melt, for he got that letter and read it. He hid it away among his papers and never told a soul. A few months ago he died. When his elder son went to settle his business, he found the letter almost the first thing. He dropped everything, and came, with his wife, to hunt that baby, because he always had loved his brother dearly, and wanted him back. He had hunted for him all he dared all these years, but when he got here you were gone—I mean the baby was gone, and I had to tell you, Freckles, for you see, it might have happened to you like that just as easy as to that other lost boy."

Freckles reached up and turned the Angel's face until he compelled her eyes to meet his.

"Angel," he asked quietly, "why don't you look at me when you are telling about that lost boy?"

"I—I didn't know I wasn't," faltered the Angel.

"It seems to me," said Freckles, his breath beginning to come in sharp wheezes, "that you got us rather mixed, and it ain't like you to be mixing things till one can't be knowing. If they were telling you so much, did they say which hand was for being off that lost boy?"

The Angel's eyes escaped again.

"It—it was the same as yours," she ventured, barely breathing in her fear.

Still Freckles lay rigid and whiter than the coverlet.

"Would that boy be as old as me?" he asked.

"Yes," said the Angel faintly.

"Angel," said Freckles at last, catching her wrist, "are you trying to tell me that there is somebody hunting a boy that you're thinking might be me? Are you belavin' you've found me relations?"

Then the Angel's eyes came home. The time had come. She pinioned Freckles's arms to his sides and bent above him.

"How strong are you, dear heart?" she breathed. "How brave are you? Can you bear it? Dare I tell you that?"

"No!" gasped Freckles. "Not if you're sure! I can't bear it! I'll die if you do!"

The day had been one unremitting strain with the Angel. Nerve tension was drawn to the finest thread. It snapped suddenly.

"Die!" she flamed. "Die, if I tell you that! You said this morning that you would die if you *didn't* know your name, and if your people were honorable. Now I've gone and found you a name that stands for ages of honor, a mother who loved you enough to go into the fire and die for you, and the nicest kind of relatives, and you turn round and say you'll die over that! YOU JUST TRY DYING AND YOU'LL GET A GOOD SLAP!"

The Angel stood glaring at him. One second Freckles lay paralyzed and dumb with astonishment. The next the Irish in his soul arose above everything. A laugh burst from him. The terrified Angel caught him in her arms and tried to stifle the sound. She implored and commanded. When he was too worn to utter another sound, his eyes laughed silently.

After a long time, when he was quiet and rested, the Angel commenced talking to him gently, and this time her big eyes, humid with tenderness and mellow with happiness, seemed as if they could not leave his face.

"Dear Freckles," she was saying, "across your knees there is the face of the mother who went into the fire for you, and I know the name—old and full of honor—to which you were born. Dear heart, which will you have first?"

Freckles was very tired; the big drops of perspiration ran together on his temples; but the watching Angel caught the words his lips formed, "Me mother!"

She lifted the lovely pictured face and set it in the nook of his arm. Freckles caught her hand and drew her beside him, and together they gazed at the picture while the tears slid over their cheeks.

"Me mother! Oh, me mother! Can you ever be forgiving me? Oh, me beautiful little mother!" chanted Freckles over and over in exalted wonder, until he was so completely exhausted that his lips refused to form the question in his weary eyes.

"Wait!" cried the Angel with inborn refinement, for she could no more answer that question than he could ask. "Wait, I will write it!"

She hurried to the table, caught up the nurse's pencil, and on the back of a prescription tablet scrawled it: "Terence Maxwell O'More, Dunderry House, County Clare, Ireland."

Before she had finished came Freckles's voice: "Angel, are you hurrying?"

"Yes," said the Angel; "I am. But there is a good deal of it. I have to put in your house and country, so that you will feel located."

"Me house?" marveled Freckles.

"Of course," said the Angel. "Your uncle says your grandmother left your father her dower house and estate, because she knew his father would cut him off. You get that, and all your share of your grandfather's property besides. It is all set off for you and waiting. Lord O'More told me so. I suspect you are richer than McLean, Freckles."

She closed his fingers over the slip and straightened his hair.

"Now you are all right, dear Limberlost guard," she said. "You go to sleep and don't think of a thing but just pure joy, joy, joy! I'll keep your people until you wake up. You are too tired to see anyone else just now!"

Freckles caught her skirt as she turned from him.

"I'll go to sleep in five minutes," he said, "if you will be doing just one thing more for me. Send for your father! Oh, Angel, send for him quick! How will I ever be waiting until he comes?"

One instant the Angel stood looking at him. The next a crimson wave darkly stained her lovely face. Her chin began a spasmodic quivering and the tears sprang into her eyes. Her hands caught at her chest as if she were stifling. Freckles's grasp on her tightened until he drew her beside him. He slipped his arm around her and drew her face to his pillow.

"Don't, Angel; for the love of mercy don't be doing that," he implored. "I can't be bearing it. Tell me. You must tell me."

The Angel shook her head.

"That ain't fair, Angel," said Freckles. "You made me tell you when it was like tearing the heart raw from me breast. And you was for making everything heaven—just heaven and nothing else for me. If I'm so much more now than I was an hour ago, maybe I can be thinking of some way to fix things. You will be telling me?" he coaxed, moving his cheek against her hair.

The Angel's head moved in negation. Freckles did a moment of intent thinking.

"Maybe I can be guessing," he whispered. "Will you be giving me three chances?"

There was the faintest possible assent.

"You didn't want me to be knowing me name," guessed Freckles.

The Angel's head sprang from the pillow and her tear-stained face flamed with outraged indignation.

"Why, I did too!" she cried angrily.

"One gone," said Freckles calmly. "You didn't want me to have relatives, a home, and money."

"I did!" exclaimed the Angel. "Didn't I go myself, all alone, into the city, and find them when I was afraid as death? I did too!"

"Two gone," said Freckles. "You didn't want the beautifulest girl in the world to be telling me—"

Down went the Angel's face and a heavy sob shook her. Freckles's clasp tightened around her shoulders, while his face, in its conflicting emotions, was a study. He was so stunned and bewildered by the miracle that had been performed in bringing to light his name and relatives that he had no strength left for elaborate mental processes. Despite all it meant to him to know his name at last, and that he was of honorable birth—knowledge without which life was an eternal disgrace and burden the one thing that was hammering in Freckles's heart and beating in his brain, past any attempted expression, was the fact that, while nameless and possibly born in shame, the Angel had told him that she loved him. He could find no word with which to begin to voice the rapture of his heart over that. But if she regretted it—if it had been a thing done out of her pity for his condition, or her feeling of responsibility, if it killed him after all, there was only one thing left to do. Not for McLean, not for the Bird Woman, not for the Duncans would Freckles have done it—but for the Angel—if it would make her happy—he would do anything.

"Angel," whispered Freckles, with his lips against her hair, "you haven't learned your history book very well, or else you've forgotten."

"Forgotten what?" sobbed the Angel.

"Forgotten about the real knight, Ladybird," breathed Freckles. "Don't you know that, if anything happened that made his lady sorry, a real knight just simply couldn't be remembering it? Angel, darling little Swamp Angel, you be listening to me. There was one night on the trail, one solemn, grand, white night, that there wasn't ever any other like before or since, when the dear Boss put his arm around me and told me that he loved me; but if you care, Angel, if you don't want it that way, why, I ain't remembering that anyone else ever did—not in me whole life."

The Angel lifted her head and looked into the depths of Freckles's honest gray eyes, and they met hers unwaveringly; but the pain in them was pitiful.

"Do you mean," she demanded, "that you don't remember that a brazen, forward girl told you, when you hadn't asked her, that she"—the Angel choked on it a second, but she gave a gulp and brought it out bravely "that she loved you?"

"No!" cried Freckles. "No! I don't remember anything of the kind!"

But all the songbirds of his soul burst into melody over that one little clause: "When you hadn't asked her."

"But you will," said the Angel. "You may live to be an old, old man, and then you will."

"I will not!" cried Freckles. "How can you think it, Angel?"

"You won't even *look* as if you remember?"

"I will not!" persisted Freckles. "I'll be swearing to it if you want me to. If you wasn't too tired to think this thing out straight, you'd be seeing that I couldn't—that I just simply couldn't! I'd rather give it all up now and go into eternity alone, without ever seeing a soul of me same blood, or me home, or hearing another man call me by the name I was born to, than to remember anything that would be hurting you, Angel. I should think you'd be understanding that it ain't no ways possible for me to do it."

The Angel's tear-stained face flashed into dazzling beauty. A half-hysterical little laugh broke from her heart and bubbled over her lips.

"Oh, Freckles, forgive me!" she cried. "I've been through so much that I'm scarcely myself, or I wouldn't be here bothering you when you should be sleeping. Of course you couldn't! I knew it all the time! I was just scared! I was forgetting that you were you! You're too good a knight to remember a thing like that. Of course you are! And when you don't remember, why, then it's the same as if it never happened. I was almost killed because I'd gone and spoiled everything, but now it will be all right. Now you can go on and do things like other men, and I can have some flowers, and letters, and my sweetheart coming, and when you are SURE, why, then YOU can tell ME things, can't you? Oh, Freckles, I'm so glad! Oh, I'm so happy! It's dear of you not to remember, Freckles; perfectly dear! It's no wonder I love you so. The wonder would be if I did not. Oh, I should like to know how I'm ever going to make you understand how much I love you!"

Pillow and all, she caught him to her breast one long second; then she was gone.

Freckles lay dazed with astonishment. At last his amazed eyes searched the room for something approaching the human to which he could appeal, and falling on his mother's portrait, he set it before him.

"For the love of life! Me little mother," he panted, "did you hear that? Did you hear it! Tell me, am I living, or am I dead and all heaven come true this minute? Did you hear it?"

He shook the frame in his impatience at receiving no answer.

"You are only a pictured face," he said at last, "and of course you can't talk; but the soul of you must be somewhere, and surely in this hour you are close enough to be hearing. Tell me, did you hear that? I can't ever be telling a living soul; but darling little mother, who gave your life for mine, I can always be talking of it to you! Every day we'll talk it over and try to understand the miracle of it. Tell me, are all women like that? Were you like me Swamp Angel? If you were, then I'm understanding why me father followed across the ocean and went into the fire."

Chapter 20

Wherein Freckles Returns to the Limberlost, and Lord O'More Sails for Ireland without Him

Freckles's voice ceased, his eyes closed, and his head rolled back from exhaustion. Later in the day he insisted on seeing Lord and Lady O'More, but he fainted before the resemblance of another man to him, and gave all of his friends a terrible fright.

The next morning, the Man of Affairs, with a heart filled with misgivings, undertook the interview on which Freckles insisted. His fears were without cause. Freckles was the soul of honor and simplicity.

"Have they been telling you what's come to me?" he asked without even waiting for a greeting.

"Yes," said the Angel's father.

"Do you think you have the very worst of it clear to your understanding?"

Under Freckles's earnest eyes the Man of Affairs answered soberly: "I think I have, Mr. O'More."

That was the first time Freckles heard his name from the lips of another. One second he lay overcome; the next, tears filled his eyes, and he reached out his hand. Then the Angel's father understood, and he clasped that hand and held it in a strong, firm grasp.

"Terence, my boy," he said, "let me do the talking. I came here with the understanding that you wanted to ask me for my only child. I should like, at the proper time, to regard her marriage, if she has found the man she desires to marry, not as losing all I have, but as gaining a man on whom I can depend to love as a son and to take charge of my affairs for her when I retire from business. Bend all of your energies toward rapid recovery, and from this hour understand that my daughter and my home are yours."

"You're not forgetting this?"

Freckles lifted his right arm.

"Terence, I'm sorrier than I have words to express about that," said the Man of Affairs. "It's a damnable pity! But if it's for me to choose whether I give all I have left in this world to a man lacking a hand, or to one of these gambling, tippling, immoral spendthrifts of today, with both hands and feet off their souls, and a rotten spot in the core, I choose you; and it seems that my daughter does the same. Put what is left you of that right arm to the best uses you can in this world, and never again mention or feel that it is defective so long as you live. Good day, sir!"

"One minute more," said Freckles. "Yesterday the Angel was telling me that there was money coming to me from two sources. She said that me grandmother had left me father all of her fortune and her house, because she knew that his father would be cutting him off, and also that me uncle had set aside for me what would be me father's interest in his father's estate.

"Whatever the sum is that me grandmother left me father, because she loved him and wanted him to be having it, that I'll be taking. 'Twas hers from her father, and she had the right to be giving it as she chose. Anything from the man that knowingly left me father and me mother to go cold and hungry, and into the fire in misery, when just a little would have made life so beautiful to them, and saved me this crippled body—money that he willed from me when he knew I was living, of his blood and on charity among strangers, I don't touch, not if I freeze, starve, and burn too! If there ain't enough besides that, and I can't be earning enough to fix things for the Angel—"

"We are not discussing money!" burst in the Man of Affairs. "We don't want any blood-money! We have all we need without it. If you don't feel right and easy over it, don't you touch a cent of any of it."

"It's right I should have what me grandmother intinded for me father, and I want it," said Freckles, "but I'd die before I'd touch a cent of me grandfather's money!"

"Now," said the Angel, "we are all going home. We have done all we can for Freckles. His people are here. He should know them. They are very anxious to become acquainted with him. We'll resign him to them. When he is well, why, then he will be perfectly free to go to Ireland or come to the Limberlost, just as he chooses. We will go at once."

McLean held out for a week, and then he could endure it no longer. He was heart hungry for Freckles. Communing with himself in the long, soundful nights of the swamp, he had learned to his astonishment that for the past year his heart had been circling the Limberlost with Freckles. He began to wish that he had not left him. Perhaps the boy—his boy by first right, after all—was being neglected.

If the Boss had been a nervous old woman, he scarcely could have imagined more things that might be going wrong.

He started for Chicago, loaded with a big box of goldenrod, asters, fringed gentians, and crimson leaves, that the Angel carefully had gathered from Freckles's room, and a little, long slender package. He traveled with biting, stinging jealousy in his heart. He would not admit it even to himself, but he was unable to remain longer away from Freckles and leave him to the care of Lord O'More.

In a few minutes' talk, while McLean awaited admission to Freckles's room, his lordship had chatted genially of Freckles's rapid recovery, of his delight that he was unspotted by his early surroundings, and his desire to visit the Limberlost with Freckles before they sailed; he expressed the hope that he could prevail upon the Angel's father to place her in his wife's care and have her education finished in Paris. He said they were anxious to do all they could to help bind Freckles's arrangements with the Angel, as both he and Lady O'More regarded her as the most promising girl they knew, and one who could be fitted to fill the high position in which Freckles would place her.

Every word he uttered was pungent with bitterness to McLean. The swamp had lost its flavor without Freckles; and yet, as Lord O'More talked, McLean fervently wished himself in the heart of it. As he entered Freckles's room he almost lost his breath. Everything was changed.

Freckles lay beside a window where he could follow Lake Michigan's blue until the horizon dipped into it. He could see big soft clouds, white-capped waves, shimmering sails, and puffing steamers trailing billowing banners of lavender and gray across the sky. Gulls and curlews wheeled over the water and dipped their wings in the foam. The room was filled with every luxury that taste and money could introduce.

All the tan and sunburn had been washed from Freckles's face in sweats of agony. It was a smooth, even white, its brown rift scarcely showing. What the nurses and Lady O'More had done to Freckles's hair McLean could not guess, but it was the most beautiful that he ever had seen. Fine as floss, bright in color, waving and crisp, it fell around the white face.

They had gotten his arms into and his chest covered with a finely embroidered, pale-blue silk shirt, with soft, white tie at the throat. Among the many changes that had taken place during his absence, the fact that Freckles was most attractive and barely escaped being handsome remained almost unnoticed by the Boss, so great was his astonishment at seeing both cuffs turned back and the right arm in view. Freckles was using the maimed arm that previously he always had hidden.

"Oh Lord, sir, but I'm glad to see you!" cried Freckles, almost rolling from the bed as he reached toward McLean. "Tell me quick, is the Angel well and happy? Can me Little Chicken spread six feet of wing and sail to his mother? How's me new father, the Bird Woman, Duncans, and Nellie—darling little high-stepping Nellie? Me Aunt Alice is going to choose the hat just as soon as I'm mended enough to be going with her. How are all the gang? Have they found any more good trees? I've been thinking a lot, sir. I believe I can find others near that last one. Me Aunt Alice thinks maybe I can, and Uncle Terence says it's likely. Golly, but they're nice, ilegant people. I tell you I'm proud to be same blood with them! Come closer, quick! I was going to do this yesterday, and somehow I just felt that you'd surely be coming today and I waited. I'm selecting the Angel's ring stone. The ring she ordered for me is finished and they sent it to keep me company. See? It's an emerald—just me color, Lord O'More says."

Freckles flourished his hand.

"Ain't that fine? Never took so much comfort with anything in me life. Every color of the old swamp is in it. I asked the Angel to have a little shamrock leaf cut on it, so every time I saw it I'd be thinking of the 'love, truth, and valor' of that song she was teaching me. Ain't that a beautiful song? Some of these days I'm going to make it echo. I'm a little afraid to be doing it with me voice yet, but me heart's tuning away on it every blessed hour. Will you be looking at these now?"

Freckles tilted a tray of unset stones from Peacock's that would have ransomed several valuable kings. He held them toward McLean, stirring them with his right arm.

"I tell you I'm glad to see you, sir," he said. "I tried to tell me uncle what I wanted, but this ain't for him to be mixed up in, anyway, and I don't think I made it clear to him. I couldn't seem to say the words I wanted. I can be telling you, sir."

McLean's heart began to thump as a lover's.

"Go on, Freckles," he said assuringly.

"It's this," said Freckles. "I told him that I would pay only three hundred dollars for the Angel's stone. I'm thinking that with what he has laid up for me, and the bigness of things that the Angel did for me, it seems like a stingy little sum to him. I know he thinks I should be giving much more, but I feel as if I just had to be buying that stone with money I earned meself; and that is all I have saved of me wages. I don't mind paying for the muff, or the drexing table, or Mrs. Duncan's things, from that other money, and later the Angel can have every last cent of me grandmother's, if she'll take it; but just now—oh, sir, can't you see that I have to be buying this stone with what I have in the bank? I'm feeling that I couldn't do any other way, and don't you think the Angel would rather have the best stone I can buy with the money I earned meself than a finer one paid for with other money?"

"In other words, Freckles," said the Boss in a husky voice, "you don't want to buy the Angel's ring with money. You want to give for it your first awful fear of the swamp. You want to pay for it with the loneliness and heart hunger you have suffered there, with last winter's freezing on the line and this summer's burning in the sun. You want it to stand to her for every hour in which you risked your life to fulfill your contract honorably. You want the price of that stone to be the fears that have chilled your heart—the sweat and blood of your body."

Freckles's eyes were filled with tears and his face quivering with feeling.

"Dear Mr. McLean," he said, reaching with a caress over the Boss's black hair and his cheek. "Dear Boss, that's why I've wanted you so. I knew you would know. Now you will be looking at these? I don't want emeralds, because that's what she gave me."

He pushed the green stones into a little heap of rejected ones. Then he singled out all the pearls.

"Ain't they pretty things?" he said. "I'll be getting her some of those later. They are like lily faces, turtle-head flowers, dewdrops in the shade or moonlight; but they haven't the life in them that I want in the stone I give to the Angel right now."

Freckles heaped the pearls with the emeralds. He studied the diamonds a long time.

"These things are so fascinating like they almost tempt one, though they ain't quite the proper thing," he said. "I've always dearly loved to be watching yours, sir. I must get her some of these big ones, too, some day. They're like the Limberlost in January, when it's all ice-coated, and the sun is in the west and shines through and makes all you can see of the whole world look like fire and ice; but fire and ice ain't like the Angel."

The diamonds joined the emeralds and pearls. There was left a little red heap, and Freckles' fingers touched it with a new tenderness. His eyes were flashing.

"I'm thinking here's me Angel's stone," he exulted. "The Limberlost, and me with it, grew in mine; but it's going to bloom, and her with it, in this! There's the red of the wild poppies, the cardinal-flowers, and the little bunch of crushed foxfire that we found where she put it to save me. There's the light of the campfire, and the sun setting over Sleepy Snake Creek. There's the red of the blood we were willing to give for each other. It's like her lips, and like the drops that dried on her beautiful arm that first day, and I'm thinking it must be like the brave, tender, clean, red heart of her."

Freckles lifted the ruby to his lips and handed it to McLean.

"I'll be signing me cheque and you have it set," he said. "I want you to draw me money and pay for it with those very same dollars, sir."

Again the heart of McLean took hope.

"Freckles, may I ask you something?" he said.

"Why, sure," said Freckles. "There's nothing you would be asking that it wouldn't be giving me joy to be telling you."

McLean's eyes traveled to Freckles's right arm with which he was moving the jewels.

"Oh, that!" cried Freckles with a laugh. "You're wanting to know where all the bitterness is gone? Well sir, 'twas carried from me soul, heart, and body on the lips of an Angel. Seems that hurt was necessary in the beginning to make today come true. The wound had always been raw, but the Angel was healing it. If she doesn't care, I don't. Me dear new father doesn't, nor me aunt and uncle, and you never did. Why should I be fretting all me life about what can't be helped. The real truth is, that since what happened to it last week, I'm so everlastingly proud of it I catch meself sticking it out on display a bit."

Freckles looked the Boss in the eyes and began to laugh.

"Well thank heaven!" said McLean.

"Now it's me turn," said Freckles. "I don't know as I ought to be asking you, and yet I can't see a reason good enough to keep me from it. It's a thing I've had on me mind every hour since I've had time to straighten things out a little. May I be asking you a question?"

McLean reached over and took Freckles's hand. His voice was shaken with feeling as he replied: "Freckles, you almost hurt me. Will you never learn how much you are to me—how happy you make me in coming to me with anything, no matter what?"

"Then it's this," said Freckles, gripping the hand of McLean strongly. "If this accident, and all that's come to me since, had never happened, where was it you had planned to send me to school? What was it you meant for me to do?"

"Why, Freckles," answered McLean, "I'm scarcely prepared to state definitely. My ideas were rather hazy. I thought we would make a beginning and see which way things went. I figured on taking you to Grand Rapids first, and putting you in the care of my mother. I had an idea it would be best to secure a private tutor to coach you for a year or two, until you were ready to enter Ann Arbor or the Chicago University in good shape. Then I thought we'd finish in this country at Yale or Harvard, and end with Oxford, to get a good, all-round flavor."

"Is that all?" asked Freckles.

"No; that's leaving the music out," said McLean. "I intended to have your voice tested by some master, and if you really were endowed for a career as a great musician, and had inclinations that way, I wished to have you drop some of the college work and make music your chief study. Finally, I wanted us to take a trip through Europe and clear around the circle together."

"And then what?" queried Freckles breathlessly.

"Why, then," said McLean, "you know that my heart is hopelessly in the woods. I never will quit the timber business while there is timber to handle and breath in my body. I thought if you didn't make a profession of music, and had any inclination my way, we would stretch the partnership one more and take you into the firm, placing your work with me. Those plans may sound jumbled in the telling, but they have grown steadily on me, Freckles, as you have grown dear to me."

Freckles lifted anxious and eager eyes to McLean.

"You told me once on the trail, and again when we thought that I was dying, that you loved me. Do these things that have come to me make any difference in any way with your feeing toward me?"

"None," said McLean. "How could they, Freckles? Nothing could make me love you more, and you never will do anything that will make me love you less."

"Glory be to God!" cried Freckles. "Glory to the Almighty! Hurry and be telling your mother I'm coming! Just as soon as I can get on me feet I'll be taking that ring to me Angel, and then I'll go to Grand Rapids and be making me start just as you planned, only that I can be paying me own way. When I'm educated enough, we'll all—the Angel and her father, the Bird Woman, you, and me—all of us will go together and see me house and me relations and be taking that trip. When we get back, we'll add O'More to the Lumber Company, and golly, sir, but we'll make things hum! Good land, sir! Don't do that! Why, Mr. McLean, dear Boss, dear father, don't be doing that! What is it?"

"Nothing, nothing!" boomed McLean's deep bass. "Nothing at all!"

He abruptly turned, and hurried to the window.

"This is a mighty fine view," he said. "Lake's beautiful this morning. No wonder Chicago people are so proud of their city's location on its shore. But, Freckles, what is Lord O'More going to say to this?"

"I don't know," said Freckles. "I am going to be cut deep if he cares, for he's been more than good to me, and Lady Alice is next to me Angel. He's made me feel me blood and race me own possession. She's talked to me by the hour of me father and mother and me grandmother. She's made them all that real I can lay claim to them and feel that they are mine. I'm very sorry to be hurting them, if it will, but it can't be changed. Nobody ever puts the width of the ocean between me and the Angel. From here to the Limberlost is all I can be bearing peaceable. I want the education, and then I want to work and live here in the country where I was born, and where the ashes of me father and mother rest.

"I'll be glad to see Ireland, and glad especial to see those little people who are my kin, but I ain't ever staying long. All me heart is the Angel's, and the Limberlost is calling every minute. You're thinking, sir, that when I look from that window I see the beautiful water, ain't you? I'm not.

"I see soft, slow clouds oozing across the blue, me big black chickens hanging up there, and a great feather softly sliding down. I see mighty trees, swinging vines, bright flowers, and always masses of the wild roses, with the wild rose face of me Ladybird looking through. I see the swale rocking, smell the sweetness of the blooming things, and the damp, mucky odor of the swamp; and I hear me birds sing, me squirrels bark, the rattlers hiss, and the step of Wessner or Black Jack coming; and whether it's the things that I loved or the things that I feared, it's all a part of the day.

"Me heart's all me Swamp Angel's, and me love is all hers, and I have her and the swamp so confused in me mind I never can be separating them. When I look at her, I see blue sky, the sun rifting through the leaves and pink and red flowers; and when I look at the Limberlost I see a pink face with blue eyes, gold hair, and red lips, and, it's the truth, sir, they're mixed till they're one to me!

"I'm afraid it will be hurting some, but I have the feeing that I can be making my dear people understand, so that they will be willing to let me come back home. Send Lady O'More to put these flowers God made in the place of these glass-house ilegancies, and please be cutting the string of this little package the Angel's sent me."

As Freckles held up the package, the lights of the Limberlost flashed from the emerald on his finger. On the cover was printed: "To the Limberlost Guard!" Under it was a big, crisp, iridescent black feather.

A Girl of the Limberlost

To all girls of the Limberlost
in general
and one Jeanette Helen Porter
in particular

Contents

Chapter 1

Wherein Elnora Goes to High School and Learns Many Lessons Not Found in Her Books

"Elnora Comstock, have you lost your senses?" demanded the angry voice of Katharine Comstock while she glared at her daughter.

"Why mother!" faltered the girl.

"Don't you 'why mother' me!" cried Mrs. Comstock. "You know very well what I mean. You've given me no peace until you've had your way about this going to school business; I've fixed you good enough, and you're ready to start. But no child of mine walks the streets of Onabasha looking like a play-actress woman. You wet your hair and comb it down modest and decent and then be off, or you'll have no time to find where you belong."

Elnora gave one despairing glance at the white face, framed in a most becoming riot of reddish-brown hair, which she saw in the little kitchen mirror. Then she untied the narrow black ribbon, wet the comb and plastered the waving curls close to her head, bound them fast, pinned on the skimpy black hat and opened the back door.

"You've gone so plumb daffy you are forgetting your dinner," jeered her mother.

"I don't want anything to eat," replied Elnora.

"You'll take your dinner or you'll not go one step. Are you crazy? Walk almost three miles and no food from six in the morning until six at night. A pretty figure you'd cut if you had your way! And after I've gone and bought you this nice new pail and filled it especial to start on!"

Elnora came back with a face still whiter and picked up the lunch. "Thank you, mother! Good-bye!" she said. Mrs. Comstock did not reply. She watched the girl follow the long walk to the gate and go from sight on the road, in the bright sunshine of the first Monday of September.

"I bet a dollar she gets enough of it by night!" commented Mrs. Comstock.

Elnora walked by instinct, for her eyes were blinded with tears. She left the road where it turned south, at the corner of the Limberlost, climbed a snake fence and entered a path worn by her own feet. Dodging under willow and scrub oak branches she came at last to the faint outline of an old trail made in the days when the precious timber of the swamp was guarded by armed men. This path she followed until she reached a thick clump of bushes. From the debris in the end of a hollow log she took a key that unlocked the padlock of a large weatherbeaten old box, inside of which lay several books, a butterfly apparatus, and a small cracked mirror. The walls were lined thickly with gaudy butterflies, dragonflies, and moths. She set up the mirror and once more pulling the ribbon from her hair, she shook the bright mass over her shoulders, tossing it dry in the sunshine. Then she straightened it, bound it loosely, and replaced her hat. She tugged vainly at the low brown calico collar and gazed despairingly at the generous length of the narrow skirt. She lifted it as she would have cut it if possible. That disclosed the heavy high leather shoes, at sight of which she seemed positively ill, and hastily dropped the skirt. She opened the pail, removed the lunch, wrapped it in the napkin, and placed it in a small pasteboard box. Locking the case again she hid the key and hurried down the trail.

She followed it around the north end of the swamp and then entered a footpath crossing a farm leading in the direction of the spires of the city to the northeast. Again she climbed a fence and was on the open road. For an instant she leaned against the fence staring before her, then turned and looked back. Behind her lay the land on which she had been born to drudgery and a mother who made no pretence of loving her; before her lay the city through whose schools she hoped to find means of escape and the way to reach the things for which she cared. When she thought of how she appeared she leaned more heavily against the fence and groaned; when she thought of turning back and wearing such clothing in ignorance all the days of her life she set her teeth firmly and went hastily toward Onabasha.

On the bridge crossing a deep culvert at the suburbs she glanced around, and then kneeling she thrust the lunch box between the foundation and the flooring. This left her empty-handed as she approached the big stone high school building. She entered bravely and inquired her way to the office of the superintendent. There she learned that she should have come the previous week and arranged about her classes. There were many things incident to the opening of school, and one man unable to cope with all of them.

"Where have you been attending school?" he asked, while he advised the teacher of Domestic Science not to telephone for groceries until she knew how many she would have in her classes; wrote an order for chemicals for the students of science; and advised the leader of the orchestra to hire a professional to take the place of the bass violist, reported suddenly ill.

"I finished last spring at Brushwood school, district number nine," said Elnora. "I have been studying all summer. I am quite sure I can do the first year work, if I have a few days to get started."

"Of course, of course," assented the superintendent. "Almost invariably country pupils do good work. You may enter first year, and if it is too difficult, we will find it out speedily. Your teachers will tell you the list of books you must have, and if you will come with me I will show you the way to the auditorium. It is now time for opening exercises. Take any seat you find vacant."

Elnora stood before the entrance and stared into the largest room she ever had seen. The floor sloped to a yawning stage on which a band of musicians, grouped around a grand piano, were tuning their instruments. She had two fleeting impressions. That it was all a mistake; this was no school, but a grand display of enormous ribbon bows; and the second, that she was sinking, and had forgotten how to walk. Then a burst from the orchestra nerved her while a bevy of daintily clad, sweet-smelling things that might have been birds, or flowers, or possibly gaily dressed, happy young girls, pushed her forward. She found herself plodding across the back of the auditorium, praying for guidance, to an empty seat.

As the girls passed her, vacancies seemed to open to meet them. Their friends were moving over, beckoning and whispering invitations. Every one else was seated, but no one paid any attention to the white-faced girl stumbling half blindly down the aisle next the farthest wall. So she went on to the very end facing the stage. No one moved, and she could not summon courage to crowd past others to several empty seats she saw. At the end of the aisle she paused in desperation, while she stared back at the whole forest of faces most of which were now turned upon her.

In a flash came the full realization of her scanty dress, her pitiful little hat and ribbon, her big, heavy shoes, her ignorance of where to go or what to do; and from a sickening wave which crept over her, she felt she was going to become very ill. Then out of the mass she saw a pair of big, brown boy eyes, three seats from her, and there was a message in them. Without moving his body he reached forward and with a pencil touched the back of the seat before him. Instantly Elnora took another step which brought her to a row of vacant front seats.

She heard laughter behind her; the knowledge that she wore the only hat in the room burned her; every matter of moment, and some of none at all, cut and stung. She had no books. Where should she go when this was over? What would she give to be on the trail going home! She was shaking with a nervous chill when the music ceased, and the superintendent arose, and coming down to the front of the flower-decked platform, opened a Bible and began to read. Elnora did not know what he was reading, and she felt that she did not care. Wildly she was racking her brain to decide whether she should sit still when the others left the room or follow, and ask some one where the Freshmen went first.

In the midst of the struggle one sentence fell on her ear. "Hide me under the shadow of Thy wings."

Elnora began to pray frantically. "Hide me, O God, hide me, under the shadow of Thy wings."

Again and again she implored that prayer, and before she realized what was coming, every one had arisen and the room was emptying rapidly. Elnora hurried after the nearest girl and in the press at the door touched her sleeve timidly.

"Will you please tell me where the Freshmen go?" she asked huskily.

The girl gave her one surprised glance, and drew away.

"Same place as the fresh women," she answered, and those nearest her laughed.

Elnora stopped praying suddenly and the colour crept into her face. "I'll wager you are the first person I meet when I find it," she said and stopped short. "Not that! Oh, I must not do that!" she thought in dismay. "Make an enemy the first thing I do. Oh, not that!"

She followed with her eyes as the young people separated in the hall, some climbing stairs, some disappearing down side halls, some entering adjoining doors. She saw the girl overtake the brown-eyed boy and speak to him. He glanced back at Elnora with a scowl on his face. Then she stood alone in the hall.

Presently a door opened and a young woman came out and entered another room. Elnora waited until she returned, and hurried to her. "Would you tell me where the Freshmen are?" she panted.

"Straight down the hall, three doors to your left," was the answer, as the girl passed.

"One minute please, oh please," begged Elnora: "Should I knock or just open the door?"

"Go in and take a seat," replied the teacher.

"What if there aren't any seats?" gasped Elnora.

"Classrooms are never half-filled, there will be plenty," was the answer.

Elnora removed her hat. There was no place to put it, so she carried it in her hand. She looked infinitely better without it. After several efforts she at last opened the door and stepping inside faced a smaller and more concentrated battery of eyes.

"The superintendent sent me. He thinks I belong here," she said to the professor in charge of the class, but she never before heard the voice with which she spoke. As she stood waiting, the girl of the hall passed on her way to the blackboard, and suppressed laughter told Elnora that her thrust had been repeated.

"Be seated," said the professor, and then because he saw Elnora was desperately embarrassed he proceeded to lend her a book and to ask her if she had studied algebra. She said she had a little, but not the same book they were using. He asked her if she felt that she could do the work they were beginning, and she said she did.

That was how it happened, that three minutes after entering the room she was told to take her place beside the girl who had gone last to the board, and whose flushed face and angry eyes avoided meeting Elnora's. Being compelled to concentrate on her proposition she forgot herself. When the professor asked that all pupils sign their work she firmly wrote "Elnora Comstock" under her demonstration. Then she took her seat and waited with white lips and trembling limbs, as one after another professor called the names on the board, while their owners arose and explained their propositions, or "flunked" if they had not found a correct solution. She was so eager to catch their forms of expression and prepare herself for her recitation, that she never looked from the work on the board, until clearly and distinctly, "Elnora Cornstock," called the professor.

The dazed girl stared at the board. One tiny curl added to the top of the first curve of the m in her name, had transformed it from a good old English patronymic that any girl might bear proudly, to Cornstock. Elnora sat speechless. When and how did it happen? She could feel the wave of smothered laughter in the air around her. A rush of anger turned her face scarlet and her soul sick. The voice of the professor addressed her directly.

"This proposition seems to be beautifully demonstrated, Miss Cornstalk," he said. "Surely, you can tell us how you did it."

That word of praise saved her. She could do good work. They might wear their pretty clothes, have their friends and make life a greater misery than it ever before had been for her, but not one of them should do better work or be more womanly. That lay with her. She was tall, straight, and handsome as she arose.

"Of course I can explain my work," she said in natural tones. "What I can't explain is how I happened to be so stupid as to make a mistake in writing my own name. I must have been a little nervous. Please excuse me."

She went to the board, swept off the signature with one stroke, then rewrote it plainly. "My name is Comstock," she said distinctly. She returned to her seat and following the formula used by the others made her first high school recitation.

As Elnora resumed her seat Professor Henley looked at her steadily. "It puzzles me," he said deliberately, "how you can write as beautiful a demonstration, and explain it as clearly as ever has been done in any of my classes and still be so disturbed as to make a mistake in your own name. Are you very sure you did that yourself, Miss Comstock?"

"It is impossible that any one else should have done it," answered Elnora.

"I am very glad you think so," said the professor. "Being Freshmen, all of you are strangers to me. I should dislike to begin the year with you feeling there was one among you small enough to do a trick like that. The next proposition, please."

When the hour had gone the class filed back to the study room and Elnora followed in desperation, because she did not know where else to go. She could not study as she had no books, and when the class again left the room to go to another professor for the next recitation, she went also. At least they could put her out if she did not belong there. Noon came at last, and she kept with the others until they dispersed on the sidewalk. She was so abnormally self-conscious she fancied all the hundreds of that laughing, throng saw and jested at her. When she passed the brown-eyed boy walking with the girl of her encounter, she knew, for she heard him say: "Did you really let that gawky piece of calico get ahead of you?" The answer was indistinct.

Elnora hurried from the city. She intended to get her lunch, eat it in the shade of the first tree, and then decide whether she would go back or go home. She knelt on the bridge and reached for her box, but it was so very light that she was prepared for the fact that it was empty, before opening it. There was one thing for which to be thankful. The boy or tramp who had seen her hide it, had left the napkin. She would not have to face her mother and account for its loss. She put it in her pocket, and threw the box into the ditch. Then she sat on the bridge and tried to think, but her brain was confused.

"Perhaps the worst is over," she said at last. "I will go back. What would mother say to me if I came home now?"

So she returned to the high school, followed some other pupils to the coat room, hung her hat, and found her way to the study where she had been in the morning. Twice that afternoon, with aching head and empty stomach, she faced strange professors, in different branches. Once she escaped notice; the second time the worst happened. She was asked a question she could not answer.

"Have you not decided on your course, and secured your books?" inquired the professor.

"I have decided on my course," replied Elnora, "I do not know where to ask for my books."

"Ask?" the professor was bewildered.

"I understood the books were furnished," faltered Elnora.

"Only to those bringing an order from the township trustee," replied the Professor.

"No! Oh no!" cried Elnora. "I will have them to-morrow," and gripped her desk for support for she knew that was not true. Four books, ranging perhaps at a dollar and a half apiece; would her mother buy them? Of course she would not—could not.

Did not Elnora know the story of old. There was enough land, but no one to do clearing and farm. Tax on all those acres, recently the new gravel road tax added, the expense of living and only the work of two women to meet all of it. She was insane to think she could come to the city to school. Her mother had been right. The girl decided that if only she lived to reach home, she would stay there and lead any sort of life to avoid more of this torture. Bad as what she wished to escape had been, it was nothing like this. She never could live down the movement that went through the class when she inadvertently revealed the fact that she had expected books to be furnished. Her mother would not secure them; that settled the question.

But the end of misery is never in a hurry to come; before the day was over the superintendent entered the room and explained that pupils from the country were charged a tuition of twenty dollars a year. That really was the end. Previously Elnora had canvassed a dozen methods for securing the money for books, ranging all the way from offering to wash the superintendent's dishes to breaking into the bank. This additional expense made her plans so wildly impossible, there was nothing to do but hold up her head until she was from sight.

Down the long corridor alone among hundreds, down the long street alone among thousands, out into the country she came at last. Across the fence and field, along the old trail once trodden by a boy's bitter agony, now stumbled a white-faced girl, sick at heart. She sat on a log and began to sob in spite of her efforts at self-control. At first it was physical breakdown, later, thought came crowding.

Oh the shame, the mortification! Why had she not known of the tuition? How did she happen to think that in the city books were furnished? Perhaps it was because she had read they were in several states. But why did she not know? Why did not her mother go with her? Other mothers—but when had her mother ever been or done anything at all like other mothers? Because she never had been it was useless to blame her now. Elnora realized she should have gone to town the week before, called on some one and learned all these things herself. She should have remembered how her clothing would look, before she wore it in public places. Now she knew, and her dreams were over. She must go home to feed chickens, calves, and pigs, wear calico and coarse shoes, and with averted head, pass a library all her life. She sobbed again.

"For pity's sake, honey, what's the matter?" asked the voice of the nearest neighbour, Wesley Sinton, as he seated himself beside Elnora. "There, there," he continued, smearing tears all over her face in an effort to dry them. "Was it as bad as that, now? Maggie has been just wild over you all day. She's got nervouser every minute. She said we were foolish to let you go. She said your clothes were not right, you ought not to carry that tin pail, and that they would laugh at you. By gum, I see they did!"

"Oh, Uncle Wesley," sobbed the girl, "why didn't she tell me?"

"Well, you see, Elnora, she didn't like to. You got such a way of holding up your head, and going through with things. She thought some way that you'd make it, till you got started, and then she begun to see a hundred things we should have done. I reckon you hadn't reached that building before she remembered that your skirt should have been pleated instead of gathered, your shoes been low, and lighter for hot September weather, and a new hat. Were your clothes right, Elnora?"

The girl broke into hysterical laughter. "Right!" she cried. "Right! Uncle Wesley, you should have seen me among them! I was a picture! They'll never forget me. No, they won't get the chance, for they'll see me again to-morrow!

"Now that is what I call spunk, Elnora! Downright grit," said Wesley Sinton. "Don't you let them laugh you out. You've helped Margaret and me for years at harvest and busy times, what you've earned must amount to quite a sum. You can get yourself a good many clothes with it."

"Don't mention clothes, Uncle Wesley," sobbed Elnora, "I don't care now how I look. If I don't go back all of them will know it's because I am so poor I can't buy my books."

"Oh, I don't know as you are so dratted poor," said Sinton meditatively. "There are three hundred acres of good land, with fine timber as ever grew on it."

"It takes all we can earn to pay the tax, and mother wouldn't cut a tree for her life."

"Well then, maybe, I'll be compelled to cut one for her," suggested Sinton. "Anyway, stop tearing yourself to pieces and tell me. If it isn't clothes, what is it?"

"It's books and tuition. Over twenty dollars in all."

"Humph! First time I ever knew you to be stumped by twenty dollars, Elnora," said Sinton, patting her hand.

"It's the first time you ever knew me to want money," answered Elnora. "This is different from anything that ever happened to me. Oh, how can I get it, Uncle Wesley?"

"Drive to town with me in the morning and I'll draw it from the bank for you. I owe you every cent of it."

"You know you don't owe me a penny, and I wouldn't touch one from you, unless I really could earn it. For anything that's past I owe you and Aunt Margaret for all the home life and love I've ever known. I know how you work, and I'll not take your money."

"Just a loan, Elnora, just a loan for a little while until you can earn it. You can be proud with all the rest of the world, but there are no secrets between us, are there, Elnora?"

"No," said Elnora, "there are none. You and Aunt Margaret have given me all the love there has been in my life. That is the one reason above all others why you shall not give me charity. Hand me money because you find me crying for it! This isn't the first time this old trail has known tears and heartache. All of us know that story. Freckles stuck to what he undertook and won out. I stick, too. When Duncan moved away he gave me all Freckles left in the swamp, and as I have inherited his property maybe his luck will come with it. I won't touch your money, but I'll win some way. First, I'm going home and try mother. It's just possible I could find second-hand books, and perhaps all the tuition need not be paid at once. Maybe they would accept it quarterly. But oh, Uncle Wesley, you and Aunt Margaret keep on loving me! I'm so lonely, and no one else cares!"

Wesley Sinton's jaws met with a click. He swallowed hard on bitter words and changed what he would have liked to say three times before it became articulate.

"Elnora," he said at last, "if it hadn't been for one thing I'd have tried to take legal steps to make you ours when you were three years old. Maggie said then it wasn't any use, but I've always held on. You see, I was the first man there, honey, and there are things you see, that you can't ever make anybody else understand. She loved him Elnora, she just made an idol of him. There was that oozy green hole, with the thick scum broke, and two or three big bubbles slowly rising that were the breath of his body. There she was in spasms of agony, and beside her the great heavy log she'd tried to throw him. I can't ever forgive her for turning against you, and spoiling your childhood as she has, but I couldn't forgive anybody else for abusing her. Maggie has got no mercy on her, but Maggie didn't see what I did, and I've never tried to make it very clear to her. It's been a little too plain for me ever since. Whenever I look at your mother's face, I see what she saw, so I hold my tongue and say, in my heart, 'Give her a mite more time.' Some day it will come. She does love you, Elnora. Everybody does, honey. It's just that she's feeling so much, she can't express herself. You be a patient girl and wait a little longer. After all, she's your mother, and you're all she's got, but a memory, and it might do her good to let her know that she was fooled in that."

"It would kill her!" cried the girl swiftly. "Uncle Wesley, it would kill her! What do you mean?"

"Nothing," said Wesley Sinton soothingly. "Nothing, honey. That was just one of them fool things a man says, when he is trying his best to be wise. You see, she loved him mightily, and they'd been married only a year, and what she was loving was what she thought he was. She hadn't really got acquainted with the man yet. If it had been even one more year, she could have borne it, and you'd have got justice. Having been a teacher she was better educated and smarter than the rest of us, and so she was more sensitive like. She can't understand she was loving a dream. So I say it might do her good if somebody that knew, could tell her, but I swear to gracious, I never could. I've heard her out at the edge of that quagmire calling in them wild spells of hers off and on for the last sixteen years, and imploring the swamp to give him back to her, and I've got out of bed when I was pretty tired, and come down to see she didn't go in herself, or harm you. What she feels is too deep for me. I've got to respectin' her grief, and I can't get over it. Go home and tell your ma, honey, and ask her nice and kind to help you. If she won't, then you got to swallow that little lump of pride in your neck, and come to Aunt Maggie, like you been a-coming all your life."

"I'll ask mother, but I can't take your money, Uncle Wesley, indeed I can't. I'll wait a year, and earn some, and enter next year."

"There's one thing you don't consider, Elnora," said the man earnestly. "And that's what you are to Maggie. She's a little like your ma. She hasn't given up to it, and she's struggling on brave, but when we buried our second little girl the light went out of Maggie's eyes, and it's not come back. The only time I ever see a hint of it is when she thinks she's done something that makes you happy, Elnora. Now, you go easy about refusing her anything she wants to do for you. There's times in this world when it's our bounden duty to forget ourselves, and think what will help other people. Young woman, you owe me and Maggie all the comfort we can get out of you. There's the two of our own we can't ever do anything for. Don't you get the idea into your head that a fool thing you call pride is going to cut us out of all the pleasure we have in life beside ourselves."

"Uncle Wesley, you are a dear," said Elnora. "Just a dear! If I can't possibly get that money any way else on earth, I'll come and borrow it of you, and then I'll pay it back if I must dig ferns from the swamp and sell them from door to door in the city. I'll even plant them, so that they will be sure to come up in the spring. I have been sort of panic stricken all day and couldn't think. I can gather nuts and sell them. Freckles sold moths and butterflies, and I've a lot collected. Of course,

I am going back to-morrow! I can find a way to get the books. Don't you worry about me. I am all right!

"Now, what do you think of that?" inquired Wesley Sinton of the swamp in general. "Here's our Elnora come back to stay. Head high and right as a trivet! You've named three ways in three minutes that you could earn ten dollars, which I figure would be enough, to start you. Let's go to supper and stop worrying!"

Elnora unlocked the case, took out the pail, put the napkin in it, pulled the ribbon from her hair, binding it down tightly again and followed to the road. From afar she could see her mother in the doorway. She blinked her eyes, and tried to smile as she answered Wesley Sinton, and indeed she did feel better. She knew now what she had to expect, where to go, and what to do. Get the books she must; when she had them, she would show those city girls and boys how to prepare and recite lessons, how to walk with a brave heart; and they could show her how to wear pretty clothes and have good times.

As she neared the door her mother reached for the pail. "I forgot to tell you to bring home your scraps for the chickens," she said.

Elnora entered. "There weren't any scraps, and I'm hungry again as I ever was in my life."

"I thought likely you would be," said Mrs. Comstock, "and so I got supper ready. We can eat first, and do the work afterward. What kept you so? I expected you an hour ago."

Elnora looked into her mother's face and smiled. It was a queer sort of a little smile, and would have reached the depths with any normal mother.

"I see you've been bawling," said Mrs. Comstock. "I thought you'd get your fill in a hurry. That's why I wouldn't go to any expense. If we keep out of the poor-house we have to cut the corners close. It's likely this Brushwood road tax will eat up all we've saved in years. Where the land tax is to come from I don't know. It gets bigger every year. If they are going to dredge the swamp ditch again they'll just have to take the land to pay for it. I can't, that's all! We'll get up early in the morning and gather and hull the beans for winter, and put in the rest of the day hoeing the turnips."

Elnora again smiled that pitiful smile.

"Do you think I didn't know that I was funny and would be laughed at?" she asked.

"Funny?" cried Mrs. Comstock hotly.

"Yes, funny! A regular caricature," answered Elnora. "No one else wore calico, not even one other. No one else wore high heavy shoes, not even one. No one else had such a funny little old hat; my hair was not right, my ribbon invisible compared with the others, I did not know where to go, or what to do, and I had no books. What a spectacle I made for them!" Elnora laughed nervously at her own picture. "But there are always two sides! The professor said in the algebra class that he never had a better solution and explanation than mine of the proposition he gave me, which scored one for me in spite of my clothes."

"Well, I wouldn't brag on myself!"

"That was poor taste," admitted Elnora. "But, you see, it is a case of whistling to keep up my courage. I honestly could see that I would have looked just as well as the rest of them if I had been dressed as they were. We can't afford that, so I have to find something else to brace me. It was rather bad, mother!"

"Well, I'm glad you got enough of it!"

"Oh, but I haven't," hurried in Elnora. "I just got a start. The hardest is over. To-morrow they won't be surprised. They will know what to expect. I am sorry to hear about the dredge. Is it really going through?"

"Yes. I got my notification today. The tax will be something enormous. I don't know as I can spare you, even if you are willing to be a laughing-stock for the town."

With every bite Elnora's courage returned, for she was a healthy young thing.

"You've heard about doing evil that good might come from it," she said. "Well, mother mine, it's something like that with me. I'm willing to bear the hard part to pay for what I'll learn. Already I have selected the ward building in which I shall teach in about four years. I am going to ask for a room with a south exposure so that the flowers and moths I take in from the swamp to show the children will do well."

"You little idiot!" said Mrs. Comstock. "How are you going to pay your expenses?"

"Now that is just what I was going to ask you!" said Elnora. "You see, I have had two startling pieces of news to-day. I did not know I would need any money. I thought the city furnished the books, and there is an out-of-town tuition, also. I need ten dollars in the morning. Will you please let me have it?"

"Ten dollars!" cried Mrs. Comstock. "Ten dollars! Why don't you say a hundred and be done with it! I could get one as easy as the other. I told you! I told you I couldn't raise a cent. Every year expenses grow bigger and bigger. I told you not to ask for money!"

"I never meant to," replied Elnora. "I thought clothes were all I needed and I could bear them. I never knew about buying books and tuition."

"Well, I did!" said Mrs. Comstock. "I knew what you would run into! But you are so bull-dog stubborn, and so set in your way, I thought I would just let you try the world a little and see how you liked it!"

Elnora pushed back her chair and looked at her mother.

"Do you mean to say," she demanded, "that you knew, when you let me go into a city classroom and reveal the fact before all of them that I expected to have my books handed out to me; do you mean to say that you knew I had to pay for them?"

Mrs. Comstock evaded the direct question.

"Anybody but an idiot mooning over a book or wasting time prowling the woods would have known you had to pay. Everybody has to pay for everything. Life is made up of pay, pay, pay! It's always and forever pay! If you don't pay one way you do another! Of course, I knew you had to pay. Of course, I knew you would come home blubbering! But you don't get a penny! I haven't one cent, and can't get one! Have your way if you are determined, but I think you will find the road somewhat rocky."

"Swampy, you mean, mother," corrected Elnora. She arose white and trembling. "Perhaps some day God will teach me how to understand you. He knows I do not now. You can't possibly realize just what you let me go through to-day, or how you let me go, but I'll tell you this: You understand enough that if you had the money, and would offer it to me, I wouldn't touch it now. And I'll tell you this much more. I'll get it myself. I'll raise it, and do it some honest way. I am going back to-morrow, the next day, and the next. You need not come out, I'll do the night work, and hoe the turnips."

It was ten o'clock when the chickens, pigs, and cattle were fed, the turnips hoed, and a heap of bean vines was stacked beside the back door.

Chapter 2

Wherein Wesley and Margaret Go Shopping, and Elnora's Wardrobe Is Replenished

Wesley Sinton walked down the road half a mile and turned at the lane leading to his home. His heart was hot and filled with indignation. He had told Elnora he did not blame her mother, but he did. His wife met him at the door.

"Did you see anything of Elnora?" she questioned.

"Most too much, Maggie," he answered. "What do you say to going to town? There's a few things has to be got right away."

"Where did you see her, Wesley?"

"Along the old Limberlost trail, my girl, torn to pieces sobbing. Her courage always has been fine, but the thing she met to-day was too much for her. We ought to have known better than to let her go that way. It wasn't only clothes; there were books, and entrance fees for out-of-town people, that she didn't know about; while there must have been jeers, whispers, and laughing. Maggie, I feel as if I'd been a traitor to those girls of ours. I ought to have gone in and seen about this school business. Don't cry, Maggie. Get me some supper, and I'll hitch up and see what we can do now."

"What can we do, Wesley?"

"I don't just know. But we've got to do something. Kate Comstock will be a handful, while Elnora will be two, but between us we must see that the girl is not too hard pressed about money, and that she is dressed so she is not ridiculous. She's saved us the wages of a woman many a day, can't you make her some decent dresses?"

"Well, I'm not just what you call expert, but I could beat Kate Comstock all to pieces. I know that skirts should be pleated to the band instead of gathered, and full enough to sit in, and short enough to walk in. I could try. There are patterns for sale. Let's go right away, Wesley."

"Set me a bit of supper, while I hitch up."

Margaret built a fire, made coffee, and fried ham and eggs. She set out pie and cake and had enough for a hungry man by the time the carriage was at the door, but she had no appetite. She dressed while Wesley ate, put away the food while he dressed, and then they drove toward the city through the beautiful September evening, and as they went they planned for Elnora. The trouble was, not whether they were generous enough to buy what she needed, but whether she would accept their purchases, and what her mother would say.

They went to a drygoods store and when a clerk asked what they wanted to see neither of them knew, so they stepped aside and held a whispered consultation.

"What had we better get, Wesley?"

"Dresses," said Wesley promptly,

"But how many dresses, and what kind?"

"Blest if I know!" exclaimed Wesley. "I thought you would manage that. I know about some things I'm going to get."

At that instant several high school girls came into the store and approached them.

"There!" exclaimed Wesley breathlessly. "There, Maggie! Like them! That's what she needs! Buy like they have!"

Margaret stared. What did they wear? They were rapidly passing; they seemed to have so much, and she could not decide so quickly. Before she knew it she was among them.

"I beg your pardon, but won't you wait one minute?" she asked.

The girls stopped with wondering faces.

"It's your clothes," explained Mrs. Sinton. "You look just beautiful to me. You look exactly as I should have wanted to see my girls. They both died of diphtheria when they were little, but they had yellow hair, dark eyes, and pink cheeks, and everybody thought they were lovely. If they had lived, they'd been near your age now, and I'd want them to look like you."

There was sympathy on every girl face.

"Why thank you!" said one of them. "We are very sorry for you."

"Of course you are," said Margaret. "Everybody always has been. And because I can't ever have the joy of a mother in thinking for my girls and buying pretty things for them, there is nothing left for me, but to do what I can for some one who has no mother to care for her. I know a girl, who would be just as pretty as any of you, if she had the clothes, but her mother does not think about her, so I mother her some myself."

"She must be a lucky girl," said another.

"Oh, she loves me," said Margaret, "and I love her. I want her to look just like you do. Please tell me about your clothes. Are these the dresses and hats you wear to school? What kind of goods are they, and where do you buy them?"

The girls began to laugh and cluster around Margaret. Wesley strode down the store with his head high through pride in her, but his heart was sore over the memory of two little faces under Brushwood sod. He inquired his way to the shoe department.

"Why, every one of us have on gingham or linen dresses," they said, "and they are our school clothes."

For a few moments there was a babel of laughing voices explaining to the delighted Margaret that school dresses should be bright and pretty, but simple and plain, and until cold weather they should wash.

"I'll tell you," said Ellen Brownlee, "my father owns this store, I know all the clerks. I'll take you to Miss Hartley. You tell her just how much you want to spend, and what you want to buy, and she will know how to get the most for your money. I've heard papa say she was the best clerk in the store for people who didn't know precisely what they wanted."

"That's the very thing," agreed Margaret. "But before you go, tell me about your hair. Elnora's hair is bright and wavy, but yours is silky as hackled flax. How do you do it?"

"Elnora?" asked four girls in concert.

"Yes, Elnora is the name of the girl I want these things for."

"Did she come to the high school to-day?" questioned one of them.

"Was she in your classes?" demanded Margaret without reply.

Four girls stood silent and thought fast. Had there been a strange girl among them, and had she been overlooked and passed by with indifference, because she was so very shabby? If she had appeared as much better than they, as she had looked worse, would her reception have been the same?

"There was a strange girl from the country in the Freshman class to-day," said Ellen Brownlee, "and her name was Elnora."

"That was the girl," said Margaret.

"Are her people so very poor?" questioned Ellen.

"No, not poor at all, come to think of it," answered Margaret. "It's a peculiar case. Mrs. Comstock had a great trouble and she let it change her whole life and make a different woman of her. She used to be lovely; now she is forever saving and scared to death for fear they will go to the poorhouse; but there is a big farm, covered with lots of good timber. The taxes are high for women who can't manage to clear and work the land. There ought to be enough to keep two of them in good shape all their lives, if they only knew how to do it. But no one ever told Kate Comstock anything, and never will, for she won't listen. All she does is droop all day, and walk the edge of the swamp half the night, and neglect Elnora. If you girls would make life just a little easier for her it would be the finest thing you ever did."

All of them promised they would.

"Now tell me about your hair," persisted Margaret Sinton.

So they took her to a toilet counter, and she bought the proper hair soap, also a nail file, and cold cream, for use after windy days. Then they left her with the experienced clerk, and when at last Wesley found her she was loaded with bundles and the light of other days was in her beautiful eyes. Wesley also carried some packages.

"Did you get any stockings?" he whispered.

"No, I didn't," she said. "I was so interested in dresses and hair ribbons and a—a hat—" she hesitated and glanced at Wesley. "Of course, a hat!" prompted Wesley. "That I forgot all about those horrible shoes. She's got to have decent shoes, Wesley."

"Sure!" said Wesley. "She's got decent shoes. But the man said some brown stockings ought to go with them. Take a peep, will you!"

Wesley opened a box and displayed a pair of thick-soled, beautifully shaped brown walking shoes of low cut. Margaret cried out with pleasure.

"But do you suppose they are the right size, Wesley? What did you get?"

"I just said for a girl of sixteen with a slender foot."

"Well, that's about as near as I could come. If they don't fit when she tries them, we will drive straight in and change them. Come on now, let's get home."

All the way they discussed how they should give Elnora their purchases and what Mrs. Comstock would say.

"I am afraid she will be awful mad," said Margaret.

"She'll just rip!" replied Wesley graphically. "But if she wants to leave the raising of her girl to the neighbours, she needn't get fractious if they take some pride in doing a good job. From now on I calculate Elnora shall go to school; and she shall have all the clothes and books she needs, if I go around on the back of Kate Comstock's land and cut a tree, or drive off a calf to pay for them. Why I know one tree she owns that would put Elnora in heaven for a year. Just think of it, Margaret! It's not fair. One-third of what is there belongs to Elnora by law, and if Kate Comstock raises a row I'll tell her so, and see that the girl gets it. You go to see Kate in the morning, and I'll go with you. Tell her you want Elnora's pattern, that you are going to make her a dress, for helping us. And sort of hint at a few more things. If Kate balks, I'll take a hand and settle her. I'll go to law for Elnora's share of that land and sell enough to educate her."

"Why, Wesley Sinton, you're perfectly wild."

"I'm not! Did you ever stop to think that such cases are so frequent there have been laws made to provide for them? I can bring it up in court and force Kate to educate Elnora, and board and clothe her till she's of age, and then she can take her share."

"Wesley, Kate would go crazy!"

"She's crazy now. The idea of any mother living with as sweet a girl as Elnora and letting her suffer till I find her crying like a funeral. It makes me fighting mad. All uncalled for. Not a grain of sense in it. I've offered and offered to oversee clearing her land and working her fields. Let her sell a good tree, or a few acres. Something is going to be done, right now. Elnora's been fairly happy up to this, but to spoil the school life she's planned, is to ruin all her life. I won't have it! If Elnora won't take these things, so help me, I'll tell her what she is worth, and loan her the money and she can pay me back when she comes of age. I am going to have it out with Kate Comstock in the morning. Here we are! You open up what you got while I put away the horses, and then I'll show you."

When Wesley came from the barn Margaret had four pieces of crisp gingham, a pale blue, a pink, a gray with green stripes and a rich brown and blue plaid. On each of them lay a yard and a half of wide ribbon to match. There were handkerchiefs and a brown leather belt. In her hands she held a wide-brimmed tan straw hat, having a high crown banded with velvet strips each of which fastened with a tiny gold buckle.

"It looks kind of bare now," she explained. "It had three quills on it here."

"Did you have them taken off?" asked Wesley.

"Yes, I did. The price was two and a half for the hat, and those things were a dollar and a half apiece. I couldn't pay that."

"It does seem considerable," admitted Wesley, "but will it look right without them?"

"No, it won't!" said Margaret. "It's going to have quills on it. Do you remember those beautiful peacock wing feathers that Phoebe Simms gave me? Three of them go on just where those came off, and nobody will ever know the difference. They match the hat to a moral, and they are just a little longer and richer than the ones that I had taken off. I was wondering whether I better sew them on to-night while I remember how they set, or wait till morning."

"Don't risk it!" exclaimed Wesley anxiously. "Don't you risk it! Sew them on right now!"

"Open your bundles, while I get the thread," said Margaret.

Wesley unwrapped the shoes. Margaret took them up and pinched the leather and stroked them.

"My, but they are fine!" she cried.

Wesley picked up one and slowly turned it in his big hands. He glanced at his foot and back to the shoe.

"It's a little bit of a thing, Margaret," he said softly. "Like as not I'll have to take it back. It seems as if it couldn't fit."

"It seems as if it didn't dare do anything else," said Margaret. "That's a happy little shoe to get the chance to carry as fine a girl as Elnora to high school. Now what's in the other box?"

Wesley looked at Margaret doubtfully.

"Why," he said, "you know there's going to be rainy days, and those things she has now ain't fit for anything but to drive up the cows—"

"Wesley, did you get high shoes, too?"

"Well, she ought to have them! The man said he would make them cheaper if I took both pairs at once."

Margaret laughed aloud. "Those will do her past Christmas," she exulted. "What else did you buy?"

"Well sir," said Wesley, "I saw something to-day. You told me about Kate getting that tin pail for Elnora to carry to high school and you said you told her it was a shame. I guess Elnora was ashamed all right, for to-night she stopped at the old case Duncan gave her, and took out that pail, where it had been all day, and put a napkin inside it. Coming home she confessed she was half starved because she hid her dinner under a culvert, and a tramp took it. She hadn't had a bite to eat the whole day. But she never complained at all, she was pleased that she hadn't lost the napkin. So I just inquired around till I found this, and I think it's about the ticket."

Wesley opened the package and laid a brown leather lunch box on the table. "Might be a couple of books, or drawing tools or most anything that's neat and genteel. You see, it opens this way."

It did open, and inside was a space for sandwiches, a little porcelain box for cold meat or fried chicken, another for salad, a glass with a lid which screwed on, held by a ring in a corner, for custard or jelly, a flask for tea or milk, a beautiful little knife, fork, and spoon fastened in holders, and a place for a napkin.

Margaret was almost crying over it.

"How I'd love to fill it!" she exclaimed

"Do it the first time, just to show Kate Comstock what love is!" said Wesley. "Get up early in the morning and make one of those dresses to-morrow. Can't you make a plain gingham dress in a day? I'll pick a chicken, and you fry it and fix a little custard for the cup, and do it up brown. Go on, Maggie, you do it!"

"I never can," said Margaret. "I am slow as the itch about sewing, and these are not going to be plain dresses when it comes to making them. There are going to be edgings of plain green, pink, and brown to the bias strips, and tucks and pleats around the hips, fancy belts and collars, and all of it takes time."

"Then Kate Comstock's got to help," said Wesley. "Can the two of you make one, and get that lunch to-morrow?"

"Easy, but she'll never do it!"

"You see if she doesn't!" said Wesley. "You get up and cut it out, and soon as Elnora is gone I'll go after Kate myself. She'll take what I'll say better alone. But she'll come, and she'll help make the dress. These other things are our Christmas gifts to Elnora. She'll no doubt need them more now than she will then, and we can give them just as well. That's yours, and this is mine, or whichever way you choose."

Wesley untied a good brown umbrella and shook out the folds of a long, brown raincoat. Margaret dropped the hat, arose and took the coat. She tried it on, felt it, cooed over it and matched it with the umbrella.

"Did it look anything like rain to-night?" she inquired so anxiously that Wesley laughed.

"And this last bundle?" she said, dropping back in her chair, the coat still over her shoulders.

"I couldn't buy this much stuff for any other woman and nothing for my own," said Wesley. "It's Christmas for you, too, Margaret!" He shook out fold after fold of soft gray satiny goods that would look lovely against Margaret's pink cheeks and whitening hair.

"Oh, you old darling!" she exclaimed, and fled sobbing into his arms.

But she soon dried her eyes, raked together the coals in the cooking stove and boiled one of the dress patterns in salt water for half an hour. Wesley held the lamp while she hung the goods on the line to dry. Then she set the irons on the stove so they would be hot the first thing in the morning.

Chapter 3

Wherein Elnora Visits the Bird Woman, and Opens a Bank Account

Four o'clock the following morning Elnora was shelling beans. At six she fed the chickens and pigs, swept two of the rooms of the cabin, built a fire, and put on the kettle for breakfast. Then she climbed the narrow stairs to the attic she had occupied since a very small child, and dressed in the hated shoes and brown calico, plastered down her crisp curls, ate what breakfast she could, and pinning on her hat started for town.

"There is no sense in your going for an hour yet," said her mother.

"I must try to discover some way to earn those books," replied Elnora. "I am perfectly positive I shall not find them lying beside the road wrapped in tissue paper, and tagged with my name."

She went toward the city as on yesterday. Her perplexity as to where tuition and books were to come from was worse but she did not feel quite so badly. She never again would have to face all of it for the first time. There had been times yesterday when she had prayed to be hidden, or to drop dead, and neither had happened. "I believe the best way to get an answer to prayer is to work for it," muttered Elnora grimly.

Again she followed the trail to the swamp, rearranged her hair and left the tin pail. This time she folded a couple of sandwiches in the napkin, and tied them in a neat light paper parcel which she carried in her hand. Then she hurried along the road to Onabasha and found a book-store. There she asked the prices of the list of books that she needed, and learned that six dollars would not quite supply them. She anxiously inquired for second-hand books, but was told that the only way to secure them was from the last year's Freshmen. Just then Elnora felt that she positively could not approach any of those she supposed to be Sophomores and ask to buy their old books. The only balm the girl could see for the humiliation of yesterday was to appear that day with a set of new books.

"Do you wish these?" asked the clerk hurriedly, for the store was rapidly filling with school children wanting anything from a dictionary to a pen.

"Yes," gasped Elnora, "Oh, yes! But I cannot pay for them just now. Please let me take them, and I will pay for them on Friday, or return them as perfect as they are. Please trust me for them a few days."

"I'll ask the proprietor," he said. When he came back Elnora knew the answer before he spoke.

"I'm sorry," he said, "but Mr. Hann doesn't recognize your name. You are not a customer of ours, and he feels that he can't take the risk."

Elnora clumped out of the store, the thump of her heavy, shoes beating as a hammer on her brain. She tried two other dealers with the same result, and then in sick despair came into the street. What could she do? She was too frightened to think. Should she stay from school that day and canvass the homes appearing to belong to the wealthy, and try to sell beds of wild ferns, as she had suggested to Wesley Sinton? What would she dare ask for bringing in and planting a clump of ferns? How could she carry them? Would people buy them? She slowly moved past the hotel and then glanced around to see if there were a clock anywhere, for she felt sure the young people passing her constantly were on their way to school.

There it stood in a bank window in big black letters staring straight at her: WANTED: CATERPILLARS, COCOONS, CHRYSALIDES, PUPAE CASES, BUTTERFLIES, MOTHS, INDIAN RELICS OF ALL KINDS. HIGHEST SCALE OF PRICES PAID IN CASH

Elnora caught the wicket at the cashier's desk with both hands to brace herself against disappointment.

"Who is it wants to buy cocoons, butterflies, and moths?" she panted.

"The Bird Woman," answered the cashier. "Have you some for sale?"

"I have some, I do not know if they are what she would want."

"Well, you had better see her," said the cashier. "Do you know where she lives?"

"Yes," said Elnora. "Would you tell me the time?"

"Twenty-one after eight," was the answer.

She had nine minutes to reach the auditorium or be late. Should she go to school, or to the Bird Woman? Several girls passed her walking swiftly and she remembered their faces. They were hurrying to school. Elnora caught the infection. She would see the Bird Woman at noon. Algebra came first, and that professor was kind. Perhaps she could slip to the superintendent and ask him for a book for the next lesson, and at noon—"Oh, dear Lord make it come true," prayed Elnora, at noon possibly she could sell some of those wonderful shining-winged things she had been collecting all her life around the outskirts of the Limberlost.

As she went down the long hall she noticed the professor of mathematics standing in the door of his recitation room. When she passed him he smiled and spoke to her.

"I have been watching for you," he said, and Elnora stopped bewildered.

"For me?" she questioned.

"Yes," said Professor Henley. "Step inside."

Elnora followed him into the room and closed the door behind them.

"At teachers' meeting last evening, one of the professors mentioned that a pupil had betrayed in class that she had expected her books to be furnished by the city. I thought possibly it was you. Was it?"

"Yes," breathed Elnora.

"That being the case," said Professor Henley, "it just occurred to me as you had expected that, you might require a little time to secure them, and you are too fine a mathematician to fall behind for want of supplies. So I telephoned one of our Sophomores to bring her last year's books this morning. I am sorry to say they are somewhat abused, but the text is all here. You can have them for two dollars, and pay when you are ready. Would you care to take them?"

Elnora sat suddenly, because she could not stand another instant. She reached both hands for the books, and said never a word. The professor was silent also. At last Eleanor arose, hugging those books to her heart as a mother clasps a baby.

"One thing more," said the professor. "You may pay your tuition quarterly. You need not bother about the first instalment this month. Any time in October will do."

It seemed as if Elnora's gasp of relief must have reached the soles of her brogans.

"Did any one ever tell you how beautiful you are!" she cried.

As the professor was lank, tow-haired, and so near-sighted that he peered at his pupils through spectacles, no one ever had.

"No," said Professor Henley, "I've waited some time for that; for which reason I shall appreciate it all the more. Come now, or we shall be late for opening exercises."

So Elnora entered the auditorium a second time. Her face was like the brightest dawn that ever broke over the Limberlost. No matter about the lumbering shoes and skimpy dress. No matter about anything, she had the books. She could take them home. In her garret she could commit them to memory, if need be. She could prove that clothes were not all. If the Bird Woman did not want any of the many different kinds of specimens she had collected, she was quite sure now she could sell ferns, nuts, and a great many things. Then, too, a girl made a place for her that morning, and several smiled and bowed. Elnora forgot everything save her books, and that she was where she could use them intelligently—everything except one little thing away back in her head. Her mother had known about the books and the tuition, and had not told her when she agreed to her coming.

At noon Elnora took her little parcel of lunch and started to the home of the Bird Woman. She must know about the specimens first and then she would walk to the suburbs somewhere and eat a few bites. She dropped the heavy iron knocker on the door of a big red log cabin, and her heart thumped at the resounding stroke.

"Is the Bird Woman at home?" she asked of the maid.

"She is at lunch," was the answer.

"Please ask her if she will see a girl from the Limberlost about some moths?" inquired Elnora.

"I never need ask, if it's moths," laughed the girl. "Orders are to bring any one with specimens right in. Come this way."

Elnora followed down the hall and entered a long room with high panelled wainscoting, old English fireplace with an overmantel and closets of peculiar china filling the corners. At a bare table of oak, yellow as gold, sat a woman Elnora often had watched and followed covertly around the Limberlost. The Bird Woman was holding out a hand of welcome.

"I heard!" she laughed. "A little pasteboard box, or just the mere word 'specimen,' passes you at my door. If it is moths I hope you have hundreds. I've been very busy all summer and unable to collect, and I need so many. Sit down and lunch with me, while we talk it over. From the Limberlost, did you say?"

"I live near the swamp," replied Elnora. "Since it's so cleared I dare go around the edge in daytime, though we are all afraid at night."

"What have you collected?" asked the Bird Woman, as she helped Elnora to sandwiches unlike any she ever before had tasted, salad that seemed to be made of many familiar things, and a cup of hot chocolate that would have delighted any hungry schoolgirl.

"I am afraid I am bothering you for nothing, and imposing on you," she said. "That 'collected' frightens me. I've only gathered. I always loved everything outdoors, so I made friends and playmates of them. When I learned that the moths die so soon, I saved them especially, because there seemed no wickedness in it."

"I have thought the same thing," said the Bird Woman encouragingly. Then because the girl could not eat until she learned about the moths, the Bird Woman asked Elnora if she knew what kinds she had.

"Not all of them," answered Elnora. "Before Mr. Duncan moved away he often saw me near the edge of the swamp and he showed me the box he had fixed for Freckles, and gave me the key. There were some books and things, so from that time on I studied and tried to take moths right, but I am afraid they are not what you want."

"Are they the big ones that fly mostly in June nights?" asked the Bird Woman.

"Yes," said Elnora. "Big gray ones with reddish markings, pale blue-green, yellow with lavender, and red and yellow."

"What do you mean by 'red and yellow?'" asked the Bird Woman so quickly that the girl almost jumped.

"Not exactly red," explained Elnora, with tremulous voice. "A reddish, yellowish brown, with canary-coloured spots and gray lines on their wings."

"How many of them?" It was the same quick question.

"I had over two hundred eggs," said Elnora, "but some of them didn't hatch, and some of the caterpillars died, but there must be at least a hundred perfect ones."

"Perfect! How perfect?" cried the Bird Woman.

"I mean whole wings, no down gone, and all their legs and antennae," faltered Elnora.

"Young woman, that's the rarest moth in America," said the Bird Woman solemnly. "If you have a hundred of them, they are worth a hundred dollars according to my list. I can use all that are not damaged."

"What if they are not pinned right," quavered Elnora.

"If they are perfect, that does not make the slightest difference. I know how to soften them so that I can put them into any shape I choose. Where are they? When may I see them?"

"They are in Freckles's old case in the Limberlost," said Elnora. "I couldn't carry many for fear of breaking them, but I could bring a few after school."

"You come here at four," said the Bird Woman, "and we will drive out with some specimen boxes, and a price list, and see what you have to sell. Are they your very own? Are you free to part with them?"

"They are mine," said Elnora. "No one but God knows I have them. Mr. Duncan gave me the books and the box. He told Freckles about me, and Freckles told him to give me all he left. He said for me to stick to the swamp and be brave, and my hour would come, and it has! I know most of them are all right, and oh, I do need the money!"

"Could you tell me?" asked the Bird Woman softly.

"You see the swamp and all the fields around it are so full," explained Elnora. "Every day I felt smaller and smaller, and I wanted to know more and more, and pretty soon I grew desperate, just as Freckles did. But I am better off than he was, for I have his books, and I have a mother; even if she doesn't care for me as other girls' mothers do for them, it's better than no one."

The Bird Woman's glance fell, for the girl was not conscious of how much she was revealing. Her eyes were fixed on a black pitcher filled with goldenrod in the centre of the table and she was saying what she thought.

"As long as I could go to the Brushwood school I was happy, but I couldn't go further just when things were the most interesting, so I was determined I'd come to high school and mother wouldn't consent. You see there's plenty of land, but father was drowned when I was a baby, and mother and I can't make money as men do. The taxes are higher every year, and she said it was too expensive. I wouldn't give her any rest, until at last she bought me this dress, and these shoes, and I came. It was awful!"

"Do you live in that beautiful cabin at the northwest end of the swamp?" asked the Bird Woman.

"Yes," said Elnora.

"I remember the place and a story about it, now. You entered the high school yesterday?"

"Yes."

"It was rather bad?"

"Rather bad!" echoed Elnora.

The Bird Woman laughed.

"You can't tell me anything about that," she said. "I once entered a city school straight from the country. My dress was brown calico, and my shoes were heavy."

The tears began to roll down Elnora's cheeks.

"Did they—?" she faltered.

"They did!" said the Bird Woman. "All of it. I am sure they did not miss one least little thing."

Then she wiped away some tears that began coursing her cheeks, and laughed at the same time.

"Where are they now?" asked Elnora suddenly.

"They are widely scattered, but none of them have attained heights out of range. Some of the rich are poor, and some of the poor are rich. Some of the brightest died insane, and some of the dullest worked out high positions; some of the very worst to bear have gone out, and I frequently hear from others. Now I am here, able to remember it, and mingle laughter with what used to be all tears; for every day I have my beautiful work, and almost every day God sends some one like you to help me. What is your name, my girl?"

216

"Elnora Comstock," answered Elnora. "Yesterday on the board it changed to Cornstock, and for a minute I thought I'd die, but I can laugh over that already."

The Bird Woman arose and kissed her. "Finish your lunch," she said, "and I will bring my price lists, and make a memorandum of what you think you have, so I will know how many boxes to prepare. And remember this: What you are lies with you. If you are lazy, and accept your lot, you may live in it. If you are willing to work, you can write your name anywhere you choose, among the only ones who live beyond the grave in this world, the people who write books that help, make exquisite music, carve statues, paint pictures, and work for others. Never mind the calico dress, and the coarse shoes. Work at your books, and before long you will hear yesterday's tormentors boasting that they were once classmates of yours. 'I could a tale unfold'—!"

She laughingly left the room and Elnora sat thinking, until she remembered how hungry she was, so she ate the food, drank the hot chocolate and began to feel better.

Then the Bird Woman came back and showed Elnora a long printed slip giving a list of graduated prices for moths, butterflies, and dragonflies.

"Oh, do you want them!" exulted Elnora. "I have a few and I can get more by the thousand, with every colour in the world on their wings."

"Yes," said the Bird Woman, "I will buy them, also the big moth caterpillars that are creeping everywhere now, and the cocoons that they will spin just about this time. I have a sneaking impression that the mystery, wonder, and the urge of their pure beauty, are going to force me to picture and paint our moths and put them into a book for all the world to see and know. We Limberlost people must not be selfish with the wonders God has given to us. We must share with those poor cooped-up city people the best we can. To send them a beautiful book, that is the way, is it not, little new friend of mine?"

"Yes, oh yes!" cried Elnora. "And please God they find a way to earn the money to buy the books, as I have those I need so badly."

"I will pay good prices for all the moths you can find." said the Bird Woman, "because you see I exchange them with foreign collectors. I want a complete series of the moths of America to trade with a German scientist, another with a man in India, and another in Brazil. Others I can exchange with home collectors for those of California and Canada, so you see I can use all you can raise, or find. The banker will buy stone axes, arrow points, and Indian pipes. There was a teacher from the city grade schools here to-day for specimens. There is a fund to supply the ward buildings. I'll help you get in touch with that. They want leaves of different trees, flowers, grasses, moths, insects, birds' nests, and anything about birds."

Elnora's eyes were blazing. "Had I better go back to school or open a bank account and begin being a millionaire? Uncle Wesley and I have a bushel of arrow points gathered, a stack of axes, pipes, skin-dressing tools, tubes, and mortars. I don't know how I ever shall wait three hours."

"You must go, or you will be late," said the Bird Woman. "I will be ready at four."

After school closed Elnora, seated beside the Bird Woman, drove to Freckles's room in the Limberlost. One at a time the beautiful big moths were taken from the interior of the old black case. Not a fourth of them could be moved that night and it was almost dark when the last box was closed, the list figured, and into Elnora's trembling fingers were paid fifty-nine dollars and sixteen cents. Elnora clasped the money closely.

"Oh you beautiful stuff!" she cried. "You are going to buy the books, pay the tuition, and take me to high school."

Then because she was a woman, she sat on a log and looked at her shoes. Long after the Bird Woman drove away Elnora remained. She had her problem, and it was a big one. If she told her mother, would she take the money to pay the taxes? If she did not tell her, how could she account for the books, and things for which she would spend it. At last she counted out what she needed for the next day, placed the remainder in the farthest corner of the case, and locked the door. She then filled the front of her skirt from a heap of arrow points beneath the case and started home.

Chapter 4

Wherein the Sintons Are Disappointed, and Mrs. Comstock Learns that She Can Laugh

With the first streak of red above the Limberlost Margaret Sinton was busy with the gingham and the intricate paper pattern she had purchased. Wesley cooked the breakfast and worked until he thought Elnora would be gone, then he started to bring her mother.

"Now you be mighty careful," cautioned Margaret. "I don't know how she will take it."

"I don't either," said Wesley philosophically, "but she's got to take it some way. That dress has to be finished by school time in the morning."

Wesley had not slept well that night. He had been so busy framing diplomatic speeches to make to Mrs. Comstock that sleep had little chance with him. Every step nearer to her he approached his position seemed less enviable. By the time he reached the front gate and started down the walk between the rows of asters and lady slippers he was perspiring, and every plausible and convincing speech had fled his brain. Mrs. Comstock helped him. She met him at the door.

"Good morning," she said. "Did Margaret send you for something?"

"Yes," said Wesley. "She's got a job that's too big for her, and she wants you to help."

"Of course I will," said Mrs. Comstock. It was no one's affair how lonely the previous day had been, or how the endless hours of the present would drag. "What is she doing in such a rush?"

Now was his chance.

"She's making a dress for Elnora," answered, Wesley. He saw Mrs. Comstock's form straighten, and her face harden, so he continued hastily. "You see Elnora has been helping us at harvest time, butchering, and with unexpected visitors for years. We've made out that she's saved us a considerable sum, and as she wouldn't ever touch any pay for anything, we just went to town and got a few clothes we thought would fix her up a little for the high school. We want to get a dress done to-day mighty bad, but Margaret is slow about sewing, and she never can finish alone, so I came after you."

"And it's such a simple little matter, so dead easy; and all so between old friends like, that you can't look above your boots while you explain it," sneered Mrs. Comstock. "Wesley Sinton, what put the idea into your head that Elnora would take things bought with money, when she wouldn't take the money?"

Then Sinton's eyes came up straightly.

"Finding her on the trail last night sobbing as hard as I ever saw any one at a funeral. She wasn't complaining at all, but she's come to me all her life with her little hurts, and she couldn't hide how she'd been laughed at, twitted, and run face to face against the fact that there were books and tuition, unexpected, and nothing will ever make me believe you didn't know that, Kate Comstock."

"If any doubts are troubling you on that subject, sure I knew it! She was so anxious to try the world, I thought I'd just let her take a few knocks and see how she liked them."

"As if she'd ever taken anything but knocks all her life!" cried Wesley Sinton. "Kate Comstock, you are a heartless, selfish woman. You've never shown Elnora any real love in her life. If ever she finds out that thing you'll lose her, and it will serve you right."

"She knows it now," said Mrs. Comstock icily, "and she'll be home to-night just as usual."

"Well, you are a brave woman if you dared put a girl of Elnora's make through what she suffered yesterday, and will suffer again to-day, and let her know you did it on purpose. I admire your nerve. But I've watched this since Elnora was born, and I got enough. Things have come to a pass where they go better for her, or I interfere."

"As if you'd ever done anything but interfere all her life! Think I haven't watched you? Think I, with my heart raw in my breast, and too numb to resent it openly, haven't seen you and Mag Sinton trying to turn Elnora against me day after day? When did you ever tell her what her father meant to me? When did you ever try to make her see the wreck of my life, and what I've suffered? No indeed! Always it's been poor little abused Elnora, and cakes, kissing, extra clothes, and encouraging her to run to you with a pitiful mouth every time I tried to make a woman of her."

"Kate Comstock, that's unjust," cried Sinton. "Only last night I tried to show her the picture I saw the day she was born. I begged her to come to you and tell you pleasant what she needed, and ask you for what I happen to know you can well afford to give her."

"I can't!" cried Mrs. Comstock. "You know I can't!"

"Then get so you can!" said Wesley Sinton. "Any day you say the word you can sell six thousand worth of rare timber off this place easy. I'll see to clearing and working the fields cheap as dirt, for Elnora's sake. I'll buy you more cattle to fatten. All you've got to do is sign a lease, to pull thousands from the ground in oil, as the rest of us are doing all around you!"

"Cut down Robert's trees!" shrieked Mrs. Comstock. "Tear up his land! Cover everything with horrid, greasy oil! I'll die first."

"You mean you'll let Elnora go like a beggar, and hurt and mortify her past bearing. I've got to the place where I tell you plain what I am going to do. Maggie and I went to town last night, and we bought what things Elnora needs most urgent to make her look a little like the rest of the high school girls. Now here it is in plain English. You can help get these things ready, and let us give them to her as we want—"

"She won't touch them!" cried Mrs. Comstock.

"Then you can pay us, and she can take them as her right—"

"I won't!"

"Then I will tell Elnora just what you are worth, what you can afford, and how much of this she owns. I'll loan her the money to buy books and decent clothes, and when she is of age she can sell her share and pay me."

Mrs. Comstock gripped a chair-back and opened her lips, but no words came.

"And," Sinton continued, "if she is so much like you that she won't do that, I'll go to the county seat and lay complaint against you as her guardian before the judge. I'll swear to what you are worth, and how you are raising her, and have you discharged, or have the judge appoint some man who will see that she is comfortable, educated, and decent looking!"

"You—you wouldn't!" gasped Kate Comstock.

"I won't need to, Kate!" said Sinton, his heart softening the instant the hard words were said. "You won't show it, but you do love Elnora! You can't help it! You must see how she needs things; come help us fix them, and be friends. Maggie and I couldn't live without her, and you couldn't either. You've got to love such a fine girl as she is; let it show a little!"

"You can hardly expect me to love her," said Mrs. Comstock coldly. "But for her a man would stand back of me now, who would beat the breath out of your sneaking body for the cowardly thing with which you threaten me. After all I've suffered you'd drag me to court and compel me to tear up Robert's property. If I ever go they carry me. If they touch one tree, or put down one greasy old oil well, it will be over all I can shoot, before they begin. Now, see how quick you can clear out of here!"

"You won't come and help Maggie with the dress?"

For answer Mrs. Comstock looked around swiftly for some object on which to lay her hands. Knowing her temper, Wesley Sinton left with all the haste consistent with dignity. But he did not go home. He crossed a field, and in an hour brought another neighbour who was skilful with her needle. With sinking heart Margaret saw them coming.

"Kate is too busy to help to-day, she can't sew before to-morrow," said Wesley cheerfully as they entered.

That quieted Margaret's apprehension a little, though she had some doubts. Wesley prepared the lunch, and by four o'clock the dress was finished as far as it possibly could be until it was fitted on Elnora. If that did not entail too much work, it could be completed in two hours.

Then Margaret packed their purchases into the big market basket. Wesley took the hat, umbrella, and raincoat, and they went to Mrs. Comstock's. As they reached the step, Margaret spoke pleasantly to Mrs. Comstock, who sat reading just inside the door, but she did not answer and deliberately turned a leaf without looking up.

Wesley Sinton opened the door and went in followed by Margaret.

"Kate," he said, "you needn't take out your mad over our little racket on Maggie. I ain't told her a word I said to you, or you said to me. She's not so very strong, and she's sewed since four o'clock this morning to get this dress ready for to-morrow. It's done and we came down to try it on Elnora."

"Is that the truth, Mag Sinton?" demanded Mrs. Comstock.

"You heard Wesley say so," proudly affirmed Mrs. Sinton.

"I want to make you a proposition," said Wesley. "Wait till Elnora comes. Then we'll show her the things and see what she says."

"How would it do to see what she says without bribing her," sneered Mrs. Comstock.

"If she can stand what she did yesterday, and will to-day, she can bear 'most anything," said Wesley. "Put away the clothes if you want to, till we tell her."

"Well, you don't take this waist I'm working on," said Margaret, "for I have to baste in the sleeves and set the collar. Put the rest out of sight if you like."

Mrs. Comstock picked up the basket and bundles, placed them inside her room and closed the door.

Margaret threaded her needle and began to sew. Mrs. Comstock returned to her book, while Wesley fidgeted and raged inwardly. He could see that Margaret was nervous and almost in tears, but the lines in Mrs. Comstock's impassive face were set and cold. So they sat while the clock ticked off the time—one hour, two, dusk, and no Elnora. Just when Margaret and Wesley were discussing whether he had not better go to town to meet Elnora, they heard her coming up the walk. Wesley dropped his tilted chair and squared himself. Margaret gripped her sewing, and turned pleading eyes toward the door. Mrs. Comstock closed her book and grimly smiled.

"Mother, please open the door," called Elnora.

Mrs. Comstock arose, and swung back the screen. Elnora stepped in beside her, bent half double, the whole front of her dress gathered into a sort of bag filled with a heavy load, and one arm stacked high with books. In the dim light she did not see the Sintons.

"Please hand me the empty bucket in the kitchen, mother," she said. "I just had to bring these arrow points home, but I'm scared for fear I've spoiled my dress and will have to wash it. I'm to clean them, and take them to the banker in the morning, and oh, mother, I've sold enough stuff to pay for my books, my tuition, and maybe a dress and some lighter shoes besides. Oh, mother I'm so happy! Take the books and bring the bucket!"

Then she saw Margaret and Wesley. "Oh, glory!" she exulted. "I was just wondering how I'd ever wait to tell you, and here you are! It's too perfectly splendid to be true!"

"Tell us, Elnora," said Sinton.

"Well sir," said Elnora, doubling down on the floor and spreading out her skirt, "set the bucket here, mother. These points are brittle, and should be put in one at a time. If they are chipped I can't sell them. Well sir! I've had a time! You know I just had to have books. I tried three stores, and they wouldn't trust me, not even three days, I didn't know what in this world I could do quickly enough. Just when I was almost frantic I saw a sign in a bank window asking for caterpillars, cocoons, butterflies, arrow points, and everything. I went in, and it was this Bird Woman who wants the insects, and the banker wants the stones. I had to go to school then, but, if you'll believe it"—Elnora beamed on all of them in turn as she talked and slipped the arrow points from her dress to the pail—"if you'll believe it—but you won't, hardly, until you look at the books—there was the mathematics teacher, waiting at his door, and he had a set of books for me that he had telephoned a Sophomore to bring."

"How did he happen to do that, Elnora?" interrupted Sinton.

Elnora blushed.

"It was a fool mistake I made yesterday in thinking books were just handed out to one. There was a teachers' meeting last night and the history teacher told about that. Professor Henley thought of me. You know I told you what he said about my algebra, mother. Ain't I glad I studied out some of it myself this summer! So he telephoned and a girl brought the books. Because they are marked and abused some I get the whole outfit for two dollars. I can erase most of the marks, paste down the covers, and fix them so they look better. But I must hurry to the joy part. I didn't stop to eat, at noon, I just ran to the Bird Woman's, and I had lunch with her. It was salad, hot chocolate, and lovely things, and she wants to buy most every old scrap I ever gathered. She wants dragonflies, moths, butterflies, and he—the banker, I mean—wants everything Indian. This very night she came to the swamp with me and took away enough stuff to pay for the books and tuition, and to-morrow she is going to buy some more."

Elnora laid the last arrow point in the pail and arose, shaking leaves and bits of baked earth from her dress. She reached into her pocket, produced her money and waved it before their wondering eyes.

"And that's the joy part!" she exulted. "Put it up in the clock till morning, mother. That pays for the books and tuition and—" Elnora hesitated, for she saw the nervous grasp with which her mother's fingers closed on the bills. Then she continued, but more slowly and thinking before she spoke.

"What I get to-morrow pays for more books and tuition, and maybe a few, just a few, things to wear. These shoes are so dreadfully heavy and hot, and they make such a noise on the floor. There isn't another calico dress in the whole building, not among hundreds of us. Why, what is that? Aunt Margaret, what are you hiding in your lap?"

She snatched the waist and shook it out, and her face was beaming. "Have you taken to waists all fancy and buttoned in the back? I bet you this is mine!"

"I bet you so too," said Margaret Sinton. "You undress right away and try it on, and if it fits, it will be done for morning. There are some low shoes, too!"

Elnora began to dance. "Oh, you dear people!" she cried. "I can pay for them to-morrow night! Isn't it too splendid! I was just thinking on the way home that I certainly would be compelled to have cooler shoes until later, and I was wondering what I'd do when the fall rains begin."

"I meant to get you some heavy dress skirts and a coat then," said Mrs. Comstock.

"I know you said so!" cried Elnora. "But you needn't, now! I can buy every single stitch I need myself. Next summer I can gather up a lot more stuff, and all winter on the way to school. I am sure I can sell ferns, I know I can nuts, and the Bird Woman says the grade rooms want leaves, grasses, birds' nests, and cocoons. Oh, isn't this world lovely! I'll be helping with the tax, next, mother!"

Elnora waved the waist and started for the bedroom. When she opened the door she gave a little cry.

"What have you people been doing?" she demanded. "I never saw so many interesting bundles in all my life. I'm 'skeered' to death for fear I can't pay for them, and will have to give up something."

"Wouldn't you take them, if you could not pay for them, Elnora?" asked her mother instantly.

"Why, not unless you did," answered Elnora. "People have no right to wear things they can't afford, have they?"

"But from such old friends as Maggie and Wesley!" Mrs. Comstock's voice was oily with triumph.

"From them least of all," cried Elnora stoutly. "From a stranger sooner than from them, to whom I owe so much more than I ever can pay now."

"Well, you don't have to," said Mrs. Comstock. "Maggie just selected these things, because she is more in touch with the world, and has got such good taste. You can pay as long as your money holds out, and if there's more necessary, maybe I can sell the butcher a calf, or if things are too costly for us, of course, they can take them back. Put on the waist now, and then you can look over the rest and see if they are suitable, and what you want."

Elnora stepped into the adjoining room and closed the door. Mrs. Comstock picked up the bucket and started for the well with it. At the bedroom she paused.

"Elnora, were you going to wash these arrow points?"

"Yes. The Bird Woman says they sell better if they are clean, so it can be seen that there are no defects in them."

"Of course," said Mrs. Comstock. "Some of them seem quite baked. Shall I put them to soak? Do you want to take them in the morning?"

"Yes, I do," answered Elnora. "If you would just fill the pail with water."

Mrs. Comstock left the room. Wesley Sinton sat with his back to the window in the west end of the cabin which overlooked the well. A suppressed sound behind him caused him to turn quickly. Then he arose and leaned over Margaret.

"She's out there laughing like a blamed monkey!" he whispered indignantly.

"Well, she can't help it!" exclaimed Margaret.

"I'm going home!" said Wesley.

"Oh no, you are not!" retorted Margaret. "You are missing the point. The point is not how you look, or feel. It is to get these things in Elnora's possession past dispute. You go now, and to-morrow Elnora will wear calico, and Kate Comstock will return these goods. Right here I stay until everything we bought is Elnora's."

"What are you going to do?" asked Wesley.

"I don't know yet, myself," said Margaret.

Then she arose and peered from the window. At the well curb stood Katharine Comstock. The strain of the day was finding reaction. Her chin was in the air, she was heaving, shaking and strangling to suppress any sound. The word that slipped between Margaret Sinton's lips shocked Wesley until he dropped on his chair, and recalled her to her senses. She was fairly composed as she turned to Elnora, and began the fitting. When she had pinched, pulled, and patted she called, "Come see if you think this fits, Kate."

Mrs. Comstock had gone around to the back door and answered from the kitchen. "You know more about it than I do. Go ahead! I'm getting supper. Don't forget to allow for what it will shrink in washing!"

"I set the colours and washed the goods last night; it can be made to fit right now," answered Margaret.

When she could find nothing more to alter she told Elnora to heat some water. After she had done that the girl began opening packages.

The hat came first.

"Mother!" cried Elnora. "Mother, of course, you have seen this, but you haven't seen it on me. I must try it on."

"Don't you dare put that on your head until your hair is washed and properly combed," said Margaret.

"Oh!" cried Elnora. "Is that water to wash my hair? I thought it was to set the colour in another dress."

"Well, you thought wrong," said Margaret simply. "Your hair is going to be washed and brushed until it shines like copper. While it dries you can eat your supper, and this dress will be finished. Then you can put on your new ribbon, and your hat. You can try your shoes now, and if they don't fit, you and Wesley can drive to town and change them. That little round bundle on the top of the basket is your stockings."

Margaret sat down and began sewing swiftly, and a little later opened the machine, and ran several long seams.

Elnora returned in a few minutes holding up her skirts and stepping daintily in the new shoes.

"Don't soil them, honey, else you're sure they fit," cautioned Wesley.

"They seem just a trifle large, maybe," said Elnora dubiously, and Wesley knelt to feel. He and Margaret thought them a fit, and then Elnora appealed to her mother. Mrs. Comstock appeared wiping her hands on her apron. She examined the shoes critically.

"They seem to fit," she said, "but they are away too fine to walk country roads."

"I think so, too," said Elnora instantly. "We had better take these back and get a cheaper pair."

"Oh, let them go for this time," said Mrs. Comstock. "They are so pretty, I hate to part with them. You can get cheaper ones after this."

Wesley and Margaret scarcely breathed for a long time.

When Wesley went to do the feeding. Elnora set the table. When the water was hot, Margaret pinned a big towel around Elnora's shoulders and washed and dried the lovely hair according to the instructions she had been given the previous night. As the hair began to dry it billowed out in a sparkling sheen that caught the light and gleamed and flashed.

"Now, the idea is to let it stand naturally, just as the curl will make it. Don't you do any of that nasty, untidy snarling, Elnora," cautioned Margaret. "Wash it this way every two weeks while you are in school, shake it out, and dry it. Then part it in the middle and turn a front quarter on each side from your face. You tie the back at your neck with a string—so, and the ribbon goes in a big, loose bow. I'll show you." One after another Margaret Sinton tied the ribbons, creasing each of them so they could not be returned, as she explained that she was trying to find the colour most becoming. Then she produced the raincoat which carried Elnora into transports.

Mrs. Comstock objected. "That won't be warm enough for cold weather, and you can't afford it and a coat, too."

"I'll tell you what I thought," said Elnora. "I was planning on the way home. These coats are fine because they keep you dry. I thought I would get one, and a warm sweater to wear under it cold days. Then I always would be dry, and warm. The sweater only costs three dollars, so I could get it and the raincoat both for half the price of a heavy cloth coat."

"You are right about that," said Mrs. Comstock. "You can change more with the weather, too. Keep the raincoat, Elnora."

"Wear it until you try the hat," said Margaret. "It will have to do until the dress is finished."

Elnora picked up the hat dubiously. "Mother, may I wear my hair as it is now?" she asked.

"Let me take a good look," said Katharine Comstock.

Heaven only knows what she saw. To Wesley and to Margaret the bright young face of Elnora, with its pink tints, its heavy dark brows, its bright blue-gray eyes, and its frame of curling reddish-brown hair was the sweetest sight on earth, and at that instant Elnora was radiant.

"So long as it's your own hair, and combed back as plain as it will go, I don't suppose it cuts much ice whether it's tied a little tighter or looser," conceded Mrs. Comstock. "If you stop right there, you may let it go at that."

Elnora set the hat on her head. It was only a wide tan straw with three exquisite peacock quills at one side. Margaret Sinton cried out, Wesley slapped his knee and sighed deeply while Mrs. Comstock stood speechless for a second.

"I wish you had asked the price before you put that on," she said impatiently. "We never can afford it."

"It's not so much as you think," said Margaret. "Don't you see what I did? I had them take off the quills, and put on some of those Phoebe Simms gave me from her peacocks. The hat will only cost you a dollar and a half."

She avoided Wesley's eyes, and looked straight at Mrs. Comstock. Elnora removed the hat to examine it.

"Why, they are those reddish-tan quills of yours!" she cried. "Mother, look how beautifully they are set on! I'd much rather have them than those from the store."

"So would I," said Mrs. Comstock. "If Margaret wants to spare them, that will make you a beautiful hat; dirt cheap, too! You must go past Mrs. Simms and show her. She would be pleased to see them."

Elnora sank into a chair and contemplated her toe. "Landy, ain't I a queen?" she murmured. "What else have I got?"

"Just a belt, some handkerchiefs, and a pair of top shoes for rainy days and colder weather," said Margaret.

"About those high shoes, that was my idea," said Wesley. "Soon as it rains, low shoes won't do, and by taking two pairs at once I could get them some cheaper. The low ones are two and the high ones two fifty, together three seventy-five. Ain't that cheap?"

"That's a real bargain," said Mrs. Comstock, "if they are good shoes, and they look it."

"This," said Wesley, producing the last package, "is your Christmas present from your Aunt Maggie. I got mine, too, but it's at the house. I'll bring it up in the morning."

He handed Margaret the umbrella, and she passed it over to Elnora who opened it and sat laughing under its shelter. Then she kissed both of them. She brought a pencil and a slip of paper to set down the prices they gave her of everything they had brought except the umbrella, added the sum, and said laughingly: "Will you please wait till to-morrow for the money? I will have it then, sure."

"Elnora," said Wesley Sinton. "Wouldn't you—"

"Elnora, hustle here a minute!" called Mrs. Comstock from the kitchen. "I need you!"

"One second, mother," answered Elnora, throwing off the coat and hat, and closing the umbrella as she ran. There were several errands to do in a hurry, and then supper. Elnora chattered incessantly, Wesley and Margaret talked all they could, while Mrs. Comstock said a word now and then, which was all she ever did. But Wesley Sinton was watching her, and time and again he saw a peculiar little twist around her mouth. He knew that for the first time in sixteen years she really was laughing over something. She had all she could do to preserve her usually sober face. Wesley knew what she was thinking.

After supper the dress was finished, the pattern for the next one discussed, and then the Sintons went home. Elnora gathered her treasures. When she started upstairs she stopped. "May I kiss you good-night, mother?" she asked lightly.

"Never mind any slobbering," said Mrs. Comstock. "I should think you'd lived with me long enough to know that I don't care for it."

"Well, I'd love to show you in some way how happy I am, and how I thank you."

"I wonder what for?" said Mrs. Comstock. "Mag Sinton chose that stuff and brought it here and you pay for it."

"Yes, but you seemed willing for me to have it, and you said you would help me if I couldn't pay all."

"Maybe I did," said Mrs. Comstock. "Maybe I did. I meant to get you some heavy dress skirts about Thanksgiving, and I still can get them. Go to bed, and for any sake don't begin mooning before a mirror, and make a dunce of yourself."

Mrs. Comstock picked up several papers and blew out the kitchen light. She stood in the middle of the sitting-room floor for a time and then went into her room and closed the door. Sitting on the edge of the bed she thought for a few minutes and then suddenly buried her face in the pillow and again heaved with laughter.

Down the road plodded Margaret and Wesley Sinton. Neither of them had words to utter their united thought.

"Done!" hissed Wesley at last. "Done brown! Did you ever feel like a bloomin', confounded donkey? How did the woman do it?"

"She didn't do it!" gulped Margaret through her tears "She didn't do anything. She trusted to Elnora's great big soul to bring her out right, and really she was right, and so it had to bring her. She's a darling, Wesley! But she's got a time before her. Did you see Kate Comstock grab that money? Before six months she'll be out combing the Limberlost for bugs and arrow points to help pay the tax. I know her."

"Well, I don't!" exclaimed Sinton, "she's too many for me. But there is a laugh left in her yet! I didn't s'pose there was. Bet you a dollar, if we could see her this minute, she'd be chuckling over the way we got left."

Both of them stopped in the road and looked back.

"There's Elnora's light in her room," said Margaret. "The poor child will feel those clothes, and pore over her books till morning, but she'll look decent to go to school, anyway. Nothing is too big a price to pay for that."

"Yes, if Kate lets her wear them. Ten to one, she makes her finish the week with that old stuff!"

"No, she won't," said Margaret. "She'll hardly dare. Kate made some concessions, all right; big ones for her—if she did get her way in the main. She bent some, and if Elnora proves that she can walk out barehanded in the morning and come back with that much money in her pocket, an armful of books, and buy a turnout like that, she proves that she is of some consideration, and Kate's smart enough. She'll think twice before she'll do that. Elnora won't wear a calico dress to high school again. You watch and see if she does. She may have the best clothes she'll get for a time, for the least money, but she won't know it until she tries to buy goods herself at the same rates. Wesley, what about those prices? Didn't they shrink considerable?"

"You began it," said Wesley. "Those prices were all right. We didn't say what the goods cost us, we said what they would cost her. Surely, she's mistaken about being able to pay all that. Can she pick up stuff of that value around the Limberlost? Didn't the Bird Woman see her trouble, and just give her the money?"

"I don't think so," said Margaret. "Seems to me I've heard of her paying, or offering to pay those who would take the money, for bugs and butterflies, and I've known people who sold that banker Indian stuff. Once I heard that his pipe collection beat that of the Government at the Philadelphia Centennial. Those things have come to have a value."

"Well, there's about a bushel of that kind of valuables piled up in the woodshed, that belongs to Elnora. At least, I picked them up because she said she wanted them. Ain't it queer that she'd take to stones, bugs, and butterflies, and save them. Now they are going to bring her the very thing she wants the worst. Lord, but this is a funny world when you get to studying! Looks like things didn't all come by accident. Looks as if there was a plan back of it, and somebody driving that knows the road, and how to handle the lines. Anyhow, Elnora's in the wagon, and when I get out in the night and the dark closes around me, and I see the stars, I don't feel so cheap. Maggie, how the nation did Kate Comstock do that?"

"You will keep on harping, Wesley. I told you she didn't do it. Elnora did it! She walked in and took things right out of our hands. All Kate had to do was to enjoy having it go her way, and she was cute enough to put in a few questions that sort of guided Elnora. But I don't know, Wesley. This thing makes me think, too. S'pose we'd taken Elnora when she was a baby, and we'd heaped on her all the love we can't on our own, and we'd coddled, petted, and shielded her, would she have made the woman that living alone, learning to think for herself, and taking all the knocks Kate Comstock could give, have made of her?"

"You bet your life!" cried Wesley, warmly. "Loving anybody don't hurt them. We wouldn't have done anything but love her. You can't hurt a child loving it. She'd have learned to work, to study, and grown into a woman with us, without suffering like a poor homeless dog."

"But you don't see the point, Wesley. She would have grown into a fine woman with us; but as we would have raised her, would her heart ever have known the world as it does now? Where's the anguish, Wesley, that child can't comprehend? Seeing what she's seen of her mother hasn't hardened her. She can understand any mother's sorrow. Living life from the rough side has only broadened her. Where's the girl or boy burning with shame, or struggling to find a way, that will cross Elnora's path and not get a lift from her? She's had the knocks, but there'll never be any of the thing you call 'false pride' in her. I guess we better keep out. Maybe Kate Comstock knows what she's doing. Sure as you live, Elnora has grown bigger on knocks than she would on love."

"I don't s'pose there ever was a very fine point to anything but I missed it," said Wesley, "because I am blunt, rough, and have no book learning to speak of. Since you put it into words I see what you mean, but it's dinged hard on Elnora, just the same. And I don't keep out. I keep watching closer than ever. I got my slap in the face, but if I don't miss my guess, Kate Comstock learned her lesson, same as I did. She learned that I was in earnest, that I would haul her to court if she didn't loosen up a bit, and she'll loosen. You see if she doesn't. It may come hard, and the hinges creak, but she'll fix Elnora decent after this, if Elnora doesn't prove that she can fix herself. As for me, I found out that what I was doing was as much for myself as for Elnora. I wanted her to take those things from us, and love us for giving them. It didn't work, and but for you, I'd messed the whole thing and stuck like a pig in crossing a bridge. But you helped me out; Elnora's got the clothes, and by morning, maybe I won't grudge Kate the only laugh she's had in sixteen years. You been showing me the way quite a spell now, ain't you, Maggie?"

In her attic Elnora lighted two candles, set them on her little table, stacked the books, and put away the precious clothes. How lovingly she hung the hat and umbrella, folded the raincoat, and spread the new dress over a chair. She fingered the ribbons, and tried to smooth the creases from them. She put away the hose neatly folded, touched the handkerchiefs, and tried the belt. Then she slipped into her white nightdress, shook down her hair that it might become thoroughly dry, set a chair before the table, and reverently opened one of the books. A stiff draught swept the attic, for it stretched the length of the cabin, and had a window in each end. Elnora arose and going to the east window closed it. She stood for a minute looking at the stars, the sky, and the dark outline of the straggling trees of the rapidly dismantling Limberlost. In the region of her case a tiny point of light flashed and disappeared. Elnora straightened and wondered. Was it wise to leave her precious money there? The light flashed once more, wavered a few seconds, and died out. The girl waited. She did not see it again, so she turned to her books.

In the Limberlost the hulking figure of a man sneaked down the trail.

"The Bird Woman was at Freckles's room this evening," he muttered. "Wonder what for?"

He left the trail, entered the enclosure still distinctly outlined, and approached the case. The first point of light flashed from the tiny electric lamp on his vest. He took a duplicate key from his pocket, felt for the padlock and opened it. The door swung wide. The light flashed the second time. Swiftly his glance swept the interior.

"'Bout a fourth of her moths gone. Elnora must have been with the Bird Woman and given them to her." Then he stood tense. His keen eyes discovered the roll of bills hastily thrust back in the bottom of the case. He snatched them up, shut off the light, relocked the case by touch, and swiftly went down the trail. Every few seconds he paused and listened intently. Just as he reached the road, a second figure approached him.

"Is it you, Pete?" came the whispered question.

"Yes," said the first man.

"I was coming down to take a peep, when I saw your flash," he said. "I heard the Bird Woman had been at the case to-day. Anything doing?"

"Not a thing," said Pete. "She just took away about a fourth of the moths. Probably had the Comstock girl getting them for her. Heard they were together. Likely she'll get the rest to-morrow. Ain't picking gettin' bare these days?"

"Well, I should say so," said the second man, turning back in disgust. "Coming home, now?"

"No, I am going down this way," answered Pete, for his eyes caught the gleam from the window of the Comstock cabin, and he had a desire to learn why Elnora's attic was lighted at that hour.

He slouched down the road, occasionally feeling the size of the roll he had not taken time to count.

The attic was too long, the light too near the other end, and the cabin stood much too far back from the road. He could see nothing although he climbed the fence and walked back opposite the window. He knew Mrs. Comstock was probably awake, and that she sometimes went to the swamp behind her home at night. At times a cry went up from that locality that paralyzed any one near, or sent them fleeing as if for life. He did not care to cross behind the cabin. He returned to the road, passed, and again climbed the fence. Opposite the west window he could see Elnora. She sat before a small table reading from a book between two candles. Her hair fell in a bright sheen around her, and with one hand she lightly shook, and tossed it as she studied. The man stood out in the night and watched.

For a long time a leaf turned at intervals and the hair-drying went on. The man drew nearer. The picture grew more beautiful as he approached. He could not see so well as he desired, for the screen was of white mosquito netting, and it angered him. He cautiously crept closer. The elevation shut off his view. Then he remembered the large willow tree shading the well and branching across the window fit the west end of the cabin. From childhood Elnora had stepped from the sill to a limb and slid down the slanting trunk of the tree. He reached it and noiselessly swung himself up. Three steps out on the big limb the man shuddered. He was within a few feet of the girl.

He could see the throb of her breast under its thin covering and smell the fragrance of the tossing hair. He could see the narrow bed with its pieced calico cover, the whitewashed walls with gay lithographs, and every crevice stuck full of twigs with dangling cocoons. There were pegs for the few clothes, the old chest, the little table, the two chairs, the uneven floor covered with rag rugs and braided corn husk. But nothing was worth a glance except the perfect face and form within reach by one spring through the rotten mosquito bar. He gripped the limb above that on which he stood, licked his lips, and breathed through his throat to be sure he was making no sound. Elnora closed the book and laid it aside. She picked up a towel, and turning the gathered ends of her hair rubbed them across it, and dropping the towel on her lap, tossed the hair again. Then she sat in deep thought. By and by words began to come softly. Near as he was the man could not hear at first. He bent closer and listened intently.

"—ever could be so happy," murmured the soft voice. "The dress is so pretty, such shoes, the coat, and everything. I won't have to be ashamed again, not ever again, for the Limberlost is full of precious moths, and I always can collect them. The Bird Woman will buy more to-morrow, and the next day, and the next. When they are all gone, I can spend every minute gathering cocoons, and hunting other things I can sell. Oh, thank God, for my precious, precious money. Why, I didn't pray in vain after all! I thought when I asked the Lord to hide me, there in that big hall, that He wasn't doing it, because I wasn't covered from sight that instant. But I'm hidden now, I feel that." Elnora lifted her eyes to the beams above her. "I don't know much about praying properly," she muttered, "but I do thank you, Lord, for hiding me in your own time and way."

Her face was so bright that it shone with a white radiance. Two big tears welled from her eyes, and rolled down her smiling cheeks. "Oh, I do feel that you have hidden me," she breathed. Then she blew out the lights, and the little wooden bed creaked under her weight.

Pete Corson dropped from the limb and found his way to the road. He stood still a long time, then started back to the Limberlost. A tiny point of light flashed in the region of the case. He stopped with an oath.

"Another hound trying to steal from a girl," he exclaimed. "But it's likely he thinks if he gets anything it will be from a woman who can afford it, as I did."

He went on, but beside the fences, and very cautiously.

"Swamp seems to be alive to-night," he muttered. "That's three of us out."

He entered a deep place at the northwest corner, sat on the ground and taking a pencil from his pocket, he tore a leaf from a little notebook, and laboriously wrote a few lines by the light he carried. Then he went back to the region of the case and waited. Before his eyes swept the vision of the slender white creature with tossing hair. He smiled, and worshipped it, until a distant rooster faintly announced dawn.

Then he unlocked the case again, and replaced the money, laid the note upon it, and went back to concealment, where he remained until Elnora came down the trail in the morning, appearing very lovely in her new dress and hat.

Chapter 5

Wherein Elnora Receives a Warning, and Billy Appears on the Scene

It would be difficult to describe how happy Elnora was that morning as she hurried through her work, bathed and put on the neat, dainty gingham dress, and the tan shoes. She had a struggle with her hair. It crinkled, billowed, and shone, and she could not avoid seeing the becoming frame it made around her face. But in deference to her mother's feelings the girl set her teeth, and bound her hair closely to her head with a shoe-string. "Not to be changed at the case," she told herself.

That her mother was watching she was unaware. Just as she picked up the beautiful brown ribbon Mrs. Comstock spoke.

"You had better let me tie that. You can't reach behind yourself and do it right."

Elnora gave a little gasp. Her mother never before had proposed to do anything for the girl that by any possibility she could do herself. Her heart quaked at the thought of how her mother would arrange that bow, but Elnora dared not refuse. The offer was too precious. It might never be made again.

"Oh thank you!" said the girl, and sitting down she held out the ribbon.

Her mother stood back and looked at her critically.

"You haven't got that like Mag Sinton had it last night," she announced. "You little idiot! You've tried to plaster it down to suit me, and you missed it. I liked it away better as Mag fixed it, after I saw it. You didn't look so peeled."

"Oh mother, mother!" laughed Elnora, with a half sob in her voice.

"Hold still, will you?" cried Mrs. Comstock. "You'll be late, and I haven't packed your dinner yet."

She untied the string and shook out the hair. It rose with electricity and clung to her fingers and hands. Mrs. Comstock jumped back as if bitten. She knew that touch. Her face grew white, and her eyes angry.

"Tie it yourself," she said shortly, "and then I'll put on the ribbon. But roll it back loose like Mag did. It looked so pretty that way."

Almost fainting Elnora stood before the glass, divided off the front parts of her hair, and rolled them as Mrs. Sinton had done; tied it at the nape of her neck, then sat while her mother arranged the ribbon.

"If I pull it down till it comes tight in these creases where she had it, it will be just right, won't it?" queried Mrs. Comstock, and the amazed Elnora stammered,

"Yes."

When she looked in the glass the bow was perfectly tied, and how the gold tone of the brown did match the lustre of the shining hair! "That's pretty," commented Mrs. Comstock's soul, but her stiff lips had said all that could be forced from them for once. Just then Wesley Sinton came to the door.

"Good morning," he cried heartily. "Elnora, you look a picture! My, but you're sweet! If any of the city boys get sassy you tell your Uncle Wesley, and he'll horsewhip them. Here's your Christmas present from me." He handed Elnora the leather lunch box, with her name carved across the strap in artistic lettering.

"Oh Uncle Wesley!" was all Elnora could say.

"Your Aunt Maggie filled it for me for a starter," he said. "Now, if you are ready, I'm going to drive past your way and you can ride almost to Onabasha with me, and save the new shoes that much."

Elnora was staring at the box. "Oh I hope it isn't impolite to open it before you," she said. "I just feel as if I must see inside."

"Don't you stand on formality with the neighbours," laughed Sinton. "Look in your box if you want to!"

Elnora slipped the strap and turned back the lid.

This disclosed the knife, fork, napkin, and spoon, the milk flask, and the interior packed with dainty sandwiches wrapped in tissue paper, and the little compartments for meat, salad, and the custard cup.

"Oh mother!" cried Elnora. "Oh mother, isn't it fine? What made you think of it, Uncle Wesley? How will I ever thank you? No one will have a finer lunch box than I. Oh I do thank you! That's the nicest gift I ever had. How I love Christmas in September!"

"It's a mighty handy thing," assented Mrs. Comstock, taking in every detail with sharp eyes. "I guess you are glad now you went and helped Mag and Wesley when you could, Elnora?"

"Deedy, yes," laughed Elnora, "and I'm going again first time they have a big day if I stay from school to do it."

"You'll do no such thing!" said the delighted Sinton. "Come now, if you're going!"

"If I ride, can you spare me time to run into the swamp to my box a minute?" asked Elnora.

The light she had seen the previous night troubled her.

"Sure," said Wesley largely. So they drove away and left a white-faced woman watching them from the door, her heart a little sorer than usual.

"I'd give a pretty to hear what he'll say to her!" she commented bitterly. "Always sticking in, always doing things I can't ever afford. Where on earth did he get that thing and what did it cost?"

Then she entered the cabin and began the day's work, but mingled with the brooding bitterness of her soul was the vision of a sweet young face, glad with a gladness never before seen on it, and over and over she repeated: "I wonder what he'll say to her!"

What he said was that she looked as fresh and sweet as a posy, and to be careful not to step in the mud or scratch her shoes when she went to the case.

Elnora found her key and opened the door. Not where she had placed it, but conspicuously in front lay her little heap of bills, and a crude scrawl of writing beside it. Elnora picked up the note in astonishment.

DERE ELNORY,

the lord amighty is hiding you all right done you ever dout it this money of yourn was took for some time las nite but it is returned with intres for god sake done ever come to the swamp at nite or late evnin or mornin or far in any time sompin worse an you know could git you

A FREND.

Elnora began to tremble. She hastily glanced around. The damp earth before the case had been trodden by large, roughly shod feet. She caught up the money and the note, thrust them into her guimpe, locked the case, and ran to the road.

She was so breathless and her face so white Sinton noticed it.

"What in the world's the matter, Elnora?" he asked.

"I am half afraid!" she panted

"Tut, tut, child!" said Wesley Sinton. "Nothing in the world to be afraid of. What happened?"

"Uncle Wesley," said Elnora, "I had more money than I brought home last night, and I put it in my case. Some one has been there. The ground is all trampled, and they left this note."

"And took your money, I'll wager," said Sinton angrily.

"No," answered Elnora. "Read the note, and oh Uncle Wesley, tell me what it means!"

Sinton's face was a study. "I don't know what it means," he said. "Only one thing is clear. It means some beast who doesn't really want to harm you has got his eye on you, and he is telling you plain as he can, not to give him a chance. You got to keep along the roads, in the open, and not let the biggest moth that ever flew toll you out of hearing of us, or your mother. It means that, plain and distinct."

"Just when I can sell them! Just when everything is so lovely on account of them! I can't! I can't stay away from the swamp. The Limberlost is going to buy the books, the clothes, pay the tuition, and even start a college fund. I just can't!"

"You've got to," said Sinton. "This is plain enough. You go far in the swamp at your own risk, even in daytime."

"Uncle Wesley," said the girl, "last night before I went to bed, I was so happy I tried to pray, and I thanked God for hiding me 'under the shadow of His wing.' But how in the world could any one know it?"

Wesley Sinton's heart leaped in his breast. His face was whiter than the girl's now.

"Were you praying out loud, honey?" he almost whispered.

"I might have said words," answered Elnora. "I know I do sometimes. I've never had any one to talk with, and I've played with and talked to myself all my life. You've caught me at it often, but it always makes mother angry when she does. She says it's silly. I forget and do it, when I'm alone. But Uncle Wesley, if I said anything last night, you know it was the merest whisper, because I'd have been so afraid of waking mother. Don't you see? I sat up late, and studied two lessons."

Sinton was steadying himself. "I'll stop and examine the case as I come back," he said. "Maybe I can find some clue. That other—that was just accidental. It's a common expression. All the preachers use it. If I tried to pray, that would be the very first thing I'd say."

The colour returned to Elnora's face.

"Did you tell your mother about this money, Elnora?" he asked.

"No, I didn't," said Elnora. "It's dreadful not to, but I was afraid. You see they are clearing the swamp so fast. Every year it grows more difficult to find things, and Indian stuff becomes scarcer. I want to graduate, and that's four years unless I can double on the course. That means twenty dollars tuition each year, and new books, and clothes. There won't ever be so much at one time again, that I know. I just got to hang to my money. I was afraid to tell her, for fear she would want it for taxes, and she really must sell a tree or some cattle for that, mustn't she, Uncle Wesley?"

"On your life, she must!" said Wesley. "You put your little wad in the bank all safe, and never mention it to a living soul. It doesn't seem right, but your case is peculiar. Every word you say is a true word. Each year you will find less in the swamp, and things everywhere will be scarcer. If you ever get a few dollars ahead, that can start your college fund. You know you are going to college, Elnora!"

"Of course I am," said Elnora. "I settled that as soon as I knew what a college was. I will put all my money in the bank, except what I owe you. I'll pay that now."

"If your arrows are heavy," said Wesley, "I'll drive on to Onabasha with you."

"But they are not. Half of them were nicked, and this little box held all the good ones. It's so surprising how many are spoiled when you wash them."

"What does he pay?"

"Ten cents for any common perfect one, fifty for revolvers, a dollar for obsidian, and whatever is right for enormous big ones."

"Well, that sounds fair," said Sinton. "You can come down Saturday and wash the stuff at our house, and I'll take it in when we go marketing in the afternoon."

Elnora jumped from the carriage. She soon found that with her books, her lunch box, and the points she had a heavy load. She had almost reached the bridge crossing the culvert when she heard distressed screams of a child. Across an orchard of the suburbs came a small boy, after him a big dog, urged by a man in the background. Elnora's heart was with the small fleeing figure in any event whatever. She dropped her load on the bridge, and with practised hand flung a stone at the dog. The beast curled double with a howl. The boy reached the fence, and Elnora was there to help him over. As he touched the top she swung him to the ground, but he clung to her, clasping her tightly, sobbing with fear. Elnora helped him to the bridge, and sat with him in her arms. For a time his replies to her questions were indistinct, but at last he became quieter and she could understand.

He was a mite of a boy, nothing but skin-covered bones, his burned, freckled face in a mortar of tears and dust, his clothing unspeakably dirty, one great toe in a festering mass from a broken nail, and sores all over the visible portions of the small body.

"You won't let the mean old thing make his dog get me!" he wailed.

"Indeed no," said Elnora, holding him closely.

"You wouldn't set a dog on a boy for just taking a few old apples when you fed 'em to pigs with a shovel every day, would you?"

"No, I would not," said Elnora hotly.

"You'd give a boy all the apples he wanted, if he hadn't any breakfast, and was so hungry he was all twisty inside, wouldn't you?"

"Yes, I would," said Elnora.

"If you had anything to eat you would give me something right now, wouldn't you?"

"Yes," said Elnora. "There's nothing but just stones in the package. But my dinner is in that case. I'll gladly divide."

She opened the box. The famished child gave a little cry and reached both hands. Elnora caught them back.

"Did you have any supper?"

"No."

"Any dinner yesterday?"

"An apple and some grapes I stole."

"Whose boy are you?"

"Old Tom Billings's."

"Why doesn't your father get you something to eat?"

"He does most days, but he's drunk now."

"Hush, you must not!" said Elnora. "He's your father!"

"He's spent all the money to get drunk, too," said the boy, "and Jimmy and Belle are both crying for breakfast. I'd a got out all right with an apple for myself, but I tried to get some for them and the dog got too close. Say, you can throw, can't you?"

"Yes," admitted Elnora. She poured half the milk into the cup. "Drink this," she said, holding it to him.

The boy gulped the milk and swore joyously, gripping the cup with shaking fingers.

"Hush!" cried Elnora. "That's dreadful!"

"What's dreadful?"

"To say such awful words."

"Huh! Pa says worser 'an that every breath he draws."

Elnora saw that the child was older than she had thought. He might have been forty judging by his hard, unchildish expression.

"Do you want to be like your father?"

"No, I want to be like you. Couldn't a angel be prettier 'an you. Can I have more milk?"

Elnora emptied the flask. The boy drained the cup. He drew a breath of satisfaction as he gazed into her face.

"You wouldn't go off and leave your little boy, would you?" he asked.

"Did some one go away and leave you?"

"Yes, my mother went off and left me, and left Jimmy and Belle, too," said the boy. "You wouldn't leave your little boy, would you?"

"No."

The boy looked eagerly at the box. Elnora lifted a sandwich and uncovered the fried chicken. The boy gasped with delight.

"Say, I could eat the stuff in the glass and the other box and carry the bread and the chicken to Jimmy and Belle," he offered.

Elnora silently uncovered the custard with preserved cherries on top and handed it and the spoon to the child. Never did food disappear faster. The salad went next, and a sandwich and half a chicken breast followed.

"I better leave the rest for Jimmy and Belle," he said, "they're 'ist fightin' hungry."

Elnora gave him the remainder of the carefully prepared lunch. The boy clutched it and ran with a sidewise hop like a wild thing. She covered the dishes and cup, polished the spoon, replaced it, and closed the case. She caught her breath in a tremulous laugh.

"If Aunt Margaret knew that, she'd never forgive me," she said. "It seems as if secrecy is literally forced upon me, and I hate it. What shall I do for lunch? I'll have to sell my arrows and keep enough money for a restaurant sandwich."

So she walked hurriedly into town, sold her points at a good price, deposited her funds, and went away with a neat little bank book and the note from the Limberlost carefully folded inside. Elnora passed down the hall that morning, and no one paid the slightest attention to her. The truth was she looked so like every one else that she was perfectly inconspicuous. But in the coat room there were members of her class. Surely no one intended it, but the whisper was too loud.

"Look at the girl from the Limberlost in the clothes that woman gave her!"

Elnora turned on them. "I beg your pardon," she said unsteadily, "I couldn't help hearing that! No one gave me these clothes. I paid for them myself."

Some one muttered, "Pardon me," but incredulous faces greeted her.

Elnora felt driven. "Aunt Margaret selected them, and she meant to give them to me," she explained, "but I wouldn't take them. I paid for them myself." There was silence.

"Don't you believe me?" panted Elnora.

"Really, it is none of our affair," said another girl. "Come on, let's go."

Elnora stepped before the girl who had spoken. "You have made this your affair," she said, "because you told a thing which was not true. No one gave me what I am wearing. I paid for my clothes myself with money I earned selling moths to the Bird Woman. I just came from the bank where I deposited what I did not use. Here is my credit." Elnora drew out and offered the little red book. "Surely you will believe that," she said.

"Why of course," said the girl who first had spoken. "We met such a lovely woman in Brownlee's store, and she said she wanted our help to buy some things for a girl, and that's how we came to know."

"Dear Aunt Margaret," said Elnora, "it was like her to ask you. Isn't she splendid?"

"She is indeed," chorused the girls. Elnora set down her lunch box and books, unpinned her hat, hanging it beside the others, and taking up the books she reached to set the box in its place and dropped it. With a little cry she snatched at it and caught the strap on top. That pulled from the fastening, the cover unrolled, the box fell away as far as it could, two porcelain lids rattled on the floor, and the one sandwich rolled like a cartwheel across the room. Elnora lifted a ghastly face. For once no one laughed. She stood an instant staring.

"It seems to be my luck to be crucified at every point of the compass," she said at last. "First two days you thought I was a pauper, now you will think I'm a fraud. All of you will believe I bought an expensive box, and then was too poor to put anything but a restaurant sandwich in it. You must stop till I prove to you that I'm not."

Elnora gathered up the lids, and kicked the sandwich into a corner.

"I had milk in that bottle, see! And custard in the cup. There was salad in the little box, fried chicken in the large one, and nut sandwiches in the tray. You can see the crumbs of all of them. A man set a dog on a child who was so starved he was stealing apples. I talked with him, and I thought I could bear hunger better, he was such a little boy, so I gave him my lunch, and got the sandwich at the restaurant."

Elnora held out the box. The girls were laughing by that time. "You goose," said one, "why didn't you give him the money, and save your lunch?"

"He was such a little fellow, and he really was hungry," said Elnora. "I often go without anything to eat at noon in the fields and woods, and never think of it."

She closed the box and set it beside the lunches of other country pupils. While her back was turned, into the room came the girl of her encounter on the first day, walked to the rack, and with an exclamation of approval took down Elnora's hat.

"Just the thing I have been wanting!" she said. "I never saw such beautiful quills in all my life. They match my new broadcloth to perfection. I've got to have that kind of quills for my hat. I never saw the like! Whose is it, and where did it come from?"

No one said a word, for Elnora's question, the reply, and her answer, had been repeated. Every one knew that the Limberlost girl had come out ahead and Sadie Reed had not been amiable, when the little flourish had been added to Elnora's name in the algebra class. Elnora's swift glance was pathetic, but no one helped her. Sadie Reed glanced from the hat to the faces around her and wondered.

"Why, this is the Freshman section, whose hat is it?" she asked again, this time impatiently.

"That's the tassel of the cornstock," said Elnora with a forced laugh.

The response was genuine. Every one shouted. Sadie Reed blushed, but she laughed also.

"Well, it's beautiful," she said, "especially the quills. They are exactly what I want. I know I don't deserve any kindness from you, but I do wish you would tell me at whose store you found those quills."

"Gladly!" said Elnora. "You can't buy quills like those at a store. They are from a living bird. Phoebe Simms gathers them in her orchard as her peacocks shed them. They are wing quills from the males."

Then there was perfect silence. How was Elnora to know that not a girl there would have told that?

"I haven't a doubt but I can get you some," she offered. "She gave Aunt Margaret a large bunch, and those are part of them. I am quite sure she has more, and would spare some."

Sadie Reed laughed shortly. "You needn't trouble," she said, "I was fooled. I thought they were expensive quills. I wanted them for a twenty-dollar velvet toque to match my new suit. If they are gathered from the ground, really, I couldn't use them."

"Only in spots!" said Elnora. "They don't just cover the earth. Phoebe Simms's peacocks are the only ones within miles of Onabasha, and they moult but once a year. If your hat cost only twenty dollars, it's scarcely good enough for those quills. You see, the Almighty made and coloured those Himself; and He puts the same kind on Phoebe Simms's peacocks that He put on the head of the family in the forests of Ceylon, away back in the beginning. Any old manufactured quill from New York or Chicago will do for your little twenty-dollar hat. You should have something infinitely better than that to be worthy of quills that are made by the Creator."

How those girls did laugh! One of them walked with Elnora to the auditorium, sat beside her during exercises, and tried to talk whenever she dared, to keep Elnora from seeing the curious and admiring looks bent upon her.

For the brown-eyed boy whistled, and there was pantomime of all sorts going on behind Elnora's back that day. Happy with her books, no one knew how much she saw, and from her absorption in her studies it was evident she cared too little to notice.

After school she went again to the home of the Bird Woman, and together they visited the swamp and carried away more specimens. This time Elnora asked the Bird Woman to keep the money until noon of the next day, when she would call for it and have it added to her bank account. She slowly walked home, for the visit to the swamp had brought back full force the experience of the morning. Again and again she examined the crude little note, for she did not know what it meant, yet it bred vague fear. The only thing of which Elnora knew herself afraid was her mother; when with wild eyes and ears deaf to childish pleading, she sometimes lost control of herself in the night and visited the pool where her husband had sunk before her, calling his name in unearthly tones and begging of the swamp to give back its dead.

Chapter 6

Wherein Mrs. Comstock Indulges in "Frills," and Billy Reappears

It was Wesley Sinton who really wrestled with Elnora's problem while he drove about his business. He was not forced to ask himself what it meant; he knew. The old Corson gang was still holding together. Elder members who had escaped the law had been joined by a younger brother of Jack's, and they met in the thickest of the few remaining fast places of the swamp to drink, gamble, and loaf. Then suddenly, there would be a robbery in some country house where a farmer that day had sold his wheat or corn and not paid a visit to the bank, or in some neighbouring village.

The home of Mrs. Comstock and Elnora adjoined the swamp. Sinton's land lay next, and not another residence or man easy to reach in case of trouble. Whoever wrote that note had some human kindness in his breast, but the fact stood revealed that he feared his strength if Elnora were delivered into his hands. Where had he been the previous night when he heard that prayer? Was that the first time he had been in such proximity? Sinton drove fast, for he wished to reach the swamp before Elnora and the Bird Woman would go there.

At almost four he came to the case, and dropping on his knees studied the ground, every sense alert. He found two or three little heel prints. Those were made by Elnora or the Bird Woman. What Sinton wanted to learn was whether all the remainder were the footprints of one man. It was easily seen, they were not. There were deep, even tracks made by fairly new shoes, and others where a well-worn heel cut deeper on the inside of the print than at the outer edge. Undoubtedly some of Corson's old gang were watching the case, and the visits of the women to it. There was no danger that any one would attack the Bird Woman. She never went to the swamp at night, and on her trips in the daytime, every one knew that she carried a revolver, understood how to use it, and pursued her work in a fearless manner.

Elnora, prowling around the swamp and lured into the interior by the flight of moths and butterflies; Elnora, without father, money, or friends save himself, to defend her—Elnora was a different proposition. For this to happen just when the Limberlost was bringing the very desire of her heart to the girl, it was too bad.

Sinton was afraid for her, yet he did not want to add the burden of fear to Katharine Comstock's trouble, or to disturb the joy of Elnora in her work. He stopped at the cabin and slowly went up the walk. Mrs. Comstock was sitting on the front steps with some sewing. The work seemed to Sinton as if she might be engaged in putting a tuck in a petticoat. He thought of how Margaret had shortened Elnora's dress to the accepted length for girls of her age, and made a mental note of Mrs. Comstock's occupation.

She dropped her work on her lap, laid her hands on it and looked into his face with a sneer.

"You didn't let any grass grow under your feet," she said.

Sinton saw her white, drawn face and comprehended.

"I went to pay a debt and see about this opening of the ditch, Kate."

"You said you were going to prosecute me."

"Good gracious, Kate!" cried Sinton. "Is that what you have been thinking all day? I told you before I left yesterday that I would not need do that. And I won't! We can't afford to quarrel over Elnora. She's all we've got. Now that she has proved that if you don't do just what I think you ought by way of clothes and schooling, she can take care of herself, I put that out of my head. What I came to see you about is a kind of scare I've had to-day. I want to ask you if you ever see anything about the swamp that makes you think the old Corson gang is still at work?"

"Can't say that I do," said Mrs. Comstock. "There's kind of dancing lights there sometimes, but I supposed it was just people passing along the road with lanterns. Folks hereabout are none too fond of the swamp. I hate it like death. I've never stayed here a night in my life without Robert's revolver, clean and loaded, under my pillow, and the shotgun, same condition, by the bed. I can't say that I'm afraid here at home. I'm not. I can take care of myself. But none of the swamp for me!"

"Well, I'm glad you are not afraid, Kate, because I must tell you something. Elnora stopped at the case this morning, and somebody had been into it in the night."

"Broke the lock?"

"No. Used a duplicate key. To-day I heard there was a man here last night. I want to nose around a little."

Sinton went to the east end of the cabin and looked up at the window. There was no way any one could have reached it without a ladder, for the logs were hewed and mortar filled the cracks even. Then he went to the west end, the willow faced him as he turned the corner. He examined the trunk carefully. There was no mistake about small particles of black swamp muck adhering to the sides of the tree. He reached the low branches and climbed the willow. There was earth on the large limb crossing Elnora's window. He stood on it, holding the branch as had been done the night before, and looked into the room. He could see very little, but he knew that if it had been dark outside and sufficiently light for Elnora to study inside he could have seen vividly. He brought his face close to the netting, and he could see the bed with its head to the east, at its foot the table with the candles and the chair before it, and then he knew where the man had been who had heard Elnora's prayer.

Mrs. Comstock had followed around the corner and stood watching him. "Do you think some slinking hulk was up there peekin' in at Elnora?" she demanded indignantly.

"There is muck on the trunk, and plenty on the limb," said Sinton. "Hadn't you better get a saw and let me take this branch off?"

"No, I hadn't," said Mrs. Comstock. "First place, Elnora's climbed from that window on that limb all her life, and it's hers. Second place, no one gets ahead of me after I've had warning. Any crow that perches on that roost again will get its feathers somewhat scattered. Look along the fence, there, and see if you can find where he came in."

The place was easy to find as was a trail leading for some distance west of the cabin.

"You just go home, and don't fret yourself," said Mrs. Comstock. "I'll take care of this. If you should hear the dinner bell at any time in the night you come down. But I wouldn't say anything to Elnora. She better keep her mind on her studies, if she's going to school."

When the work was finished that night Elnora took her books and went to her room to prepare some lessons, but every few minutes she looked toward the swamp to see if there were lights near the case. Mrs. Comstock raked together the coals in the cooking stove, got out the lunch box, and sitting down she studied it grimly. At last she arose.

"Wonder how it would do to show Mag Sinton a frill or two," she murmured.

She went to her room, knelt before a big black-walnut chest and hunted through its contents until she found an old-fashioned cook book. She tended the fire as she read and presently was in action. She first sawed an end from a fragrant, juicy, sugar-cured ham and put it to cook. Then she set a couple of eggs boiling, and after long hesitation began creaming butter and sugar in a crock. An hour later the odour of the ham, mingled with some of the richest spices of "happy Araby," in a combination that could mean nothing save spice cake, crept up to Elnora so strongly that she lifted her head and sniffed amazedly. She would have given all her precious money to have gone down and thrown her arms around her mother's neck, but she did not dare move.

Mrs. Comstock was up early, and without a word handed Elnora the case as she left the next morning.

"Thank you, mother," said Elnora, and went on her way.

She walked down the road looking straight ahead until she came to the corner, where she usually entered the swamp. She paused, glanced that way and smiled. Then she turned and looked back. There was no one coming in any direction. She followed the road until well around the corner, then she stopped and sat on a grassy spot, laid her books beside her and opened the lunch box. Last night's odours had in a measure prepared her for what she would see, but not quite. She scarcely could believe her senses. Half the bread compartment was filled with dainty sandwiches of bread and butter sprinkled with the yolk of egg and the remainder with three large slices of the most fragrant spice cake imaginable. The meat dish contained shaved cold ham, of which she knew the quality, the salad was tomatoes and celery, and the cup held preserved pear, clear as amber. There was milk in the bottle, two tissue-wrapped cucumber pickles in the folding drinking-cup, and a fresh napkin in the ring. No lunch was ever daintier or more palatable; of that Elnora was perfectly sure. And her mother had prepared it for her! "She does love me!" cried the happy girl. "Sure as you're born she loves me; only she hasn't found it out yet!"

She touched the papers daintily, and smiled at the box as if it were a living thing. As she began closing it a breath of air swept by, lifting the covering of the cake. It was like an invitation, and breakfast was several hours away. Elnora picked up a piece and ate it. That cake tasted even better than it looked. Then she tried a sandwich. How did her mother come to think of making them that way. They never had any at home. She slipped out the fork, sampled the salad, and one-quarter of pear. Then she closed the box and started down the road nibbling one of the pickles and trying to decide exactly how happy she was, but she could find no standard high enough for a measure.

She was to go to the Bird Woman's after school for the last load from the case. Saturday she would take the arrow points and specimens to the bank. That would exhaust her present supplies and give her enough money ahead to pay for books, tuition, and clothes for at least two years. She would work early and late gathering nuts. In October she would sell all the ferns she could find. She must collect specimens of all tree leaves before they fell, gather nests and cocoons later, and keep her eyes wide open for anything the grades could use. She would see the superintendent that night about selling specimens to the ward buildings. She must be ahead of any one else if she wanted to furnish these things. So she approached the bridge.

That it was occupied could be seen from a distance. As she came up she found the small boy of yesterday awaiting her with a confident smile.

"We brought you something!" he announced without greeting. "This is Jimmy and Belle—and we brought you a present."

He offered a parcel wrapped in brown paper.

"Why, how lovely of you!" said Elnora. "I supposed you had forgotten me when you ran away so fast yesterday."

"Naw, I didn't forget you," said the boy. "I wouldn't forget you, not ever! Why, I was ist a-hurrying to take them things to Jimmy and Belle. My they was glad!"

Elnora glanced at the children. They sat on the edge of the bridge, obviously clad in a garment each, very dirty and unkept, a little boy and a girl of about seven and nine. Elnora's heart began to ache.

"Say," said the boy. "Ain't you going to look what we have gave you?"

"I thought it wasn't polite to look before people," answered Elnora. "Of course, I will, if you would like to have me."

Elnora opened the package. She had been presented with a quarter of a stale loaf of baker's bread, and a big piece of ancient bologna.

"But don't you want this yourselves?" she asked in surprise.

"Gosh, no! I mean ist no," said the boy. "We always have it. We got stacks this morning. Pa's come out of it now, and he's so sorry he got more 'an ever we can eat. Have you had any before?"

"No," said Elnora, "I never did!"

The boy's eyes brightened and the girl moved restlessly

"We thought maybe you hadn't," said the boy. "First you ever have, you like it real well; but when you don't have anything else for a long time, years an' years, you git so tired." He hitched at the string which held his trousers and watched Elnora speculatively.

"I don't s'pose you'd trade what you got in that box for ist old bread and bologna now, would you? Mebby you'd like it! And I know, I ist know, what you got would taste like heaven to Jimmy and Belle. They never had nothing like that! Not even Belle, and she's most ten! No, sir-ee, they never tasted things like you got!"

It was in Elnora's heart to be thankful for even a taste in time, as she knelt on the bridge, opened the box and divided her lunch into three equal parts, the smaller boy getting most of the milk. Then she told them it was school time and she must go.

"Why don't you put your bread and bologna in the nice box?" asked the boy.

"Of course," said Elnora. "I didn't think."

When the box was arranged to the children's satisfaction all of them accompanied Elnora to the corner where she turned toward the high school.

"Billy," said Elnora, "I would like you much better if you were cleaner. Surely, you have water! Can't you children get some soap and wash yourselves? Gentlemen are never dirty. You want to be a gentleman, don't you?"

"Is being clean all you have to do to be a gentleman?"

"No," said Elnora. "You must not say bad words, and you must be kind and polite to your sister."

"Must Belle be kind and polite to me, else she ain't a lady?"

"Yes."

"Then Belle's no lady!" said Billy succinctly.

Elnora could say nothing more just then, and she bade them good-bye and started them home.

"The poor little souls!" she mused. "I think the Almighty put them in my way to show me real trouble. I won't be likely to spend much time pitying myself while I can see them." She glanced at the lunchbox. "What on earth do I carry this for? I never had anything that was so strictly ornamental! One sure thing! I can't take this stuff to the high school. You never seem to know exactly what is going to happen to you while you are there."

As if to provide a way out of her difficulty a big dog arose from a lawn, and came toward the gate wagging his tail. "If those children ate the stuff, it can't possibly kill him!" thought Elnora, so she offered the bologna. The dog accepted it graciously, and being a beast of pedigree he trotted around to a side porch and laid the bologna before his mistress. The woman snatched it, screaming: "Come, quick! Some one is trying to poison Pedro!" Her daughter came running from the house. "Go see who is on the street. Hurry!" cried the excited mother.

Ellen Brownlee ran and looked. Elnora was half a block away, and no one nearer. Ellen called loudly, and Elnora stopped. Ellen came running toward her.

"Did you see any one give our dog something?" she cried as she approached.

Elnora saw no escape.

"I gave it a piece of bologna myself," she said. "It was fit to eat. It wouldn't hurt the dog."

Ellen stood and looked at her. "Of course, I didn't know it was your dog," explained Elnora. "I had something I wanted to throw to some dog, and that one looked big enough to manage it."

Ellen had arrived at her conclusions. "Pass over that lunch box," she demanded.

"I will not!" said Elnora.

"Then I will have you arrested for trying to poison our dog," laughed the girl as she took the box.

"One chunk of stale bread, one half mile of antique bologna contributed for dog feed; the remains of cake, salad and preserves in an otherwise empty lunch box. One ham sandwich yesterday. I think it's lovely you have the box. Who ate your lunch to-day?"

"Same," confessed Elnora, "but there were three of them this time."

"Wait, until I run back and tell mother about the dog, and get my books."

Elnora waited. That morning she walked down the hall and into the auditorium beside one of the very nicest girls in Onabasha, and it was the fourth day. But the surprise came at noon when Ellen insisted upon Elnora lunching at the Brownlee home, and convulsed her parents and family, and overwhelmed Elnora with a greatly magnified, but moderately accurate history of her lunch box.

"Gee! but it's a box, daddy!" cried the laughing girl. "It's carved leather and fastens with a strap that has her name on it. Inside are trays for things all complete, and it bears evidence of having enclosed delicious food, but Elnora never gets any. She's carried it two days now, and both times it has been empty before she reached school. Isn't that killing?"

"It is, Ellen, in more ways than one. No girl is going to eat breakfast at six o'clock, walk three miles, and do good work without her lunch. You can't tell me anything about that box. I sold it last Monday night to Wesley Sinton, one of my good country customers. He told me it was a present for a girl who was worthy of it, and I see he was right."

"He's so good to me," said Elnora. "Sometimes I look at him and wonder if a neighbour can be so kind to one, what a real father would be like. I envy a girl with a father unspeakably."

"You have cause," said Ellen Brownlee. "A father is the very dearest person in the whole round world, except a mother, who is just a dear." The girl, starting to pay tribute to her father, saw that she must include her mother, and said the thing before she remembered what Mrs. Sinton had told the girls in the store. She stopped in dismay. Elnora's face paled a trifle, but she smiled bravely.

"Then I'm fortunate in having a mother," she said.

Mr. Brownlee lingered at the table after the girls had excused themselves and returned to school.

"There's a girl Ellen can't see too much of, in my opinion," he said. "She is every inch a lady, and not a foolish notion or action about her. I can't understand just what combination of circumstances produced her in this day."

"It has been an unusual case of repression, for one thing. She waits on her elders and thinks before she speaks," said Mrs. Brownlee.

"She's mighty pretty. She looks so sound and wholesome, and she's neatly dressed."

"Ellen says she was a fright the first two days. Long brown calico dress almost touching the floor, and big, lumbering shoes. Those Sinton people bought her clothes. Ellen was in the store, and the woman stopped her crowd and asked them about their dresses. She said the girl was not poor, but her mother was selfish and didn't care for her. But Elnora showed a bank book the next day, and declared that she paid for the things herself, so the Sinton people must just have selected them. There's something peculiar about it, but nothing wrong I am sure. I'll encourage Ellen to ask her again."

"I should say so, especially if she is going to keep on giving away her lunch."

"She lunched with the Bird Woman one day this week."

"She did!"

"Yes, she lives out by the Limberlost. You know the Bird Woman works there a great deal, and probably knows her that way. I think the girl gathers specimens for her. Ellen says she knows more than the teachers about any nature question that comes up, and she is going to lead all of them in mathematics, and make them work in any branch."

When Elnora entered the coat room after having had luncheon with Ellen Brownlee there was such a difference in the atmosphere that she could feel it.

"I am almost sorry I have these clothes," she said to Ellen.

"In the name of sense, why?" cried the astonished girl.

"Every one is so nice to me in them, it sets me to wondering if in time I could have made them be equally friendly in the others."

Ellen looked at her introspectively. "I believe you could," she announced at last. "But it would have taken time and heartache, and your mind would have been less free to work on your studies. No one is happy without friends, and I just simply can't study when I am unhappy."

That night the Bird Woman made the last trip to the swamp. Every specimen she possibly could use had been purchased at a fair price, and three additions had been made to the bank book, carrying the total a little past two hundred dollars.

There remained the Indian relics to sell on Saturday, and Elnora had secured the order to furnish material for nature work for the grades. Life suddenly grew very full. There was the most excitingly interesting work for every hour, and that work was to pay high school expenses and start the college fund. There was one little rift in her joy. All of it would have been so much better if she could have told her mother, and given the money into her keeping; but the struggle to get a start had been so terrible, Elnora was afraid to take the risk. When she reached home, she only told her mother that the last of the things had been sold that evening.

"I think," said Mrs. Comstock, "that we will ask Wesley to move that box over here back of the garden for you. There you are apt to get tolled farther into the swamp than you intend to go, and you might mire or something. There ought to be just the same things in our woods, and along our swampy places, as there are in the Limberlost. Can't you hunt your stuff here?"

"I can try," said Elnora. "I don't know what I can find until I do. Our woods are undisturbed, and there is a possibility they might be even better hunting than the swamp. But I wouldn't have Freckles's case moved for the world. He might come back some day, and not like it. I've tried to keep his room the best I could, and taking out the box would make a big hole in one side of it. Store boxes don't cost much. I will have Uncle Wesley buy me one, and set it up wherever hunting looks the best, early in the spring. I would feel safer at home."

"Shall we do the work or have supper first?"

"Let's do the work," said Elnora. "I can't say that I'm hungry now. Doesn't seem as if I ever could be hungry again with such a lunch. I am quite sure no one carried more delicious things to eat than I."

Mrs. Comstock was pleased. "I put in a pretty good hunk of cake. Did you divide it with any one?"

"Why, yes, I did," admitted Elnora.

"Who?"

This was becoming uncomfortable. "I ate the biggest piece myself," said Elnora, "and gave the rest to a couple of boys named Jimmy and Billy and a girl named Belle. They said it was the very best cake they ever tasted in all their lives."

Mrs. Comstock sat straight. "I used to be a master hand at spice cake," she boasted. "But I'm a little out of practice. I must get to work again. With the very weeds growing higher than our heads, we should raise plenty of good stuff to eat on this land, if we can't afford anything else but taxes."

Elnora laughed and hurried up stairs to change her dress. Margaret Sinton came that night bringing a beautiful blue one in its place, and carried away the other to launder.

"Do you mean to say those dresses are to be washed every two days?" questioned Mrs. Comstock.

"They have to be, to look fresh," replied Margaret. "We want our girl sweet as a rose."

"Well, of all things!" cried Mrs. Comstock. "Every two days! Any girl who can't keep a dress clean longer than that is a dirty girl. You'll wear the goods out and fade the colours with so much washing."

"We'll have a clean girl, anyway."

"Well, if you like the job you can have it," said Mrs. Comstock. "I don't mind the washing, but I'm so inconvenient with an iron."

Elnora sat late that night working over her lessons. The next morning she put on her blue dress and ribbon and in those she was a picture. Mrs. Comstock caught her breath with a queer stirring around her heart, and looked twice to be sure of what she saw. As Elnora gathered her books her mother silently gave her the lunch box.

"Feels heavy," said Elnora gaily. "And smelly! Like as not I'll be called upon to divide again."

"Then you divide!" said Mrs. Comstock. "Eating is the one thing we don't have to economize on, Elnora. Spite of all I can do food goes to waste in this soil every day. If you can give some of those city children a taste of the real thing, why, don't be selfish."

Elnora went down the road thinking of the city children with whom she probably would divide. Of course, the bridge would be occupied again. So she stopped and opened the box.

"I don't want to be selfish," murmured Elnora, "but it really seems as if I can't give away this lunch. If mother did not put love into it, she's substituted something that's likely to fool me."

She almost felt her steps lagging as she approached the bridge. A very hungry dog had been added to the trio of children. Elnora loved all dogs, and as usual, this one came to her in friendliness. The children said "Good morning!" with alacrity, and another paper parcel lay conspicuous.

"How are you this morning?" inquired Elnora.

"All right!" cried the three, while the dog sniffed ravenously at the lunch box, and beat a perfect tattoo with his tail.

"How did you like the bologna?" questioned Billy eagerly.

"One of the girls took me to lunch at her home yesterday," answered Elnora.

Dawn broke beautifully over Billy's streaked face. He caught the package and thrust it toward Elnora.

"Then maybe you'd like to try the bologna to-day!"

The dog leaped in glad apprehension of something, and Belle scrambled to her feet and took a step forward. The look of famished greed in her eyes was more than Elnora could endure. It was not that she cared for the food so much. Good things to eat had been in abundance all her life. She wanted with this lunch to try to absorb what she felt must be an expression of some sort from her mother, and if it were not a manifestation of love, she did not know what to think it. But it was her mother who had said "be generous." She knelt on the bridge. "Keep back the dog!" she warned the elder boy.

She opened the box and divided the milk between Billy and the girl. She gave each a piece of cake leaving one and a sandwich. Billy pressed forward eagerly, bitter disappointment on his face, and the elder boy forgot his charge.

"Aw, I thought they'd be meat!" lamented Billy.

Elnora could not endure that.

"There is!" she said gladly. "There is a little pigeon bird. I want a teeny piece of the breast, for a sort of keepsake, just one bite, and you can have the rest among you."

Elnora drew the knife from its holder and cut off the wishbone. Then she held the bird toward the girl.

"You can divide it," she said. The dog made a bound and seizing the squab sprang from the bridge and ran for life. The girl and boy hurried after him. With awful eyes Billy stared and swore tempestuously. Elnora caught him and clapped her hand over the little mouth. A delivery wagon came tearing down the street, the horse running full speed, passed the fleeing dog with the girl and boy in pursuit, and stopped at the bridge. High school girls began to roll from all sides of it.

"A rescue! A rescue!" they shouted.

It was Ellen Brownlee and her crowd, and every girl of them carried a big parcel. They took in the scene as they approached. The fleeing dog with something in its mouth, the half-naked girl and boy chasing it told the story. Those girls screamed with laughter as they watched the pursuit.

"Thank goodness, I saved the wishbone!" said Elnora "As usual, I can prove that there was a bird." She turned toward the box. Billy had improved the time. He had the last piece of cake in one hand, and the last bite of salad disappeared in one great gulp. Then the girls shouted again.

"Let's have a sample ourselves," suggested one. She caught up the box and handed out the remaining sandwich. Another girl divided it into bites each little over an inch square, and then she lifted the cup lid and deposited a preserved strawberry on each bite. "One, two, three, altogether now!" she cried.

"You old mean things!" screamed Billy.

In an instant he was down in the road and handfuls of dust began to fly among them. The girls scattered before him.

"Billy!" cried Elnora. "Billy! I'll never give you another bite, if you throw dust on any one!"

Then Billy dropped the dust, bored both fists into his eyes, and fled sobbing into Elnora's new blue skirt. She stooped to meet him and consolation began. Those girls laughed on. They screamed and shouted until the little bridge shook.

"To-morrow might as well be a clear day," said Ellen, passing around and feeding the remaining berries to the girls as they could compose themselves enough to take them. "Billy, I admire your taste more than your temper."

Elnora looked up. "The little soul is nothing but skin and bones," she said. "I never was really hungry myself; were any of you?"

"Well, I should say so," cried a plump, rosy girl. "I'm famished right now. Let's have breakfast immediate!"

"We got to refill this box first!" said Ellen Brownlee. "Who's got the butter?" A girl advanced with a wooden tray.

"Put it in the preserve cup, a little strawberry flavour won't hurt it. Next!" called Ellen.

A loaf of bread was produced and Ellen cut off a piece which filled the sandwich box.

"Next!" A bottle of olives was unwrapped. The grocer's boy who was waiting opened that, and Ellen filled the salad dish.

"Next!"

A bag of macaroons was produced and the cake compartment filled.

"Next!"

"I don't suppose this will make quite as good dog feed as a bird," laughed a girl holding open a bag of sliced ham while Ellen filled the meat dish.

"Next!"

A box of candy was handed her and she stuffed every corner of the lunch box with chocolates and nougat. Then it was closed and formally presented to Elnora. The girls each helped themselves to candy and olives, and gave Billy the remainder of the food. Billy took one bite of ham, and approved. Belle and Jimmy had given up chasing the dog, and angry and ashamed, stood waiting half a block away.

"Come back!" cried Billy. "You great big dunces, come back! They's a new kind of meat, and cake and candy."

The boy delayed, but the girl joined Billy. Ellen wiped her fingers, stepped to the cement abutment and began reciting "Horatio at the Bridge!" substituting Elnora wherever the hero appeared in the lines.

Elnora gathered up the sacks, and gave them to Belle, telling her to take the food home, cut and spread the bread, set things on the table, and eat nicely.

Then Elnora was taken into the wagon with the girls, and driven on the run to the high school. They sang a song beginning—

"Elnora, please give me a sandwich.
I'm ashamed to ask for cake!"

as they went. Elnora did not know it, but that was her initiation. She belonged to "the crowd." She only knew that she was happy, and vaguely wondered what her mother and Aunt Margaret would have said about the proceedings.

Chapter 7

Wherein Mrs. Comstock Manipulates Margaret and Billy Acquires a Residence

Saturday morning Elnora helped her mother with the work. When she had finished Mrs. Comstock told her to go to Sintons' and wash her Indian relics, so that she would be ready to accompany Wesley to town in the afternoon. Elnora hurried down the road and was soon at the cistern with a tub busily washing arrow points, stone axes, tubes, pipes, and skin-cleaning implements.

Then she went home, dressed and was waiting when the carriage reached the gate. She stopped at the bank with the box, and Sinton went to do his marketing and some shopping for his wife.

At the dry goods store Mr. Brownlee called to him, "Hello, Sinton! How do you like the fate of your lunch box?" Then he began to laugh—

"I always hate to see a man laughing alone," said Sinton. "It looks so selfish! Tell me the fun, and let me help you."

Mr. Brownlee wiped his eyes.

"I supposed you knew, but I see she hasn't told."

Then the three days' history of the lunch box was repeated with particulars which included the dog.

"Now laugh!" concluded Mr. Brownlee.

"Blest if I see anything funny!" replied Wesley Sinton. "And if you had bought that box and furnished one of those lunches yourself, you wouldn't either. I call such a work a shame! I'll have it stopped."

"Some one must see to that, all right. They are little leeches. Their father earns enough to support them, but they have no mother, and they run wild. I suppose they are crazy for cooked food. But it is funny, and when you think it over you will see it, if you don't now."

"About where would a body find that father?" inquired Wesley Sinton grimly. Mr. Brownlee told him and he started, locating the house with little difficulty.

House was the proper word, for of home there was no sign. Just a small empty house with three unkept little children racing through and around it. The girl and the elder boy hung back, but dirty little Billy greeted Sinton with: "What you want here?"

"I want to see your father," said Sinton.

"Well, he's asleep," said Billy.

"Where?" asked Sinton.

"In the house," answered Billy, "and you can't wake him."

"Well, I'll try," said Wesley.

Billy led the way. "There he is!" he said. "He is drunk again."

On a dirty mattress in a corner lay a man who appeared to be strong and well. Billy was right. You could not awake him. He had gone the limit, and a little beyond.

He was now facing eternity. Sinton went out and closed the door.

"Your father is sick and needs help," he said. "You stay here, and I will send a man to see him."

"If you just let him 'lone, he'll sleep it off," volunteered Billy. "He's that way all the time, but he wakes up and gets us something to eat after awhile. Only waitin' twists you up inside pretty bad."

The boy wore no air of complaint. He was merely stating facts.

Wesley Sinton looked intently at Billy. "Are you twisted up inside now?" he asked.

Billy laid a grimy hand on the region of his stomach and the filthy little waist sank close to the backbone. "Bet yer life, boss," he said cheerfully.

"How long have you been twisted?" asked Sinton.

Billy appealed to the others. "When was it we had the stuff on the bridge?"

"Yesterday morning," said the girl.

"Is that all gone?" asked Sinton.

"She went and told us to take it home," said Billy ruefully, "and 'cos she said to, we took it. Pa had come back, he was drinking some more, and he ate a lot of it—almost the whole thing, and it made him sick as a dog, and he went and wasted all of it. Then he got drunk some more, and now he's asleep again. We didn't get hardly none."

"You children sit on the steps until the man comes," said Sinton. "I'll send you some things to eat with him. What's your name, sonny?"

"Billy," said the boy.

"Well, Billy, I guess you better come with me. I'll take care of him," Sinton promised the others. He reached a hand to Billy.

"I ain't no baby, I'm a boy!" said Billy, as he shuffled along beside Sinton, taking a kick at every movable object without regard to his battered toes.

Once they passed a Great Dane dog lolling after its master, and Billy ascended Sinton as if he were a tree, and clung to him with trembling hot hands.

"I ain't afraid of that dog," scoffed Billy, as he was again placed on the walk, "but onc't he took me for a rat or somepin' and his teeth cut into my back. If I'd a done right, I'd a took the law on him."

Sinton looked down into the indignant little face. The child was bright enough, he had a good head, but oh, such a body!

"I 'bout got enough of dogs," said Billy. "I used to like 'em, but I'm getting pretty tired. You ought to seen the lickin' Jimmy and Belle and me give our dog when we caught him, for taking a little bird she gave us. We waited 'till he was asleep 'nen laid a board on him and all of us jumped on it to onc't. You could a heard him yell a mile. Belle said mebbe we could squeeze the bird out of him. But, squeeze nothing! He was holler as us, and that bird was lost long 'fore it got to his stummick. It was ist a little one, anyway. Belle said it wouldn't 'a' made a bite apiece for three of us nohow, and the dog got one good swaller. We didn't get much of the meat, either. Pa took most of that. Seems like pas and dogs gets everything."

Billy laughed dolefully. Involuntarily Wesley Sinton reached his hand. They were coming into the business part of Onabasha and the streets were crowded. Billy understood it to mean that he might lose his companion and took a grip. That little hot hand clinging tight to his, the sore feet recklessly scouring the walk, the hungry child panting for breath as he tried to keep even, the brave soul jesting in the face of hard luck, caught Sinton in a tender, empty spot.

"Say, son," he said. "How would you like to be washed clean, and have all the supper your skin could hold, and sleep in a good bed?"

"Aw, gee!" said Billy. "I ain't dead yet! Them things is in heaven! Poor folks can't have them. Pa said so."

"Well, you can have them if you want to go with me and get them," promised Sinton.

"Honest?"

"Yes, honest."

"Crost yer heart?"

"Yes," said Sinton.

"Kin I take some to Jimmy and Belle?"

"If you'll come with me and be my boy, I'll see that they have plenty."

"What will Pa say?"

"Your pa is in that kind of sleep now where he won't wake up, Billy," said Sinton. "I am pretty sure the law will give you to me, if you want to come."

"When people don't ever wake up they're dead," announced Billy. "Is my pa dead?"

"Yes, he is," answered Sinton.

"And you'll take care of Jimmy and Belle, too?"

"I can't adopt all three of you," said Sinton. "I'll take you, and see that they are well provided for. Will you come?"

"Yep, I'll come," said Billy. "Let's eat, first thing we do."

"All right," agreed Sinton. "Come into this restaurant." He lifted Billy to the lunch counter and ordered the clerk to give him as many glasses of milk as he wanted, and a biscuit. "I think there's going to be fried chicken when we get home, Billy," he said, "so you just take the edge off now, and fill up later."

While Billy lunched Sinton called up the different departments and notified the proper authorities ending with the Women's Relief Association. He sent a basket of food to Belle and Jimmy, bought Billy a pair of trousers, and a shirt, and went to bring Elnora.

"Why, Uncle Wesley!" cried the girl. "Where did you find Billy?"

"I've adopted him for the time being, if not longer," replied Wesley Sinton.

"Where did you get him?"

"Well, young woman," said Wesley Sinton, "Mr. Brownlee told me the history of your lunch box. It didn't seem so funny to me as it does to the rest of them; so I went to look up the father of Billy's family, and make him take care of them, or allow the law to do it for him. It will have to be the law."

"He's deader than anything!" broke in Billy. "He can't ever take all the meat any more."

"Billy!" gasped Elnora.

"Never you mind!" said Sinton. "A child doesn't say such things about a father who loved and raised him right. When it happens, the father alone is to blame. You won't hear Billy talk like that about me when I cross over."

"You don't mean you are going to take him to keep!"

"I'll soon need help," said Wesley. "Billy will come in just about right ten years from now, and if I raise him I'll have him the way I want him."

"But Aunt Margaret doesn't like boys," objected Elnora.

"Well, she likes me, and I used to be a boy. Anyway, as I remember she has had her way about everything at our house ever since we were married. I am going to please myself about Billy. Hasn't she always done just as she chose so far as you know? Honest, Elnora!"

"Honest!" replied Elnora. "You are beautiful to all of us, Uncle Wesley; but Aunt Margaret won't like Billy. She won't want him in her home."

"In our home," corrected Wesley.

"What makes you want him?" marvelled Elnora.

"God only knows," said Sinton. "Billy ain't so beautiful, and he ain't so smart, I guess it's because he's so human. My heart goes out to him."

"So did mine," said Elnora. "I love him. I'd rather see him eat my lunch than have it myself any time."

"What makes you like him?" asked Wesley.

"Why, I don't know," pondered Elnora. "He's so little, he needs so much, he's got such splendid grit, and he's perfectly unselfish with his brother and sister. But we must wash him before Aunt Margaret sees him. I wonder if mother—"

"You needn't bother. I'm going to take him home the way he is," said Sinton. "I want Maggie to see the worst of it."

"I'm afraid—" began Elnora.

"So am I," said Wesley, "but I won't give him up. He's taken a sort of grip on my heart. I've always been crazy for a boy. Don't let him hear us."

"Don't let him be killed!" cried Elnora. During their talk Billy had wandered to the edge of the walk and barely escaped the wheels of a passing automobile in an effort to catch a stray kitten that seemed in danger.

Wesley drew Billy back to the walk, and held his hand closely. "Are you ready, Elnora?"

"Yes; you were gone a long time," she said.

Wesley glanced at a package she carried. "Have to have another book?" he asked.

"No, I bought this for mother. I've had such splendid luck selling my specimens, I didn't feel right about keeping all the money for myself, so I saved enough from the Indian relics to get a few things I wanted. I would have liked to have gotten her a dress, but I didn't dare, so I compromised on a book."

"What did you select, Elnora?" asked Wesley wonderingly.

"Well," said she, "I have noticed mother always seemed interested in anything Mark Twain wrote in the newspapers, and I thought it would cheer her up a little, so I just got his 'Innocents Abroad.' I haven't read it myself, but I've seen mention made of it all my life, and the critics say it's genuine fun."

"Good!" cried Sinton. "Good! You've made a splendid choice. It will take her mind off herself a lot. But she will scold you."

"Of course," assented Elnora. "But, possibly she will read it, and feel better. I'm going to serve her a trick. I am going to hide it until Monday, and set it on her little shelf of books the last thing before I go away. She must have all of them by heart. When she sees a new one she can't help being glad, for she loves to read, and if she has all day to become interested, maybe she'll like it so she won't scold so much."

"We are both in for it, but I guess we are prepared. I don't know what Margaret will say, but I'm going to take Billy home and see. Maybe he can win with her, as he did with us."

Elnora had doubts, but she did not say anything more. When they started home Billy sat on the front seat. He drove with the hitching strap tied to the railing of the dash-board, flourished the whip, and yelled with delight. At first Sinton laughed with him, but by the time he left Elnora with several packages at her gate, he was looking serious enough.

Margaret was at the door as they drove up the lane. Wesley left Billy in the carriage, hitched the horses and went to explain to her. He had not reached her before she cried, "Look, Wesley, that child! You'll have a runaway!"

Wesley looked and ran. Billy was standing in the carriage slashing the mettlesome horses with the whip.

"See me make 'em go!" he shouted as the whip fell a second time.

He did make them go. They took the hitching post and a few fence palings, which scraped the paint from a wheel. Sinton missed the lines at the first effort, but the dragging post impeded the horses, and he soon caught them. He led them to the barn, and ordered Billy to remain in the carriage while he unhitched. Then leading Billy and carrying his packages he entered the yard.

"You run play a few minutes, Billy," he said. "I want to talk to the nice lady."

The nice lady was looking rather stupefied as Wesley approached her.

"Where in the name of sense did you get that awful child?" she demanded.

"He is a young gentleman who has been stopping Elnora and eating her lunch every day, part of the time with the assistance of his brother and sister, while our girl went hungry. Brownlee told me about it at the store. It's happened three days running. The first time she went without anything, the second time Brownlee's girl took her to lunch, and the third a crowd of high school girls bought a lot of stuff and met them at the bridge. The youngsters seemed to think they could rob her every day, so I went to see their father about having it stopped."

"Well, I should think so!" cried Margaret.

"There were three of them, Margaret," said Wesley, "that little fellow—"

"Hyena, you mean," interpolated Margaret.

"Hyena," corrected Wesley gravely, "and another boy and a girl, all equally dirty and hungry. The man was dead. They thought he was in a drunken sleep, but he was stone dead. I brought the little boy with me, and sent the officers and other help to the house. He's half starved. I want to wash him, and put clean clothes on him, and give him some supper."

"Have you got anything to put on him?"

"Yes."

"Where did you get it?"

"Bought it. It ain't much. All I got didn't cost a dollar."

"A dollar is a good deal when you work and save for it the way we do."

"Well, I don't know a better place to put it. Have you got any hot water? I'll use this tub at the cistern. Please give me some soap and towels."

Instead Margaret pushed by him with a shriek. Billy had played by producing a cord from his pocket, and having tied the tails of Margaret's white kittens together, he had climbed on a box and hung them across the clothes line. Wild with fright the kittens were clawing each other to death, and the air was white with fur. The string had twisted and the frightened creatures could not recognize friends. Margaret stepped back with bleeding hands. Sinton cut the cord with his knife and the poor little cats raced under the house bleeding and disfigured. Margaret white with wrath faced Wesley.

"If you don't hitch up and take that animal back to town," she said, "I will."

Billy threw himself on the grass and began to scream.

"You said I could have fried chicken for supper," he wailed. "You said she was a nice lady!"

Wesley lifted him and something in his manner of handling the child infuriated Margaret. His touch was so gentle. She reached for Billy and gripped his shirt collar in the back. Wesley's hand closed over hers.

"Gently, girl!" he said. "This little body is covered with sores."

"Sores!" she ejaculated. "Sores? What kind of sores?"

"Oh, they might be from bruises made by fists or boot toes, or they might be bad blood, from wrong eating, or they might be pure filth. Will you hand me some towels?"

"No, I won't!" said Margaret.

"Well, give me some rags, then."

Margaret compromised on pieces of old tablecloth. Wesley led Billy to the cistern, pumped cold water into the tub, poured in a kettle of hot, and beginning at the head scoured him. The boy shut his little teeth, and said never a word though he twisted occasionally when the soap struck a raw spot. Margaret watched the process from the window in amazed and ever-increasing anger. Where did Wesley learn it? How could his big hands be so gentle? He came to the door.

"Have you got any peroxide?" he asked.

"A little," she answered stiffly.

"Well, I need about a pint, but I'll begin on what you have."

Margaret handed him the bottle. Wesley took a cup, weakened the drug and said to Billy: "Man, these sores on you must be healed. Then you must eat the kind of food that's fit for little men. I am going to put some medicine on you, and it is going to sting like fire. If it just runs off, I won't use any more. If it boils, there is poison in these places, and they must be tied up, dosed every day, and you must be washed, and kept mighty clean. Now, hold still, because I am going to put it on."

"I think the one on my leg is the worst," said the undaunted Billy, holding out a raw place. Sinton poured on the drug. Billy's body twisted and writhed, but he did not run.

"Gee, look at it boil!" he cried. "I guess they's poison. You'll have to do it to all of them."

Wesley's teeth were set, as he watched the boy's face. He poured the drug, strong enough to do effective work, on a dozen places over that little body and bandaged all he could. Billy's lips quivered at times, and his chin jumped, but he did not shed a tear or utter a sound other than to take a deep interest in the boiling. As Wesley put the small shirt on the boy, and fastened the trousers, he was ready to reset the hitching post and mend the fence without a word.

"Now am I clean?" asked Billy.

"Yes, you are clean outside," said Wesley. "There is some dirty blood in your body, and some bad words in your mouth, that we have to get out, but that takes time. If we put right things to eat into your stomach that will do away with the sores, and if you know that I don't like bad words you won't say them any oftener than you can help, will you Billy?"

Billy leaned against Wesley in apparent indifference.

"I want to see me!" he demanded.

Wesley led the boy into the house, and lifted him to a mirror.

"My, I'm purty good-looking, ain't I?" bragged Billy. Then as Wesley stooped to set him on the floor Billy's lips passed close to the big man's ear and hastily whispered a vehement "No!" as he ran for the door.

"How long until supper, Margaret?" asked Wesley as he followed.

"You are going to keep him for supper?" she asked

"Sure!" said Wesley. "That's what I brought him for. It's likely he never had a good square meal of decent food in his life. He's starved to the bone."

Margaret arose deliberately, removed the white cloth from the supper table and substituted an old red one she used to wrap the bread. She put away the pretty dishes they commonly used and set the table with old plates for pies and kitchen utensils. But she fried the chicken, and was generous with milk and honey, snowy bread, gravy, potatoes, and fruit.

Wesley repainted the scratched wheel. He mended the fence, with Billy holding the nails and handing the pickets. Then he filled the old hole, digged a new one and set the hitching post.

Billy hopped on one foot at his task of holding the post steady as the earth was packed around it. There was not the shadow of a trouble on his little freckled face.

Sinton threw in stones and pounded the earth solid around the post. The sound of a gulping sob attracted him to Billy. The tears were rolling down his cheeks. "If I'd a knowed you'd have to get down in a hole, and work so hard I wouldn't 'a' hit the horses," he said.

"Never you mind, Billy," said Wesley. "You will know next time, so you can think over it, and make up your mind whether you really want to before you strike."

Wesley went to the barn to put away the tools. He thought Billy was at his heels, but the boy lagged on the way. A big snowy turkey gobbler resented the small intruder in his especial preserves, and with spread tail and dragging wings came toward him threateningly. If that turkey gobbler had known the sort of things with which Billy was accustomed to holding his own, he never would have issued the challenge. Billy accepted instantly. He danced around with stiff arms at his sides and imitated the gobbler. Then came his opportunity, and he jumped on the big turkey's back. Wesley heard Margaret's scream in time to see the flying leap and admire its dexterity. The turkey tucked its tail and scampered. Billy slid from its back and as he fell he clutched wildly, caught the folded tail, and instinctively clung to it. The turkey gave one scream and relaxed its muscles. Then it fled in disfigured defeat to the haystack. Billy scrambled to his feet holding the tail, while his eyes were bulging.

"Why, the blasted old thing came off!" he said to Wesley, holding out the tail in amazed wonder.

The man, caught suddenly, forgot everything and roared. Seeing which, Billy thought a turkey tail of no account and flung that one high above him shouting in wild childish laughter, when the feathers scattered and fell.

Margaret, watching, began to cry. Wesley had gone mad. For the first time in her married life she wanted to tell her mother. When Wesley had waited until he was so hungry he could wait no longer he invaded the kitchen to find a cooked supper baking on the back of the stove, while Margaret with red eyes nursed a pair of demoralized white kittens.

"Is supper ready?" he asked.

"It has been for an hour," answered Margaret.

"Why didn't you call us?"

That "us" had too much comradeship in it. It irritated Margaret.

"I supposed it would take you even longer than this to fix things decent again. As for my turkey, and my poor little kittens, they don't matter."

"I am mighty sorry about them, Margaret, you know that. Billy is very bright, and he will soon learn—"

"Soon learn!" cried Margaret. "Wesley Sinton, you don't mean to say that you think of keeping that creature here for some time?"

"No, I think of keeping a well-behaved little boy."

Margaret set the supper on the table. Seeing the old red cloth Wesley stared in amazement. Then he understood. Billy capered around in delight.

"Ain't that pretty?" he exulted. "I wish Jimmy and Belle could see. We, why we ist eat out of our hands or off a old dry goods box, and when we fix up a lot, we have newspaper. We ain't ever had a nice red cloth like this."

Wesley looked straight at Margaret, so intently that she turned away, her face flushing. He stacked the dictionary and the geography of the world on a chair, and lifted Billy beside him. He heaped a plate generously, cut the food, put a fork into Billy's little fist, and made him eat slowly and properly. Billy did his best. Occasionally greed overcame him, and he used his left hand to pop a bite into his mouth with his fingers. These lapses Wesley patiently overlooked, and went on with his general instructions. Luckily Billy did not spill anything on his clothing or the cloth. After supper Wesley took him to the barn while he finished the night work. Then he went and sat beside Margaret on the front porch. Billy appropriated the hammock, and swung by pulling a rope tied around a tree. The very energy with which he went at the work of swinging himself appealed to Wesley.

"Mercy, but he's an active little body," he said. "There isn't a lazy bone in him. See how he works to pay for his fun."

"There goes his foot through it!" cried Margaret. "Wesley, he shall not ruin my hammock."

"Of course he shan't!" said Wesley. "Wait, Billy, let me show you."

Thereupon he explained to Billy that ladies wearing beautiful white dresses sat in hammocks, so little boys must not put their dusty feet in them. Billy immediately sat, and allowed his feet to swing.

"Margaret," said Wesley after a long silence on the porch, "isn't it true that if Billy had been a half-starved sore cat, dog, or animal of any sort, that you would have pitied, and helped care for it, and been glad to see me get any pleasure out of it I could?"

"Yes," said Margaret coldly.

"But because I brought a child with an immortal soul, there is no welcome."

"That isn't a child, it's an animal."

"You just said you would have welcomed an animal."

"Not a wild one. I meant a tame beast."

"Billy is not a beast!" said Wesley hotly. "He is a very dear little boy. Margaret, you've always done the church-going and Bible reading for this family. How do you reconcile that 'Suffer little children to come unto Me' with the way you are treating Billy?"

Margaret arose. "I haven't treated that child. I have only let him alone. I can barely hold myself. He needs the hide tanned about off him!"

"If you'd cared to look at his body, you'd know that you couldn't find a place to strike without cutting into a raw spot," said Wesley. "Besides, Billy has not done a thing for which a child should be punished. He is only full of life, no training, and with a boy's love of mischief. He did abuse your kittens, but an hour before I saw him risk his life to save one from being run over. He minds what you tell him, and doesn't do anything he is told not to. He thinks of his brother and sister right away when anything pleases him. He took that stinging medicine with the grit of a bulldog. He is just a bully little chap, and I love him."

"Oh good heavens!" cried Margaret, going into the house as she spoke.

Sinton sat still. At last Billy tired of the swing, came to him and leaned his slight body against the big knee.

"Am I going to sleep here?" he asked.

"Sure you are!" said Sinton.

Billy swung his feet as he laid across Wesley's knee. "Come on," said Wesley, "I must clean you up for bed."

"You have to be just awful clean here," announced Billy. "I like to be clean, you feel so good, after the hurt is over."

Sinton registered that remark, and worked with especial tenderness as he redressed the ailing places and washed the dust from Billy's feet and hands.

"Where can he sleep?" he asked Margaret.

"I'm sure I don't know," she answered.

"Oh, I can sleep ist any place," said Billy. "On the floor or anywhere. Home, I sleep on pa's coat on a store-box, and Jimmy and Belle they sleep on the storebox, too. I sleep between them, so's I don't roll off and crack my head. Ain't you got a storebox and a old coat?"

Wesley arose and opened a folding lounge. Then he brought an armload of clean horse blankets from a closet.

"These don't look like the nice white bed a little boy should have, Billy," he said, "but we'll make them do. This will beat a storebox all hollow."

Billy took a long leap for the lounge. When he found it bounced, he proceeded to bounce, until he was tired. By that time the blankets had to be refolded. Wesley had Billy take one end and help, while both of them seemed to enjoy the job. Then Billy lay down and curled up in his clothes like a small dog. But sleep would not come.

Finally he sat up. He stared around restlessly. Then he arose, went to Wesley, and leaned against his knee. He picked up the boy and folded his arms around him. Billy sighed in rapturous content.

"That bed feels so lost like," he said. "Jimmy always jabbed me on one side, and Belle on the other, and so I knew I was there. Do you know where they are?"

"They are with kind people who gave them a fine supper, a clean bed, and will always take good care of them."

"I wisht I was—" Billy hesitated and looked earnestly at Wesley. "I mean I wish they was here."

"You are about all I can manage, Billy," said Wesley.

Billy sat up. "Can't she manage anything?" he asked, waving toward Margaret.

"Indeed, yes," said Wesley. "She has managed me for twenty years."

"My, but she made you nice!" said Billy. "I just love you. I wisht she'd take Jimmy and Belle and make them nice as you."

"She isn't strong enough to do that, Billy. They will grow into a good boy and girl where they are."

Billy slid from Wesley's arms and walked toward Margaret until he reached the middle of the room. Then he stopped, and at last sat on the floor. Finally he lay down and closed his eyes. "This feels more like my bed; if only Jimmy and Belle was here to crowd up a little, so it wasn't so alone like."

"Won't I do, Billy?" asked Wesley in a husky voice.

Billy moved restlessly. "Seems like—seems like toward night as if a body got kind o' lonesome for a woman person—like her."

Billy indicated Margaret and then closed his eyes so tight his small face wrinkled.

Soon he was up again. "Wisht I had Snap," he said. "Oh, I ist wisht I had Snap!"

"I thought you laid a board on Snap and jumped on it," said Wesley.

"We did!" cried Billy. "Oh, you ought to heard him squeal!" Billy laughed loudly, then his face clouded.

"But I want Snap to lay beside me so bad now—that if he was here I'd give him a piece of my chicken, 'fore I ate any. Do you like dogs?"

"Yes, I do," said Wesley.

Billy was up instantly. "Would you like Snap?"

"I am sure I would," said Wesley.

"Would she?" Billy indicated Margaret. And then he answered his own question. "But of course, she wouldn't, cos she likes cats, and dogs chases cats. Oh, dear, I thought for a minute maybe Snap could come here." Billy lay down and closed his eyes resolutely.

Suddenly they flew open. "Does it hurt to be dead?" he demanded.

"Nothing hurts you after you are dead, Billy," said Wesley.

"Yes, but I mean does it hurt getting to be dead?"

"Sometimes it does. It did not hurt your father, Billy. It came softly while he was asleep."

"It ist came softly?"

"Yes."

"I kind o' wisht he wasn't dead!" said Billy. "'Course I like to stay with you, and the fried chicken, and the nice soft bed, and—and everything, and I like to be clean, but he took us to the show, and he got us gum, and he never hurt us when he wasn't drunk."

Billy drew a deep breath, and tightly closed his eyes. But very soon they opened. Then he sat up. He looked at Wesley pitifully, and then he glanced at Margaret. "You don't like boys, do you?" he questioned.

"I like good boys," said Margaret.

Billy was at her knee instantly. "Well say, I'm a good boy!" he announced joyously.

"I do not think boys who hurt helpless kittens and pull out turkeys' tails are good boys."

"Yes, but I didn't hurt the kittens," explained Billy. "They got mad 'bout ist a little fun and scratched each other. I didn't s'pose they'd act like that. And I didn't pull the turkey's tail. I ist held on to the first thing I grabbed, and the turkey pulled. Honest, it was the turkey pulled." He turned to Wesley. "You tell her! Didn't the turkey pull? I didn't know its tail was loose, did I?"

"I don't think you did, Billy," said Wesley.

Billy stared into Margaret's cold face. "Sometimes at night, Belle sits on the floor, and I lay my head in her lap. I could pull up a chair and lay my head in your lap. Like this, I mean." Billy pulled up a chair, climbed on it and laid his head on Margaret's lap. Then he shut his eyes again. Margaret could have looked little more repulsed if he had been a snake. Billy was soon up.

"My, but your lap is hard," he said. "And you are a good deal fatter 'an Belle, too!" He slid from the chair and came back to the middle of the room.

"Oh but I wisht he wasn't dead!" he cried. The flood broke and Billy screamed in desperation.

Out of the night a soft, warm young figure flashed through the door and with a swoop caught him in her arms. She dropped into a chair, nestled him closely, drooped her fragrant brown head over his little bullet-eyed red one, and rocked softly while she crooned over him—

"Billy, boy, where have you been?
Oh, I have been to seek a wife,
She's the joy of my life,
But then she's a young thing and she can't leave her mammy!"

Billy clung to her frantically. Elnora wiped his eyes, kissed his face, swayed, and sang.

"Why aren't you asleep?" she asked at last.

"I don't know," said Billy. "I tried. I tried awful hard cos I thought he wanted me to, but it ist wouldn't come. Please tell her I tried." He appealed to Margaret.

"He did try to go to sleep," admitted Margaret.

"Maybe he can't sleep in his clothes," suggested Elnora. "Haven't you an old dressing sacque? I could roll the sleeves."

Margaret got an old sacque, and Elnora put it on Billy. Then she brought a basin of water and bathed his face and head. She gathered him up and began to rock again.

"Have you got a pa?" asked Billy.

"No," said Elnora.

"Is he dead like mine?"

"Yes."

"Did it hurt him to die?"

"I don't know."

Billy was wide awake again. "It didn't hurt my pa," he boasted. "He ist died while he was asleep. He didn't even know it was coming."

"I am glad of that," said Elnora, pressing the small head against her breast again.

Billy escaped her hand and sat up. "I guess I won't go to sleep," he said. "It might 'come softly' and get me."

"It won't get you, Billy," said Elnora, rocking and singing between sentences. "It doesn't get little boys. It just takes big people who are sick."

"Was my pa sick?"

"Yes," said Elnora. "He had a dreadful sickness inside him that burned, and made him drink things. That was why he would forget his little boys and girl. If he had

271

been well, he would have gotten you good things to eat, clean clothes, and had the most fun with you."

Billy leaned against her and closed his eyes, and Elnora rocked hopefully.

"If I was dead would you cry?" he was up again.

"Yes, I would," said Elnora, gripping him closer until Billy almost squealed with the embrace.

"Do you love me tight as that?" he questioned blissfully.

"Yes, bushels and bushels," said Elnora. "Better than any little boy in the whole world."

Billy looked at Margaret. "She don't!" he said. "She'd be glad if it would get me 'softly,' right now. She don't want me here 't all."

Elnora smothered his face against her breast and rocked.

"You love me, don't you?"

"I will, if you will go to sleep."

"Every single day you will give me your dinner for the bologna, won't you," said Billy.

"Yes, I will," replied Elnora. "But you will have as good lunch as I do after this. You will have milk, eggs, chicken, all kinds of good things, little pies, and cakes, maybe."

Billy shook his head. "I am going back home soon as it is light," he said. "She don't want me. She thinks I'm a bad boy. She's going to whip me—if he lets her. She said so. I heard her. Oh, I wish he hadn't died! I want to go home." Billy shrieked again.

Mrs. Comstock had started to walk slowly to meet Elnora. The girl had been so late that her mother reached the Sinton gate and followed the path until the picture inside became visible. Elnora had told her about Wesley taking Billy home. Mrs. Comstock had some curiosity to see how Margaret bore the unexpected addition to her family. Billy's voice, raised with excitement, was plainly audible. She could see Elnora holding him, and hear his excited wail. Wesley's face was drawn and haggard, and Margaret's set and defiant. A very imp of perversity entered the breast of Mrs. Comstock.

"Hoity, toity!" she said as she suddenly appeared in the door. "Blest if I ever heard a man making sounds like that before!"

Billy ceased suddenly. Mrs. Comstock was tall, angular, and her hair was prematurely white. She was only thirty-six, although she appeared fifty. But there was an expression on her usually cold face that was attractive just then, and Billy was in search of attractions.

"Have I stayed too late, mother?" asked Elnora anxiously. "I truly intended to come straight back, but I thought I could rock Billy to sleep first. Everything is strange, and he's so nervous."

"Is that your ma?" demanded Billy.

"Yes."

"Does she love you?"

"Of course!"

"My mother didn't love me," said Billy. "She went away and left me, and never came back. She don't care what happens to me. You wouldn't go away and leave your little girl, would you?" questioned Billy.

"No," said Katharine Comstock, "and I wouldn't leave a little boy, either."

Billy began sliding from Elnora's knees.

"Do you like boys?" he questioned.

"If there is anything I love it is a boy," said Mrs. Comstock assuringly. Billy was on the floor.

"Do you like dogs?"

"Yes. Almost as well as boys. I am going to buy a dog as soon as I can find a good one."

Billy swept toward her with a whoop.

"Do you want a boy?" he shouted.

Katharine Comstock stretched out her arms, and gathered him in.

"Of course, I want a boy!" she rejoiced.

"Maybe you'd like to have me?" offered Billy.

"Sure I would," triumphed Mrs. Comstock. "Any one would like to have you. You are just a real boy, Billy."

"Will you take Snap?"

"I'd like to have Snap almost as well as you."

"Mother!" breathed Elnora imploringly. "Don't! Oh, don't! He thinks you mean it!"

"And so I do mean it," said Mrs. Comstock. "I'll take him in a jiffy. I throw away enough to feed a little tyke like him every day. His chatter would be great company while you are gone. Blood soon can be purified with right food and baths, and as for Snap, I meant to buy a bulldog, but possibly Snap will serve just as well. All I ask of a dog is to bark at the right time. I'll do the rest. Would you like to come and be my boy, Billy?"

Billy leaned against Mrs. Comstock, reached his arms around her neck and gripped her with all his puny might. "You can whip me all you want to," he said. "I won't make a sound."

Mrs. Comstock held him closely and her hard face was softening; of that there could be no doubt.

"Now, why would any one whip a nice little boy like you?" she asked wonderingly.

"She"—Billy from his refuge waved toward Margaret—"she was going to whip me 'cause her cats fought, when I tied their tails together and hung them over the line to dry. How did I know her old cats would fight?"

Mrs. Comstock began to laugh suddenly, and try as she would she could not stop so soon as she desired. Billy studied her.

"Have you got turkeys?" he demanded.

"Yes, flocks of them," said Mrs. Comstock, vainly struggling to suppress her mirth, and settle her face in its accustomed lines.

"Are their tails fast?" demanded Billy.

"Why, I think so," marvelled Mrs. Comstock.

"Hers ain't!" said Billy with the wave toward Margaret that was becoming familiar. "Her turkey pulled, and its tail comed right off. She's going to whip me if he lets her. I didn't know the turkey would pull. I didn't know its tail would come off. I won't ever touch one again, will I?"

"Of course, you won't," said Mrs. Comstock. "And what's more, I don't care if you do! I'd rather have a fine little man like you than all the turkeys in the country. Let them lose their old tails if they want to, and let the cats fight. Cats and turkeys don't compare with boys, who are going to be fine big men some of these days."

Then Billy and Mrs. Comstock hugged each other rapturously, while their audience stared in silent amazement.

"You like boys!" exulted Billy, and his head dropped against Mrs. Comstock in unspeakable content.

"Yes, and if I don't have to carry you the whole way home, we must start right now," said Mrs. Comstock. "You are going to be asleep before you know it."

Billy opened his eyes and braced himself. "I can walk," he said proudly.

"All right, we must start. Come, Elnora! Good-night, folks!" Mrs. Comstock set Billy on the floor, and arose gripping his hand. "You take the other side, Elnora, and we will help him as much as we can," she said.

Elnora stared piteously at Margaret, then at Wesley, and arose in white-faced bewilderment.

"Billy, are you going to leave without even saying good-bye to me?" asked Wesley, with a gulp.

Billy held tight to Mrs. Comstock and Elnora.

"Good-bye!" he said casually. "I'll come and see you some time."

Wesley Sinton gave a smothered sob, and strode from the room.

Mrs. Comstock started toward the door, dragging at Billy while Elnora pulled back, but Mrs. Sinton was before them, her eyes flashing.

"Kate Comstock, you think you are mighty smart, don't you?" she cried.

"I ain't in the lunatic asylum, where you belong, anyway," said Mrs. Comstock. "I am smart enough to tell a dandy boy when I see him, and I'm good and glad to get him. I'll love to have him!"

"Well, you won't have him!" exclaimed Margaret Sinton. "That boy is Wesley's! He found him, and brought him here. You can't come in and take him like that! Let go of him!"

"Not much, I won't!" cried Mrs. Comstock. "Leave the poor sick little soul here for you to beat, because he didn't know just how to handle things! Of course, he'll make mistakes. He must have a lot of teaching, but not the kind he'll get from you! Clear out of my way!"

"You let go of our boy," ordered Margaret.

"Why? Do you want to whip him, before he can go to sleep?" jeered Mrs. Comstock.

"No, I don't!" said Margaret. "He's Wesley's, and nobody shall touch him. Wesley!"

Wesley Sinton appeared behind Margaret in the doorway, and she turned to him. "Make Kate Comstock let go of our boy!" she demanded.

"Billy, she wants you now," said Wesley Sinton. "She won't whip you, and she won't let any one else. You can have stacks of good things to eat, ride in the carriage, and have a great time. Won't you stay with us?"

Billy drew away from Mrs. Comstock and Elnora.

He faced Margaret, his eyes shrewd with unchildish wisdom. Necessity had taught him to strike the hot iron, to drive the hard bargain.

"Can I have Snap to live here always?" he demanded.

"Yes, you can have all the dogs you want," said Margaret Sinton.

"Can I sleep close enough so's I can touch you?"

"Yes, you can move your lounge up so that you can hold my hand," said Margaret.

"Do you love me now?" questioned Billy.

"I'll try to love you, if you are a good boy," said Margaret.

"Then I guess I'll stay," said Billy, walking over to her.

Out in the night Elnora and her mother went down the road in the moonlight; every few rods Mrs. Comstock laughed aloud.

"Mother, I don't understand you," sobbed Elnora.

"Well, maybe when you have gone to high school longer you will," said Mrs. Comstock. "Anyway, you saw me bring Mag Sinton to her senses, didn't you?"

"Yes, I did," answered Elnora, "but I thought you were in earnest. So did Billy, and Uncle Wesley, and Aunt Margaret."

"Well, wasn't I?" inquired Mrs. Comstock.

"But you just said you brought Aunt Margaret to!"

"Well, didn't I?"

"I don't understand you."

"That's the reason I am recommending more schooling!"

Elnora took her candle and went to bed. Mrs. Comstock was feeling too good to sleep. Twice of late she really had enjoyed herself for the first in sixteen years, and greediness for more of the same feeling crept into her blood like intoxication. As she sat brooding alone she knew the truth. She would have loved to have taken Billy. She would not have minded his mischief, his chatter, or his dog. He would have meant a distraction from herself that she greatly needed; she was even sincere about the dog. She had intended to tell Wesley to buy her one at the very first opportunity. Her last thought was of Billy. She chuckled softly, for she was not saintly, and now she knew how she could even a long score with Margaret and Wesley in a manner that would fill her soul with grim satisfaction.

Chapter 8

Wherein the Limberlost Tempts Elnora, and Billy Buries His Father

Immediately after dinner on Sunday Wesley Sinton stopped at the Comstock gate to ask if Elnora wanted to go to town with them. Billy sat beside him and he did not appear as if he were on his way to a funeral. Elnora said she had to study and could not go, but she suggested that her mother take her place. Mrs. Comstock put on her hat and went at once, which surprised Elnora. She did not know that her mother was anxious for an opportunity to speak with Sinton alone. Elnora knew why she was repeatedly cautioned not to leave their land, if she went specimen hunting.

She studied two hours and was several lessons ahead of her classes. There was no use to go further. She would take a walk and see if she could gather any caterpillars or find any freshly spun cocoons. She searched the bushes and low trees behind the garden and all around the edge of the woods on their land, and having little success, at last came to the road. Almost the first thorn bush she examined yielded a Polyphemus cocoon. Elnora lifted her head with the instinct of a hunter on the chase, and began work. She reached the swamp before she knew it, carrying five fine cocoons of different species as her reward. She pushed back her hair and gazed around longingly. A few rods inside she thought she saw cocoons on a bush, to which she went, and found several. Sense of caution was rapidly vanishing; she was in a fair way to forget everything and plunge into the swamp when she thought she heard footsteps coming down the trail. She went back, and came out almost facing Pete Corson.

That ended her difficulty. She had known him since childhood. When she sat on the front bench of the Brushwood schoolhouse, Pete had been one of the big boys at the back of the room. He had been rough and wild, but she never had been afraid of him, and often he had given her pretty things from the swamp.

"What luck!" she cried. "I promised mother I would not go inside the swamp alone, and will you look at the cocoons I've found! There are more just screaming for me to come get them, because the leaves will fall with the first frost, and then the jays and crows will begin to tear them open. I haven't much time, since I'm going to school. You will go with me, Pete! Please say yes! Just a little way!"

"What are those things?" asked the man, his keen black eyes staring at her.

"They are the cases these big caterpillars spin for winter, and in the spring they come out great night moths, and I can sell them. Oh, Pete, I can sell them for enough to take me through high school and dress me so like the others that I don't look different, and if I have very good luck I can save some for college. Pete, please go with me?"

"Why don't you go like you always have?"

"Well, the truth is, I had a little scare," said Elnora. "I never did mean to go alone; sometimes I sort of wandered inside farther than I intended, chasing things. You know Duncan gave me Freckles's books, and I have been gathering moths like he did. Lately I found I could sell them. If I can make a complete collection, I can get three hundred dollars for it. Three such collections would take me almost through college, and I've four years in the high school yet. That's a long time. I might collect them."

"Can every kind there is be found here?"

"No, not all of them, but when I get more than I need of one kind, I can trade them with collectors farther north and west, so I can complete sets. It's the only way I see to earn the money. Look what I have already. Big gray Cecropias come from this kind; brown Polyphemus from that, and green Lunas from these. You aren't working on Sunday. Go with me only an hour, Pete!"

The man looked at her narrowly. She was young, wholesome, and beautiful. She was innocent, intensely in earnest, and she needed the money, he knew that.

"You didn't tell me what scared you," he said.

"Oh, I thought I did! Why you know I had Freckles's box packed full of moths and specimens, and one evening I sold some to the Bird Woman. Next morning I found a note telling me it wasn't safe to go inside the swamp. That sort of scared me. I think I'll go alone, rather than miss the chance, but I'd be so happy if you would take care of me. Then I could go anywhere I chose, because if I mired you could pull me out. You will take care of me, Pete?"

"Yes, I'll take care of you," promised Pete Corson.

"Goody!" said Elnora. "Let's start quick! And Pete, you look at these closely, and when you are hunting or going along the road, if one dangles under your nose, you cut off the little twig and save it for me, will you?"

"Yes, I'll save you all I see," promised Pete. He pushed back his hat and followed Elnora. She plunged fearlessly among bushes, over underbrush, and across dead logs. One minute she was crying wildly, that here was a big one, the next she was reaching for a limb above her head or on her knees overturning dead leaves under a hickory or oak tree, or working aside black muck with her bare hands as she searched for buried pupae cases. For the first hour Pete bent back bushes and followed, carrying what Elnora discovered. Then he found one.

"Is this the kind of thing you are looking for?" he asked bashfully, as he presented a wild cherry twig.

"Oh Pete, that's a Promethea! I didn't even hope to find one."

"What's the bird like?" asked Pete.

"Almost black wings," said Elnora, "with clay-coloured edges, and the most wonderful wine-coloured flush over the under side if it's a male, and stronger wine above and below if it's a female. Oh, aren't I happy!"

"How would it do to make what you have into a bunch that we could leave here, and come back for them?"

"That would be all right."

Relieved of his load Pete began work. First, he narrowly examined the cocoons Elnora had found. He questioned her as to what other kinds would be like. He began to use the eyes of a trained woodman and hunter in her behalf. He saw several so easily, and moved through the forest so softly, that Elnora forgot the moths in watching him. Presently she was carrying the specimens, and he was making the trips of investigation to see which was a cocoon and which a curled leaf, or he was on his knees digging around stumps. As he worked he kept asking questions. What kind of logs were best to look beside, what trees were pupae cases most likely to be under; on what bushes did caterpillars spin most frequently? Time passed, as it always does when one's occupation is absorbing.

When the Sintons took Mrs. Comstock home, they stopped to see Elnora. She was not there. Mrs Comstock called at the edge of her woods and received no reply. Then Wesley turned and drove back to the Limberlost. He left Margaret and Mrs. Comstock holding the team and entertaining Billy, while he entered the swamp.

Elnora and Pete had made a wide trail behind them. Before Sinton had thought of calling, he heard voices and approached with some caution. Soon he saw Elnora, her flushed face beaming as she bent with an armload of twigs and branches and talked to a kneeling man.

"Now go cautiously!" she was saying. "I am just sure we will find an Imperialis here. It's their very kind of a place. There! What did I tell you! Isn't that splendid? Oh, I am so glad you came with me!"

Wesley stood staring in speechless astonishment, for the man had arisen, brushed the dirt from his hands, and held out to Elnora a small shining dark pupa case. As his face came into view Sinton almost cried out, for he was the one man of all others Wesley knew with whom he most feared for Elnora's safety. She had him on his knees digging pupae cases for her from the swamp.

"Elnora!" called Sinton. "Elnora!"

"Oh, Uncle Wesley!" cried the girl. "See what luck we've had! I know we have a dozen and a half cocoons and we have three pupae cases. It's much harder to get the cases because you have to dig for them, and you can't see where to look. But Pete is fine at it! He's found three, and he says he will keep watch beside the roads, and through the woods while he hunts. Isn't that splendid of him? Uncle Wesley, there is a college over there on the western edge of the swamp. Look closely, and you can see the great dome up among the clouds."

"I should say you have had luck," said Wesley, striving to make his voice natural. "But I thought you were not coming to the swamp?"

"Well, I wasn't," said Elnora, "but I couldn't find many anywhere else, honest, I couldn't, and just as soon as I came to the edge I began to see them here. I kept my promise. I didn't come in alone. Pete came with me. He's so strong, he isn't afraid of anything, and he's perfectly splendid to locate cocoons! He's found half of these. Come on, Pete, it's getting dark now, and we must go."

They started toward the trail, Pete carrying the cocoons. He left them at the case, while Elnora and Wesley went on to the carriage together.

"Elnora Comstock, what does this mean?" demanded her mother.

"It's all right, one of the neighbours was with her, and she got several dollars' worth of stuff," interposed Wesley.

"You oughter seen my pa," shouted Billy. "He was ist all whited out, and he laid as still as anything. They put him away deep in the ground."

"Billy!" breathed Margaret in a prolonged groan.

"Jimmy and Belle are going to be together in a nice place. They are coming to see me, and Snap is right down here by the wheel. Here, Snap! My, but he'll be tickled to get something to eat! He's 'most twisted as me. They get new clothes, and all they want to eat, too, but they'll miss me. They couldn't have got along without me. I took care of them. I had a lot of things give to me 'cause I was the littlest, and I always divided with them. But they won't need me now."

When she left the carriage Mrs. Comstock gravely shook hands with Billy. "Remember," she said to him, "I love boys, and I love dogs. Whenever you don't have a good time up there, take your dog and come right down and be my little boy. We will just have loads of fun. You should hear the whistles I can make. If you aren't treated right you come straight to me."

Billy wagged his head sagely. "You ist bet I will!" he said.

"Mother, how could you?" asked Elnora as they walked up the path.

"How could I, missy? You better ask how couldn't I? I just couldn't! Not for enough to pay, my road tax! Not for enough to pay the road tax, and the dredge tax, too!"

"Aunt Margaret always has been lovely to me, and I don't think it's fair to worry her."

"I choose to be lovely to Billy, and let her sweat out her own worries just as she has me, these sixteen years. There is nothing in all this world so good for people as taking a dose of their own medicine. The difference is that I am honest. I just say in plain English, 'if they don't treat you right, come to me.' They have only said it in actions and inferences. I want to teach Mag Sinton how her own doses taste, but she begins to sputter before I fairly get the spoon to her lips. Just you wait!"

"When I think what I owe her—" began Elnora.

"Well, thank goodness, I don't owe her anything, and so I'm perfectly free to do what I choose. Come on, and help me get supper. I'm hungry as Billy!"

Margaret Sinton rocked slowly back and forth in her chair. On her breast lay Billy's red head, one hand clutched her dress front with spasmodic grip, even after he was unconscious.

"You mustn't begin that, Margaret," said Sinton. "He's too heavy. And it's bad for him. He's better off to lie down and go to sleep alone."

"He's very light, Wesley. He jumps and quivers so. He has to be stronger than he is now, before he will sleep soundly."

Chapter 9

Wherein Elnora Discovers a Violin, and Billy Disciplines Margaret

Elnora missed the little figure at the bridge the following morning. She slowly walked up the street and turned in at the wide entrance to the school grounds. She scarcely could comprehend that only a week ago she had gone there friendless, alone, and so sick at heart that she was physically ill. To-day she had decent clothing, books, friends, and her mind was at ease to work on her studies.

As she approached home that night the girl paused in amazement. Her mother had company, and she was laughing. Elnora entered the kitchen softly and peeped into the sitting-room. Mrs. Comstock sat in her chair holding a book and every few seconds a soft chuckle broke into a real laugh. Mark Twain was doing his work; while Mrs. Comstock was not lacking in a sense of humour. Elnora entered the room before her mother saw her. Mrs. Comstock looked up with flushed face.

"Where did you get this?" she demanded.

"I bought it," said Elnora.

"Bought it! With all the taxes due!"

"I paid for it out of my Indian money, mother," said Elnora. "I couldn't bear to spend so much on myself and nothing at all on you. I was afraid to buy the dress I should have liked to, and I thought the book would be company, while I was gone. I haven't read it, but I do hope it's good."

"Good! It's the biggest piece of foolishness I have read in all my life. I've laughed all day, ever since I found it. I had a notion to go out and read some of it to the cows and see if they wouldn't laugh."

"If it made you laugh, it's a wise book," said Elnora.

"Wise!" cried Mrs. Comstock. "You can stake your life it's a wise book. It takes the smartest man there is to do this kind of fooling," and she began laughing again.

Elnora, highly satisfied with her purchase, went to her room and put on her working clothes. Thereafter she made a point of bringing a book that she thought would interest her mother, from the library every week, and leaving it on the sitting-room table. Each night she carried home at least two school books and studied until she had mastered the points of her lessons. She did her share of the work faithfully, and every available minute she was in the fields searching for cocoons, for the moths promised to become her largest source of income.

She gathered baskets of nests, flowers, mosses, insects, and all sorts of natural history specimens and sold them to the grade teachers. At first she tried to tell these instructors what to teach their pupils about the specimens; but recognizing how much more she knew than they, one after another begged her to study at home, and use her spare hours in school to exhibit and explain nature subjects to their pupils. Elnora loved the work, and she needed the money, for every few days some matter of expense arose that she had not expected.

From the first week she had been received and invited with the crowd of girls in her class, and it was their custom in passing through the business part of the city to stop at the confectioners' and take turns in treating to expensive candies, ice cream sodas, hot chocolate, or whatever they fancied. When first Elnora was asked she accepted without understanding. The second time she went because she seldom had tasted these things, and they were so delicious she could not resist. After that she went because she knew all about it, and had decided to go.

She had spent half an hour on the log beside the trail in deep thought and had arrived at her conclusions. She worked harder than usual for the next week, but she seemed to thrive on work. It was October and the red leaves were falling when her first time came to treat. As the crowd flocked down the broad walk that night Elnora called, "Girls, it's my treat to-night! Come on!"

She led the way through the city to the grocery they patronized when they had a small spread, and entering came out with a basket, which she carried to the bridge on her home road. There she arranged the girls in two rows on the cement abutments and opening her basket she gravely offered each girl an exquisite little basket of bark, lined with red leaves, in one end of which nestled a juicy big red apple and in the other a spicy doughnut not an hour from Margaret Sinton's frying basket.

Another time she offered big balls of popped corn stuck together with maple sugar, and liberally sprinkled with beechnut kernels. Again it was hickory-nut kernels glazed with sugar, another time maple candy, and once a basket of warm pumpkin pies. She never made any apology, or offered any excuse. She simply gave what she could afford, and the change was as welcome to those city girls accustomed to sodas and French candy, as were these same things to Elnora surfeited on popcorn and pie. In her room was a little slip containing a record of the number of weeks in the school year, the times it would be her turn to treat and the dates on which such occasions would fall, with a number of suggestions beside each. Once the girls almost fought over a basket lined with yellow leaves, and filled with fat, very ripe red haws. In late October there was a riot over one which was lined with red leaves and contained big fragrant pawpaws frost-bitten to a perfect degree. Then hazel nuts were ripe, and once they served. One day Elnora at her wits' end, explained to her mother that the girls had given her things and she wanted to treat them. Mrs. Comstock, with characteristic stubbornness, had said she would leave a basket at the grocery for her, but firmly declined to say what would be in it. All day Elnora struggled to keep her mind on her books. For hours she wavered in tense uncertainty. What would her mother do? Should she take the girls to the confectioner's that night or risk the basket? Mrs. Comstock could make delicious things to eat, but would she?

As they left the building Elnora made a final rapid mental calculation. She could not see her way clear to a decent treat for ten people for less than two dollars and if the basket proved to be nice, then the money would be wasted. She decided to risk it. As they went to the bridge the girls were betting on what the treat would be, and crowding near Elnora like spoiled small children. Elnora set down the basket.

"Girls," she said, "I don't know what this is myself, so all of us are going to be surprised. Here goes!"

She lifted the cover and perfumes from the land of spices rolled up. In one end of the basket lay ten enormous sugar cakes the tops of which had been liberally dotted with circles cut from stick candy. The candy had melted in baking and made small transparent wells of waxy sweetness and in the centre of each cake was a fat turtle made from a raisin with cloves for head and feet. The remainder of the basket was filled with big spiced pears that could be held by their stems while they were eaten. The girls shrieked and attacked the cookies, and of all the treats Elnora offered perhaps none was quite so long remembered as that.

When Elnora took her basket, placed her books in it, and started home, all the girls went with her as far as the fence where she crossed the field to the swamp. At parting they kissed her good-bye. Elnora was a happy girl as she hurried home to thank her mother. She was happy over her books that night, and happy all the way to school the following morning.

When the music swelled from the orchestra her heart almost broke with throbbing joy. For music always had affected her strangely, and since she had been comfortable enough in her surroundings to notice things, she had listened to every note to find what it was that literally hurt her heart, and at last she knew. It was the talking of the violins. They were human voices, and they spoke a language Elnora understood. It seemed to her that she must climb up on the stage, take the instruments from the fingers of the players and make them speak what was in her heart.

That night she said to her mother, "I am perfectly crazy for a violin. I am sure I could play one, sure as I live. Did any one—" Elnora never completed that sentence.

"Hush!" thundered Mrs. Comstock. "Be quiet! Never mention those things before me again—never as long as you live! I loathe them! They are a snare of the very devil himself! They were made to lure men and women from their homes and their honour. If ever I see you with one in your fingers I will smash it in pieces."

Naturally Elnora hushed, but she thought of nothing else after she had finished her lessons. At last there came a day when for some reason the leader of the orchestra left his violin on the grand piano. That morning Elnora made her first mistake in algebra. At noon, as soon as the building was empty, she slipped into the auditorium, found the side door which led to the stage, and going through the musicians' entrance she took the violin. She carried it back into the little side room where the orchestra assembled, closed all the doors, opened the case and lifted out the instrument.

She laid it on her breast, dropped her chin on it and drew the bow softly across the strings. One after another she tested the open notes. Gradually her stroke ceased to tremble and she drew the bow firmly. Then her fingers began to fall and softly, slowly she searched up and down those strings for sounds she knew. Standing in the middle of the floor, she tried over and over. It seemed scarcely a minute before the hall was filled with the sound of hurrying feet, and she was forced to put away the violin and go to her classes. The next day she prayed that the violin would be left again, but her petition was not answered. That night when she returned from the school she made an excuse to go down to see Billy. He was engaged in hulling walnuts by driving them through holes in a board. His hands were protected by a pair of Margaret's old gloves, but he had speckled his face generously. He appeared well, and greeted Elnora hilariously.

"Me an' the squirrels are laying up our winter stores," he shouted. "Cos the cold is coming, an' the snow an' if we have any nuts we have to fix 'em now. But I'm ahead, cos Uncle Wesley made me this board, and I can hull a big pile while the old squirrel does only ist one with his teeth."

Elnora picked him up and kissed him. "Billy, are you happy?" she asked.

"Yes, and so's Snap," answered Billy. "You ought to see him make the dirt fly when he gets after a chipmunk. I bet you he could dig up Pa, if anybody wanted him to."

"Billy!" gasped Margaret as she came out to them.

"Well, me and Snap don't want him up, and I bet you Jimmy and Belle don't, either. I ain't been twisty inside once since I been here, and I don't want to go away, and Snap don't, either. He told me so."

"Billy! That is not true. Dogs can't talk," cautioned Margaret.

"Then what makes you open the door when he asks you to?" demanded Billy.

"Scratching and whining isn't talking."

"Anyway, it's the best Snap can talk, and you get up and do things he wants done. Chipmunks can talk too. You ought to hear them damn things holler when Snap gets them!"

"Billy! When you want a cooky for supper and I don't give it to you it is because you said a wrong word."

"Well, for—" Billy clapped his hand over his mouth and stained his face in swipes. "Well, for—anything! Did I go an' forget again! The cookies will get all hard, won't they? I bet you ten dollars I don't say that any more."

He espied Wesley and ran to show him a walnut too big to go through the holes, and Elnora and Margaret entered the house.

They talked of many things for a time and then Elnora said suddenly: "Aunt Margaret, I like music."

"I've noticed that in you all your life," answered Margaret.

"If dogs can't talk, I can make a violin talk," announced Elnora, and then in amazement watched the face of Margaret Sinton grow pale.

"A violin!" she wavered. "Where did you get a violin?"

"They fairly seemed to speak to me in the orchestra. One day the conductor left his in the auditorium, and I took it, and Aunt Margaret, I can make it do the wind in the swamp, the birds, and the animals. I can make any sound I ever heard on it. If I had a chance to practise a little, I could make it do the orchestra music, too. I don't know how I know, but I do."

"Did—did you ever mention it to your mother?" faltered Margaret.

"Yes, and she seems prejudiced against them. But oh, Aunt Margaret, I never felt so about anything, not even going to school. I just feel as if I'd die if I didn't have one. I could keep it at school, and practise at noon a whole hour. Soon they'd ask me to play in the orchestra. I could keep it in the case and practise in the woods in summer. You'd let me play over here Sunday. Oh, Aunt Margaret, what does one cost? Would it be wicked for me to take of my money, and buy a very cheap one? I could play on the least expensive one made."

"Oh, no you couldn't! A cheap machine makes cheap music. You got to have a fine fiddle to make it sing. But there's no sense in your buying one. There isn't a decent reason on earth why you shouldn't have your fa—"

"My father's!" cried Elnora. She caught Margaret Sinton by the arm. "My father had a violin! He played it. That's why I can! Where is it! Is it in our house? Is it in mother's room?"

"Elnora!" panted Margaret. "Your mother will kill me! She always hated it."

"Mother dearly loves music," said Elnora.

"Not when it took the man she loved away from her to make it!"

"Where is my father's violin?"

"Elnora!"

"I've never seen a picture of my father. I've never heard his name mentioned. I've never had a scrap that belonged to him. Was he my father, or am I a charity child like Billy, and so she hates me?"

"She has good pictures of him. Seems she just can't bear to hear him talked about. Of course, he was your father. They lived right there when you were born. She doesn't dislike you; she merely tries to make herself think she does. There's no sense in the world in you not having his violin. I've a great notion—"

"Has mother got it?"

"No. I've never heard her mention it. It was not at home when he—when he died."

"Do you know where it is?"

"Yes. I'm the only person on earth who does, except the one who has it."

"Who is that?"

"I can't tell you, but I will see if they have it yet, and get it if I can. But if your mother finds it out she will never forgive me."

"I can't help it," said Elnora. "I want that violin."

"I'll go to-morrow, and see if it has been destroyed."

"Destroyed! Oh, Aunt Margaret! Would any one dare?"

"I hardly think so. It was a good instrument. He played it like a master."

"Tell me!" breathed Elnora.

"His hair was red and curled more than yours, and his eyes were blue. He was tall, slim, and the very imp of mischief. He joked and teased all day until he picked up that violin. Then his head bent over it, and his eyes got big and earnest. He seemed to listen as if he first heard the notes, and then copied them. Sometimes he drew the bow trembly, like he wasn't sure it was right, and he might have to try again. He could almost drive you crazy when he wanted to, and no man that ever lived could make you dance as he could. He made it all up as he went. He seemed to listen for his dancing music, too. It appeared to come to him; he'd begin to play and you had to keep time. You couldn't be still; he loved to sweep a crowd around with that bow of his. I think it was the thing you call inspiration. I can see him now, his handsome head bent, his cheeks red, his eyes snapping, and that bow going across the strings, and driving us like sheep. He always kept his body swinging, and he loved to play. He often slighted his work shamefully, and sometimes her a little; that is why she hated it—Elnora, what are you making me do?"

The tears were rolling down Elnora's cheeks. "Oh, Aunt Margaret," she sobbed. "Why haven't you told me about him sooner? I feel as if you had given my father to me living, so that I could touch him. I can see him, too! Why didn't you ever tell me before? Go on! Go on!"

"I can't, Elnora! I'm scared silly. I never meant to say anything. If I hadn't promised her not to talk of him to you she wouldn't have let you come here. She made me swear it."

"But why? Why? Was he a shame? Was he disgraced?"

"Maybe it was that unjust feeling that took possession of her when she couldn't help him from the swamp. She had to blame some one, or go crazy, so she took it out on you. At times, those first ten years, if I had talked to you, and you had repeated anything to her, she might have struck you too hard. She was not master of herself. You must be patient with her, Elnora. God only knows what she has gone through, but I think she is a little better, lately."

"So do I," said Elnora. "She seems more interested in my clothes, and she fixes me such delicious lunches that the girls bring fine candies and cake and beg to trade. I gave half my lunch for a box of candy one day, brought it home to her, and told her. Since, she has wanted me to carry a market basket and treat the crowd every day, she was so pleased. Life has been too monotonous for her. I think she enjoys even the little change made by my going and coming. She sits up half the night to read the library books I bring, but she is so stubborn she won't even admit that she touches them. Tell me more about my father."

"Wait until I see if I can find the violin."

So Elnora went home in suspense, and that night she added to her prayers: "Dear Lord, be merciful to my father, and oh, do help Aunt Margaret to get his violin."

Wesley and Billy came in to supper tired and hungry. Billy ate heartily, but his eyes often rested on a plate of tempting cookies, and when Wesley offered them to the boy he reached for one. Margaret was compelled to explain that cookies were forbidden that night.

"What!" said Wesley. "Wrong words been coming again. Oh Billy, I do wish you could remember! I can't sit and eat cookies before a little boy who has none. I'll have to put mine back, too." Billy's face twisted in despair.

"Aw go on!" he said gruffly, but his chin was jumping, for Wesley was his idol.

"Can't do it," said Wesley. "It would choke me."

Billy turned to Margaret. "You make him," he appealed.

"He can't, Billy," said Margaret. "I know how he feels. You see, I can't myself."

Then Billy slid from his chair, ran to the couch, buried his face in the pillow and cried heart-brokenly. Wesley hurried to the barn, and Margaret to the kitchen. When the dishes were washed Billy slipped from the back door.

Wesley piling hay into the mangers heard a sound behind him and inquired, "That you, Billy?"

"Yes," answered Billy, "and it's all so dark you can't see me now, isn't it?"

"Well, mighty near," answered Wesley.

"Then you stoop down and open your mouth."

Sinton had shared bites of apple and nuts for weeks, for Billy had not learned how to eat anything without dividing with Jimmy and Belle. Since he had been separated from them, he shared with Wesley and Margaret. So he bent over the boy and received an instalment of cooky that almost choked him.

"Now you can eat it!" shouted Billy in delight. "It's all dark! I can't see what you're doing at all!"

Wesley picked up the small figure and set the boy on the back of a horse to bring his face level so that they could talk as men. He never towered from his height above Billy, but always lifted the little soul when important matters were to be discussed.

"Now what a dandy scheme," he commented. "Did you and Aunt Margaret fix it up?"

"No. She ain't had hers yet. But I got one for her. Ist as soon as you eat yours, I am going to take hers, and feed her first time I find her in the dark."

"But Billy, where did you get the cookies? You know Aunt Margaret said you were not to have any."

"I ist took them," said Billy, "I didn't take them for me. I ist took them for you and her."

Wesley thought fast. In the warm darkness of the barn the horses crunched their corn, a rat gnawed at a corner of the granary, and among the rafters the white pigeon cooed a soft sleepy note to his dusky mate.

"Did—did—I steal?" wavered Billy.

Wesley's big hands closed until he almost hurt the boy.

"No!" he said vehemently. "That is too big a word. You made a mistake. You were trying to be a fine little man, but you went at it the wrong way. You only made a mistake. All of us do that, Billy. The world grows that way. When we make mistakes we can see them; that teaches us to be more careful the next time, and so we learn."

"How wouldn't it be a mistake?"

"If you had told Aunt Margaret what you wanted to do, and asked her for the cookies she would have given them to you."

"But I was 'fraid she wouldn't, and you ist had to have it."

"Not if it was wrong for me to have it, Billy. I don't want it that much."

"Must I take it back?"

"You think hard, and decide yourself."

"Lift me down," said Billy, after a silence, "I got to put this in the jar, and tell her."

Wesley set the boy on the floor, but as he did so he paused one second and strained him close to his breast.

Margaret sat in her chair sewing; Billy slipped in and crept beside her. The little face was lined with tragedy.

"Why Billy, whatever is the matter?" she cried as she dropped her sewing and held out her arms. Billy stood back. He gripped his little fists tight and squared his shoulders. "I got to be shut up in the closet," he said.

"Oh Billy! What an unlucky day! What have you done now?"

"I stold!" gulped Billy. "He said it was ist a mistake, but it was worser 'an that. I took something you told me I wasn't to have."

"Stole!" Margaret was in despair. "What, Billy?"

"Cookies!" answered Billy in equal trouble.

"Billy!" wailed Margaret. "How could you?"

"It was for him and you," sobbed Billy. "He said he couldn't eat it 'fore me, but out in the barn it's all dark and I couldn't see. I thought maybe he could there. Then we might put out the light and you could have yours. He said I only made it worse, cos I mustn't take things, so I got to go in the closet. Will you hold me tight a little bit first? He did."

Margaret opened her arms and Billy rushed in and clung to her a few seconds, with all the force of his being, then he slipped to the floor and marched to the closet. Margaret opened the door. Billy gave one glance at the light, clinched his fists and, walking inside, climbed on a box. Margaret closed the door.

Then she sat and listened. Was the air pure enough? Possibly he might smother. She had read something once. Was it very dark? What if there should be a mouse in the closet and it should run across his foot and frighten him into spasms. Somewhere she had heard—Margaret leaned forward with tense face and listened. Something dreadful might happen. She could bear it no longer. She arose hurriedly and opened the door. Billy was drawn up on the box in a little heap, and he lifted a disapproving face to her.

"Shut that door!" he said. "I ain't been in here near long enough yet!"

Chapter 10

Wherein Elnora Has More Financial Troubles, and Mrs. Comstock Again Hears the Song of the Limberlost

The following night Elnora hurried to Sintons'. She threw open the back door and with anxious eyes searched Margaret's face.

"You got it!" panted Elnora. "You got it! I can see by your face that you did. Oh, give it to me!"

"Yes, I got it, honey, I got it all right, but don't be so fast. It had been kept in such a damp place it needed glueing, it had to have strings, and a key was gone. I knew how much you wanted it, so I sent Wesley right to town with it. They said they could fix it good as new, but it should be varnished, and that it would take several days for the glue to set. You can have it Saturday."

"You found it where you thought it was? You know it's his?"

"Yes, it was just where I thought, and it's the same violin I've seen him play hundreds of times. It's all right, only laying so long it needs fixing."

"Oh Aunt Margaret! Can I ever wait?"

"It does seem a long time, but how could I help it? You couldn't do anything with it as it was. You see, it had been hidden away in a garret, and it needed cleaning and drying to make it fit to play again. You can have it Saturday sure. But Elnora, you've got to promise me that you will leave it here, or in town, and not let your mother get a hint of it. I don't know what she'd do."

"Uncle Wesley can bring it here until Monday. Then I will take it to school so that I can practise at noon. Oh, I don't know how to thank you. And there's more than the violin for which to be thankful. You've given me my father. Last night I saw him plainly as life."

"Elnora you were dreaming!"

"I know I was dreaming, but I saw him. I saw him so closely that a tiny white scar at the corner of his eyebrow showed. I was just reaching out to touch him when he disappeared."

"Who told you there was a scar on his forehead?"

"No one ever did in all my life. I saw it last night as he went down. And oh, Aunt Margaret! I saw what she did, and I heard his cries! No matter what she does, I don't believe I ever can be angry with her again. Her heart is broken, and she can't help it. Oh, it was terrible, but I am glad I saw it. Now, I will always understand."

"I don't know what to make of that," said Margaret. "I don't believe in such stuff at all, but you couldn't make it up, for you didn't know."

"I only know that I played the violin last night, as he played it, and while I played he came through the woods from the direction of Carneys'. It was summer and all the flowers were in bloom. He wore gray trousers and a blue shirt, his head was bare, and his face was beautiful. I could almost touch him when he sank."

Margaret stood perplexed. "I don't know what to think of that!" she ejaculated. "I was next to the last person who saw him before he was drowned. It was late on a June afternoon, and he was dressed as you describe. He was bareheaded because he had found a quail's nest before the bird began to brood, and he gathered the eggs in his hat and left it in a fence corner to get on his way home; they found it afterward."

"Was he coming from Carneys'?"

"He was on that side of the quagmire. Why he ever skirted it so close as to get caught is a mystery you will have to dream out. I never could understand it."

"Was he doing something he didn't want my mother to know?"

"Why?"

"Because if he had been, he might have cut close the swamp so he couldn't be seen from the garden. You know, the whole path straight to the pool where he sank can be seen from our back door. It's firm on our side. The danger is on the north and east. If he didn't want mother to know, he might have tried to pass on either of those sides and gone too close. Was he in a hurry?"

"Yes, he was," said Margaret. "He had been away longer than he expected, and he almost ran when he started home."

"And he'd left his violin somewhere that you knew, and you went and got it. I'll wager he was going to play, and didn't want mother to find it out!"

"It wouldn't make any difference to you if you knew every little thing, so quit thinking about it, and just be glad you are to have what he loved best of anything."

"That's true. Now I must hurry home. I am dreadfully late."

Elnora sprang up and ran down the road, but when she approached the cabin she climbed the fence, crossed the open woods pasture diagonally and entered at the back garden gate. As she often came that way when she had been looking for cocoons her mother asked no questions.

Elnora lived by the minute until Saturday, when, contrary to his usual custom, Wesley went to town in the forenoon, taking her along to buy some groceries. Wesley drove straight to the music store, and asked for the violin he had left to be mended.

In its new coat of varnish, with new keys and strings, it seemed much like any other violin to Sinton, but to Elnora it was the most beautiful instrument ever made, and a priceless treasure. She held it in her arms, touched the strings softly and then she drew the bow across them in whispering measure. She had no time to think what a remarkably good bow it was for sixteen years' disuse. The tan leather case might have impressed her as being in fine condition also, had she been in a state to question anything. She did remember to ask for the bill and she was gravely presented with a slip calling for four strings, one key, and a coat of varnish, total, one dollar fifty. It seemed to Elnora she never could put the precious instrument in the case and start home. Wesley left her in the music store where the proprietor showed her all he could about tuning, and gave her several beginners' sheets of notes and scales. She carried the violin in her arms as far as the crossroads at the corner of their land, then reluctantly put it under the carriage seat.

As soon as her work was done she ran down to Sintons' and began to play, and on Monday the violin went to school with her. She made arrangements with the superintendent to leave it in his office and scarcely took time for her food at noon, she was so eager to practise. Often one of the girls asked her to stay in town all night for some lecture or entertainment. She could take the violin with her, practise, and secure help. Her skill was so great that the leader of the orchestra offered to give her lessons if she would play to pay for them, so her progress was rapid in technical work. But from the first day the instrument became hers, with perfect faith that she could play as her father did, she spent half her practice time in imitating the sounds of all outdoors and improvising the songs her happy heart sang in those days.

So the first year went, and the second and third were a repetition; but the fourth was different, for that was the close of the course, ending with graduation and all its attendant ceremonies and expenses. To Elnora these appeared mountain high. She had hoarded every cent, thinking twice before she parted with a penny, but teaching natural history in the grades had taken time from her studies in school which must be made up outside. She was a conscientious student, ranking first in most of her classes, and standing high in all branches. Her interest in her violin had grown with the years. She went to school early and practised half an hour in the little room adjoining the stage, while the orchestra gathered. She put in a full hour at noon, and remained another half hour at night. She carried the violin to Sintons' on Saturday and practised all the time she could there, while Margaret watched the road to see that Mrs. Comstock was not coming. She had become so skilful that it was a delight to hear her play music of any composer, but when she played her own, that was joy inexpressible, for then the wind blew, the water rippled, the Limberlost sang her songs of sunshine, shadow, black storm, and white night.

Since her dream Elnora had regarded her mother with peculiar tenderness. The girl realized, in a measure, what had happened. She avoided anything that possibly could stir bitter memories or draw deeper a line on the hard, white face. This cost many sacrifices, much work, and sometimes delayed progress, but the horror of that awful dream remained with Elnora. She worked her way cheerfully, doing all she could to interest her mother in things that happened in school, in the city, and by carrying books that were entertaining from the public library.

Three years had changed Elnora from the girl of sixteen to the very verge of womanhood. She had grown tall, round, and her face had the loveliness of perfect complexion, beautiful eyes and hair and an added touch from within that might have been called comprehension. It was a compound of self-reliance, hard knocks, heart hunger, unceasing work, and generosity. There was no form of suffering with which the girl could not sympathize, no work she was afraid to attempt, no subject she had investigated she did not understand. These things combined to produce a breadth and depth of character altogether unusual. She was so absorbed in her classes and her music that she had not been able to gather many specimens. When she realized this and hunted assiduously, she soon found that changing natural conditions had affected such work. Men all around were clearing available land. The trees fell wherever corn would grow. The swamp was broken by several gravel roads, dotted in places around the edge with little frame houses, and the machinery of oil wells; one especially low place around the region of Freckles's room was nearly all that remained of the original. Wherever the trees fell the moisture dried, the creeks ceased to flow, the river ran low, and at times the bed was dry. With unbroken sweep the winds of the west came, gathering force with every mile and howled and raved; threatening to tear the shingles from the roof, blowing the surface from the soil in clouds of fine dust and rapidly changing everything. From coming in with two or three dozen rare moths in a day, in three years' time Elnora had grown to be delighted with finding two or three. Big pursy caterpillars could not be picked from their favourite bushes, when there were no bushes. Dragonflies would not hover over dry places, and butterflies became scarce in proportion to the flowers, while no land yields over three crops of Indian relics.

All the time the expense of books, clothing and incidentals had continued. Elnora added to her bank account whenever she could, and drew out when she was compelled, but she omitted the important feature of calling for a balance. So, one early spring morning in the last quarter of the fourth year, she almost fainted when she learned that her funds were gone. Commencement with its extra expense was coming, she had no money, and very few cocoons to open in June, which would be too late. She had one collection for the Bird Woman complete to a pair of Imperialis moths, and that was her only asset. On the day she added these big Yellow Emperors she had been promised a check for three hundred dollars, but she would not get it until these specimens were secured. She remembered that she never had found an Emperor before June.

Moreover, that sum was for her first year in college. Then she would be of age, and she meant to sell enough of her share of her father's land to finish. She knew her mother would oppose her bitterly in that, for Mrs. Comstock had clung to every acre and tree that belonged to her husband. Her land was almost complete forest where her neighbours owned cleared farms, dotted with wells that every hour sucked oil from beneath her holdings, but she was too absorbed in the grief she nursed to know or care. The Brushwood road and the redredging of the big Limberlost ditch had been more than she could pay from her income, and she had trembled before the wicket as she asked the banker if she had funds to pay it, and wondered why he laughed when he assured her she had. For Mrs. Comstock had spent no time on compounding interest, and never added the sums she had been depositing through nearly twenty years. Now she thought her funds were almost gone, and every day she worried over expenses. She could see no reason in going through the forms of graduation when pupils had all in their heads that was required to graduate. Elnora knew she had to have her diploma in order to enter the college she wanted to attend, but she did not dare utter the word, until high school was finished, for, instead of softening as she hoped her mother had begun to do, she seemed to remain very much the same.

When the girl reached the swamp she sat on a log and thought over the expense she was compelled to meet. Every member of her particular set was having a large photograph taken to exchange with the others. Elnora loved these girls and boys, and to say she could not have their pictures to keep was more than she could endure. Each one would give to all the others a handsome graduation present. She knew they would prepare gifts for her whether she could make a present in return or not. Then it was the custom for each graduating class to give a great entertainment and use the funds to present the school with a statue for the entrance hall. Elnora had been cast for and was practising a part in that performance. She was expected to furnish her dress and personal necessities. She had been told that she must have a green gauze dress, and where was it to come from?

Every girl of the class would have three beautiful new frocks for Commencement: one for the baccalaureate sermon, another, which could be plain, for graduation exercises, and a handsome one for the banquet and ball. Elnora faced the past three years and wondered how she could have spent so much money and not kept account of it. She did not realize where it had gone. She did not know what she could do now. She thought over the photographs, and at last settled that question to her satisfaction. She studied longer over the gifts, ten handsome ones there must be, and at last decided she could arrange for them. The green dress came first. The lights would be dim in the scene, and the setting deep woods. She could manage that. She simply could not have three dresses. She would have to get a very simple one for the sermon and do the best she could for graduation. Whatever she got for that must be made with a guimpe that could be taken out to make it a little more festive for the ball. But where could she get even two pretty dresses?

The only hope she could see was to break into the collection of the man from India, sell some moths, and try to replace them in June. But in her soul she knew that never would do. No June ever brought just the things she hoped it would. If she spent the college money she knew she could not replace it. If she did not, the only way was to secure a room in the grades and teach a year. Her work there had been so appreciated that Elnora felt with the recommendation she knew she could get from the superintendent and teachers she could secure a position. She was sure she could pass the examinations easily. She had once gone on Saturday, taken them and secured a license for a year before she left the Brushwood school.

She wanted to start to college when the other girls were going. If she could make the first year alone, she could manage the remainder. But make that first year herself, she must. Instead of selling any of her collection, she must hunt as she never before had hunted and find a Yellow Emperor. She had to have it, that was all. Also, she had to have those dresses. She thought of Wesley and dismissed it. She thought of the Bird Woman, and knew she could not tell her. She thought of every way in which she ever had hoped to earn money and realized that with the play, committee meetings, practising, and final examinations she scarcely had time to live, much less to do more than the work required for her pictures and gifts. Again Elnora was in trouble, and this time it seemed the worst of all.

It was dark when she arose and went home.

"Mother," she said, "I have a piece of news that is decidedly not cheerful."

"Then keep it to yourself!" said Mrs. Comstock. "I think I have enough to bear without a great girl like you piling trouble on me."

"My money is all gone!" said Elnora.

"Well, did you think it would last forever? It's been a marvel to me that it's held out as well as it has, the way you've dressed and gone."

"I don't think I've spent any that I was not compelled to," said Elnora. "I've dressed on just as little as I possibly could to keep going. I am heartsick. I thought I had over fifty dollars to put me through Commencement, but they tell me it is all gone."

"Fifty dollars! To put you through Commencement! What on earth are you proposing to do?"

"The same as the rest of them, in the very cheapest way possible."

"And what might that be?"

Elnora omitted the photographs, the gifts and the play. She told only of the sermon, graduation exercises, and the ball.

"Well, I wouldn't trouble myself over that," sniffed Mrs. Comstock. "If you want to go to a sermon, put on the dress you always use for meeting. If you need white for the exercises wear the new dress you got last spring. As for the ball, the best thing for you to do is to stay a mile away from such folly. In my opinion you'd best bring home your books, and quit right now. You can't be fixed like the rest of them, don't be so foolish as to run into it. Just stay here and let these last few days go. You can't learn enough more to be of any account."

"But, mother," gasped Elnora. "You don't understand!"

"Oh, yes, I do!" said Mrs. Comstock. "I understand perfectly. So long as the money lasted, you held up your head, and went sailing without even explaining how you got it from the stuff you gathered. Goodness knows I couldn't see. But now it's gone, you come whining to me. What have I got? Have you forgot that the ditch and the road completely strapped me? I haven't any money. There's nothing for you to do but get out of it."

"I can't!" said Elnora desperately. "I've gone on too long. It would make a break in everything. They wouldn't let me have my diploma!"

"What's the difference? You've got the stuff in your head. I wouldn't give a rap for a scrap of paper. That don't mean anything!"

"But I've worked four years for it, and I can't enter—I ought to have it to help me get a school, when I want to teach. If I don't have my grades to show, people will think I quit because I couldn't pass my examinations. I must have my diploma!"

"Then get it!" said Mrs. Comstock.

"The only way is to graduate with the others."

"Well, graduate if you are bound to!"

"But I can't, unless I have things enough like the class, that I don't look as I did that first day."

"Well, please remember I didn't get you into this, and I can't get you out. You are set on having your own way. Go on, and have it, and see how you like it!"

Elnora went upstairs and did not come down again that night, which her mother called pouting.

"I've thought all night," said the girl at breakfast, "and I can't see any way but to borrow the money of Uncle Wesley and pay it back from some that the Bird Woman will owe me, when I get one more specimen. But that means that I can't go to—that I will have to teach this winter, if I can get a city grade or a country school."

"Just you dare go dinging after Wesley Sinton for money," cried Mrs. Comstock. "You won't do any such a thing!"

"I can't see any other way. I've got to have the money!"

"Quit, I tell you!"

"I can't quit!—I've gone too far!"

"Well then, let me get your clothes, and you can pay me back."

"But you said you had no money!"

"Maybe I can borrow some at the bank. Then you can return it when the Bird Woman pays you."

"All right," said Elnora. "I don't need expensive things. Just some kind of a pretty cheap white dress for the sermon, and a white one a little better than I had last summer, for Commencement and the ball. I can use the white gloves and shoes I got myself for last year, and you can get my dress made at the same place you did that one. They have my measurements, and do perfect work. Don't get expensive things. It will be warm so I can go bareheaded."

Then she started to school, but was so tired and discouraged she scarcely could walk. Four years' plans going in one day! For she felt that if she did not start to college that fall she never would. Instead of feeling relieved at her mother's offer, she was almost too ill to go on. For the thousandth time she groaned: "Oh, why didn't I keep account of my money?"

After that the days passed so swiftly she scarcely had time to think, but several trips her mother made to town, and the assurance that everything was all right, satisfied Elnora. She worked very hard to pass good final examinations and perfect herself for the play. For two days she had remained in town with the Bird Woman in order to spend more time practising and at her work.

Often Margaret had asked about her dresses for graduation, and Elnora had replied that they were with a woman in the city who had made her a white dress for last year's Commencement when she was a junior usher, and they would be all right.

So Margaret, Wesley, and Billy concerned themselves over what they would give her for a present. Margaret suggested a beautiful dress. Wesley said that would look to every one as if she needed dresses. The thing was to get a handsome gift like all the others would have. Billy wanted to present her a five-dollar gold piece to buy music for her violin. He was positive Elnora would like that best of anything.

It was toward the close of the term when they drove to town one evening to try to settle this important question. They knew Mrs. Comstock had been alone several days, so they asked her to accompany them. She had been more lonely than she would admit, filled with unusual unrest besides, and so she was glad to go. But before they had driven a mile Billy had told that they were going to buy Elnora a graduation present, and Mrs. Comstock devoutly wished that she had remained at home. She was prepared when Billy asked: "Aunt Kate, what are you going to give Elnora when she graduates?"

"Plenty to eat, a good bed to sleep in, and do all the work while she trollops," answered Mrs. Comstock dryly.

Billy reflected. "I guess all of them have that," he said. "I mean a present you buy at the store, like Christmas?"

"It is only rich folks who buy presents at stores," replied Mrs. Comstock. "I can't afford it."

"Well, we ain't rich," he said, "but we are going to buy Elnora something as fine as the rest of them have if we sell a corner of the farm. Uncle Wesley said so."

"A fool and his land are soon parted," said Mrs. Comstock tersely. Wesley and Billy laughed, but Margaret did not enjoy the remark.

While they were searching the stores for something on which all of them could decide, and Margaret was holding Billy to keep him from saying anything before Mrs. Comstock about the music on which he was determined, Mr. Brownlee met Wesley and stopped to shake hands.

"I see your boy came out finely," he said.

"I don't allow any boy anywhere to be finer than Billy," said Wesley.

"I guess you don't allow any girl to surpass Elnora," said Mr. Brownlee. "She comes home with Ellen often, and my wife and I love her. Ellen says she is great in her part to-night. Best thing in the whole play! Of course, you are in to see it! If you haven't reserved seats, you'd better start pretty soon, for the high school auditorium only seats a thousand. It's always jammed at these home-talent plays. All of us want to see how our children perform."

"Why yes, of course," said the bewildered Wesley. Then he hurried to Margaret. "Say," he said, "there is going to be a play at the high school to-night; and Elnora is in it. Why hasn't she told us?"

"I don't know," said Margaret, "but I'm going."

"So am I," said Billy.

"Me too!" said Wesley, "unless you think for some reason she doesn't want us. Looks like she would have told us if she had. I'm going to ask her mother."

"Yes, that's what's she's been staying in town for," said Mrs. Comstock. "It's some sort of a swindle to raise money for her class to buy some silly thing to stick up in the school house hall to remember them by. I don't know whether it's now or next week, but there's something of the kind to be done."

"Well, it's to-night," said Wesley, "and we are going. It's my treat, and we've got to hurry or we won't get in. There are reserved seats, and we have none, so it's the gallery for us, but I don't care so I get to take one good peep at Elnora."

"S'pose she plays?" whispered Margaret in his ear.

"Aw, tush! She couldn't!" said Wesley.

"Well, she's been doing it three years in the orchestra, and working like a slave at it."

"Oh, well that's different. She's in the play to-night. Brownlee told me so. Come on, quick! We'll drive and hitch closest place we can find to the building."

Margaret went in the excitement of the moment, but she was troubled.

When they reached the building Wesley tied the team to a railing and Billy sprang out to help Margaret. Mrs. Comstock sat still.

"Come on, Kate," said Wesley, reaching his hand.

"I'm not going anywhere," said Mrs. Comstock, settling comfortably back against the cushions.

All of them begged and pleaded, but it was no use. Not an inch would Mrs. Comstock budge. The night was warm and the carriage comfortable, the horses were securely hitched. She did not care to see what idiotic thing a pack of school children were doing, she would wait until the Sintons returned. Wesley told her it might be two hours, and she said she did not care if it were four, so they left her.

"Did you ever see such—?"

"Cookies!" cried Billy.

"Such blamed stubbornness in all your life?" demanded Wesley. "Won't come to see as fine a girl as Elnora in a stage performance. Why, I wouldn't miss it for fifty dollars!"

"I think it's a blessing she didn't," said Margaret placidly. "I begged unusually hard so she wouldn't. I'm scared of my life for fear Elnora will play."

They found seats near the door where they could see fairly well. Billy stood at the back of the hall and had a good view. By and by, a great volume of sound welled from the orchestra, but Elnora was not playing.

301

"Told you so!" said Sinton. "Got a notion to go out and see if Kate won't come now. She can take my seat, and I'll stand with Billy."

"You sit still!" said Margaret emphatically. "This is not over yet."

So Wesley remained in his seat. The play opened and progressed very much as all high school plays have gone for the past fifty years. But Elnora did not appear in any of the scenes.

Out in the warm summer night a sour, grim woman nursed an aching heart and tried to justify herself. The effort irritated her intensely. She felt that she could not afford the things that were being done. The old fear of losing the land that she and Robert Comstock had purchased and started clearing was strong upon her. She was thinking of him, how she needed him, when the orchestra music poured from the open windows near her. Mrs. Comstock endured it as long as she could, and then slipped from the carriage and fled down the street.

She did not know how far she went or how long she stayed, but everything was still, save an occasional raised voice when she wandered back. She stood looking at the building. Slowly she entered the wide gates and followed up the walk. Elnora had been coming here for almost four years. When Mrs. Comstock reached the door she looked inside. The wide hall was lighted with electricity, and the statuary and the decorations of the walls did not seem like pieces of foolishness. The marble appeared pure, white, and the big pictures most interesting. She walked the length of the hall and slowly read the titles of the statues and the names of the pupils who had donated them. She speculated on where the piece Elnora's class would buy could be placed to advantage.

Then she wondered if they were having a large enough audience to buy marble. She liked it better than the bronze, but it looked as if it cost more. How white the broad stairway was! Elnora had been climbing those stairs for years and never told her they were marble. Of course, she thought they were wood. Probably the upper hall was even grander than this. She went over to the fountain, took a drink, climbed to the first landing and looked around her, and then without thought to the second. There she came opposite the wide-open doors and the entrance to the auditorium packed with people and a crowd standing outside. When they noticed a tall woman with white face and hair and black dress, one by one they stepped a little aside, so that Mrs. Comstock could see the stage. It was covered with curtains, and no one was doing anything. Just as she turned to go a sound so faint that every one leaned forward and listened, drifted down the auditorium. It was difficult to tell just what it was; after one instant half the audience looked toward the windows, for it seemed only a breath of wind rustling freshly opened leaves; merely a hint of stirring air.

Then the curtains were swept aside swiftly. The stage had been transformed into a lovely little corner of creation, where trees and flowers grew and moss carpeted the earth. A soft wind blew and it was the gray of dawn. Suddenly a robin began to sing, then a song sparrow joined him, and then several orioles began talking at once. The light grew stronger, the dew drops trembled, flower perfume began to creep out to the audience; the air moved the branches gently and a rooster crowed. Then all the scene was shaken with a babel of bird notes in which you could hear a cardinal whistling, and a blue finch piping. Back somewhere among the high branches a dove cooed and then a horse neighed shrilly. That set a blackbird crying, "T'check," and a whole flock answered it. The crows began to caw and a lamb bleated. Then the grosbeaks, chats, and vireos had something to say, and the sun rose higher, the light grew stronger and the breeze rustled the treetops loudly; a cow bawled and the whole barnyard answered. The guineas were clucking, the turkey gobbler strutting, the hens calling, the chickens cheeping, the light streamed down straight overhead and the bees began to hum. The air stirred strongly, and away in an unseen field a reaper clacked and rattled through ripening wheat while the driver whistled. An uneasy mare whickered to her colt, the colt answered, and the light began to decline. Miles away a rooster crowed for twilight, and dusk was coming down. Then a catbird and a brown thrush sang against a grosbeak and a hermit thrush. The air was tremulous with heavenly notes, the lights went out in the hall, dusk swept across the stage, a cricket sang and a katydid answered, and a wood pewee wrung the heart with its lonesome cry. Then a night hawk screamed, a whip-poor-will complained, a belated killdeer swept the sky, and the night wind sang a louder song. A little screech owl tuned up in the distance, a barn owl replied, and a great horned owl drowned both their voices. The moon shone and the scene was warm with mellow light. The bird voices died and soft exquisite melody began to swell and roll. In the centre of the stage, piece by piece the grasses, mosses and leaves dropped from an embankment, the foliage softly blew away, while plainer and plainer came the outlines of a lovely girl figure draped in soft clinging green. In her shower of bright hair a few green leaves and white blossoms clung, and they fell over her robe down to her feet. Her white throat and arms were bare, she leaned forward a little and swayed with the melody, her eyes fast on the clouds above her, her lips parted, a pink tinge of exercise in her cheeks as she drew her bow. She played as only a peculiar chain of circumstances puts it in the power of a very few to play. All nature had grown still, the violin sobbed, sang, danced and quavered on alone, no voice in particular; the soul of the melody of all nature combined in one great outpouring.

At the doorway, a white-faced woman endured it as long as she could and then fell senseless. The men nearest carried her down the hall to the fountain, revived her, and then placed her in the carriage to which she directed them. The girl played on and never knew. When she finished, the uproar of applause sounded a block down the street, but the half-senseless woman scarcely realized what it meant. Then the girl came to the front of the stage, bowed, and lifting the violin she played her conception of an invitation to dance. Every living soul within sound of her notes strained their nerves to sit still and let only their hearts dance with her. When that began the woman ran toward the country. She never stopped until the carriage overtook her half-way to her cabin. She said she had grown tired of sitting, and walked on ahead. That night she asked Billy to remain with her and sleep on Elnora's bed. Then she pitched headlong upon her own, and suffered agony of soul such as she never before had known. The swamp had sent back the soul of her loved dead and put it into the body of the daughter she resented, and it was almost more than she could endure and live.

Chapter 11

Wherein Elnora Graduates, and Freckles and the Angel Send Gifts

That was Friday night. Elnora came home Saturday morning and began work. Mrs. Comstock asked no questions, and the girl only told her that the audience had been large enough to more than pay for the piece of statuary the class had selected for the hall. Then she inquired about her dresses and was told they would be ready for her. She had been invited to go to the Bird Woman's to prepare for both the sermon and Commencement exercises. Since there was so much practising to do, it had been arranged that she should remain there from the night of the sermon until after she was graduated. If Mrs. Comstock decided to attend she was to drive in with the Sintons. When Elnora begged her to come she said she cared nothing about such silliness.

It was almost time for Wesley to come to take Elnora to the city, when fresh from her bath, and dressed to her outer garment, she stood with expectant face before her mother and cried: "Now my dress, mother!"

Mrs. Comstock was pale as she replied: "It's on my bed. Help yourself."

Elnora opened the door and stepped into her mother's room with never a misgiving. Since the night Margaret and Wesley had brought her clothing, when she first started to school, her mother had selected all of her dresses, with Mrs. Sinton's help made most of them, and Elnora had paid the bills. The white dress of the previous spring was the first made at a dressmaker's. She had worn that as junior usher at Commencement; but her mother had selected the material, had it made, and it had fitted perfectly and had been suitable in every way. So with her heart at rest on that point, Elnora hurried to the bed to find only her last summer's white dress, freshly washed and ironed. For an instant she stared at it, then she picked up the garment, looked at the bed beneath it, and her gaze slowly swept the room.

It was unfamiliar. Perhaps this was the third time she had been in it since she was a very small child. Her eyes ranged over the beautiful walnut dresser, the tall bureau, the big chest, inside which she never had seen, and the row of masculine attire hanging above it. Somewhere a dainty lawn or mull dress simply must be hanging: but it was not. Elnora dropped on the chest because she felt too weak to stand. In less than two hours she must be in the church, at Onabasha. She could not wear a last year's washed dress. She had nothing else. She leaned against the wall and her father's overcoat brushed her face. She caught the folds and clung to it with all her might.

"Oh father! Father!" she moaned. "I need you! I don't believe you would have done this!" At last she opened the door.

"I can't find my dress," she said.

"Well, as it's the only one there I shouldn't think it would be much trouble."

"You mean for me to wear an old washed dress to-night?"

"It's a good dress. There isn't a hole in it! There's no reason on earth why you shouldn't wear it."

"Except that I will not," said Elnora. "Didn't you provide any dress for Commencement, either?"

"If you soil that to-night, I've plenty of time to wash it again."

Wesley's voice called from the gate.

"In a minute," answered Elnora.

She ran upstairs and in an incredibly short time came down wearing one of her gingham school dresses. Her face cold and hard, she passed her mother and went into the night. Half an hour later Margaret and Billy stopped for Mrs. Comstock with the carriage. She had determined fully that she would not go before they called. With the sound of their voices a sort of horror of being left seized her, so she put on her hat, locked the door and went out to them.

"How did Elnora look?" inquired Margaret anxiously.

"Like she always does," answered Mrs. Comstock curtly.

"I do hope her dresses are as pretty as the others," said Margaret. "None of them will have prettier faces or nicer ways."

Wesley was waiting before the big church to take care of the team. As they stood watching the people enter the building, Mrs. Comstock felt herself growing ill. When they went inside among the lights, saw the flower-decked stage, and the masses of finely dressed people, she grew no better. She could hear Margaret and Billy softly commenting on what was being done.

"That first chair in the very front row is Elnora's," exulted Billy, "cos she's got the highest grades, and so she gets to lead the procession to the platform."

"The first chair!" "Lead the procession!" Mrs. Comstock was dumbfounded. The notes of the pipe organ began to fill the building in a slow rolling march. Would Elnora lead the procession in a gingham dress? Or would she be absent and her chair vacant on this great occasion? For now, Mrs. Comstock could see that it was a great occasion. Every one would remember how Elnora had played a few nights before, and they would miss her and pity her. Pity? Because she had no one to care for her. Because she was worse off than if she had no mother. For the first time in her life, Mrs. Comstock began to study herself as she would appear to others. Every time a junior girl came fluttering down the aisle, leading some one to a seat, and Mrs. Comstock saw a beautiful white dress pass, a wave of positive illness swept over her. What had she done? What would become of Elnora?

As Elnora rode to the city, she answered Wesley's questions in monosyllables so that he thought she was nervous or rehearsing her speech and did not care to talk. Several times the girl tried to tell him and realized that if she said the first word it would bring uncontrollable tears. The Bird Woman opened the screen and stared unbelievingly.

"Why, I thought you would be ready; you are so late!" she said. "If you have waited to dress here, we must hurry."

"I have nothing to put on," said Elnora.

In bewilderment the Bird Woman drew her inside.

"Did—did—" she faltered. "Did you think you would wear that?"

"No. I thought I would telephone Ellen that there had been an accident and I could not come. I don't know yet how to explain. I'm too sick to think. Oh, do you suppose I can get something made by Tuesday, so that I can graduate?"

"Yes; and you'll get something on you to-night, so that you can lead your class, as you have done for four years. Go to my room and take off that gingham, quickly. Anna, drop everything, and come help me."

The Bird Woman ran to the telephone and called Ellen Brownlee.

"Elnora has had an accident. She will be a little late," she said. "You have got to make them wait. Have them play extra music before the march."

Then she turned to the maid. "Tell Benson to have the carriage at the gate, just as soon as he can get it there. Then come to my room. Bring the thread box from the sewing-room, that roll of wide white ribbon on the cutting table, and gather all the white pins from every dresser in the house. But first come with me a minute."

"I want that trunk with the Swamp Angel's stuff in it, from the cedar closet," she panted as they reached the top of the stairs.

They hurried down the hall together and dragged the big trunk to the Bird Woman's room. She opened it and began tossing out white stuff.

"How lucky that she left these things!" she cried. "Here are white shoes, gloves, stockings, fans, everything!"

"I am all ready but a dress," said Elnora.

The Bird Woman began opening closets and pulling out drawers and boxes. "I think I can make it this way," she said.

She snatched up a creamy lace yoke with long sleeves that recently had been made for her and held it out. Elnora slipped into it, and the Bird Woman began smoothing out wrinkles and sewing in pins. It fitted very well with a little lapping in the back. Next, from among the Angel's clothing she caught up a white silk waist with low neck and elbow sleeves, and Elnora put it on. It was large enough, but distressingly short in the waist, for the Angel had worn it at a party when she was sixteen. The Bird Woman loosened the sleeves and pushed them to a puff on the shoulders, catching them in places with pins. She began on the wide draping of the yoke, fastening it front, back and at each shoulder. She pulled down the waist and pinned it. Next came a soft white dress skirt of her own. By pinning her waist band quite four inches above Elnora's, the Bird Woman could secure a perfect Empire sweep, with the clinging silk. Then she began with the wide white ribbon that was to trim a new frock for herself, bound it three times around the high waist effect she had managed, tied the ends in a knot and let them fall to the floor in a beautiful sash.

"I want four white roses, each with two or three leaves," she cried.

Anna ran to bring them, while the Bird Woman added pins.

"Elnora," she said, "forgive me, but tell me truly. Is your mother so poor as to make this necessary?"

"No," answered Elnora. "Next year I am heir to my share of over three hundred acres of land covered with almost as valuable timber as was in the Limberlost. We adjoin it. There could be thirty oil wells drilled that would yield to us the thousands our neighbours are draining from under us, and the bare land is worth over one hundred dollars an acre for farming. She is not poor, she is—I don't know what she is. A great trouble soured and warped her. It made her peculiar. She does not in the least understand, but it is because she doesn't care to, instead of ignorance. She does not—"

Elnora stopped.

"She is—is different," finished the girl.

Anna came with the roses. The Bird Woman set one on the front of the draped yoke, one on each shoulder and the last among the bright masses of brown hair. Then she turned the girl facing the tall mirror.

"Oh!" panted Elnora. "You are a genius! Why, I will look as well as any of them."

"Thank goodness for that!" cried the Bird Woman. "If it wouldn't do, I should have been ill. You are lovely; altogether lovely! Ordinarily I shouldn't say that; but when I think of how you are carpentered, I'm admiring the result."

The organ began rolling out the march as they came in sight. Elnora took her place at the head of the procession, while every one wondered. Secretly they had hoped that she would be dressed well enough, that she would not appear poor and neglected. What this radiant young creature, gowned in the most recent style, her smooth skin flushed with excitement, and a rose-set coronet of red gold on her head, had to do with the girl they knew was difficult to decide. The signal was given and Elnora began the slow march across the vestry and down the aisle. The music welled softly, and Margaret began to sob without knowing why.

Mrs. Comstock gripped her hands together and shut her eyes. It seemed an eternity to the suffering woman before Margaret caught her arm and whispered, "Oh, Kate! For any sake look at her! Here! The aisle across!"

Mrs. Comstock opened her eyes and directing them where she was told, gazed intently, and slid down in her seat close to collapse. She was saved by Margaret's tense clasp and her command: "Here! Idiot! Stop that!"

In the blaze of light Elnora climbed the steps to the palm-embowered platform, crossed it and took her place. Sixty young men and women, each of them dressed the best possible, followed her. There were manly, fine-looking men in that class which Elnora led. There were girls of beauty and grace, but not one of them was handsomer or clothed in better taste than she.

Billy thought the time never would come when Elnora would see him, but at last she met his eye, then Margaret and Wesley had faint signs of recognition in turn, but there was no softening of the girl's face and no hint of a smile when she saw her mother.

Heartsick, Katharine Comstock tried to prove to herself that she was justified in what she had done, but she could not. She tried to blame Elnora for not saying that she was to lead a procession and sit on a platform in the sight of hundreds of people; but that was impossible, for she realized that she would have scoffed and not understood if she had been told. Her heart pained until she suffered with every breath.

When at last the exercises were over she climbed into the carriage and rode home without a word. She did not hear what Margaret and Billy were saying. She scarcely heard Wesley, who drove behind, when he told her that Elnora would not be home until Wednesday. Early the next morning Mrs. Comstock was on her way to Onabasha. She was waiting when the Brownlee store opened. She examined ready-made white dresses, but they had only one of the right size, and it was marked forty dollars. Mrs. Comstock did not hesitate over the price, but whether the dress would be suitable. She would have to ask Elnora. She inquired her way to the home of the Bird Woman and knocked.

"Is Elnora Comstock here?" she asked the maid.

"Yes, but she is still in bed. I was told to let her sleep as long as she would."

"Maybe I could sit here and wait," said Mrs. Comstock. "I want to see about getting her a dress for to-morrow. I am her mother."

"Then you don't need wait or worry," said the girl cheerfully. "There are two women up in the sewing-room at work on a dress for her right now. It will be done in time, and it will be a beauty."

Mrs. Comstock turned and trudged back to the Limberlost. The bitterness in her soul became a physical actuality, which water would not wash from her lips. She was too late! She was not needed. Another woman was mothering her girl. Another woman would prepare a beautiful dress such as Elnora had worn the previous night. The girl's love and gratitude would go to her. Mrs. Comstock tried the old process of blaming some one else, but she felt no better. She nursed her grief as closely as ever in the long days of the girl's absence. She brooded over Elnora's possession of the forbidden violin and her ability to play it until the performance could not have been told from her father's. She tried every refuge her mind could conjure, to quiet her heart and remove the fear that the girl never would come home again, but it persisted. Mrs. Comstock could neither eat nor sleep. She wandered around the cabin and garden. She kept far from the pool where Robert Comstock had sunk from sight for she felt that it would entomb her also if Elnora did not come home Wednesday morning. The mother told herself that she would wait, but the waiting was as bitter as anything she ever had known.

When Elnora awoke Monday another dress was in the hands of a seamstress and was soon fitted. It had belonged to the Angel, and was a soft white thing that with a little alteration would serve admirably for Commencement and the ball. All that day Elnora worked, helping prepare the auditorium for the exercises, rehearsing the march and the speech she was to make in behalf of the class. The following day was even busier. But her mind was at rest, for the dress was a soft delicate lace easy to change, and the marks of alteration impossible to detect.

The Bird Woman had telephoned to Grand Rapids, explained the situation and asked the Angel if she might use it. The reply had been to give the girl the contents of the chest. When the Bird Woman told Elnora, tears filled her eyes.

"I will write at once and thank her," she said. "With all her beautiful gowns she does not need them, and I do. They will serve for me often, and be much finer than anything I could afford. It is lovely of her to give me the dress and of you to have it altered for me, as I never could."

The Bird Woman laughed. "I feel religious to-day," she said. "You know the first and greatest rock of my salvation is 'Do unto others.' I'm only doing to you what there was no one to do for me when I was a girl very like you. Anna tells me your mother was here early this morning and that she came to see about getting you a dress."

"She is too late!" said Elnora coldly. "She had over a month to prepare my dresses, and I was to pay for them, so there is no excuse."

"Nevertheless, she is your mother," said the Bird Woman, softly. "I think almost any kind of a mother must be better than none at all, and you say she has had great trouble."

"She loved my father and he died," said Elnora. "The same thing, in quite as tragic a manner, has happened to thousands of other women, and they have gone on with calm faces and found happiness in life by loving others. There was something else I am afraid I never shall forget; this I know I shall not, but talking does not help. I must deliver my presents and photographs to the crowd. I have a picture and I made a present for you, too, if you would care for them."

"I shall love anything you give me," said the Bird Woman. "I know you well enough to know that whatever you do will be beautiful."

Elnora was pleased over that, and as she tried on her dress for the last fitting she was really happy. She was lovely in the dainty gown: it would serve finely for the ball and many other like occasions, and it was her very own.

The Bird Woman's driver took Elnora in the carriage and she called on all the girls with whom she was especially intimate, and left her picture and the package containing her gift to them. By the time she returned parcels for her were arriving. Friends seemed to spring from everywhere. Almost every one she knew had some gift for her, while because they so loved her the members of her crowd had made her beautiful presents. There were books, vases, silver pieces, handkerchiefs, fans, boxes of flowers and candy. One big package settled the trouble at Sinton's, for it contained a dainty dress from Margaret; a five-dollar gold piece, conspicuously labelled, "I earned this myself," from Billy, with which to buy music; and a gorgeous cut-glass perfume bottle, it would have cost five dollars to fill with even a moderate-priced scent, from Wesley.

In an expressed crate was a fine curly-maple dressing table, sent by Freckles. The drawers were filled with wonderful toilet articles from the Angel. The Bird Woman added an embroidered linen cover and a small silver vase for a few flowers, so no girl of the class had finer gifts. Elnora laid her head on the table sobbing happily, and the Bird Woman was almost crying herself. Professor Henley sent a butterfly book, the grade rooms in which Elnora had taught gave her a set of volumes covering every phase of life afield, in the woods, and water. Elnora had no time to read so she carried one of these books around with her hugging it as she went. After she had gone to dress a queer-looking package was brought by a small boy who hopped on one foot as he handed it in and said: "Tell Elnora that is from her ma."

"Who are you?" asked the Bird Woman as she took the bundle.

"I'm Billy!" announced the boy. "I gave her the five dollars. I earned it myself dropping corn, sticking onions, and pulling weeds. My, but you got to drop, and stick, and pull a lot before it's five dollars' worth."

"Would you like to come in and see Elnora's gifts?"

"Yes, ma'am!" said Billy, trying to stand quietly.

"Gee-mentley!" he gasped. "Does Elnora get all this?"

"Yes."

"I bet you a thousand dollars I be first in my class when I graduate. Say, have the others got a lot more than Elnora?"

"I think not."

"Well, Uncle Wesley said to find out if I could, and if she didn't have as much as the rest, he'd buy till she did, if it took a hundred dollars. Say, you ought to know him! He's just scrumptious! There ain't anybody any where finer 'an he is. My, he's grand!"

"I'm very sure of it!" said the Bird Woman. "I've often heard Elnora say so."

"I bet you nobody can beat this!" he boasted. Then he stopped, thinking deeply. "I don't know, though," he began reflectively. "Some of them are awful rich; they got big families to give them things and wagon loads of friends, and I haven't seen what they have. Now, maybe Elnora is getting left, after all!"

"Don't worry, Billy," she said. "I will watch, and if I find Elnora is 'getting left' I'll buy her some more things myself. But I'm sure she is not. She has more beautiful gifts now than she will know what to do with, and others will come. Tell your Uncle Wesley his girl is bountifully remembered, very happy, and she sends her dearest love to all of you. Now you must go, so I can help her dress. You will be there to-night of course?"

"Yes, sir-ee! She got me a seat, third row from the front, middle section, so I can see, and she's going to wink at me, after she gets her speech off her mind. She kissed me, too! She's a perfect lady, Elnora is. I'm going to marry her when I am big enough."

"Why isn't that splendid!" laughed the Bird Woman as she hurried upstairs.

"Dear!" she called. "Here is another gift for you."

Elnora was half disrobed as she took the package and, sitting on a couch, opened it. The Bird Woman bent over her and tested the fabric with her fingers.

"Why, bless my soul!" she cried. "Hand-woven, hand-embroidered linen, fine as silk. It's priceless; I haven't seen such things in years. My mother had garments like those when I was a child, but my sisters had them cut up for collars, belts, and fancy waists while I was small. Look at the exquisite work!"

"Where could it have come from?" cried Elnora.

She shook out a petticoat, with a hand-wrought ruffle a foot deep, then an old-fashioned chemise the neck and sleeve work of which was elaborate and perfectly wrought. On the breast was pinned a note that she hastily opened.

"I was married in these," it read, "and I had intended to be buried in them, but perhaps it would be more sensible for you to graduate and get married in them yourself, if you like. Your mother."

"From my mother!" Wide-eyed, Elnora looked at the Bird Woman. "I never in my life saw the like. Mother does things I think I never can forgive, and when I feel hardest, she turns around and does something that makes me think she just must love me a little bit, after all. Any of the girls would give almost anything to graduate in hand-embroidered linen like that. Money can't buy such things. And they came when I was thinking she didn't care what became of me. Do you suppose she can be insane?"

"Yes," said the Bird Woman. "Wildly insane, if she does not love you and care what becomes of you."

Elnora arose and held the petticoat to her. "Will you look at it?" she cried. "Only imagine her not getting my dress ready, and then sending me such a petticoat as this! Ellen would pay fifty dollars for it and never blink. I suppose mother has had it all my life, and I never saw it before."

"Go take your bath and put on those things," said the Bird Woman. "Forget everything and be happy. She is not insane. She is embittered. She did not understand how things would be. When she saw, she came at once to provide you a dress. This is her way of saying she is sorry she did not get the other. You notice she has not spent any money, so perhaps she is quite honest in saying she has none."

"Oh, she is honest!" said Elnora. "She wouldn't care enough to tell an untruth. She'd say just how things were, no matter what happened."

Soon Elnora was ready for her dress. She never had looked so well as when she again headed the processional across the flower and palm decked stage of the high school auditorium. As she sat there she could have reached over and dropped a rose she carried into the seat she had occupied that September morning when she entered the high school. She spoke the few words she had to say in behalf of the class beautifully, had the tiny wink ready for Billy, and the smile and nod of recognition for Wesley and Margaret. When at last she looked into the eyes of a white-faced woman next them, she slipped a hand to her side and raised her skirt the fraction of an inch, just enough to let the embroidered edge of a petticoat show a trifle. When she saw the look of relief which flooded her mother's face, Elnora knew that forgiveness was in her heart, and that she would go home in the morning.

It was late afternoon before she arrived, and a dray followed with a load of packages. Mrs. Comstock was overwhelmed. She sat half dazed and made Elnora show her each costly and beautiful or simple and useful gift, tell her carefully what it was and from where it came. She studied the faces of Elnora's particular friends. The gifts from them had to be set in a group. Several times she started to speak and then stopped. At last, between her dry lips, came a harsh whisper.

"Elnora, what did you give back for these things?"

"I'll show you," said Elnora cheerfully. "I made the same gifts for the Bird Woman, Aunt Margaret, and you if you care for it. But I have to run upstairs to get it."

When she returned she handed her mother an oblong frame, hand carved, enclosing Elnora's picture, taken by a schoolmate's camera. She wore her storm-coat and carried a dripping umbrella. From under it looked her bright face; her books and lunchbox were on her arm, and across the bottom of the frame was carved, "Your Country Classmate."

Then she offered another frame.

"I am strong on frames," she said. "They seemed to be the best I could do without money. I located the maple and the black walnut myself, in a little corner that had been overlooked between the river and the ditch. They didn't seem to belong to any one so I just took them. Uncle Wesley said it was all right, and he cut and hauled them for me. I gave the mill half of each tree for sawing and curing the remainder. Then I gave the wood-carver half of that for making my frames. A photographer gave me a lot of spoiled plates, and I boiled off the emulsion, and took the specimens I framed from my stuff. The man said the white frames were worth three and a half, and the black ones five. I exchanged those little framed pictures for the photographs of the others. For presents, I gave each one of my crowd one like this, only a different moth. The Bird Woman gave me the birch bark. She got it up north last summer."

Elnora handed her mother a handsome black-walnut frame a foot and a half wide by two long. It finished a small, shallow glass-covered box of birch bark, to the bottom of which clung a big night moth with delicate pale green wings and long exquisite trailers.

"So you see I did not have to be ashamed of my gifts," said Elnora. "I made them myself and raised and mounted the moths."

"Moth, you call it," said Mrs. Comstock. "I've seen a few of the things before."

"They are numerous around us every June night, or at least they used to be," said Elnora. "I've sold hundreds of them, with butterflies, dragonflies, and other specimens. Now, I must put away these and get to work, for it is almost June and there are a few more I want dreadfully. If I find them I will be paid some money for which I have been working."

She was afraid to say college at that time. She thought it would be better to wait a few days and see if an opportunity would not come when it would work in more naturally. Besides, unless she could secure the Yellow Emperor she needed to complete her collection, she could not talk college until she was of age, for she would have no money.

Chapter 12

Wherein Margaret Sinton Reveals a Secret, and Mrs. Comstock Possesses the Limberlost

"Elnora, bring me the towel, quick!" cried Mrs. Comstock.

"In a minute, mother," mumbled Elnora.

She was standing before the kitchen mirror, tying the back part of her hair, while the front turned over her face.

"Hurry! There's a varmint of some kind!"

Elnora ran into the sitting-room and thrust the heavy kitchen towel into her mother's hand. Mrs. Comstock swung open the screen door and struck at some object, Elnora tossed the hair from her face so that she could see past her mother. The girl screamed wildly.

"Don't! Mother, don't!"

Mrs. Comstock struck again. Elnora caught her arm. "It's the one I want! It's worth a lot of money! Don't! Oh, you shall not!"

"Shan't, missy?" blazed Mrs. Comstock. "When did you get to bossing me?"

The hand that held the screen swept a half-circle and stopped at Elnora's cheek. She staggered with the blow, and across her face, paled with excitement, a red mark arose rapidly. The screen slammed shut, throwing the creature on the floor before them. Instantly Mrs. Comstock crushed it with her foot. Elnora stepped back. Excepting the red mark, her face was very white.

"That was the last moth I needed," she said, "to complete a collection worth three hundred dollars. You've ruined it before my eyes!"

"Moth!" cried Mrs. Comstock. "You say that because you are mad. Moths have big wings. I know a moth!"

"I've kept things from you," said Elnora, "because I didn't dare confide in you. You had no sympathy with me. But you know I never told you untruths in all my life."

"It's no moth!" reiterated Mrs. Comstock.

"It is!" cried Elnora. "It's from a case in the ground. Its wings take two or three hours to expand and harden."

"If I had known it was a moth—" Mrs. Comstock wavered.

"You did know! I told you! I begged you to stop! It meant just three hundred dollars to me."

"Bah! Three hundred fiddlesticks!"

"They are what have paid for books, tuition, and clothes for the past four years. They are what I could have started on to college. You've ruined the very one I needed. You never made any pretence of loving me. At last I'll be equally frank with you. I hate you! You are a selfish, wicked woman! I hate you!"

Elnora turned, went through the kitchen and from the back door. She followed the garden path to the gate and walked toward the swamp a short distance when reaction overtook her. She dropped on the ground and leaned against a big log. When a little child, desperate as now, she had tried to die by holding her breath. She had thought in that way to make her mother sorry, but she had learned that life was a thing thrust upon her and she could not leave it at her wish.

She was so stunned over the loss of that moth, which she had childishly named the Yellow Emperor, that she scarcely remembered the blow. She had thought no luck in all the world would be so rare as to complete her collection; now she had been forced to see a splendid Imperialis destroyed before her. There was a possibility that she could find another, but she was facing the certainty that the one she might have had and with which she undoubtedly could have attracted others, was spoiled by her mother. How long she sat there Elnora did not know or care. She simply suffered in dumb, abject misery, an occasional dry sob shaking her. Aunt Margaret was right. Elnora felt that morning that her mother never would be any different. The girl had reached the place where she realized that she could endure it no longer.

As Elnora left the room, Mrs. Comstock took one step after her.

"You little huzzy!" she gasped.

But Elnora was gone. Her mother stood staring.

"She never did lie to me," she muttered. "I guess it was a moth. And the only one she needed to get three hundred dollars, she said. I wish I hadn't been so fast! I never saw anything like it. I thought it was some deadly, stinging, biting thing. A body does have to be mighty careful here. But likely I've spilt the milk now. Pshaw! She can find another! There's no use to be foolish. Maybe moths are like snakes, where there's one, there are two."

Mrs. Comstock took the broom and swept the moth out of the door. Then she got down on her knees and carefully examined the steps, logs and the earth of the flower beds at each side. She found the place where the creature had emerged from the ground, and the hard, dark-brown case which had enclosed it, still wet inside. Then she knew Elnora had been right. It was a moth. Its wings had been damp and not expanded. Mrs. Comstock never before had seen one in that state, and she did not know how they originated. She had thought all of them came from cases spun on trees or against walls or boards. She had seen only enough to know that there were such things; as a flash of white told her that an ermine was on her premises, or a sharp "buzzzzz" warned her of a rattler.

So it was from creatures like that Elnora had secured her school money. In one sickening sweep there rushed into the heart of the woman a full realization of the width of the gulf that separated her from her child. Lately many things had pointed toward it, none more plainly than when Elnora, like a reincarnation of her father, had stood fearlessly before a large city audience and played with even greater skill than he, on what Mrs. Comstock felt very certain was his violin. But that little crawling creature of earth, crushed by her before its splendid yellow and lavender wings could spread and carry it into the mystery of night, had performed a miracle.

"We are nearer strangers to each other than we are with any of the neighbours," she muttered.

So one of the Almighty's most delicate and beautiful creations was sacrificed without fulfilling the law, yet none of its species ever served so glorious a cause, for at last Mrs. Comstock's inner vision had cleared. She went through the cabin mechanically. Every few minutes she glanced toward the back walk to see if Elnora were coming. She knew arrangements had been made with Margaret to go to the city some time that day, so she grew more nervous and uneasy every moment. She was haunted by the fear that the blow might discolour Elnora's cheek; that she would tell Margaret. She went down the back walk, looking intently in all directions, left the garden and followed the swamp path. Her step was noiseless on the soft, black earth, and soon she came close enough to see Elnora. Mrs. Comstock stood looking at the girl in troubled uncertainty. Not knowing what to say, at last she turned and went back to the cabin.

Noon came and she prepared dinner, calling, as she always did, when Elnora was in the garden, but she got no response, and the girl did not come. A little after one o'clock Margaret stopped at the gate.

"Elnora has changed her mind. She is not going," called Mrs. Comstock.

She felt that she hated Margaret as she hitched her horse and came up the walk instead of driving on.

"You must be mistaken," said Margaret. "I was going on purpose for her. She asked me to take her. I had no errand. Where is she?"

"I will call her," said Mrs. Comstock.

She followed the path again, and this time found Elnora sitting on the log. Her face was swollen and discoloured, and her eyes red with crying. She paid no attention to her mother.

"Mag Sinton is here," said Mrs. Comstock harshly. "I told her you had changed your mind, but she said you asked her to go with you, and she had nothing to go for herself."

Elnora arose, recklessly waded through the deep swamp grasses and so reached the path ahead of her mother. Mrs. Comstock followed as far as the garden, but she could not enter the cabin. She busied herself among the vegetables, barely looking up when the back-door screen slammed noisily. Margaret Sinton approached colourless, her eyes so angry that Mrs. Comstock shrank back.

"What's the matter with Elnora's face?" demanded Margaret.

Mrs. Comstock made no reply.

"You struck her, did you?"

"I thought you wasn't blind!"

"I have been, for twenty long years now, Kate Comstock," said Margaret Sinton, "but my eyes are open at last. What I see is that I've done you no good and Elnora a big wrong. I had an idea that it would kill you to know, but I guess you are tough enough to stand anything. Kill or cure, you get it now!"

"What are you frothing about?" coolly asked Mrs. Comstock.

"You!" cried Margaret. "You! The woman who doesn't pretend to love her only child. Who lets her grow to a woman, as you have let Elnora, and can't be satisfied with every sort of neglect, but must add abuse yet; and all for a fool idea about a man who wasn't worth his salt!"

Mrs. Comstock picked up a hoe.

"Go right on!" she said. "Empty yourself. It's the last thing you'll ever do!"

"Then I'll make a tidy job of it," said Margaret. "You'll not touch me. You'll stand there and hear the truth at last, and because I dare face you and tell it, you will know in your soul it is truth. When Robert Comstock shaved that quagmire out there so close he went in, he wanted to keep you from knowing where he was coming from. He'd been to see Elvira Carney. They had plans to go to a dance that night——"

"Close your lips!" said Mrs. Comstock in a voice of deadly quiet.

"You know I wouldn't dare open them if I wasn't telling you the truth. I can prove what I say. I was coming from Reeds. It was hot in the woods and I stopped at Carney's as I passed for a drink. Elvira's bedridden old mother heard me, and she was so crazy for some one to talk with, I stepped in a minute. I saw Robert come down the path. Elvira saw him, too, so she ran out of the house to head him off. It looked funny, and I just deliberately moved where I could see and hear. He brought her his violin, and told her to get ready and meet him in the woods with it that night, and they would go to a dance. She took it and hid it in the loft to the well-house and promised she'd go."

"Are you done?" demanded Mrs. Comstock.

"No. I am going to tell you the whole story. You don't spare Elnora anything. I shan't spare you. I hadn't been here that day, but I can tell you just how he was dressed, which way he went and every word they said, though they thought I was busy with her mother and wouldn't notice them. Put down your hoe, Kate. I went to Elvira, told her what I knew and made her give me Comstock's violin for Elnora over three years ago. She's been playing it ever since. I won't see her slighted and abused another day on account of a man who would have broken your heart if he had lived. Six months more would have showed you what everybody else knew. He was one of those men who couldn't trust himself, and so no woman was safe with him. Now, will you drop grieving over him, and do Elnora justice?"

Mrs. Comstock grasped the hoe tighter and turning she went down the walk, and started across the woods to the home of Elvira Carney. With averted head she passed the pool, steadily pursuing her way. Elvira Carney, hanging towels across the back fence, saw her coming and went toward the gate to meet her. Twenty years she had dreaded that visit. Since Margaret Sinton had compelled her to produce the violin she had hidden so long, because she was afraid to destroy it, she had come closer expectation than dread. The wages of sin are the hardest debts on earth to pay, and they are always collected at inconvenient times and unexpected places. Mrs. Comstock's face and hair were so white, that her dark eyes seemed burned into their setting. Silently she stared at the woman before her a long time.

"I might have saved myself the trouble of coming," she said at last, "I see you are guilty as sin!"

"What has Mag Sinton been telling you?" panted the miserable woman, gripping the fence.

"The truth!" answered Mrs. Comstock succinctly. "Guilt is in every line of your face, in your eyes, all over your wretched body. If I'd taken a good look at you any time in all these past years, no doubt I could have seen it just as plain as I can now. No woman or man can do what you've done, and not get a mark set on them for every one to read."

"Mercy!" gasped weak little Elvira Carney. "Have mercy!"

"Mercy?" scoffed Mrs. Comstock. "Mercy! That's a nice word from you! How much mercy did you have on me? Where's the mercy that sent Comstock to the slime of the bottomless quagmire, and left me to see it, and then struggle on in agony all these years? How about the mercy of letting me neglect my baby all the days of her life? Mercy! Do you really dare use the word to me?"

"If you knew what I've suffered!"

"Suffered?" jeered Mrs. Comstock. "That's interesting. And pray, what have you suffered?"

"All the neighbours have suspected and been down on me. I ain't had a friend. I've always felt guilty of his death! I've seen him go down a thousand times, plain as ever you did. Many's the night I've stood on the other bank of that pool and listened to you, and I tried to throw myself in to keep from hearing you, but I didn't dare. I knew God would send me to burn forever, but I'd better done it; for now, He has set the burning on my body, and every hour it is slowly eating the life out of me. The doctor says it's a cancer—"

Mrs. Comstock exhaled a long breath. Her grip on the hoe relaxed and her stature lifted to towering height.

"I didn't know, or care, when I came here, just what I did," she said. "But my way is beginning to clear. If the guilt of your soul has come to a head, in a cancer on your body, it looks as if the Almighty didn't need any of my help in meting out His punishments. I really couldn't fix up anything to come anywhere near that. If you are going to burn until your life goes out with that sort of fire, you don't owe me anything!"

"Oh, Katharine Comstock!" groaned Elvira Carney, clinging to the fence for support.

"Looks as if the Bible is right when it says, 'The wages of sin is death,' doesn't it?" asked Mrs. Comstock. "Instead of doing a woman's work in life, you chose the smile of invitation, and the dress of unearned cloth. Now you tell me you are marked to burn to death with the unquenchable fire. And him! It was shorter with him, but let me tell you he got his share! He left me with an untruth on his lips, for he told me he was going to take his violin to Onabasha for a new key, when he carried it to you. Every vow of love and constancy he ever made me was a lie, after he touched your lips, so when he tried the wrong side of the quagmire, to hide from me the direction in which he was coming, it reached out for him, and it got him. It didn't hurry, either! It sucked him down, slow and deliberate."

"Mercy!" groaned Elvira Carney. "Mercy!"

"I don't know the word," said Mrs. Comstock. "You took all that out of me long ago. The past twenty years haven't been of the sort that taught mercy. I've never had any on myself and none on my child. Why in the name of justice, should I have mercy on you, or on him? You were both older than I, both strong, sane people, you deliberately chose your course when you lured him, and he, when he was unfaithful to me. When a Loose Man and a Light Woman face the end the Almighty ordained for them, why should they shout at me for mercy? What did I have to do with it?"

Elvira Carney sobbed in panting gasps.

"You've got tears, have you?" marvelled Mrs. Comstock. "Mine all dried long ago. I've none left to shed over my wasted life, my disfigured face and hair, my years of struggle with a man's work, my wreck of land among the tilled fields of my neighbours, or the final knowledge that the man I so gladly would have died to save, wasn't worth the sacrifice of a rattlesnake. If anything yet could wring a tear from me, it would be the thought of the awful injustice I always have done my girl. If I'd lay hand on you for anything, it would be for that."

"Kill me if you want to," sobbed Elvira Carney. "I know that I deserve it, and I don't care."

"You are getting your killing fast enough to suit me," said Mrs. Comstock. "I wouldn't touch you, any more than I would him, if I could. Once is all any man or woman deceives me about the holiest things of life. I wouldn't touch you any more than I would the black plague. I am going back to my girl."

Mrs. Comstock turned and started swiftly through the woods, but she had gone only a few rods when she stopped, and leaning on the hoe, she stood thinking deeply. Then she turned back. Elvira still clung to the fence, sobbing bitterly.

"I don't know," said Mrs. Comstock, "but I left a wrong impression with you. I don't want you to think that I believe the Almighty set a cancer to burning you as a punishment for your sins. I don't! I think a lot more of the Almighty. With a whole sky-full of worlds on His hands to manage, I'm not believing that He has time to look down on ours, and pick you out of all the millions of us sinners, and set a special kind of torture to eating you. It wouldn't be a gentlemanly thing to do, and first of all, the Almighty is bound to be a gentleman. I think likely a bruise and bad blood is what caused your trouble. Anyway, I've got to tell you that the cleanest housekeeper I ever knew, and one of the noblest Christian women, was slowly eaten up by a cancer. She got hers from the careless work of a poor doctor. The Almighty is to forgive sin and heal disease, not to invent and spread it."

She had gone only a few steps when she again turned back.

"If you will gather a lot of red clover bloom, make a tea strong as lye of it, and drink quarts, I think likely it will help you, if you are not too far gone. Anyway, it will cool your blood and make the burning easier to bear."

Then she swiftly went home. Enter the lonely cabin she could not, neither could she sit outside and think. She attacked a bed of beets and hoed until the perspiration ran from her face and body, then she began on the potatoes. When she was too tired to take another stroke she bathed and put on dry clothing. In securing her dress she noticed her husband's carefully preserved clothing lining one wall. She gathered it in an armload and carried it to the swamp. Piece by piece she pitched into the green maw of the quagmire all those articles she had dusted carefully and fought moths from for years, and stood watching as it slowly sucked them down. She went back to her room and gathered every scrap that had in any way belonged to Robert Comstock, excepting his gun and revolver, and threw it into the swamp. Then for the first time she set her door wide open.

She was too weary now to do more, but an urging unrest drove her. She wanted Elnora. It seemed to her she never could wait until the girl came and delivered her judgment. At last in an effort to get nearer to her, Mrs. Comstock climbed the stairs and stood looking around Elnora's room. It was very unfamiliar. The pictures were strange to her. Commencement had filled it with packages and bundles. The walls were covered with cocoons; moths and dragonflies were pinned everywhere. Under the bed she could see half a dozen large white boxes. She pulled out one and lifted the lid. The bottom was covered with a sheet of thin cork, and on long pins sticking in it were large, velvet-winged moths. Each one was labelled, always there were two of a kind, in many cases four, showing under and upper wings of both male and female. They were of every colour and shape.

Mrs. Comstock caught her breath sharply. When and where had Elnora found them? They were the most exquisite sight the woman ever had seen, so she opened all the boxes to feast on their beautiful contents. As she did so there came more fully a sense of the distance between her and her child. She could not understand how Elnora had gone to school, and performed so much work secretly. When it was finished, to the last moth, she, the mother who should have been the first confidant and helper, had been the one to bring disappointment. Small wonder Elnora had come to hate her.

Mrs. Comstock carefully closed and replaced the boxes; and again stood looking around the room. This time her eyes rested on some books she did not remember having seen before, so she picked up one and found that it was a moth book. She glanced over the first pages and was soon eagerly reading. When the text reached the classification of species, she laid it down, took up another and read the introductory chapters. By that time her brain was in a confused jumble of ideas about capturing moths with differing baits and bright lights.

She went down stairs thinking deeply. Being unable to sit still and having nothing else to do she glanced at the clock and began preparing supper. The work dragged. A chicken was snatched up and dressed hurriedly. A spice cake sprang into being. Strawberries that had been intended for preserves went into shortcake. Delicious odours crept from the cabin. She put many extra touches on the table and then commenced watching the road. Everything was ready, but Elnora did not come. Then began the anxious process of trying to keep cooked food warm and not spoil it. The birds went to bed and dusk came. Mrs. Comstock gave up the fire and set the supper on the table. Then she went out and sat on the front-door step watching night creep around her. She started eagerly as the gate creaked, but it was only Wesley Sinton coming.

"Katharine, Margaret and Elnora passed where I was working this afternoon, and Margaret got out of the carriage and called me to the fence. She told me what she had done. I've come to say to you that I am sorry. She has heard me threaten to do it a good many times, but I never would have got it done. I'd give a good deal if I could undo it, but I can't, so I've come to tell you how sorry I am."

"You've got something to be sorry for," said Mrs. Comstock, "but likely we ain't thinking of the same thing. It hurts me less to know the truth, than to live in ignorance. If Mag had the sense of a pewee, she'd told me long ago. That's what hurts me, to think that both of you knew Robert was not worth an hour of honest grief, yet you'd let me mourn him all these years and neglect Elnora while I did it. If I have anything to forgive you, that is what it is."

Wesley removed his hat and sat on a bench.

"Katharine," he said solemnly, "nobody ever knows how to take you."

"Would it be asking too much to take me for having a few grains of plain common sense?" she inquired. "You've known all this time that Comstock got what he deserved, when he undertook to sneak in an unused way across a swamp, with which he was none too familiar. Now I should have thought that you'd figure that knowing the same thing would be the best method to cure me of pining for him, and slighting my child."

"Heaven only knows we have thought of that, and talked of it often, but we were both too big cowards. We didn't dare tell you."

"So you have gone on year after year, watching me show indifference to Elnora, and yet a little horse-sense would have pointed out to you that she was my salvation. Why look at it! Not married quite a year. All his vows of love and fidelity made to me before the Almighty forgotten in a few months, and a dance and a Light Woman so alluring he had to lie and sneak for them. What kind of a prospect is that for a life? I know men and women. An honourable man is an honourable man, and a liar is a liar; both are born and not made. One cannot change to the other any more than that same old leopard can change its spots. After a man tells a woman the first untruth of that sort, the others come piling thick, fast, and mountain high. The desolation they bring in their wake overshadows anything I have suffered completely. If he had lived six months more I should have known him for what he was born to be. It was in the blood of him. His father and grandfather before him were fiddling, dancing people; but I was certain of him. I thought we could leave Ohio and come out here alone, and I could so love him and interest him in his work, that he would be a man. Of all the fool, fruitless jobs, making anything of a creature that begins by deceiving her, is the foolest a sane woman ever undertook. I am more than sorry you and Margaret didn't see your way clear to tell me long ago. I'd have found it out in a few more months if he had lived, and I wouldn't have borne it a day. The man who breaks his vows to me once, doesn't get the second chance. I give truth and honour. I have a right to ask it in return. I am glad I understand at last. Now, if Elnora will forgive me, we will take a new start and see what we can make out of what is left of life. If she won't, then it will be my time to learn what suffering really means."

"But she will," said Wesley. "She must! She can't help it when things are explained."

"I notice she isn't hurrying any about coming home. Do you know where she is or what she is doing?"

"I do not. But likely she will be along soon. I must go help Billy with the night work. Good-bye, Katharine. Thank the Lord you have come to yourself at last!"

They shook hands and Wesley went down the road while Mrs. Comstock entered the cabin. She could not swallow food. She stood in the back door watching the sky for moths, but they did not seem to be very numerous. Her spirits sank and she breathed unevenly. Then she heard the front screen. She reached the middle door as Elnora touched the foot of the stairs.

"Hurry, and get ready, Elnora," she said. "Your supper is almost spoiled now."

Elnora closed the stair door behind her, and for the first time in her life, threw the heavy lever which barred out anyone from down stairs. Mrs. Comstock heard the thud, and knew what it meant. She reeled slightly and caught the doorpost for support. For a few minutes she clung there, then sank to the nearest chair. After a long time she arose and stumbling half blindly, she put the food in the cupboard and covered the table. She took the lamp in one hand, the butter in the other, and started to the spring house. Something brushed close by her face, and she looked just in time to see a winged creature rise above the cabin and sail away.

"That was a night bird," she muttered. As she stopped to set the butter in the water, came another thought. "Perhaps it was a moth!" Mrs. Comstock dropped the butter and hurried out with the lamp; she held it high above her head and waited until her arms ached. Small insects of night gathered, and at last a little dusty miller, but nothing came of any size.

"I must go where they are, if I get them," muttered Mrs. Comstock.

She went to the barn after the stout pair of high boots she used in feeding stock in deep snow. Throwing these beside the back door she climbed to the loft over the spring house, and hunted an old lard oil lantern and one of first manufacture for oil. Both these she cleaned and filled. She listened until everything up stairs had been still for over half an hour. By that time it was past eleven o'clock. Then she took the lantern from the kitchen, the two old ones, a handful of matches, a ball of twine, and went from the cabin, softly closing the door.

Sitting on the back steps, she put on the boots, and then stood gazing into the perfumed June night, first in the direction of the woods on her land, then toward the Limberlost. Its outline was so dark and forbidding she shuddered and went down the garden, following the path toward the woods, but as she neared the pool her knees wavered and her courage fled. The knowledge that in her soul she was now glad Robert Comstock was at the bottom of it made a coward of her, who fearlessly had mourned him there, nights untold. She could not go on. She skirted the back of the garden, crossed a field, and came out on the road. Soon she reached the Limberlost. She hunted until she found the old trail, then followed it stumbling over logs and through clinging vines and grasses. The heavy boots clumped on her feet, overhanging branches whipped her face and pulled her hair. But her eyes were on the sky as she went straining into the night, hoping to find signs of a living creature on wing.

By and by she began to see the wavering flight of something she thought near the right size. She had no idea where she was, but she stopped, lighted a lantern and hung it as high as she could reach. A little distance away she placed the second and then the third. The objects came nearer and sick with disappointment she saw that they were bats. Crouching in the damp swamp grasses, without a thought of snakes or venomous insects, she waited, her eyes roving from lantern to lantern. Once she thought a creature of high flight dropped near the lard oil light, so she arose breathlessly waiting, but either it passed or it was an illusion. She glanced at the old lantern, then at the new, and was on her feet in an instant creeping close. Something large as a small bird was fluttering around. Mrs. Comstock began to perspire, while her hand shook wildly. Closer she crept and just as she reached for it, something similar swept past and both flew away together.

Mrs. Comstock set her teeth and stood shivering. For a long time the locusts rasped, the whip-poor-wills cried and a steady hum of night life throbbed in her ears. Away in the sky she saw something coming when it was no larger than a falling leaf. Straight toward the light it flew. Mrs. Comstock began to pray aloud.

"This way, O Lord! Make it come this way! Please! O Lord, send it lower!"

The moth hesitated at the first light, then slowly, easily it came toward the second, as if following a path of air. It touched a leaf near the lantern and settled. As Mrs. Comstock reached for it a thin yellow spray wet her hand and the surrounding leaves. When its wings raised above its back, her fingers came together. She held the moth to the light. It was nearer brown than yellow, and she remembered having seen some like it in the boxes that afternoon. It was not the one needed to complete the collection, but Elnora might want it, so Mrs. Comstock held on. Then the Almighty was kind, or nature was sufficient, as you look at it, for following the law of its being when disturbed, the moth again threw the spray by which some suppose it attracts its kind, and liberally sprinkled Mrs. Comstock's dress front and arms. From that instant, she became the best moth bait ever invented. Every Polyphemus in range hastened to her, and other fluttering creatures of night followed. The influx came her way. She snatched wildly here and there until she had one in each hand and no place to put them. She could see more coming, and her aching heart, swollen with the strain of long excitement, hurt pitifully. She prayed in broken exclamations that did not always sound reverent, but never was human soul in more intense earnest.

Moths were coming. She had one in each hand. They were not yellow, and she did not know what to do. She glanced around to try to discover some way to keep what she had, and her throbbing heart stopped and every muscle stiffened. There was the dim outline of a crouching figure not two yards away, and a pair of eyes their owner thought hidden, caught the light in a cold stream. Her first impulse was to scream and fly for life. Before her lips could open a big moth alighted on her breast while she felt another walking over her hair. All sense of caution deserted her. She did not care to live if she could not replace the yellow moth she had killed. She turned her eyes to those among the leaves.

"Here, you!" she cried hoarsely. "I need you! Get yourself out here, and help me. These critters are going to get away from me. Hustle!"

Pete Corson parted the bushes and stepped into the light.

"Oh, it's you!" said Mrs. Comstock. "I might have known! But you gave me a start. Here, hold these until I make some sort of bag for them. Go easy! If you break them I don't guarantee what will happen to you!"

"Pretty fierce, ain't you!" laughed Pete, but he advanced and held out his hands. "For Elnora, I s'pose?"

"Yes," said Mrs. Comstock. "In a mad fit, I trampled one this morning, and by the luck of the old boy himself it was the last moth she needed to complete a collection. I got to get another one or die."

"Then I guess it's your funeral," said Pete. "There ain't a chance in a dozen the right one will come. What colour was it?"

"Yellow, and big as a bird."

"The Emperor, likely," said Pete. "You dig for that kind, and they are not numerous, so's 'at you can smash 'em for fun."

"Well, I can try to get one, anyway," said Mrs. Comstock. "I forgot all about bringing anything to put them in. You take a pinch on their wings until I make a poke."

Mrs. Comstock removed her apron, tearing off the strings. She unfastened and stepped from the skirt of her calico dress. With one apron string she tied shut the band and placket. She pulled a wire pin from her hair, stuck it through the other string, and using it as a bodkin ran it around the hem of her skirt, so shortly she had a large bag. She put several branches inside to which the moths could cling, closed the mouth partially and held it toward Pete.

"Put your hand well down and let the things go!" she ordered. "But be careful, man! Don't run into the twigs! Easy! That's one. Now the other. Is the one on my head gone? There was one on my dress, but I guess it flew. Here comes a kind of a gray-looking one."

Pete slipped several more moths into the bag.

"Now, that's five, Mrs. Comstock," he said. "I'm sorry, but you'll have to make that do. You must get out of here lively. Your lights will be taken for hurry calls, and inside the next hour a couple of men will ride here like fury. They won't be nice Sunday-school men, and they won't hold bags and catch moths for you. You must go quick!"

Mrs. Comstock laid down the bag and pulled one of the lanterns lower.

"I won't budge a step," she said. "This land doesn't belong to you. You have no right to order me off it. Here I stay until I get a Yellow Emperor, and no little petering thieves of this neighbourhood can scare me away."

"You don't understand," said Pete. "I'm willing to help Elnora, and I'd take care of you, if I could, but there will be too many for me, and they will be mad at being called out for nothing."

"Well, who's calling them out?" demanded Mrs. Comstock. "I'm catching moths. If a lot of good-for-nothings get fooled into losing some sleep, why let them, they can't hurt me, or stop my work."

"They can, and they'll do both."

"Well, I'll see them do it!" said Mrs. Comstock. "I've got Robert's revolver in my dress, and I can shoot as straight as any man, if I'm mad enough. Any one who interferes with me to-night will find me mad a-plenty. There goes another!"

She stepped into the light and waited until a big brown moth settled on her and was easily taken. Then in light, airy flight came a delicate pale green thing, and Mrs. Comstock started in pursuit. But the scent was not right. The moth fluttered high, then dropped lower, still lower, and sailed away. With outstretched hands Mrs.

Comstock pursued it. She hurried one way and another, then ran over an object which tripped her and she fell. She regained her feet in an instant, but she had lost sight of the moth. With livid face she turned to the crouching man.

"You nasty, sneaking son of Satan!" she cried. "Why are you hiding there? You made me lose the one I wanted most of any I've had a chance at yet. Get out of here! Go this minute, or I'll fill your worthless carcass so full of holes you'll do to sift cornmeal. Go, I say! I'm using the Limberlost to-night, and I won't be stopped by the devil himself! Cut like fury, and tell the rest of them they can just go home. Pete is going to help me, and he is all of you I need. Now go!"

The man turned and went. Pete leaned against a tree, held his mouth shut and shook inwardly. Mrs. Comstock came back panting.

"The old scoundrel made me lose that!" she said. "If any one else comes snooping around here I'll just blow them up to start with. I haven't time to talk. Suppose that had been yellow! I'd have killed that man, sure! The Limberlost isn't safe to-night, and the sooner those whelps find it out, the better it will be for them."

Pete stopped laughing to look at her. He saw that she was speaking the truth. She was quite past reason, sense, or fear. The soft night air stirred the wet hair around her temples, the flickering lanterns made her face a ghastly green. She would stop at nothing, that was evident. Pete suddenly began catching moths with exemplary industry. In putting one into the bag, another escaped.

"We must not try that again," said Mrs. Comstock. "Now, what will we do?"

"We are close to the old case," said Pete. "I think I can get into it. Maybe we could slip the rest in there."

"That's a fine idea!" said Mrs. Comstock. "They'll have so much room there they won't be likely to hurt themselves, and the books say they don't fly in daytime unless they are disturbed, so they will settle when it's light, and I can come with Elnora to get them."

They captured two more, and then Pete carried them to the case.

"Here comes a big one!" he cried as he returned.

Mrs. Comstock looked up and stepped out with a prayer on her lips. She could not tell the colour at that distance, but the moth appeared different from the others. On it came, dropping lower and darting from light to light. As it swept near her, "O Heavenly Father!" exulted Mrs. Comstock, "it's yellow! Careful Pete! Your hat, maybe!"

Pete made a long sweep. The moth wavered above the hat and sailed away. Mrs. Comstock leaned against a tree and covered her face with her shaking hands.

"That is my punishment!" she cried. "Oh, Lord, if you will give a moth like that into my possession, I'll always be a better woman!"

The Emperor again came in sight. Pete stood tense and ready. Mrs. Comstock stepped into the light and watched the moth's course. Then a second appeared in pursuit of the first. The larger one wavered into the radius of light once more. The perspiration rolled down the man's face. He half lifted the hat.

"Pray, woman! Pray now!" he panted.

"I guess I best get over by that lard oil light and go to work," breathed Mrs. Comstock. "The Lord knows this is all in prayer, but it's no time for words just now. Ready, Pete! You are going to get a chance first!"

Pete made another long, steady sweep, but the moth darted beneath the hat. In its flight it came straight toward Mrs. Comstock. She snatched off the remnant of apron she had tucked into her petticoat band and held the calico before her. The moth struck full against it and clung to the goods. Pete crept up stealthily. The second moth followed the first, and the spray showered the apron.

"Wait!" gasped Mrs. Comstock. "I think they have settled. The books say they won't leave now."

The big pale yellow creature clung firmly, lowering and raising its wings. The other came nearer. Mrs. Comstock held the cloth with rigid hands, while Pete could hear her breathing in short gusts.

"Shall I try now?" he implored.

"Wait!" whispered the woman. "Something seems to say wait!"

The night breeze stiffened and gently waved the apron. Locusts rasped, mosquitoes hummed and frogs sang uninterruptedly. A musky odour slowly filled the air.

"Now shall I?" questioned Pete.

"No. Leave them alone. They are safe now. They are mine. They are my salvation. God and the Limberlost gave them to me! They won't move for hours. The books all say so. O Heavenly Father, I am thankful to You, and you, too, Pete Corson! You are a good man to help me. Now, I can go home and face my girl."

Instead, Mrs. Comstock dropped suddenly. She spread the apron across her knees. The moths remained undisturbed. Then her tired white head dropped, the tears she had thought forever dried gushed forth, and she sobbed for pure joy.

"Oh, I wouldn't do that now, you know!" comforted Pete. "Think of getting two! That's more than you ever could have expected. A body would think you would cry, if you hadn't got any. Come on, now. It's almost morning. Let me help you home."

Pete took the bag and the two old lanterns. Mrs. Comstock carried her moths and the best lantern and went ahead to light the way.

Elnora had sat beside her window far into the night. At last she undressed and went to bed, but sleep would not come. She had gone to the city to talk with members of the School Board about a room in the grades. There was a possibility that she might secure the moth, and so be able to start to college that fall, but if she did not, then she wanted the school. She had been given some encouragement, but she was so unhappy that nothing mattered. She could not see the way open to anything in life, save a long series of disappointments, while she remained with her mother. Yet Margaret Sinton had advised her to go home and try once more. Margaret had seemed so sure there would be a change for the better, that Elnora had consented, although she had no hope herself. So strong is the bond of blood, she could not make up her mind to seek a home elsewhere, even after the day that had passed. Unable to sleep she arose at last, and the room being warm, she sat on the floor close the window. The lights in the swamp caught her eye. She was very uneasy, for quite a hundred of her best moths were in the case. However, there was no money, and no one ever had touched a book or any of her apparatus. Watching the lights set her thinking, and before she realized it, she was in a panic of fear.

She hurried down the stairway softly calling her mother. There was no answer. She lightly stepped across the sitting-room and looked in at the open door. There was no one, and the bed had not been used. Her first thought was that her mother had gone to the pool; and the Limberlost was alive with signals. Pity and fear mingled in the heart of the girl. She opened the kitchen door, crossed the garden and ran back to the swamp. As she neared it she listened, but she could hear only the usual voices of night.

"Mother!" she called softly. Then louder, "Mother!"

There was not a sound. Chilled with fright she hurried back to the cabin. She did not know what to do. She understood what the lights in the Limberlost meant. Where was her mother? She was afraid to enter, while she was growing very cold and still more fearful about remaining outside. At last she went to her mother's room, picked up the gun, carried it into the kitchen, and crowding in a little corner behind the stove, she waited in trembling anxiety. The time was dreadfully long before she heard her mother's voice. Then she decided some one had been ill and sent for her, so she took courage, and stepping swiftly across the kitchen she unbarred the door and drew back from sight beside the table.

Mrs. Comstock entered dragging her heavy feet. Her dress skirt was gone, her petticoat wet and drabbled, and the waist of her dress was almost torn from her body. Her hair hung in damp strings; her eyes were red with crying. In one hand she held the lantern, and in the other stiffly extended before her, on a wad of calico reposed a magnificent pair of Yellow Emperors. Elnora stared, her lips parted.

"Shall I put these others in the kitchen?" inquired a man's voice.

The girl shrank back to the shadows.

"Yes, anywhere inside the door," replied Mrs. Comstock as she moved a few steps to make way for him. Pete's head appeared. He set down the moths and was gone.

"Thank you, Pete, more than ever woman thanked you before!" said Mrs. Comstock.

She placed the lantern on the table and barred the door. As she turned Elnora came into view. Mrs. Comstock leaned toward her, and held out the moths. In a voice vibrant with tones never before heard she said: "Elnora, my girl, mother's found you another moth!"

Chapter 13

Wherein Mother Love Is Bestowed on Elnora, and She Finds an Assistant in Moth Hunting

Elnora awoke at dawn and lay gazing around the unfamiliar room. She noticed that every vestige of masculine attire and belongings was gone, and knew, without any explanation, what that meant. For some reason every tangible evidence of her father was banished, and she was at last to be allowed to take his place. She turned to look at her mother. Mrs. Comstock's face was white and haggard, but on it rested an expression of profound peace Elnora never before had seen. As she studied the features on the pillow beside her, the heart of the girl throbbed in tenderness. She realized as fully as any one else could what her mother had suffered. Thoughts of the night brought shuddering fear. She softly slipped from the bed, went to her room, dressed and entered the kitchen to attend the Emperors and prepare breakfast. The pair had been left clinging to the piece of calico. The calico was there and a few pieces of beautiful wing. A mouse had eaten the moths!

"Well, of all the horrible luck!" gasped Elnora.

With the first thought of her mother, she caught up the remnants of the moths, burying them in the ashes of the stove. She took the bag to her room, hurriedly releasing its contents, but there was not another yellow one. Her mother had said some had been confined in the case in the Limberlost. There was still a hope that an Emperor might be among them. She peeped at her mother, who still slept soundly.

Elnora took a large piece of mosquito netting, and ran to the swamp. Throwing it over the top of the case, she unlocked the door. She reeled, faint with distress. The living moths that had been confined there in their fluttering to escape to night and the mates they sought not only had wrecked the other specimens of the case, but torn themselves to fringes on the pins. A third of the rarest moths of the collection for the man of India were antennaless, legless, wingless, and often headless. Elnora sobbed aloud.

"This is overwhelming," she said at last. "It is making a fatalist of me. I am beginning to think things happen as they are ordained from the beginning, this plainly indicating that there is to be no college, at least, this year, for me. My life is all mountain-top or canon. I wish some one would lead me into a few days of 'green pastures.' Last night I went to sleep on mother's arm, the moths all secured, love and college, certainties. This morning I wake to find all my hopes wrecked. I simply don't dare let mother know that instead of helping me, she has ruined my collection. Everything is gone—unless the love lasts. That actually seemed true. I believe I will go see."

The love remained. Indeed, in the overflow of the long-hardened, pent-up heart, the girl was almost suffocated with tempestuous caresses and generous offerings. Before the day was over, Elnora realized that she never had known her mother. The woman who now busily went through the cabin, her eyes bright, eager, alert, constantly planning, was a stranger. Her very face was different, while it did not seem possible that during one night the acid of twenty years could disappear from a voice and leave it sweet and pleasant.

For the next few days Elnora worked at mounting the moths her mother had taken. She had to go to the Bird Woman and tell about the disaster, but Mrs. Comstock was allowed to think that Elnora delivered the moths when she made the trip. If she had told her what actually happened, the chances were that Mrs. Comstock again would have taken possession of the Limberlost, hunting there until she replaced all the moths that had been destroyed. But Elnora knew from experience what it meant to collect such a list in pairs. It would require steady work for at least two summers to replace the lost moths. When she left the Bird Woman she went to the president of the Onabasha schools and asked him to do all in his power to secure her a room in one of the ward buildings.

The next morning the last moth was mounted, and the housework finished. Elnora said to her mother, "If you don't mind, I believe I will go into the woods pasture beside Sleepy Snake Creek and see if I can catch some dragonflies or moths."

"Wait until I get a knife and a pail and I will go along," answered Mrs. Comstock. "The dandelions are plenty tender for greens among the deep grasses, and I might just happen to see something myself. My eyes are pretty sharp."

"I wish you could realize how young you are," said Elnora. "I know women in Onabasha who are ten years older than you, yet they look twenty years younger. So could you, if you would dress your hair becomingly, and wear appropriate clothes."

"I think my hair puts me in the old woman class permanently," said Mrs. Comstock.

"Well, it doesn't!" cried Elnora. "There is a woman of twenty-eight who has hair as white as yours from sick headaches, but her face is young and beautiful. If your face would grow a little fuller and those lines would go away, you'd be lovely!"

"You little pig!" laughed Mrs. Comstock. "Any one would think you would be satisfied with having a splinter new mother, without setting up a kick on her looks, first thing. Greedy!"

"That is a good word," said Elnora. "I admit the charge. I am greedy over every wasted year. I want you young, lovely, suitably dressed, and enjoying life like the other girls' mothers."

Mrs. Comstock laughed softly as she pushed back her sunbonnet so that shrubs and bushes beside the way could be scanned closely. Elnora walked ahead with a case over her shoulder, a net in her hand. Her head was bare, the rolling collar of her lavender gingham dress was cut in a V at the throat, the sleeves only reached the elbows. Every few steps she paused and examined the shrubbery carefully, while Mrs. Comstock was watching until her eyes ached, but there were no dandelions in the pail she carried.

Early June was rioting in fresh grasses, bright flowers, bird songs, and gay-winged creatures of air. Down the footpath the two went through the perfect morning, the love of God and all nature in their hearts. At last they reached the creek, following it toward the bridge. Here Mrs. Comstock found a large bed of tender dandelions and stopped to fill her pail. Then she sat on the bank, picking over the greens, while she listened to the creek softly singing its June song.

Elnora remained within calling distance, and was having good success. At last she crossed the creek, following it up to a bridge. There she began a careful examination of the under sides of the sleepers and flooring for cocoons. Mrs. Comstock could see her and the creek for several rods above. The mother sat beating the long green leaves across her hand, carefully picking out the white buds, because Elnora liked them, when a splash up the creek attracted her attention.

Around the bend came a man. He was bareheaded, dressed in a white sweater, and waders which reached his waist. He walked on the bank, only entering the water when forced. He had a queer basket strapped on his hip, and with a small rod he sent a long line spinning before him down the creek, deftly manipulating with it a little floating object. He was closer Elnora than her mother, but Mrs. Comstock thought possibly by hurrying she could remain unseen and yet warn the girl that a stranger was coming. As she approached the bridge, she caught a sapling and leaned over the water to call Elnora. With her lips parted to speak she hesitated a second to watch a sort of insect that flashed past on the water, when a splash from the man attracted the girl.

She was under the bridge, one knee planted in the embankment and a foot braced to support her. Her hair was tousled by wind and bushes, her face flushed, and she lifted her arms above her head, working to loosen a cocoon she had found. The call Mrs. Comstock had intended to utter never found voice, for as Elnora looked down at the sound, "Possibly I could get that for you," suggested the man.

Mrs. Comstock drew back. He was a young man with a wonderfully attractive face, although it was too white for robust health, broad shoulders, and slender, upright frame.

"Oh, I do hope you can!" answered Elnora. "It's quite a find! It's one of those lovely pale red cocoons described in the books. I suspect it comes from having been in a dark place and screened from the weather."

"Is that so?" cried the man. "Wait a minute. I've never seen one. I suppose it's a Cecropia, from the location."

"Of course," said Elnora. "It's so cool here the moth hasn't emerged. The cocoon is a big, baggy one, and it is as red as fox tail."

"What luck!" he cried. "Are you making a collection?"

He reeled in his line, laid his rod across a bush and climbed the embankment to Elnora's side, produced a knife and began the work of whittling a deep groove around the cocoon.

"Yes. I paid my way through the high school in Onabasha with them. Now I am starting a collection which means college."

"Onabasha!" said the man. "That is where I am visiting. Possibly you know my people—Dr. Ammon's? The doctor is my uncle. My home is in Chicago. I've been having typhoid fever, something fierce. In the hospital six weeks. Didn't gain strength right, so Uncle Doc sent for me. I am to live out of doors all summer, and exercise until I get in condition again. Do you know my uncle?"

"Yes. He is Aunt Margaret's doctor, and he would be ours, only we are never ill."

"Well, you look it!" said the man, appraising Elnora at a glance.

"Strangers always mention it," sighed Elnora. "I wonder how it would seem to be a pale, languid lady and ride in a carriage."

"Ask me!" laughed the man. "It feels like the—dickens! I'm so proud of my feet. It's quite a trick to stand on them now. I have to keep out of the water all I can and stop to baby every half-mile. But with interesting outdoor work I'll be myself in a week."

"Do you call that work?" Elnora indicated the creek.

"I do, indeed! Nearly three miles, banks too soft to brag on and never a strike. Wouldn't you call that hard labour?"

"Yes," laughed Elnora. "Work at which you might kill yourself and never get a fish. Did any one tell you there were trout in Sleepy Snake Creek?"

"Uncle said I could try."

"Oh, you can," said Elnora. "You can try no end, but you'll never get a trout. This is too far south and too warm for them. If you sit on the bank and use worms you might catch some perch or catfish."

"But that isn't exercise."

"Well, if you only want exercise, go right on fishing. You will have a creel full of invisible results every night."

"I object," said the man emphatically. He stopped work again and studied Elnora. Even the watching mother could not blame him. In the shade of the bridge Elnora's bright head and her lavender dress made a picture worthy of much contemplation.

"I object!" repeated the man. "When I work I want to see results. I'd rather exercise sawing wood, making one pile grow little and the other big than to cast all day and catch nothing because there is not a fish to take. Work for work's sake doesn't appeal to me."

He digged the groove around the cocoon with skilled hand. "Now there is some fun in this!" he said. "It's going to be a fair job to cut it out, but when it comes, it is not only beautiful, but worth a price; it will help you on your way. I think I'll put up my rod and hunt moths. That would be something like! Don't you want help?"

Elnora parried the question. "Have you ever hunted moths, Mr. Ammon?"

"Enough to know the ropes in taking them and to distinguish the commonest ones. I go wild on Catocalae. There's too many of them, all too much alike for Philip, but I know all these fellows. One flew into my room when I was about ten years old, and we thought it a miracle None of us ever had seen one so we took it over to the museum to Dr. Dorsey. He said they were common enough, but we didn't see them because they flew at night. He showed me the museum collection, and I was so interested I took mine back home and started to hunt them. Every year after that we went to our cottage a month earlier, so I could find them, and all my family helped. I stuck to it until I went to college. Then, keeping the little moths out of the big ones was too much for the mater, so father advised that I donate mine to the museum. He bought a fine case for them with my name on it, which constitutes my sole contribution to science. I know enough to help you all right."

"Aren't you going north this year?"

"All depends on how this fever leaves me. Uncle says the nights are too cold and the days too hot there for me. He thinks I had better stay in an even temperature until I am strong again. I am going to stick pretty close to him until I know I am. I wouldn't admit it to any one at home, but I was almost gone. I don't believe anything can eat up nerve much faster than the burning of a slow fever. No, thanks, I have enough. I stay with Uncle Doc, so if I feel it coming again he can do something quickly."

"I don't blame you," said Elnora. "I never have been sick, but it must be dreadful. I am afraid you are tiring yourself over that. Let me take the knife awhile."

"Oh, it isn't so bad as that! I wouldn't be wading creeks if it were. I only need a few more days to get steady on my feet again. I'll soon have this out."

"It is kind of you to get it," said Elnora. "I should have had to peel it, which would spoil the cocoon for a specimen and ruin the moth."

"You haven't said yet whether I may help you while I am here."

Elnora hesitated.

"You better say 'yes,'" he persisted. "It would be a real kindness. It would keep me outdoors all day and give an incentive to work. I'm good at it. I'll show you if I am not in a week or so. I can 'sugar,' manipulate lights, and mirrors, and all the expert methods. I'll wager, moths are numerous in the old swamp over there."

"They are," said Elnora. "Most I have I took there. A few nights ago my mother caught a number, but we don't dare go alone."

"All the more reason why you need me. Where do you live? I can't get an answer from you, I'll go tell your mother who I am and ask her if I may help you. I warn you, young lady, I have a very effective way with mothers. They almost never turn me down."

"Then it's probable you will have a new experience when you meet mine," said Elnora. "She never was known to do what any one expected she surely would."

The cocoon came loose. Philip Ammon stepped down the embankment turning to offer his hand to Elnora. She ran down as she would have done alone, and taking the cocoon turned it end for end to learn if the imago it contained were alive. Then Ammon took back the cocoon to smooth the edges. Mrs. Comstock gave them one long look as they stood there, and returned to her dandelions. While she worked she paused occasionally, listening intently. Presently they came down the creek, the man carrying the cocoon as if it were a jewel, while Elnora made her way along the bank, taking a lesson in casting. Her face was flushed with excitement, her eyes shining, the bushes taking liberties with her hair. For a picture of perfect loveliness she scarcely could have been surpassed, and the eyes of Philip Ammon seemed to be in working order.

"Moth-er!" called Elnora.

There was an undulant, caressing sweetness in the girl's voice, as she sung out the call in perfect confidence that it would bring a loving answer, that struck deep in Mrs. Comstock's heart. She never had heard that word so pronounced before and a lump arose in her throat.

"Here!" she answered, still cleaning dandelions.

"Mother, this is Mr. Philip Ammon, of Chicago," said Elnora. "He has been ill and he is staying with Dr. Ammon in Onabasha. He came down the creek fishing and cut this cocoon from under the bridge for me. He feels that it would be better to hunt moths than to fish, until he is well. What do you think about it?"

Philip Ammon extended his hand. "I am glad to know you," he said.

"You may take the hand-shaking for granted," replied Mrs. Comstock. "Dandelions have a way of making fingers sticky, and I like to know a man before I take his hand, anyway. That introduction seems mighty comprehensive on your part, but it still leaves me unclassified. My name is Comstock."

Philip Ammon bowed.

"I am sorry to hear you have been sick," said Mrs. Comstock. "But if people will live where they have such vile water as they do in Chicago, I don't see what else they are to expect."

Philip studied her intently.

"I am sure I didn't have a fever on purpose," he said.

"You do seem a little wobbly on your legs," she observed. "Maybe you had better sit and rest while I finish these greens. It's late for the genuine article, but in the shade, among long grass they are still tender."

"May I have a leaf?" he asked, reaching for one as he sat on the bank, looking from the little creek at his feet, away through the dim cool spaces of the June forest on the opposite side. He drew a deep breath. "Glory, but this is good after almost two months inside hospital walls!"

He stretched on the grass and lay gazing up at the leaves, occasionally asking the interpretation of a bird note or the origin of an unfamiliar forest voice. Elnora began helping with the dandelions.

"Another, please," said the young man, holding out his hand.

"Do you suppose this is the kind of grass Nebuchadnezzar ate?" Elnora asked, giving the leaf.

"He knew a good thing if it is."

"Oh, you should taste dandelions boiled with bacon and served with mother's cornbread."

"Don't! My appetite is twice my size now. While it is—how far is it to Onabasha, shortest cut?"

"Three miles."

The man lay in perfect content, nibbling leaves.

"This surely is a treat," he said. "No wonder you find good hunting here. There seems to be foliage for almost every kind of caterpillar. But I suppose you have to exchange for northern species and Pacific Coast kinds?"

"Yes. And every one wants Regalis in trade. I never saw the like. They consider a Cecropia or a Polyphemus an insult, and a Luna is barely acceptable."

"What authorities have you?"

Elnora began to name text-books which started a discussion. Mrs. Comstock listened. She cleaned dandelions with greater deliberation than they ever before were examined. In reality she was taking stock of the young man's long, well-proportioned frame, his strong hands, his smooth, fine-textured skin, his thick shock of dark hair, and making mental notes of his simple manly speech and the fact that he evidently did know much about moths. It pleased her to think that if he had been a neighbour boy who had lain beside her every day of his life while she worked, he could have been no more at home. She liked the things he said, but she was proud that Elnora had a ready answer which always seemed appropriate.

At last Mrs. Comstock finished the greens.

"You are three miles from the city and less than a mile from where we live," she said. "If you will tell me what you dare eat, I suspect you had best go home with us and rest until the cool of the day before you start back. Probably some one that you can ride in with will be passing before evening."

"That is mighty kind of you," said Philip. "I think I will. It doesn't matter so much what I eat, the point is that I must be moderate. I am hungry all the time."

"Then we will go," said Mrs. Comstock, "and we will not allow you to make yourself sick with us."

Philip Ammon arose: picking up the pail of greens and his fishing rod, he stood waiting. Elnora led the way. Mrs. Comstock motioned Philip to follow and she walked in the rear. The girl carried the cocoon and the box of moths she had taken, searching every step for more. The young man frequently set down his load to join in the pursuit of a dragonfly or moth, while Mrs. Comstock watched the proceedings with sharp eyes. Every time Philip picked up the pail of greens she struggled to suppress a smile.

Elnora proceeded slowly, chattering about everything beside the trail. Philip was interested in all the objects she pointed out, noticing several things which escaped her. He carried the greens as casually when they took a short cut down the roadway as on the trail. When Elnora turned toward the gate of her home Philip Ammon stopped, took a long look at the big hewed log cabin, the vines which clambered over it, the flower garden ablaze with beds of bright bloom interspersed with strawberries and tomatoes, the trees of the forest rising north and west like a green wall and exclaimed: "How beautiful!"

Mrs. Comstock was pleased. "If you think that," she said, "perhaps you will understand how, in all this present-day rush to be modern, I have preferred to remain as I began. My husband and I took up this land, and enough trees to build the cabin, stable, and outbuildings are nearly all we ever cut. Of course, if he had lived, I suppose we should have kept up with our neighbours. I hear considerable about the value of the land, the trees which are on it, and the oil which is supposed to be under it, but as yet I haven't brought myself to change anything. So we stand for one of the few remaining homes of first settlers in this region. Come in. You are very welcome to what we have."

Mrs. Comstock stepped forward and took the lead. She had a bowl of soft water and a pair of boots to offer for the heavy waders, for outer comfort, a glass of cold buttermilk and a bench on which to rest, in the circular arbour until dinner was ready. Philip Ammon splashed in the water. He followed to the stable and exchanged boots there. He was ravenous for the buttermilk, and when he stretched on the bench in the arbour the flickering patches of sunlight so tantalized his tired eyes, while the bees made such splendid music, he was soon sound asleep. When Elnora and her mother came out with a table they stood a short time looking at him. It is probable Mrs. Comstock voiced a united thought when she said: "What a refined, decent looking young man! How proud his mother must be of him! We must be careful what we let him eat."

Then they returned to the kitchen where Mrs. Comstock proceeded to be careful. She broiled ham of her own sugar-curing, creamed potatoes, served asparagus on toast, and made a delicious strawberry shortcake. As she cooked dandelions with bacon, she feared to serve them to him, so she made an excuse that it took too long to prepare them, blanched some and made a salad. When everything was ready she touched Philip's sleeve.

"Best have something to eat, lad, before you get too hungry," she said.

"Please hurry!" he begged laughingly as he held a plate toward her to be filled. "I thought I had enough self-restraint to start out alone, but I see I was mistaken. If you would allow me, just now, I am afraid I should start a fever again. I never did smell food so good as this. It's mighty kind of you to take me in. I hope I will be man enough in a few days to do something worth while in return."

Spots of sunshine fell on the white cloth and blue china, the bees and an occasional stray butterfly came searching for food. A rose-breasted grosbeak, released from a three hours' siege of brooding, while his independent mate took her bath and recreation, mounted the top branch of a maple in the west woods from which he serenaded the dinner party with a joyful chorus in celebration of his freedom. Philip's eyes strayed to the beautiful cabin, to the mixture of flowers and vegetables stretching down to the road, and to the singing bird with his red-splotched breast of white and he said: "I can't realize now that I ever lay in ice packs in a hospital. How I wish all the sick folks could come here to grow strong!"

The grosbeak sang on, a big Turnus butterfly sailed through the arbour and poised over the table. Elnora held up a lump of sugar and the butterfly, clinging to her fingers, tasted daintily. With eager eyes and parted lips, the girl held steadily. When at last it wavered away, "That made a picture!" said Philip. "Ask me some other time how I lost my illusions concerning butterflies. I always thought of them in connection with sunshine, flower pollen, and fruit nectar, until one sad day."

"I know!" laughed Elnora. "I've seen that, too, but it didn't destroy any illusion for me. I think quite as much of the butterflies as ever."

Then they talked of flowers, moths, dragonflies, Indian relics, and all the natural wonders the swamp afforded, straying from those subjects to books and school work. When they cleared the table Philip assisted, carrying several tray loads to the kitchen. He and Elnora mounted specimens while Mrs. Comstock washed the dishes. Then she came out with a ruffle she was embroidering.

"I wonder if I did not see a picture of you in Onabasha last night," Philip said to Elnora. "Aunt Anna took me to call on Miss Brownlee. She was showing me her crowd—of course, it was you! But it didn't half do you justice, although it was the nearest human of any of them. Miss Brownlee is very fond of you. She said the finest things."

Then they talked of Commencement, and at last Philip said he must go or his friends would become anxious about him.

Mrs. Comstock brought him a blue bowl of creamy milk and a plate of bread. She stopped a passing team and secured a ride to the city for him, as his exercise of the morning had been too violent, and he was forced to admit he was tired.

"May I come to-morrow afternoon and hunt moths awhile?" he asked Mrs. Comstock as he arose. "We will 'sugar' a tree and put a light beside it, if I can get stuff to make the preparation. Possibly we can take some that way. I always enjoy moth hunting, I'd like to help Miss Elnora, and it would be a charity to me. I've got to remain outdoors some place, and I'm quite sure I'd get well faster here than anywhere else. Please say I may come."

"I have no objections, if Elnora really would like help," said Mrs. Comstock.

In her heart she wished he would not come. She wanted her newly found treasure all to herself, for a time, at least. But Elnora's were eager, shining eyes. She thought it would be splendid to have help, and great fun to try book methods for taking moths, so it was arranged. As Philip rode away, Mrs. Comstock's eyes followed him. "What a nice young man!" she said.

"He seems fine," agreed Elnora.

"He comes of a good family, too. I've often heard of his father. He is a great lawyer."

"I am glad he likes it here. I need help. Possibly—"

"Possibly what?"

"We can find many moths."

"What did he mean about the butterflies?"

"That he always had connected them with sunshine, flowers, and fruits, and thought of them as the most exquisite of creations; then one day he found some clustering thickly over carrion."

"Come to think of it, I have seen butterflies—"

"So had he," laughed Elnora. "And that is what he meant."

Chapter 14

Wherein a New Position Is Tendered Elnora, and Philip Ammon Is Shown Limberlost Violets

The next morning Mrs. Comstock called to Elnora, "The mail carrier stopped at our box."

Elnora ran down the walk and came back carrying an official letter. She tore it open and read:

MY DEAR MISS COMSTOCK:

At the weekly meeting of the Onabasha School Board last night, it was decided to add the position of Lecturer on Natural History to our corps of city teachers. It will be the duty of this person to spend two hours a week in each of the grade schools exhibiting and explaining specimens of the most prominent objects in nature: animals, birds, insects, flowers, vines, shrubs, bushes, and trees. These specimens and lectures should be appropriate to the seasons and the comprehension of the grades. This position was unanimously voted to you. I think you will find the work delightful and much easier than the routine grind of the other teachers. It is my advice that you accept and begin to prepare yourself at once. Your salary will be $750 a year, and you will be allowed $200 for expenses in procuring specimens and books. Let us know at once if you want the position, as it is going to be difficult to fill satisfactorily if you do not.

Very truly yours,

DAVID THOMPSON, President, Onabasha Schools.

"I hardly understand," marvelled Mrs. Comstock.

"It is a new position. They never have had anything like it before. I suspect it arose from the help I've been giving the grade teachers in their nature work. They are trying to teach the children something, and half the instructors don't know a blue jay from a king-fisher, a beech leaf from an elm, or a wasp from a hornet."

"Well, do you?" anxiously inquired Mrs. Comstock.

"Indeed, I do!" laughed Elnora. "And several other things beside. When Freckles bequeathed me the swamp, he gave me a bigger inheritance than he knew. While you have thought I was wandering aimlessly, I have been following a definite plan, studying hard, and storing up the stuff that will earn these seven hundred and fifty dollars. Mother dear, I am going to accept this, of course. The work will be a delight. I'd love it most of anything in teaching. You must help me. We must find nests, eggs, leaves, queer formations in plants and rare flowers. I must have flower boxes made for each of the rooms and filled with wild things. I should begin to gather specimens this very day."

Elnora's face was flushed and her eyes bright.

"Oh, what great work that will be!" she cried. "You must go with me so you can see the little faces when I tell them how the goldfinch builds its nest, and how the bees make honey."

So Elnora and her mother went into the woods behind the cabin to study nature.

"I think," said Elnora, "the idea is to begin with fall things in the fall, keeping to the seasons throughout the year."

"What are fall things?" inquired Mrs. Comstock.

"Oh, fringed gentians, asters, ironwort, every fall flower, leaves from every tree and vine, what makes them change colour, abandoned bird nests, winter quarters of caterpillars and insects, what becomes of the butterflies and grasshoppers—myriads of stuff. I shall have to be very wise to select the things it will be most beneficial for the children to learn."

"Can I really help you?" Mrs. Comstock's strong face was pathetic.

"Indeed, yes!" cried Elnora. "I never can get through it alone. There will be an immense amount of work connected with securing and preparing specimens."

Mrs. Comstock lifted her head proudly and began doing business at once. Her sharp eyes ranged from earth to heaven. She investigated everything, asking innumerable questions. At noon Mrs. Comstock took the specimens they had collected, and went to prepare dinner, while Elnora followed the woods down to the Sintons' to show her letter.

She had to explain what became of her moths, and why college would have to be abandoned for that year, but Margaret and Wesley vowed not to tell. Wesley waved the letter excitedly, explaining it to Margaret as if it were a personal possession. Margaret was deeply impressed, while Billy volunteered first aid in gathering material.

"Now anything you want in the ground, Snap can dig it out," he said. "Uncle Wesley and I found a hole three times as big as Snap, that he dug at the roots of a tree."

"We will train him to hunt pupae cases," said Elnora.

"Are you going to the woods this afternoon?" asked Billy.

"Yes," answered Elnora. "Dr. Ammon's nephew from Chicago is visiting in Onabasha. He is going to show me how men put some sort of compound on a tree, hang a light beside it, and take moths that way. It will be interesting to watch and learn."

"May I come?" asked Billy.

"Of course you may come!" answered Elnora.

"Is this nephew of Dr. Ammon a young man?" inquired Margaret.

"About twenty-six, I should think," said Elnora. "He said he had been out of college and at work in his father's law office three years."

"Does he seem nice?" asked Margaret, and Wesley smiled.

"Finest kind of a person," said Elnora. "He can teach me so much. It is very interesting to hear him talk. He knows considerable about moths that will be a help to me. He had a fever and he has to stay outdoors until he grows strong again."

"Billy, I guess you better help me this afternoon," said Margaret. "Maybe Elnora had rather not bother with you."

"There's no reason on earth why Billy should not come!" cried Elnora, and Wesley smiled again.

"I must hurry home or I won't be ready," she added.

Hastening down the road she entered the cabin, her face glowing.

"I thought you never would come," said Mrs. Comstock. "If you don't hurry Mr. Ammon will be here before you are dressed."

"I forgot about him until just now," said Elnora. "I am not going to dress. He's not coming to visit. We are only going to the woods for more specimens. I can't wear anything that requires care. The limbs take the most dreadful liberties with hair and clothing."

Mrs. Comstock opened her lips, looked at Elnora and closed them. In her heart she was pleased that the girl was so interested in her work that she had forgotten Philip Ammon's coming. But it did seem to her that such a pleasant young man should have been greeted by a girl in a fresh dress. "If she isn't disposed to primp at the coming of a man, heaven forbid that I should be the one to start her," thought Mrs. Comstock.

Philip came whistling down the walk between the cinnamon pinks, pansies, and strawberries. He carried several packages, while his face flushed with more colour than on the previous day.

"Only see what has happened to me!" cried Elnora, offering her letter.

"I'll wager I know!" answered Philip. "Isn't it great! Every one in Onabasha is talking about it. At last there is something new under the sun. All of them are pleased. They think you'll make a big success. This will give an incentive to work. In a few days more I'll be myself again, and we'll overturn the fields and woods around here."

He went on to congratulate Mrs. Comstock.

"Aren't you proud of her, though?" he asked. "You should hear what folks are saying! They say she created the necessity for the position, and every one seems to feel that it is a necessity. Now, if she succeeds, and she will, all of the other city schools will have such departments, and first thing you know she will have made the whole world a little better. Let me rest a few seconds; my feet are acting up again. Then we will cook the moth compound and put it to cool."

He laughed as he sat breathing shortly.

"It doesn't seem possible that a fellow could lose his strength like this. My knees are actually trembling, but I'll be all right in a minute. Uncle Doc said I could come. I told him how you took care of me, and he said I would be safe here."

Then he began unwrapping packages and explaining to Mrs. Comstock how to cook the compound to attract the moths. He followed her into the kitchen, kindled the fire, and stirred the preparation as he talked. While the mixture cooled, he and Elnora walked through the vegetable garden behind the cabin and strayed from there into the woods.

"What about college?" he asked. "Miss Brownlee said you were going."

"I had hoped to," replied Elnora, "but I had a streak of dreadful luck, so I'll have to wait until next year. If you won't speak of it, I'll tell you."

Philip promised, so Elnora recited the history of the Yellow Emperor. She was so interested in doing the Emperor justice she did not notice how many personalities went into the story. A few pertinent questions told him the remainder. He looked at the girl in wonder. In face and form she was as lovely as any one of her age and type he ever had seen. Her school work far surpassed that of most girls of her age he knew. She differed in other ways. This vast store of learning she had gathered from field and forest was a wealth of attraction no other girl possessed. Her frank, matter-of-fact manner was an inheritance from her mother, but there was something more. Once, as they talked he thought "sympathy" was the word to describe it and again "comprehension." She seemed to possess a large sense of brotherhood for all human and animate creatures. She spoke to him as if she had known him all her life. She talked to the grosbeak in exactly the same manner, as she laid strawberries and potato bugs on the fence for his family. She did not swerve an inch from her way when a snake slid past her, while the squirrels came down from the trees and took corn from her fingers. She might as well have been a boy, so lacking was she in any touch of feminine coquetry toward him. He studied her wonderingly. As they went along the path they reached a large slime-covered pool surrounded by decaying stumps and logs thickly covered with water hyacinths and blue flags. Philip stopped.

"Is that the place?" he asked.

Elnora assented. "The doctor told you?"

"Yes. It was tragic. Is that pool really bottomless?"

"So far as we ever have been able to discover."

Philip stood looking at the water, while the long, sweet grasses, thickly sprinkled with blue flag bloom, over which wild bees clambered, swayed around his feet. Then he turned to the girl. She had worked hard. The same lavender dress she had worn the previous day clung to her in limp condition. But she was as evenly coloured and of as fine grain as a wild rose petal, her hair was really brown, but never was such hair touched with a redder glory, while her heavy arching brows added a look of strength to her big gray-blue eyes.

"And you were born here?"

He had not intended to voice that thought.

"Yes," she said, looking into his eyes. "Just in time to prevent my mother from saving the life of my father. She came near never forgiving me."

"Ah, cruel!" cried Philip.

"I find much in life that is cruel, from our standpoints," said Elnora. "It takes the large wisdom of the Unfathomable, the philosophy of the Almighty, to endure some of it. But there is always right somewhere, and at last it seems to come."

"Will it come to you?" asked Philip, who found himself deeply affected.

"It has come," said the girl serenely. "It came a week ago. It came in fullest measure when my mother ceased to regret that I had been born. Now, work that I love has come—that should constitute happiness. A little farther along is my violet bed. I want you to see it."

As Philip Ammon followed he definitely settled upon the name of the unusual feature of Elnora's face. It should be called "experience." She had known bitter experiences early in life. Suffering had been her familiar more than joy. He watched her earnestly, his heart deeply moved. She led him into a swampy half-open space in the woods, stopped and stepped aside. He uttered a cry of surprised delight.

A few decaying logs were scattered around, the grass grew in tufts long and fine. Blue flags waved, clusters of cowslips nodded gold heads, but the whole earth was purple with a thick blanket of violets nodding from stems a foot in length.

Elnora knelt and slipping her fingers between the leaves and grasses to the roots, gathered a few violets and gave them to Philip.

"Can your city greenhouses surpass them?" she asked.

He sat on a log to examine the blooms.

"They are superb!" he said. "I never saw such length of stem or such rank leaves, while the flowers are the deepest blue, the truest violet I ever saw growing wild. They are coloured exactly like the eyes of the girl I am going to marry."

Elnora handed him several others to add to those he held. "She must have wonderful eyes," she commented.

"No other blue eyes are quite so beautiful," he said. "In fact, she is altogether lovely."

"Is it customary for a man to think the girl he is going to marry lovely? I wonder if I should find her so."

"You would," said Philip. "No one ever fails to. She is tall as you, very slender, but perfectly rounded; you know about her eyes; her hair is black and wavy— while her complexion is clear and flushed with red."

"Why, she must be the most beautiful girl in the whole world!" she cried.

"No, indeed!" he said. "She is not a particle better looking in her way than you are in yours. She is a type of dark beauty, but you are equally as perfect. She is unusual in her combination of black hair and violet eyes, although every one thinks them black at a little distance. You are quite as unusual with your fair face, black brows, and brown hair; indeed, I know many people who would prefer your bright head to her dark one. It's all a question of taste—and being engaged to the girl," he added.

"That would be likely to prejudice one," laughed Elnora.

"Edith has a birthday soon; if these last will you let me have a box of them to send her?"

"I will help gather and pack them for you, so they will carry nicely. Does she hunt moths with you?"

Back went Philip Ammon's head in a gale of laughter.

"No!" he cried. "She says they are 'creepy.' She would go into a spasm if she were compelled to touch those caterpillars I saw you handling yesterday."

"Why would she?" marvelled Elnora. "Haven't you told her that they are perfectly clean, helpless, and harmless as so much animate velvet?"

"No, I have not told her. She wouldn't care enough about caterpillars to listen."

"In what is she interested?"

"What interests Edith Carr? Let me think! First, I believe she takes pride in being a little handsomer and better dressed than any girl of her set. She is interested in having a beautiful home, fine appointments, in being petted, praised, and the acknowledged leader of society.

"She likes to find new things which amuse her, and to always and in all circumstances have her own way about everything."

"Good gracious!" cried Elnora, staring at him. "But what does she do? How does she spend her time?"

"Spend her time!" repeated Philip. "Well, she would call that a joke. Her days are never long enough. There is endless shopping, to find the pretty things; regular visits to the dressmakers, calls, parties, theatres, entertainments. She is always rushed. I never am able to be with her half as much as I would like."

"But I mean work," persisted Elnora. "In what is she interested that is useful to the world?"

"Me!" cried Philip promptly.

"I can understand that," laughed Elnora. "What I can't understand is how you can be in—" She stopped in confusion, but she saw that he had finished the sentence as she had intended. "I beg your pardon!" she cried. "I didn't intend to say that. But I cannot understand these people I hear about who live only for their own amusement. Perhaps it is very great; I'll never have a chance to know. To me, it seems the only pleasure in this world worth having is the joy we derive from living for those we love, and those we can help. I hope you are not angry with me."

Philip sat silently looking far away, with deep thought in his eyes.

"You are angry," faltered Elnora.

His look came back to her as she knelt before him among the flowers and he gazed at her steadily.

"No doubt I should be," he said, "but the fact is I am not. I cannot understand a life purely for personal pleasure myself. But she is only a girl, and this is her playtime. When she is a woman in her own home, then she will be different, will she not?"

Elnora never resembled her mother so closely as when she answered that question.

"I would have to be well acquainted with her to know, but I should hope so. To make a real home for a tired business man is a very different kind of work from that required to be a leader of society. It demands different talent and education. Of course, she means to change, or she would not have promised to make a home for you. I suspect our dope is cool now, let's go try for some butterflies."

As they went along the path together Elnora talked of many things but Philip answered absently. Evidently he was thinking of something else. But the moth bait recalled him and he was ready for work as they made their way back to the woods. He wanted to try the Limberlost, but Elnora was firm about remaining on home ground. She did not tell him that lights hung in the swamp would be a signal to call up a band of men whose presence she dreaded. So they started, Ammon carrying the dope, Elnora the net, Billy and Mrs. Comstock following with cyanide boxes and lanterns.

First they tried for butterflies and captured several fine ones without trouble. They also called swarms of ants, bees, beetles, and flies. When it grew dusk, Mrs. Comstock and Philip went to prepare supper. Elnora and Billy remained until the butterflies disappeared. Then they lighted the lanterns, repainted the trees and followed the home trail.

"Do you 'spec you'll get just a lot of moths?" asked Billy, as he walked beside Elnora.

"I am sure I hardly know," said the girl. "This is a new way for me. Perhaps they will come to the lights, but few moths eat; and I have some doubt about those which the lights attract settling on the right trees. Maybe the smell of that dope will draw them. Between us, Billy, I think I like my old way best. If I can find a hidden moth, slip up and catch it unawares, or take it in full flight, it's my captive, and I can keep it until it dies naturally. But this way you seem to get it under false pretences, it has no chance, and it will probably ruin its wings struggling for freedom before morning."

"Well, any moth ought to be proud to be taken anyway, by you," said Billy. "Just look what you do! You can make everybody love them. People even quit hating caterpillars when they see you handle them and hear you tell all about them. You must have some to show people how they are. It's not like killing things to see if you can, or because you want to eat them, the way most men kill birds. I think it is right for you to take enough for collections, to show city people, and to illustrate the Bird Woman's books. You go on and take them! The moths don't care. They're glad to have you. They like it!"

"Billy, I see your future," said Elnora. "We will educate you and send you up to Mr. Ammon to make a great lawyer. You'd beat the world as a special pleader. You actually make me feel that I am doing the moths a kindness to take them."

"And so you are!" cried Billy. "Why, just from what you have taught them Uncle Wesley and Aunt Margaret never think of killing a caterpillar until they look whether it's the beautiful June moth kind, or the horrid tent ones. That's what you can do. You go straight ahead!"

"Billy, you are a jewel!" cried Elnora, throwing her arm across his shoulders as they came down the path.

"My, I was scared!" said Billy with a deep breath.

"Scared?" questioned Elnora.

"Yes sir-ee! Aunt Margaret scared me. May I ask you a question?"

"Of course, you may!"

"Is that man going to be your beau?"

"Billy! No! What made you think such a thing?"

"Aunt Margaret said likely he would fall in love with you, and you wouldn't want me around any more. Oh, but I was scared! It isn't so, is it?"

"Indeed, no!"

"I am your beau, ain't I?"

"Surely you are!" said Elnora, tightening her arm.

"I do hope Aunt Kate has ginger cookies," said Billy with a little skip of delight.

Chapter 15

Wherein Mrs. Comstock Faces the Almighty, and Philip Ammon Writes a Letter

Mrs. Comstock and Elnora were finishing breakfast the following morning when they heard a cheery whistle down the road. Elnora with surprised eyes looked at her mother.

"Could that be Mr. Ammon?" she questioned.

"I did not expect him so soon," commented Mrs. Comstock.

It was sunrise, but the musician was Philip Ammon. He appeared stronger than on yesterday.

"I hope I am not too early," he said. "I am consumed with anxiety to learn if we have made a catch. If we have, we should beat the birds to it. I promised Uncle Doc to put on my waders and keep dry for a few days yet, when I go to the woods. Let's hurry! I am afraid of crows. There might be a rare moth."

The sun was topping the Limberlost when they started. As they neared the place Philip stopped.

"Now we must use great caution," he said. "The lights and the odours always attract numbers that don't settle on the baited trees. Every bush, shrub, and limb may hide a specimen we want."

So they approached with much care.

"There is something, anyway!" cried Philip.

"There are moths! I can see them!" exulted Elnora.

"Those you see are fast enough. It's the ones for which you must search that will escape. The grasses are dripping, and I have boots, so you look beside the path while I take the outside," suggested Ammon.

Mrs. Comstock wanted to hunt moths, but she was timid about making a wrong movement, so she wisely sat on a log and watched Philip and Elnora to learn how they proceeded. Back in the deep woods a hermit thrush was singing his chant to the rising sun. Orioles were sowing the pure, sweet air with notes of gold, poured out while on wing. The robins were only chirping now, for their morning songs had awakened all the other birds an hour ago. Scolding red-wings tilted on half the bushes. Excepting late species of haws, tree bloom was almost gone, but wild flowers made the path border and all the wood floor a riot of colour. Elnora, born among such scenes, worked eagerly, but to the city man, recently from a hospital, they seemed too good to miss. He frequently stooped to examine a flower face, paused to listen intently to the thrush or lifted his head to see the gold flash which accompanied the oriole's trailing notes. So Elnora uttered the first cry, as she softly lifted branches and peered among the grasses.

"My find!" she called. "Bring the box, mother!"

Philip came hurrying also. When they reached her she stood on the path holding a pair of moths. Her eyes were wide with excitement, her cheeks pink, her red lips parted, and on the hand she held out to them clung a pair of delicate blue-green moths, with white bodies, and touches of lavender and straw colour. All around her lay flower-brocaded grasses, behind the deep green background of the forest, while the sun slowly sifted gold from heaven to burnish her hair. Mrs. Comstock heard a sharp breath behind her.

"Oh, what a picture!" exulted Philip at her shoulder. "She is absolutely and altogether lovely! I'd give a small fortune for that faithfully set on canvas!"

He picked the box from Mrs. Comstock's fingers and slowly advanced with it. Elnora held down her hand and transferred the moths. Philip closed the box carefully, but the watching mother saw that his eyes were following the girl's face. He was not making the slightest attempt to conceal his admiration.

"I wonder if a woman ever did anything lovelier than to find a pair of Luna moths on a forest path, early on a perfect June morning," he said to Mrs. Comstock, when he returned the box.

She glanced at Elnora who was intently searching the bushes.

"Look here, young man," said Mrs. Comstock. "You seem to find that girl of mine about right."

"I could suggest no improvement," said Philip. "I never saw a more attractive girl anywhere. She seems absolutely perfect to me."

"Then suppose you don't start any scheme calculated to spoil her!" proposed Mrs. Comstock dryly. "I don't think you can, or that any man could, but I'm not taking any risks. You asked to come here to help in this work. We are both glad to have you, if you confine yourself to work; but it's the least you can do to leave us as you find us."

"I beg your pardon!" said Philip. "I intended no offence. I admire her as I admire any perfect creation."

"And nothing in all this world spoils the average girl so quickly and so surely," said Mrs. Comstock. She raised her voice. "Elnora, fasten up that tag of hair over your left ear. These bushes muss you so you remind me of a sheep poking its nose through a hedge fence."

Mrs. Comstock started down the path toward the log again, when she reached it she called sharply: "Elnora, come here! I believe I have found something myself."

The "something" was a Citheronia Regalis which had emerged from its case on the soft earth under the log. It climbed up the wood, its stout legs dragging a big pursy body, while it wildly flapped tiny wings the size of a man's thumb-nail. Elnora gave one look and a cry which brought Philip.

"That's the rarest moth in America!" he announced. "Mrs. Comstock, you've gone up head. You can put that in a box with a screen cover to-night, and attract half a dozen, possibly."

"Is it rare, Elnora?" inquired Mrs. Comstock, as if no one else knew.

"It surely is," answered Elnora. "If we can find it a mate to-night, it will lay from two hundred and fifty to three hundred eggs to-morrow. With any luck at all I can raise two hundred caterpillars from them. I did once before. And they are worth a dollar apiece."

"Was the one I killed like that?"

"No. That was a different moth, but its life processes were the same as this. The Bird Woman calls this the King of the Poets."

"Why does she?"

"Because it is named for Citheron who was a poet, and regalis refers to a king. You mustn't touch it or you may stunt wing development. You watch and don't let that moth out of sight, or anything touch it. When the wings are expanded and hardened we will put it in a box."

"I am afraid it will race itself to death," objected Mrs. Comstock.

"That's a part of the game," said Philip. "It is starting circulation now. When the right moment comes, it will stop and expand its wings. If you watch closely you can see them expand."

Presently the moth found a rough projection of bark and clung with its feet, back down, its wings hanging. The body was an unusual orange red, the tiny wings were gray, striped with the red and splotched here and there with markings of canary yellow. Mrs. Comstock watched breathlessly. Presently she slipped from the log and knelt to secure a better view.

"Are its wings developing?" called Elnora.

"They are growing larger and the markings coming stronger every minute."

"Let's watch, too," said Elnora to Philip.

They came and looked over Mrs. Comstock's shoulder. Lower drooped the gay wings, wider they spread, brighter grew the markings as if laid off in geometrical patterns. They could hear Mrs. Comstock's tense breath and see her absorbed expression.

"Young people," she said solemnly, "if your studying science and the elements has ever led you to feel that things just happen, kind of evolve by chance, as it were, this sight will be good for you. Maybe earth and air accumulate, but it takes the wisdom of the Almighty God to devise the wing of a moth. If there ever was a miracle, this whole process is one. Now, as I understand it, this creature is going to keep on spreading those wings, until they grow to size and harden to strength sufficient to bear its body. Then it flies away, mates with its kind, lays its eggs on the leaves of a certain tree, and the eggs hatch tiny caterpillars which eat just that kind of leaves, and the worms grow and grow, and take on different forms and colours until at last they are big caterpillars six inches long, with large horns. Then they burrow into the earth, build a water-proof house around themselves from material which is inside them, and lie through rain and freezing cold for months. A year from egg laying they come out like this, and begin the process all over again. They don't eat, they don't see distinctly, they live but a few days, and fly only at night; then they drop off easy, but the process goes on."

A shivering movement went over the moth. The wings drooped and spread wider. Mrs. Comstock sank into soft awed tones.

"There never was a moment in my life," she said, "when I felt so in the Presence, as I do now. I feel as if the Almighty were so real, and so near, that I could reach out and touch Him, as I could this wonderful work of His, if I dared. I feel like saying to Him: 'To the extent of my brain power I realize Your presence, and all it is in me to comprehend of Your power. Help me to learn, even this late, the lessons of Your wonderful creations. Help me to unshackle and expand my soul to the fullest realization of Your wonders. Almighty God, make me bigger, make me broader!'"

The moth climbed to the end of the projection, up it a little way, then suddenly reversed its wings, turned the hidden sides out and dropped them beside its abdomen, like a large fly. The upper side of the wings, thus exposed, was far richer colour, more exquisite texture than the under, and they slowly half lifted and drooped again. Mrs. Comstock turned her face to Philip.

"Am I an old fool, or do you feel it, too?" she half whispered.

"You are wiser than you ever have been before," answered he. "I feel it, also."

"And I," breathed Elnora.

The moth spread its wings, shivered them tremulously, opening and closing them rapidly. Philip handed the box to Elnora.

She shook her head.

"I can't take that one," she said. "Give her freedom."

"But, Elnora," protested Mrs. Comstock, "I don't want to let her go. She's mine. She's the first one I ever found this way. Can't you put her in a big box, and let her live, without hurting her? I can't bear to let her go. I want to learn all about her."

"Then watch while we gather these on the trees," said Elnora. "We will take her home until night and then decide what to do. She won't fly for a long time yet."

Mrs. Comstock settled on the ground, gazing at the moth. Elnora and Philip went to the baited trees, placing several large moths and a number of smaller ones in the cyanide jar, and searching the bushes beyond where they found several paired specimens of differing families. When they returned Elnora showed her mother how to hold her hand before the moth so that it would climb upon her fingers. Then they started back to the cabin, Elnora and Philip leading the way; Mrs. Comstock followed slowly, stepping with great care lest she stumble and injure the moth. Her face wore a look of comprehension, in her eyes was an exalted light. On she came to the blue-bordered pool lying beside her path.

A turtle scrambled from a log and splashed into the water, while a red-wing shouted, "O-ka-lee!" to her. Mrs. Comstock paused and looked intently at the slime-covered quagmire, framed in a flower riot and homed over by sweet-voiced birds. Then she gazed at the thing of incomparable beauty clinging to her fingers and said softly: "If you had known about wonders like these in the days of your youth, Robert Comstock, could you ever have done what you did?"

Elnora missed her mother, and turning to look for her, saw her standing beside the pool. Would the old fascination return? A panic of fear seized the girl. She went back swiftly.

"Are you afraid she is going?" Elnora asked. "If you are, cup your other hand over her for shelter. Carrying her through this air and in the hot sunshine will dry her wings and make them ready for flight very quickly. You can't trust her in such air and light as you can in the cool dark woods."

While she talked she took hold of her mother's sleeve, anxiously smiling a pitiful little smile that Mrs. Comstock understood. Philip set his load at the back door, returning to hold open the garden gate for Elnora and Mrs. Comstock. He reached it in time to see them standing together beside the pool. The mother bent swiftly and kissed the girl on the lips. Philip turned and was busily hunting moths on the raspberry bushes when they reached the gate. And so excellent are the rewards of attending your own business, that he found a Promethea on a lilac in a corner; a moth of such rare wine-coloured, velvety shades that it almost sent Mrs. Comstock to her knees again. But this one was fully developed, able to fly, and had to be taken into the cabin hurriedly. Mrs. Comstock stood in the middle of the room holding up her Regalis.

"Now what must I do?" she asked.

Elnora glanced at Philip Ammon. Their eyes met and both of them smiled; he with amusement at the tall, spare figure, with dark eyes and white crown, asking the childish question so confidingly; and Elnora with pride. She was beginning to appreciate the character of her mother.

"How would you like to sit and see her finish development? I'll get dinner," proposed the girl.

After they had dined, Philip and Elnora carried the dishes to the kitchen, brought out boxes, sheets of cork, pins, ink, paper slips, and everything necessary for mounting and classifying the moths they had taken. When the housework was finished Mrs. Comstock with her ruffle sat near, watching and listening. She remembered all they said that she understood, and when uncertain she asked questions. Occasionally she laid down her work to straighten some flower which needed attention or to search the garden for a bug for the grosbeak. In one of these absences Elnora said to Philip: "These replace quite a number of the moths I lost for the man of India. With a week of such luck, I could almost begin to talk college again."

"There is no reason why you should not have the week and the luck," said he. "I have taken moths until the middle of August, though I suspect one is more likely to find late ones in the north where it is colder than here. The next week is hay-time, but we can count on a few double-brooders and strays, and by working the exchange method for all it is worth, I think we can complete the collection again."

"You almost make me hope," said Elnora, "but I must not allow myself. I don't truly think I can replace all I lost, not even with your help. If I could, I scarcely see my way clear to leave mother this winter. I have found her so recently, and she is so precious, I can't risk losing her again. I am going to take the nature position in the Onabasha schools, and I shall be most happy doing the work. Only, these are a temptation."

"I wish you might go to college this fall with the other girls," said Philip. "I feel that if you don't you never will. Isn't there some way?"

"I can't see it if there is, and I really don't want to leave mother."

"Well, mother is mighty glad to hear it," said Mrs. Comstock, entering the arbour.

Philip noticed that her face was pale, her lips quivering, her voice cold.

"I was telling your daughter that she should go to college this winter," he explained, "but she says she doesn't want to leave you."

"If she wants to go, I wish she could," said Mrs. Comstock, a look of relief spreading over her face.

"Oh, all girls want to go to college," said Philip. "It's the only proper place to learn bridge and embroidery; not to mention midnight lunches of mixed pickles and fruit cake, and all the delights of the sororities."

"I have thought for years of going to college," said Elnora, "but I never thought of any of those things."

"That is because your education in fudge and bridge has been sadly neglected," said Philip. "You should hear my sister Polly! This was her final year! Lunches and sororities were all I heard her mention, until Tom Levering came on deck; now he is the leading subject. I can't see from her daily conversation that she knows half as much really worth knowing as you do, but she's ahead of you miles on fun."

"Oh, we had some good times in the high school," said Elnora. "Life hasn't been all work and study. Is Edith Carr a college girl?"

"No. She is the very selectest kind of a private boarding-school girl."

"Who is she?" asked Mrs. Comstock.

Philip opened his lips.

"She is a girl in Chicago, that Mr. Ammon knows very well," said Elnora. "She is beautiful and rich, and a friend of his sister's. Or, didn't you say that?"

"I don't remember, but she is," said Philip. "This moth needs an alcohol bath to remove the dope."

"Won't the down come, too?" asked Elnora anxiously.

"No. You watch and you will see it come out, as Polly would say, 'a perfectly good' moth."

"Is your sister younger than you?" inquired Elnora.

"Yes," said Philip, "but she is three years older than you. She is the dearest sister in all the world. I'd love to see her now."

"Why don't you send for her," suggested Elnora. "Perhaps she'd like to help us catch moths."

"Yes, I think Polly in a Virot hat, Picot embroidered frock, and three-inch heels would take more moths than any one who ever tried the Limberlost," laughed Philip.

"Well, you find many of them, and you are her brother."

"Yes, but that is different. Father was reared in Onabasha, and he loved the country. He trained me his way and mother took charge of Polly. I don't quite understand it.

Mother is a great home body herself, but she did succeed in making Polly strictly ornamental."

"Does Tom Levering need a 'strictly ornamental' girl?"

"You are too matter of fact! Too 'strictly' material. He needs a darling girl who will love him plenty, and Polly is that."

"Well, then, does the Limberlost need a 'strictly ornamental' girl?"

"No!" cried Philip. "You are ornament enough for the Limberlost. I have changed my mind. I don't want Polly here. She would not enjoy catching moths, or anything we do."

"She might," persisted Elnora. "You are her brother, and surely you care for these things."

"The argument does not hold," said Philip. "Polly and I do not like the same things when we are at home, but we are very fond of each other. The member of my family who would go crazy about this is my father. I wish he could come, if only for a week. I'd send for him, but he is tied up in preparing some papers for a great corporation case this summer. He likes the country. It was his vote that brought me here."

Philip leaned back against the arbour, watching the grosbeak as it hunted food between a tomato vine and a day lily. Elnora set him to making labels, and when he finished them he asked permission to write a letter. He took no pains to conceal his page, and from where she sat opposite him, Elnora could not look his way without reading: "My dearest Edith." He wrote busily for a time and then sat staring across the garden.

"Have you run out of material so quickly?" asked Elnora.

"That's about it," said Philip. "I have said that I am getting well as rapidly as possible, that the air is fine, the folks at Uncle Doc's all well, and entirely too good to me; that I am spending most of my time in the country helping catch moths for a collection, which is splendid exercise; now I can't think of another thing that will be interesting."

There was a burst of exquisite notes in the maple.

"Put in the grosbeak," suggested Elnora. "Tell her you are so friendly with him you feed him potato bugs."

Philip lowered the pen to the sheet, bent forward, then hesitated.

"Blest if I do!" he cried. "She'd think a grosbeak was a depraved person with a large nose. She'd never dream that it was a black-robed lover, with a breast of snow and a crimson heart. She doesn't care for hungry babies and potato bugs. I shall write that to father. He will find it delightful."

Elnora deftly picked up a moth, pinned it and placed its wings. She straightened the antennae, drew each leg into position and set it in perfectly lifelike manner.

As she lifted her work to see if she had it right, she glanced at Philip. He was still frowning and hesitating over the paper.

"I dare you to let me dictate a couple of paragraphs."

"Done!" cried Philip. "Go slowly enough that I can write it."

Elnora laughed gleefully.

"I am writing this," she began, "in an old grape arbour in the country, near a log cabin where I had my dinner. From where I sit I can see directly into the home of the next-door neighbour on the west. His name is R. B. Grosbeak. From all I have seen of him, he is a gentleman of the old school; the oldest school there is, no doubt. He always wears a black suit and cap and a white vest, decorated with one large red heart, which I think must be the emblem of some ancient order. I have been here a number of times, and I never have seen him wear anything else, or his wife appear in other than a brown dress with touches of white.

"It has appealed to me at times that she was a shade neglectful of her home duties, but he does not seem to feel that way. He cheerfully stays in the sitting-room, while she is away having a good time, and sings while he cares for the four small children. I must tell you about his music. I am sure he never saw inside a conservatory. I think he merely picked up what he knows by ear and without vocal training, but there is a tenderness in his tones, a depth of pure melody, that I never have heard surpassed. It may be that I think more of his music than that of some other good vocalists hereabout, because I see more of him and appreciate his devotion to his home life.

"I just had an encounter with him at the west fence, and induced him to carry a small gift to his children. When I see the perfect harmony in which he lives, and the depth of content he and the brown lady find in life, I am almost persuaded to— Now this is going to be poetry," said Elnora. "Move your pen over here and begin with a quote and a cap."

Philip's face had been an interesting study while he wrote her sentences. Now he gravely set the pen where she indicated, and Elnora dictated—

"*Buy a nice little home in the country,*
And settle down there for life."

"That's the truth!" cried Philip. "It's as big a temptation as I ever had. Go on!"

"That's all," said Elnora. "You can finish. The moths are done. I am going hunting for whatever I can find for the grades."

"Wait a minute," begged Philip. "I am going, too."

"No. You stay with mother and finish your letter."

"It is done. I couldn't add anything to that."

"Very well! Sign your name and come on. But I forgot to tell you all the bargain. Maybe you won't send the letter when you hear that. The remainder is that you show me the reply to my part of it."

"Oh, that's easy! I wouldn't have the slightest objection to showing you the whole letter."

He signed his name, folded the sheets and slipped them into his pocket.

"Where are we going and what do we take?"

"Will you go, mother?" asked Elnora.

"I have a little work that should be done," said Mrs. Comstock. "Could you spare me? Where do you want to go?"

"We will go down to Aunt Margaret's and see her a few minutes and get Billy. We will be back in time for supper."

Mrs. Comstock smiled as she watched them down the road. What a splendid-looking pair of young creatures they were! How finely proportioned, how full of vitality! Then her face grew troubled as she saw them in earnest conversation. Just as she was wishing she had not trusted her precious girl with so much of a stranger, she saw Elnora stoop to lift a branch and peer under. The mother grew content. Elnora was thinking only of her work. She was to be trusted utterly.

Chapter 16

Wherein the Limberlost Sings for Philip, and the Talking Trees Tell Great Secrets

A few days later Philip handed Elnora a sheet of paper and she read: "In your condition I should think the moth hunting and life at that cabin would be very good for you, but for any sake keep away from that Grosbeak person, and don't come home with your head full of granger ideas. No doubt he has a remarkable voice, but I can't bear untrained singers, and don't you get the idea that a June song is perennial. You are not hearing the music he will make when the four babies have the scarlet fever and the measles, and the gadding wife leaves him at home to care for them then. Poor soul, I pity her! How she exists where rampant cows bellow at you, frogs croak, mosquitoes consume you, the butter goes to oil in summer and bricks in winter, while the pump freezes every day, and there is no earthly amusement, and no society! Poor things! Can't you influence him to move? No wonder she gads when she has a chance! I should die. If you are thinking of settling in the country, think also of a woman who is satisfied with white and brown to accompany you! Brown! Of all deadly colours! I should go mad in brown."

Elnora laughed while she read. Her face was dimpling, as she returned the sheet. "Who's ahead?" she asked.

"Who do you think?" he parried.

"She is," said Elnora. "Are you going to tell her in your next that R. B. Grosbeak is a bird, and that he probably will spend the winter in a wild plum thicket in Tennessee?"

"No," said Philip. "I shall tell her that I understand her ideas of life perfectly, and, of course, I never shall ask her to deal with oily butter and frozen pumps—"

"—and measley babies," interpolated Elnora.

"Exactly!" said Philip. "At the same time I find so much to counterbalance those things, that I should not object to bearing them myself, in view of the recompense. Where do we go and what do we do to-day?"

"We will have to hunt beside the roads and around the edge of the Limberlost to-day," said Elnora. "Mother is making strawberry preserves, and she can't come until she finishes. Suppose we go down to the swamp and I'll show you what is left of the flower-room that Terence O'More, the big lumber man of Great Rapids, made when he was a homeless boy here. Of course, you have heard the story?"

"Yes, and I've met the O'Mores who are frequently in Chicago society. They have friends there. I think them one ideal couple."

"That sounds as if they might be the only one," said Elnora, "and, indeed, they are not. I know dozens. Aunt Margaret and Uncle Wesley are another, the Brownlees another, and my mathematics professor and his wife. The world is full of happy people, but no one ever hears of them. You must fight and make a scandal to get into the papers. No one knows about all the happy people. I am happy myself, and look how perfectly inconspicuous I am."

"You only need go where you will be seen," began Philip, when he remembered and finished. "What do we take to-day?"

"Ourselves," said Elnora. "I have a vagabond streak in my blood and it's in evidence. I am going to show you where real flowers grow, real birds sing, and if I feel quite right about it, perhaps I shall raise a note or two myself."

"Oh, do you sing?" asked Philip politely.

"At times," answered Elnora. "'As do the birds; because I must,' but don't be scared. The mood does not possess me often. Perhaps I shan't raise a note."

They went down the road to the swamp, climbed the snake fence, followed the path to the old trail and then turned south upon it. Elnora indicated to Philip the trail with remnants of sagging barbed wire.

"It was ten years ago," she said. "I was a little school girl, but I wandered widely even then, and no one cared. I saw him often. He had been in a city institution all his life, when he took the job of keeping timber thieves out of this swamp, before many trees had been cut. It was a strong man's work, and he was a frail boy, but he grew hardier as he lived out of doors. This trail we are on is the path his feet first wore, in those days when he was insane with fear and eaten up with loneliness, but he stuck to his work and won out. I used to come down to the road and creep among the bushes as far as I dared, to watch him pass. He walked mostly, at times he rode a wheel.

"Some days his face was dreadfully sad, others it was so determined a little child could see the force in it, and once he was radiant. That day the Swamp Angel was with him. I can't tell you what she was like. I never saw any one who resembled her. He stopped close here to show her a bird's nest. Then they went on to a sort of flower-room he had made, and he sang for her. By the time he left,

I had gotten bold enough to come out on the trail, and I met the big Scotchman Freckles lived with. He saw me catching moths and butterflies, so he took me to the flower-room and gave me everything there. I don't dare come alone often, so I can't keep it up as he did, but you can see something of how it was."

Elnora led the way and Philip followed. The outlines of the room were not distinct, because many of the trees were gone, but Elnora showed how it had been as nearly as she could.

"The swamp is almost ruined now," she said. "The maples, walnuts, and cherries are all gone. The talking trees are the only things left worth while."

"The 'talking trees!' I don't understand," commented Philip.

"No wonder!" laughed Elnora. "They are my discovery. You know all trees whisper and talk during the summer, but there are two that have so much to say they keep on the whole winter, when the others are silent. The beeches and oaks so love to talk, they cling to their dead, dry leaves. In the winter the winds are stiffest and blow most, so these trees whisper, chatter, sob, laugh, and at times roar until the sound is deafening. They never cease until new leaves come out in the spring to push off the old ones. I love to stand beneath them with my ear to the trunks, interpreting what they say to fit my moods. The beeches branch low, and their leaves are small so they only know common earthly things; but the oaks run straight above almost all other trees before they branch, their arms are mighty, their leaves large. They meet the winds that travel around the globe, and from them learn the big things."

Philip studied the girl's face. "What do the beeches tell you, Elnora?" he asked gently.

"To be patient, to be unselfish, to do unto others as I would have them do to me."

"And the oaks?"

"They say 'be true,' 'live a clean life,' 'send your soul up here and the winds of the world will teach it what honour achieves.'"

"Wonderful secrets, those!" marvelled Philip. "Are they telling them now? Could I hear?"

"No. They are only gossiping now. This is play-time. They tell the big secrets to a white world, when the music inspires them."

"The music?"

"All other trees are harps in the winter. Their trunks are the frames, their branches the strings, the winds the musicians. When the air is cold and clear, the world very white, and the harp music swelling, then the talking trees tell the strengthening, uplifting things."

"You wonderful girl!" cried Philip. "What a woman you will be!"

"If I am a woman at all worth while, it will be because I have had such wonderful opportunities," said Elnora. "Not every girl is driven to the forest to learn what God has to say there. Here are the remains of Freckles's room. The time the Angel came here he sang to her, and I listened. I never heard music like that. No wonder she loved him. Every one who knew him did, and they do yet. Try that log, it makes a fairly good seat. This old store box was his treasure house, just as it's now mine. I will show you my dearest possession. I do not dare take it home because mother can't overcome her dislike for it. It was my father's, and in some ways I am like him. This is the strongest."

Elnora lifted the violin and began to play. She wore a school dress of green gingham, with the sleeves rolled to the elbows. She seemed a part of the setting all around her. Her head shone like a small dark sun, and her face never had seemed so rose-flushed and fair. From the instant she drew the bow, her lips parted and her eyes turned toward something far away in the swamp, and never did she give more of that impression of feeling for her notes and repeating something audible only to her. Philip was too close to get the best effect. He arose and stepped back several yards, leaning against a large tree, looking and listening intently.

As he changed positions he saw that Mrs. Comstock had followed them, and was standing on the trail, where she could not have helped hearing everything Elnora had said.

So to Philip before her and the mother watching on the trail, Elnora played the Song of the Limberlost. It seemed as if the swamp hushed all its other voices and spoke only through her dancing bow. The mother out on the trail had heard it all, once before from the girl, many times from her father. To the man it was a revelation. He stood so stunned he forgot Mrs. Comstock. He tried to realize what a city audience would say to that music, from such a player, with a similar background, and he could not imagine.

He was wondering what he dared say, how much he might express, when the last note fell and the girl laid the violin in the case, closed the door, locked it and hid the key in the rotting wood at the end of a log. Then she came to him. Philip stood looking at her curiously.

"I wonder," he said, "what people would say to that?"

"I played that in public once," said Elnora. "I think they liked it, fairly well. I had a note yesterday offering me the leadership of the high school orchestra in Onabasha. I can take it as well as not. None of my talks to the grades come the first thing in the morning. I can play a few minutes in the orchestra and reach the rooms in plenty of time. It will be more work that I love, and like finding the money. I would gladly play for nothing, merely to be able to express myself."

"With some people it makes a regular battlefield of the human heart—this struggle for self-expression," said Philip. "You are going to do beautiful work in the world, and do it well. When I realize that your violin belonged to your father, that he played it before you were born, and it no doubt affected your mother strongly, and then couple with that the years you have roamed these fields and swamps finding in nature all you had to lavish your heart upon, I can see how you evolved. I understand what you mean by self-expression. I know something of what you have to express. The world never so wanted your message as it does now. It is hungry for the things you know. I can see easily how your position came to you. What you have to give is taught in no college, and I am not sure but you would spoil yourself if you tried to run your mind through a set groove with hundreds of others. I never thought I should say such a thing to any one, but I do say to you, and I honestly believe it; give up the college idea. Your mind does not need that sort of development. Stick close to your work in the woods. You are becoming so infinitely greater on it, than the best college girl I ever knew, that there is no comparison. When you have money to spend, take that violin and go to one of the world's great masters and let the Limberlost sing to him; if he thinks he can improve it, very well. I have my doubts."

"Do you really mean that you would give up all idea of going to college, in my place?"

"I really mean it," said Philip. "If I now held the money in my hands to send you, and could give it to you in some way you would accept I would not. I do not know why it is the fate of the world always to want something different from what life gives them. If you only could realize it, my girl, you are in college, and have been always. You are in the school of experience, and it has taught you to think, and given you a heart. God knows I envy the man who wins it! You have been in the college of the Limberlost all your life, and I never met a graduate from any other institution who could begin to compare with you in sanity, clarity, and interesting knowledge. I wouldn't even advise you to read too many books on your lines. You acquire your material first hand, and you know that you are right. What you should do is to begin early to practise self-expression. Don't wait too long to tell us about the woods as you know them."

"Follow the course of the Bird Woman, you mean?" asked Elnora.

"In your own way; with your own light. She won't live forever. You are younger, and you will be ready to begin where she ends. The swamp has given you all you need so far; now you give it to the world in payment. College be confounded! Go to work and show people what there is in you!"

Not until then did he remember Mrs. Comstock.

"Should we go out to the trail and see if your mother is coming?" he asked.

"Here she is now," said Elnora. "Gracious, it's a mercy I got that violin put away in time! I didn't expect her so soon," whispered the girl as she turned and went toward her mother. Mrs. Comstock's expression was peculiar as she looked at Elnora.

"I forgot that you were making sun-preserves and they didn't require much cooking," she said. "We should have waited for you."

"Not at all!" answered Mrs. Comstock. "Have you found anything yet?"

"Nothing that I can show you," said Elnora. "I am almost sure I have found an idea that will revolutionize the whole course of my work, thought, and ambitions."

"'Ambitions!' My, what a hefty word!" laughed Mrs. Comstock. "Now who would suspect a little red-haired country girl of harbouring such a deadly germ in her body? Can you tell mother about it?"

"Not if you talk to me that way, I can't," said Elnora.

"Well, I guess we better let ambition lie. I've always heard it was safest asleep. If you ever get a bona fide attack, it will be time to attend it. Let's hunt specimens. It is June. Philip and I are in the grades. You have an hour to put an idea into our heads that will stick for a lifetime, and grow for good. That's the way I look at your job. Now, what are you going to give us? We don't want any old silly stuff that has been hashed over and over, we want a big new idea to plant in our hearts. Come on, Miss Teacher, what is the boiled-down, double-distilled essence of June? Give it to us strong. We are large enough to furnish it developing ground. Hurry up! Time is short and we are waiting. What is the miracle of June? What one thing epitomizes the whole month, and makes it just a little different from any other?"

"The birth of these big night moths," said Elnora promptly.

Philip clapped his hands. The tears started to Mrs. Comstock's eyes. She took Elnora in her arms, and kissed her forehead.

"You'll do!" she said. "June is June, not because it has bloom, bird, fruit, or flower, exclusive to it alone.

"It's half May and half July in all of them. But to me, it's just June, when it comes to these great, velvet-winged night moths which sweep its moonlit skies, consummating their scheme of creation, and dropping like a bloomed-out flower. Give them moths for June. Then make that the basis of your year's work. Find the distinctive feature of each month, the one thing which marks it a time apart, and hit them squarely between the eyes with it. Even the babies of the lowest grades can comprehend moths when they see a few emerge, and learn their history, as it can be lived before them. You should show your specimens in pairs, then their eggs, the growing caterpillars, and then the cocoons. You want to dig out the red heart of every month in the year, and hold it pulsing before them.

"I can't name all of them off-hand, but I think of one more right now. February belongs to our winter birds. It is then the great horned owl of the swamp courts his mate, the big hawks pair, and even the crows begin to take notice. These are truly our birds. Like the poor we have them always with us. You should hear the musicians of this swamp in February, Philip, on a mellow night. Oh, but they are in earnest! For twenty-one years I've listened by night to the great owls, all the smaller sizes, the foxes, coons, and every resident left in these woods, and by day to the hawks, yellow-hammers, sap-suckers, titmice, crows, and other winter birds. Only just now it's come to me that the distinctive feature of February is not linen bleaching, nor sugar making; it's the love month of our very own birds. Give them hawks and owls for February, Elnora."

With flashing eyes the girl looked at Philip. "How's that?" she said. "Don't you think I will succeed, with such help? You should hear the concert she is talking about! It is simply indescribable when the ground is covered with snow, and the moonlight white."

"It's about the best music we have," said Mrs. Comstock. "I wonder if you couldn't copy that and make a strong, original piece out of it for your violin, Elnora?"

There was one tense breath, then— "I could try," said Elnora simply.

Philip rushed to the rescue. "We must go to work," he said, and began examining a walnut branch for Luna moth eggs. Elnora joined him while Mrs. Comstock drew her embroidery from her pocket and sat on a log. She said she was tired, they could come for her when they were ready to go. She could hear their voices around her until she called them at supper time. When they came to her she stood waiting on the trail, the sewing in one hand, the violin in the other. Elnora became very white, but followed the trail without a word. Philip, unable to see a woman carry a heavier load than he, reached for the instrument. Mrs. Comstock shook her head. She carried the violin home, took it into her room and closed the door. Elnora turned to Philip.

"If she destroys that, I shall die!" cried the girl.

"She won't!" said Philip. "You misunderstand her. She wouldn't have said what she did about the owls, if she had meant to. She is your mother. No one loves you as she does. Trust her! Myself—I think she's simply great!"

Mrs. Comstock returned with serene face, and all of them helped with the supper. When it was over Philip and Elnora sorted and classified the afternoon's specimens, and made a trip to the woods to paint and light several trees for moths. When they came back Mrs. Comstock sat in the arbour, and they joined her.

The moonlight was so intense, print could have been read by it. The damp night air held odours near to earth, making flower and tree perfume strong. A thousand insects were serenading, and in the maple the grosbeak occasionally said a reassuring word to his wife, while she answered that all was well. A whip-poor-will wailed in the swamp and beside the blue-bordered pool a chat complained disconsolately. Mrs. Comstock went into the cabin, but she returned immediately, laying the violin and bow across Elnora's lap. "I wish you would give us a little music," she said.

Chapter 17

Wherein Mrs. Comstock Dances in the Moonlight, and Elnora Makes a Confession

Billy was swinging in the hammock, at peace with himself and all the world, when he thought he heard something. He sat bolt upright, his eyes staring. Once he opened his lips, then thought again and closed them. The sound persisted. Billy vaulted the fence, and ran down the road with his queer sidewise hop. When he neared the Comstock cabin, he left the warm dust of the highway and stepped softly at slower pace over the rank grasses of the roadside. He had heard aright. The violin was in the grape arbour, singing a perfect jumble of everything, poured out in an exultant tumult. The strings were voicing the joy of a happy girl heart.

Billy climbed the fence enclosing the west woods and crept toward the arbour. He was not a spy and not a sneak. He merely wanted to satisfy his child-heart as to whether Mrs. Comstock was at home, and Elnora at last playing her loved violin with her mother's consent. One peep sufficed. Mrs. Comstock sat in the moonlight, her head leaning against the arbour; on her face was a look of perfect peace and contentment. As he stared at her the bow hesitated a second and Mrs. Comstock spoke:

"That's all very melodious and sweet," she said, "but I do wish you could play 'Money Musk' and some of the tunes I danced as a girl."

Elnora had been carefully avoiding every note that might be reminiscent of her father. At the words she laughed softly and began "Turkey in the Straw." An instant later Mrs. Comstock was dancing in the moonlight. Ammon sprang to her side, caught her in his arms, while to Elnora's laughter and the violin's impetus they danced until they dropped panting on the arbour bench.

Billy scarcely knew when he reached the road. His light feet barely touched the soft way, so swiftly he flew. He vaulted the fence and burst into the house.

"Aunt Margaret! Uncle Wesley!" he screamed. "Listen! Listen! She's playing it! Elnora's playing her violin at home! And Aunt Kate is dancing like anything before the arbour! I saw her in the moonlight! I ran down! Oh, Aunt Margaret!"

Billy fled sobbing to Margaret's breast.

"Why Billy!" she chided. "Don't cry, you little dunce! That's what we've all prayed for these many years; but you must be mistaken about Kate. I can't believe it."

Billy lifted his head. "Well, you just have to!" he said. "When I say I saw anything, Uncle Wesley knows I did. The city man was dancing with her. They danced together and Elnora laughed. But it didn't look funny to me; I was scared."

"Who was it said 'wonders never cease,'" asked Wesley. "You mark my word, once you get Kate Comstock started, you can't stop her. There's a wagon load of penned-up force in her. Dancing in the moonlight! Well, I'll be hanged!"

Billy was at his side instantly. "Whoever does it will have to hang me, too," he cried.

Sinton threw his arm around Billy and drew him closely. "Tell us all about it, son," he said. Billy told. "And when Elnora just stopped a breath, 'Can't you play some of the old things I knew when I was a girl?' said her ma. Then Elnora began to do a thing that made you want to whirl round and round, and quicker 'an scat there was her ma a-whirling. The city man, he ups and grabs her and whirls, too, and back in the woods I was going just like they did. Elnora begins to laugh, and I ran to tell you, cos I knew you'd like to know. Now, all the world is right, ain't it?" ended Billy in supreme satisfaction.

"You just bet it is!" said Wesley.

Billy looked steadily at Margaret. "Is it, Aunt Margaret?"

Margaret Sinton smiled at him bravely.

An hour later when Billy was ready to climb the stairs to his room, he went to Margaret to say good night. He leaned against her an instant, then brought his lips to her ear. "Wish I could get your little girls back for you!" he whispered and dashed toward the stairs.

Down at the Comstock cabin the violin played on until Elnora was so tired she scarcely could lift the bow. Then Philip went home. The women walked to the gate with him, and stood watching him from sight.

"That's what I call one decent young man!" said Mrs. Comstock. "To see him fit in with us, you'd think he'd been brought up in a cabin; but it's likely he's always had the very cream o' the pot."

"Yes, I think so," laughed Elnora, "but it hasn't hurt him. I've never seen anything I could criticise. He's teaching me so much, unconsciously. You know he graduated from Harvard, and has several degrees in law. He's coming in the morning, and we are going to put in a big day on Catocalae."

"Which is—?"

"Those gray moths with wings that fold back like big flies, and they appear as if they had been carved from old wood. Then, when they fly, the lower wings flash out and they are red and black, or gold and black, or pink and black, or dozens of bright, beautiful colours combined with black. No one ever has classified all of them and written their complete history, unless the Bird Woman is doing it now. She wants everything she can get about them."

"I remember," said Mrs. Comstock. "They are mighty pretty things. I've started up slews of them from the vines covering the logs, all my life. I must be cautious and catch them after this, but they seem powerful spry. I might get hold of something rare." She thought intently and added, "And wouldn't know it if I did. It would just be my luck. I've had the rarest thing on earth in reach this many a day and only had the wit to cinch it just as it was going. I'll bet I don't let anything else escape me."

Next morning Philip came early, and he and Elnora went at once to the fields and woods. Mrs. Comstock had come to believe so implicitly in him that she now stayed at home to complete the work before she joined them, and when she did she often sat sewing, leaving them wandering hours at a time. It was noon before she finished, and then she packed a basket of lunch. She found Elnora and Philip near the violet patch, which was still in its prime. They all lunched together in the shade of a wild crab thicket, with flowers spread at their feet, and the gold orioles streaking the air with flashes of light and trailing ecstasy behind them, while the red-wings, as always, asked the most impertinent questions. Then Mrs. Comstock carried the basket back to the cabin, and Philip and Elnora sat on a log, resting a few minutes. They had unexpected luck, and both were eager to continue the search.

"Do you remember your promise about these violets?" asked he. "To-morrow is Edith's birthday, and if I'd put them special delivery on the morning train, she'd get them in the late afternoon. They ought to keep that long. She leaves for the North next day."

"Of course, you may have them," said Elnora. "We will quit long enough before supper to gather a large bunch. They can be packed so they will carry all right. They should be perfectly fresh, especially if we gather them this evening and let them drink all night."

Then they went back to hunt Catocalae. It was a long and a happy search. It led them into new, unexplored nooks of the woods, past a red-poll nest, and where goldfinches prospected for thistledown for the cradles they would line a little later. It led them into real forest, where deep, dark pools lay, where the hermit thrush and the wood robin extracted the essence from all other bird melody, and poured it out in their pure bell-tone notes. It seemed as if every old gray tree-trunk, slab of loose bark, and prostrate log yielded the flashing gray treasures; while of all others they seemed to take alarm most easily, and be most difficult to capture.

Philip came to Elnora at dusk, daintily holding one by the body, its dark wings showing and its long slender legs trying to clasp his fingers and creep from his hold.

"Oh for mercy's sake!" cried Elnora, staring at him.

"I half believe it!" exulted Ammon.

"Did you ever see one?"

"Only in collections, and very seldom there."

Elnora studied the black wings intently. "I surely believe that's Sappho," she marvelled. "The Bird Woman will be overjoyed."

"We must get the cyanide jar quickly," said Philip.

"I wouldn't lose her for anything. Such a chase as she led me!"

Elnora brought the jar and began gathering up paraphernalia.

"When you make a find like that," she said, "it's the right time to quit and feel glorious all the rest of that day. I tell you I'm proud! We will go now. We have barely time to carry out our plans before supper. Won't mother be pleased to see that we have a rare one?"

"I'd like to see any one more pleased than I am!" said Philip Ammon. "I feel as if I'd earned my supper to-night. Let's go."

He took the greater part of the load and stepped aside for Elnora to precede him. She followed the path, broken by the grazing cattle, toward the cabin and nearest the violet patch she stopped, laid down her net, and the things she carried. Philip passed her and hurried straight toward the back gate.

"Aren't you going to—?" began Elnora.

"I'm going to get this moth home in a hurry," he said. "This cyanide has lost its strength, and it's not working well. We need some fresh in the jar."

He had forgotten the violets! Elnora stood looking after him, a curious expression on her face. One second so—then she picked up the net and followed. At the blue-bordered pool she paused and half turned back, then she closed her lips firmly and went on. It was nine o'clock when Philip said good-bye, and started to town. His gay whistle floated to them from the farthest corner of the Limberlost. Elnora complained of being tired, so she went to her room and to bed. But sleep would not come. Thought was racing in her brain and the longer she lay the wider awake she grew. At last she softly slipped from bed, lighted her lamp and began opening boxes. Then she went to work. Two hours later a beautiful birch bark basket, strongly and artistically made, stood on her table. She set a tiny alarm clock at three, returned to bed and fell asleep instantly with a smile on her lips.

She was on the floor with the first tinkle of the alarm, and hastily dressing, she picked up the basket and a box to fit it, crept down the stairs, and out to the violet patch. She was unafraid as it was growing light, and lining the basket with damp mosses she swiftly began picking, with practised hands, the best of the flowers. She scarcely could tell which were freshest at times, but day soon came creeping over the Limberlost and peeped at her. The robins awoke all their neighbours, and a babel of bird notes filled the air. The dew was dripping, while the first strong rays of light fell on a world in which Elnora worshipped. When the basket was filled to overflowing, she set it in the stout pasteboard box, packed it solid with mosses, tied it firmly and slipped under the cord a note she had written the previous night.

Then she took a short cut across the woods and walked swiftly to Onabasha. It was after six o'clock, but all of the city she wished to avoid were asleep. She had no trouble in finding a small boy out, and she stood at a distance waiting while he rang Dr. Ammon's bell and delivered the package for Philip to a maid, with the note which was to be given him at once.

On the way home through the woods passing some baited trees she collected the captive moths. She entered the kitchen with them so naturally that Mrs. Comstock made no comment. After breakfast Elnora went to her room, cleared away all trace of the night's work and was out in the arbour mounting moths when Philip came down the road. "I am tired sitting," she said to her mother. "I think I will walk a few rods and meet him."

"Who's a trump?" he called from afar.

"Not you!" retorted Elnora. "Confess that you forgot!"

"Completely!" said Philip. "But luckily it would not have been fatal. I wrote Polly last week to send Edith something appropriate to-day, with my card. But that touch from the woods will be very effective. Thank you more than I can say. Aunt Anna and I unpacked it to see the basket, and it was a beauty. She says you are always doing such things."

"Well, I hope not!" laughed Elnora. "If you'd seen me sneaking out before dawn, not to awaken mother and coming in with moths to make her think I'd been to the trees, you'd know it was a most especial occasion."

Then Philip understood two things: Elnora's mother did not know of the early morning trip to the city, and the girl had come to meet him to tell him so.

"You were a brick to do it!" he whispered as he closed the gate behind them. "I'll never forget you for it. Thank you ever so much."

"I did not do that for you," said Elnora tersely. "I did it mostly to preserve my own self-respect. I saw you were forgetting. If I did it for anything besides that, I did it for her."

"Just look what I've brought!" said Philip, entering the arbour and greeting Mrs. Comstock. "Borrowed it of the Bird Woman. And it isn't hers. A rare edition of Catocalae with coloured plates. I told her the best I could, and she said to try for Sappho here. I suspect the Bird Woman will be out presently. She was all excitement."

Then they bent over the book together and with the mounted moth before them determined her family. The Bird Woman did come later, and carried the moth away, to put into a book and Elnora and Philip were freshly filled with enthusiasm.

So these days were the beginning of the weeks that followed. Six of them flying on Time's wings, each filled to the brim with interest. After June, the moth hunts grew less frequent; the fields and woods were searched for material for Elnora's grade work. The most absorbing occupation they found was in carrying out Mrs. Comstock's suggestion to learn the vital thing for which each month was distinctive, and make that the key to the nature work. They wrote out a list of the months, opposite each the things all of them could suggest which seemed to pertain to that month alone, and then tried to sift until they found something typical. Mrs. Comstock was a great help. Her mother had been Dutch and had brought from Holland numerous quaint sayings and superstitions easily traceable to Pliny's Natural History; and in Mrs. Comstock's early years in Ohio she had heard much Indian talk among her elders, so she knew the signs of each season, and sometimes they helped. Always her practical thought and sterling common sense were useful. When they were afield until exhausted they came back to the cabin for food, to prepare specimens and classify them, and to talk over the day. Sometimes Philip brought books and read while Elnora and her mother worked, and every night Mrs. Comstock asked for the violin. Her perfect hunger for music was sufficient evidence of how she had suffered without it. So the days crept by, golden, filled with useful work and pure pleasure.

The grosbeak had led the family in the maple abroad and a second brood, in a wild grape vine clambering over the well, was almost ready for flight. The dust lay thick on the country roads, the days grew warmer; summer was just poising to slip into fall, and Philip remained, coming each day as if he had belonged there always.

One warm August afternoon Mrs. Comstock looked up from the ruffle on which she was engaged to see a blue-coated messenger enter the gate.

"Is Philip Ammon here?" asked the boy.

"He is," said Mrs. Comstock.

"I have a message for him."

"He is in the woods back of the cabin. I will ring the bell. Do you know if it is important?"

"Urgent," said the boy. "I rode hard."

Mrs. Comstock stepped to the back door and clanged the dinner bell sharply, paused a second, and rang again. In a short time Philip and Elnora ran down the path.

"Are you ill, mother?" cried Elnora.

Mrs. Comstock indicated the boy. "There is an important message for Philip," she said.

He muttered an excuse and tore open the telegram. His colour faded slightly. "I have to take the first train," he said. "My father is ill and I am needed."

He handed the sheet to Elnora. "I have about two hours, as I remember the trains north, but my things are all over Uncle Doc's house, so I must go at once."

"Certainly," said Elnora, giving back the message. "Is there anything I can do to help? Mother, bring Philip a glass of buttermilk to start on. I will gather what you have here."

"Never mind. There is nothing of importance. I don't want to be hampered. I'll send for it if I miss anything I need."

Philip drank the milk, said good-bye to Mrs. Comstock, thanked her for all her kindness, and turned to Elnora.

"Will you walk to the edge of the Limberlost with me?" he asked. Elnora assented. Mrs. Comstock followed to the gate, urged him to come again soon, and repeated her good-bye. Then she went back to the arbour to await Elnora's return. As she watched down the road she smiled softly.

"I had an idea he would speak to me first," she thought, "but this may change things some. He hasn't time. Elnora will come back a happy girl, and she has good reason. He is a model young man. Her lot will be very different from mine."

She picked up her embroidery and began setting dainty precise little stitches, possible only to certain women.

On the road Elnora spoke first. "I do hope it is nothing serious," she said. "Is he usually strong?"

"Quite strong," said Philip. "I am not at all alarmed but I am very much ashamed. I have been well enough for the past month to have gone home and helped him with some critical cases that were keeping him at work in this heat. I was enjoying myself so I wouldn't offer to go, and he would not ask me to come, so long as he could help it. I have allowed him to overtax himself until he is down, and mother and Polly are north at our cottage. He's never been sick before, and it's probable I am to blame that he is now."

"He intended you to stay this long when you came," urged Elnora.

"Yes, but it's hot in Chicago. I should have remembered him. He is always thinking of me. Possibly he has needed me for days. I am ashamed to go to him in splendid condition and admit that I was having such a fine time I forgot to come home."

"You have had a fine time, then?" asked Elnora.

They had reached the fence. Philip vaulted over to take a short cut across the fields. He turned and looked at her.

"The best, the sweetest, and most wholesome time any man ever had in this world," he said. "Elnora, if I talked hours I couldn't make you understand what a girl I think you are. I never in all my life hated anything as I hate leaving you. It seems to me that I have not strength to do it."

"If you have learned anything worth while from me," said Elnora, "that should be it. Just to have strength to go to your duty, and to go quickly."

He caught the hand she held out to him in both his. "Elnora, these days we have had together, have they been sweet to you?"

"Beautiful days!" said Elnora. "Each like a perfect dream to be thought over and over all my life. Oh, they have been the only really happy days I've ever known; these days rich with mother's love, and doing useful work with your help. Good-bye! You must hurry!"

Philip gazed at her. He tried to drop her hand, only clutched it closer. Suddenly he drew her toward him. "Elnora," he whispered, "will you kiss me good-bye?"

Elnora drew back and stared at him with wide eyes. "I'd strike you sooner!" she said. "Have I ever said or done anything in your presence that made you feel free to ask that, Philip Ammon?"

"No!" panted Philip. "No! I think so much of you I wanted to touch your lips once before I left you. You know, Elnora—"

"Don't distress yourself," said Elnora calmly. "I am broad enough to judge you sanely. I know what you mean. It would be no harm to you. It would not matter to me, but here we will think of some one else. Edith Carr would not want your lips to-morrow if she knew they had touched mine to-day. I was wise to say: 'Go quickly!'"

Philip still clung to her. "Will you write me?" he begged.

"No," said Elnora. "There is nothing to say, save good-bye. We can do that now."

He held on. "Promise that you will write me only one letter," he urged. "I want just one message from you to lock in my desk, and keep always. Promise you will write once, Elnora."

She looked into his eyes, and smiled serenely. "If the talking trees tell me this winter, the secret of how a man may grow perfect, I will write you what it is, Philip. In all the time I have known you, I never have liked you so little. Good-bye."

She drew away her hand and swiftly turned back to the road. Philip Ammon, wordless, started toward Onabasha on a run.

Elnora crossed the road, climbed the fence and sought the shelter of their own woods. She chose a diagonal course and followed it until she came to the path leading past the violet patch. She went down this hurriedly. Her hands were clenched at her side, her eyes dry and bright, her cheeks red-flushed, and her breath coming fast. When she reached the patch she turned into it and stood looking around her.

The mosses were dry, the flowers gone, weeds a foot high covered it. She turned away and went on down the path until she was almost in sight of the cabin.

Mrs. Comstock smiled and waited in the arbour until it occurred to her that Elnora was a long time coming, so she went to the gate. The road stretched away toward the Limberlost empty and lonely. Then she knew that Elnora had gone into their own woods and would come in the back way. She could not understand why the girl did not hurry to her with what she would have to tell. She went out and wandered around the garden. Then she stepped into the path and started along the way leading to the woods, past the pool now framed in a thick setting of yellow lilies. Then she saw, and stopped, gasping for breath. Her hands flew up and her lined face grew ghastly. She stared at the sky and then at the prostrate girl figure. Over and over she tried to speak, but only a dry breath came. She turned and fled back to the garden.

In the familiar enclosure she gazed around her like a caged animal seeking escape. The sun beat down on her bare head mercilessly, and mechanically she moved to the shade of a half-grown hickory tree that voluntarily had sprouted beside the milk house. At her feet lay an axe with which she made kindlings for fires. She stooped and picked it up. The memory of that prone figure sobbing in the grass caught her with a renewed spasm. She shut her eyes as if to close it out. That made hearing so acute she felt certain she heard Elnora moaning beside the path. The eyes flew open. They looked straight at a few spindling tomato plants set too near the tree and stunted by its shade. Mrs. Comstock whirled on the hickory and swung the axe. Her hair shook down, her clothing became disarranged, in the heat the perspiration streamed, but stroke fell on stroke until the tree crashed over, grazing a corner of the milk house and smashing the garden fence on the east.

At the sound Elnora sprang to her feet and came running down the garden walk. "Mother!" she cried. "Mother! What in the world are you doing?"

Mrs. Comstock wiped her ghastly face on her apron. "I've laid out to cut that tree for years," she said. "It shades the beets in the morning, and the tomatoes in the afternoon!"

Elnora uttered one wild little cry and fled into her mother's arms. "Oh mother!" she sobbed. "Will you ever forgive me?"

Mrs. Comstock's arms swept together in a tight grip around Elnora.

"There isn't a thing on God's footstool from a to izzard I won't forgive you, my precious girl!" she said. "Tell mother what it is!"

Elnora lifted her wet face. "He told me," she panted, "just as soon as he decently could—that second day he told me. Almost all his life he's been engaged to a girl at home. He never cared anything about me. He was only interested in the moths and growing strong."

Mrs. Comstock's arms tightened. With a shaking hand she stroked the bright hair.

"Tell me, honey," she said. "Is he to blame for a single one of these tears?"

"Not one!" sobbed Elnora. "Oh mother, I won't forgive you if you don't believe that. Not one! He never said, or looked, or did anything all the world might not have known. He likes me very much as a friend. He hated to go dreadfully!"

"Elnora!" the mother's head bent until the white hair mingled with the brown. "Elnora, why didn't you tell me at first?"

Elnora caught her breath in a sharp snatch. "I know I should!" she sobbed. "I will bear any punishment for not, but I didn't feel as if I possibly could. I was afraid."

"Afraid of what?" the shaking hand was on the hair again.

"Afraid you wouldn't let him come!" panted Elnora. "And oh, mother, I wanted him so!"

Chapter 18

Wherein Mrs. Comstock Experiments with Rejuvenation, and Elnora Teaches Natural History

For the following week Mrs. Comstock and Elnora worked so hard there was no time to talk, and they were compelled to sleep from physical exhaustion. Neither of them made any pretence of eating, for they could not swallow without an effort, so they drank milk and worked. Elnora kept on setting bait for Catacolae and Sphinginae, which, unlike the big moths of June, live several months. She took all the dragonflies and butterflies she could, and when she went over the list for the man of India, she found, to her amazement, that with Philip's help she once more had it complete save a pair of Yellow Emperors.

This circumstance was so surprising she had a fleeting thought of writing Philip and asking him to see if he could not secure her a pair. She did tell the Bird Woman, who from every source at her command tried to complete the series with these moths, but could not find any for sale.

"I think the mills of the Gods are grinding this grist," said Elnora, "and we might as well wait patiently until they choose to send a Yellow Emperor."

Mrs. Comstock invented work. When she had nothing more to do, she hoed in the garden although the earth was hard and dry and there were no plants that really needed attention. Then came a notification that Elnora would be compelled to attend a week's session of the Teachers' Institute held at the county seat twenty miles north of Onabasha the following week. That gave them something of which to think and real work to do. Elnora was requested to bring her violin. As she was on the programme of one of the most important sessions for a talk on nature work in grade schools, she was driven to prepare her speech, also to select and practise some music. Her mother turned her attention to clothing.

They went to Onabasha together and purchased a simple and appropriate fall suit and hat, goods for a dainty little coloured frock, and a dress skirt and several fancy waists. Margaret Sinton came down and the sewing began. When everything was finished and packed, Elnora kissed her mother good-bye at the depot, and entered the train. Mrs. Comstock went into the waiting-room and dropped into a seat to rest. Her heart was so sore her whole left side felt tender. She was half starved for the food she had no appetite to take. She had worked in dogged determination until she was exhausted. For a time she simply sat and rested. Then she began to think. She was glad Elnora had gone where she would be compelled to fix her mind on other matters for a few days. She remembered the girl had said she wanted to go.

School would begin the following week. She thought over what Elnora would have to do to accomplish her work successfully. She would be compelled to arise at six o'clock, walk three miles through varying weather, lead the high school orchestra, and then put in the remainder of the day travelling from building to building over the city, teaching a specified length of time every week in each room. She must have her object lessons ready, and she must do a certain amount of practising with the orchestra. Then a cold lunch at noon, and a three-mile walk at night.

"Humph!" said Mrs. Comstock. "To get through that the girl would have to be made of cast-iron. I wonder how I can help her best?"

She thought deeply.

"The less she sees of what she's been having all summer, the sooner she'll feel better about it," she muttered.

She arose, went to the bank and inquired for the cashier.

"I want to know just how I am fixed here," she said.

The cashier laughed. "You haven't been in a hurry," he replied. "We have been ready for you any time these twenty years, but you didn't seem to pay much attention. Your account is rather flourishing. Interest, when it gets to compounding, is quite a money breeder. Come back here to a table and I will show you your balances."

Mrs. Comstock sank into a chair and waited while the cashier read a jumble of figures to her. It meant that her deposits had exceeded her expenses from one to three hundred dollars a year, according to the cattle, sheep, hogs, poultry, butter, and eggs she had sold. The aggregate of these sums had been compounding interest throughout the years. Mrs. Comstock stared at the total with dazed and unbelieving eyes. Through her sick heart rushed the realization, that if she merely had stood before that wicket and asked one question, she would have known that all those bitter years of skimping for Elnora and herself had been unnecessary. She arose and went back to the depot.

"I want to send a message," she said. She picked up the pencil, and with rash extravagance, wrote, "Found money at bank didn't know about. If you want to go to college, come on first train and get ready." She hesitated a second and then she said to herself grimly, "Yes, I'll pay for that, too," and recklessly added, "With love, Mother." Then she sat waiting for the answer. It came in less than an hour. "Will teach this winter. With dearest love, Elnora."

Mrs. Comstock held the message a long time. When she arose she was ravenously hungry, but the pain in her heart was a little easier. She went to a restaurant and ate some food, then to a dressmaker where she ordered four dresses: two very plain every-day ones, a serviceable dark gray cloth suit, and a soft light gray silk with touches of lavender and lace. She made a heavy list of purchases at Brownlee's, and the remainder of the day she did business in her direct and spirited way. At night she was so tired she scarcely could walk home, but she built a fire and cooked and ate a hearty meal.

Later she went out beside the west fence and gathered an armful of tansy which she boiled to a thick green tea. Then she stirred in oatmeal until it was a stiff paste. She spread a sheet over her bed and began tearing strips of old muslin. She bandaged each hand and arm with the mixture and plastered the soggy, evil-smelling stuff in a thick poultice over her face and neck. She was so tired she went to sleep, and when she awoke she was half skinned. She bathed her face and hands, did the work and went back to town, coming home at night to go through the same process.

By the third morning she was a raw even red, the fourth she had faded to a brilliant pink under the soothing influence of a cream recommended. That day came a letter from Elnora saying that she would remain where she was until Saturday morning, and then come to Ellen Brownlee's at Onabasha and stay for the Saturday's session of teachers to arrange their year's work. Sunday was Ellen's last day at home, and she wanted Elnora very much. She had to call together the orchestra and practise them Sunday; and could not come home until after school Monday night. Mrs. Comstock at once answered the letter saying those arrangements suited her.

The following day she was a pale pink, later a delicate porcelain white. Then she went to a hairdresser and had the rope of snowy hair which covered her scalp washed, dressed, and fastened with such pins and combs as were decided to be most becoming. She took samples of her dresses, went to a milliner, and bought a street hat to match her suit, and a gray satin with lavender orchids to wear with the silk dress. Her last investment was a loose coat of soft gray broadcloth with white lining, and touches of lavender on the embroidered collar, and gray gloves to match.

Then she went home, rested and worked by turns until Monday. When school closed on that evening, Elnora, so tired she almost trembled, came down the long walk after a late session of teachers' meeting, to be stopped by a messenger boy.

"There's a lady wants to see you most important. I am to take you to the place," he said.

Elnora groaned. She could not imagine who wanted her, but there was nothing to do but find out; tired and anxious to see her mother as she was.

"This is the place," said the boy, and went his way whistling. Elnora was three blocks from the high school building on the same street. She was before a quaint old house, fresh with paint and covered with vines. There was a long wide lot, grass-covered, closely set with trees, and a barn and chicken park at the back that seemed to be occupied. Elnora stepped on the veranda which was furnished with straw rugs, bent-hickory chairs, hanging baskets, and a table with a work-box and magazines, and knocked at the screen door.

Inside she could see polished floors, walls freshly papered in low-toned harmonious colours, straw rugs and madras curtains. It seemed to be a restful, homelike place to which she had come. A second later down an open stairway came a tall, dark-eyed woman with cheeks faintly pink and a crown of fluffy snow-white hair. She wore a lavender gingham dress with white collar and cuffs, and she called as she advanced: "That screen isn't latched! Open it and come see your brand-new mother, my girl."

Elnora stepped inside the door. "Mother!" she cried. "You my mother! I don't believe it!"

"Well, you better!" said Mrs. Comstock. "Because it's true! You said you wished I were like the other girls' mothers, and I've shot as close the mark as I could without any practice. I thought that walk would be too much for you this winter, so I just rented this house and moved in, to be near you, and help more in case I'm needed. I've only lived here a day, but I like it so well I've a mortal big notion to buy the place."

"But mother!" protested Elnora, clinging to her wonderingly. "You are perfectly beautiful, and this house is a little paradise, but how will we ever pay for it? We can't afford it!"

"Humph! Have you forgotten I telegraphed you I'd found some money I didn't know about? All I've done is paid for, and plenty more to settle for all I propose to do."

Mrs. Comstock glanced around with satisfaction.

"I may get homesick as a pup before spring," she said, "but if I do I can go back. If I don't, I'll sell some timber and put a few oil wells where they don't show much. I can have land enough cleared for a few fields and put a tenant on our farm, and we will buy this and settle here. It's for sale."

"You don't look it, but you've surely gone mad!"

"Just the reverse, my girl," said Mrs. Comstock, "I've gone sane. If you are going to undertake this work, you must be convenient to it. And your mother should be where she can see that you are properly dressed, fed, and cared for. This is our—let me think—reception-room. How do you like it? This door leads to your workroom and study. I didn't do much there because I wasn't sure of my way. But I knew you would want a rug, curtains, table, shelves for books, and a case for your specimens, so I had a carpenter shelve and enclose that end of it. Looks pretty neat to me. The dining-room and kitchen are back, one of the cows in the barn, and some chickens in the coop. I understand that none of the other girls' mothers milk a cow, so a neighbour boy will tend to ours for a third of the milk. There are three bedrooms, and a bath upstairs. Go take one, put on some fresh clothes, and come to supper. You can find your room because your things are in it."

Elnora kissed her mother over and over, and hurried upstairs. She identified her room by the dressing-case. There were a pretty rug, and curtains, white iron bed, plain and rocking chairs to match her case, a shirtwaist chest, and the big closet was filled with her old clothing and several new dresses. She found the bathroom, bathed, dressed in fresh linen and went down to a supper that was an evidence of Mrs. Comstock's highest art in cooking. Elnora was so hungry she ate her first real meal in two weeks. But the bites went down slowly because she forgot about them in watching her mother.

"How on earth did you do it?" she asked at last. "I always thought you were naturally brown as a nut."

"Oh, that was tan and sunburn!" explained Mrs. Comstock. "I always knew I was white underneath it. I hated to shade my face because I hadn't anything but a sunbonnet, and I couldn't stand for it to touch my ears, so I went bareheaded and took all the colour I accumulated. But when I began to think of moving you in to your work, I saw I must put up an appearance that wouldn't disgrace you, so I thought I'd best remove the crust. It took some time, and I hope I may die before I ever endure the feel and the smell of the stuff I used again, but it skinned me nicely. What you now see is my own with a little dust of rice powder, for protection. I'm sort of tender yet."

"And your lovely, lovely hair?" breathed Elnora.

"Hairdresser did that!" said Mrs. Comstock. "It cost like smoke. But I watched her, and with a little help from you I can wash it alone next time, though it will be hard work. I let her monkey with it until she said she had found 'my style.' Then I tore it down and had her show me how to build it up again three times. I thought my arms would drop. When I paid the bill for her work, the time I'd taken, the pins, and combs she'd used, I nearly had heart failure, but I didn't turn a hair before her. I just smiled at her sweetly and said, 'How reasonable you are!' Come to think of it, she was! She might have charged me ten dollars for what she did quite as well as nine seventy-five. I couldn't have helped myself. I had made no bargain to begin on."

Then Elnora leaned back in her chair and shouted, in a gust of hearty laughter, so a little of the ache ceased in her breast. There was no time to think, the remainder of that evening, she was so tired she had to sleep, while her mother did not awaken her until she barely had time to dress, breakfast, and reach school. There was nothing in the new life to remind her of the old. It seemed as if there never came a minute for retrospection, but her mother appeared on the scene with more work, or some entertaining thing to do.

Mrs. Comstock invited Elnora's friends to visit her, and proved herself a bright and interesting hostess. She digested a subject before she spoke; and when she advanced a view, her point was sure to be original and tersely expressed. Before three months people waited to hear what she had to say. She kept her appearance so in mind that she made a handsome and a distinguished figure.

Elnora never mentioned Philip Ammon, neither did Mrs. Comstock. Early in December came a note and a big box from him. It contained several books on nature subjects which would be of much help in school work, a number of conveniences Elnora could not afford, and a pair of glass-covered plaster casts, for each large moth she had. In these the upper and underwings of male and female showed. He explained that she would break her specimens easily, carrying them around in boxes. He had seen these and thought they would be of use. Elnora was delighted with them, and at once began the tedious process of softening the mounted moths and fitting them to the casts moulded to receive them. Her time was so taken in school, she progressed slowly, so her mother undertook this work. After trying one or two very common ones she learned to handle the most delicate with ease. She took keen pride in relaxing the tense moths, fitting them to the cases, polishing the glass covers to the last degree and sealing them. The results were beautiful to behold.

Soon after Elnora wrote to Philip:

DEAR FRIEND:

I am writing to thank you for the books, and the box of conveniences sent me for my work. I can use everything with fine results. Hope I am giving good satisfaction in my posi-

tion. You will be interested to learn that when the summer's work was classified and pinned, I again had my complete collection for the man of India, save a Yellow Emperor. I have tried everywhere I know, so has the Bird Woman. We cannot find a pair for sale. Fate is against me, at least this season. I shall have to wait until next year and try again.

Thank you very much for helping me with my collection and for the books and cases. Sincerely yours,

ELNORA COMSTOCK.

Philip was disappointed over that note and instead of keeping it he tore it into bits and dropped them into the waste basket.

That was precisely what Elnora had intended he should do. Christmas brought beautiful cards of greeting to Mrs. Comstock and Elnora, Easter others, and the year ran rapidly toward spring. Elnora's position had been intensely absorbing, while she had worked with all her power. She had made a wonderful success and won new friends. Mrs. Comstock had helped in every way she could, so she was very popular also.

Throughout the winter they had enjoyed the city thoroughly, and the change of life it afforded, but signs of spring did wonderful things to the hearts of the country-bred women. A restlessness began on bright February days, calmed during March storms and attacked full force in April. When neither could bear it any longer they were forced to discuss the matter and admit they were growing ill with pure homesickness. They decided to keep the city house during the summer, but to return to the farm to live as soon as school closed.

So Mrs. Comstock would prepare breakfast and lunch and then slip away to the farm to make up beds in her ploughed garden, plant seeds, trim and tend her flowers, and prepare the cabin for occupancy. Then she would go home and make the evening as cheerful as possible for Elnora; in these days she lived only for the girl.

Both of them were glad when the last of May came and the schools closed. They packed the books and clothing they wished to take into a wagon and walked across the fields to the old cabin. As they approached it, Mrs. Comstock said to Elnora: "You are sure you won't be lonely here?"

Elnora knew what she really meant.

"Quite sure," she said. "For a time last fall I was glad to be away, but that all wore out with the winter. Spring made me homesick as I could be. I can scarcely wait until we get back again."

So they began that summer as they had begun all others—with work. But both of them took a new joy in everything, and the violin sang by the hour in the twilight.

Chapter 19

Wherein Philip Ammon Gives a Ball in Honour of Edith Carr, and Hart Henderson Appears on the Scene

Edith Carr stood in a vine-enclosed side veranda of the Lake Shore Club House waiting while Philip Ammon gave some important orders. In a few days she would sail for Paris to select a wonderful trousseau she had planned for her marriage in October. To-night Philip was giving a club dance in her honour. He had spent days in devising new and exquisite effects in decorations, entertainment, and supper. Weeks before the favoured guests had been notified. Days before they had received the invitations asking them to participate in this entertainment by Philip Ammon in honour of Miss Carr. They spoke of it as "Phil's dance for Edith!"

She could hear the rumble of carriages and the panting of automobiles as in a steady stream they rolled to the front entrance. She could catch glimpses of floating draperies of gauze and lace, the flash of jewels, and the passing of exquisite colour. Every one was newly arrayed in her honour in the loveliest clothing, and the most expensive jewels they could command. As she thought of it she lifted her head a trifle higher and her eyes flashed proudly.

She was robed in a French creation suggested and designed by Philip. He had said to her: "I know a competent judge who says the distinctive feature of June is her exquisite big night moths. I want you to be the very essence of June that night, as you will be the embodiment of love. Be a moth. The most beautiful of them is either the pale-green Luna or the Yellow Imperialis. Be my moon lady, or my gold Empress."

He took her to the museum and showed her the moths. She instantly decided on the yellow. Because she knew the shades would make her more startlingly beautiful than any other colour. To him she said: "A moon lady seems so far away and cold. I would be of earth and very near on that night. I choose the Empress."

So she matched the colours exactly, wrote out the idea and forwarded the order to Paquin. To-night when Philip Ammon came for her, he stood speechless a minute and then silently kissed her hands.

For she stood tall, lithe, of grace inborn, her dark waving hair high piled and crossed by gold bands studded with amethyst and at one side an enamelled lavender orchid rimmed with diamonds, which flashed and sparkled. The soft yellow robe of lightest weight velvet fitted her form perfectly, while from each shoulder fell a great velvet wing lined with lavender, and flecked with embroidery of that colour in imitation of the moth. Around her throat was a wonderful necklace and on her arms were bracelets of gold set with amethyst and rimmed with diamonds. Philip had said that her gloves, fan, and slippers must be lavender, because the feet of the moth were that colour. These accessories had been made to order and embroidered with gold. It had been arranged that her mother, Philip's, and a few best friends should receive his guests. She was to appear when she led the grand march with Philip Ammon. Miss Carr was positive that she would be the most beautiful, and most exquisitely gowned woman present. In her heart she thought of herself as "Imperialis Regalis," as the Yellow Empress. In a few moments she would stun her world into feeling it as Philip Ammon had done, for she had taken pains that the history of her costume should be whispered to a few who would give it circulation. She lifted her head proudly and waited, for was not Philip planning something unusual and unsurpassed in her honour? Then she smiled.

But of all the fragmentary thoughts crossing her brain the one that never came was that of Philip Ammon as the Emperor. Philip the king of her heart; at least her equal in all things. She was the Empress—yes, Philip was but a mere man, to devise entertainments, to provide luxuries, to humour whims, to kiss hands!

"Ah, my luck!" cried a voice behind her.

Edith Carr turned and smiled.

"I thought you were on the ocean," she said.

"I only reached the dock," replied the man, "when I had a letter that recalled me by the first limited."

"Oh! Important business?"

"The only business of any importance in all the world to me. I'm triumphant that I came. Edith, you are the most superb woman in every respect that I have ever seen. One glimpse is worth the whole journey."

"You like my dress?" She moved toward him and turned, lifting her arms. "Do you know what it is intended to represent?"

"Yes, Polly Ammon told me. I knew when I heard about it how you would look, so I started a sleuth hunt, to get the first peep. Edith, I can become intoxicated merely with looking at you to-night."

He half-closed his eyes and smilingly stared straight at her. He was taller than she, a lean man, with close-cropped light hair, steel-gray eyes, a square chin and "man of the world" written all over him.

Edith Carr flushed. "I thought you realized when you went away that you were to stop that, Hart Henderson," she cried.

"I did, but this letter of which I tell you called me back to start it all over again."

She came a step closer. "Who wrote that letter, and what did it contain concerning me?" she demanded.

"One of your most intimate chums wrote it. It contained the hazard that possibly I had given up too soon. It said that in a fit of petulance you had broken your engagement with Ammon twice this winter, and he had come back because he knew you did not really mean it. I thought deeply there on the dock when I read that, and my boat sailed without me. I argued that anything so weak as an engagement twice broken and patched up again was a mighty frail affair indeed, and likely to smash completely at any time, so I came on the run. I said once I would not see you marry any other man. Because I could not bear it, I planned to go into exile of any sort to escape that. I have changed my mind. I have come back to haunt you until the ceremony is over. Then I go, not before. I was insane!"

The girl laughed merrily. "Not half so insane as you are now, Hart!" she cried gaily. "You know that Philip Ammon has been devoted to me all my life. Now I'll tell you something else, because this looks serious for you. I love him with all my heart. Not while he lives shall he know it, and I will laugh at him if you tell him, but the fact remains: I intend to marry him, but no doubt I shall tease him constantly. It's good for a man to be uncertain. If you could see Philip's face at the quarterly return of his ring, you would understand the fun of it. You had better have taken your boat."

"Possibly," said Henderson calmly. "But you are the only woman in the world for me, and while you are free, as I now see my light, I remain near you. You know the old adage."

"But I'm not 'free!'" cried Edith Carr. "I'm telling you I am not. This night is my public acknowledgment that Phil and I are promised, as our world has surmised since we were children. That promise is an actual fact, because of what I just have told you. My little fits of temper don't count with Phil. He's been reared on them. In fact, I often invent one in a perfect calm to see him perform. He is the most amusing spectacle. But, please, please, do understand that I love him, and always shall, and that we shall be married."

"Just the same, I'll wait and see it an accomplished fact," said Henderson. "And Edith, because I love you, with the sort of love it is worth a woman's while to inspire, I want your happiness before my own. So I am going to say this to you, for I never dreamed you were capable of the feeling you have displayed for Phil. If you do love him, and have loved him always, a disappointment would cut you deeper than you know. Go careful from now on! Don't strain that patched engagement of yours any further. I've known Philip all my life. I've known him through boyhood, in college, and since. All men respect him. Where the rest of us confess our sins, he stands clean. You can go to his arms with nothing to forgive. Mark this thing! I have heard him say, 'Edith is my slogan,' and I have seen him march home strong in the strength of his love for you, in the face of temptations before which every other man of us fell. Before the gods! that ought to be worth something to a girl, if she really is the delicate, sensitive, refined thing she would have man believe. It would take a woman with the organism of an ostrich to endure some of the men here to-night, if she knew them as I do; but Phil is sound to the core. So this is what I would say to you: first, your instincts are right in loving him, why not let him feel it in the ways a woman knows? Second, don't break your engagement again. As men know the man, any of us would be afraid to the soul. He loves you, yes! He is long-suffering for you, yes! But men know he has a limit. When the limit is reached, he will stand fast, and all the powers can't move him. You don't seem to think it, but you can go too far!"

"Is that all?" laughed Edith Carr sarcastically.

"No, there is one thing more," said Henderson. "Here or here-after, now and so long as I breathe, I am your slave. You can do anything you choose and know that I will kneel before you again. So carry this in the depths of your heart; now or at any time, in any place or condition, merely lift your hand, and I will come. Anything you want of me, that thing will I do. I am going to wait; if you need me, it is not necessary to speak; only give me the faintest sign. All your life I will be somewhere near you waiting for it."

"Idjit! You rave!" laughed Edith Carr. "How you would frighten me! What a bugbear you would raise! Be sensible and go find what keeps Phil. I was waiting patiently, but my patience is going. I won't look nearly so well as I do now when it is gone."

At that instant Philip Ammon entered. He was in full evening dress and exceptionally handsome. "Everything is ready," he said. "They are waiting for us to lead the march. It is formed."

Edith Carr smiled entrancingly. "Do you think I am ready?"

Philip looked what he thought, and offered his arm. Edith Carr nodded carelessly to Hart Henderson, and moved away. Attendants parted the curtains and the Yellow Empress bowing right and left, swept the length of the ballroom and took her place at the head of the formed procession. The large open dancing pavilion was draped with yellow silk caught up with lilac flowers. Every corner was filled with bloom of those colours. The music was played by harpers dressed in yellow and violet, so the ball opened.

The midnight supper was served with the same colours and the last half of the programme was being danced. Never had girl been more complimented and petted in the same length of time than Edith Carr. Every minute she seemed to grow more worthy of praise. A partners' dance was called and the floor was filled with couples waiting for the music. Philip stood whispering delightful things to Edith facing him. From out of the night, in at the wide front entrance to the pavilion, there swept in slow wavering flight a large yellow moth and fluttered toward the centre cluster of glaring electric lights. Philip Ammon and Edith Carr saw it at the same instant.

"Why, isn't that—?" she began excitedly.

"It's a Yellow Emperor! This is fate!" cried Philip. "The last one Elnora needs for her collection. I must have it! Excuse me!"

He ran toward the light. "Hats! Handkerchiefs! Fans! Anything!" he panted. "Every one hold up something and stop that! It's a moth; I've got to catch it!"

"It's yellow! He wants it for Edith!" ran in a murmur around the hall. The girl's face flushed, while she bit her lips in vexation.

Instantly every one began holding up something to keep the moth from flying back into the night. One fan held straight before it served, and the moth gently settled on it.

"Hold steady!" cried Philip. "Don't move for your life!" He rushed toward the moth, made a quick sweep and held it up between his fingers. "All right!" he called. "Thanks, every one! Excuse me a minute."

He ran to the office.

"An ounce of gasolene, quick!" he ordered. "A cigar box, a cork, and the glue bottle."

He poured some glue into the bottom of the box, set the cork in it firmly, dashed the gasolene over the moth repeatedly, pinned it to the cork, poured the remainder of the liquid over it, closed the box, and fastened it. Then he laid a bill on the counter.

"Pack that box with cork around it, in one twice its size, tie securely and express to this address at once."

He scribbled on a sheet of paper and shoved it over.

"On your honour, will you do that faithfully as I say?" he asked the clerk.

"Certainly," was the reply.

"Then keep the change," called Philip as he ran back to the pavilion.

Edith Carr stood where he left her, thinking rapidly. She heard the murmur that arose when Philip started to capture the exquisite golden creature she was impersonating. She saw the flash of surprise that went over unrestrained faces when he ran from the room, without even showing it to her. "The last one Elnora needs," rang in her ears. He had told her that he helped collect moths the previous summer, but she had understood that the Bird Woman, with whose work Miss Carr was familiar, wanted them to put in a book.

He had spoken of a country girl he had met who played the violin wonderfully, and at times, he had shown a disposition to exalt her as a standard of womanhood. Miss Carr had ignored what he said, and talked of something else. But that girl's name had been Elnora. It was she who was collecting moths! No doubt she was the competent judge who was responsible for the yellow costume Philip had devised. Had Edith Carr been in her room, she would have torn off the dress at the thought.

Being in a circle of her best friends, which to her meant her keenest rivals and harshest critics, she grew rigid with anger. Her breath hurt her paining chest. No one thought to speak to the musicians, and seeing the floor filled, they began the waltz. Only part of the guests could see what had happened, and at once the others formed and commenced to dance. Gay couples came whirling past her.

Edith Carr grew very white as she stood alone. Her lips turned pale, while her dark eyes flamed with anger. She stood perfectly still where Philip had left her, and the approaching men guided their partners around her, while the girls, looking back, could be seen making exclamations of surprise.

The idolized only daughter of the Carr family hoped that she would drop dead from mortification, but nothing happened. She was too perverse to step aside and say that she was waiting for Philip. Then came Tom Levering dancing with Polly Ammon. Being in the scales with the Ammon family, Tom scented trouble from afar, so he whispered to Polly: "Edith is standing in the middle of the floor, and she's awful mad about something."

"That won't hurt her," laughed Polly. "It's an old pose of hers. She knows she looks superb when she is angry, so she keeps herself furious half the time on purpose."

"She looks like the mischief!" answered Tom. "Hadn't we better steer over and wait with her? She's the ugliest sight I ever saw!"

"Why, Tom!" cried Polly. "Stop, quickly!"

They hurried to Edith.

"Come dear," said Polly. "We are going to wait with you until Phil returns. Let's go after a drink. I am so thirsty!"

"Yes, do!" begged Tom, offering his arm. "Let's get out of here until Phil comes."

There was the opportunity to laugh and walk away, but Edith Carr would not accept it.

"My betrothed left me here," she said. "Here I shall remain until he returns for me, and then—he will be my betrothed no longer!"

Polly grasped Edith's arm.

"Oh, Edith!" she implored. "Don't make a scene here, and to-night. Edith, this has been the loveliest dance ever given at the club house. Every one is saying so. Edith! Darling, do come! Phil will be back in a second. He can explain! It's only a breath since I saw him go out. I thought he had returned."

As Polly panted these disjointed ejaculations, Tom Levering began to grow angry on her account.

"He has been gone just long enough to show every one of his guests that he will leave me standing alone, like a neglected fool, for any passing whim of his. Explain! His explanation would sound well! Do you know for whom he caught that moth? It is being sent to a girl he flirted with all last summer. It has just occurred to me that the dress I am wearing is her suggestion. Let him try to explain!"

Speech unloosed the fountain. She stripped off her gloves to free her hands. At that instant the dancers parted to admit Philip. Instinctively they stopped as they approached and with wondering faces walled in Edith and Philip, Polly and Tom.

"Mighty good of you to wait!" cried Philip, his face showing his delight over his success in capturing the Yellow Emperor. "I thought when I heard the music you were going on."

"How did you think I was going on?" demanded Edith Carr in frigid tones.

"I thought you would step aside and wait a few seconds for me, or dance with Henderson. It was most important to have that moth. It completes a valuable collection for a person who needs the money. Come!"

He held out his arms.

"I 'step aside' for no one!" stormed Edith Carr. "I await no other girl's pleasure! You may 'complete the collection' with that!"

She drew her engagement ring from her finger and reached to place it on one of Philip's outstretched hands. He saw and drew back. Instantly Edith dropped the ring. As it fell, almost instinctively Philip caught it in air. With amazed face he looked closely at Edith Carr. Her distorted features were scarcely recognizable. He held the ring toward her.

"Edith, for the love of mercy, wait until I can explain," he begged. "Put on your ring and let me tell you how it is."

"I know perfectly 'how it is,'" she answered. "I never shall wear that ring again."

"You won't even hear what I have to say? You won't take back your ring?" he cried.

"Never! Your conduct is infamous!"

"Come to think of it," said Philip deliberately, "it is 'infamous' to cut a girl, who has danced all her life, out of a few measures of a waltz. As for asking forgiveness for so black a sin as picking up a moth, and starting it to a friend who lives by collecting them, I don't see how I could! I have not been gone three minutes by the clock, Edith. Put on your ring and finish the dance like a dear girl."

He thrust the glittering ruby into her fingers and again held out his arms. She dropped the ring, and it rolled some distance from them. Hart Henderson followed its shining course, and caught it before it was lost.

"You really mean it?" demanded Philip in a voice as cold as hers ever had been.

"You know I mean it!" cried Edith Carr.

"I accept your decision in the presence of these witnesses," said Philip Ammon. "Where is my father?" The elder Ammon with a distressed face hurried to him. "Father, take my place," said Philip. "Excuse me to my guests. Ask all my friends to forgive me. I am going away for awhile."

He turned and walked from the pavilion. As he went Hart Henderson rushed to Edith Carr and forced the ring into her fingers. "Edith, quick. Come, quick!" he implored. "There's just time to catch him. If you let him go that way, he never will return in this world. Remember what I told you."

"Great prophet! Aren't you, Hart?" she sneered. "Who wants him to return? If that ring is thrust upon me again I shall fling it into the lake. Signal the musicians to begin, and dance with me."

Henderson put the ring into his pocket, and began the dance. He could feel the muscular spasms of the girl in his arms, her face was cold and hard, but her breath burned with the scorch of fever. She finished the dance and all others, taking Phil's numbers with Henderson, who had arrived too late to arrange a programme. She left with the others, merely inclining her head as she passed Ammon's father taking his place, and entered the big touring car for which Henderson had telephoned. She sank limply into a seat and moaned softly.

"Shall I drive awhile in the night air?" asked Henderson.

She nodded. He instructed the chauffeur.

She raised her head in a few seconds. "Hart, I'm going to pieces," she said. "Won't you put your arm around me a little while?"

Henderson gathered her into his arms and her head fell on his shoulder. "Closer!" she cried.

Henderson held her until his arms were numb, but he did not know it. The tricks of fate are cruel enough, but there scarcely could have been a worse one than that: To care for a woman as he loved Edith Carr and have her given into his arms because she was so numb with misery over her trouble with another man that she did not know or care what she did. Dawn was streaking the east when he spoke to her.

"Edith, it is growing light."

"Take me home," she said.

Henderson helped her up the steps and rang the bell.

"Miss Carr is ill," he said to the footman. "Arouse her maid instantly, and have her prepare something hot as quickly as possible."

"Edith," he cried, "just a word. I have been thinking. It isn't too late yet. Take your ring and put it on. I will go find Phil at once and tell him you have, that you are expecting him, and he will come."

"Think what he said!" she cried. "He accepted my decision as final, 'in the presence of witnesses,' as if it were court. He can return it to me, if I ever wear it again."

"You think that now, but in a few days you will find that you feel very differently. Living a life of heartache is no joke, and no job for a woman. Put on your ring and send me to tell him to come."

"No."

"Edith, there was not a soul who saw that, but sympathized with Phil. It was ridiculous for you to get so angry over a thing which was never intended for the slightest offence, and by no logical reasoning could have been so considered."

"Do you think that?" she demanded.

"I do!" said Henderson. "If you had laughed and stepped aside an instant, or laughed and stayed where you were, Phil would have been back; or, if he needed punishment in your eyes, to have found me having one of his dances would have been enough. I was waiting. You could have called me with one look. But to publicly do and say what you did, my lady—I know Phil, and I know you went too far. Put on that ring, and send him word you are sorry, before it is too late."

"I will not! He shall come to me."

"Then God help you!" said Henderson, "for you are plunging into misery whose depth you do not dream. Edith, I beg of you—"

She swayed where she stood. Her maid opened the door and caught her. Henderson went down the hall and out to his car.

Chapter 20

Wherein the Elder Ammon
Offers Advice, and Edith Carr Experiences
Regrets

Philip Ammon walked from among his friends a humiliated and a wounded man. Never before had Edith Carr appeared quite so beautiful. All evening she had treated him with unusual consideration. Never had he loved her so deeply. Then in a few seconds everything was different. Seeing the change in her face, and hearing her meaningless accusations, killed something in his heart. Warmth went out and a cold weight took its place. But even after that, he had offered the ring to her again, and asked her before others to reconsider. The answer had been further insult.

He walked, paying no heed to where he went. He had traversed many miles when he became aware that his feet had chosen familiar streets. He was passing his home. Dawn was near, but the first floor was lighted. He staggered up the steps and was instantly admitted. The library door stood open, while his father sat with a book pretending to read. At Philip's entrance the father scarcely glanced up.

"Come on!" he called. "I have just told Banks to bring me a cup of coffee before I turn in. Have one with me!"

Philip sat beside the table and leaned his head on his hands, but he drank a cup of steaming coffee and felt better.

"Father," he said, "father, may I talk with you a little while?"

"Of course," answered Mr. Ammon. "I am not at all tired. I think I must have been waiting in the hope that you would come. I want no one's version of this but yours. Tell me the straight of the thing, Phil."

Philip told all he knew, while his father sat in deep thought.

"On my life I can't see any occasion for such a display of temper, Phil. It passed all bounds of reason and breeding. Can't you think of anything more?"

"I cannot!"

"Polly says every one expected you to carry the moth you caught to Edith. Why didn't you?"

"She screams if a thing of that kind comes near her. She never has taken the slightest interest in them. I was in a big hurry. I didn't want to miss one minute of my dance with her. The moth was not so uncommon, but by a combination of bad luck it had become the rarest in America for a friend of mine, who is making a collection to pay college expenses. For an instant last June the series was completed; when a woman's uncontrolled temper ruined this specimen and the search for it began over. A few days later a pair was secured, and again the money was in sight for several hours. Then an accident wrecked one-fourth of the collection. I helped replace those last June, all but this Yellow Emperor which we could not secure, and we haven't been able to find, buy, or trade for one since. So my friend was compelled to teach this past winter instead of going to college. When that moth came flying in there to-night, it seemed to me like fate. All I thought of was, that to secure it would complete the collection and secure the money. So I caught the Emperor and started it to Elnora. I declare to you that I was not out of the pavilion over three minutes at a liberal estimate. If I only had thought to speak to the orchestra! I was sure I would be back before enough couples gathered and formed for the dance."

The eyes of the father were very bright.

"The friend for whom you wanted the moth is a girl?" he asked indifferently, as he ran the book leaves through his fingers.

"The girl of whom I wrote you last summer, and told you about in the fall. I helped her all the time I was away."

"Did Edith know of her?"

"I tried many times to tell her, to interest her, but she was so indifferent that it was insulting. She would not hear me."

"We are neither one in any condition to sleep. Why don't you begin at the first and tell me about this girl? To think of other matters for a time may clear our vision for a sane solution of this. Who is she, just what is she doing, and what is she like? You know I was reared among those Limberlost people, I can understand readily. What is her name and where does she live?"

Philip gave a man's version of the previous summer, while his father played with the book industriously.

"You are very sure as to her refinement and education?"

"In almost two months' daily association, could a man be mistaken? She can far and away surpass Polly, Edith, or any girl of our set on any common, high school, or supplementary branch, and you know high schools have French, German, and physics now. Besides, she is a graduate of two other institutions. All her life she has been in the school of Hard Knocks. She has the biggest, tenderest, most human heart I ever knew in a girl. She has known life in its most cruel phases, and instead of hardening her, it has set her trying to save other people suffering. Then this nature position of which I told you; she graduated in the School of the Woods, before she secured that. The Bird Woman, whose work you know, helped her there. Elnora knows more interesting things in a minute than any other girl I ever met knew in an hour, provided you are a person who cares to understand plant and animal life."

The book leaves slid rapidly through his fingers as the father drawled: "What sort of looking girl is she?"

"Tall as Edith, a little heavier, pink, even complexion, wide open blue-gray eyes with heavy black brows, and lashes so long they touch her cheeks. She has a rope of waving, shining hair that makes a real crown on her head, and it appears almost red in the light. She is as handsome as any fair woman I ever saw, but she doesn't know it. Every time any one pays her a compliment, her mother, who is a caution, discovers that, for some reason, the girl is a fright, so she has no appreciation of her looks."

"And you were in daily association two months with a girl like that! How about it, Phil?"

"If you mean, did I trifle with her, no!" cried Philip hotly. "I told her the second time I met her all about Edith. Almost every day I wrote to Edith in her presence. Elnora gathered violets and made a fancy basket to put them in for Edith's birthday. I started to err in too open admiration for Elnora, but her mother brought me up with a whirl I never forgot. Fifty times a day in the swamps and forests Elnora made a perfect picture, but I neither looked nor said anything. I never met any girl so down-right noble in bearing and actions. I never hated anything as I hated leaving her, for we were dear friends, like two wholly congenial men. Her mother was almost always with us. She knew how much I admired Elnora, but so long as I concealed it from the girl, the mother did not care."

"Yet you left such a girl and came back whole-hearted to Edith Carr!"

"Surely! You know how it has been with me about Edith all my life."

"Yet the girl you picture is far her superior to an unprejudiced person, when thinking what a man would require in a wife to be happy."

"I never have thought what I would 'require' to be happy! I only thought whether I could make Edith happy. I have been an idiot! What I've borne you'll never know! To-night is only one of many outbursts like that, in varying and lesser degrees."

"Phil, I love you, when you say you have thought only of Edith! I happen to know that it is true. You are my only son, and I have had a right to watch you closely. I believe you utterly. Any one who cares for you as I do, and has had my years of experience in this world over yours, knows that in some ways, to-night would be a blessed release, if you could take it; but you cannot! Go to bed now, and rest. To-morrow, go back to her and fix it up."

"You heard what I said when I left her! I said it because something in my heart died a minute before that, and I realized that it was my love for Edith Carr. Never again will I voluntarily face such a scene. If she can act like that at a ball, before hundreds, over a thing of which I thought nothing at all, she would go into actual physical fits and spasms, over some of the household crises I've seen the mater meet with a smile. Sir, it is truth that I have thought only of her up to the present. Now, I will admit I am thinking about myself. Father, did you see her? Life is too short, and it can be too sweet, to throw it away in a battle with an unrestrained woman. I am no fighter—where a girl is concerned, anyway. I respect and love her or I do nothing. Never again is either respect or love possible between me and Edith Carr. Whenever I think of her in the future, I will see her as she was to-night. But I can't face the crowd just yet. Could you spare me a few days?"

"It is only ten days until you were to go north for the summer, go now."

"I don't want to go north. I don't want to meet people I know. There, the story would precede me. I do not need pitying glances or rough condolences. I wonder if I could not hide at Uncle Ed's in Wisconsin for awhile?"

The book closed suddenly. The father leaned across the table and looked into the son's eyes.

"Phil, are you sure of what you just have said?"

"Perfectly sure!"

"Do you think you are in any condition to decide to-night?"

"Death cannot return to life, father. My love for Edith Carr is dead. I hope never to see her again."

"If I thought you could be certain so soon! But, come to think of it, you are very like me in many ways. I am with you in this. Public scenes and disgraces I would not endure. It would be over with me, were I in your position, that I know."

"It is done for all time," said Philip Ammon. "Let us not speak of it further."

"Then, Phil," the father leaned closer and looked at the son tenderly, "Phil, why don't you go to the Limberlost?"

"Father!"

"Why not? No one can comfort a hurt heart like a tender woman; and, Phil, have you ever stopped to think that you may have a duty in the Limberlost, if you are free? I don't know! I only suggest it. But, for a country schoolgirl, unaccustomed to men, two months with a man like you might well awaken feelings of which you do not think. Because you were safe-guarded is no sign the girl was. She might care to see you. You can soon tell. With you, she comes next to Edith, and you have made it clear to me that you appreciate her in many ways above. So I repeat it, why not go to the Limberlost?"

A long time Philip Ammon sat in deep thought. At last he raised his head.

"Well, why not!" he said. "Years could make me no surer than I am now, and life is short. Please ask Banks to get me some coffee and toast, and I will bathe and dress so I can take the early train."

"Go to your bath. I will attend to your packing and everything. And Phil, if I were you, I would leave no addresses."

"Not an address!" said Philip. "Not even Polly."

When the train pulled out, the elder Ammon went home to find Hart Henderson waiting.

"Where is Phil?" he demanded.

"He did not feel like facing his friends at present, and I am just back from driving him to the station. He said he might go to Siam, or Patagonia. He would leave no address."

Henderson almost staggered. "He's not gone? And left no address? You don't mean it! He'll never forgive her!"

"Never is a long time, Hart," said Mr. Ammon. "And it seems even longer to those of us who are well acquainted with Phil. Last night was not the last straw. It was the whole straw-stack. It crushed Phil so far as she is concerned. He will not see her again voluntarily, and he will not forget if he does. You can take it from him, and from me, we have accepted the lady's decision. Will you have a cup of coffee?"

Twice Henderson opened his lips to speak of Edith Carr's despair. Twice he looked into the stern, inflexible face of Mr. Ammon and could not betray her. He held out the ring.

"I have no instructions as to that," said the elder Ammon, drawing back. "Possibly Miss Carr would have it as a keepsake."

"I am sure not," said Henderson curtly.

"Then suppose you return it to Peacock. I will phone him. He will give you the price of it, and you might add it to the children's Fresh Air Fund. We would be obliged if you would do that. No one here cares to handle the object."

"As you choose," said Henderson. "Good morning!"

Then he went to his home, but he could not think of sleep. He ordered breakfast, but he could not eat. He paced the library for a time, but it was too small. Going on the streets he walked until exhausted, then he called a hansom and was driven to his club. He had thought himself familiar with every depth of suffering; that night had taught him that what he felt for himself was not to be compared with the anguish which wrung his heart over the agony of Edith Carr. He tried to blame Philip Ammon, but being an honest man, Henderson knew that was unjust. The fault lay wholly with her, but that only made it harder for him, as he realized it would in time for her.

As he sauntered into the room an attendant hurried to him.

"You are wanted most urgently at the 'phone, Mr. Henderson," he said. "You have had three calls from Main 5770."

Henderson shivered as he picked down the receiver and gave the call.

"Is that you, Hart?" came Edith's voice.

"Yes."

"Did you find Phil?"

"No."

"Did you try?"

"Yes. As soon as I left you I went straight there."

"Wasn't he home yet?"

"He has been home and gone again."

"Gone!"

The cry tore Henderson's heart.

"Shall I come and tell you, Edith?"

"No! Tell me now."

"When I reached the house Banks said Mr. Ammon and Phil were out in the motor, so I waited. Mr. Ammon came back soon. Edith, are you alone?"

"Yes. Go on!"

"Call your maid. I can't tell you until some one is with you."

"Tell me instantly!"

"Edith, he said he had been to the station. He said Phil had started to Siam or Patagonia, he didn't know which, and left no address. He said—"

Distinctly Henderson heard her fall. He set the buzzer ringing, and in a few seconds heard voices, so he knew she had been found. Then he crept into a private den and shook with a hard, nervous chill.

The next day Edith Carr started on her trip to Europe. Henderson felt certain she hoped to meet Philip there. He was sure she would be disappointed, though he had no idea where Ammon could have gone. But after much thought he decided he would see Edith soonest by remaining at home, so he spent the summer in Chicago.

Chapter 21

Wherein Philip Ammon Returns to the Limberlost, and Elnora Studies the Situation

"We must be thinking about supper, mother," said Elnora, while she set the wings of a Cecropia with much care. "It seems as if I can't get enough to eat, or enough of being at home. I enjoyed that city house. I don't believe I could have done my work if I had been compelled to walk back and forth. I thought at first I never wanted to come here again. Now, I feel as if I could not live anywhere else."

"Elnora," said Mrs. Comstock, "there's some one coming down the road."

"Coming here, do you think?"

"Yes, coming here, I suspect."

Elnora glanced quickly at her mother and then turned to the road as Philip Ammon reached the gate.

"Careful, mother!" the girl instantly warned. "If you change your treatment of him a hair's breadth, he will suspect. Come with me to meet him."

She dropped her work and sprang up.

"Well, of all the delightful surprises!" she cried.

She was a trifle thinner than during the previous summer. On her face there was a more mature, patient look, but the sun struck her bare head with the same ray of red gold. She wore one of the old blue gingham dresses, open at the throat and rolled to the elbows. Mrs. Comstock did not appear at all the same woman, but Philip saw only Elnora; heard only her greeting. He caught both hands where she offered but one.

"Elnora," he cried, "if you were engaged to me, and we were at a ball, among hundreds, where I offended you very much, and didn't even know I had done anything, and if I asked you before all of them to allow me to explain, to forgive me, to wait, would your face grow distorted and unfamiliar with anger? Would you drop my ring on the floor and insult me repeatedly? Oh Elnora, would you?"

Elnora's big eyes seemed to leap, while her face grew very white. She drew away her hands.

"Hush, Phil! Hush!" she protested. "That fever has you again! You are dreadfully ill. You don't know what you are saying."

"I am sleepless and exhausted; I'm heartsick; but I am well as I ever was. Answer me, Elnora, would you?"

"Answer nothing!" cried Mrs. Comstock. "Answer nothing! Hang your coat there on your nail, Phil, and come split some kindling. Elnora, clean away that stuff, and set the table. Can't you see the boy is starved and tired? He's come home to rest and eat a decent meal. Come on, Phil!"

Mrs. Comstock marched away, and Philip hung his coat in its old place and followed. Out of sight and hearing she turned on him.

"Do you call yourself a man or a hound?" she flared.

"I beg your pardon—" stammered Philip Ammon.

"I should think you would!" she ejaculated. "I'll admit you did the square thing and was a man last summer, though I'd liked it better if you'd faced up and told me you were promised; but to come back here babying, and take hold of Elnora like that, and talk that way because you have had a fuss with your girl, I don't tolerate. Split that kindling and I'll get your supper, and then you better go. I won't have you working on Elnora's big heart, because you have quarrelled with some one else. You'll have it patched up in a week and be gone again, so you can go right away."

"Mrs. Comstock, I came to ask Elnora to marry me."

"The more fool you, then!" cried Mrs. Comstock. "This time yesterday you were engaged to another woman, no doubt. Now, for some little flare-up you come racing here to use Elnora as a tool to spite the other girl. A week of sane living, and you will be sorry and ready to go back to Chicago, or, if you really are man enough to be sure of yourself, she will come to claim you. She has her rights. An engagement of years is a serious matter, and not broken for a whim. If you don't go, she'll come. Then, when you patch up your affairs and go sailing away together, where does my girl come in?"

"I am a lawyer, Mrs. Comstock," said Philip. "It appeals to me as beneath your ordinary sense of justice to decide a case without hearing the evidence. It is due me that you hear me first."

"Hear your side!" flashed Mrs. Comstock. "I'd a heap sight rather hear the girl!"

"I wish to my soul that you had heard and seen her last night, Mrs. Comstock," said Ammon. "Then, my way would be clear. I never even thought of coming here to-day. I'll admit I would have come in time, but not for many months. My father sent me."

"Your father sent you! Why?"

"Father, mother, and Polly were present last night. They, and all my friends, saw me insulted and disgraced in the worst exhibition of uncontrolled temper any of us ever witnessed. All of them knew it was the end. Father liked what I had told him of Elnora, and he advised me to come here, so I came. If she does not want me, I can leave instantly, but, oh I hoped she would understand!"

"You people are not splitting wood," called Elnora.

"Oh yes we are!" answered Mrs. Comstock. "You set out the things for biscuit, and lay the table." She turned again to Philip. "I know considerable about your father," she said. "I have met your Uncle's family frequently this winter. I've heard your Aunt Anna say that she didn't at all like Miss Carr, and that she and all your family secretly hoped that something would happen to prevent your marrying her. That chimes right in with your saying that your father sent you here. I guess you better speak your piece."

Philip gave his version of the previous night.

"Do you believe me?" he finished.

"Yes," said Mrs. Comstock.

"May I stay?"

"Oh, it looks all right for you, but what about her?"

"Nothing, so far as I am concerned. Her plans were all made to start to Europe to-day. I suspect she is on the way by this time. Elnora is very sensible, Mrs. Comstock. Hadn't you better let her decide this?" .

"The final decision rests with her, of course," admitted Mrs. Comstock. "But look you one thing! She's all I have. As Solomon says, 'she is the one child, the only child of her mother.' I've suffered enough in this world that I fight against any suffering which threatens her. So far as I know you've always been a man, and you may stay. But if you bring tears and heartache to her, don't have the assurance to think I'll bear it tamely. I'll get right up and fight like a catamount, if things go wrong for Elnora!"

"I have no doubt but you will," replied Philip, "and I don't blame you in the least if you do. I have the utmost devotion to offer Elnora, a good home, fair social position, and my family will love her dearly. Think it over. I know it is sudden, but my father advised it."

"Yes, I reckon he did!" said Mrs. Comstock dryly. "I guess instead of me being the catamount, you had the genuine article up in Chicago, masquerading in peacock feathers, and posing as a fine lady, until her time came to scratch. Human nature seems to be the same the world over. But I'd give a pretty to know that secret thing you say you don't, that set her raving over your just catching a moth for Elnora. You might get that crock of strawberries in the spring house."

They prepared and ate supper. Afterward they sat in the arbour and talked, or Elnora played until time for Philip to go.

"Will you walk to the gate with me?" he asked Elnora as he arose.

"Not to-night," she answered lightly. "Come early in the morning if you like, and we will go over to Sleepy Snake Creek and hunt moths and gather dandelions for dinner."

Philip leaned toward her. "May I tell you to-morrow why I came?" he asked.

"I think not," replied Elnora. "The fact is, I don't care why you came. It is enough for me that we are your very good friends, and that in trouble, you have found us a refuge. I fancy we had better live a week or two before you say anything. There is a possibility that what you have to say may change in that length of time.

"It will not change one iota!" cried Philip.

"Then it will have the grace of that much age to give it some small touch of flavour," said the girl. "Come early in the morning."

She lifted the violin and began to play.

"Well bless my soul!" ejaculated the astounded Mrs. Comstock. "To think I was worrying for fear you couldn't take care of yourself!"

Elnora laughed while she played.

"Shall I tell you what he said?"

"Nope! I don't want to hear it!" said Elnora. "He is only six hours from Chicago. I'll give her a week to find him and fix it up, if he stays that long. If she doesn't put in an appearance then, he can tell me what he wants to say, and I'll take my time to think it over. Time in plenty, too! There are three of us in this, and one must be left with a sore heart for life. If the decision rests with me I propose to be very sure that it is the one who deserves such hard luck."

The next morning Philip came early, dressed in the outing clothing he had worn the previous summer, and aside from a slight paleness seemed very much the same as when he left. Elnora met him on the old footing, and for a week life went on exactly as it had the previous summer. Mrs. Comstock made mental notes and watched in silence. She could see that Elnora was on a strain, though she hoped Philip would not. The girl grew restless as the week drew to a close. Once when the gate clicked she suddenly lost colour and moved nervously. Billy came down the walk.

Philip leaned toward Mrs. Comstock and said: "I am expressly forbidden to speak to Elnora as I would like. Would you mind telling her for me that I had a letter from my father this morning saying that Miss Carr is on her way to Europe for the summer?"

"Elnora," said Mrs. Comstock promptly, "I have just heard that Carr woman is on her way to Europe, and I wish to my gracious stars she'd stay there!"

Philip Ammon shouted, but Elnora arose hastily and went to meet Billy. They came into the arbour together and after speaking to Mrs. Comstock and Philip, Billy said: "Uncle Wesley and I found something funny, and we thought you'd like to see."

"I don't know what I should do without you and Uncle Wesley to help me," said Elnora. "What have you found now?"

"Something I couldn't bring. You have to come to it. I tried to get one and I killed it. They are a kind of insecty things, and they got a long tail that is three fine hairs. They stick those hairs right into the hard bark of trees, and if you pull, the hairs stay fast and it kills the bug."

"We will come at once," laughed Elnora. "I know what they are, and I can use some in my work."

"Billy, have you been crying?" inquired Mrs. Comstock.

Billy lifted a chastened face. "Yes, ma'am," he replied. "This has been the worst day."

"What's the matter with the day?"

"The day is all right," admitted Billy. "I mean every single thing has gone wrong with me."

"Now that is too bad!" sympathized Mrs. Comstock. .

"Began early this morning," said Billy. "All Snap's fault, too."

"What has poor Snap been doing?" demanded Mrs. Comstock, her eyes beginning to twinkle.

"Digging for woodchucks, like he always does. He gets up at two o'clock to dig for them. He was coming in from the woods all tired and covered thick with dirt. I was going to the barn with the pail of water for Uncle Wesley to use in milking. I had to set down the pail to shut the gate so the chickens wouldn't get into the flower beds, and old Snap stuck his dirty nose into the water and began to lap it down. I knew Uncle Wesley wouldn't use that, so I had to go 'way back to the cistern for more, and it pumps awful hard. Made me mad, so I threw the water on Snap."

"Well, what of it?"

"Nothing, if he'd stood still. But it scared him awful, and when he's afraid he goes a-humping for Aunt Margaret. When he got right up against her he stiffened out and gave a big shake. You oughter seen the nice blue dress she had put on to go to Onabasha!"

Mrs. Comstock and Philip laughed, but Elnora put her arms around the boy. "Oh Billy!" she cried. "That was too bad!"

"She got up early and ironed that dress to wear because it was cool. Then, when it was all dirty, she wouldn't go, and she wanted to real bad." Billy wiped his eyes. "That ain't all, either," he added.

"We'd like to know about it, Billy," suggested Mrs. Comstock, struggling with her face.

"Cos she couldn't go to the city, she's most worked herself to death. She's done all the dirty, hard jobs she could find. She's fixing her grape juice now."

"Sure!" cried Mrs. Comstock. "When a woman is disappointed she always works like a dog to gain sympathy!"

"Well, Uncle Wesley and I are sympathizing all we know how, without her working so. I've squeezed until I almost busted to get the juice out from the seeds and skins. That's the hard part. Now, she has to strain it through white flannel and seal it in bottles, and it's good for sick folks. Most wish I'd get sick myself, so I could have a glass. It's so good!"

Elnora glanced swiftly at her mother.

"I worked so hard," continued Billy, "that she said if I would throw the leavings in the woods, then I could come after you to see about the bugs. Do you want to go?"

"We will all go," said Mrs. Comstock. "I am mightily interested in those bugs myself."

From afar commotion could be seen at the Sinton home. Wesley and Margaret were running around wildly and peculiar sounds filled the air.

"What's the trouble?" asked Philip, hurrying to Wesley.

"Cholera!" groaned Sinton. "My hogs are dying like flies."

Margaret was softly crying. "Wesley, can't I fix something hot? Can't we do anything? It means several hundred dollars and our winter meat."

"I never saw stock taken so suddenly and so hard," said Wesley. "I have 'phoned for the veterinary to come as soon as he can get here."

All of them hurried to the feeding pen into which the pigs seemed to be gathering from the woods. Among the common stock were big white beasts of pedigree which were Wesley's pride at county fairs. Several of these rolled on their backs, pawing the air feebly and emitting little squeaks. A huge Berkshire sat on his haunches, slowly shaking his head, the water dropping from his eyes, until he, too, rolled over with faint grunts. A pair crossing the yard on wavering legs collided, and attacked each other in anger, only to fall, so weak they scarcely could squeal. A fine snowy Plymouth Rock rooster, after several attempts, flew to the fence, balanced with great effort, wildly flapped his wings and started a guttural crow, but fell sprawling among the pigs, too helpless to stand.

"Did you ever see such a dreadful sight?" sobbed Margaret.

Billy climbed on the fence, took one long look and turned an astounded face to Wesley.

"Why them pigs is drunk!" he cried. "They act just like my pa!"

Wesley turned to Margaret.

"Where did you put the leavings from that grape juice?" he demanded.

"I sent Billy to throw it in the woods."

"Billy—" began Wesley.

"Threw it just where she told me to," cried Billy. "But some of the pigs came by there coming into the pen, and some were close in the fence corners."

"Did they eat it?" demanded Wesley.

"They just chanked into it," replied Billy graphically. "They pushed, and squealed, and fought over it. You couldn't blame 'em! It was the best stuff I ever tasted!"

"Margaret," said Wesley, "run 'phone that doctor he won't be needed. Billy, take Elnora and Mr. Ammon to see the bugs. Katharine, suppose you help me a minute."

Wesley took the clothes basket from the back porch and started in the direction of the cellar. Margaret returned from the telephone.

"I just caught him," she said. "There's that much saved. Why Wesley, what are you going to. do?"

"You go sit on the front porch a little while," said Wesley. "You will feel better if you don't see this."

"Wesley," cried Margaret aghast. "Some of that wine is ten years old. There are days and days of hard work in it, and I couldn't say how much sugar. Dr. Ammon keeps people alive with it when nothing else will stay on their stomachs."

"Let 'em die, then!" said Wesley. "You heard the boy, didn't you?"

"It's a cold process. There's not a particle of fermentation about it."

"Not a particle of fermentation! Great day, Margaret! Look at those pigs!"

Margaret took a long look. "Leave me a few bottles for mince-meat," she wavered.

"Not a smell for any use on this earth! You heard the boy! He shan't say, when he grows to manhood, that he learned to like it here!"

Wesley threw away the wine, Mrs. Comstock cheerfully assisting. Then they walked to the woods to see and learn about the wonderful insects. The day ended with a big supper at Sintons', and then they went to the Comstock cabin for a concert. Elnora played beautifully that night. When the Sintons left she kissed Billy with particular tenderness. She was so moved that she was kinder to Philip than she had intended to be, and Elnora as an antidote to a disappointed lover was a decided success in any mood.

However strong the attractions of Edith Carr had been, once the bond was finally broken, Philip Ammon could not help realizing that Elnora was the superior woman, and that he was fortunate to have escaped, when he regarded his ties strongest. Every day, while working with Elnora, he saw more to admire. He grew very thankful that he was free to try to win her, and impatient to justify himself to her.

Elnora did not evince the slightest haste to hear what he had to say, but waited the week she had set, in spite of Philip's hourly manifest impatience. When she did consent to listen, Philip felt before he had talked five minutes, that she was putting herself in Edith Carr's place, and judging him from what the other girl's standpoint would be. That was so disconcerting, he did not plead his cause nearly so well as he had hoped, for when he ceased Elnora sat in silence.

"You are my judge," he said at last. "What is your verdict?"

"If I could hear her speak from her heart as I just have heard you, then I could decide," answered Elnora.

"She is on the ocean," said Philip. "She went because she knew she was wholly in the wrong. She had nothing to say, or she would have remained."

"That sounds plausible," reasoned Elnora, "but it is pretty difficult to find a woman in an affair that involves her heart with nothing at all to say. I fancy if I could meet her, she would say several things. I should love to hear them. If I could talk with her three minutes, I could tell what answer to make you."

"Don't you believe me, Elnora?"

"Unquestioningly," answered Elnora. "But I would believe her also. If only I could meet her I soon would know."

"I don't see how that is to be accomplished," said Philip, "but I am perfectly willing. There is no reason why you should not meet her, except that she probably would lose her temper and insult you."

"Not to any extent," said Elnora calmly. "I have a tongue of my own, while I am not without some small sense of personal values."

Philip glanced at her and began to laugh. Very different of facial formation and colouring, Elnora at times closely resembled her mother. She joined in his laugh ruefully.

"The point is this," she said. "Some one is going to be hurt, most dreadfully. If the decision as to whom it shall be rests with me, I must know it is the right one.

Of course, no one ever hinted it to you, but you are a very attractive man, Philip. You are mighty good to look at, and you have a trained, refined mind, that makes you most interesting. For years Edith Carr has felt that you were hers. Now, how is she going to change? I have been thinking—thinking deep and long, Phil. If I were in her place, I simply could not give you up, unless you had made yourself unworthy of love. Undoubtedly, you never seemed so desirable to her as just now, when she is told she can't have you. What I think is that she will come to claim you yet."

"You overlook the fact that it is not in a woman's power to throw away a man and pick him up at pleasure," said Philip with some warmth. "She publicly and repeatedly cast me off. I accepted her decision as publicly as it was made. You have done all your thinking from a wrong viewpoint. You seem to have an idea that it lies with you to decide what I shall do, that if you say the word, I shall return to Edith. Put that thought out of your head! Now, and for all time to come, she is a matter of indifference to me. She killed all feeling in my heart for her so completely that I do not even dread meeting her.

"If I hated her, or was angry with her, I could not be sure the feeling would not die. As it is, she has deadened me into a creature of indifference. So you just revise your viewpoint a little, Elnora. Cease thinking it is for you to decide what I shall do, and that I will obey you. I make my own decisions in reference to any woman, save you. The question you are to decide is whether I may remain here, associating with you as I did last summer; but with the difference that it is understood that I am free; that it is my intention to care for you all I please, to make you return my feeling for you if I can. There is just one question for you to decide, and it is not triangular. It is between us. May I remain? May I love you? Will you give me the chance to prove what I think of you?"

"You speak very plainly," said Elnora.

"This is the time to speak plainly," said Philip Ammon. "There is no use in allowing you to go on threshing out a problem which does not exist. If you do not want me here, say so and I will go. Of course, I warn you before I start, that I will come back. I won't yield without the stiffest fight it is in me to make. But drop thinking it lies in your power to send me back to Edith Carr. If she were the last woman in the world, and I the last man, I'd jump off the planet before I would give her further opportunity to exercise her temper on me. Narrow this to us, Elnora. Will you take the place she vacated? Will you take the heart she threw away? I'd give my right hand and not flinch, if I could offer you my life, free from any contact with hers, but that is not possible. I can't undo things which are done. I can only profit by experience and build better in the future."

"I don't see how you can be sure of yourself," said Elnora. "I don't see how I could be sure of you. You loved her first, you never can care for me anything like that. Always I'd have to be afraid you were thinking of her and regretting."

"Folly!" cried Philip. "Regretting what? That I was not married to a woman who was liable to rave at me any time or place, without my being conscious of having given offence? A man does relish that! I am likely to pine for more!"

"You'd be thinking she'd learned a lesson. You would think it wouldn't happen again."

"No, I wouldn't be 'thinking,'" said, Philip. "I'd be everlastingly sure! I wouldn't risk what I went through that night again, not to save my life! Just you and me, Elnora. Decide for us."

"I can't!" cried Elnora. "I am afraid!"

"Very well," said Philip. "We will wait until you feel that you can. Wait until fear vanishes. Just decide now whether you would rather have me go for a few months, or remain with you. Which shall it be, Elnora?"

"You can never love me as you did her," wailed Elnora.

"I am happy to say I cannot," replied he. "I've cut my matrimonial teeth. I'm cured of wanting to swell in society. I'm over being proud of a woman for her looks alone. I have no further use for lavishing myself on a beautiful, elegantly dressed creature, who thinks only of self. I have learned that I am a common man. I admire beauty and beautiful clothing quite as much as I ever did; but, first, I want an understanding, deep as the lowest recess of my soul, with the woman I marry. I want to work for you, to plan for you, to build you a home with every comfort, to give you all good things I can, to shield you from every evil. I want to interpose my body between yours and fire, flood, or famine. I want to give you everything; but I hate the idea of getting nothing at all on which I can depend in return. Edith Carr had only good looks to offer, and when anger overtook her, beauty went out like a snuffed candle.

"I want you to love me. I want some consideration. I even crave respect. I've kept myself clean. So far as I know how to be, I am honest and scrupulous. It wouldn't hurt me to feel that you took some interest in these things. Rather fierce temptations strike a man, every few days, in this world. I can keep decent, for a woman who cares for decency, but when I do, I'd like to have the fact recognized, by just enough of a show of appreciation that I could see it. I am tired of this one-sided business. After this, I want to get a little in return for what I give. Elnora, you have love, tenderness, and honest appreciation of the finest in life. Take what I offer, and give what I ask."

"You do not ask much," said Elnora.

"As for not loving you as I did Edith," continued Philip, "as I said before, I hope not! I have a newer and a better idea of loving. The feeling I offer you was inspired by you. It is a Limberlost product. It is as much bigger, cleaner, and more wholesome than any feeling I ever had for Edith Carr, as you are bigger than she, when you stand before your classes and in calm dignity explain the marvels of the Almighty, while she stands on a ballroom floor, and gives way to uncontrolled temper. Ye gods, Elnora, if you could look into my soul, you would see it leap and rejoice over my escape! Perhaps it isn't decent, but it's human; and I'm only a common human being. I'm the gladdest man alive that I'm free! I would turn somersaults and yell if I dared. What an escape! Stop straining after Edith Carr's viewpoint and take a look from mine. Put yourself in my place and try to study out how I feel.

"I am so happy I grow religious over it. Fifty times a day I catch myself whispering, 'My soul is escaped!' As for you, take all the time you want. If you prefer to be alone, I'll take the next train and stay away as long as I can bear it, but I'll come back. You can be most sure of that. Straight as your pigeons to their loft, I'll come back to you, Elnora. Shall I go?"

"Oh, what's the use to be extravagant?" murmured Elnora.

Chapter 22

Wherein Philip Ammon Kneels to Elnora, and Strangers Come to the Limberlost

The month which followed was a reproduction of the previous June. There were long moth hunts, days of specimen gathering, wonderful hours with great books, big dinners all of them helped to prepare, and perfect nights filled with music. Everything was as it had been, with the difference that Philip was now an avowed suitor. He missed no opportunity to advance himself in Elnora's graces. At the end of the month he was no nearer any sort of understanding with her than he had been at the beginning. He revelled in the privilege of loving her, but he got no response. Elnora believed in his love, yet she hesitated to accept him, because she could not forget Edith Carr.

One afternoon early in July, Philip came across the fields, through the Comstock woods, and entered the garden. He inquired for Elnora at the back door and was told that she was reading under the willow. He went around the west end of the cabin to her. She sat on a rustic bench they had made and placed beneath a drooping branch. He had not seen her before in the dress she was wearing. It was clinging mull of pale green, trimmed with narrow ruffles and touched with knots of black velvet; a simple dress, but vastly becoming. Every tint of her bright hair, her luminous eyes, her red lips, and her rose-flushed face, neck, and arms grew a little more vivid with the delicate green setting.

He stopped short. She was so near, so temptingly sweet, he lost control. He went to her with a half-smothered cry after that first long look, dropped on one knee beside her and reached an arm behind her to the bench back, so that he was very near. He caught her hands.

"Elnora!" he cried tensely. "End it now! Say this strain is over. I pledge you that you will be happy. You don't know! If you only would say the word, you would awake to new life and great joy! Won't you promise me now, Elnora?"

The girl sat staring into the west woods, while strong in her eyes was her father's look of seeing something invisible to others. Philip's arm slipped from the bench around her. His fingers closed firmly over hers. "Elnora," he pleaded, "you know me well enough. You have had time in plenty. End it now. Say you will be mine!" He gathered her closer, pressing his face against hers, his breath on her cheek. "Can't you quite promise yet, my girl of the Limberlost?"

Elnora shook her head. Instantly he released her.

"Forgive me," he begged. "I had no intention of thrusting myself upon you, but, Elnora, you are the veriest Queen of Love this afternoon. From the tips of your toes to your shining crown, I worship you. I want no woman save you. You are so wonderful this afternoon, I couldn't help urging. Forgive me. Perhaps it was something that came this morning for you. I wrote Polly to send it. May we try if it fits? Will you tell me if you like it?"

He drew a little white velvet box from his pocket and showed her a splendid emerald ring.

"It may not be right," he said. "The inside of a glove finger is not very accurate for a measure, but it was the best I could do. I wrote Polly to get it, because she and mother are home from the East this week, but next they will go on to our cottage in the north, and no one knows what is right quite so well as Polly." He laid the ring in Elnora's hand. "Dearest," he said, "don't slip that on your finger; put your arms around my neck and promise me, all at once and abruptly, or I'll keel over and die of sheer joy."

Elnora smiled.

"I won't! Not all those venturesome things at once; but, Phil, I'm ashamed to confess that ring simply fascinates me. It is the most beautiful one I ever saw, and do you know that I never owned a ring of any kind in my life? Would you think me unwomanly if I slip it on for a second, before I can say for sure? Phil, you know I care! I care very much! You know I will tell you the instant I feel right about it."

"Certainly you will," agreed Philip promptly. "It is your right to take all the time you choose. I can't put that ring on you until it means a bond between us. I'll shut my eyes and you try it on, so we can see if it fits." Philip turned his face toward the west woods and tightly closed his eyes. It was a boyish thing to do, and it caught the hesitating girl in the depths of her heart as the boy clement in a man ever appeals to a motherly woman. Before she quite realized what she was doing, the ring slid on her finger. With both arms she caught Philip and drew him to her breast, holding him closely. Her head drooped over his, her lips were on his hair. So an instant, then her arms dropped. He lifted a convulsed, white face.

"Dear Lord!" he whispered. "You—you didn't mean that, Elnora! You—What made you do it?"

"You—you looked so boyish!" panted Elnora. "I didn't mean it! I—I forgot that you were older than Billy. Look—look at the ring!"

"'The Queen can do no wrong,'" quoted Philip between his set teeth. "But don't you do that again, Elnora, unless you do mean it. Kings are not so good as queens, and there is a limit with all men. As you say, we will look at your ring. It seems very lovely to me. Suppose you leave it on until time for me to go. Please do! I have heard of mute appeals; perhaps it will plead for me. I am wild for your lips this afternoon. I am going to take your hands."

He caught both of them and covered them with kisses.

"Elnora," he said. "Will you be my wife?"

"I must have a little more time," she whispered. "I must be absolutely certain, for when I say yes, and give myself to you, only death shall part us. I would not give you up. So I want a little more time—but, I think I will."

"Thank you," said Philip. "If at any time you feel that you have reached a decision, will you tell me? Will you promise me to tell me instantly, or shall I keep asking you until the time comes?"

"You make it difficult," said Elnora. "But I will promise you that. Whenever the last doubt vanishes, I will let you know instantly—if I can."

"Would it be difficult for you?" whispered Ammon.

"I—I don't know," faltered Elnora.

"It seems as if I can't be man enough to put this thought aside and give up this afternoon," said Philip. "I am ashamed of myself, but I can't help it. I am going to ask God to make that last doubt vanish before I go this night. I am going to believe that ring will plead for me. I am going to hope that doubt will disappear suddenly. I will be watching. Every second I will be watching. If it happens and you can't speak, give me your hand. Just the least movement toward me, I will understand. Would it help you to talk this over with your mother? Shall I call her? Shall I—?"

Honk! Honk! Honk! Hart Henderson set the horn of the big automobile going as it shot from behind the trees lining the Brushwood road. The picture of a vine-covered cabin, a large drooping tree, a green-clad girl and a man bending over her very closely flashed into view. Edith Carr caught her breath with a snap. Polly Ammon gave Tom Levering a quick touch and wickedly winked at him.

Several days before, Edith had returned from Europe suddenly. She and Henderson had called at the Ammon residence saying that they were going to motor down to the Limberlost to see Philip a few hours, and urged that Polly and Tom accompany them. Mrs. Ammon knew that her husband would disapprove of the trip, but it was easy to see that Edith Carr had determined on going. So the mother thought it better to have Polly along to support Philip than to allow him to confront Edith unexpectedly and alone. Polly was full of spirit. She did not relish the thought of Edith as a sister. Always they had been in the same set, always

Edith, because of greater beauty and wealth, had patronized Polly. Although it had rankled, she had borne it sweetly. But two days before, her father had extracted a promise of secrecy, given her Philip's address and told her to send him the finest emerald ring she could select. Polly knew how that ring would be used. What she did not know was that the girl who accompanied her went back to the store afterward, made an excuse to the clerk that she had been sent to be absolutely sure that the address was right, and so secured it for Edith Carr.

Two days later Edith had induced Hart Henderson to take her to Onabasha. By the aid of maps they located the Comstock land and passed it, merely to see the place. Henderson hated that trip, and implored Edith not to take it, but she made no effort to conceal from him what she suffered, and it was more than he could endure. He pointed out that Philip had gone away without leaving an address, because he did not wish to see her, or any of them. But Edith was so sure of her power, she felt certain Philip needed only to see her to succumb to her beauty as he always had done, while now she was ready to plead for forgiveness. So they came down the Brushwood road, and Henderson had just said to Edith beside him: "This should be the Comstock land on our left."

A minute later the wood ended, while the sunlight, as always pitiless, etched with distinctness the scene at the west end of the cabin. Instinctively, to save Edith, Henderson set the horn blowing. He had thought to drive to the city, but Polly Ammon arose crying: "Phil! Phil!" Tom Levering was on his feet shouting and waving, while Edith in her most imperial manner ordered him to turn into the lane leading through the woods beside the cabin.

"Find some way for me to have a minute alone with her," she commanded as he stopped the car.

"That is my sister Polly, her fiancé Tom Levering, a friend of mine named Henderson, and—" began Philip,

"—and Edith Carr," volunteered Elnora.

"And Edith Carr," repeated Philip Ammon. "Elnora, be brave, for my sake. Their coming can make no difference in any way. I won't let them stay but a few minutes. Come with me!"

"Do I seem scared?" inquired Elnora serenely. "This is why you haven't had your answer. I have been waiting just six weeks for that motor. You may bring them to me at the arbour."

Philip glanced at her and broke into a laugh. She had not lost colour. Her self-possession was perfect. She deliberately turned and walked toward the grape arbour, while he sprang over the west fence and ran to the car.

Elnora standing in the arbour entrance made a perfect picture, framed in green leaves and tendrils. No matter how her heart ached, it was good to her, for it pumped steadily, and kept her cheeks and lips suffused with colour. She saw Philip reach the car and gather his sister into his arms. Past her he reached a hand to Levering, then to Edith Carr and Henderson. He lifted his sister to the ground, and assisted Edith to alight. Instantly, she stepped beside him, and Elnora's heart played its first trick.

She could see that Miss Carr was splendidly beautiful, while she moved with the hauteur and grace supposed to be the prerogatives of royalty. And she had instantly taken possession of Philip. But he also had a brain which was working with rapidity. He knew Elnora was watching, so he turned to the others.

"Give her up, Tom!" he cried. "I didn't know I wanted to see the little nuisance so badly, but I do. How are father and mother? Polly, didn't the mater send me something?"

"She did!" said Polly Ammon, stopping on the path and lifting her chin as a little child, while she drew away her veil.

Philip caught her in his arms and stooped for his mother's kiss.

"Be good to Elnora!" he whispered.

"Umhu!" assented Polly. And aloud—"Look at that ripping green and gold symphony! I never saw such a beauty! Thomas Asquith Levering, you come straight here and take my hand!"

Edith's move to compel Philip to approach Elnora beside her had been easy to see; also its failure. Henderson stepped into Philip's place as he turned to his sister. Instead of taking Polly's hand Levering ran to open the gate. Edith passed through first, but Polly darted in front of her on the run, with Phil holding her arm, and swept up to Elnora. Polly looked for the ring and saw it. That settled matters with her.

"You lovely, lovely, darling girl!" she cried, throwing her arms around Elnora and kissing her. With her lips close Elnora's ear, Polly whispered, "Sister! Dear, dear sister!"

Elnora drew back, staring at Polly in confused amazement. She was a beautiful girl, her eyes were sparkling and dancing, and as she turned to make way for the others, she kept one of Elnora's hands in hers. Polly would have dropped dead in that instant if Edith Carr could have killed with a look, for not until then did she realize that Polly would even many a slight, and that it had been a great mistake to bring her.

Edith bowed low, muttered something, and touched Elnora's fingers. Tom took his cue from Polly.

"I always follow a good example," he said, and before any one could divine his intention he kissed Elnora as he gripped her hand and cried: "Mighty glad to meet you! Like to meet you a dozen times a day, you know!"

Elnora laughed and her heart pumped smoothly. They had accomplished their purpose. They had let her know they were there through compulsion, but on her side. In that instant only pity was in Elnora's breast for the flashing dark beauty, standing with smiling face while her heart must have been filled with exceeding bitterness. Elnora stepped back from the entrance.

"Come into the shade," she urged. "You must have found it warm on these country roads. Won't you lay aside your dust-coats and have a cool drink? Philip, would you ask mother to come, and bring that pitcher from the spring house?"

They entered the arbour exclaiming at the dim, green coolness. There was plenty of room and wide seats around the sides, a table in the centre, on which lay a piece of embroidery, magazines, books, the moth apparatus, and the cyanide jar containing several specimens. Polly rejoiced in the cooling shade, slipped off her duster, removed her hat, rumpled her pretty hair and seated herself to indulge in the delightful occupation of paying off old scores. Tom Levering followed her example. Edith took a seat but refused to remove her hat and coat, while Henderson stood in the entrance.

"There goes something with wings! Should you have that?" cried Levering.

He seized a net from the table and raced across the garden after a butterfly. He caught it and came back mightily pleased with himself. As the creature struggled in the net, Elnora noted a repulsed look on Edith Carr's face. Levering helped the situation beautifully.

"Now what have I got?" he demanded. "Is it just a common one that every one knows and you don't keep, or is it the rarest bird off the perch?"

"You must have had practice, you took that so perfectly," said Elnora. "I am sorry, but it is quite common and not of a kind I keep. Suppose all of you see how beautiful it is and then it may go nectar hunting again."

She held the butterfly where all of them could see, showed its upper and under wing colours, answered Polly's questions as to what it ate, how long it lived, and how it died. Then she put it into Polly's hand saying: "Stand there in the light and loosen your hold slowly and easily."

Elnora caught a brush from the table and began softly stroking the creature's sides and wings. Delighted with the sensation the butterfly opened and closed its wings, clinging to Polly's soft little fingers, while every one cried out in surprise. Elnora laid aside the brush, and the butterfly sailed away.

"Why, you are a wizard! You charm them!" marvelled Levering.

"I learned that from the Bird Woman," said Elnora. "She takes soft brushes and coaxes butterflies and moths into the positions she wants for the illustrations of a book she is writing. I have helped her often. Most of the rare ones I find go to her."

"Then you don't keep all you take?" questioned Levering.

"Oh, dear, no!" cried Elnora. "Not a tenth! For myself, a pair of each kind to use in illustrating the lectures I give in the city schools in the winter, and one pair for each collection I make. One might as well keep the big night moths of June, for they only live four or five days anyway. For the Bird Woman, I only save rare ones she has not yet secured. Sometimes I think it is cruel to take such creatures from freedom, even for an hour, but it is the only way to teach the masses of people how to distinguish the pests they should destroy, from the harmless ones of great beauty. Here comes mother with something cool to drink."

Mrs. Comstock came deliberately, talking to Philip as she approached. Elnora gave her one searching look, but could discover only an extreme brightness of eye to denote any unusual feeling. She wore one of her lavender dresses, while her snowy hair was high piled. She had taken care of her complexion, and her face had grown fuller during the winter. She might have been any one's mother with pride, and she was perfectly at ease.

Polly instantly went to her and held up her face to be kissed. Mrs. Comstock's eyes twinkled and she made the greeting hearty.

The drink was compounded of the juices of oranges and berries from the garden. It was cool enough to frost glasses and pitcher and delicious to dusty tired travellers. Soon the pitcher was empty, and Elnora picked it up and went to refill it. While she was gone Henderson asked Philip about some trouble he was having with his car. They went to the woods and began a minute examination to find a defect which did not exist. Polly and Levering were having an animated conversation with Mrs. Comstock. Henderson saw Edith arise, follow the garden path next the woods and stand waiting under the willow which Elnora would pass on her return. It was for that meeting he had made the trip. He got down on the ground, tore up the car, worked, asked for help, and kept Philip busy screwing bolts and applying the oil can. All the time Henderson kept an eye on Edith and Elnora under the willow. But he took pains to lay the work he asked Philip to do where that scene would be out of his sight. When Elnora came around the corner with the pitcher, she found herself facing Edith Carr.

"I want a minute with you," said Miss Carr.

"Very well," replied Elnora, walking on.

"Set the pitcher on the bench there," commanded Edith Carr, as if speaking to a servant.

"I prefer not to offer my visitors a warm drink," said Elnora. "I'll come back if you really wish to speak with me."

"I came solely for that," said Edith Carr.

"It would be a pity to travel so far in this dust and heat for nothing. I'll only be gone a second."

Elnora placed the pitcher before her mother. "Please serve this," she said. "Miss Carr wishes to speak with me."

"Don't you pay the least attention to anything she says," cried Polly. "Tom and I didn't come here because we wanted to. We only came to checkmate her. I hoped I'd get the opportunity to say a word to you, and now she has given it to me. I just want to tell you that she threw Phil over in perfectly horrid way. She hasn't any right to lay the ghost of a claim to him, has she, Tom?"

"Nary a claim," said Tom Levering earnestly. "Why, even you, Polly, couldn't serve me as she did Phil, and ever get me back again. If I were you, Miss Comstock, I'd send my mother to talk with her and I'd stay here."

Tom had gauged Mrs. Comstock rightly. Polly put her arms around Elnora. "Let me go with you, dear," she begged.

"I promised I would speak with her alone," said Elnora, "and she must be considered. But thank you, very much."

"How I shall love you!" exulted Polly, giving Elnora a parting hug.

The girl slowly and gravely walked back to the willow. She could not imagine what was coming, but she was promising herself that she would be very patient and control her temper.

"Will you be seated?" she asked politely.

Edith Carr glanced at the bench, while a shudder shook her.

"No. I prefer to stand," she said. "Did Mr. Ammon give you the ring you are wearing, and do you consider yourself engaged to him?"

"By what right do you ask such personal questions as those?" inquired Elnora.

"By the right of a betrothed wife. I have been promised to Philip Ammon ever since I wore short skirts. All our lives we have expected to marry. An agreement of years cannot be broken in one insane moment. Always he has loved me devotedly. Give me ten minutes with him and he will be mine for all time."

"I seriously doubt that," said Elnora. "But I am willing that you should make the test. I will call him."

"Stop!" commanded Edith Carr. "I told you that it was you I came to see."

"I remember," said Elnora.

"Mr. Ammon is my betrothed," continued Edith Carr. "I expect to take him back to Chicago with me."

"You expect considerable," murmured Elnora. "I will raise no objection to your taking him, if you can—but, I tell you frankly, I don't think it possible."

"You are so sure of yourself as that," scoffed Edith Carr. "One hour in my presence will bring back the old spell, full force. We belong to each other. I will not give him up."

"Then it is untrue that you twice rejected his ring, repeatedly insulted him, and publicly renounced him?"

"That was through you!" cried Edith Carr. "Phil and I never had been so near and so happy as we were on that night. It was your clinging to him for things that caused him to desert me among his guests, while he tried to make me await your pleasure. I realize the spell of this place, for a summer season. I understand what you and your mother have done to inveigle him. I know that your hold on him is quite real. I can see just how you have worked to ensnare him!"

"Men would call that lying," said Elnora calmly. "The second time I met Philip Ammon he told me of his engagement to you, and I respected it. I did by you as I would want you to do by me. He was here parts of each day, almost daily last summer. The Almighty is my witness that never once, by word or look, did I ever make the slightest attempt to interest him in my person or personality. He wrote you frequently in my presence. He forgot the violets for which he asked to send you. I gathered them and carried them to him. I sent him back to you in unswerving devotion, and the Almighty is also my witness that I could have changed his heart last summer, if I had tried. I wisely left that work for you. All my life I shall be glad that I lived and worked on the square. That he ever would come back to me free, by your act, I never dreamed. When he left me I did not hope or expect to see him again," Elnora's voice fell soft and low, "and, behold! You sent him—and free!"

"You exult in that!" cried Edith Carr. "Let me tell you he is not free! We have belonged for years. We always shall. If you cling to him, and hold him to rash things he has said and done, because he thought me still angry and unforgiving with him, you will ruin all our lives. If he married you, before a month you would read heart-hunger for me in his eyes. He could not love me as he has done, and give me up for a little scene like that!"

"There is a great poem," said Elnora, "one line of which reads, 'For each man kills the thing he loves.' Let me tell you that a woman can do that also. He did love you—that I concede. But you killed his love everlastingly, when you disgraced him in public. Killed it so completely he does not even feel resentment toward you. To-day, he would do you a favour, if he could; but love you, no! That is over!"

Edith Carr stood truly regal and filled with scorn. "You are mistaken! Nothing on earth could kill that!" she cried, and Elnora saw that the girl really believed what she said.

"You are very sure of yourself!" said Elnora.

"I have reason to be sure," answered Edith Carr. "We have lived and loved too long. I have had years with him to match against your days. He is mine! His work, his ambitions, his friends, his place in society are with me. You may have a summer charm for a sick man in the country; if he tried placing you in society, he soon would see you as others will. It takes birth to position, schooling, and endless practice to meet social demands gracefully. You would put him to shame in a week."

"I scarcely think I should follow your example so far," said Elnora dryly. "I have a feeling for Philip that would prevent my hurting him purposely, either in public or private. As for managing a social career for him he never mentioned that he desired such a thing. What he asked of me was that I should be his wife. I understood that to mean that he desired me to keep him a clean house, serve him digestible food, mother his children, and give him loving sympathy and tenderness."

"Shameless!" cried Edith Carr.

"To which of us do you intend that adjective to apply?" inquired Elnora. "I never was less ashamed in all my life. Please remember I am in my own home, and your presence here is not on my invitation."

Miss Carr lifted her head and struggled with her veil. She was very pale and trembling violently, while Elnora stood serene, a faint smile on her lips.

"Such vulgarity!" panted Edith Carr. "How can a man like Philip endure it?"

"Why don't you ask him?" inquired Elnora. "I can call him with one breath; but, if he judged us as we stand, I should not be the one to tremble at his decision. Miss Carr, you have been quite plain. You have told me in carefully selected words what you think of me. You insult my birth, education, appearance, and home. I assure you I am legitimate. I will pass a test examination with you on any high school or supplementary branch, or French or German. I will take a physical examination beside you. I will face any social emergency you can mention with you. I am acquainted with a whole world in which Philip Ammon is keenly interested, that you scarcely know exists. I am not afraid to face any audience you can get together anywhere with my violin. I am not repulsive to look at, and I have a wholesome regard for the proprieties and civilities of life. Philip Ammon never asked anything more of me, why should you?"

"It is plain to see," cried Edith Carr, "that you took him when he was hurt and angry and kept his wound wide open. Oh, what have you not done against me?"

"I did not promise to marry him when an hour ago he asked me, and offered me this ring, because there was so much feeling in my heart for you, that I knew I never could be happy, if I felt that in any way I had failed in doing justice to your interests. I did slip on this ring, which he had just brought, because I never owned one, and it is very beautiful, but I made him no promise, nor shall I make any, until I am quite, quite sure, that you fully realize he never would marry you if I sent him away this hour."

"You know perfectly that if your puny hold on him were broken, if he were back in his home, among his friends, and where he was meeting me, in one short week he would be mine again, as he always has been. In your heart you don't believe what you say. You don't dare trust him in my presence. You are afraid to allow him out of your sight, because you know what the results would be. Right or wrong, you have made up your mind to ruin him and me, and you are going to be selfish enough to do it. But—"

"That will do!" said Elnora. "Spare me the enumeration of how I will regret it. I shall regret nothing. I shall not act until I know there will be nothing to regret. I have decided on my course. You may return to your friends."

"What do you mean?" demanded Edith Carr.

"That is my affair," replied Elnora. "Only this! When your opportunity comes, seize it! Any time you are in Philip Ammon's presence, exert the charms of which you boast, and take him. I grant you are justified in doing it if you can. I want nothing more than I want to see you marry Philip if he wants you. He is just across the fence under that automobile. Go spread your meshes and exert your wiles. I won't stir to stop you. Take him to Onabasha, and to Chicago with you. Use every art you possess. If the old charm can be revived I will be the first to wish both of you well. Now, I must return to my visitors. Kindly excuse me."

Elnora turned and went back to the arbour. Edith Carr followed the fence and passed through the gate into the west woods where she asked Henderson about the car. As she stood near him she whispered: "Take Phil back to Onabasha with us."

"I say, Ammon, can't you go to the city with us and help me find a shop where I can get this pinion fixed?" asked Henderson. "We want to lunch and start back by five. That will get us home about midnight. Why don't you bring your automobile here?"

"I am a working man," said Philip. "I have no time to be out motoring. I can't see anything the matter with your car, myself; but, of course you don't want to break down in the night, on strange roads, with women on your hands. I'll see."

Philip went into the arbour, where Polly took possession of his lap, fingered his hair, and kissed his forehead and lips.

"When are you coming to the cottage, Phil?" she asked. "Come soon, and bring Miss Comstock for a visit. All of us will be so glad to have her."

Philip beamed on Polly. "I'll see about that," he said. "Sounds pretty good. Elnora, Henderson is in trouble with his automobile. He wants me to go to

Onabasha with him to show him where the doctor lives, and make repairs so he can start back this evening. It will take about two hours. May I go?"

"Of course, you must go," she said, laughing lightly. "You can't leave your sister. Why don't you return to Chicago with them? There is plenty of room, and you could have a fine visit."

"I'll be back in just two hours," said Philip. "While I am gone, you be thinking over what we were talking of when the folks came."

"Miss Comstock can go with us as well as not," said Polly. "That back seat was made for three, and I can sit on your lap."

"Come on! Do come!" urged Philip instantly, and Tom Levering joined him, but Henderson and Edith silently waited at the gate.

"No, thank you," laughed Elnora. "That would crowd you, and it's warm and dusty. We will say good-bye here."

She offered her hand to all of them, and when she came to Philip she gave him one long steady look in the eyes, then shook hands with him also.

Chapter 23

Wherein Elnora Reaches a Decision, and Freckles and the Angel Appear

"Well, she came, didn't she?" remarked Mrs. Comstock to Elnora as they watched the automobile speed down the road. As it turned the Limberlost corner, Philip arose and waved to them.

"She hasn't got him yet, anyway," said Mrs. Comstock, taking heart. "What's that on your finger, and what did she say to you?"

Elnora explained about the ring as she drew it off.

"I have several letters to write, then I am going to change my dress and walk down toward Aunt Margaret's for a little exercise. I may meet some of them, and I don't want them to see this ring. You keep it until Philip comes," said Elnora. "As for what Miss Carr said to me, many things, two of importance: one, that I lacked every social requirement necessary for the happiness of Philip Ammon, and that if I married him I would see inside a month that he was ashamed of me—"

"Aw, shockins!" scorned Mrs. Comstock. "Go on!"

"The other was that she has been engaged to him for years, that he belongs to her, and she refuses to give him up. She said that if he were in her presence one hour, she would have him under a mysterious thing she calls 'her spell' again; if he were where she could see him for one week, everything would be made up. It is her opinion that he is suffering from wounded pride, and that the slightest concession on her part will bring him to his knees before her."

Mrs. Comstock giggled. "I do hope the boy isn't weak-kneed," she said. "I just happened to be passing the west window this afternoon—"

Elnora laughed. "Nothing save actual knowledge ever would have made me believe there was a girl in all this world so infatuated with herself. She speaks casually of her power over men, and boasts of 'bringing a man to his knees' as complacently as I would pick up a net and say: 'I am going to take a butterfly.' She honestly believes that if Philip were with her a short time she could rekindle his love for her and awaken in him every particle of the old devotion. Mother, the girl

426

is honest! She is absolutely sincere! She so believes in herself and the strength of Phil's love for her, that all her life she will believe in and brood over that thought, unless she is taught differently. So long as she thinks that, she will nurse wrong ideas and pine over her blighted life. She must be taught that Phil is absolutely free, and yet he will not go to her."

"But how on earth are you proposing to teach her that?"

"The way will open."

"Lookey here, Elnora!" cried Mrs. Comstock. "That Carr girl is the handsomest dark woman I ever saw. She's got to the place where she won't stop at anything. Her coming here proves that. I don't believe there was a thing the matter with that automobile. I think that was a scheme she fixed up to get Phil where she could see him alone, as she worked to see you. If you are going deliberately to put Philip under her influence again, you've got to brace yourself for the possibility that she may win. A man is a weak mortal, where a lovely woman is concerned, and he never denied that he loved her once. You may make yourself downright miserable."

"But mother, if she won, it wouldn't make me half so miserable as to marry Phil myself, and then read hunger for her in his eyes! Some one has got to suffer over this. If it proves to be me, I'll bear it, and you'll never hear a whisper of complaint from me. I know the real Philip Ammon better in our months of work in the fields than she knows him in all her years of society engagements. So she shall have the hour she asked, many, many of them, enough to make her acknowledge that she is wrong. Now I am going to write my letters and take my walk."

Elnora threw her arms around her mother and kissed her repeatedly. "Don't you worry about me," she said. "I will get along all right, and whatever happens, I always will be your girl and you my darling mother."

She left two sealed notes on her desk. Then she changed her dress, packed a small bundle which she dropped with her hat from the window beside the willow, and softly went down stairs. Mrs. Comstock was in the garden. Elnora picked up the hat and bundle, hurried down the road a few rods, then climbed the fence and entered the woods. She took a diagonal course, and after a long walk reached a road two miles west and one south. There she straightened her clothing, put on her hat and a thin dark veil and waited the passing of the next trolley. She left it at the first town and took a train for Fort Wayne. She made that point just in time to climb on the evening train north, as it pulled from the station. It was after midnight when she left the car at Grand Rapids, and went into the depot to await the coming of day.

Tired out, she laid her head on her bundle and fell asleep on a seat in the women's waiting-room. Long after light she was awakened by the roar and rattle of trains. She washed, re-arranged her hair and clothing, and went into the general waiting-room to find her way to the street. She saw him as he entered the door. There was no mistaking the tall, lithe figure, the bright hair, the lean, brown-splotched face, the steady gray eyes. He was dressed for travelling, and carried a light overcoat and a bag. Straight to him Elnora went speeding.

"Oh, I was just starting to find you!" she cried.

"Thank you!" he said.

"You are going away?" she panted.

"Not if I am needed. I have a few minutes. Can you be telling me briefly?"

"I am the Limberlost girl to whom your wife gave the dress for Commencement last spring, and both of you sent lovely gifts. There is a reason, a very good reason, why I must be hidden for a time, and I came straight to you—as if I had a right."

"You have!" answered Freckles. "Any boy or girl who ever suffered one pang in the Limberlost has a claim to the best drop of blood in my heart. You needn't be telling me anything more. The Angel is at our cottage on Mackinac. You shall tell her and play with the babies while you want shelter. This way!"

They breakfasted in a luxurious car, talked over the swamp, the work of the Bird Woman; Elnora told of her nature lectures in the schools, and soon they were good friends. In the evening they left the train at Mackinaw City and crossed the Straits by boat. Sheets of white moonlight flooded the water and paved a molten path across the breast of it straight to the face of the moon.

The island lay a dark spot on the silver surface, its tall trees sharply outlined on the summit, and a million lights blinked around the shore. The night guns boomed from the white fort and a dark sentinel paced the ramparts above the little city tucked down close to the water. A great tenor summering in the north came out on the upper deck of the big boat, and baring his head, faced the moon and sang: "Oh, the moon shines bright on my old Kentucky home!" Elnora thought of the Limberlost, of Philip, and her mother, and almost choked with the sobs that would arise in her throat. On the dock a woman of exquisite beauty swept into the arms of Terence O'More.

"Oh, Freckles!" she cried. "You've been gone a month!"

"Four days, Angel, only four days by the clock," remonstrated Freckles. "Where are the children?"

"Asleep! Thank goodness! I'm worn to a thread. I never saw such inventive, active children. I can't keep track of them!"

"I have brought you help," said Freckles. "Here is the Limberlost girl in whom the Bird Woman is interested. Miss Comstock needs a rest before beginning her school work for next year, so she came to us."

"You dear thing! How good of you!" cried the Angel. "We shall be so happy to have you!"

In her room that night, in a beautiful cottage furnished with every luxury, Elnora lifted a tired face to the Angel.

"Of course, you understand there is something back of this?" she said. "I must tell you."

"Yes," agreed the Angel. "Tell me! If you get it out of your system, you will stand a better chance of sleeping."

Elnora stood brushing the copper-bright masses of her hair as she talked. When she finished the Angel was almost hysterical.

"You insane creature!" she cried. "How crazy of you to leave him to her! I know both of them. I have met them often. She may be able to make good her boast. But it is perfectly splendid of you! And, after all, really it is the only way. I can see that. I think it is what I should have done myself, or tried to do. I don't know that I could have done it! When I think of walking away and leaving Freckles with a woman he once loved, to let her see if she can make him love her again, oh, it gives me a graveyard heart. No, I never could have done it! You are bigger than I ever was. I should have turned coward, sure."

"I am a coward," admitted Elnora. "I am soul-sick! I am afraid I shall lose my senses before this is over. I didn't want to come! I wanted to stay, to go straight into his arms, to bind myself with his ring, to love him with all my heart. It wasn't my fault that I came. There was something inside that just pushed me. She is beautiful—"

"I quite agree with you!"

"You can imagine how fascinating she can be. She used no arts on me. Her purpose was to cower me. She found she could not do that, but she did a thing which helped her more: she proved that she was honest, perfectly sincere in what she thought. She believes that if she merely beckons to Philip, he will go to her. So I am giving her the opportunity to learn from him what he will do. She never will believe it from any one else. When she is satisfied, I shall be also."

"But, child! Suppose she wins him back!"

"That is the supposition with which I shall eat and sleep for the coming few weeks. Would one dare ask for a peep at the babies before going to bed?"

"Now, you are perfect!" announced the Angel. "I never should have liked you all I can, if you had been content to go to sleep in this house without asking to see the babies. Come this way. We named the first boy for his father, of course, and the girl for Aunt Alice. The next boy is named for my father, and the baby for the Bird Woman. After this we are going to branch out."

Elnora began to laugh.

"Oh, I suspect there will be quite a number of them," said the Angel serenely. "I am told the more there are the less trouble they make. The big ones take care of the little ones. We want a large family. This is our start."

She entered a dark room and held aloft a candle. She went to the side of a small white iron bed in which lay a boy of eight and another of three. They were perfectly formed, rosy children, the elder a replica of his mother, the other very like. Then they came to a cradle where a baby girl of almost two slept soundly, and made a picture.

"But just see here!" said the Angel. She threw the light on a sleeping girl of six. A mass of red curls swept the pillow. Line and feature the face was that of Freckles. Without asking, Elnora knew the colour and expression of the closed eyes. The Angel handed Elnora the candle, and stooping, straightened the child's body. She ran her fingers through the bright curls, and lightly touched the aristocratic little nose.

"The supply of freckles holds out in my family, you see!" she said. "Both of the girls will have them, and the second boy a few."

She stood an instant longer, then bending, ran her hand caressingly down a rosy bare leg, while she kissed the babyish red mouth. There had been some reason for touching all of them, the kiss fell on the lips which were like Freckles's.

To Elnora she said a tender good-night, whispering brave words of encouragement and making plans to fill the days to come. Then she went away. An hour later there was a light tap on the girl's door.

"Come!" she called as she lay staring into the dark.

The Angel felt her way to the bedside, sat down and took Elnora's hands.

"I just had to come back to you," she said. "I have been telling Freckles, and he is almost hurting himself with laughing. I didn't think it was funny, but he does. He thinks it's the funniest thing that ever happened. He says that to run away from Mr. Ammon, when you had made him no promise at all, when he wasn't sure of you, won't send him home to her; it will set him hunting you! He says if you had combined the wisdom of Solomon, Socrates, and all the remainder of the wise men, you couldn't have chosen any course that would have sealed him to you so surely. He feels that now Mr. Ammon will perfectly hate her for coming down there and driving you away. And you went to give her the chance she wanted. Oh, Elnora! It is becoming funny! I see it, too!"

The Angel rocked on the bedside. Elnora faced the dark in silence.

"Forgive me," gulped the Angel. "I didn't mean to laugh. I didn't think it was funny, until all at once it came to me. Oh, dear! Elnora, it *is* funny! I've got to laugh!"

"Maybe it is," admitted Elnora, "to others; but it isn't very funny to me. And it won't be to Philip, or to mother."

That was very true. Mrs. Comstock had been slightly prepared for stringent action of some kind, by what Elnora had said. The mother instantly had guessed where the girl would go, but nothing was said to Philip. That would have been to invalidate Elnora's test in the beginning, and Mrs. Comstock knew her child well enough to know that she never would marry Philip unless she felt it right that she should. The only way was to find out, and Elnora had gone to seek the information. There was nothing to do but wait until she came back, and her mother was not in the least uneasy but that the girl would return brave and self-reliant, as always.

Philip Ammon hurried back to the Limberlost, strong in the hope that now he might take Elnora into his arms and receive her promise to become his wife. His first shock of disappointment came when he found her gone. In talking with Mrs. Comstock he learned that Edith Carr had made an opportunity to speak with Elnora alone. He hastened down the road to meet her, coming back alone, an agitated man. Then search revealed the notes. His read:

DEAR PHILIP:

I find that I am never going to be able to answer your question of this afternoon fairly to all of us, when you are with me. So I am going away a few weeks to think over matters alone. I shall not tell you, or even mother, where I am going, but I shall be safe, well cared for, and happy. Please go back home and live among your friends, just as you always have done, and on or before the first of September, I will write you where I am, and what I have decided. Please do not blame Edith Carr for this, and do not avoid her. I hope you will call on her and be friends. I think she is very sorry, and covets your friendship at least. Until September, then, as ever,

ELNORA.

Mrs. Comstock's note was much the same. Philip was ill with disappointment. In the arbour he laid his head on the table, among the implements of Elnora's loved work, and gulped down dry sobs he could not restrain. Mrs. Comstock never had liked him so well. Her hand involuntarily crept toward his dark head, then she drew back. Elnora would not want her to do anything whatever to influence him.

"What am I going to do to convince Edith Carr that I do not love her, and Elnora that I am hers?" he demanded.

"I guess you have to figure that out yourself," said Mrs. Comstock. "I'd be glad to help you if I could, but it seems to be up to you."

Philip sat a long time in silence. "Well, I have decided!" he said abruptly. "Are you perfectly sure Elnora had plenty of money and a safe place to go?"

"Absolutely!" answered Mrs. Comstock. "She has been taking care of herself ever since she was born, and she always has come out all right, so far; I'll stake all I'm worth on it, that she always will. I don't know where she is, but I'm not going to worry about her safety."

"I can't help worrying!" cried Philip. "I can think of fifty things that may happen to her when she thinks she is safe. This is distracting! First, I am going to run up to see my father. Then, I'll let you know what we have decided. Is there anything I can do for you?"

"Nothing!" said Mrs. Comstock.

But the desire to do something for him was so strong with her she scarcely could keep her lips closed or her hands quiet. She longed to tell him what Edith Carr had said, how it had affected Elnora, and to comfort him as she felt she could. But loyalty to the girl held her. If Elnora truly felt that she could not decide until Edith Carr was convinced, then Edith Carr would have to yield or triumph. It rested with Philip. So Mrs. Comstock kept silent, while Philip took the night limited, a bitterly disappointed man.

By noon the next day he was in his father's offices. They had a long conference, but did not arrive at much until the elder Ammon suggested sending for Polly. Anything that might have happened could be explained after Polly had told of the private conference between Edith and Elnora.

"Talk about lovely woman!" cried Philip Ammon. "One would think that after such a dose as Edith gave me, she would be satisfied to let me go my way, but no! Not caring for me enough herself to save me from public disgrace, she must now pursue me to keep any other woman from loving me. I call that too much! I am going to see her, and I want you to go with me, father."

"Very well," said Mr. Ammon, "I will go."

When Edith Carr came into her reception-room that afternoon, gowned for conquest, she expected only Philip, and him penitent. She came hurrying toward him, smiling, radiant, ready to use every allurement she possessed, and paused in dismay when she saw his cold face and his father. "Why, Phil!" she cried. "When did you come home?"

"I am not at home," answered Philip. "I merely ran up to see my father on business, and to inquire of you what it was you said to Miss Comstock yesterday that caused her to disappear before I could return to the Limberlost."

"Miss Comstock disappear! Impossible!" cried Edith Carr. "Where could she go?"

"I thought perhaps you could answer that, since it was through you that she went."

"Phil, I haven't the faintest idea where she is," said the girl gently.

"But you know perfectly why she went! Kindly tell me that."

"Let me see you alone, and I will."

"Here and now, or not at all."

"Phil!"

"What did you say to the girl I love?"

Then Edith Carr stretched out her arms.

"Phil, I am the girl you love!" she cried. "All your life you have loved me. Surely it cannot be all gone in a few weeks of misunderstanding. I was jealous of her! I did not want you to leave me an instant that night for any other girl living. That was the moth I was representing. Every one knew it! I wanted you to bring it to me. When you did not, I knew instantly it had been for her that you worked last summer, she who suggested my dress, she who had power to take you from me, when I wanted you most. The thought drove me mad, and I said and did those insane things. Phil, I beg your pardon! I ask your forgiveness. Yesterday she said that you had told her of me at once. She vowed both of you had been true to me and Phil, I couldn't look into her eyes and not see that it was the truth. Oh, Phil, if you understood how I have suffered you would forgive me. Phil, I never knew how much I cared for you! I will do anything—anything!"

"Then tell me what you said to Elnora yesterday that drove her, alone and friendless, into the night, heaven knows where!"

"You have no thought for any one save her?"

"Yes," said Philip. "I have. Because I once loved you, and believed in you, my heart aches for you. I will gladly forgive anything you ask. I will do anything you want, except to resume our former relations. That is impossible. It is hopeless and useless to ask it."

"You truly mean that!"

"Yes."

"Then find out from her what I said!"

"Come, father," said Philip, rising.

"You were going to show Miss Comstock's letter to Edith!" suggested Mr. Ammon.

"I have not the slightest interest in Miss Comstock's letter," said Edith Carr.

"You are not even interested in the fact that she says you are not responsible for her going, and that I am to call on you and be friends with you?"

"That is interesting, indeed!" sneered Miss Carr.

She took the letter, read, and returned it.

"She has done what she could for my cause, it seems," she said coldly. "How very generous of her! Do you propose calling out Pinkertons and instituting a general search?"

"No," replied Philip. "I simply propose to go back to the Limberlost and live with her mother, until Elnora becomes convinced that I am not courting you, and never shall be. Then, perhaps, she will come home to us. Good-bye. Good luck to you always!"

Chapter 24

Wherein Edith Carr Wages a Battle, and Hart Henderson Stands Guard

Many people looked, a few followed, when Edith Carr slowly came down the main street of Mackinac, pausing here and there to note the glow of colour in one small booth after another, overflowing with gay curios. That street of packed white sand, winding with the curves of the shore, outlined with brilliant shops, and thronged with laughing, bare-headed people in outing costumes was a picturesque and fascinating sight. Thousands annually made long journeys and paid exorbitant prices to take part in that pageant.

As Edith Carr passed, she was the most distinguished figure of the old street. Her clinging black gown was sufficiently elaborate for a dinner dress. On her head was a large, wide, drooping-brimmed black hat, with immense floating black plumes, while on the brim, and among the laces on her breast glowed velvety, deep red roses. Some way these made up for the lack of colour in her cheeks and lips, and while her eyes seemed unnaturally bright, to a close observer they appeared weary. Despite the effort she made to move lightly she was very tired, and dragged her heavy feet with an effort.

She turned at the little street leading to the dock, and went to meet the big lake steamer ploughing up the Straits from Chicago. Past the landing place, on to the very end of the pier she went, then sat down, leaned against a dock support and closed her tired eyes. When the steamer came very close she languidly watched the people lining the railing. Instantly she marked one lean anxious face turned toward hers, and with a throb of pity she lifted a hand and waved to Hart Henderson. He was the first man to leave the boat, coming to her instantly. She spread her trailing skirts and motioned him to sit beside her. Silently they looked across the softly lapping water. At last she forced herself to speak to him.

"Did you have a successful trip?"

"I accomplished my purpose."

"You didn't lose any time getting back."

"I never do when I am coming to you."

"Do you want to go to the cottage for anything?"

"No."

"Then let us sit here and wait until the Petoskey steamer comes in. I like to watch the boats. Sometimes I study the faces, if I am not too tired."

"Have you seen any new types to-day?"

She shook her head. "This has not been an easy day, Hart."

"And it's going to be worse," said Henderson bitterly. "There's no use putting it off. Edith, I saw some one to-day."

"You should have seen thousands," she said lightly.

"I did. But of them all, only one will be of interest to you."

"Man or woman?"

"Man."

"Where?"

"Lake Shore private hospital."

"An accident?"

"No. Nervous and physical breakdown."

"Phil said he was going back to the Limberlost."

"He went. He was there three weeks, but the strain broke him. He has an old letter in his hands that he has handled until it is ragged. He held it up to me and said: 'You can see for yourself that she says she will be well and happy, but we can't know until we see her again, and that may never be. She may have gone too near that place her father went down, some of that Limberlost gang may have found her in the forest, she may lie dead in some city morgue this instant, waiting for me to find her body.'"

"Hart! For pity sake stop!"

"I can't," cried Henderson desperately. "I am forced to tell you. They are fighting brain fever. He did go back to the swamp and he prowled it night and day. The days down there are hot now, and the nights wet with dew and cold. He paid no attention and forgot his food. A fever started and his uncle brought him home. They've never had a word from her, or found a trace of her. Mrs. Comstock thought she had gone to O'Mores' at Great Rapids, so when Phil broke down she telegraphed there. They had been gone all summer, so her mother is as anxious as Phil."

"The O'Mores are here," said Edith. "I haven't seen any of them, because I haven't gone out much in the few days since we came, but this is their summer home."

"Edith, they say at the hospital that it will take careful nursing to save Phil. He is surrounded by stacks of maps and railroad guides. He is trying to frame up a plan to set the entire detective agency of the country to work. He says he will stay there just two days longer. The doctors say he will kill himself when he goes. He is a sick man, Edith. His hands are burning and shaky and his breath was hot against my face."

"Why are you telling me?" It was a cry of acute anguish.

"He thinks you know where she is."

"I do not! I haven't an idea! I never dreamed she would go away when she had him in her hand! I should not have done it!"

"He said it was something you said to her that made her go."

"That may be, but it doesn't prove that I know where she went."

Henderson looked across the water and suffered keenly. At last he turned to Edith and laid a firm, strong hand over hers.

"Edith," he said, "do you realize how serious this is?"

"I suppose I do."

"Do you want as fine a fellow as Philip driven any further? If he leaves that hospital now, and goes out to the exposure and anxiety of a search for her, there will be a tragedy that no after regrets can avert. Edith, what did you say to Miss Comstock that made her run away from Phil?"

The girl turned her face from him and sat still, but the man gripping her hands and waiting in agony could see that she was shaken by the jolting of the heart in her breast.

"Edith, what did you say?"

"What difference can it make?"

"It might furnish some clue to her action."

"It could not possibly."

"Phil thinks so. He has thought so until his brain is worn enough to give way. Tell me, Edith!"

"I told her Phil was mine! That if he were away from her an hour and back in my presence, he would be to me as he always has been."

"Edith, did you believe that?"

"I would have staked my life, my soul on it!"

"Do you believe it now?"

There was no answer. Henderson took her other hand and holding both of them firmly he said softly: "Don't mind me, dear. I don't count! I'm just old Hart! You can tell me anything. Do you still believe that?"

The beautiful head barely moved in negation. Henderson gathered both her hands in one of his and stretched an arm across her shoulders to the post to support her. She dragged her hands from him and twisted them together.

"Oh, Hart!" she cried. "It isn't fair! There is a limit! I have suffered my share. Can't you see? Can't you understand?"

"Yes," he panted. "Yes, my girl! Tell me just this one thing yet, and I'll cheerfully kill any one who annoys you further. Tell me, Edith!"

Then she lifted her big, dull, pain-filled eyes to his and cried: "No! I do not believe it now! I know it is not true! I killed his love for me. It is dead and gone forever. Nothing will revive it! Nothing in all this world. And that is not all. I did not know how to touch the depths of his nature. I never developed in him those things he was made to enjoy. He admired me. He was proud to be with me. He thought, and I thought, that he worshipped me; but I know now that he never did care for me as he cares for her. Never! I can see it! I planned to lead society, to make his home a place sought for my beauty and popularity. She plans to advance his political ambitions, to make him comfortable physically, to stimulate his intellect, to bear him a brood of red-faced children. He likes her and her plans as he never did me and mine. Oh, my soul! Now, are you satisfied?"

She dropped back against his arm exhausted. Henderson held her and learned what suffering truly means. He fanned her with his hat, rubbed her cold hands and murmured broken, incoherent things. By and by slow tears slipped from under her closed lids, but when she opened them her eyes were dull and hard.

"What a rag one is when the last secret of the soul is torn out and laid bare!" she cried.

Henderson thrust his handkerchief into her fingers and whispered, "Edith, the boat has been creeping up. It's very close. Maybe some of our crowd are on it. Hadn't we better slip away from here before it lands?"

"If I can walk," she said. "Oh, I am so dead tired, Hart!"

"Yes, dear," said Henderson soothingly. "Just try to pass the landing before the boat anchors. If I only dared carry you!"

They struggled through the waiting masses, but directly opposite the landing there was a backward movement in the happy, laughing crowd, the gang-plank came down with a slam, and people began hurrying from the boat. Crowded against the fish house on the dock, Henderson could only advance a few steps at a time. He was straining every nerve to protect and assist Edith. He saw no one he recognized near them, so he slipped his arm across her back to help support her. He felt her stiffen against him and catch her breath. At the same instant, the clearest, sweetest male voice he ever had heard called: "Be careful there, little men!"

Henderson sent a swift glance toward the boat. Terence O'More had stepped from the gang-plank, leading a little daughter, so like him, it was comical. There followed a picture not easy to describe. The Angel in the full flower of her beauty, richly dressed, a laugh on her cameo face, the setting sun glinting on her gold hair, escorted by her eldest son, who held her hand tightly and carefully watched her steps. Next came Elnora, dressed with equal richness, a trifle taller and slenderer, almost the same type of colouring, but with different eyes and hair, facial lines and expression. She was led by the second O'More boy who convulsed the crowd by saying: "Tareful, Elnora! Don't 'oo be 'teppin' in de water!"

People surged around them, purposely closing them in.

"What lovely women! Who are they? It's the O'Mores. The lightest one is his wife. Is that her sister? No, it is his! They say he has a title in England."

Whispers ran fast and audible. As the crowd pressed around the party an opening was left beside the fish sheds. Edith ran down the dock. Henderson sprang after her, catching her arm and assisting her to the street.

"Up the shore! This way!" she panted. "Every one will go to dinner the first thing they do."

They left the street and started around the beach, but Edith was breathless from running, while the yielding sand made difficult walking.

"Help me!" she cried, clinging to Henderson. He put his arm around her, almost carrying her from sight into a little cove walled by high rocks at the back, while there was a clean floor of white sand, and logs washed from the lake for seats. He found one of these with a back rest, and hurrying down to the water he soaked his handkerchief and carried it to her. She passed it across her lips, over her eyes, and then pressed the palms of her hands upon it. Henderson removed the heavy hat, fanned her with his, and wet the handkerchief again.

"Hart, what makes you?" she said wearily. "My mother doesn't care. She says this is good for me. Do you think this is good for me, Hart?"

"Edith, you know I would give my life if I could save you this," he said, and could not speak further.

She leaned against him, closed her eyes and lay silent so long the man fell into panic.

"Edith, you are not unconscious?" he whispered, touching her.

"No, just resting. Please don't leave me."

He held her carefully, gently fanning her. She was suffering almost more than either of them could endure.

"I wish you had your boat," she said at last. "I want to sail with the wind in my face."

"There is no wind. I can bring my motor around in a few minutes."

"Then get it."

"Lie on the sand. I can 'phone from the first booth. It won't take but a little while."

Edith lay on the white sand, and Henderson covered her face with her hat. Then he ran to the nearest booth and talked imperatively. Presently he was back bringing a hot drink that was stimulating. Shortly the motor ran close to the beach and stopped. Henderson's servant brought a row-boat ashore and took them to the launch. It was filled with cushions and wraps. Henderson made a couch and soon, warmly covered, Edith sped out over the water in search of peace.

Hour after hour the boat ran up and down the shore. The moon arose and the night air grew very chilly. Henderson put on an overcoat and piled more covers on Edith.

"You must take me home," she said at last. "The folks will be uneasy."

He was compelled to take her to the cottage with the battle still raging. He went back early the next morning, but already she had wandered out over the island. Instinctively Henderson felt that the shore would attract her. There was something in the tumult of rough little Huron's waves that called to him. It was there he found her, crouching so close the water the foam was dampening her skirts.

"May I stay?" he asked.

"I have been hoping you would come," she answered. "It's bad enough when you are here, but it is a little easier than bearing it alone."

"Thank God for that!" said Henderson sitting beside her. "Shall I talk to you?"

She shook her head. So they sat by the hour. At last she spoke: "Of course, you know there is something I have got to do, Hart!"

"You have not!" cried Henderson, violently. "That's all nonsense! Give me just one word of permission. That is all that is required of you."

"'Required?' You grant, then, that there is something 'required?'"

"One word. Nothing more."

"Did you ever know one word could be so big, so black, so desperately bitter? Oh, Hart!"

"No."

"But you know it now, Hart!"

"Yes."

"And still you say that it is 'required?'"

Henderson suffered unspeakably. At last he said: "If you had seen and heard him, Edith, you, too, would feel that it is 'required.' Remember—"

"No! No! No!" she cried. "Don't ask me to remember even the least of my pride and folly. Let me forget!"

She sat silent for a long time.

"Will you go with me?" she whispered.

"Of course."

At last she arose.

"I might as well give up and have it over," she faltered.

That was the first time in her life that Edith Carr ever had proposed to give up anything she wanted.

"Help me, Hart!"

Henderson started around the beach assisting her all he could. Finally he stopped.

"Edith, there is no sense in this! You are too tired to go. You know you can trust me. You wait in any of these lovely places and send me. You will be safe, and I'll run. One word is all that is necessary."

"But I've got to say that word myself, Hart!"

"Then write it, and let me carry it. The message is not going to prove who went to the office and sent it."

"That is quite true," she said, dropping wearily, but she made no movement to take the pen and paper he offered.

"Hart, you write it," she said at last.

Henderson turned away his face. He gripped the pen, while his breath sucked between his dry teeth.

"Certainly!" he said when he could speak. "Mackinac, August 27, 1908. Philip Ammon, Lake Shore Hospital, Chicago." He paused with suspended pen and glanced at Edith. Her white lips were working, but no sound came. "Miss Comstock is with the Terence O'Mores, on Mackinac Island," prompted Henderson.

Edith nodded.

"Signed, Henderson," continued the big man.

Edith shook her head.

"Say, 'She is well and happy,' and sign, Edith Carr!" she panted.

"Not on your life!" flashed Henderson.

"For the love of mercy, Hart, don't make this any harder! It is the least I can do, and it takes every ounce of strength in me to do it."

"Will you wait for me here?" he asked.

She nodded, and, pulling his hat lower over his eyes, Henderson ran around the shore. In less than an hour he was back. He helped her a little farther to where the Devil's Kitchen lay cut into the rocks; it furnished places to rest, and cool water. Before long his man came with the boat. From it they spread blankets on the sand for her, and made chafing-dish tea. She tried to refuse it, but the fragrance overcame her for she drank ravenously. Then Henderson cooked several dishes and spread an appetizing lunch. She was young, strong, and almost famished for food. She was forced to eat. That made her feel much better. Then Henderson helped her into the boat and ran it through shady coves of the shore, where there were refreshing breezes. When she fell asleep the girl did not know, but the man did. Sadly in need of rest himself, he ran that boat for five hours through quiet bays, away from noisy parties, and where the shade was cool and deep. When she awoke he took her home, and as they went she knew that she had been mistaken. She would not die. Her heart was not even broken. She had suffered horribly; she would suffer more; but eventually the pain must wear out. Into her head crept a few lines of an old opera:

> *"Hearts do not break, they sting and ache,*
> *For old love's sake, but do not die,*
> *As witnesseth the living I."*

That evening they were sailing down the Straits before a stiff breeze and Henderson was busy with the tiller when she said to him: "Hart, I want you to do something more for me."

"You have only to tell me," he said.

"Have I only to tell you, Hart?" she asked softly.

"Haven't you learned that yet, Edith?"

"I want you to go away."

"Very well," he said quietly, but his face whitened visibly.

"You say that as if you had been expecting it."

"I have. I knew from the beginning that when this was over you would dislike me for having seen you suffer. I have grown my Gethsemane in a full realization of what was coming, but I could not leave you, Edith, so long as it seemed to me that I was serving you. Does it make any difference to you where I go?"

"I want you where you will be loved, and good care taken of you."

"Thank you!" said Henderson, smiling grimly. "Have you any idea where such a spot might be found?"

"It should be with your sister at Los Angeles. She always has seemed very fond of you."

"That is quite true," said Henderson, his eyes brightening a little. "I will go to her. When shall I start?"

"At once."

Henderson began to tack for the landing, but his hands shook until he scarcely could manage the boat. Edith Carr sat watching him indifferently, but her heart was throbbing painfully. "Why is there so much suffering in the world?" she kept whispering to herself. Inside her door Henderson took her by the shoulders almost roughly.

"For how long is this, Edith, and how are you going to say good-bye to me?"

She raised tired, pain-filled eyes to his.

"I don't know for how long it is," she said. "It seems now as if it had been a slow eternity. I wish to my soul that God would be merciful to me and make something 'snap' in my heart, as there did in Phil's, that would give me rest. I don't know for how long, but I'm perfectly shameless with you, Hart. If peace ever comes and I want you, I won't wait for you to find it out yourself, I'll cable, Marconigraph, anything. As for how I say good-bye; any way you please, I don't care in the least what happens to me."

Henderson studied her intently.

"In that case, we will shake hands," he said. "Good-bye, Edith. Don't forget that every hour I am thinking of you and hoping all good things will come to you soon."

Chapter 25

Wherein Philip Finds Elnora, and Edith Carr Offers a Yellow Emperor

"Oh, I need my own violin," cried Elnora. "This one may be a thousand times more expensive, and much older than mine; but it wasn't inspired and taught to sing by a man who knew how. It doesn't know 'beans,' as mother would say, about the Limberlost."

The guests in the O'More music-room laughed appreciatively.

"Why don't you write your mother to come for a visit and bring yours?" suggested Freckles.

"I did that three days ago," acknowledged Elnora. "I am half expecting her on the noon boat. That is one reason why this violin grows worse every minute. There is nothing at all the matter with me."

"Splendid!" cried the Angel. "I've begged and begged her to do it. I know how anxious these mothers become. When did you send? What made you? Why didn't you tell me?"

"'When?' Three days ago. 'What made me?' You. 'Why didn't I tell you?' Because I can't be sure in the least that she will come. Mother is the most individual person. She never does what every one expects she will. She may not come, and I didn't want you to be disappointed."

"How did I make you?" asked the Angel.

"Loving Alice. It made me realize that if you cared for your girl like that, with Mr. O'More and three other children, possibly my mother, with no one, might like to see me. I know I want to see her, and you had told me to so often, I just sent for her. Oh, I do hope she comes! I want her to see this lovely place."

"I have been wondering what you thought of Mackinac," said Freckles.

"Oh, it is a perfect picture, all of it! I should like to hang it on the wall, so I could see it whenever I wanted to; but it isn't real, of course; it's nothing but a picture."

"These people won't agree with you," smiled Freckles.

"That isn't necessary," retorted Elnora. "They know this, and they love it; but you and I are acquainted with something different. The Limberlost is life. Here it is a carefully kept park. You motor, sail, and golf, all so secure and fine. But what I like is the excitement of choosing a path carefully, in the fear that the quagmire may reach out and suck me down; to go into the swamp naked-handed and wrest from it treasures that bring me books and clothing, and I like enough of a fight for things that I always remember how I got them. I even enjoy seeing a canny old vulture eyeing me as if it were saying: 'Ware the sting of the rattler, lest I pick your bones as I did old Limber's.' I like sufficient danger to put an edge on life. This is so tame. I should have loved it when all the homes were cabins, and watchers for the stealthy Indian canoes patrolled the shores. You wait until mother comes, and if my violin isn't angry with me for leaving it, to-night we shall sing you the Song of the Limberlost. You shall hear the big gold bees over the red, yellow, and purple flowers, bird song, wind talk, and the whispers of Sleepy Snake Creek, as it goes past you. You will know!" Elnora turned to Freckles.

He nodded. "Who better?" he asked. "This is secure while the children are so small, but when they grow larger, we are going farther north, into real forest, where they can learn self-reliance and develop backbone."

Elnora laid away the violin. "Come along, children," she said. "We must get at that backbone business at once. Let's race to the playhouse."

With the brood at her heels Elnora ran, and for an hour lively sounds stole from the remaining spot of forest on the Island, which lay beside the O'More cottage. Then Terry went to the playroom to bring Alice her doll. He came racing back, dragging it by one leg, and crying: "There's company! Someone has come that mamma and papa are just tearing down the house over. I saw through the window."

"It could not be my mother, yet," mused Elnora. "Her boat is not due until twelve. Terry, give Alice that doll—"

"It's a man-person, and I don't know him, but my father is shaking his hand right straight along, and my mother is running for a hot drink and a cushion. It's a kind of a sick person, but they are going to make him well right away, any one can see that. This is the best place."

"I'll go tell him to come lie on the pine needles in the sun and watch the sails go by. That will fix him!"

"Watch sails go by," chanted Little Brother. "'A fix him! Elnora fix him, won't you?"

"I don't know about that," answered Elnora. "What sort of person is he, Terry?"

"A beautiful white person; but my father is going to 'colour him up,' I heard him say so. He's just out of the hospital, and he is a bad person, 'cause he ran away from the doctors and made them awful angry. But father and mother are going to doctor him better. I didn't know they could make sick people well."

"'Ey do anyfing!" boasted Little Brother.

Before Elnora missed her, Alice, who had gone to investigate, came flying across the shadows and through the sunshine waving a paper. She thrust it into Elnora's hand.

"There is a man-person—a stranger-person!" she shouted. "But he knows you! He sent you that! You are to be the doctor! He said so! Oh, do hurry! I like him heaps!"

Elnora read Edith Carr's telegram to Philip Ammon and understood that he had been ill, that she had been located by Edith who had notified him. In so doing she had acknowledged defeat. At last Philip was free. Elnora looked up with a radiant face.

"I like him 'heaps' myself!" she cried. "Come on children, we will go tell him so."

Terry and Alice ran, but Elnora had to suit her steps to Little Brother, who was her loyal esquire, and would have been heartbroken over desertion and insulted at being carried. He was rather dragged, but he was arriving, and the emergency was great, he could see that.

"She's coming!" shouted Alice.

"She's going to be the doctor!" cried Terry.

"She looked just like she'd seen angels when she read the letter," explained Alice.

"She likes you 'heaps!' She said so!" danced Terry. "Be waiting! Here she is!"

Elnora helped Little Brother up the steps, then deserted him and came at a rush. The stranger-person stood holding out trembling arms.

"Are you sure, at last, runaway?" asked Philip Ammon.

"Perfectly sure!" cried Elnora.

"Will you marry me now?"

"This instant! That is, any time after the noon boat comes in."

"Why such unnecessary delay?" demanded Ammon.

"It is almost September," explained Elnora. "I sent for mother three days ago. We must wait until she comes, and we either have to send for Uncle Wesley and Aunt Margaret, or go to them. I couldn't possibly be married properly without those dear people."

"We will send," decided Ammon. "The trip will be a treat for them. O'More, would you get off a message at once?"

Every one met the noon boat. They went in the motor because Philip was too weak to walk so far. As soon as people could be distinguished at all Elnora and Philip sighted an erect figure, with a head like a snowdrift. When the gang-plank fell the first person across it was a lean, red-haired boy of eleven, carrying a violin in one hand and an enormous bouquet of yellow marigolds and purple asters in the other. He was beaming with broad smiles until he saw Philip. Then his expression changed.

"Aw, say!" he exclaimed reproachfully. "I bet you Aunt Margaret is right. He is going to be your beau!"

Elnora stooped to kiss Billy as she caught her mother.

"There, there!" cried Mrs. Comstock. "Don't knock my headgear into my eye. I'm not sure I've got either hat or hair. The wind blew like bizzem coming up the river."

She shook out her skirts, straightened her hat, and came forward to meet Philip, who took her into his arms and kissed her repeatedly. Then he passed her along to Freckles and the Angel to whom her greetings were mingled with scolding and laughter over her wind-blown hair.

"No doubt I'm a precious spectacle!" she said to the Angel. "I saw your pa a little before I started, and he sent you a note. It's in my satchel. He said he was coming up next week. What a lot of people there are in this world! And what on earth are all of them laughing about? Did none of them ever hear of sickness, or sorrow, or death? Billy, don't you go to playing Indian or chasing woodchucks until you get out of those clothes. I promised Margaret I'd bring back that suit good as new."

Then the O'More children came crowding to meet Elnora's mother.

"Merry Christmas!" cried Mrs. Comstock, gathering them in. "Got everything right here but the tree, and there seems to be plenty of them a little higher up. If this wind would stiffen just enough more to blow away the people, so one could see this place, I believe it would be right decent looking."

"See here," whispered Elnora to Philip. "You must fix this with Billy I can't have his trip spoiled."

"Now, here is where I dust the rest of 'em!" complacently remarked Mrs. Comstock, as she climbed into the motor car for her first ride, in company with Philip and Little Brother. "I have been the one to trudge the roads and hop out of the way of these things for quite a spell."

She sat very erect as the car rolled into the broad main avenue, where only stray couples were walking. Her eyes began to twinkle and gleam. Suddenly she leaned forward and touched the driver on the shoulder.

"Young man," she said, "just you toot that horn suddenly and shave close enough a few of those people, so that I can see how I look when I leap for ragweed and snake fences."

The amazed chauffeur glanced questioningly at Philip who slightly nodded. A second later there was a quick "honk!" and a swerve at a corner. A man engrossed in conversation grabbed the woman to whom he was talking and dashed for the safety of a lawn. The woman tripped in her skirts, and as she fell the man caught and dragged her. Both of them turned red faces to the car and berated the driver. Mrs. Comstock laughed in unrestrained enjoyment. Then she touched the chauffeur again.

"That's enough," she said. "It seems a mite risky." A minute later she added to Philip, "If only they had been carrying six pounds of butter and ten dozen eggs apiece, wouldn't that have been just perfect?"

Billy had wavered between Elnora and the motor, but his loyal little soul had been true to her, so the walk to the cottage began with him at her side. Long before they arrived the little O'Mores had crowded around and captured Billy, and he was giving them an expurgated version of Mrs. Comstock's tales of Big Foot and Adam Poe, boasting that Uncle Wesley had been in the camps of Me-shin-go-me-sia and knew Wa-ca-co-nah before he got religion and dressed like white men; while the mighty prowess of Snap as a woodchuck hunter was done full justice. When they reached the cottage Philip took Billy aside, showed him the emerald ring and gravely asked his permission to marry Elnora. Billy struggled to be just, but it was going hard with him, when Alice, who kept close enough to hear, intervened.

"Why don't you let them get married?" she asked. "You are much too small for her. You wait for me!"

Billy studied her intently. At last he turned to Ammon. "Aw, well! Go on, then!" he said gruffly. "I'll marry Alice!"

Alice reached her hand. "If you got that settled let's put on our Indian clothes, call the boys, and go to the playhouse."

"I haven't got any Indian clothes," said Billy ruefully.

"Yes, you have," explained Alice. "Father bought you some coming from the dock. You can put them on in the playhouse. The boys do."

Billy examined the playhouse with gleaming eyes.

Never had he encountered such possibilities. He could see a hundred amusing things to try, and he could not decide which to do first. The most immediate attraction seemed to be a dead pine, held perpendicularly by its fellows, while its bark had decayed and fallen, leaving a bare, smooth trunk.

"If we just had some grease that would make the dandiest pole to play Fourth of July with!" he shouted.

The children remembered the Fourth. It had been great fun.

"Butter is grease. There is plenty in the 'frigerator," suggested Alice, speeding away.

Billy caught the cold roll and began to rub it against the tree excitedly.

"How are you going to get it greased to the top?" inquired Terry.

Billy's face lengthened. "That's so!" he said. "The thing is to begin at the top and grease down. I'll show you!"

Billy put the butter in his handkerchief and took the corners between his teeth. He climbed the pole, greasing it as he slid down.

"Now, I got to try first," he said, "because I'm the biggest and so I have the best chance; only the one that goes first hasn't hardly any chance at all, because he has to wipe off the grease on himself, so the others can get up at last. See?"

"All right!" said Terry. "You go first and then I will and then Alice. Phew! It's slick. He'll never get up."

Billy wrestled manfully, and when he was exhausted he boosted Terry, and then both of them helped Alice, to whom they awarded a prize of her own doll. As they rested Billy remembered.

"Do your folks keep cows?" he asked.

"No, we buy milk," said Terry.

"Gee! Then what about the butter? Maybe your ma needs it for dinner!"

"No, she doesn't!" cried Alice. "There's stacks of it! I can have all the butter I want."

"Well, I'm mighty glad of it!" said Billy. "I didn't just think. I'm afraid we've greased our clothes, too."

"That's no difference," said Terry. "We can play what we please in these things."

"Well, we ought to be all dirty, and bloody, and have feathers on us to be real Indians," said Billy.

Alice tried a handful of dirt on her sleeve and it streaked beautifully. Instantly all of them began smearing themselves.

"If we only had feathers," lamented Billy.

Terry disappeared and shortly returned from the garage with a feather duster. Billy fell on it with a shriek. Around each one's head he firmly tied a twisted handkerchief, and stuck inside it a row of stiffly upstanding feathers.

"Now, if we just only had some pokeberries to paint us red, we'd be real, for sure enough Indians, and we could go on the warpath and fight all the other tribes and burn a lot of them at the stake."

Alice sidled up to him. "Would huckleberries do?" she asked softly.

"Yes!" shouted Terry, wild with excitement. "Anything that's a colour."

Alice made another trip to the refrigerator. Billy crushed the berries in his hands and smeared and streaked all their faces liberally.

"Now are we ready?" asked Alice.

Billy collapsed. "I forgot the ponies! You got to ride ponies to go on the warpath!"

"You ain't neither!" contradicted Terry. "It's the very latest style to go on the warpath in a motor. Everybody does! They go everywhere in them. They are much faster and better than any old ponies."

Billy gave one genuine whoop. "Can we take your motor?"

Terry hesitated.

"I suppose you are too little to run it?" said Billy.

"I am not!" flashed Terry. "I know how to start and stop it, and I drive lots for Stephens. It is hard to turn over the engine when you start."

"I'll turn it," volunteered Billy. "I'm strong as anything."

"Maybe it will start without. If Stephens has just been running it, sometimes it will. Come on, let's try."

Billy straightened up, lifted his chin and cried: "Houpe! Houpe! Houpe!"

The little O'Mores stared in amazement.

"Why don't you come on and whoop?" demanded Billy. "Don't you know how? You are great Indians! You got to whoop before you go on the warpath. You ought to kill a bat, too, and see if the wind is right. But maybe the engine won't run if we wait to do that. You can whoop, anyway. All together now!"

They did whoop, and after several efforts the cry satisfied Billy, so he led the way to the big motor, and took the front seat with Terry. Alice and Little Brother climbed into the back.

"Will it go?" asked Billy. "Or do we have to turn it?"

"It will go," said Terry as the machine gently slid out into the avenue and started under his guidance.

"This is no warpath!" scoffed Billy. "We got to go a lot faster than this, and we got to whoop. Alice, why don't you whoop?"

Alice arose, took hold of the seat in front and whooped.

"If I open the throttle, I can't squeeze the bulb to scare people out of our way," said Terry. "I can't steer and squeeze, too."

"We'll whoop enough to get them out of the way. Go faster!" urged Billy.

Billy also stood, lifted his chin and whooped like the wildest little savage that ever came out of the West. Alice and Little Brother added their voices, and when he was not absorbed with the steering gear, Terry joined in.

"Faster!" shouted Billy.

Intoxicated with the speed and excitement, Terry threw the throttle wider and the big car leaped forward and sped down the avenue. In it four black, feather-bedecked children whooped in wild glee until suddenly Terry's war cry changed to a scream of panic.

"The lake is coming!"

"Stop!" cried Billy. "Stop! Why don't you stop?"

Paralyzed with fear Terry clung to the steering gear and the car sped onward.

"You little fool! Why don't you stop?" screamed Billy, catching Terry's arm. "Tell me how to stop!"

A bicycle shot beside them and Freckles standing on the pedals shouted: "Pull out the pin in that little circle at your feet!"

Billy fell on his knees and tugged and the pin yielded at last. Just as the wheels struck the white sand the bicycle sheered close, Freckles caught the lever and with one strong shove set the brake. The water flew as the car struck Huron, but luckily it was shallow and the beach smooth. Hub deep the big motor stood quivering as Freckles climbed in and backed it to dry sand.

Then he drew a deep breath and stared at his brood.

"Terence, would you kindly be explaining?" he said at last.

Billy looked at the panting little figure of Terry.

"I guess I better," he said. "We were playing Indians on the warpath, and we hadn't any ponies, and Terry said it was all the style to go in automobiles now, so we—"

Freckles's head went back, and he did some whooping himself.

"I wonder if you realize how nearly you came to being four drowned children?" he said gravely, after a time.

"Oh, I think I could swim enough to get most of us out," said Billy. "Anyway, we need washing."

"You do indeed," said Freckles. "I will head this procession to the garage, and there we will remove the first coat." For the remainder of Billy's visit the nurse, chauffeur, and every servant of the O'More household had something of importance on their minds, and Billy's every step was shadowed.

"I have Billy's consent," said Philip to Elnora, "and all the other consent you have stipulated. Before you think of something more, give me your left hand, please."

Elnora gave it gladly, and the emerald slipped on her finger. Then they went together into the forest to tell each other all about it, and talk it over.

"Have you seen Edith?" asked Philip.

"No," answered Elnora. "But she must be here, or she may have seen me when we went to Petoskey a few days ago. Her people have a cottage over on the bluff, but the Angel never told me until to-day. I didn't want to make that trip, but the folks were so anxious to entertain me, and it was only a few days until I intended to let you know myself where I was."

"And I was going to wait just that long, and if I didn't hear then I was getting ready to turn over the country. I can scarcely realize yet that Edith sent me that telegram."

"No wonder! It's a difficult thing to believe. I can't express how I feel for her."

"Let us never speak of it again," said Philip. "I came nearer feeling sorry for her last night than I have yet. I couldn't sleep on that boat coming over, and I couldn't put away the thought of what sending that message cost her. I never would have believed it possible that she would do it. But it is done. We will forget it."

"I scarcely think I shall," said Elnora. "It is something I like to remember. How suffering must have changed her! I would give anything to bring her peace."

"Henderson came to see me at the hospital a few days ago. He's gone a rather wild pace, but if he had been held from youth by the love of a good woman he might have lived differently. There are things about him one cannot help admiring."

"I think he loves her," said Elnora softly.

"He does! He always has! He never made any secret of it. He will cut in now and do his level best, but he told me that he thought she would send him away. He understands her thoroughly."

Edith Carr did not understand herself. She went to her room after her good-bye to Henderson, lay on her bed and tried to think why she was suffering as she was.

"It is all my selfishness, my unrestrained temper, my pride in my looks, my ambition to be first," she said. "That is what has caused this trouble."

Then she went deeper.

"How does it happen that I am so selfish, that I never controlled my temper, that I thought beauty and social position the vital things of life?" she muttered. "I think that goes a little past me. I think a mother who allows a child to grow up as I did, who educates it only for the frivolities of life, has a share in that child's ending. I think my mother has some responsibility in this," Edith Carr whispered to the night. "But she will recognize none. She would laugh at me if I tried to tell her what I have suffered and the bitter, bitter lesson I have learned. No one really cares, but Hart. I've sent him away, so there is no one! No one!"

Edith pressed her fingers across her burning eyes and lay still.

"He is gone!" she whispered at last. "He would go at once. He would not see me again. I should think he never would want to see me any more. But I will want to see him! My soul! I want him now! I want him every minute! He is all I have. And I've sent him away. Oh, these dreadful days to come, alone! I can't bear it. Hart! Hart!" she cried aloud. "I want you! No one cares but you. No one understands but you. Oh, I want you!"

She sprang from her bed and felt her way to her desk.

"Get me some one at the Henderson cottage," she said to Central, and waited shivering.

"They don't answer."

"They are there! You must get them. Turn on the buzzer."

After a time the sleepy voice of Mrs. Henderson answered.

"Has Hart gone?" panted Edith Carr.

"No! He came in late and began to talk about starting to California. He hasn't slept in weeks to amount to anything. I put him to bed. There is time enough to start to California when he awakens. Edith, what are you planning to do next with that boy of mine?"

"Will you tell him I want to see him before he goes?"

"Yes, but I won't wake him."

"I don't want you to. Just tell him in the morning."

"Very well."

"You will be sure?"

"Sure!"

Hart was not gone. Edith fell asleep. She arose at noon the next day, took a cold bath, ate her breakfast, dressed carefully, and leaving word that she had gone to the forest, she walked slowly across the leaves. It was cool and quiet there, so she sat where she could see him coming, and waited. She was thinking deep and fast

Henderson came swiftly down the path. A long sleep, food, and Edith's message had done him good. He had dressed in new light flannels that were becoming. Edith arose and went to meet him.

"Let us walk in the forest," she said.

They passed the old Catholic graveyard, and entered the deepest wood of the Island, where all shadows were green, all voices of humanity ceased, and there was no sound save the whispering of the trees, a few bird notes and squirrel rustle. There Edith seated herself on a mossy old log, and Henderson studied her. He could detect a change. She was still pale and her eyes tired, but the dull, strained look was gone. He wanted to hope, but he did not dare. Any other man would have forced her to speak. The mighty tenderness in Henderson's heart shielded her in every way.

"What have you thought of that you wanted yet, Edith?" he asked lightly as he stretched himself at her feet.

"You!"

Henderson lay tense and very still.

"Well, I am here!"

"Thank Heaven for that!"

Henderson sat up suddenly, leaning toward her with questioning eyes. Not knowing what he dared say, afraid of the hope which found birth in his heart, he tried to shield her and at the same time to feel his way.

"I am more thankful than I can express that you feel so," he said. "I would be of use, of comfort, to you if I knew how, Edith."

"You are my only comfort," she said. "I tried to send you away. I thought I didn't want you. I thought I couldn't bear the sight of you, because of what you have seen me suffer. But I went to the root of this thing last night, Hart, and with self in mind, as usual, I found that I could not live without you."

Henderson began breathing lightly. He was afraid to speak or move.

"I faced the fact that all this is my own fault," continued Edith, "and came through my own selfishness. Then I went farther back and realized that I am as I was reared. I don't want to blame my parents, but I was carefully trained into what I am. If Elnora Comstock had been like me, Phil would have come back to me. I can see how selfish I seem to him, and how I appear to you, if you would admit it."

"Edith," said Henderson desperately, "there is no use to try to deceive you. You have known from the first that I found you wrong in this. But it's the first time in your life I ever thought you wrong about anything—and it's the only time I ever shall. Understand, I think you the bravest, most beautiful woman on earth, the one most worth loving."

"I'm not to be considered in the same class with her."

"I don't grant that, but if I did, you, must remember how I compare with Phil. He's my superior at every point. There's no use in discussing that. You wanted to see me, Edith. What did you want?"

"I wanted you to not go away."

"Not at all?"

"Not at all! Not ever! Not unless you take me with you, Hart."

She slightly extended one hand to him. Henderson took that hand, kissing it again and again.

"Anything you want, Edith," he said brokenly. "Just as you wish it. Do you want me to stay here, and go on as we have been?"

"Yes, only with a difference."

"Can you tell me, Edith?"

"First, I want you to know that you are the dearest thing on earth to me, right now. I would give up everything else, before I would you. I can't honestly say that I love you with the love you deserve. My heart is too sore. It's too soon to know. But I love you some way. You are necessary to me. You are my comfort, my shield. If you want me, as you know me to be, Hart, you may consider me yours. I give you my word of honour I will try to be as you would have me, just as soon as I can."

Henderson kissed her hand passionately. "Don't, Edith," he begged. "Don't say those things. I can't bear it. I understand. Everything will come right in time. Love like mine must bring a reward. You will love me some day. I can wait. I am the most patient fellow."

"But I must say it," cried Edith. "I—I think, Hart, that I have been on the wrong road to find happiness. I planned to finish life as I started it with Phil; and you see how glad he was to change. He wanted the other sort of girl far more than he ever wanted me. And you, Hart, honest, now—I'll know if you don't tell me the truth! Would you rather have a wife as I planned to live life with Phil, or would you rather have her as Elnora Comstock intends to live with him?"

"Edith!" cried the man, "Edith!"

"Of course, you can't say it in plain English," said the girl. "You are far too chivalrous for that. You needn't say anything. I am answered. If you could have your choice you wouldn't have a society wife, either. In your heart you'd like the smaller home of comfort, the furtherance of your ambitions, the palatable meals regularly served, and little children around you. I am sick of all we have grown up to, Hart. When your hour of trouble comes, there is no comfort for you. I am tired to death. You find out what you want to do, and he, that is a man's work in the world, and I will plan our home, with no thought save your comfort. I'll be the other kind of a girl, as fast as I can learn. I can't correct all my faults in one day, but I'll change as rapidly as I can."

"God knows, I will be different, too, Edith. You shall not be the only generous one. I will make all the rest of life worthy of you. I will change, too!"

"Don't you dare!" said Edith Carr, taking his head between her hands and holding it against her knees, while the tears slid down her cheeks. "Don't you dare change, you big-hearted, splendid lover! I am little and selfish. You are the very finest, just as you are!"

Henderson was not talking then, so they sat through a long silence. At last he heard Edith draw a quick breath, and lifting his head he looked where she pointed.

Up a fern stalk climbed a curious looking object. They watched breathlessly. By lavender feet clung a big, pursy, lavender-splotched, yellow body. Yellow and lavender wings began to expand and take on colour. Every instant great beauty became more apparent. It was one of those double-brooded freaks, which do occur on rare occasions, or merely an Eacles Imperialis moth that in the cool damp northern forest had failed to emerge in June. Edith Carr drew back with a long, shivering breath. Henderson caught her hands and gripped them firmly. Steadily she looked the thought of her heart into his eyes.

"By all the powers, you shall not!" swore the man. "You have done enough. I will smash that thing!"

"Oh no you won't!" cried the girl, clinging to his hands. "I am not big enough yet, Hart, but before I leave this forest I shall have grown to breadth and strength to carry that to her. She needs two of each kind. Phil only sent her one!"

"Edith I can't bear it! That's not demanded! Let me take it!"

"You may go with me. I know where the O'More cottage is. I have been there often."

"I'll say you sent it!"

"You may watch me deliver it!"

"Phil may be there by now."

"I hope he is! I should like him to see me do one decent thing by which to remember me."

"I tell you that is not necessary!"

"'Not necessary!'" cried the girl, her big eyes shining. "Not necessary? Then what on earth is the thing doing here? I just have boasted that I would change, that I would be like her, that I would grow bigger and broader. As the words are spoken God gives me the opportunity to prove whether I am sincere. This is my test, Hart! Don't you see it? If I am big enough to carry that to her, you will believe that there is some good in me. You will not be loving me in vain. This is an especial Providence, man! Be my strength! Help me, as you always have done!"

Henderson arose and shook the leaves from his clothing. He drew Edith Carr to her feet and carefully picked the mosses from her skirts. He went to the water and moistened his handkerchief to bathe her face.

"Now a dust of powder," he said when the tears were washed away.

From a tiny book Edith tore leaves that she passed over her face.

"All gone!" cried Henderson, critically studying her. "You look almost half as lovely as you really are!"

Edith Carr drew a wavering breath. She stretched one hand to him.

"Hold tight, Hart!" she said. "I know they handle these things, but I would quite as soon touch a snake."

Henderson clenched his teeth and held steadily. The moth had emerged too recently to be troublesome. It climbed on her fingers quietly and obligingly clung there without moving. So hand in hand they went down the dark forest path. When they came to the avenue, the first person they met paused with an ejaculation of wonder. The next stopped also, and every one following. They could make little progress on account of marvelling, interested people. A strange excitement took possession of Edith. She began to feel proud of the moth.

"Do you know," she said to Henderson, "this is growing easier every step. Its clinging is not disagreeable as I thought it would be. I feel as if I were saving it, protecting it. I am proud that we are taking it to be put into a collection or a book. It seems like doing a thing worth while. Oh, Hart, I wish we could work together at something for which people would care as they seem to for this. Hear what they say! See them lift their little children to look at it!"

"Edith, if you don't stop," said Henderson, "I will take you in my arms here on the avenue. You are adorable!"

"Don't you dare!" laughed Edith Carr. The colour rushed to her cheeks and a new light leaped in her eyes.

"Oh, Hart!" she cried. "Let's work! Let's do something! That's the way she makes people love her so. There's the place, and thank goodness, there is a crowd."

"You darling!" whispered Henderson as they passed up the walk. Her face was rose-flushed with excitement and her eyes shone.

"Hello, everyone!" she cried as she came on the wide veranda. "Only see what we found up in the forest! We thought you might like to have it for some of your collections."

She held out the moth as she walked straight to Elnora, who arose to meet her, crying: "How perfectly splendid! I don't even know how to begin to thank you."

Elnora took the moth. Edith shook hands with all of them and asked Philip if he were improving. She said a few polite words to Freckles and the Angel, declined to remain on account of an engagement, and went away, gracefully.

"Well bully for her!" said Mrs. Comstock. "She's a little thoroughbred after all!"

"That was a mighty big thing for her to be doing," said Freckles in a hushed voice.

"If you knew her as well as I do," said Philip Ammon, "you would have a better conception of what that cost."

"It was a terror!" cried the Angel. "I never could have done it."

"'Never could have done it!'" echoed Freckles. "Why, Angel, dear, that is the one thing of all the world you would have done!"

"I have to take care of this," faltered Elnora, hurrying toward the door to hide the tears which were rolling down her cheeks.

"I must help," said Philip, disappearing also. "Elnora," he called, catching up with her, "take me where I may cry, too. Wasn't she great?"

"Superb!" exclaimed Elnora. "I have no words. I feel so humbled!"

"So do I," said Philip. "I think a brave deed like that always makes one feel so. Now are you happy?"

"Unspeakably happy!" answered Elnora.

The Harvester

This portion of the life of a man of today is offered in the hope that in cleanliness, poetic temperament, and mental force, a likeness will be seen to Henry David Thoreau.

Contents

Chapter 1

Belshazzar's Decision

"Bel, come here!" The Harvester sat in the hollow worn in the hewed log stoop by the feet of his father and mother and his own sturdier tread, and rested his head against the casing of the cabin door when he gave the command. The tip of the dog's nose touched the gravel between his paws as he crouched flat on earth, with beautiful eyes steadily watching the master, but he did not move a muscle.

"Bel, come here!"

Twinkles flashed in the eyes of the man when he repeated the order, while his voice grew more imperative as he stretched a lean, wiry hand toward the dog. The animal's eyes gleamed and his sensitive nose quivered, yet he lay quietly.

"Belshazzar, kommen Sie hier!"

The body of the dog arose on straightened legs and his muzzle dropped in the outstretched palm. A wind slightly perfumed with the odour of melting snow and unsheathing buds swept the lake beside them, and lifted a waving tangle of light hair on the brow of the man, while a level ray of the setting sun flashed across the water and illumined the graven, sensitive face, now alive with keen interest in the game being played.

"Bel, dost remember the day?" inquired the Harvester.

The eager attitude and anxious eyes of the dog betrayed that he did not, but was waiting with every sense alert for a familiar word that would tell him what was expected.

"Surely you heard the killdeers crying in the night," prompted the man. "I called your attention when the ecstasy of the first bluebird waked the dawn. All day you have seen the gold-yellow and blood-red osiers, the sap-wet maples and spring tracing announcements of her arrival on the sunny side of the levee."

The dog found no clew, but he recognized tones he loved in the suave, easy voice, and his tail beat his sides in vigorous approval. The man nodded gravely.

"Ah, so! Then you realize this day to be the most important of all the coming year to me; this hour a solemn one that influences my whole after life. It is time for your annual decision on my fate for a twelve-month. Are you sure you are fully alive to the gravity of the situation, Bel?"

The dog felt himself safe in answering a rising inflection ending in his name uttered in that tone, and wagged eager assent.

"Well then," said the man, "which shall it be? Do I leave home for the noise and grime of the city, open an office and enter the money-making scramble?"

Every word was strange to the dog, almost breathlessly waiting for a familiar syllable. The man gazed steadily into the animal's eyes. After a long pause he continued:

"Or do I remain at home to harvest the golden seal, mullein, and ginseng, not to mention an occasional hour with the black bass or tramps for partridge and cotton-tails?"

The dog recognized each word of that. Before the voice ceased, his sleek sides were quivering, his nostrils twitching, his tail lashing, and at the pause he leaped up and thrust his nose against the face of the man. The Harvester leaned back laughing in deep, full-chested tones; then he patted the dog's head with one hand and renewed his grip with the other.

"Good old Bel!" he cried exultantly. "Six years you have decided for me, and right—every time! We are of the woods, Bel, born and reared here as our fathers before us. What would we of the camp fire, the long trail, the earthy search, we harvesters of herbs the famous chemists require, what would we do in a city? And when the sap is rising, the bass splashing, and the wild geese honking in the night! We never could endure it, Bel.

"When we delivered that hemlock at the hospital to-day, did you hear that young doctor talking about his 'lid'? Well up there is ours, old fellow! Just sky and clouds overhead for us, forest wind in our faces, wild perfume in our nostrils, muck on our feet, that's the life for us. Our blood was tainted to begin with, and we've lived here so long it is now a passion in our hearts. If ever you sentence us to life in the city, you'll finish both of us, that's what you'll do! But you won't, will you? You realize what God made us for and what He made for us, don't you, Bel?"

As he lovingly patted the dog's head the man talked and the animal trembled with delight. Then the voice of the Harvester changed and dropped to tones of gravest import.

"Now how about that other matter, Bel? You always decide that too. The time has come again. Steady now! This is far more important than the other. Just to be wiped out, Bel, pouf! That isn't anything and it concerns no one save ourselves.

But to bring misery into our lives and live with it daily, that would be a condition to rend the soul. So careful, Bel! Cautious now!"

The voice of the man dropped to a whisper as he asked the question.

"What about the girl business?"

Trembling with eagerness to do the thing that would bring more caressing, bewildered by unfamiliar words and tones, the dog hesitated.

"Do I go on as I have ever since mother left me, rustling for grub, living in untrammelled freedom? Do I go on as before, Bel?"

The Harvester paused and waited the answer, with anxiety in his eyes as he searched the beast face. He had talked to that dog, as most men commune with their souls, for so long and played the game in such intense earnest that he felt the results final with him. The animal was immovable now, lost again, his anxious eyes watching the face of the master, his eager ears waiting for words he recognized. After a long time the man continued slowly and hesitantly, as if fearing the out-come. He did not realize that there was sufficient anxiety in his voice to change its tones.

"Or do I go courting this year? Do I rig up in uncomfortable store-clothes, and parade before the country and city girls and try to persuade the one I can get, probably—not the one I would want—to marry me, and come here and spoil all our good times? Do we want a woman around scolding if we are away from home, whining because she is lonesome, fretting for luxuries we cannot afford to give her? Are you going to let us in for a scrape like that, Bel?"

The bewildered dog could bear the unusual scene no longer. Taking the rising inflection, that sounded more familiar, for a cue, and his name for a certainty, he sprang forward, his tail waving as his nose touched the face of the Harvester. Then he shot across the driveway and lay in the spice thicket, half the ribs of one side aching, as he howled from the lowest depths of dog misery.

"You ungrateful cur!" cried the Harvester. "What has come over you? Six years I have trusted you, and the answer has been right, every time! Confound your picture! Sentence me to tackle the girl proposition! I see myself! Do you know what it would mean? For the first thing you'd be chained, while I pranced over the country like a half-broken colt, trying to attract some girl. I'd have to waste time I need for my work and spend money that draws good interest while we sleep, to tempt her with presents. I'd have to rebuild the cabin and there's not a chance in ten she would not fret the life out of me whining to go to the city to live, arrange for her here the best I could. Of all the fool, unreliable dogs that ever trod a man's tracks, you are the limit! And you never before failed me! You blame, degenerate pup, you!"

The Harvester paused for breath and the dog subsided to a pitiful whimper. He was eager to return to the man who had struck him the first blow his pampered body ever had received; but he could not understand a kick and harsh words for him, so he lay quivering with anxiety and fear.

"You howling, whimpering idiot!" exclaimed the Harvester. "Choose a day like this to spoil! Air to intoxicate a mummy! Roots swelling! Buds bursting! Harvest close and you'd call me off and put me at work like that, would you? If I ever had supposed lost all your senses, I never would have asked you. Six years you have decided my fate, when the first bluebird came, and you've been true blue every time. If I ever trust you again! But the mischief is done now.

"Have you forgotten that your name means 'to protect'? Don't you remember it is because of that, it is your name? Protect! I'd have trusted you with my life, Bell! You gave it to me the time you pointed that rattler within six inches of my fingers in the blood-root bed. You saw the falling limb in time to warn me. You always know where the quicksands lie. But you are protecting me now, like sin, ain't you? Bring a girl here to spoil both our lives! Not if I know myself! Protect!"

The man arose and going inside the cabin closed the door. After that the dog lay in abject misery so deep that two big tears squeezed from his eyes and rolled down his face. To be shut out was worse than the blow. He did not take the trouble to arise from the wet leaves covering the cold earth, but closing his eyes went to sleep.

The man leaned against the door and ran his fingers through his hair as he anathematized the dog. Slowly his eyes travelled around the room. He saw his tumbled bed by the open window facing the lake, the small table with his writing material, the crude rack on the wall loaded with medical works, botanies, drug encyclopaedias, the books of the few authors who interested him, and the bare, muck-tracked floor. He went to the kitchen, where he built a fire in the cook stove, and to the smoke-house, from which he returned with a slice of ham and some eggs. He set some potatoes boiling and took bread, butter and milk from the pantry. Then he laid a small note-book on the table before him and studied the transactions of the day.

"Not so bad," he muttered, bending over the figures. "I wonder if any of my neighbours who harvest the fields average as well at this season. I'll wager they don't. That's pretty fair! Some days I don't make it, and then when a consignment of seeds go or ginseng is wanted the cash comes in right properly. I could waste half of it on a girl and yet save money. But where is the woman who would be content with half? She'd want all and fret because there wasn't more. Blame that dog!"

10 lbs.	wild cherry bark	6 cents	$.60
5 "	wahoo root bark	25 "	1.25
20 "	witch hazel bark	5 "	1.00
5 "	blue flag root	12 "	.60
10 "	snake root	18 "	1.80
10 "	blood root	12 "	1.20
15 "	hoarhound	10 "	1.50
			$7.95

He put the book in his pocket, prepared and ate his supper, heaped a plate generously, placed it on the floor beneath the table, and set away the food that remained.

"Not that you deserve it," he said to space. "You get this in honour of your distinguished name and the faithfulness with which you formerly have lived up to its import. If you hadn't been a dog with more sense than some men, I wouldn't take your going back on me now so hard. One would think an animal of your intelligence might realize that you would get as much of a dose as I. Would she permit you to eat from a plate on the kitchen floor? Not on your life, Belshazzar! Frozen scraps around the door for you! Would she allow you to sleep across the foot of the bed? Ho, ho, ho! Would she have you tracking on her floor? It would be the barn, and growling you didn't do at that. If I'd serve you right, I'd give you a dose and allow you to see how you like it. But it's cutting off my nose to spite my face, as the old adage goes, for whatever she did to a dog, she'd probably do worse to a man. I think not!"

He entered the front room and stood before a long shelf on which were arranged an array of partially completed candlesticks carved from wood. There were black and white walnut, red, white, and golden oak, cherry and curly maple, all in original designs. Some of them were oddities, others were failures, but most of them were unusually successful. He selected one of black walnut, carved until the outline of his pattern was barely distinguishable. He was imitating the trunk of a tree with the bark on, the spreading, fern-covered roots widening for the base, from which a vine sprang. Near the top was the crude outline of a big night moth climbing toward the light. He stood turning this stick with loving hands and holding it from him for inspection.

"I am going to master you!" he exulted. "Your lines are right. The design balances and it's graceful. If I have any trouble it will be with the moth, and I think I can manage. I've got to decide whether to use cecropia or polyphemus before long. Really, on a walnut, and in the woods, it should be a luna, according to the eternal fitness of things—but I'm afraid of the trailers. They turn over and half curl and I believe I had better not tackle them for a start. I'll use the easiest to begin on, and if I succeed I'll duplicate the pattern and try a luna then. The beauties!"

The Harvester selected a knife from the box and began carving the stick slowly and carefully. His brain was busy, for presently he glanced at the floor.

"She'd object to that!" he said emphatically. "A man could no more sit and work where he pleased than he could fly. At least I know mother never would have it, and she was no nagger, either. What a mother she was! If one only could stop the lonely feeling that will creep in, and the aching hunger born with the body, for a mate; if a fellow only could stop it with a woman like mother! How she revelled in sunshine and beauty! How she loved earth and air! How she went straight to the marrow of the finest line in the best book I could bring from the library! How clean and true she was and how unyielding! I can hear her now, holding me with her last breath to my promise. If I could marry a girl like mother—great Caesar! You'd see me buying an automobile to make the run to the county clerk. Wouldn't that be great! Think of coming in from a long, difficult day, to find a hot supper, and a girl such as she must have been, waiting for me! Bel, if I thought there was a woman similar to her in all the world, and I had even the ghost of a chance to win her, I'd call you in and forgive you. But I know the girls of to-day. I pass them on the roads, on the streets, see them in the cafe's, stores, and at the library. Why even the nurses at the hospital, for all the gravity of their positions, are a giggling, silly lot; and they never know that the only time they look and act presentably to me is when they stop their chatter, put on their uniforms, and go to work. Some of them are pretty, then. There's a little blue-eyed one, but all she needs is feathers to make her a 'ha! ha! bird.' Drat that dog!"

The Harvester took the candlestick and the box of knives, opened the door, and returned to the stoop. Belshazzar arose, pleading in his eyes, and cautiously advanced a few steps. The man bent over his work and paid not the slightest heed, so the discouraged dog sank to earth and fixedly watched the unresponsive master. The carving of the candlestick went on steadily. Occasionally the Harvester lifted his head and repeatedly sucked his lungs full of air. Sometimes for an instant he scanned the surface of the lake for signs of breaking fish or splash of migrant water bird. Again his gaze wandered up the steep hill, crowned with giant trees, whose swelling buds he could see and smell. Straight before him lay a low marsh, through which the little creek that gurgled and tumbled down hill curved, crossed the drive some distance below, and entered the lake of Lost Loons.

While the trees were bare, and when the air was clear as now, he could see the spires of Onabasha, five miles away, intervening cultivated fields, stretches of wood, the long black line of the railway, and the swampy bottom lands gradually rising to the culmination of the tree-crowned summit above him. His cocks were crowing warlike challenges to rivals on neighbouring farms. His hens were carolling their spring egg-song. In the barn yard ganders were screaming stridently. Over the lake and the cabin, with clapping snowy wings, his white doves circled in a last joy-flight before seeking their cotes in the stable loft. As the light grew fainter, the Harvester worked slower. Often he leaned against the casing, and closed his eyes to rest them. Sometimes he whistled snatches of old songs to which his mother had cradled him, and again bits of opera and popular music he had heard on the streets of Onabasha. As he worked, the sun went down and a half moon appeared above the wood across the lake. Once it seemed as if it were a silver bowl set on the branch of a giant oak; higher, it rested a tilted crescent on the rim of a cloud.

The dog waited until he could endure it no longer, and straightening from his crouching position, he took a few velvet steps forward, making faint, whining sounds in his throat. When the man neither turned his head nor gave him a glance, Belshazzar sank to earth again, satisfied for the moment with being a little closer. Across Loon Lake came the wavering voice of a night love song. The Harvester remembered that as a boy he had shrunk from those notes until his mother explained that they were made by a little brown owl asking for a mate to come and live in his hollow tree. Now he rather liked the sound. It was eloquent of earnest pleading. With the lonely bird on one side, and the reproachful dog eyes on the other, the man grinned rather foolishly.

Between two fires, he thought. If that dog ever catches my eye he will come tearing as a cyclone, and I would not kick him again for a hundred dollars. First time I ever struck him, and didn't intend to then. So blame mad and disappointed my foot just shot out before I knew it. There he lies half dead to make up, but I'm blest if I forgive him in a hurry. And there is that insane little owl screeching for a mate. If I'd start out making sounds like that, all the girls would line up and compete for possession of my happy home.

The Harvester laughed and at the sound Belshazzar took courage and advanced five steps before he sank belly to earth again. The owl continued its song. The Harvester imitated the cry and at once it responded. He called again and leaned back waiting. The notes came closer. The Harvester cried once more and peered across the lake, watching for the shadow of silent wings. The moon was high above the trees now, the knife dropped in the box, the long fingers closed around the stick, the head rested against the casing, and the man intoned the cry with all his skill, and then watched and waited. He had been straining his eyes over the carving until they were tired, and when he watched for the bird the moonlight tried them; for it touched the lightly rippling waves of the lake in a line of yellow light that stretched straight across the water from the opposite bank, directly to the gravel bed below, where lay the bathing pool. It made a path of gold that wavered and shimmered as the water moved gently, but it appeared sufficiently material to resemble a bridge spanning the lake.

"Seems as if I could walk it," muttered the Harvester.

The owl cried again and the man intently watched the opposite bank. He could not see the bird, but in the deep wood where he thought it might be he began to discern a misty, moving shimmer of white. Marvelling, he watched closer. So slowly he could not detect motion it advanced, rising in height and taking shape.

"Do I end this day by seeing a ghost?" he queried.

He gazed intently and saw that a white figure really moved in the woods of the opposite bank.

"Must be some boys playing fool pranks!" exclaimed the Harvester.

He watched fixedly with interested face, and then amazement wiped out all other expression and he sat motionless, breathless, looking, intently looking. For the white object came straight toward the water and at the very edge unhesitatingly stepped upon the bridge of gold and lightly, easily advanced in his direction. The man waited. On came the figure and as it drew closer he could see that it was a very tall, extremely slender woman, wrapped in soft robes of white. She stepped along the slender line of the gold bridge with grace unequalled.

From the water arose a shining mist, and behind the advancing figure a wall of light outlined and rimmed her in a setting of gold. As she neared the shore the Harvester's blood began to race in his veins and his lips parted in wonder. First she was like a slender birch trunk, then she resembled a wild lily, and soon she was close enough to prove that she was young and very lovely. Heavy braids of dark hair rested on her head as a coronet. Her forehead was low and white. Her eyes were wide-open wells of darkness, her rounded cheeks faintly pink, and her red lips smiling invitation. Her throat was long, very white, and the hands that caught up the fleecy robe around her were rose-coloured and slender. In a panic the Harvester saw that the trailing robe swept the undulant gold water, but was not wet; the feet that alternately showed as she advanced were not purple with cold, but warm with a pink glow.

She was coming straight toward him, wonderful, alluring, lovely beyond any woman the Harvester ever had seen. Straightway the fountains of twenty-six years' repression overflowed in the breast of the man and all his being ran toward her in a wave of desire. On she came, and now her tender feet were on the white gravel. When he could see clearly she was even more beautiful than she had appeared at a distance. He opened his lips, but no sound came. He struggled to rise, but his legs would not bear his weight. Helpless, he sank against the casing. The girl walked to his feet, bent, placed a hand on each of his shoulders, and smiled into his eyes. He could scent the flower-like odour of her body and wrapping, even her hair. He struggled frantically to speak to her as she leaned closer, yet closer, and softly but firmly laid lips of pulsing sweetness on his in a deliberate kiss.

The Harvester was on his feet now. Belshazzar shrank into the shadows.

"Come back!" cried the man. "Come back! For the love of mercy, where are you?"

He ran stumblingly toward the lake. The bridge of gold was there, the little owl cried lonesomely; and did he see or did he only dream he saw a mist of white vanishing in the opposite wood?

His breath came between dry lips, and he circled the cabin searching eagerly, but he could find nothing, hear nothing, save the dog at his heels. He hurried to the stoop and stood gazing at the molten path of moonlight. One minute he was half frozen, the next a rosy glow enfolded him. Slowly he lifted a hand and touched his lips. Then he raised his eyes from the water and swept the sky in a penetrant gaze.

"My gracious Heavenly Father," said the Harvester reverently. "Would it be like that?"

Chapter 2

The Effect of a Dream

.

Fully convinced at last that he had been dreaming, the Harvester picked up his knives and candlestick and entered the cabin. He placed them on a shelf and turned away, but after a second's hesitation he closed the box and arranged the sticks neatly. Then he set the room in order and carefully swept the floor. As he replaced the broom he thought for an instant, then opened the door and whistled softly. Belshazzar came at a rush. The Harvester pushed the plate of food toward the hungry dog and he ate greedily. The man returned to the front room and closed the door.

He stood a long time before his shelf of books, at last selected a volume of "Medicinal Plants" and settled to study. His supper finished, Belshazzar came scratching and whining at the door. Several times the man lifted his head and glanced in that direction, but he only returned to his book and read again. Tired and sleepy, at last, he placed the volume on the shelf, went to a closet for a pair of bath towels, and hung them across a chair. Then he undressed, opened the door, and ran for the lake. He plunged with a splash and swam vigorously for a few minutes, his white body growing pink under the sting of the chilled water. Over and over he scanned the golden bridge to the moon, and stood an instant dripping on the gravel of the landing to make sure that no dream woman was crossing the wavering floor! He rubbed to a glow and turned back the covers of his bed. The door and window stood wide. Before he lay down, the Harvester paused in arrested motion a second, then stepped to the kitchen door and lifted the latch.

As the man drew the covers over him, the dog's nose began making an opening, and a little later he quietly walked into the room. The Harvester rested, facing the lake. The dog sniffed at his shoulder, but the man was rigid. Then the click of nails could be heard on the floor as Belshazzar went to the opposite side. At his accustomed place he paused and set one foot on the bed. There was not a sound, so he lifted the other. Then one at a time he drew up his hind feet and crouched as he had on the gravel. The man lay watching the bright bridge. The moonlight entered the window and flooded the room. The strong lines on the weather-beaten face of the Harvester were mellowed in the light, and he appeared young and good to see. His lithe figure stretched the length of the bed, his hair appeared almost white, and his face, touched by the glorifying light of the moon, was a study.

One instant his countenance was swept with ultimate scorn; then gradually that would fade and the lines soften, until his lips curved in child-like appeal and his eyes were filled with pleading. Several times he lifted a hand and gently touched his lips, as if a kiss were a material thing and would leave tangible evidence of having been given. After a long time his eyes closed and he scarcely was unconscious before Belshazzar's cold nose touched the outstretched hand and the Harvester lifted and laid it on the dog's head.

"Forgive me, Bel," he muttered. "I never did that. I wouldn't have hurt you for anything. It happened before I had time to think."

They both fell asleep. The clear-cut lines of manly strength on the face of the Harvester were touched to tender beauty. He lay smiling softly. Far in the night he realized the frost-chill and divided the coverlet with the happy Belshazzar.

The golden dream never came again. There was no need. It had done its perfect work. The Harvester awoke the next morning a different man. His face was youthful and alive with alert anticipation. He began his work with eager impetuosity, whistling and singing the while, and he found time to play with and talk to Belshazzar, until that glad beast almost wagged off his tail in delight. They breakfasted together and arranged the rooms with unusual care.

"You see," explained the Harvester to the dog, "we must walk neatly after this. Maybe there is such a thing as fate. Possibly your answer was right. There might be a girl in the world for me. I don't expect it, but there is a possibility that she may find us before we locate her. Anyway, we should work and be ready. All the old stock in the store-house goes out as soon as we can cart it. A new cabin shall rise as fast as we can build it. There must be a basement and furnace, too. Dream women don't have cold feet, but if there is a girl living like that, and she is coming to us or waiting for us to come to her, we must have a comfortable home to offer. There should be a bathroom, too. She couldn't dip in the lake as we do. And until we build the new house we must keep the old one clean, just on the chance of her happening on us. She might be visiting some of the neighbours or come from town with some one or I might see her on the street or at the library or hospital or in some of the stores. For the love of mercy, help me watch for her, Bel! The half of my kingdom if you will point her for me!"

The Harvester worked as he talked. He set the rooms in order, put away the remains of breakfast, and started to the stable. He turned back and stood for a long time, scanning the face in the kitchen mirror. Once he went to the door, then he hesitated, and finally took out his shaving set and used it carefully and washed vigorously. He pulled his shirt together at the throat, and hunting among his clothing, found an old red tie that he knotted around his neck. This so changed his every-day appearance that he felt wonderfully dressed and whistled gaily on his way to the barn. There he confided in the old gray mare as he curried and harnessed her to the spring wagon.

"Hardly know me, do you, Betsy?" he inquired. "Well, I'll explain. Our friend Bel, here, has doomed me to go courting this year. Wouldn't that durnfound you? I was mad as hornets at first, but since I've slept on the idea, I rather like it. Maybe we are too lonely and dull. Perhaps the right woman would make life a very different matter. Last night I saw her, Betsy, and between us, I can't tell even you. She was the loveliest, sweetest girl on earth, and that is all I can say. We are going to watch for her to-day, and every trip we make, until we find her, if it requires a hundred years. Then some glad time we are going to locate her, and when we do, well, you just keep your eye on us, Betsy, and you'll see how courting straight from the heart is done, even if we lack experience."

Intoxicated with new and delightful sensations his tongue worked faster than his hands.

"I don't mind telling you, old faithful, that I am in love this morning," he said. "In love heels over, Betsy, for the first time in all my life. If any man ever was a bigger fool than I am to-day, it would comfort me to know about it. I am acting like an idiot, Betsy. I know that, but I wish you could understand how I feel. Power! I am the head-waters of Niagara! I could pluck down the stars and set them in different places! I could twist the tail from the comet! I could twirl the globe on my palm and topple mountains and wipe lakes from the surface! I am a live man, Betsy. Existence is over. So don't you go at any tricks or I might pull off your head. Betsy, if you see the tallest girl you ever saw, and she wears a dark diadem, and has big black eyes and a face so lovely it blinds you, why you have seen Her, and you balk, right on the spot, and stand like the rock of Gibraltar, until you make me see her, too. As if I wouldn't know she was coming a mile away! There's more I could tell you, but that is my secret, and it's too precious to talk about, even to my best friends. Bel, bring Betsy to the store-room."

The Harvester tossed the hitching strap to the dog and walked down the driveway to a low structure built on the embankment beside the lake. One end of it was a dry-house of his own construction. Here, by an arrangement of hot water pipes, he evaporated many of the barks, roots, seeds, and leaves he grew to supply large concerns engaged in the manufacture of drugs. By his process crude stock was thoroughly cured, yet did not lose in weight and colour as when dried in the sun or outdoor shade.

So the Harvester was enabled to send his customers big packages of brightly coloured raw material, and the few cents per pound he asked in advance of the catalogued prices were paid eagerly. He lived alone, and never talked of his work; so none of the harvesters of the fields adjoining dreamed of the extent of his reaping. The idea had been his own. He had been born in the cabin in which he now lived. His father and grandfather were old-time hunters of skins and game. They had added to their earnings by gathering in spring and fall the few medicinal seeds, leaves, and barks they knew. His mother had been of different type. She had loved and married the picturesque young hunter, and gone to live with him on the section of land taken by his father. She found life, real life, vastly different from her girlhood dreams, but she was one of those changeless, unyielding women who suffer silently, but never rue a bargain, no matter how badly they are cheated. Her only joy in life had been her son. For him she had worked and saved unceasingly, and when he was old enough she sent him to the city to school and kept pace with him in the lessons he brought home at night.

Using what she knew of her husband's work as a guide, and profiting by pamphlets published by the government, every hour of the time outside school and in summer vacations she worked in the woods with the boy, gathering herbs and roots to pay for his education and clothing. So the son passed the full high-school course, and then, selecting such branches as interested him, continued his studies alone.

From books and drug pamphlets he had learned every medicinal plant, shrub, and tree of his vicinity, and for years roamed far afield and through the woods collecting. After his father's death expenses grew heavier and the boy saw that he must earn more money. His mother frantically opposed his going to the city, so he thought out the plan of transplanting the stuff he gathered, to the land they owned and cultivating it there. This work was well developed when he was twenty, but that year he lost his mother.

From that time he went on steadily enlarging his species, transplanting trees, shrubs, vines, and medicinal herbs from such locations as he found them to similar conditions on his land. Six years he had worked cultivating these beds, and hunting through the woods on the river banks, government land, the great Limberlost Swamp, and neglected corners of earth for barks and roots. He occasionally made long trips across the country for rapidly diminishing plants he found in the woodland of men who did not care to bother with a few specimens, and many big beds of profitable herbs, extinct for miles around, now flourished on the banks of Loon Lake, in the marsh, and through the forest rising above. To what extent and value his venture had grown, no one save the Harvester knew. When his neighbours twitted him with being too lazy to plow and sow, of "mooning" over books, and derisively sneered when they spoke of him as the Harvester of the Woods or the Medicine Man, David Langston smiled and went his way.

How lonely he had been since the death of his mother he never realized until that morning when a new idea really had taken possession of him. From the store-house he heaped packages of seeds, dried leaves, barks, and roots into the wagon. But he kept a generous supply of each, for he prided himself on being able to fill all orders that reached him. Yet the load he took to the city was much larger than usual. As he drove down the hill and passed the cabin he studied the location.

"The drainage is perfect," he said to Belshazzar beside him on the seat. "So is the situation. We get the cool breezes from the lake in summer and the hillside warmth in winter. View down the valley can't be surpassed. We will grub out that thicket in front, move over the driveway, and build a couple of two-story rooms, with basement for cellar and furnace, and a bathroom in front of the cabin and use it with some fixing over for a dining-room and kitchen. Then we will deepen and widen Singing Water, stick a bushel of bulbs and roots and sow a peck of flower seeds in the marsh, plant a hedge along the drive, and straighten the lake shore a little. I can make a beautiful wild-flower garden and arrange so that with one season's work this will appear very well. We will express this stuff and then select and fell some trees to-night. Soon as the frost is out of the ground we will dig our basement and lay the foundations. The neighbours will help me raise the logs; after that I can finish the inside work. I've got some dried maple, cherry, and walnut logs that would work into beautiful furniture. I haven't forgotten the prices McLean offered me. I can use it as well as he. Plain way the best things are built now, I believe I could make tables and couches myself. I can see plans in the magazines at the library. I'll take a look when I get this off. I feel strong enough to do all of it in a few days and I am crazy to commence. But I scarcely know where to begin. There are about fifty things I'd like to do. But to fell and dry the trees and get the walls up come first, I believe. What do you think, old unreliable?"

Belshazzar thought the world was a place of beauty that morning. He sniffed the icy, odorous air and with tilted head watched the birds. A wearied band of ducks had settled on Loon Lake to feed and rest, for there was nothing to disturb them. Signs were numerous everywhere prohibiting hunters from firing over the Harvester's land. Beside the lake, down the valley, crossing the railroad, and in the farther lowlands, the dog was a nervous quiver, as he constantly scented game or saw birds he wanted to point. But when they neared the city, he sat silently watching everything with alert eyes. As they reached the outer fringe of residences the Harvester spoke to him.

"Now remember, Bel," he said. "Point me the tallest girl you ever saw, with a big braid of dark hair, shining black eyes, and red velvet lips, sweeter than wild crab apple blossoms. Make a dead set! Don't allow her to pass us. Heaven is going to begin in Medicine Woods when we find her and prove to her that there lies her happy home.

"When we find her," repeated the Harvester softly and exultantly. "When we find her!"

He said it again and again, pronouncing the words with tender modulations. Because he was chanting it in his soul, in his heart, in his brain, with his lips, he had a hasty glance for every woman he passed. Light hair, blue eyes, and short figures got only casual inspection: but any tall girl with dark hair and eyes endured rather close scrutiny that morning. He drove to the express office and delivered his packages and then to the hospital. In the hall the blue-eyed nurse met him and cried gaily, "Good morning, Medicine Man!"

"Ugh! I scalp pale-faces!" threatened the Harvester, but the girl was not afraid and stood before him laughing. She might have gone her way quite as well. She could not have differed more from the girl of the newly begun quest. The man merely touched his wide-brimmed hat as he walked around her and entered the office of the chief surgeon.

A slender, gray-eyed man with white hair turned from his desk, smiled warmly, pushed a chair, and reached a welcoming hand.

"Ah good-morning, David," he cried. "You bring the very breath of spring with you. Are you at the maples yet?"

"Begin to-morrow," was the answer. "I want to get all my old stock off hands. Sugar water comes next, and then the giddy sassafras and spring roots rush me, and after that, harvest begins full force, and all my land is teeming. This is going to be a big year. Everything is sufficiently advanced to be worth while. I have decided to enlarge the buildings."

"Store-room too small?"

"Everything!" said the Harvester comprehensively. "I am crowded everywhere."

The keen gray eyes bent on him searchingly.

"Ho, ho!" laughed the doctor. "'Crowded everywhere.' I had not heard of cramped living quarters before. When did you meet her?"

"Last night," replied the Harvester. "Her home is already in construction. I chose seven trees as I drove here that are going to fall before night."

So casual was the tone the doctor was disarmed.

"I am trying your nerve remedy," he said.

Instantly the Harvester tingled with interest.

"How does it work?" he inquired.

"Finely! Had a case that presented just the symptoms you mentioned. High-school girl broken down from trying to lead her classes, lead her fraternity, lead her parents, lead society—the Lord only knows what else. Gone all to pieces! Pretty a case of nervous prostration as you ever saw in a person of fifty. I began on fractional doses with it, and at last got her where she can rest. It did precisely what you claimed it would, David."

"Good!" cried the Harvester. "Good! I hoped it would be effective. Thank you for the test. It will give me confidence when I go before the chemists with it. I've got a couple more compounds I wish you would try when you have safe cases where you can do no harm."

"You are cautious for a young man, son!"

"The woods do that. You not only discover miracles and marvels in them, you not only trace evolution and the origin of species, but you get the greatest lessons taught in all the world ground into you early and alone—courage, caution, and patience."

"Those are the rocks on which men are stranded as a rule. You think you can breast them, David?"

The Harvester laughed.

"Aside from breaking a certain promise mother rooted in the blood and bones of me, if I am afraid of anything, I don't know it. You don't often see me going head-long, do you? As to patience! Ten years ago I began removing every tree, bush, vine, and plant of medicinal value from the woods around to my land; I set and sowed acres in ginseng, knowing I must nurse, tend, and cultivate seven years. If my neighbours had understood what I was attempting, what do you think they would have said? Cranky and lazy would have become adjectives too mild. Lunatic would have expressed it better. That's close the general opinion, anyway. Because I will not fell my trees, and the woods hide the work I do, it is generally conceded that I spend my time in the sun reading a book. I do, as often as I have an opportunity. But the point is that this fall, when I harvest that ginseng bed, I will clear more money than my stiffest detractor ever saw at one time. I'll wager my bank account won't compare so unfavourably with the best of them now. I did well this morning. Yes, I'll admit this much: I am reasonably cautious, I'm a pattern for patience, and my courage never has failed me yet, anyway. But I must rap on wood; for that boast is a sign that I probably will meet my Jonah soon."

"David, you are a man after my own heart," said the doctor. "I love you more than any other friend I have; I wouldn't see a hair of your head changed for the world. Now I've got to hurry to my operation. Remain as long as you please if there is anything that interests you; but don't let the giggling little nurse that always haunts the hall when you come make any impression. She is not up to your standard."

"Don't!" said the Harvester. "I've learned one of the big lessons of life since last I saw you, Doc. I have no standard. There is just one woman in all the world for me, and when I find her I will know her, and I will be happy for even a glance; as for that talk of standards, I will be only too glad to take her as she is."

"David! I supposed what you said about enlarged buildings was nonsense or applied to store-rooms."

"Go to your operation!"

"David, if you send me in suspense, I may operate on the wrong man. What has happened?"

"Nothing!" said the Harvester. "Nothing!"

"David, it is not like you to evade. What happened?"

"Nothing! On my word! I merely saw a vision and dreamed a dream."

"You! A rank materialist! Saw a vision and dreamed a dream! And you call it nothing. Worst thing that could happen! Whenever a man of common-sense goes to seeing things that don't exist, and dreaming dreams, why look out! What did you see? What did you dream?"

"You woman!" laughed the Harvester. "Talk about curiosity! I'd have to be a poet to describe my vision, and the dream was strictly private. I couldn't tell it, not for any price you could mention. Go to your operation."

The doctor paused on the threshold.

"You can't fool me," he said. "I can diagnose you all right. You are poet enough, but the vision was sacred, and when a man won't tell, it's always and forever a woman. I know all now I ever will, because I know you, David. A man with a loose mouth and a low mind drags the women of his acquaintance through whatever mire he sinks in; but you couldn't tell, David, not even about a dream woman. Come again soon! You are my elixir of life, lad! I revel in the atmosphere you bring. Wish me success now, I am going to a difficult, delicate operation."

"I do!" cried the Harvester heartily. "I do! But you can't fail. You never have and that proves you cannot! Good-bye!"

Down the street went the Harvester, passing over city pave with his free, swinging stride, his head high, his face flushed with vivid outdoor tints, going somewhere to do something worth while, the impression always left behind him. Men envied his robust appearance and women looked twice, always twice, and sometimes oftener if there was any opportunity; but twice at least was the rule. He left a little roll of bills at the bank and started toward the library. When he entered the reading room an attendant with an eager smile hastily came toward him.

"What will you have this morning, Mr. Langston?" she asked in the voice of one who would render willing service.

"Not the big books to-day," laughed the Harvester. "I've only a short time. I'll glance through the magazines."

He selected several from a table and going to a corner settled with them and for two hours was deeply engrossed. He took an envelope from his pocket, traced lines, and read intently. He studied the placing of rooms, the construction of furniture, and all attractive ideas were noted. When at last he arose the attendant went to replace the magazines on the table. They had been opened widely, and as she turned the leaves they naturally fell apart at the plans for houses or articles of furniture.

The Harvester slowly went down the street. Before every furniture store he paused and studied the designs displayed in the windows. Then he untied Betsy and drove to a lumber mill on the outskirts of the city and made arrangements to have some freshly felled logs of black walnut and curly maple sawed into different sizes and put through a course in drying.

He drove back to Medicine Woods whistling, singing, and talking to Belshazzar beside him. He ate a hasty lunch and at three o'clock was in the forest, blazing and felling slender, straight-trunked oak and ash of the desired proportions.

Chapter 3

Harvesting the Forest

The forest is never so wonderful as when spring wrestles with winter for supremacy. While the earth is yet ice bound, while snows occasionally fly, spring breathes her warmer breath of approach, and all nature responds. Sunny knolls, embankments, and cleared spaces become bare, while shadow spots and sheltered nooks remain white. This perfumes the icy air with a warmer breath of melting snow. The sap rises in the trees and bushes, sets buds swelling, and they distil a faint, intangible odour. Deep layers of dead leaves cover the frozen earth, and the sun shining on them raises a steamy vapour unlike anything else in nature. A different scent rises from earth where the sun strikes it. Lichen faces take on the brightest colours they ever wear, and rough, coarse mosses emerge in rank growth from their cover of snow and add another perfume to mellowing air. This combination has breathed a strange intoxication into the breast of mankind in all ages, and bird and animal life prove by their actions that it makes the same appeal to them.

Crows caw supremacy from tall trees; flickers, drunk on the wine of nature, flash their yellow-lined wings and red crowns among trees in a search for suitable building places; nut-hatches run head foremost down rough trunks, spying out larvae and early emerging insects; titmice chatter; the bold, clear whistle of the cardinal sounds never so gaily; and song sparrows pipe from every wayside shrub and fence post. Coons and opossums stir in their dens, musk-rat and ground-hog inspect the weather, while squirrels race along branches and bound from tree to tree like winged folk.

All of them could have outlined the holdings of the Harvester almost as well as any surveyor. They understood where the bang of guns and the snap of traps menaced life. Best of all, they knew where cracked nuts, handfuls of wheat, oats, and crumbs were scattered on the ground, and where suet bones dangled from bushes. Here, too, the last sheaf from the small wheat field at the foot of the hill was stoutly fixed on a high pole, so that the grain was free to all feathered visitors.

When the Harvester hitched Betsy, loaded his spiles and sap buckets into the wagon, and started to the woods to gather the offering the wet maples were pouring down their swelling sides, almost his entire family came to see him. They knew who fed and passed every day among them, and so were unafraid.

After the familiarity of a long, cold winter, when it had been easier to pick up scattered food than to search for it, they became so friendly with the man, the dog, and the gray horse that they hastily snatched the food offered at the barn and then followed through the woods. The Harvester always was particular to wear large pockets, for it was good company to have living creatures flocking after him, trusting to his bounty. Ajax, a shimmering wonder of gorgeous feathers, sunned on the ridge pole of the old log stable, preened, spread his train, and uttered the peacock cry of defiance, to exercise his voice or to express his emotions at all times. But at feeding hour he descended to the park and snatched bites from the biggest turkey cocks and ganders and reigned in power absolute over ducks, guineas, and chickens. Then he followed to the barn and tried to frighten crows and jays, and the gentle white doves under the eaves.

The Harvester walked through deep leaves and snow covering the road that only a forester could have distinguished. Over his shoulder he carried a mattock, and in the wagon were his clippers and an ax. Behind him came Betsy drawing the sap buckets and big evaporating kettles. Through the wood ranged Belshazzar, the craziest dog in all creation. He always went wild at sap time. Here was none of the monotony of trapping for skins around the lake. This marked the first full day in the woods for the season. He ranged as he pleased and came for a pat or a look of confidence when he grew lonely, while the Harvester worked.

At camp the man unhitched Betsy and tied her to the wagon and for several hours distributed buckets. Then he hung the kettles and gathered wood for the fire. At noon he returned to the cabin for lunch and brought back a load of empty syrup cans, and barrels in which to collect the sap. While the buckets filled at the dripping trees, he dug roots in the sassafras thicket to fill orders and supply the demand of Onabasha for tea. Several times he stopped to cut an especially fine tree.

"You know I hate to kill you," he apologized to the first one he felled. "But it certainly must be legitimate for a man to take enough of his trees to build a home. And no other house is possible for a creature of the woods but a cabin, is there? The birds use of the material they find here; surely I have the right to do the same. Seems as if nothing else would serve, at least for me. I was born and reared here, I've always loved you; of course, I can't use anything else for my home."

He swung the ax and the chips flew as he worked on a straight half-grown oak. After a time he paused an instant and rested, and as he did so he looked speculatively at his work.

"I wonder where she is to-day," he said. "I wonder what she is going to think of a log cabin in the woods. Maybe she has been reared in the city and is afraid of a forest. She may not like houses made of logs. Possibly she won't want to marry a Medicine Man. She may dislike the man, not to mention his occupation. She may think it coarse and common to work out of doors with your hands, although I'd have to argue there is a little brain in the combination. I must figure out all these things. But there is one on the lady: She should have settled these points before she became quite so familiar. I have that for a foundation anyway, so I'll go on cutting wood, and the remainder will be up to her when I find her. When I find her," repeated the Harvester slowly. "But I am not going to locate her very soon monkeying around in these woods. I should be out where people are, looking for her right now."

He chopped steadily until the tree crashed over, and then, noticing a rapidly filling bucket, he struck the ax in the wood and began gathering sap. When he had made the round, he drove to the camp, filled the kettles, and lighted the fire. While it started he cut and scraped sassafras roots, and made clippings of tag alder, spice brush and white willow into big bundles that were ready to have the bark removed during the night watch, and then cured in the dry-house.

He went home at evening to feed the poultry and replenish the ever-burning fire of the engine and to keep the cabin warm enough that food would not freeze. With an oilcloth and blankets he returned to camp and throughout the night tended the buckets and boiling sap, and worked or dozed by the fire between times. Toward the end of boiling, when the sap was becoming thick, it had to be watched with especial care so it would not scorch. But when the kettles were freshly filled the Harvester sat beside them and carefully split tender twigs of willow and slipped off the bark ready to be spread on the trays.

"You are a good tonic," he mused as he worked, "and you go into some of the medicine for rheumatism. If she ever has it we will give her some of you, and then she will be all right again. Strange that I should be preparing medicinal bark by the sugar camp fire, but I have to make this hay, not while the sun shines, but when the bark is loose, while the sap is rising. Wonder who will use this. Depends largely on where I sell it. Anyway, I hope it will take the pain out of some poor body. Prices so low now, not worth gathering unless I can kill time on it while waiting for something else. Never got over seven cents a pound for the best I ever sold, and it takes a heap of these little quills to make a pound when they are dry. That's all of you—about twenty-five cents' worth. But even that is better than doing nothing while I wait, and some one has to keep the doctors supplied with salicin and tannin, so, if I do, other folks needn't bother."

He arose and poured more sap into the kettles as it boiled away and replenished the fire. He nibbled a twig when he began on the spice brush. As he sat on the piled wood, and bent over his work he was an attractive figure. His face shone with health and was bright with anticipation. While he split the tender bark and slipped out the wood he spoke his thoughts slowly:

"The five cents a pound I'll get for you is even less, but I love the fragrance and taste. You don't peel so easy as the willow, but I like to prepare you better, because you will make some miserable little sick child well or you may cool some one's fevered blood. If ever she has a fever, I hope she will take medicine made from my bark, because it will be strong and pure. I've half a notion to set some one else gathering the stuff and tending the plants and spend my time in the little laboratory compounding different combinations. I don't see what bigger thing a man can do than to combine pure, clean, unadulterated roots and barks into medicines that will cool fevers, stop chills, and purify bad blood. The doctors may be all right, but what are they going to do if we men behind the prescription cases don't supply them with unadulterated drugs. Answer me that, Mr. Sapsucker. Doc says I've done mighty well so far as I have gone. I can't think of a thing on earth I'd rather do, and there's money no end in it. I could get too rich for comfort in short order. I wouldn't be too wealthy to live just the way I do for any consideration. I don't know about her, though. She is lovely, and handsome women usually want beautiful clothing, and a quantity of things that cost no end of money. I may need all I can get, for her. One never can tell."

He arose to stir the sap and pour more from the barrels to the kettles before he began on the tag alder he had gathered.

"If it is all the same to you, I'll just keep on chewing spice brush while I work," he muttered. "You are entirely too much of an astringent to suit my taste and you bring a cent less a pound. But you are thicker and dry heavier, and you grow in any quantity around the lake and on the marshy places, so I'll make the size of the bundle atone for the price. If I peel you while I wait on the sap I'm that much ahead. I can spread you on drying trays in a few seconds and there you are. Howl your head off, Bel, I don't care what you have found. I wouldn't shoot anything to-day, unless the cupboard was bare and I was starvation hungry. In that case I think a man comes first, and I'd kill a squirrel or quail in season, but blest if I'd butcher a lot or do it often. Vegetables and bread are better anyway. You peel easier even than the willow. What jolly whistles father used to make!

"There was about twenty cents' worth of spice, and I'll easy raise it to a dollar on this. I'll get a hundred gallons of syrup in the coming two weeks and it will bring one fifty if I boil and strain it carefully and can guarantee it contains no hickory bark and brown sugar. And it won't! Straight for me or not at all. Pure is the word at Medicine Woods; syrup or drugs it's the same thing. Between times I can fell every tree I'll need for the new cabin, and average a dollar a day besides on spice, alder, and willow, and twice that for sassafras for the Onabasha markets; not to mention the quantities I can dry this year. Aside from spring tea, they seem to use it for everything. I never yet have had enough. It goes into half the tonics, anodyne, and stimulants; also soap and candy. I see where I grow rich in spite of myself, and also where my harvest is going to spoil before I can garner it, if I don't step lively and double even more than I am now. Where the cabin is to come in— well it must come if everything else goes.

"The roots can wait and I'll dig them next year and get more and larger pieces. I won't really lose anything, and if she should come before I am ready to start to find her, why then I'll have her home prepared. How long before you begin your house, old fire-fly?" he inquired of a flaming cardinal tilting on a twig.

He arose to make the round of the sap buckets again, then resumed his work peeling bark, and so the time passed. In the following ten days he collected and boiled enough sap to make more syrup than he had expected. His earliest spring store of medicinal twigs, that were peeled to dry in quills, were all collected and on the trays; he had digged several wagon loads of sassafras and felled all the logs of stout, slender oak he would require for his walls. Choice timber he had been curing for candlestick material he hauled to the saw-mills to have cut properly, for the thought of trying his hand at tables and chairs had taken possession of him. He was sure he could make furniture that would appear quite as well as the mission pieces he admired on display in the store windows of the city. To him, chairs and tables made from trees that grew on land that had belonged for three generations to his ancestors, trees among which he had grown, played, and worked, trees that were so much his friends that he carefully explained the situation to them before using an ax or saw, trees that he had cut, cured, and fashioned into designs of his own, would make vastly more valuable furnishings in his home than anything that could be purchased in the city.

As he drove back and forth he watched constantly for her. He was working so desperately, planning far ahead, doubling and trebling tasks, trying to do everything his profession demanded in season, and to prepare timber and make plans for the new cabin, as well as to start a pair of candlesticks of marvellous design for her, that night was one long, unbroken sleep of the thoroughly tired man, but day had become a delightful dream.

He fed the chickens to produce eggs for her. He gathered barks and sluiced roots on the raft in the lake, for her. He grubbed the spice thicket before the door and moved it into the woods to make space for a lawn, for her. His eyes were wide open for every woven case and dangling cocoon of the big night moths that propagated around him, for her. Every night when he left the woods from one to a dozen cocoons, that he had detected with remarkable ease while the trees were bare, were stuck in his hat band. As he arranged them in a cool, dry place he talked to them.

"Of course I know you are valuable and there are collectors who would pay well for you, but I think not. You are the prettiest thing God made that I ever saw, and those of you that home with me have no price on your wings. You are much safer here than among the crows and jays of the woods. I am gathering you to protect you, and to show to her. If I don't find her by June, you may go scot free. All I want is the best pattern I can get from some of you for candlestick designs. Of everything in the whole world a candlestick should be made of wood. It should be carved by hand, and of all ornamentations on earth the moth that flies to the night light is the most appropriate. Owls are not so bad. They are of the night, and they fly to light, too, but they are so old. Nobody I ever have known used a moth. They missed the best when they neglected them. I'll make her sticks over an original pattern; I'll twine nightshade vines, with flowers and berries around them, and put a trailed luna on one, and what is the next prettiest for the other? I'll think well before if decide. Maybe she'll come by the time I get to carving and tell me what she likes. That would beat my taste or guessing a mile."

He carefully arranged the twigs bearing cocoons in a big, wire-covered box to protect them from the depredations of nibbling mice and the bolder attacks of the saucy ground squirrels that stored nuts in his loft and took possession of the attic until their scampering sometimes awoke him in the night.

Every trip he made to the city he stopped at the library to examine plans of buildings and furniture and to make notes. The oak he had hauled was being hewed into shape by a neighbour who knew how, and every wagon that carried a log to the city to be dressed at the mill brought back timber for side walls, joists, and rafters. Night after night he sat late poring over his plans for the new rooms, above all for her chamber. With poised pencil he wavered over where to put the closet and entrance to her bath. He figured on how wide to make her bed and where it should stand. He remembered her dressing table in placing windows and a space for a chest of drawers. In fact there was nothing the active mind of the Harvester did not busy itself with in those days that might make a woman a comfortable home. Every thought emanated from impulses evolved in his life in the woods, and each was executed with mighty tenderness.

A killdeer sweeping the lake close two o'clock one morning awakened him. He had planned to close the sugar camp for the season that day, but when he heard the notes of the loved bird he wondered if that would not be a good time to stake out the foundations and begin digging. There was yet ice in the ground, but the hillside was rapidly thawing, and although the work would be easier later, so eager was the Harvester to have walls up and a roof over that he decided to commence.

But when morning came and he and Belshazzar breakfasted and fed Betsy and the stock, he concluded to return to his first plan and close the camp. All the sap collected that day went into the vinegar barrel. He loaded the kettles, buckets, and spiles and stopped at the spice thicket to cut a bale of twigs as he passed. He carried one load to the wagon and returned for another. Down wind on swift wing came a bird and entered the bushes. Motionless the Harvester peered at it. A mourning dove had returned to him through snow, skiffing over cold earth. It settled on a limb and began dressing its plumage. At that instant a wavering, "Coo coo a'gh coo," broke in sobbing notes from the deep wood. Without paying the slightest heed, the dove finished a wing, ruffled and settled her feathers, and opened her bill in a human-like yawn. The Harvester smiled. The notes swelled closer in renewed pleading. The cry was beyond doubt a courting male and this an indifferent female. Her beady eyes snapped, her head turned coquettishly, a picture of self-possession, she hid among the dense twigs of the spice thicket. Around the outside circled the pleading male.

With shining eyes the Harvester watched. These were of the things that made life in the woods most worth while. More insistent grew the wavering notes of the lover. More indifferent became the beloved. She was superb in her poise as she amused herself in hiding. A perfect burst of confused, sobbing notes broke on the air. Then away in the deep wood a softly-wavering, half-questioning "Coo-ah!" answered them. Amazement flashed into the eyes of the Harvester, but his face was not nearly so expressive as that of the bird. She lifted a bewildered head and grew rigid in an attitude of tense listening. There was a pause. In quicker measure and crowding notes the male called again. Instantly the soft "Coo!" wavered in answer. The surprised little hen bird of the thicket hopped straight up and settled on her perch again, her dark eyes indignant as she uttered a short "Coo!" The muscles of the Harvester's chest were beginning to twitch and quiver. More intense grew the notes of the pleading male. Softly seductive came the reply. The clapping of his wings could be heard as he flew in search of the charmer. "A'gh coo!" cried the deserted female as she tilted off the branch and tore through the thicket in pursuit, with wings hastened by fright at the ringing laugh of the Harvester.

"Not so indifferent after all, Bel," he said to the dog standing in stiff point beside him. "That was all 'pretend!' But she waited just a trifle too long. Now she will have to fight it out with a rival. Good thing if some of the flirtatious women could have seen that. Help them to learn their own minds sooner."

He laughed as he heaped the twigs on top of the wagon and started down the hill chuckling. Belshazzar followed, leading Betsy straight in the middle of the road by the hitching strap. A few yards ahead the man stopped suddenly with lifted hand. The dog and horse stood motionless. A dove flashed across the road and settled in sight on a limb. Almost simultaneously another perched beside it, and they locked bills in a long caress, utterly heedless of a plaintive "Coo" in the deep wood.

"Settled!" said the Harvester. "Jupiter! I wish my troubles were that nearly finished! Wish I knew where she is and how to find my way to her lips! Wonder if she will come when I call her. What if I should find her, and she would have everything on earth, other lovers, and indifference worse than Madam Dove's for me. Talk about bitterness! Well I'd have the dream left anyway. And there are always two sides. There is just a possibility that she may be poor and overworked, sick and tired, and wondering why I don't come. Possibly she had a dream, too, and she wishes I would hurry. Dear Lord!"

The Harvester began to perspire as he strode down the hill. He scarcely waited to hang the harness properly. He did not stop to unload the wagon until night, but went after an ax and a board that he split into pegs. Then he took a ball of twine, a measuring line, and began laying out his foundation, when the hard earth would scarcely hold the stakes he drove into it. When he found he only would waste time in digging he put away the neatly washed kettles, peeled the spice brush, spread it to dry, and prepared his dinner. After that he began hauling stone and cement for his basement floor and foundation walls. Occasionally he helped at hewing logs when the old man paused to rest. That afternoon the first robin of the season hailed him in passing.

"Hello!" cried the Harvester. "You don't mean to tell me that you have beaten the larks! You really have! Well since I see it, I must believe, but you are early. Come around to the back door if crumbs or wheat will do or if you can make out on suet and meat bones! We are good and ready for you. Where is your mate? For any sake, don't tell me you don't know. One case of that kind at Medicine Woods is enough. Say you came ahead to see if it is too cold or to select a home and get ready for her. Say anything on earth except that you love her, and want her until your body is one quivering ache, and you don't know where she is."

Chapter 4

A Commission for the South Wind

The next morning the larks trailed ecstasy all over the valley, the following day cuckoos were calling in the thickets, a warm wind swept from the south and set swollen buds bursting, while the sun shone, causing the Harvester to rejoice. Betsy's white coat was splashed with the mud of the valley road; the feet of Belshazzar left tracks over lumber piles; and the Harvester removed his muck-covered shoes at the door and wore slippers inside. The skunk cabbage appeared around the edge of the forest, rank mullein and thistles lay over the fields in big circles of green, and even plants of delicate growth were thrusting their heads through mellowing earth and dead leaves, to reach light and air.

Then the Harvester took his mattock and began to dig. His level best fell so far short of what he felt capable of doing and desired to accomplish that the following day he put two more men on the job. Then the earth did fly, and so soon as the required space was excavated the walls were lined with stone and a smooth basement floor was made of cement. The night the new home stood, a skeleton of joists and rafters, gleaming whitely on the banks of Loon Lake, the Harvester went to the bridge crossing Singing Water and slowly came up the driveway to see how the work appeared. He caught his breath as he advanced. He had intended to stake out generous rooms, but this, compared with the cabin, seemed like a big hotel.

"I hope I haven't made it so large it will be a burden," he soliloquized. "It's huge! But while I am at it I want to build big enough, and I think I have."

He stood on the driveway, his arms folded, and looked at the structure as he occasionally voiced his thoughts.

"The next thing is to lay up the side walls and get the roof over. Got to have plenty of help, for those logs are hewed to fourteen inches square and some of them are forty feet long. That's timber! Grew with me, too. Personally acquainted with almost every tree of it. We will bed them in cement, use care with the roof, and if that doesn't make a cool house in the summer, and a warm one in winter,

I'll be disappointed. It sets among the trees, and on the hillside just right. We must have a wide porch, plenty of flowers, vines, ferns, and mosses, and when I get everything finished and she sees it—perhaps it will please her."

A great horned owl swept down the hill, crossed the lake, and hooted from the forest of the opposite bank. The Harvester thought of his dream and turned.

"Any women walking the water to-night? Come if you like," he bantered. "I don't mind in the least. In fact, I'd rather enjoy it. I'd be so happy if you would come now and tell me how this appears to you, for it's all yours. I'd have enlarged the store-room, dry-houses and laboratory for myself, but this cabin, never! The old one suited me as it was; but for you—I should have a better home."

The Harvester glanced from the shining skeleton to the bridge of gold and back again.

"Where are you to-night?" he questioned. "What are you doing? Can't you give me a hint of where to search for you when this is ready? I don't know but I am beginning wrong. My little brothers of the wood do differently. They announce their intentions the first thing, flaunt their attractions, and display their strength. They say aloud, for all the listening world to hear, what is in their hearts. They chip, chirp, and sing, warble, whistle, thrill, scream, and hoot it. They are strong on self-expression, and appreciative of their appearance. They meet, court, mate, and THEN build their home together after a mutual plan. It's a good way, too! Lots surer of getting things satisfactory."

The Harvester sat on a lumber pile and gazed questioningly at the framework.

"I wish I knew if I am going at things right," he said. "There are two sides to consider. If she is in a good home, and lovingly cared for, it would be proper to court her and get her promise, if I could—no I'm blest if I'll be so modest—get her promise, as I said, and let her wait while I build the cabin. But if she should be poor, tired, and neglected, then I ought to have this ready when I find her, so I could pick her up and bring her to it, with no more ceremony than the birds."

The Harvester's clear skin flushed crimson.

"Of course, I don't mean no wedding ceremony," he amended. "I was thinking of a long time wasted in preliminaries when in my soul I know I am going to marry my Dream Girl before I ever have seen her in reality. What would be the use in spending much time in courting? She is my wife now, by every law of God. Let me get a glimpse of her, and I'll prove it. But I've got to make tracks, for if she were here, where would I put her? I must hurry!"

He went to the work room and began polishing a table top. He had bought a chest of tools and was spending every spare minute on tables, chair seats, and legs. He had decided to make these first and carve candlesticks later when he had more time. Two hours he worked at the furniture, and then went to bed. The following morning he put eggs under several hens that wanted to set, trimmed his grape-vines, examined the precious ginseng beds, attended his stock, got breakfast for Belshazzar and himself, and was ready for work when the first carpenter arrived. Laying hewed logs went speedily, and before the Harvester believed it possible the big shingles he had ordered were being nailed on the roof. Then came the plumber and arranged for the bathroom, and the furnace man placed the heating pipes. The Harvester had intended the cabin to be mostly the work of his own hands, but when he saw how rapidly skilled carpenters worked, he changed his mind and had them finish the living-room, his room, and the upstairs, and make over the dining-room and kitchen.

Her room he worked on alone, with a little help if he did not know how to join the different parts. Every thing was plain and simple, after plans of his own, but the Harvester laid floors and made window casings, seats, and doors of wood that the big factories of Grand Rapids used in veneering their finest fur-niture. When one of his carpenters pointed out this to him, and suggested that he sell his lumber to McLean and use pine flooring from the mills the Harvester laughed at him.

"I don't say that I could afford to buy burl maple, walnut, and cherry for wood-work," said the Harvester. "I could not, but since I have it, you can stake your life I won't sell it and build my home of cheap, rapidly decaying wood. The best I have goes into this cabin and what remains will do to sell. I have an idea that when this is done it is going to appear first rate. Anyway, it will be solid enough to last a thousand years, and with every day of use natural wood grows more beauti-ful. When we get some tables, couches, and chairs made from the same timber as the casings and the floors, I think it will be fine. I want money, but I don't want it bad enough to part with the BEST of anything I have for it. Go carefully and neatly there; it will have to be changed if you don't."

So the work progressed rapidly. When the carpenters had finished the last stroke on the big veranda they remained a day more and made flower boxes, and a swinging couch, and then the greedy Harvester kept the best man with him a week longer to help on the furniture.

"Ain't you going to say a word about her, Langston?" asked this man as they put a mirror-like surface on a curly maple dressing table top.

"Her!" ejaculated the Harvester. "What do you mean?"

"I haven't seen you bathe anywhere except in the lake since I have been here," said the carpenter. "Do you want me to think that a porcelain tub, this big closet, and chest of drawers are for you?"

A wave of crimson swept over the Harvester.

"No, they are not for me," he said simply. "I don't want to be any more different from other men than I can help, although I know that life in the woods, the rigid training of my mother, and the reading of only the books that would aid in my work have made me individual in many of my thoughts and ways. I suppose most men, just now, would tell you anything you want to know. There is only one thing I can say: The best of my soul and brain, the best of my woods and store-house, the best I can buy with money is not good enough for her. That's all. For myself, I am getting ready to marry, of course. I think all normal men do and that it is a matter of plain common-sense that they should. Life with the right woman must be infinitely broader and better than alone. Are you married?"

"Yes. Got a wife and four children."

"Are you sorry?"

"Sorry!" the carpenter shrilled the word. "Sorry! Well that's the best I ever heard! Am I sorry I married Nell and got the kids? Do I look sorry?"

"I am not expecting to be, either," said the Harvester calmly. "I think I have done fairly well to stick to my work and live alone until I am twenty-six. I have thought the thing all over and made up my mind. As soon as I get this house far enough along that I feel I can proceed alone I am going to rush the marrying business just as fast as I can, and let her finish the remainder to her liking."

"Well this ought to please her."

"That's because you find your own work good," laughed the Harvester.

"Not altogether!" The carpenter polished the board and stood it on end to examine the surface as he talked. "Not altogether! Nothing but good work would suit you. I was thinking of the little creek splashing down the hill to the lake; and that old log hewer said that in a few more days things here would be a blaze of colour until fall."

"Almost all the drug plants and bushes leaf beautifully and flower brilliantly," explained the Harvester. "I studied the location suitable to each variety before I set the beds and planned how to grow plants for continuity of bloom, and as much harmony of colour as possible. Of course a landscape gardener would tear up some of it, but seen as a whole it isn't so bad. Did you ever notice that in the open, with God's blue overhead and His green for a background, He can place purple and yellow, pink, magenta, red, and blue in masses or any combination you can mention and the brighter the colour the more you like it? You don't seem to see or feel that any grouping clashes; you revel in each wonderful growth, and luxuriate in the brilliancy of the whole. Anyway, this suits me."

"I guess it will please her, too," said the carpenter. "After all the pains you've taken, she is a good one if it doesn't."

"I'll always have the consolation of having done my best," replied the Harvester. "One can't do more! Whether she likes it or not depends greatly on the way she has been reared."

"You talk as if you didn't know," commented the carpenter.

"You go on with this now," said the Harvester hastily. "I've got to uncover some beds and dig my year's supply of skunk cabbage, else folk with asthma and dropsy who depend on me will be short on relief. I ought to take my sweet flag, too, but I'm so hurried now I think I'll leave it until fall; I do when I can, because the bloom is so pretty around the lake and the bees simply go wild over the pollen. Sometimes I almost think I can detect it in their honey. Do you know I've wondered often if the honey my bees make has medicinal properties and should be kept separate in different seasons. In early spring when the plants and bushes that furnish the roots and barks of most of the tonics are in bloom, and the bees gather the pollen, that honey should partake in a degree of the same properties and be good medicine. In the summer it should aid digestion, and in the fall cure rheumatism and blood disorders."

"Say you try it!" urged the carpenter. "I want a lot of the fall kind. I'm always full of rheumatism by October. Exposure, no doubt."

"Over eating of too much rich food, you mean," laughed the Harvester. "I'd like to see any man expose his body to more differing extremes of weather than I do, and I'm never sick. It's because I am my own cook and so I live mostly on fruits, vegetables, bread, milk, and eggs, a few fish from the lake, a little game once in a great while or a chicken, and no hot drinks; plenty of fresh water, air, and continuous work out of doors. That's the prescription! I'd be ashamed to have rheumatism at your age. There's food in the cupboard if you grow hungry. I am going past one of the neighbours on my way to see about some work I want her to do."

The Harvester stopped for lunch, carried food to Belshazzar, and started straight across country, his mattock, with a bag rolled around the handle, on his shoulder. His feet sank in the damp earth at the foot of the hill, and he laughed as he leaped across Singing Water.

"You noisy chatterbox!" cried the man. "The impetus of coming down the curves of the hill keeps you talking all the way across this muck bed to the lake. With small work I can make you a thing of beauty. A few bushes grubbed, a little deepening where you spread too much, and some more mallows along the banks will do the trick. I must attend to you soon."

"Now what does the boy want?" laughed a white-haired old woman, as the Harvester entered the door. "Mebby you think I don't know what you're up to! I even can hear the hammering and the voices of the men when the wind is in the south. I've been wondering how soon you'd need me. Out with it!"

"I want you to get a woman and come over and spend a day with me. I'll come after you and bring you back. I want you to go over mother's bedding and have what needs it washed. All I want you to do is to superintend, and tell me now what I will want from town for your work."

"I put away all your mother's bedding that you were not using, clean as a ribbon."

"But it has been packed in moth preventives ever since and out only four times a year to air, as you told me. It must smell musty and be yellow. I want it fresh and clean."

"So what I been hearing is true, David?"

"Quite true!" said the Harvester.

"Whose girl is she, and when are you going to jine hands?"

The Harvester lifted his clear eyes and hesitated.

"Doc Carey laid you in my arms when you was born, David. I tended you 'fore ever your ma did. All your life you've been my boy, and I love you same as my own blood; it won't go no farther if you say so. I'll never tell a living soul. But I'm old and 'til better weather comes, house bound; and I get mighty lonely. I'd like to think about you and her, and plan for you, and love her as I always did you folks. Who is she, David? Do I know the family?"

"No. She is a stranger to these parts," said the unhappy Harvester.

"David, is she a nice girl 'at your ma would have liked?"

"She's the only girl in the world that I'd marry," said the Harvester promptly, glad of a question he could answer heartily. "Yes. She is gentle, very tender and—and affectionate," he went on so rapidly that Granny Moreland could not say a word, "and as soon as I bring her home you shall come to spend a day and get acquainted. I know you will love her! I'll come in the morning, then. I must hurry now. I am working double this spring and I'm off for the skunk cabbage bed to-day."

"You are working fit to kill, the neighbours say. Slavin' like a horse all day, and half the night I see your lights burning."

"Do I appear killed?" laughingly inquired the Harvester.

"You look peart as a struttin' turkey gobbler," said the old woman. "Go on with your work! Work don't hurt a-body. Eat a-plenty, sleep all you ort, and you CAN'T work enough to hurt you."

"So the neighbours say I'm working now? New story, isn't it? Usually I'm too lazy to make a living, if I remember."

"Only to those who don't sense your purceedings, David. I always knowed how you grubbed and slaved an' set over them fearful books o' yours."

"More interesting than the wildest fiction," said the man. "I'm making some medicine for your rheumatism, Granny. It is not fully tested yet, but you get ready for it by cutting out all the salt you can. I haven't time to explain this morning, but you remember what I say, leave out the salt, and when Doc thinks it's safe I'll bring you something that will make a new woman of you."

He went swinging down the road, and Granny Moreland looked after him.

"While he was talkin'," she muttered, "I felt full of information as a flock o' almanacs, but now since he's gone, 'pears to me I don't know a thing more 'an I did to start on."

"Close call," the Harvester was thinking. "Why the nation did I admit anything to her? People may talk as they please, so long as I don't sanction it, but I have two or three times. That's a fool trick. Suppose I can't find her? Maybe she won't look at me if I can. Then I'd have started something I couldn't finish. And if anybody thinks I'll end this by taking any girl I can get, if I can't find Her, why they think wrongly. Just the girl of my golden dream or no woman at all for me. I've lived alone long enough to know how to do it in comfort. If I can't find and win her I have no intention of starting a boarding house."

The Harvester began to laugh. "'I'd rather keep bachelor's hall in Hell than go to board in Heaven!'" he quoted gaily. "That's my sentiment too. If you can't have what you want, don't have anything. But there is no use to become discouraged before I start. I haven't begun to hunt her yet. Until I do, I might as well believe that she will walk across the bridge and take possession just as soon as I get the last chair leg polished. She might! She came in the dream, and to come actually couldn't be any more real. I'll make a stiff hunt of it before I give up, if I ever do. I never yet have made a complete failure of anything. But just now I am hunting skunk cabbage. It's precisely the time to take it."

Across the lake, in the swampy woods, close where the screech owl sang and the girl of the golden dream walked in the moonlight the Harvester began operations. He unrolled the sack, went to one end of the bed and systematically started a swath across it, lifting every other plant by the roots. Flowering time was almost past, but the bees knew where pollen ripened, and hummed incessantly over and inside the queer cone-shaped growths with their hooked beaks. It almost appeared as if the sound made inside might be to give outsiders warning not to poach on occupied territory, for the Harvester noticed that no bee entered a pre-empted plant.

With skilful hand each stroke brought up a root and he tossed it to one side. The plants were vastly peculiar things. First they seemed to be a curled leaf with no flower. In colour they shaded from yellow to almost black mahogany, and appeared as if they were a flower with no leaf. Closer examination proved there was a stout leaf with a heavy outside mid-rib, the tip of which curled over in a beak effect, that wrapped around a peculiar flower of very disagreeable odour. The handling of these plants by the hundred so intensified this smell the Harvester shook his head.

"I presume you are mostly mine," he said to the busy little workers around him. "If there is anything in my theory of honey having varying medicinal properties at different seasons, right now mine should be good for Granny's rheumatism and for nervous and dropsical people. I shouldn't think honey flavoured with skunk cabbage would be fit to eat. But, of course, it isn't all this. There is catkin pollen on the wind, hazel and sassafras are both in bloom now, and so are several of the earliest little flowers of the woods. You can gather enough of them combined to temper the disagreeable odour into a racy sweetness, and all the shrub blooms are good tonics, too, and some of the earthy ones. I'm going to try giving some of you empty cases next spring and analyzing the honey to learn if it isn't good medicine."

The Harvester straightened and leaned on the mattock to fill his lungs with fresh air and as he delightedly sniffed it he commented, "Nothing else has much of a chance since I've stirred up the cabbage bed. I can scent the catkins plainly, being so close, and as I came here I could detect the hazel and sassafras all right."

Above him a peculiar, raucous chattering for an instant hushed other wood voices. The Harvester looked up, laughing gaily.

"So you've decided to announce it to your tribe at last, have you?" he inquired. "You are waking the sleepers in their dens to-day? Well, there's nothing like waiting until you have a sure thing. The bluebirds broke the trail for the feathered folk the twenty-fourth of February. The sap oozed from the maples about the same time for the trees. The very first skunk cabbage was up quite a month ago to signal other plants to come on, and now you are rousing the furred folk. I'll write this down in my records—'When the earliest bluebird sings, when the sap wets the maples, when the skunk cabbage flowers, and the first striped squirrel barks, why then, it is spring!'"

He bent to his task and as he worked closer the water he noticed sweet-flag leaves waving two inches tall beneath the surface.

"Great day!" he cried. "There you are making signs, too! And right! Of course! Nature is always right. Just two inches high and it's harvest for you. I can use a rake, and dried in the evaporator you bring me ten cents a pound; to the folks needing a tonic you are worth a small fortune. No doubt you cost that by the time you reach them; but I fear I can't gather you just now. My head is a little preoccupied these days. What with the cabbage, and now you, and many of the bushes and trees making signs, with a new cabin to build and furnish, with a girl to find and win, I'm what you might call busy. I've covered my book shelf. I positively don't dare look Emerson or Maeterlinck in the face. One consolation! I've got the best of Thoreau in my head, and if I read Stickeen a few times more I'll be able to recite that. There's a man for you, not to mention the dog! Bel, where are you? Would you stick to me like that? I think you would. But you are a big, strong fellow. Stickeen was only such a mite of a dog. But what a man he followed! I feel as if I should put on high-heeled slippers and carry a fan and a lace handkerchief when I think of him. And yet, most men wouldn't consider my job so easy!"

The Harvester rapidly pitched the evil-smelling plants into big heaps and as he worked he imitated the sounds around him as closely as he could. The song sparrow laughed at him and flew away in disgust when he tried its notes. The jay took time to consider, but was not fooled. The nut-hatch ran head first down trees, larvae hunting, and was never a mite deceived. But the killdeer on invisible legs, circling the lake shore, replied instantly; so did the lark soaring above, and the dove of the elm thicket close beside. The glittering black birds flashing over every tree top answered the "T'check, t'chee!" of the Harvester quite as readily as their mates.

The last time he paused to rest he had studied scents. When he straightened again he was occupied with every voice of earth and air around and above him, and the notes of singing hens, exultant cocks, the scream of geese, the quack of ducks, the rasping crescendo of guineas running wild in the woods, the imperial note of Ajax sunning on the ridge pole and echoes from all of them on adjoining and distant farms.

"'Now I see the full meaning and beauty of that word sound!'" quoted the Harvester. "'I thank God for sound. It always mounts and makes me mount!'"

He breathed deeply and stood listening, a superb figure of a man, his lean face glowing with emotion.

"If she could see and hear this, she would come," he said softly, "She would come and she would love it as I do. Any one who understands, and knows how to translate, cares for this above all else earth has to offer. They who do not, fail to read as they run!"

He shifted feet mired in swamp muck, and stood as if loath to bend again to his task. He lifted a weighted mattock and scraped the earth from it, sniffing it delightedly the while. A soft south wind freighted with aromatic odours swept his warm face. The Harvester removed his hat and shook his head that the breeze might thread his thick hair.

"I've a commission for you, South Wind," he said whimsically. "Go find my Dream Girl. Go carry her this message from me. Freight your breath with spicy pollen, sun warmth, and flower nectar. Fill all her senses with delight, and then, close to her ear, whisper it softly, 'Your lover is coming!' Tell her that, O South Wind! Carry Araby to her nostrils, Heaven to her ears, and then whisper and whisper it over and over until you arouse the passion of earth in her blood. Tell her what is rioting in my heart, and brain, and soul this morning. Repeat it until she must awake to its meaning, 'Your lover is coming.'"

Chapter 5

When the
Harvester Made Good

The sassafras and skunk cabbage were harvested. The last workman was gone. There was not a sound at Medicine Woods save the babel of bird and animal notes and the never-ending accompaniment of Singing Water. The geese had gone over, some flocks pausing to rest and feed on Loon Lake, and ducks that homed there were busy among the reeds and rushes. In the deep woods the struggle to maintain and reproduce life was at its height, and the courting songs of gaily coloured birds were drowned by hawk screams and crow calls of defiance.

Every night before he plunged into the lake and went to sleep the Harvester made out a list of the most pressing work that he would undertake on the coming day. By systematizing and planning ahead he was able to accomplish an unbelievable amount. The earliest rush of spring drug gathering was over. He could be more deliberate in collecting the barks he wanted. Flowers that were to be gathered at bloom time and leaves were not yet ready. The heavy leaf coverings he had helped the winds to heap on his beds of lily of the valley, bloodroot, and sarsaparilla were removed carefully.

Inside the cabin the Harvester cleaned the glass, swept the floors with a soft cloth pinned over the broom, and hung pale yellow blinds at the windows. Every spare minute he worked on making furniture, and with each piece he grew in experience and ventured on more difficult undertakings. He had progressed so far that he now allowed himself an hour each day on the candlesticks for her. Every evening he opened her door and with soft cloths polished the furniture he had made. When her room was completed and the dining-room partially finished, the Harvester took time to stain the cabin and porch roofs the shade of the willow leaves, and on the logs and pillars he used oil that served to intensify the light yellow of the natural wood. With that much accomplished he felt better. If she came now, in a few hours he would be able to offer a comfortable room, enough conveniences to live until more could be provided, and of food there was always plenty.

His daily programme was to feed and water his animals and poultry, prepare breakfast for himself and Belshazzar, and go to the woods, dry-house or store-room to do the work most needful in his harvesting. In the afternoon he laboured over furniture and put finishing touches on the new cabin, and after supper he carved and found time to read again, as before his dream.

He was so happy he whistled and sang at his work much of the time at first, but later there came days when doubts crept in and all his will power was required to proceed steadily. As the cabin grew in better shape for occupancy each day, more pressing became the thought of how he was going to find and meet the girl of his dream. Sometimes it seemed to him that the proper way was to remain at home and go on with his work, trusting her to come to him. At such times he was happy and gaily whistled and sang:

"Stay in your chimney corner,
Don't roam the world about,
Stay in your chimney corner,
And your own true love will find you out."

But there were other days while grubbing in the forest, battling with roots in the muck and mire of the lake bank, staggering under a load for two men, scarcely taking time to eat and sleep enough to keep his condition perfect, when that plan seemed too hopeless and senseless to contemplate. Then he would think of locking the cabin, leaving the drugs to grow undisturbed by collecting, hiring a neighbour to care for his living creatures, and starting a search over the world to find her. There came times when the impulse to go was so strong that only the desire to take a day more to decide where, kept him. Every time his mind was made up to start the following day came the counter thought, what if I should go and she should come in my absence? In the dream she came. That alone held him, even in the face of the fact that if he left home some one might know of and rifle the precious ginseng bed, carefully tended these seven years for the culmination the coming fall would bring. That ginseng was worth many thousands and he had laboured over it, fighting worms and parasites, covering and uncovering it with the changing seasons, a siege of loving labour.

Sometimes a few hours of misgiving tortured him, but as a rule he was cheerful and happy in his preparations. Without intending to do it he was gradually furnishing the cabin. Every few days saw a new piece finished in the workshop. Each trip to Onabasha ended in the purchase of some article he could see would harmonize with his colour plans for one of the rooms. He had filled the flower boxes for the veranda with delicate plants that were growing luxuriantly.

Then he designed and began setting a wild-flower garden outside her door and started climbing vines over the logs and porches, but whatever he planted he found in the woods or took from beds he cultivated. Many of the medicinal vines had leaves, flowers, twining tendrils, and berries or fruits of wonderful beauty. Every trip to the forest he brought back a half dozen vines, plants, or bushes to set for her. All of them either bore lovely flowers, berries, quaint seed pods, or nuts, and beside the drive and before the cabin he used especial care to plant a hedge of bittersweet vines, burning bush, and trees of mountain ash, so that the glory of their colour would enliven the winter when days might be gloomy.

He planted wild yam under her windows that its queer rattles might amuse her, and hop trees where their castanets would play gay music with every passing wind of fall. He started a thicket along the opposite bank of Singing Water where it bubbled past her window, and in it he placed in graduated rows every shrub and small tree bearing bright flower, berry, or fruit. Those remaining he used as a border for the driveway from the lake, so that from earliest spring her eyes would fall on a procession of colour beginning with catkins and papaw lilies, and running through alders, haws, wild crabs, dogwood, plums, and cherry intermingled with forest saplings and vines bearing scarlet berries in fall and winter. In the damp soil of the same character from which they were removed, in the shade and under the skilful hand of the Harvester, few of these knew they had been transplanted, and when May brought the catbirds and orioles much of this growth was flowering quite as luxuriantly as the same species in the woods.

The Harvester was in the store-house packing boxes for shipment. His room was so small and orders so numerous that he could not keep large quantities on hand. All crude stuff that he sent straight from the drying-house was fresh and brightly coloured. His stock always was marked prime A-No. 1. There was a step behind him and the Harvester turned. A boy held out a telegram. The man opened it to find an order for some stuff to be shipped that day to a large laboratory in Toledo.

His hands deftly tied packages and he hastily packed bottles and nailed boxes. Then he ran to harness Betsy and load. As he drove down the hill to the bridge he looked at his watch and shook his head.

"What are you good for at a pinch, Betsy?" he asked as he flecked the surprised mare's flank with a switch. Belshazzar cocked his ears and gazed at the Harvester in astonishment.

"That wasn't enough to hurt her," explained the man. "She must speed up. This is important business. The amount involved is not so much, but I do love to make good. It's a part of my religion, Bel. And my religion has so precious few parts that if I fail in the observance of any of them it makes a big hole in my performances. Now we don't want to end a life full of holes, so we must get there with this stuff, not because it's worth the exertion in dollars and cents, but because these men patronize us steadily and expect us to fill orders, even by telegraph. Hustle, Betsy!"

The whip fell again and Belshazzar entered indignant protest.

"It isn't going to hurt her," said the Harvester impatiently. "She may walk all the way back. She can rest while I get these boxes billed and loaded if she can be persuaded to get them to the express office on time. The trouble with Betsy is that she wants to meander along the road with a loaded wagon as her mother and grandmother before her wandered through the woods wearing a bell to attract the deer. Father used to say that her mother was the smartest bell mare that ever entered the forest. She'd not only find the deer, but she'd make friends with them and lead them straight as a bee-line to where he was hiding. Betsy, you must travel!"

The Harvester drew the lines taut, and the whip fell smartly. The astonished Betsy snorted and pranced down the valley as fast as she could, but every step indicated that she felt outraged and abused. This was the loveliest day of the season. The sun was shining, the air was heavy with the perfume of flowering shrubs and trees, the orchards of the valley were white with bloom. Farmers were hurrying back and forth across fields, leaving up turned lines of black, swampy mould behind them, and one progressive individual rode a wheeled plow, drove three horses and enjoyed the shelter of a canopy.

"Saints preserve us, Belshazzar!" cried the Harvester. "Do you see that? He is one of the men who makes a business of calling me shiftless. Now he thinks he is working. Working! For a full-grown man, did you ever see the equal? If I were going that far I'd wear a tucked shirt, panama hat, have a pianola attachment, and an automatic fan."

The Harvester laughed as he again touched Betsy and hurried to Onabasha. He scarcely saw the delights offered on either hand, and where his eyes customarily took in every sight, and his ears were tuned for the faintest note of earth or tree top, to day he saw only Betsy and listened for a whistle he dreaded to hear at the water tank. He climbed the embankment of the railway at a slower pace, but made up time going down hill to the city.

"I am not getting a blame thing out of this," he complained to Belshazzar. "There are riches to stagger any scientist wasting to-day, and all I've got to show is one oriole. I did hear his first note and see his flash, and so unless we can take time to make up for this on the home road we will have to christen it oriole day. It's a perfumed golden day, too; I can get that in passing, but how I loathe hurrying. I don't mind planning things and working steadily, but it's not consistent with the dignity of a sane man to go rushing across country with as much appreciation of the delights offered right now as a chicken with its head off would have. We will loaf going back to pay for this! And won't we invite our souls? We will stop and gather a big bouquet of crab apple blossoms to fill the green pitcher for her. Maybe some of their wonderful perfume will linger in her room. When the petals fall we will scatter them in the drawers of her dresser, and they may distil a faint flower odour there. We could do that to all her furniture, but perhaps she doesn't like perfume. She'll be compelled to after she reaches Medicine Woods. Betsy, you must travel faster!"

The whip fell again and the Harvester stopped at the depot with a few minutes to spare. He threw the hitching strap to Belshazzar, and ran into the express office with an arm load of boxes.

"Bill them!" he cried. "It's a rush order. I want it to go on the next express. Almost due I think. I'll help you and we can book them afterward."

The expressman ran for a truck and they hastily weighed and piled on boxes. When the last one was loaded from the wagon, a heap more lying in the office were added, pitched on indiscriminately as the train pulled under the sheds of the Union Station.

"I'll push," cried the Harvester, "and help you get them on."

Hurrying as fast as he could the expressman drew the heavy truck through the iron gates and started toward the train slowing to a stop, and the Harvester pushed. As they came down the platform they passed the dining and sleeping cars of the long train and were several times delayed by descending passengers. Just opposite the day coach the expressman narrowly missed running into several women leading small children and stopped abruptly. A toppling box threatened the head of the Harvester. He peered around the truck and saw they must wait a few seconds. He put in the time watching the people. A gray-haired old man, travelling in a silk hat, wavered on the top step and went his way. A fat woman loaded with bundles puffed as she clung trembling a second in fear she would miss the step she could not see. A tall, slender girl with a face coldly white came next, and from the broken shoe she advanced, the bewildered fright of big, dark eyes glancing helplessly, the Harvester saw that she was poor, alone, ill, and in trouble. Pityingly he turned to watch her, and as he gauged her height, saw her figure, and a dark coronet of hair came into view, a ghastly pallor swept his face.

"Merciful God!" he breathed. "That's my Dream Girl!"

The truck started with a jerk. The toppling box fell, struck a passing boy, and knocked him down. The mother screamed and the Harvester sprang to pick up the child and see that he was not dangerously hurt. Then he ran after the truck, pitched on the box, and whirling, sped beside the train toward the gates of exit. There was the usual crush, but he could see the tall figure passing up the steps to the depot. He tried to force his way and was called a brute by a crowded woman. He ran down the platform to the gates he had entered with the truck. They were automatic and had locked. Then he became a primal creature being cheated of a lawful mate and climbed the high iron fence and ran for the waiting room.

He swept it at a glance, not forgetting the women's apartment and the side entrance. Then he hurried to the front exit. Up the street leading from the city there were few people and he could see no sign of the slight, white-faced girl. He crossed the sidewalk and ran down the gutter for a block and breathlessly waited the passing crowd on the corner. She was not among it. He tried one more square. Still he could not see her. Then he ran back to the depot. He thought surely he must have missed her. He again searched the woman's and general waiting room and then he thought of the conductor. From him it could be learned where she entered the car. He ran for the station, bolted the gate while the official called to him, and reached the track in time to see the train pull out within a few yards of him.

"You blooming idiot!" cried the angry expressman as the Harvester ran against him. "Where did you go? Why didn't you help me? You are white as a sheet! Have you lost your senses?"

"Worse!" groaned the Harvester. "Worse! I've lost what I prize most on earth. How could I reach the conductor of that train?"

"Telegraph him at the next station. You can have an answer in a half hour."

The Harvester ran to the office, and with shaking hand wrote this message:

"Where did a tall girl with big black eyes and wearing a gray dress take your train? Important."

Then he went out and minutely searched the depot and streets. He hired an automobile to drive him over the business part of Onabasha for three quarters of an hour. Up one street and down another he went slowly where there were crowds, faster as he could, but never a sight of her. Then he returned to the depot and found his message. It read, "Transferred to me at Fort Wayne from Chicago."

"Chicago baggage!" he cried, and hurried to the check room. He had lost almost an hour. When he reached the room he found the officials busy and unwilling to be interrupted. Finally he learned there had been a half dozen trunks from Chicago. All were taken save two, and one glance at them told the Harvester that they did not belong to the girl in gray. The others had been claimed by men having checks for them. If she had been there, the officials had not noticed a tall girl having a white face and dark eyes. When he could think of no further effort to make he drove to the hospital.

Doctor Carey was not in his office, and the Harvester sat in the revolving chair before the desk and gripped his head between his hands as he tried to think. He could not remember anything more he could have done, but since what he had done only ended in failure, he was reproaching himself wildly that he had taken his eyes from the Girl an instant after recognizing her. Yet it was in his blood to be decent and he could not have run away and left a frightened woman and a hurt child. Trusting to his fleet feet and strength he had taken time to replace the box also, and then had met the crowd and delay. Just for the instant it appeared to him as if he had done all a man could, and he had not found her. If he allowed her to return to Chicago, probably he never would. He leaned his head on his hands and groaned in discouragement.

Doctor Carey whirled the chair so that it faced him before the Harvester realized that he was not alone.

"What's the trouble, David?" he asked tersely.

The Harvester lifted a strained face.

"I came for help," he said.

"Well you will get it! All you have to do is to state what you want."

That seemed simplicity itself to the doctor. But when it came to putting his case into words, it was not easy for the Harvester.

"Go on!" said the doctor.

"You'll think me a fool."

The doctor laughed heartily.

"No doubt!" he said soothingly. "No doubt, David! Probably you are; so why shouldn't I think so. But remember this, when we make the biggest fools of ourselves that is precisely the time when we need friends, and when they stick to us the tightest, if they are worth while. I've been waiting since latter February for you to tell me. We can fix it, of course; there's always a way. Go on!"

"Well I wasn't fooling about the dream and the vision I told you of then, Doc. I did have a dream—and it was a dream of love. I did see a vision—and it was a beautiful woman."

"I hope you are not nursing that experience as something exclusive and peculiar to you," said the doctor. "There is not a normal, sane man living who has not dreamed of love and the most exquisite woman who came from the clouds or anywhere and was gracious to him. That's a part of a man's experience in this world, and it happens to most of us, not once, but repeatedly. It's a case where the wish fathers the dream."

"Well it hasn't happened to me 'on repeated occasions,' but it did one night, and by dawn I was converted. How CAN a dream be so real, Doc? How could I see as clearly as I ever saw in the daytime in my most alert moment, hear every step and garment rustle, scent the perfume of hair, and feel warm breath strike my face? I don't understand it!"

"Neither does any one else! All you need say is that your dream was real as life. Go on!"

"I built a new cabin and pretty well overturned the place and I've been making furniture I thought a woman would like, and carrying things from town ever since."

"Gee! It was reality to you, lad!"

"Nothing ever more so," said the Harvester.

"And of course, you have been looking for her?"

"And this morning I saw her!"

"David!"

"Not the ghost of a chance for a mistake. Her height, her eyes, her hair, her walk, her face; only something terrible has happened since she came to me. It was the same girl, but she is ill and in trouble now."

"Where is she?"

"Do you suppose I'd be here if I knew?"

"David, are you dreaming in daytime?"

"She got off the Chicago train this morning while I was helping Daniels load a big truck of express matter. Some of it was mine, and it was important. Just at the wrong instant a box fell and knocked down a child and I got in a jam—"

"And as it was you, of course you stopped to pick up the child and do everything decent for other folks, before you thought of yourself, and so you lost her. You needn't tell me anything more. David, if I find her, and prove to you that she has been married ten years and has an interesting family, will you thank me?"

"Can't be done!" said the Harvester calmly. "She has been married only since she gave herself to me in February, and she is not a mother. You needn't bank on that."

"You are mighty sure!"

"Why not? I told you the dream was real, and now that I have seen her, and she is in this very town, why shouldn't I be sure?"

"What have you done?"

The Harvester told him.

"What are you going to do next?"

"Talk it over with you and decide."

The doctor laughed.

"Well here are a few things that occur to me without time for thought. Talk ι the ticket agents, and leave her description with them. Make it worth their while to be on the lookout, and if she goes anywhere to find out all they can. They could make an excuse of putting her address on her ticket envelope, and get it that way. See the baggagemen. Post the day police on Main Street. There is no chance for her to escape you. A full-grown woman doesn't vanish. How did she act when she got off the car? Did she appear familiar?"

"No. She was a stranger. For an instant she looked around as if she expected some one, then she followed the crowd. There must have been an automobile waiting or she took a street car. Something whirled her out of sight in a few seconds."

"Well we will get her in range again. Now for the most minute description you can give."

The Harvester hesitated. He did not care to describe the Dream Girl to any one, much less the living, suffering face and poorly clad form of the reality.

"Cut out your scruples," laughed the doctor. "You have asked me to help you; how can I if I don't know what kind of a woman to look for?"

"Very tall and slender," said the Harvester. "Almost as tall as I am."

"Unusually tall you think?"

"I know!"

"That's a good point for identification. How about her complexion, hair, and eyes?"

"Very large, dark eyes, and a great mass of black hair."

The doctor roared.

"The eyes may help," he said. "All women have masses of hair these days. I hope ―"

"Her hair is fast to her head," said the Harvester indignantly. "I saw it at close range, and I know. It went around like a crown."

The doctor choked down a laugh. He wanted to say that every woman's hair was like a crown at present, but there were things no man ventured with David Langston; those who knew him best, least of any. So he suggested, "And her colouring?"

"She was white and rosy, a lovely thing in the dream," said the Harvester, "but something dreadful has happened. That's all wiped out now. She was very pale when she left the car."

"Car sick, maybe."

"Soul sick!" was the grim reply.

Then Doctor Carey appeared so disturbed the Harvester noticed it.

n't think I'd be here prating about her if I wasn't FORCED. If she
y and well as she was in the dream, I'd have made my hunt alone and
too. But when I saw she was sick and in trouble, it took all the cour-
of me, and I broke for help. She must be found at once, and when she is
are probably the first man I'll want. I am going to put up a pretty stiff search
myself, and if I find her I'll send or get her to you if I can. Put her in the best ward
you have and anything money will do—"

The face of the doctor was growing troubled.

"Day coach or Pullman?" he asked.

"Day."

"How was she dressed?"

"Small black hat, very plain. Gray jacket and skirt, neat as a flower."

"What you'd call expensively dressed?"

The Harvester hesitated.

"What I'd call carefully dressed, but—but poverty poor, if you will have it,
Doc."

Doctor Carey's lips closed and then opened in sudden resolution.

"David, I don't like it," he said tersely.

The Harvester met his eye and purposely misunderstood him.

"Neither do I!" he exclaimed. "I hate it! There is something wrong with the
whole world when a woman having a face full of purity, intellect, and refinement
of extreme type glances around her like a hunted thing; when her appearance
seems to indicate that she has starved her body to clothe it. I know what is in your
mind, Doc, but if I were you I wouldn't put it into words, and I wouldn't even
THINK it. Has it been your experience in this world that women not fit to know
skimp their bodies to cover them? Does a girl of light character and little brain
have the hardihood to advance a foot covered with a broken shoe? If I could tell
you that she rode in a Pullman, and wore exquisite clothing, you would be doing
something. The other side of the picture shuts you up like a clam, and makes you
appear shocked. Let me tell you this: No other woman I ever saw anywhere on
God's footstool had a face of more delicate refinement, eyes of purer intelligence.
I am of the woods, and while they don't teach me how to shine in society, they
do instil always and forever the fineness of nature and her ways. I have her lessons
so well learned they help me more than anything else to discern the qualities of
human nature. If you are my friend, and have any faith at all in my common sense,
get up and do something!"

The doctor arose promptly.

"David, I'm an ass," he said. "Unusually lop-eared, and blind in the bargain. But before I ask you to forgive me, I want you to remember two things: First, she did not visit me in my dreams; and, second, I did not see her in reality. I had nothing to judge from except what you said: you seemed reluctant to tell me, and what you did say was—was— disturbing to a friend of yours. I have not the slightest doubt if I had seen her I would agree with you. We seldom disagree, David. Now, will you forgive me?"

The Harvester suddenly faced a window. When at last he turned, "The offence lies with me," he said. "I was hasty. Are you going to help me?"

"With all my heart! Go home and work until your head clears, then come back in the morning. She did not come from Chicago for a day. You've done all I know to do at present."

"Thank you," said the Harvester.

He went to Betsy and Belshazzar, and slowly drove up and down the streets until Betsy protested and calmly turned homeward. The Harvester smiled ruefully as he allowed her to proceed.

"Go slow and take it easy," he said as they reached the country. "I want to think."

Betsy stopped at the barn, the white doves took wing, and Ajax screamed shrilly before the Harvester aroused in the slightest to anything around him. Then he looked at Belshazzar and said emphatically: "Now, partner, don't ever again interfere when I am complying with the observances of my religion. Just look what I'd have missed if I hadn't made good with that order!"

Chapter 6

To Labour and to Wait

"We have reached the 'beginning of the end,' Ajax!" said the Harvester, as the peacock ceased screaming and came to seek food from his hand. "We have seen the Girl. Now we must locate her and convince her that Medicine Woods is her happy home. I feel quite equal to the latter proposition, Ajax, but how the nation to find her sticks me. I can't make a search so open that she will know and resent it. She must have all the consideration ever paid the most refined woman, but she also has got to be found, and that speedily. When I remember that look on her face, as if horrors were snatching at her skirts, it takes all the grit out of me. I feel weak as a sapling. And she needs all my strength. I've simply got to brace up. I'll work a while and then perhaps I can think."

So the Harvester began the evening routine. He thought he did not want anything to eat, but when he opened the cupboard and smelled the food he learned that he was a hungry man and he cooked and ate a good supper. He put away everything carefully, for even the kitchen was dainty and fresh and he wanted to keep it so for her. When he finished he went into the living-room, stood before the fireplace, and studied the collection of half-finished candlesticks grouped upon it. He picked up several and examined them closely, but realized that he could not bind himself to the exactions of carving that evening. He took a key from his pocket and unlocked her door. Every day he had been going there to improve upon his work for her, and he loved the room, the outlook from its windows; he was very proud of the furniture he had made. There was no paper-thin covering on her chairs, bed, and dressing table. The tops, seats, and posts were solid wood, worth hundreds of dollars for veneer.

To-night he folded his arms and stood on the sill hesitating. While she was a dream, he had loved to linger in her room. Now that she was reality, he paused. In one golden May day the place had become sacred. Since he had seen the Girl that room was so hers that he was hesitating about entering because of this fact. It was as if the tall, slender form stood before the chest of drawers or sat at the dressing table and he did not dare enter unless he were welcome. Softly he closed the door and went away. He wandered to the dry-house and turned the bark and roots on the trays, but the air stifled him and he hurried out. He tried to work in the packing room, but walls smothered him and again he sought the open.

He espied a bundle of osier-bound, moss-covered ferns that he had found in the woods, and brought the shovel to transplant them; but the work worried him, and he hurried through with it. Then he looked for something else to do and saw an ax. He caught it up and with lusty strokes began swinging it. When he had chopped wood until he was very tired he went to bed. Sleep came to the strong, young frame and he awoke in the morning refreshed and hopeful.

He wondered why he had bothered Doctor Carey. The Harvester felt able that morning to find his Dream Girl without assistance before the day was over. It was merely a matter of going to the city and locating a woman. Yesterday, it had been a question of whether she really existed. To-day, he knew. Yesterday, it had meant a search possibly as wide as earth to find her. To-day, it was narrowed to only one location so small, compared with Chicago, that the Harvester felt he could sift its population with his fingers, and pick her from others at his first attempt. If she were visiting there probably she would rest during the night, and be on the streets to-day.

When he remembered her face he doubted it. He decided to spend part of the time on the business streets and the remainder in the residence portions of the city. Because it was uncertain when he would return, everything was fed a double portion, and Betsy was left at a livery stable with instructions to care for her until he came. He did not know where the search would lead him. For several hours he slowly walked the business district and then ranged farther, but not a sight of her. He never had known that Onabasha was so large. On its crowded streets he did not feel that he could sift the population through his fingers, nor could he open doors and search houses without an excuse.

Some small boys passed him eating bananas, and the Harvester looked at his watch and was amazed to find that the day had advanced until two o'clock in the afternoon. He was tired and hungry. He went into a restaurant and ordered lunch; as he waited a girl serving tables smiled at him. Any other time the Harvester would have returned at least a pleasant look, and gone his way. To-day he scowled at her, and ate in hurried discomfort. On the streets again, he had no idea where to go and so he went to the hospital.

"I expected you early this morning," was the greeting of Doctor Carey. "Where have you been and what have you done?"

"Nothing," said the Harvester. "I was so sure she would be on the streets I just watched, but I didn't see her."

"We will go to the depot," said the doctor. "The first thing is to keep her from leaving town."

They arranged with the ticket agents, expressmen, telegraphers, and, as they left, the Harvester stopped and tipped the train caller, offering further reward worth while if he would find the Girl.

"Now we will go to the police station," said the doctor.

"I'll see the chief and have him issue a general order to his men to watch for her, but if I were you I'd select a half dozen in the down town district, and give them a little tip with a big promise!"

"Good Lord! How I hate this," groaned the Harvester.

"Want to find her by yourself?" questioned his friend.

"Yes," said the Harvester, "I do! And I would, if it hadn't been for her ghastly face. That drives me to resort to any measures. The probabilities are that she is lying sick somewhere, and if her comfort depends on the purse that dressed her, she will suffer. Doc, do you know how awful this is?"

"I know that you've got a great imagination. If the woods make all men as sensitive as you are, those who have business to transact should stay out of them. Take a common-sense view. Look at this as I do. If she was strong enough to travel in a day coach from Chicago; she can't be so very ill to-day. Leaving life by the inch isn't that easy. She will be alive this time next year, whether you find her or not. The chances are that her stress was mental anyway, and trouble almost never overcomes any one."

"You, a doctor and say that!"

"Oh, I mean instantaneously—in a day! Of course if it grinds away for years! But youth doesn't allow it to do that. It throws it off, and grows hopeful and happy again. She won't die; put that out of your mind. If I were you I would go home now and go straight on with my work, trusting to the machinery you have set in motion. I know most of the men with whom we have talked. They will locate her in a week or less. It's their business. It isn't yours. It's your job to be ready for her, and have enough ahead to support her when they find her. Try to realize that there are now a dozen men on hunt for her, and trust them. Go back to your work, and I will come full speed in the motor when the first man sights her. That ought to satisfy you. I've told all of them to call me at the hospital, and I will tell my assistant what to do in case a call comes while I am away. Straighten your face! Go back to Medicine Woods and harvest your crops, and before you know it she will be located. Then you can put on your Sunday clothes and show yourself, and see if you can make her take notice."

"Idiot!" exclaimed the Harvester, but he started home. When he arrived he attended to his work and then sat down to think.

"Doc is right," was his ultimate conclusion. "She can't leave the city, she can't move around in it, she can't go anywhere, without being seen. There's one more point: I must tell Carey to post all the doctors to report if they have such a call. That's all I can think of. I'll go to-night, and then I'll look over the ginseng for parasites, and to-morrow I'll dive into the late spring growth and work until I haven't time to think. I've let cranesbill get a week past me now, and it can't be dispensed with."

So the following morning, when the Harvester had completed his work at the cabin and barn and breakfasted, he took a mattock and a big hempen bag, and followed the path to the top of the hill. As it ran along the lake bank he descended on the other side to several acres of cleared land, where he raised corn for his stock, potatoes, and coarser garden truck, for which there was not space in the smaller enclosure close the cabin. Around the edges of these fields, and where one of them sloped toward the lake, he began grubbing a variety of grass having tall stems already over a foot in height at half growth. From each stem waved four or five leaves of six or eight inches length and the top showed forming clusters of tiny spikelets.

"I am none too early for you," he muttered to himself as he ran the mattock through the rich earth, lifting the long, tough, jointed root stalks of pale yellow, from every section of which broke sprays of fine rootlets. "None too early for you, and as you are worth only seven cents a pound, you couldn't be considered a 'get-rich-quick' expedient, so I'll only stop long enough with you to gather what I think my customers will order, and amass a fortune a little later picking mullein flowers at seventy-five cents a pound. What a crop I've got coming!"

The Harvester glanced ahead, where in the cleared soil of the bank grew large plants with leaves like yellow-green felt and tall bloom stems rising. Close them flourished other species requiring dry sandy soil, that gradually changed as it approached the water until it became covered with rank abundance of short, wiry grass, half the blades of which appeared red. Numerous everywhere he could see the grayish-white leaves of Parnassus grass. As the season advanced it would lift heart-shaped velvet higher, and before fall the stretch of emerald would be starred with white-faced, green-striped flowers.

"Not a prettier sight on earth," commented the Harvester, "than just swale wire grass in September making a fine, thick background to set off those delicate starry flowers on their slender stems. I must remember to bring her to see that."

His eyes followed the growth to the water. As the grass drew closer moisture it changed to the rank, sweet, swamp variety, then came bulrushes, cat-tails, water smartweed, docks, and in the water blue flag lifted folded buds; at its feet arose yellow lily leaves and farther out spread the white. As the light struck the surface the Harvester imagined he could see the little green buds several inches below. Above all arose wild rice he had planted for the birds. The red wings swayed on the willows and tilted on every stem that would bear their weight, singing their melodious half-chanted notes, "O-ka-lee!"

Beneath them the ducks gobbled, splashed, and chattered; grebe and coot voices could be distinguished; king rails at times flashed into sight and out again; marsh wrens scolded and chattered; occasionally a kingfisher darted around the lake shore, rolling his rattling cry and flashing his azure coat and gleaming white collar. On a hollow tree in the woods a yellow hammer proved why he was named, because he carpentered industriously to enlarge the entrance to the home he was excavating in a dead tree; and sailing over the lake and above the woods in grace scarcely surpassed by any, a lonesome turkey buzzard awaited his mate's decision as to which hollow log was most suitable for their home.

The Harvester stuffed the grass roots in the bag until it would hold no more and stood erect to wipe his face, for the sun was growing warm. As he drew his handkerchief across his brow, the south wind struck him with enough intensity to attract attention. Instantly the Harvester removed his hat, rolled it up, and put it into his pocket. He stood an instant delighting in the wind and then spoke.

"Allow me to express my most fervent thanks for your kindness," he said. "I thought probably you would take that message, since it couldn't mean much to you, and it meant all the world to me. I thought you would carry it, but, I confess, I scarcely expected the answer so soon. The only thing that could make me more grateful to you would be to know exactly where she is: but you must understand that it's like a peep into Heaven to have her existence narrowed to one place. I'm bound to be able to say inside a few days, she lives at number—I don't know yet, on street—I'll find out soon, in the closest city, Onabasha. And I know why you brought her, South Wind. If ever a girl's cheeks need fanning with your breezes, and painting with sun kisses, I wouldn't mind, since this is strictly private, adding a few of mine; if ever any one needed flowers, birds, fresh air, water, and rest! Good Lord, South Wind, did you ever reach her before you carried that message? I think not! But Onabasha isn't so large. You and the sun should get your innings there. I do hope she is not trying to work! I can attend to that; and so there will be more time when she is found, I'd better hustle now."

He picked up the bag and returned to the dry-house, where he carefully washed the roots and spread them on the trays. Then he took the same bag and mattock and going through the woods in the opposite direction he came to a heavy growth in a cleared space of high ground. The bloom heads were forming and the plant was half matured. The Harvester dug a cylindrical, tapering root, wrinkling lengthwise, wiped it clean, broke and tasted it. He made a wry face. He stood examining the white wood with its brown-red bark and, deciding that it was in prime condition, he began digging the plants. It was common wayside "Bouncing Bet," but the Harvester called it "soapwort." He took every other plant in his way across the bed, and when he digged a heavy load he carried it home, stripped the leaves, and spread them on trays, while the roots he topped, washed, and put to dry also. Then he whistled for Belshazzar and went to lunch.

As he passed down the road to the cabin his face was a study of conflicting emotions, and his eyes had a far away appearance of deep thought. Every tree of his stretch of forest was rustling fresh leaves to shelter him; dogwood, wild crab, and hawthorn offered their flowers; earth held up her tribute in painted trillium faces, spring beauties, and violets, blue, white, and yellow. Mosses, ferns, and lichen decorated the path; all the birds greeted him in friendship, and sang their purest melodies. The sky was blue, the sun bright, the air perfumed for him; Belshazzar, always true to his name, protected every footstep; Ajax, the shimmering green and gold wonder, came up the hill to meet him; the white doves circled above his head. Stumbling half blindly, the Harvester passed unheeding among them, and went into the cabin. When he came out he stood a long time in deep study, but at last he returned to the woods.

"Perhaps they will have found her before night," he said. "I'll harvest the cranesbill yet, because it's growing late for it, and then I'll see how they are coming on. Maybe they'd know her if they met her, and maybe they wouldn't. She may wear different clothing, and freshen up after her trip. She might have been car sick, as Doc suggested, and appear very different when she feels better."

He skirted the woods around the northeast end and stopped at a big bed of exquisite growth. Tall, wiry stems sprang upward almost two feet in height; leaves six inches across were cut in ragged lobes almost to the base, and here and there, enough to colour the entire bed a delicate rose or sometimes a violet purple, the first flowers were unfolding. The Harvester lifted a root and tasted it.

"No doubt about you being astringent," he muttered. "You have enough tannin in you to pucker a mushroom. By the way, those big, corn-cobby fellows should spring up with the next warm rain, and the hotels and restaurants always pay high prices. I must gather a few bushels."

He looked over the bed of beautiful wild alum and hesitated.

"I vow I hate to touch you," he said. "You are a picture right now, and in a week you will be a miracle. It seems a shame to tear up a plant for its roots, just at flowering time, and I can't avoid breaking down half I don't take, getting the ones I do. I wish you were not so pretty! You are one of the colours I love most. You remind me of red-bud, blazing star, and all those exquisite magenta shades that poets, painters, and the Almighty who made them love so much they hesitate about using them lavishly. You are so delicate and graceful and so modest. I wish she could see you! I got to stop this or I won't be able to lift a root. I never would if the ten cents a pound I'll get out of it were the only consideration."

The Harvester gripped the mattock and advanced to the bed. "What I must be thinking is that you are indispensable to the sick folks. The steady demand for you proves your value, and of course, humanity comes first, after all. If I remain in the woods alone much longer I'll get to the place where I'm not so sure that it does. Seems as if animals, birds, flowers, trees, and insects as well, have their right to life also. But it's for me to remember the sick folks! If I thought the Girl would get some of it now, I could overturn the bed with a stout heart. If any one ever needed a tonic, I think she does. Maybe some of this will reach her. If it does, I hope it will make her cheeks just the lovely pink of the bloom. Oh Lord! If only she hadn't appeared so sick and frightened! What is there in all this world of sunshine to make a girl glance around her like that? I wish I knew! Maybe they will have found her by night."

The Harvester began work on the bed, but he knelt and among the damp leaves from the spongy black earth he lifted the roots with his fingers and carefully straightened and pressed down the plants he did not take. This required more time than usual, but his heart was so sore he could not be rough with anything, most of all a flower. So he harvested the wild alum by hand, and heaped large stacks of roots around the edges of the bed. Often he paused as he worked and on his knees stared through the forest as if he hoped perhaps she would realize his longing for her, and come to him in the wood as she had across the water. Over and over he repeated, "Perhaps they will find her by night!" and that so intensified the meaning that once he said it aloud. His face clouded and grew dark.

"Dealish nice business!" he said. "I am here in the woods digging flower roots, and a gang of men in the city are searching for the girl I love. If ever a job seemed peculiarly a man's own, it appears this would be. What business has any other man spying after my woman? Why am I not down there doing my own work, as I always have done it? Who's more likely to find her than I am? It seems as if there would be an instinct that would lead me straight to her, if I'd go. And you can wager I'll go fast enough."

The Harvester appeared as if he would start that instant, but with lips closely shut he finally forced himself to go on with his work. When he had rifled the bed, and uprooted all he cared to take during one season, he carried the roots to the lake shore below the curing house, and spread them on a platform he had built. He stepped into his boat and began dashing pails of water over them and using a brush. As he worked he washed away the woody scars of last year's growth, and the tiny buds appearing for the coming season.

Belshazzar sat on the opposite bank and watched the operation; and Ajax came down and, flying to a dead stump, erected and slowly waved his train to attract the sober-faced man who paid no heed. He left the roots to drain while he prepared supper, then placed them on the trays, now filled to overflowing, and was glad he had finished. He could not cure anything else at present if he wanted to. He was as far advanced as he had been at the same time the previous year. Then he dressed neatly and locking the Girl's room, and leaving Belshazzar to protect it, he went to Onabasha.

"Bravo!" cried Doctor Carey as the Harvester entered his office. "You are heroic to wait all day for news. How much stuff have you gathered?"

"Three crops. How many missing women have you located?"

The doctor laughed. There was no sign of a smile on the face of the Harvester.

"You didn't really expect her to come to light the first day? That would be too easy! We can't find her in a minute."

"It will be no surprise to me if you can't find her at all. I am not expecting another man to do what I don't myself."

"You are not hunting her. You are harvesting the woods. The men you employ are to find her."

"Maybe I am, and maybe I am not," said the Harvester slowly. "To me it appears to be a poor stick of a man who coolly proceeds with money making, and trusts to men who haven't even seen her to search for the girl he loves. I think a few hours of this is about all my patience will endure."

"What are you going to do?"

"I don't know," said the Harvester. "But you can bank on one thing sure—I'm going to do something! I've had my fill of this. Thank you for all you've done, and all you are going to do. My head is not clear enough yet to decide anything with any sense, but maybe I'll hit on something soon. I'm for the streets for a while."

"Better go home and go to bed. You seem very tired."

"I am," said the Harvester. "The only way to endure this is to work myself down. I'm all right, and I'll be careful, but I rather think I'll find her myself."

"Better go on with your work as we planned."

"I'll think about it," said the Harvester as he went out.

Until he was too tired to walk farther he slowly paced the streets of the city, and then followed the home road through the valley and up the hill to

Medicine Woods. When he came to Singing Water, Belshazzar heard his steps on the bridge, and came bounding to meet him. The Harvester stretched himself on a seat and turned his face to the sky. It was a deep, dark-blue bowl, closely set with stars, and a bright moon shed a soft May radiance on the young earth. The lake was flooded with light, and the big trees of the forest crowning the hill were silver coroneted. The unfolding leaves had hidden the new cabin from the bridge, but the driveway shone white, and already the upspringing bushes hedged it in. Insects were humming lazily in the perfumed night air, and across the lake a courting whip-poor-will was explaining to his sweetheart just how much and why he loved her. A few bats were wavering in air hunting insects, and occasionally an owl or a nighthawk crossed the lake. Killdeer were glorying in the moonlight and night flight, and cried in pure, clear notes as they sailed over the water. The Harvester was tired and filled with unrest as he stretched on the bridge, but the longer he lay the more the enfolding voices comforted him. All of them were waiting and working out their lives to the legitimate end; there was nothing else for him to do. He need not follow instinct or profit by chance. He was a man; he could plan and reason.

The air grew balmy and some big, soft clouds swept across the moon. The Harvester felt the dampness of rising dew, and went to the cabin. He looked at it long in the moonlight and told himself that he could see how much the plants, vines, and ferns had grown since the previous night. Without making a light, he threw himself on the bed in the outdoor room, and lay looking through the screening at the lake and sky. He was working his brain to think of some manner in which to start a search for the Dream Girl that would have some probability of success to recommend it, but he could settle on no feasible plan. At last he fell asleep, and in the night soft rain wet his face. He pulled an oilcloth sheet over the bed, and lay breathing deeply of the damp, perfumed air as he again slept. In the morning brilliant sunshine awoke him and he arose to find the earth steaming.

"If ever there was a perfect mushroom day!" he said to Belshazzar. "We must hurry and feed the stock and ourselves and gather some. They mean real money."

Chapter 7

The Quest of the Dream Girl

The Harvester breakfasted, fed the stock, hitched Betsy to the spring wagon, and went into the dripping, steamy woods. If anyone had asked him that morning concerning his idea of Heaven, he never would have dreamed of describing a place of gold-paved streets, crystal pillars, jewelled gates, and thrones of ivory. These things were beyond the man's comprehension and he would not have admired or felt at home in such magnificence if it had been materialized for him. He would have told you that a floor of last year's brown leaves, studded with myriad flower faces, big, bark-encased pillars of a thousand years, jewels on every bush, shrub, and tree, and tilting thrones on which gaudy birds almost burst themselves to voice the joy of life, while their bright-eyed little mates peered questioningly at him over nest rims—he would have told you that Medicine Woods on a damp, sunny May morning was Heaven. And he would have added that only one angel, tall and slender, with the pink of health on her cheeks and the dew of happiness in her dark eyes, was necessary to enter and establish glory. Everything spoke to him that morning, but the Harvester was silent. It had been his habit to talk constantly to Belshazzar, Ajax, his work, even the winds and perfumes; it had been his method of dissipating solitude, but to-day he had no words, even for these dear friends. He only opened his soul to beauty, and steadily climbed the hill to the crest, and then down the other side to the rich, half-shaded, half-open spaces, where big, rough mushrooms sprang in a night similar to the one just passed.

He could see them awaiting him from afar. He began work with rapid fingers, being careful to break off the heads, but not to pull up the roots. When four heaping baskets were filled he cut heavily leaved branches to spread over them, and started to Onabasha. As usual, Belshazzar rode beside him and questioned the Harvester when he politely suggested to Betsy that she make a little haste.

"Have you forgotten that mushrooms are perishable?" he asked. "If we don't get these to the city all woodsy and fresh we can't sell them.

Wonder where we can do the best? The hotels pay well. Really, the biggest prices could be had by—"

Then the Harvester threw back his head and began to laugh, and he laughed, and he laughed. A crow on the fence Joined him, and a kingfisher, heading for Loon Lake, and then Belshazzar caught the infection.

"Begorry! The very idea!" cried the Harvester. "'Heaven helps them that help themselves.' Now you just watch us manoeuvre for assistance, Belshazzar, old boy! Here we go!"

Then the laugh began again. It continued all the way to Onabasha and even into the city. The Harvester drove through the most prosperous street until he reached the residence district. At the first home he stopped, gave the lines to Belshazzar, and, taking a basket of mushrooms, went up the walk and rang the bell.

"All groceries should be delivered at the back door," snapped a pert maid, before he had time to say a word.

The Harvester lifted his hat.

"Will you kindly tell the lady of the house that I wish to speak with her?"

"What name, please?"

"I want to show her some fine mushrooms, freshly gathered," he answered.

How she did it the Harvester never knew. The first thing he realized was that the door had closed before his face, and the basket had been picked deftly from his fingers and was on the other side. After a short time the maid returned.

"What do you want for them, please?"

The last thing on earth the Harvester wanted to do was to part with those mushrooms, so he took one long, speculative look down the hall and named a price he thought would be prohibitive.

"One dollar a dozen."

"How many are there?"

"I count them as I sell them. I do not know."

The door closed again. Presently it opened and the maid knelt on the floor before him and counted the mushrooms one by one into a dish pan and in a few minutes brought back seven dollars and fifty cents. The chagrined Harvester, feeling like a thief, put the money in his pocket, and turned away.

"I was to tell you," said she, "that you are to bring all you have to sell here, and the next time please go to the kitchen door."

"Must be fond of mushrooms," said the disgruntled Harvester.

"They are a great delicacy, and there are visitors." The Harvester ached to set the girl to one side and walk through the house, but he did not dare; so he returned to the street, whistled to Betsy to come, and went to the next gate.

Here he hesitated. Should he risk further snubbing at the front door or go back at once. If he did, he only would see a maid. As he stood an instant debating, the door of the house he just had left opened and the girl ran after him. "If you have more, we will take them," she called.

The Harvester gasped for breath.

"They have to be used at once," he suggested.

"She knows that. She wants to treat her friends."

"Well she has got enough for a banquet," he said. "I—I don't usually sell more than a dozen or two in one place."

"I don't see why you can't let her have them if you have more."

"Perhaps I have orders to fill for regular customers," suggested the Harvester.

"And perhaps you haven't," said the maid. "You ought to be ashamed not to let people who are willing to pay your outrageous prices have them. It's regular highway robbery."

"Possibly that's the reason I decline to hold up one party twice," said the Harvester as he entered the gate and went up the walk to the front door.

"You should be taught your place," called the maid after him.

The Harvester again rang the bell. Another maid opened the door, and once more he asked to speak with the lady of the house. As the girl turned, a handsome old woman in cap and morning gown came down the stairs.

"What have you there?" she asked.

The Harvester lifted the leaves and exposed the musky, crimpled, big mushrooms.

"Oh!" she cried in delight. "Indeed, yes! We are very fond of them. I will take the basket, and divide with my sons. You are sure you have no poisonous ones among them?"

"Quite sure," said the Harvester faintly.

"How much do you want for the basket?"

"They are a dollar a dozen; I haven't counted them."

"Dear me! Isn't that rather expensive?"

"It is. Very!" said the Harvester. "So expensive that most people don't think of taking over a dozen. They are large and very rich, so they go a long way."

"I suppose you have to spend a great deal of time hunting them? It does seem expensive, but they are fresh, and the boys are so fond of them. I'm not often extravagant, I'll just take the lot. Sarah, bring a pan."

Again the Harvester stood and watched an entire basket counted over and carried away, and he felt the robber he had been called as he took the money.

At the next house he had learned a lesson. He carpeted a basket with leaves and counted out a dozen and a half into it, leaving the remainder in the wagon.

Three blocks on one side of the street exhausted his store and he was showered with orders. He had not seen any one that even resembled a dark-eyed girl. As he came from the last house a big, red motor shot past and then suddenly slowed and backed beside his wagon.

"What in the name of sense are you doing?" demanded Doctor Carey.

"Invading the residence district of Onabasha," said the Harvester. "Madam, would you like some nice, fresh, country mushrooms? I guarantee that there are no poisonous ones among them, and they were gathered this morning. Considering their rarity and the difficult work of collecting, they are exceedingly low at my price. I am offering these for five dollars a dozen, madam, and for mercy sake don't take them or I'll have no excuse to go to the next house."

The doctor stared, then understood, and began to laugh. When at last he could speak he said, "David, I'll bet you started with three bushels and began at the head of this street, and they are all gone."

"Put up a good one!" said the Harvester. "You win. The first house I tried they ordered me to the back door, took a market basket full away from me by force, tried to buy the load, and I didn't see any one save a maid."

The doctor lay on the steering gear and faintly groaned.

The Harvester regarded him sympathetically. "Isn't it a crime?" he questioned. "Mushrooms are no go. I can see that!—or rather they are entirely too much of a go. I never saw anything in such demand. I must seek a less popular article for my purpose. To-morrow look out for me. I shall begin where I left off to-day, but I will have changed my product."

"David, for pity sake," peeped the doctor.

"What do I care how I do it, so I locate her?" superbly inquired the Harvester.

"But you won't find her!" gasped the doctor.

"I've come as close it as you so far, anyway," said the Harvester. "Your mushrooms are on the desk in your office."

He drove slowly up and down the streets until Betsy wabbled on her legs. Then he left her to rest and walked until he wabbled; and by that time it was dark, so he went home.

At the first hint of dawn he was at work the following morning. With loaded baskets closely covered, he started to Onabasha, and began where he had quit the day before. This time he carried a small, crudely fashioned bark basket, leaf-covered, and he rang at the front door with confidence.

Every one seemed to have a maid in that part of the city, for a freshly capped and aproned girl opened the door.

"Are there any young women living here?" blandly inquired the Harvester.

"What's that of your business?" demanded the maid.

The Harvester flushed, but continued, "I am offering something especially intended for young women. If there are none, I will not trouble you."

"There are several."

"Will you please ask them if they would care for bouquets of violets, fresh from the woods?"

"How much are they, and how large are the bunches?"

"Prices differ, and they are the right size to appear well. They had better see for themselves."

The maid reached for the basket, but the Harvester drew back.

"I keep them in my possession," he said. "You may take a sample."

He lifted the leaves and drew forth a medium-sized bunch of long-stemmed blue violets with their leaves. The flowers were fresh, crisp, and strong odours of the woods arose from them.

"Oh!" cried the maid. "Oh, how lovely!"

She hurried away with them and returned carrying a purse.

"I want two more bunches," she said. "How much are they?"

"Are the girls who want them dark or fair?"

"What difference does that make?"

"I have blue violets for blondes, yellow for brunettes, and white for the others."

"Well I never! One is fair, and two have brown hair and blue eyes."

"One blue and two whites," said the Harvester calmly, as if matching women's hair and eyes with flowers were an inherited vocation. "They are twenty cents a bunch."

"Aha!" he chortled to himself as he whistled to Betsy. "At last we have it. There are no dark-eyed girls here. Now we are making headway."

Down the street he went, with varying fortune, but with patience and persistence at every house he at last managed to learn whether there was a dark-eyed girl. There did not seem to be many. Long before his store of yellow violets was gone the last blue and white had disappeared. But he calmly went on asking for dark-eyed girls, and explaining that all the blue and white were taken, because fair women were most numerous.

At one house the owner, who reminded the Harvester of his mother, came to the door. He uncovered and in his suavest tones inquired if a brunette young woman lived there and if she would like a nosegay of yellow violets.

"Well bless my soul!" cried she. "What is this world coming to? Do you mean to tell me that there are now able-bodied men offering at our doors, flowers to match our girls' complexions?"

"Yes madam," said the Harvester gravely, "and also selling them as fast as he can show them, at prices that make a profit very well worth while. I had an equal number of blue and white, but I see the dark girls are very much in the minority. The others were gone long ago, and I now have flowers to offer brunettes only."

"Well forever more! And you don't call that fiddlin' business for a big, healthy, young man?"

The Harvester's gay laugh was infectious.

"I do not," he said. "I have to start as soon as I can see, tramp long distances in wet woods and gather the violets on my knees, make them into bunches, and bring them here in water to keep them fresh. I have another occupation. I only kill time on these, but I would be ashamed to tell you what I have gotten for them this morning."

"Humph! I'm glad to hear it!" said the woman. "Shame in some form is a sign of grace. I have no use for a human being without a generous supply of it. There is a very beautiful dark-eyed girl in the house, and I will take two bunches for her. How much are they?"

"I have only three remaining," said the Harvester. "Would you like to allow her to make her own selection?"

"When I'm giving things I usually take my choice. I want that, and that one."

"As my stock is so nearly out, I'll make the two for twenty," said the Harvester. "Won't you accept the last one from me, because you remind me just a little of my mother?"

"I will indeed," said she. "Thank you very much! I shall love to have them as dearly as any of the girls. I used to gather them when I was a child, but I almost never see the blue ones any more, and I don't know as I ever expected to see a yellow violet again as long as I live. Where did you get them?"

"In my woods," said the Harvester. "You see I grow several members of the viola pedata family, bird's foot, snake, and wood violet, and three of the odorata, English, marsh, and sweet, for our big drug houses. They use the flowers in making delicate tests for acids and alkalies. The entire plant, flower, seed, leaf, and root, goes into different remedies. The beds seed themselves and spread, so I have more than I need for the chemists, and I sell a few. I don't use the white and yellow in my business; I just grow them for their beauty. I also sell my surplus lilies of the valley. Would you like to order some of them for your house or more violets for to-morrow?"

"Well bless my soul! Do you mean to tell me that lilies of the valley are medicine?"

The Harvester laughed.

"I grow immense beds of them in the woods on the banks of Loon Lake," he said. "They are the convallaris majallis of the drug houses and I scarcely know what the weak-hearted people would do without them. I use large quantities in trade, and this season I am selling a few because people so love them."

"Lilies in medicine; well dear me! Are roses good for our innards too?"

Then the Harvester did laugh.

"I imagine the roses you know go into perfumes mostly," he answered. "They do make medicine of Canadian rock rose and rose bay, laurel, and willow. I grow the bushes, but they are not what you would consider roses."

"I wonder now," said the woman studying the Harvester closely, "if you are not that queer genius I've heard of, who spends his time hunting and growing stuff in the woods and people call him the Medicine Man."

"I strongly suspect madam, I am that man," said the Harvester.

"Well bless me!" cried she. "I've always wanted to see you and here when I do, you look just like anybody else. I thought you'd have long hair, and be wild-eyed and ferocious. And your talk sounds like out of a book. Well that beats me!"

"Me too!" said the Harvester, lifting his hat. "You don't want any lilies to-morrow, then?"

"Yes I do. Medicine or no medicine, I've always liked 'em, and I'm going to keep on liking them. If you can bring me a good-sized bunch after the weak-kneed—"

"Weak-hearted," corrected the Harvester.

"Well 'weak-hearted,' then; it's all the same thing. If you've got any left, as I was saying, you can fetch them to me for the smell."

The Harvester laughed all the way down town. There he went to Doctor Carey's office, examined a directory, and got the names of all the numbers where he had sold yellow violets. A few questions when the doctor came in settled all of them, but the flower scheme was better. Because the yellow were not so plentiful as the white and blue, next day he added buttercups and cowslips to his store for the dark girls. When he had rifled his beds for the last time, after three weeks of almost daily trips to town, and had paid high prices to small boys he set searching the adjoining woods until no more flowers could be found, he drove from the outskirts of the city one day toward the hospital, and as he stopped, down the street came Doctor Carey frantically waving to him. As the big car slackened, "Come on David, quick! I've seen her!" cried the doctor.

The Harvester jumped from the wagon, threw the lines to Belshazzar, and landed in the panting car.

"For Heaven's sake where? Are you sure?"

The car went speeding down the street. A policeman beckoned and cried after it.

"It won't do any good to get arrested, Doc," cautioned the Harvester.

"Now right along here," panted Doctor Carey. "Watch both sides sharply. If I stop you jump out, and tell the blame policemen to get at their job. The party they are hired to find is right under their noses."

The Harvester began to perspire. "Doc, don't you think you should tell me? Maybe she is in some store. Maybe I could do better on foot."

"Shut up!" growled the doctor. "I am doing the best I know."

He hurried up the street for blocks and back again, and at last stopped before a large store and went in. When he returned he drove to the hospital and together they entered the office. There he turned to the Harvester.

"It isn't so hard to understand you now, my boy," he said. "Shades of Diana, but she'll be a beauty when she gets a little more flesh and colour. She came out of Whitlaw's and walked right to the crossing. I almost could have touched her, but I didn't notice. Two girls passed before me, and in hurrying, a tall, dark one knocked off one of your bunches of yellow violets. She glanced at it and laughed, but let it lay. Then your girl hesitated, stooped and picked it up. The crazy policeman yelled at me to clear the crossing and it didn't hit me for a half block how tall and white she was and how dark her eyes were. I was just thinking about her picking up the flowers, and that it was queer for her to do it, when like a brick it hit me, *That's David's girl!* I tried to turn around, but you know what Main Street is in the middle of the day. And those idiots of policemen! They ordered me on, and I couldn't turn for a street car coming, so I called to one of them that the girl we wanted was down the street, and he looked at me like an addle-pate and said, 'What girl? Move on or you'll get in a jam here.' You can use me for a football if I don't go back and smash him. Paid him five dollars myself less than two weeks ago to keep his eyes open. 'TO KEEP HIS EYES OPEN!'" panted the doctor, shaking his fist at David. "Yes sir! 'To keep his eyes open!' And he motioned for things to come along, and so I lost her too."

"I think we had better go back to the street," said the Harvester.

"Oh, I'd been back and forth along that street for nearly an hour before I gave up and came here to see if I could find you, and we've hunted it an hour more! What's the use? She's gone for this time, but by gum, I saw her! And she was worth seeing!"

"Did she appear ill to you?"

The doctor dropped on a chair and threw out his hands hopelessly.

"This was awful sudden, David," he said. "I was going along as I told you, and I noticed her stop and thought she had a good head to wait a second instead of running in before me, and there came those two girls right under the car from the other side. I only had a glimpse of her as she stooped for the flowers. I saw a big braid of hair, but I was half a block away before I got it all connected, and then came the crush in the street, and I was blocked."

The doctor broke down and wiped his face and expressed his feelings unrestrainedly.

"Don't!" said the Harvester patiently. "It's no use to feel so badly, Doc. I know what you would give to have found her for me. I know you did all you could. I let her escape me. We will find her yet. It's glorious news that she's in the city. It gives me heart to hear that. Can't you just remember if she seemed ill?"

The doctor meditated.

"She wasn't the tallest girl I ever saw," he said slowly, "but she was the tallest girl to be pretty. She had on a white waist and a gray skirt and black hat. Her eyes and hair were like you said, and she was plain, white faced, with a hue that might possibly be natural, and it might be confinement in bad light and air and poor food. She didn't seem sick, but she isn't well. There is something the matter with her, but it's not immediate or dangerous. She appeared like a flower that had got a little moisture and sprouted in a cellar."

"You saw her all right!" said the Harvester. "And I think your diagnosis is correct too. That's the way she seemed to me. I've thought she needed sun and air. I told the South Wind so the other day."

"Why you blame fool!" cried the doctor. "Is this thing going to your head? Say, I forgot! There is something else. I traced her in the store. She was at the embroidery counter and she bought some silk. If she ever comes again the clerk is going to hold her and telephone me or get her address if she has to steal it. Oh, we are getting there! We will have her pretty soon now. You ought to feel better just to know that she is in town and that I've seen her."

"I do!" said the Harvester. "Indeed I do!"

"It can't be much longer," said the doctor. "She's got to be located soon. But those policemen! I wouldn't give a nickel for the lot! I'll bet she's walked over them for two weeks. If I were you I'd discharge the bunch. They'd be peacefully asleep if she passed them. If they'd let me alone, I'd have had her. I could have turned around easily. I've been in dozens of closer places."

"Don't worry! This can't last much longer. She's of and in the city or she wouldn't have picked up the flowers. Doc, are you sure they were mine?"

"Yes. Half the girls have been tricked out in yours the past two weeks. I can spot them as far as I can see."

"Dear Lord, that's getting close!" said the Harvester intensely. "Seems as if the violets would tell her."

"Now cut out flowers talking and the South Wind!" ordered the doctor. "This is business. The violets prove something all right, though. If she was in the country, she could gather plenty herself. She is working at sewing in some room in town, either over a store or in a house. If she hadn't been starved for flowers she never would have stopped for them on the street. I could see just a flash of hesitation, but she wanted them too much. David, one bouquet will go in water and be cared for a week. Man, it's getting close! This does seem like a link."

"Since you say it, possibly I dare agree with you," said the Harvester.

"How near are you through with that canvass of yours?"

"About three fourths."

"Well I'd go on with it. After all we have got to find her ourselves. Those senile policemen!"

"I am going on with it; you needn't worry about that. But I've got to change to other flowers. I've stripped the violet beds. There's quite a crop of berries coming, but they are not ripe yet, and a tragedy to pick. The pond lilies are just beginning to open by the thousand. The lake border is blue with sweet-flag that is lovely and the marsh pale gold with cowslips. The ferns are prime and the woods solid sheets of every colour of bloom. I believe I'll go ahead with the wild flowers."

"I would too! David, you do feel better, don't you?"

"I certainly do, Doctor. Surely it won't be long now!"

The Harvester was so hopeful that he whistled and sang on the return to Medicine Woods, and that night for the first time in many days he sat long over a candlestick, and took a farewell peep into her room before he went to bed.

The next day he worked with all his might harvesting the last remnants of early spring herbs, in the dry-room and store-house, and on furniture and candlesticks.

Then he went back to flower gathering and every day offered bunches of exquisite wood and field flowers and white and gold water lilies from door to door.

Three weeks later the Harvester, perceptibly thin, pale, and worried entered the office. He sank into a chair and groaned wearily.

"Isn't this the bitterest luck!" he cried. "I've finished the town. I've almost walked off my legs. I've sold flowers by the million, but I've not had a sight of her."

"It's been almost a tragedy with me," said the doctor gloomily. "I've killed two dogs and grazed a baby, because I was watching the sidewalks instead of the street. What are you going to do now?"

"I am going home and bring up the work to the July mark. I am going to take it easy and rest a few days so I can think more clearly. I don't know what I'll try next. I've punched up the depot and the policemen again. When I get something new thought out I'll let you know."

Then he began emptying his pockets of money and heaping it on the table, small coins, bills, big and little.

"What on earth is that?"

"That," said the Harvester, giving the heap a shove of contempt, "that is the price of my pride and humiliation. That is what it cost people who allowed me to cheek my way into their homes and rob them, as one maid said, for my own purposes. Doc, where on earth does all the money come from? In almost every house I entered, women had it to waste, in many cases to throw away. I never saw so much paid for nothing in all my life. That whole heap is from mushrooms and flowers."

"What are you piling it there for?"

"For your free ward. I don't want a penny of it. I wouldn't keep it, not if I was starving."

"Why David! You couldn't compel any one to buy. You offered something they wanted, and they paid you what you asked."

"Yes, and to keep them from buying, and to make the stuff go farther, I named prices to shame a shark. When I think of that mushroom deal I can feel my face burn. I've made the search I wanted to, and I am satisfied that I can't find her that way. I have kept up my work at home between times. I am not out anything but my time, and it isn't fair to plunder the city to pay that. Take that cussed money and put it where I'll never see or hear of it. Do anything you please, except to ask me ever to profit by a cent. When I wash my hands after touching it for the last time maybe I'll feel better."

"You are a fanatic!"

"If getting rid of that is being a fanatic, I am proud of the title. You can't imagine what I've been through!"

"Can't I though?" laughed the doctor. "In work of that kind you get into every variety of place; and some of it is new to you. Never mind! No one can contaminate you. It is the law that only a man can degrade himself. Knowing things will not harm you. Doing them is a different matter. What you know will be a protection. What you do ruins—if it is wrong. You are not harmed, you are only disgusted. Think it over, and in a few days come back and get your money. It is strictly honest. You earned every cent of it."

"If you ever speak of it again or force it on me I'll take it home and throw it into the lake."

He went after Betsy and slowly drove to Medicine Woods. Belshazzar, on the seat beside him, recognized a silent, disappointed master and whimpered as he rubbed the Harvester's shoulder to attract his attention.

"This is tough luck, old boy," said the Harvester. "I had such hopes and I worked so hard. I suffered in the flesh for every hour of it, and I failed. Oh but I hate the word! If I knew where she is right now, Bel, I'd give anything I've got. But there's no use to wail and get sorry for myself. That's against the law of common decency. I'll take a swim, sleep it off, straighten up the herbs a little, and go at it again, old fellow; that's a man's way. She's somewhere, and she's got to be found, no matter what it costs."

Chapter 8

Belshazzar's Record Point

The Harvester set the neglected cabin in order; then he carefully and deftly packed all his dried herbs, barks, and roots. Next came carrying the couch grass, wild alum, and soapwort into the store-room. Then followed July herbs. He first went to his beds of foxglove, because the tender leaves of the second year should be stripped from them at flowering time, and that usually began two weeks earlier; but his bed lay in a shaded, damp location and the tall bloom stalks were only in half flower, their pale lavender making an exquisite picture. It paid to collect those leaves, so the Harvester hastily stripped the amount he wanted.

Yarrow was beginning to bloom and he gathered as much as he required, taking the whole plant. That only brought a few cents a pound, but it was used entire, so the weight made it worth while.

Catnip tops and leaves were also ready. As it grew in the open in dry soil and the beds had been weeded that spring, he could gather great arm loads of it with a sickle, but he had to watch the swarming bees. He left the male fern and mullein until the last for different reasons.

On the damp, cool, rocky hillside, beneath deep shade of big forest trees, grew the ferns, their long, graceful fronds waving softly. Tree toads sang on the cool rocks beneath them, chewinks nested under gnarled roots among them, rose-breasted grosbeaks sang in grape vines clambering over the thickets, and Singing Water ran close beside. So the Harvester left digging these roots until nearly the last, because he so disliked to disturb the bed. He could not have done it if he had not been forced. All of the demand for his fern never could be supplied. Of his products none was more important to the Harvester because this formed the basis of one of the oldest and most reliable remedies for little children. The fern had to be gathered with especial care, deteriorated quickly, and no staple was more subject to adulteration.

So he kept his bed intact, lifted the roots at the proper time, carefully cleaned without washing, rapidly dried in currents of hot air, and shipped them in bottles to the trade. He charged and received fifteen cents a pound, where careless and indifferent workers got ten.

On the banks of Singing Water, at the head of the fern bed, the Harvester stood under a gray beech tree and looked down the swaying length of delicate green. He was lean and rapidly bronzing, for he seldom remembered a head covering because he loved the sweep of the wind in his hair.

"I hate to touch you," he said. "How I wish she could see you before I begin. If she did, probably she would say it was a sin, and then I never could muster courage to do it at all. I'd give a small farm to know if those violets revived for her. I was crazy to ask Doc if they were wilted, but I hated to. If they were from the ones I gathered that morning they should have been all right."

A tree toad dared him to come on; a chipmunk grew saucy as the Harvester bent to an unloved task. If he stripped the bed as closely as he dared and not injure it, he could not fill half his orders; so, deftly and with swift, skilful fingers and an earnest face, he worked. Belshazzar came down the hill on a rush, nose to earth and began hunting among the plants. He never could understand why his loved master was so careless as to go to work before he had pronounced it safe. When the fern bed was finished, the Harvester took time to make a trip to town, but there was no word waiting him; so he went to the mullein. It lay on a sunny hillside beyond the couch grass and joined a few small fields, the only cleared land of the six hundred acres of Medicine Woods. Over rocks and little hills and hollows spread the pale, grayish-yellow of the green leaves, and from five to seven feet arose the flower stems, while the entire earth between was covered with rosettes of young plants. Belshazzar went before to give warning if any big rattlers curled in the sun on the hillside, and after him followed the Harvester cutting leaves in heaps. That was warm work and he covered his head with a floppy old straw hat, with wet grass in the crown, and stopped occasionally to rest.

He loved that yellow-faced hillside. Because so much of his reaping lay in the shade and commonly his feet sank in dead leaves and damp earth, the change was a rest. He cheerfully stubbed his toes on rocks, and endured the heat without complaint. It appeared to him as if a member of every species of butterfly he knew wavered down the hillside. There were golden-brown danais, with their black-striped wings, jetty troilus with an attempt at trailers, big asterias, velvety black with longer trails and wide bands of yellow dots. Coenia were most numerous of all and to the Harvester wonderfully attractive in rich, subdued colours with a wealth of markings and eye spots. Many small moths, with transparent wings and noses red as blood, flashed past him hunting pollen. Goldfinches, intent on thistle bloom, wavered through the air trailing mellow, happy notes behind them, and often a humming-bird visited the mullein. On the lake wild life splashed and chattered incessantly, and sometimes the Harvester paused and stood with arms heaped with leaves, to interpret some unusually appealing note of pain or anger or some very attractive melody. The red-wings were swarming, the killdeers busy, and he thought of the Dream Girl and smiled.

"I wonder if she would like this," he mused.

When the mullein leaves were deep on the trays of the dry-house he began on the bloom and that was a task he loved. Just to lay off the beds in swaths and follow them, deftly picking the stamens and yellow petals from the blooms. These he would dry speedily in hot air, bottle, and send at once to big laboratories. The listed price was seventy-five cents a pound, but the beautiful golden bottles of the Harvester always brought more. The work was worth while, and he liked the location and gathering of this particular crop: for these reasons he always left it until the last, and then revelled in the gold of sunshine, bird, butterfly, and flower. Several days were required to harvest the mullein and during the time the man worked with nimble fingers, while his brain was intensely occupied with the question of what to do next in his search for the Girl.

When the work was finished, he went to the deep wood to take a peep at acres of thrifty ginseng, and he was satisfied as he surveyed the big bed. Long years he had laboured diligently; soon came the reward. He had not realized it before, but as he studied the situation he saw that he either must begin this harvest at once or employ help If he waited until September he could not gather one third of the crop alone.

"But the roots will weigh less if I take them now," he argued, "and I can work at nothing in comfort until I have located her I will go on with my search and allow the ginseng to grow that much heavier. What a picture! It is folly to disturb this now, for I will lose the seed of every plant I dig, and that is worth almost as much as the root. It is a question whether I want to furnish the market with seed, and so raise competition for my bed. I think, be jabbers, that I'll wait for this harvest until the seed is ripe, and then bury part of a head where I dig a root, as the Indians did. That's the idea! The more I grow, the more money; and I may need considerable for her. One thing I'd like to know: Are these plants cultivated? All the books quote the wild at highest rates and all I've ever sold was wild. The start grew here naturally. What I added from the surrounding country was wild, but through and among it I've sown seed I bought, and I've tended it with every care. But this is deep wood and wild conditions. I think I have a perfect right to so label it. I'll ask Doc. And another thing I'll go through the woods west of Onabasha where I used to find ginseng, and see if I can get a little and then take the same amount of plants grown here, and make a test. That way I can discover any difference before I go to market. This is my gold mine, and that point is mighty important to me, so I'll go this very day. I used to find it in the woods northeast of town and on the land Jameson bought, west. Wonder if he lives there yet. He should have died of pure meanness long ago. I'll drive to the river and hunt along the bank."

Early the following morning the Harvester went to Onabasha and stopped at the hospital for news. Finding none, he went through town and several miles into the country on the other side, to a piece of lowland lying along the river bank, where he once had found and carried home to reset a big bed of ginseng. If he could get only a half pound of roots from there now, they would serve his purpose. He went down the bank, Belshazzar at his heels, and at last found the place. Many trees had been cut, but there remained enough for shade; the fields bore the ragged, unattractive appearance of old. The Harvester smiled grimly as he remembered that the man who lived there once had charged him for damage he might do to trees in driving across his woods, and boasted to his neighbours that a young fool was paying for the privilege of doing his grubbing. If Jameson had known what the roots he was so anxious to dispose of brought a pound on the market at that time, he would have been insane with anger. So the Harvester's eyes were dancing with fun and a wry grin twisted his lips as he clambered over the banks of the recently dredged river, and looked at its pitiful condition and straight, muddy flow.

"Appears to match the remainder of the Jameson property," he said. "I don't know who he is or where he came from, but he's no farmer. Perhaps he uses this land to corral the stock he buys until he can sell it again."

He went down the embankment and began to search for the location where he formerly had found the ginseng. When he came to the place he stood amazed, for from seed, roots, and plants he had missed, the growth had sprung up and spread, so that at a rapid estimate the Harvester thought it contained at least five pounds, allowing for what it would shrink on account of being gathered early. He hesitated an instant, and thought of coming later; but the drive was long and the loss would not amount to enough to pay for a second trip. About taking it, he never thought at all. He once had permission from the owner to dig all the shrubs, bushes, and weeds he desired from that stretch of woods, and had paid for possible damages that might occur. As he bent to the task there did come a fleeting thought that the patch was weedless and in unusual shape for wild stuff. Then, with swift strokes of his light mattock, he lifted the roots, crammed them into his sack, whistled to Belshazzar, and going back to the wagon, drove away. Reaching home he washed the ginseng, and spread it on a tray to dry. The first time he wanted the mattock he realized that he had left it lying where he had worked. It was an implement that he had directed a blacksmith to fashion to meet his requirements. No store contained anything half so useful to him. He had worked with it for years and it just suited him, so there was nothing to do but go back. Betsy was too tired to return that day, so he planned to dig his ginseng with something else, finish his work the following morning, and get the mattock in the afternoon.

"It's like a knife you've carried for years, or a gun," muttered the Harvester. "I actually don't know how to get along without it. What made me so careless I can't imagine. I never before in my life did a trick like that. I wonder if I hurried a little. I certainly was free to take it. He always wanted the stuff dug up. Of all the stupid tricks, Belshazzar, that was the worst. Now Betsy and a half day of wasted time must pay for my carelessness. Since I have to go, I'll look a little farther. Maybe there is more. Those woods used to be full of it."

According to this programme, the next afternoon the Harvester again walked down the embankment of the mourning river and through the ragged woods to the place where the ginseng had been. He went forward, stepping lightly, as men of his race had walked the forest for ages, swerving to avoid boughs, and looking straight ahead. Contrary to his usual custom of coming to heel in a strange wood, Belshazzar suddenly darted around the man and took the path they had followed the previous day. The animal was performing his office in life; he had heard or scented something unusual. The Harvester knew what that meant. He looked inquiringly at the dog, glanced around, and then at the earth. Belshazzar proceeded noiselessly at a rapid pace over the leaves: Suddenly the master saw the dog stop in a stiff point. Lifting his feet lightly and straining his eyes before him, the Harvester passed a spice thicket and came in line.

For one second he stood as rigid as Belshazzar. The next his right arm shot upward full length, and began describing circles, his open palm heavenward, and into his face leapt a glorified expression of exultation. Face down in the rifled ginseng bed lay a sobbing girl. Her frame was long and slender, a thick coil of dark hair; bound her head. A second more and the Harvester bent and softly patted Belshazzar's head. The beast broke point and looked up. The man caught the dog's chin in a caressing grip, again touched his head, moved soundless lips, and waved toward the prostrate figure. The dog hesitated. The Harvester made the same motions. Belshazzar softly stepped over the leaves, passed around the feet of the girl, and paused beside her, nose to earth, softly sniffing.

In one moment she came swiftly to a sitting posture.

"Oh!" she cried in a spasm of fright.

Belshazzar reached an investigating nose and wagged an eager tail.

"Why you are a nice friendly dog!" said the trembling voice.

He immediately verified the assertion by offering his nose for a kiss. The girl timidly laid a hand on his head.

"Heaven knows I'm lonely enough to kiss a dog," she said, "but suppose you belong to the man who stole my ginseng, and then ran away so fast he forgot his—his piece he digged with."

Belshazzar pressed closer.

"I am just killed, and I don't care whose dog you are," sobbed the girl.

She threw her arms around Belshazzar's neck and laid her white face against his satiny shoulder. The Harvester could endure no more. He took a step forward, his face convulsed with pain.

"Please don't!" he begged. "I took your ginseng. I'll bring it back to-morrow. There wasn't more than twenty-five or thirty dollars' worth. It doesn't amount to one tear."

The girl arose so quickly, the Harvester could not see how she did it. With a startled fright on her face, and the dark eyes swimming, she turned to him in one long look. Words rolled from the lips of the man in a jumble. Behind the tears there was a dull, expressionless blue in the girl's eyes and her face was so white that it appeared blank. He began talking before she could speak, in an effort to secure forgiveness without condemnation.

"You see, I grow it for a living on land I own, and I've always gathered all there was in the country and no one cared. There never was enough in one place to pay, and no other man wanted to spend the time, and so I've always felt free to take it. Every one knew I did, and no one ever objected before. Once I paid Henry Jameson for the privilege of cleaning it from these woods. That was six or seven years ago, and it didn't occur to me that I wasn't at liberty to dig what has grown since. I'll bring it back at once, and pay you for the shrinkage from gathering it too early. There won't be much over six pounds when it's dry. Please, please don't feel badly. Won't you trust me to return it, and make good the damage I've done?"

The face of the Harvester was eager and his tones appealing, as he leaned forward trying to make her understand.

"Certainly!" said the Girl as she bent to pat the dog, while she dried her eyes under cover of the movement. "Certainly! It can make no difference!"

But as the Harvester drew a deep breath of relief, she suddenly straightened to full height and looked straight at him.

"Oh what is the use to tell a pitiful lie!" she cried. "It does make a difference! It makes all the difference in the world! I need that money! I need it unspeakably. I owe a debt I must pay. What—what did I understand you to say ginseng is worth?"

"If you will take a few steps," said the Harvester, "and make yourself comfortable on this log in the shade, I will tell you all I know about it."

The girl walked swiftly to the log indicated, seated herself, and waited. The Harvester followed to a respectful distance.

"I can't tell to an ounce what wet roots would weigh," he said as easily as he could command his voice to speak with the heart in him beating wildly, "and of course they lose greatly in drying; but I've handled enough that I know the weight I carried home will come to six pounds at the very least. Then you must figure on some loss, because I dug this before it really was ready. It does not reach full growth until September, and if it is taken too soon there is a decrease in weight. I will make that up to you when I return it."

The troubled eyes were gazing on his face intently, and the Harvester studied them as he talked.

"You would think, then, there would be all of six pounds?

"Yes," said the Harvester, "closer eight. When I replace the shrinkage there is bound to be over seven."

"And how much did I understand you to say it brought a pound?"

"That all depends," answered he. "If you cure it yourself, and dry it too much, you lose in weight. If you carry it in a small lot to the druggists of Onabasha, probably you will not get over five dollars for it."

"Five?"

It was a startled cry.

"How much did you expect?" asked the Harvester gently.

"Uncle Henry said he thought he could get fifty cents a pound for all I could find."

"If your Uncle Henry has learned at last that ginseng is a salable article he should know something about the price also. Will you tell me what he said, and how you came to think of gathering roots for the market?"

"'There were men talking beneath the trees one Sunday afternoon about old times and hunting deer, and they spoke of people who made money long ago gathering roots and barks, and they mentioned one man who lived by it yet."

"Was his name Langston?"

"Yes, I remember because I liked the name. I was so eager to earn something, and I can't leave here just now because Aunt Molly is very ill, so the thought came that possibly I could gather stuff worth money, after my work was finished. I went out and asked questions. They said nothing brought enough to make it pay any one, except this ginseng plant, and the Langston man almost had stripped the country. Then uncle said he used to get stuff here, and he might have got some of that. I asked what it was like, so they told me and I hunted until I found that, and it seemed a quantity to me. Of course I didn't know it had to be dried. Uncle took a root I dug to a store, and they told him that it wasn't much used any more, but they would give him fifty cents a pound for it. What MAKES you think you can get five dollars?"

"With your permission," said the Harvester.

He seated himself on the log, drew from his pocket an old pamphlet, and spreading it before her, ran a pencil along the line of a list of schedule prices for common drug roots and herbs. Because he understood, his eyes were very bright, and his voice a trifle crisp. A latent anger springing in his breast was a good curb for his emotions. He was closely acquainted with all of the druggists of Onabasha, and he knew that not one of them had offered less than standard prices for ginseng.

"The reason I think so," he said gently, "is because growing it is the largest part of my occupation, and it was a staple with my father before me. I am David Langston, of whom you heard those men speak. Since I was a very small boy I have lived by collecting herbs and roots, and I get more for ginseng than anything else. Very early I tired of hunting other people's woods for herbs, so I began transplanting them to my own. I moved that bed out there seven years ago. What you found has grown since from roots I overlooked and seeds that fell at that time. Now do you think I am enough of an authority to trust my word on the subject?"

There was not a change of expression on her white face.

"You surely should know," she said wearily, "and you could have no possible object in deceiving me. Please go on."

"Any country boy or girl can find ginseng, gather, wash, and dry it, and get five dollars a pound. I can return yours to-morrow and you can cure and take it to a druggist I will name you, and sell for that. But if you will allow me to make a suggestion, you can get more. Your roots are now on the trays of an evaporating house. They will dry to the proper degree desired by the trade, so that they will not lose an extra ounce in weight, and if I send them with my stuff to big wholesale houses I deal with, they will be graded with the finest wild ginseng. It is worth more than the cultivated and you will get closer eight dollars a pound for it than five. There is some speculation in it, and the market fluctuates: but, as a rule, I sell for the highest price the drug brings, and, at times when the season is very dry, I set my own prices. Shall I return yours or may I cure and sell it, and bring you the money?"

"How much trouble would that make you?"

"None. The work of digging and washing is already finished. All that remains is to weigh it and make a memorandum of the amount when I sell. I should very much like to do it. It would be a comfort to see the money go into your hands.

If you are afraid to trust me, I will give you the names of several people you can ask concerning me the next time you go to the city."

She looked at him steadily.

"Never mind that," she said. "But why do you offer to do it for a stranger? It must be some trouble, no matter how small you represent it to be."

"Perhaps I am going to pay you eight and sell for ten."

"I don't think you can. Five sounds fabulous to me. I can't believe that. If you wanted to make money you needn't have told me you took it. I never would have known. That isn't your reason!"

"Possibly I would like to atone for those tears I caused," said the Harvester.

"Don't think of that! They are of no consequence to any one. You needn't do anything for me on that account."

"Don't search for a reason," said the Harvester, in his gentlest tones. "Forget that feature of the case. Say I'm peculiar, and allow me to do it because it would be a pleasure. In close two weeks I will bring you the money. Is it a bargain?"

"Yes, if you care to make it."

"I care very much. We will call that settled."

"I wish I could tell you what it will mean to me," said the Girl.

"If you only would," plead the Harvester.

"I must not burden a stranger with my troubles."

"But if it would make the stranger so happy!"

"That isn't possible. I must face life and bear what it brings me alone."

"Not unless you choose," said the Harvester. "That is, if you will pardon me, a narrow view of life. It cuts other people out of the joy of service. If you can't tell me, would you trust a very lovely and gentle woman I could bring to you?"

"No more than you. It is my affair; I must work it out myself."

"I am mighty sorry," said the Harvester. "I believe you err in that decision. Think it over a day or so, and see if two heads are not better than one. You will realize when this ginseng matter is settled that you profited by trusting me. The same will hold good along other lines, if you only can bring yourself to think so. At any rate, try. Telling a trouble makes it lighter. Sympathy should help, if nothing can be done. And as for money, I can show you how to earn sums at least worth your time, if you have nothing else you want to do."

The Girl bent toward him.

"Oh please do tell me!" she cried eagerly. "I've tried and tried to find some way ever since I have been here, but every one else I have met says I can't, and nothing seems to be worth anything. If you only would tell me something I could do!"

"If you will excuse my saying so," said the Harvester, "it appeals to me that ease, not work, is the thing you require. You appear extremely worn. Won't you let me help you find a way to a long rest first?"

"Impossible!" cried the Girl. "I know I am white and appear ill, but truly I never have been sick in all my life. I have been having trouble and working too much, but I'll be better soon. Believe me, there is no rest for me now. I must earn the money I owe first."

"There is a way, if you care to take it," said the Harvester. "In my work I have become very well acquainted with the chief surgeon of the city hospital. Through him I happen to know that he has a free bed in a beautiful room, where you could rest until you are perfectly strong again, and that room is empty just now. When you are well, I will tell you about the work."

As she arose the Harvester stood, and tall and straight she faced him.

"Impossible!" she said. "It would be brutal to leave my aunt. I cannot pay to rest in a hospital ward, and I will not accept charity. If you can put me in the way of earning, even a few cents a day, at anything I could do outside the work necessary to earn my board here, it would bring me closer to happiness than anything else on earth."

"What I suggest is not impossible," said the Harvester softly. "If you will go, inside an hour a sweet and gentle lady will come for you and take you to ease and perfect rest until you are strong again. I will see that your aunt is cared for scrupulously. I can't help urging you. It is a crime to talk of work to a woman so manifestly worn as you are."

"Then we will not speak of it," said the Girl wearily. "It is time for me to go, anyway. I see you mean to be very kind, and while I don't in the least understand it, I do hope you feel I am grateful. If half you say about the ginseng comes true, I can make a payment worth while before I had hoped to. I have no words to tell you what that will mean to me."

"If this debt you speak of were paid, could you rest then?"

"I could lie down and give up in peace, and I think I would."

"I think you wouldn't," said the Harvester, "because you wouldn't be allowed. There are people in these days who make a business of securing rest for the tired and over weary, and they would come and prevent that if you tried it. Please let me make another suggestion. If you owe money to some one you feel needs it and the debt is preying on you, let's pay it."

He drew a small check-book from his pocket and slipped a pen from a band.

"If you will name the amount and give me the address, you shall be free to go to the rest I ask for you inside an hour."

Then slowly from head to foot she looked at him.

"Why?"

"Because your face and attitude clearly indicate that you are over tired. Believe me, you do yourself wrong if you refuse."

"In what way would changing creditors rest me?"

"I thought perhaps you were owing some one who needed the money. I am not a rich man, but I have no one save myself to provide for and I have funds lying idle that I would be glad to use for you. If you make a point of it, when you are rested, you can repay me."

"My creditor needs the money, but I should prefer owing him rather than a perfect stranger. What you suggest would help me not at all. I must go now."

"Very well," said the Harvester. "If you will tell me whom to ask for and where you live, I will come to see you to-morrow and bring you some pamphlets. With these and with a little help you soon can earn any amount a girl is likely to owe. It will require but a little while. Where can I find you?"

The Girl hesitated and for the first time a hint of colour flushed her cheek. But courage appeared to be her strong point.

"Do you live in this part of the country?" she asked.

"I live ten miles from here, east of Onabasha," he answered.

"Do you know Henry Jameson?"

"By sight and by reputation."

"Did you ever know anything kind or humane of him?"

"I never did."

"My name is Ruth Jameson. At present I am indebted to him for the only shelter I have. His wife is ill through overwork and worry, and I am paying for my bed and what I don't eat, principally, by attempting her work. It scarcely would be fair to Uncle Henry to say that I do it. I stagger around as long as I can stand, then I sit through his abuse. He is a pleasant man. Please don't think I am telling you this to harrow your sympathy further. The reason I explain is because I am driven. If I do not, you will misjudge me when I say that I only can see you here. I understood what you meant when you said Uncle Henry should have known the price of ginseng if he knew it was for sale. He did. He knew what he could get for it, and what he meant to pay me. That is one of his original methods with a woman. If he thought I could earn anything worth while, he would allow me, if I killed myself doing it; and then he would take the money by force if necessary. So I can meet you here only. I can earn just what I may in secret. He buys cattle and horses and is away from home much of the day, and when Aunt Molly is comfortable I can have a few hours."

"I understand," said the Harvester. "But this is an added hardship. Why do you remain? Why subject yourself to force and work too heavy for you?"

"Because his is the only roof on earth where I feel I can pay for all I get. I don't care to discuss it, I only want you to say you understand, if I ask you to bring the pamphlets here and tell me how I can earn money."

"I do," said the Harvester earnestly, although his heart was hot in protest. "You may be very sure that I will not misjudge you. Shall I come at two o'clock to-morrow, Miss Jameson?"

"If you will be so kind."

The Harvester stepped aside and she passed him and crossing the rifled ginseng patch went toward a low brown farmhouse lying in an unkept garden, beside a ragged highway. The man sat on the log she had vacated, held his head between his hands and tried to think, but he could not for big waves of joy that swept over him when he realized that at last he had found her, had spoken with her, and had arranged a meeting for the morrow.

"Belshazzar," he said softly, "I wish I could leave you to protect her. Every day you prove to me that I need you, but Heaven knows her necessity is greater. Bel, she makes my heart ache until it feels like jelly. There seems to be just one thing to do. Get that fool debt paid like lightning, and lift her out of here quicker than that. Now, we will go and see Doc, and call off the watch-dogs of the law. Ahead of them, aren't we, Belshazzar? There is a better day coming; we feel it in our bones, don't we, old partner?"

The Harvester started through the woods on a rush, and as the exercise warmed his heart, he grew wonderfully glad. At last he had found her. Uncertainty was over. If ever a girl needed a home and care he thought she did. He was so jubilant that he felt like crying aloud, shouting for joy, but by and by the years of sober repression made their weight felt, so he climbed into the wagon and politely requested Betsy to make her best time to Onabasha. Betsy had been asked to make haste so frequently of late that she at first almost doubted the sanity of her master, the law of whose life, until recently, had been to take his time. Now he appeared to be in haste every day. She had become so accustomed to being urged to hurry that she almost had developed a gait; so at the Harvester's suggestion she did her level best to Onabasha and the hospital, where she loved to nose Belshazzar and rest near the watering tap under a big tree.

The Harvester went down the hall and into the office on the run, and his face appeared like a materialized embodiment of living joy. Doctor Carey turned at his approach and then bounded half way across the room, his hands outstretched.

"You've found her, David!"

The Harvester grabbed the hand of his friend and stood pumping it up and down while he gulped at the lump in his throat, and big tears squeezed from his eyes, but he could only nod his proud head.

"Found her!" exulted Doctor Carey. "Really found her! Well that's great! Sit down and tell me, boy! Is she sick, as we feared? Did you only see her or did you get to talk with her?"

"Well sir," said the Harvester, choking back his emotions, "you remember that ginseng I told you about getting on the old Jameson place last night. To-day, I learned I'd lost that hand-made mattock I use most, and I went back for it, and there she was."

"In the country?"

"Yes sir!"

"Well why didn't we think of it before?"

"I suppose first we would have had to satisfy ourselves that she wasn't in town, anyway."

"Sure! That would be the logical way to go at it! And so you found her?"

"Yes sir, I found her! Just Belshazzar and I! I was going along on my way to the place, and he ran past me and made a stiff point, and when I came up, there she was!"

"There she was?"

"Yes sir; there she was!"

They shook hands again.

"Then of course you spoke to her."

"Yes I spoke to her."

"Were you pleased?"

"With her speech and manner?—yes. But, Doc, if ever a woman needed everything on earth!"

"Well did you get any kind of a start made?"

"I couldn't do so very much. I had to go a little slow for fear of frightening her, but I tried to get her to come here and she won't until a debt she owes is paid, and she's in no condition to work."

"Got any idea how much it is?"

"No, but it can't be any large sum. I tried to offer to pay it, but she had no hesitation in telling me she preferred owing a man she knew to a stranger."

"Well if she is so particular, how did she come to tell you first thing that she was in debt?"

The Harvester explained.

"Oh I see!" said the doctor. "Well you'll have to baby her along with the idea that she is earning money and pay her double until you get that off her mind, and while you are at it, put in your best licks, my boy; perk right up and court her like a house afire. Women like it. All of them do. They glory in feeling that a man is crazy about them."

"Well I'm insane enough over her," said the Harvester, "but I'd hate like the nation for her to know it. Seems as if a woman couldn't respect such an addle-pate as I am lately."

"Don't you worry about that," advised the doctor. "Just you make love to her. Go at it in the good old-fashioned way."

"But maybe the 'good old-fashioned way' isn't my way."

"What's the difference whose way it is, if it wins?"

"But Kipling says: 'Each man makes love his own way!'"

"I seem to have heard you mention that name be fore," said the doctor. "Do you regard him as an authority?"

"I do!" said the Harvester. "Especially when he advises me after my own heart and reason. Miss Jameson is not a silly girl. She's a woman, and twenty-four at least. I don't want her to care for a trick or a pretence. I do want her to love me. Not that I am worth her attention, but because she needs some strong man fearfully, and I am ready and more 'willing' than the original Barkis. But, like him, I have to let her know it in my way, and court her according to the promptings of my heart."

"You deceive yourself!" said the doctor flatly. "That's all bosh! Your tongue says it for the satisfaction of your ears, and it does sound well. You will court her according to your ideas of the conventions, as you understand them, and strictly in accordance with what you consider the respect due her. If you had followed the thing you call the 'promptings of your heart,' you would have picked her up by main force and brought her to my best ward, instead of merely suggesting it and giving up when she said no. If you had followed your heart, you would have choked the name and amount out of her and paid that devilish debt. You walk away in a case like that, and then have the nerve to come here and prate to me about following your heart. I'll wager my last dollar your heart is sore because you were not allowed to help her; but on the proposition that you followed its promptings I wouldn't stake a penny. That's all tommy-rot!"

"It is," agreed the Harvester. "Utter! But what can a man do?"

"I don't know what you can do! I'd have paid that debt and brought her to the hospital."

"I'll go and ask Mrs. Carey about your courtship. I want her help on this, anyway. I can pick up Miss Jameson and bring her here if any man can, but she is nursing a sick woman who depends solely on her for care. She is above average size, and she has a very decided mind of her own. I don't think you would use force and do what you think best for her, if you were in my place. You would wait until you understood the situation better, and knew that what you did was for the best, ultimately."

"I don't know whether I would or not. One thing is sure: I'm mighty glad you have found her. May I tell my wife?"

"Please do! And ask her if I may depend on her if I need a woman's help. Now I'll call off the valiant police and go home and take a good, sound sleep. Haven't had many since I first saw her."

So Betsy trotted down the valley, up the embankment, crossed the railroad, over the levee across Singing Water, and up the hill to the cabin. As they passed it, the Harvester jumped from the wagon, tossed the hitching strap to Belshazzar, and entered. He walked straight to her door, unlocked it, and uncovering, went inside. Softly he passed from piece to piece of the furniture he had made for her, and then surveyed the walls and floor.

"It isn't half good enough," he said, "but it will have to answer until I can do better. Surely she will know I tried and care for that, anyway. I wonder how long it will take me to get her here. Oh, if I only could know she was comfortable and happy! Happy! She doesn't appear as if she ever had heard that word. Well this will be a good place to teach her. I've always enjoyed myself here. I'm going to have faith that I can win her and make her happy also. When I go to the stable to do my work for the night if I could know she was in this cabin and glad of it, and if I could hear her down here singing like a happy care-free girl, I'd scarcely be able to endure the joy of it."

Chapter 9

The Harvester Goes Courting

"She is on Henry Jameson's farm, four miles west of Onabasha," said the Harvester, as he opened his eyes next morning, and laid a caressing hand on Belshazzar's head. "At two o'clock we are going to see her, and we are going to prolong the visit to the ultimate limit, so we should make things count here before we start."

He worked in a manner that accomplished much. There seemed no end to his energy that morning. Despatching the usual routine, he gathered the herbs that were ready, spread them on the shelves of the dry-house, found time to do several things in the cabin, and polish a piece of furniture before he ate his lunch and hitched Betsy to the wagon. He also had recovered his voice, and talked almost incessantly as he worked. When it neared time to start he dressed carefully. He stood before his bookcase and selected several pamphlets published by the Department of Agriculture. He went to his beds and gathered a large arm load of plants. Then he was ready to make his first trip to see the Dream Girl, but it never occurred to him that he was going courting.

He had decided fully that there would be no use to try to make love to a girl manifestly so ill and in trouble. The first thing, it appeared to him, was to dispel the depression, improve the health, and then do the love making. So, in the most business-like manner possible and without a shade of embarrassment, the Harvester took his herbs and books and started for the Jameson woods. At times as he drove along he espied something that he used growing beside the road and stopped to secure a specimen.

He came down the river bank and reached the ginseng bed at half-past one. He was purposely early. He laid down his books and plants, and rolled the log on which she sat the day before to a more shaded location, where a big tree would serve for a back rest. He pulled away brush and windfalls, heaped dry brown leaves, and tramped them down for her feet. Then he laid the books on the log, the arm load of plants beside them, and went to the river to wash his soiled hands.

Belshazzar's short bark told him the Girl was coming, and between the trees he saw the dog race to meet her and she bent to stroke his head. She wore the same dress and appeared even paler and thinner. The Harvester hurried up the bank, wiping his hands on his handkerchief.

"Glad to see you!" he greeted her casually. "I've fixed you a seat with a back rest to-day. Don't be frightened at the stack of herbs. You needn't gather all of those. They are only suggestions. They are just common roadside plants that have some medicinal value and are worth collecting. Please try my davenport."

"Thank you!" she said as she dropped on the log and leaned her head against the tree. It appeared as if her eyes closed a few seconds in spite of her, and while they were shut the Harvester looked steadily and intently on a face of exquisite beauty, but so marred by pallor and lines of care that search was required to recognize just how handsome she was, and if he had not seen her in perfection in the dream the Harvester might have missed glorious possibilities. To bring back that vision would be a task worth while was his thought. With the first faint quiver of an eyelash the Harvester took a few steps and bent over a plant, and as he did so the Girl's eyes followed him.

He appeared so tall and strong, so bronzed by summer sun and wind, his face so keen and intense, that swift fear caught her heart. Why was he there? Why should he take so much trouble for her? With difficulty she restrained herself from springing up and running away. Turning with the plant in his hand the Harvester saw the panic in her eyes, and it troubled his heart. For an instant he was bewildered, then he understood.

"I don't want you to work when you are not able," he said in his most matter-of-fact voice, "but if you still think that you are, I'll be very glad. I need help just now, more than I can tell you, and there seem to be so few people who can be trusted. Gathering stuff for drugs is really very serious business. You see, I've a reputation to sustain with some of the biggest laboratories in the country, not to mention the fact that I sometimes try compounding a new remedy for some common complaint myself. I rather take pride in the fact that my stuff goes in so fresh and clean that I always get anywhere from three to ten cents a pound above the listed prices for it. I want that money, but I want an unbroken record for doing a job right and being square and careful, much more."

He thought the appearance of fright was fading, and a tinge of interest taking its place. She was looking straight at him, and as he talked he could see her summoning her tired forces to understand and follow him, so he continued:

"One would think that as medicines are required in cases of life and death, collectors would use extreme caution, but some of them are criminally careless. It's a common thing to gather almost any fern for male fern; to throw in anything that will increase weight, to wash imperfectly, and commit many other sins that lie with the collector; beyond that I don't like to think. I suppose there are men who deliberately adulterate pure stuff to make it go farther, but when it comes to drugs, I scarcely can speak of it calmly. I like to do a thing right. I raise most of my plants, bushes, and herbs. I gather exactly in season, wash carefully if water dare be used, clean them otherwise if not, and dry them by a hot air system in an evaporator I built purposely. Each package I put up is pure stuff, clean, properly dried, and fresh. If I caught any man in the act of adulterating any of it I'm afraid he would get hurt badly—and usually I am a peaceable man. I am explaining this to show how very careful you must be to keep things separate and collect the right plants if you are going to sell stuff to me. I am extremely particular."

The Girl was leaning toward him, watching his face, and hers was slowly changing. She was deeply interested, much impressed, and more at ease. When the Harvester saw he had talked her into confidence he crossed the leaves, and sitting on the log beside her, picked up the books and opened one.

"Oh I will be careful," said the Girl. "If you will trust me to collect for you, I will undertake only what I am sure I know, and I'll do exactly as you tell me."

"There are a dozen things that bring a price ranging from three to fifteen cents a pound, that are in season just now. I suppose you would like to begin on some common, easy things, that will bring the most money."

Without a breath of hesitation she answered, "I will commence on whatever you are short of and need most to have."

The heart of the Harvester gave a leap that almost choked him, for he was vividly conscious of a broken shoe she was hiding beneath her skirts. He wanted to say "thank you," but he was afraid to, so he turned the leaves of the book.

"I am working just now on mullein," he said.

"Oh I know mullein," she cried, with almost a hint of animation in her voice. "The tall, yellow flower stem rising from a circle of green felt leaves!"

"Good!" said the Harvester. "What a pretty way to describe it! Do you know any more plants?"

"Only a few! I had a high-school course in botany, but it was all about flower and leaf formation, nothing at all of what anything was good for. I also learned a few, drawing them for leather and embroidery designs."

"Look here!" cried the Harvester. "I came with an arm load of herbs and expected to tell you all about foxglove, mullein, yarrow, jimson, purple thorn apple, blessed thistle, hemlock, hoarhound, lobelia, and everything in season now; but if you already have a profession, why do you attempt a new one? Why don't you go on drawing? I never saw anything so stupid as most of the designs from nature for book covers and decorations, leather work and pottery. They are the same old subjects worked over and over. If you can draw enough to make original copies, I can furnish you with flowers, vines, birds, and insects, new, unused, and of exquisite beauty, for every month in the year. I've looked into the matter a little, because I am rather handy with a knife, and I carve candlesticks from suitable pieces of wood. I always have trouble getting my designs copied; securing something new and unusual, never! If you can draw just well enough to reproduce what you see, gathering drugs is too slow and tiresome. What you want to do is to reproduce the subjects I will bring, and I'll buy what I want in my work, and sell the remainder at the arts and crafts stores for you. Or I can find out what they pay for such designs at potteries and ceramic factories. You have no time to spend on herbs, when you are in the woods, if you can draw."

"I am surely in the woods," said the Girl, "and I know I can copy correctly. I often made designs for embroidery and leather for the shop mother and I worked for in Chicago."

"Won't they buy them of you now?"

"Undoubtedly."

"Do they pay anything worth while?"

"I don't know how their prices compare with others. One place was all I worked for. I think they pay what is fair."

"We will find out," said the Harvester promptly.

"I—I don't think you need waste the time," faltered the Girl. "I had better gather the plants for a while at least."

"Collecting crude drug material is not easy," said the Harvester. "Drawing may not be either, but at least you could sit while you work, and it should bring you more money. Besides, I very much want a moth copied for a candlestick I am carving. Won't you draw that for me? I have some pupae cases and the moths will be out any day now. If I'd bring you one, wouldn't you just make a copy?"

The Girl gripped her hands together and stared straight ahead of her for a second, then she turned to him.

"I'd like to," she said, "but I have nothing to work with. In Chicago they furnished my material at the shop and I drew the design and was paid for the pattern. I didn't know there would be a chance for anything like that here. I haven't even proper pencils."

"Then the way for you to do this is to strip the first mullein plants you see of the petals. I will pay you seventy-five cents a pound for them. By the time you get a few pounds I can have material you need for drawing here and you can go to work on whatever flowers, vines, and things you can find in the woods, with no thanks to any one."

"I can't see that," said the Girl. "It would appear to me that I would be under more obligations than I could repay, and to a stranger."

"I figure it this way," said the Harvester, watching from the corner of his eye. "I can sell at good prices all the mullein flowers I can secure. You collect for me, I buy them. You can use drawing tools; I get them for you, and you pay me with the mullein or out of the ginseng money I owe you. You already have that coming, and it's just as much yours as it will be ten days from now. You needn't hesitate a second about drawing on it, because I am in a hurry for the moth pattern. I find time to carve only at night, you see. As for being under obligations to a stranger, in the first place all the debt would be on my side. I'd get the drugs and the pattern I want; and, in the second place, I positively and emphatically refuse to be a stranger. It would be so much better to be mutual helpers and friends of the kind worth having; and the sooner we begin, the sooner we can work together to good advantage. Get that stranger idea out of your head right now, and replace it with thoughts of a new friend, who is willing"—the Harvester detected panic in her eyes and ended casually—"to enter a partnership that will be of benefit to both of us. Partners can't be strangers, you know," he finished.

"I don't know what to think," said the Girl.

"Never bother your head with thinking," advised the Harvester with an air of large wisdom. "It is unprofitable and very tiring. Any one can see that you are too weary now. Don't dream of such a foolish thing as thinking. Don't worry over motives and obligations. Say to yourself, 'I'll enter this partnership and if it brings me anything good, I'm that much ahead. If it fails, I have lost nothing.' That's the way to look at it."

Then before she could answer he continued: "Now I want all the mullein bloom I can get. You'll see the yellow heads everywhere. Strip the petals and bring them here, and I'll come for them every day. They must go on the trays as fresh as possible. On your part, we will make out the order now."

He took a pencil and notebook from his pocket.

"You want drawing pencils and brushes; how many, what make and size?"

The Girl hesitated for a moment as if struggling to decide what to do; then she named the articles.

"And paper?"

He wrote that down, and asked if there was more.

"I think," he said, "that I can get this order filled in Onabasha. The art stores should keep these things. And shouldn't you have water-colour paper and some paint?"

Then there was a flash across the white face.

"Oh if I only could!" she cried. "All my life I have been crazy for a box of colour, but I never could afford it, and of course, I can't now. But if this splendid plan works, and I can earn what I owe, then maybe I can."

"Well this 'splendid plan' is going to 'work,' don't you bother about that," said the Harvester. "It has begun working right now. Don't worry a minute. After things have gone wrong for a certain length of time, they always veer and go right a while as compensation. Don't think of anything save that you are at the turning. Since it is all settled that we are to be partners, would you name me the figures of the debt that is worrying you? Don't, if you mind. I just thought perhaps we could get along better if I knew. Is it—say five hundred dollars?"

"Oh dear no!" cried the Girl in a panic. "I never could face that! It is not quite one hundred, and that seems big as a mountain to me."

"Forget it!" he cried. "The ginseng will pay more than half; that I know. I can bring you the cash in a little over a week."

She started to speak, hesitated, and at last turned to him.

"Would you mind," she said, "if I asked you to keep it until I can find a way to go to town? It's too far to walk and I don't know how to send it. Would I dare put it in a letter?"

"Never!" said the Harvester. "You want a draft. That money will be too precious to run any risks. I'll bring it to you and you can write a note and explain to whom you want it paid, and I'll take it to the bank for you and get your draft. Then you can write a letter, and half your worry will be over safely."

"It must be done in a sure way," said the Girl. "If I knew I had the money to pay that much on what I owe, and then lost it, I simply could not endure it. I would lie down and give up as Aunt Molly has."

"Forget that too!" said the Harvester. "Wipe out all the past that has pain in it. The future is going to be beautifully bright. That little bird on the bush there just told me so, and you are always safe when you trust the feathered folk. If you are going to live in the country any length of time, you must know them, and they will become a great comfort. Are you planning to be here long?"

"I have no plans. After what I saw Chicago do to my mother I would rather finish life in the open than return to the city. It is horrible here, but at least I'm not hungry, and not afraid—all the time."

"Gracious Heaven!" cried the Harvester. "Do you mean to say that you are afraid any part of the time? Would you kindly tell me of whom, and why?"

"You should know without being told that when a woman born and reared in a city, and all her life confined there, steps into the woods for the first time, she's bound to be afraid. The last few weeks constitute my entire experience with the country, and I'm in mortal fear that snakes will drop from trees and bushes or spring from the ground. Some places I think I'm sinking, and whenever a bush catches my skirts it seems as if something dreadful is reaching up for me; there is a possibility of horror lurking behind every tree and—"

"Stop!" cried the Harvester. "I can't endure it! Do you mean to tell me that you are afraid here and now?"

She met his eyes squarely.

"Yes," she said. "It almost makes me ill to sit on this log without taking a stick and poking all around it first. Every minute I think something is going to strike me in the back or drop on my head."

The Harvester grew very white beneath the tan, and that developed a nice, sickly green complexion for him.

"Am I part of your tortures?" he asked tersely.

"Why shouldn't you be?" she answered. "What do I know of you or your motives or why you are here?"

"I have had no experience with the atmosphere that breeds such an attitude in a girl."

"That is a thing for which to thank Heaven. Undoubtedly it is gracious to you. My life has been different."

"Yet in mortal terror of the woods, and probably equal fear of me, you are here and asking for work that will keep you here."

"I would go through fire and flood for the money I owe. After that debt is paid—"

She threw out her hands in a hopeless gesture. The Harvester drew forth a roll of bills and tossed them into her lap.

"For the love of mercy take what you need and pay it," he said. "Then get a floor under your feet, and try, I beg of you, try to force yourself to have confidence in me, until I do something that gives you the least reason for distrusting me."

She picked up the money and gave it a contemptuous whirl that landed it at his feet.

"What greater cause of distrust could I have by any possibility than just that?" she asked.

The Harvester arose hastily, and taking several steps, he stood with folded arms, his back turned. The Girl sat watching him with wide eyes, the dull blue plain in their dusky depths. When he did not speak, she grew restless. At last she slowly arose and circling him looked into his face. It was convulsed with a struggle in which love and patience fought for supremacy over honest anger. As he saw her so close, his lips drew apart, and his breath came deeply, but he did not speak. He merely stood and looked at her, and looked; and she gazed at him as if fascinated, but uncomprehending.

"Ruth!"

The call came roaring up the hill. The Girl shivered and became paler.

"Is that your uncle?" asked the Harvester.

She nodded.

"Will you come to-morrow for your drawing materials?"

"Yes."

"Will you try to believe that there is absolutely nothing, either underfoot or overhead, that will harm you?"

"Yes."

"Will you try to think that I am not a menace to public safety, and that I would do much to help you, merely because I would be glad to be of service?"

"Yes."

"Will you try to cultivate the idea that there is nothing in all this world that would hurt you purposely?"

"Ruth!" came a splitting scream in gruff man-tones, keyed in deep anger.

"That *sounds* like it!" said the Girl, and catching up her skirts she ran through the woods, taking a different route toward the house.

The Harvester sat on the log and tried to think; but there are times when the numbed brain refuses to work, so he really sat and suffered. Belshazzar whimpered and licked his hands, and at last the man arose and went with the dog to the wagon. As they came through Onabasha, Betsy turned at the hospital corner, but the Harvester pulled her around and drove toward the country. Not until they crossed the railroad did he lift his head and then he drew a deep breath as if starved for pure air and spoke. "Not to-day Betsy! I can't face my friends just now. Someway I am making an awful fist of things. Everything I do is wrong. She no more trusts me than you would a rattlesnake, Belshazzar; and from all appearance she takes me to be almost as deadly. What must have been her experiences in life to ingrain fear and distrust in her soul at that rate? I always knew I was not handsome, but I never before regarded my appearance as alarming. And I 'fixed up,' too!"

The Harvester grinned a queer little twist of a grin that pulled and distorted his strained face. "Might as well have gone with a week's beard, a soiled shirt, and a leer! And I've always been as decent as I knew! What's the reward for clean living anyway, if the girl you love strikes you like that?"

Belshazzar reached across and kissed him. The Harvester put his arm around the dog. In the man's disappointment and heart hunger he leaned his head against the beast and said, "I've always got you to love and protect me, anyway,

Belshazzar. Maybe the man who said a dog was a man's best friend was right. You always trusted me, didn't you Bel? And you never regretted it but once, and that wasn't my fault. I never did it! If I did, I'm getting good and well paid for it. I'd rather be kicked until all the ribs of one side are broken, Bel, than to swallow the dose she just handed me. I tell you it was bitter, lad! What am I going to do? Can't you help me, Bel?"

Belshazzar quivered in anxiety to offer the comfort he could not speak.

"Of course you are right! You always are, Bel!" said the Harvester. "I know what you are trying to tell me. Sure enough, she didn't have any dream. I am afraid she had the bitterest reality. She hasn't been loving a vision of me, working and searching for me, and I don't mean to her what she does to me. Of course I see that I must be patient and bide my time. If there is anything in 'like begetting like' she is bound to care for me some day, for I love her past all expression, and for all she feels I might as well save my breath. But she has got to awake some day, Bel. She can make up her mind to that. She can't see 'why.' Over and over! I wonder what she would think if I'd up and tell her 'why' with no frills. She will drive me to it some day, then probably the shock will finish her. I wonder if Doc was only fooling or if he really would do what he said. It might wake her up, anyway, but I'm dubious as to the result. How Uncle Henry can roar! He sounded like a fog horn. I'd love to try my muscle on a man like that. No wonder she is afraid of him, if she is of me. Afraid! Well of all things I ever did expect, Belshazzar, that is the limit."

Chapter 10

The Chime of the Blue Bells

The Harvester finished his evening work and went to examine the cocoons. Many of the moths had emerged and flown, but the luna cases remained in the bottom of the box. As he stood looking at them one moved and he smiled.

"I'd give something if you would come out and be ready to work on by tomorrow afternoon," he said. "Possibly you would so interest her that she would forget her fear of me. I'd like mighty well to take you along, because she might care for you, and I do need the pattern for my candlestick. Believe I'll lay you in a warmer place."

The first thing the next morning the Harvester looked and found the open cocoon and the wet moth clinging by its feet to a twig he had placed for it.

"Luck is with me!" he exulted. "I'll carry you to her and be mighty careful what I say, and maybe she will forget about the fear."

All the forenoon he cut and spread boneset, saffron, and hemlock on the trays to dry. At noon he put on a fresh outfit, ate a hasty lunch, and drove to Onabasha. He carried the moth in a box, and as he started he picked up a rake. He went to an art store and bought the pencils and paper she had ordered. He wanted to purchase everything he saw for her, but he was fast learning a lesson of deep caution. If he took more than she ordered, she would worry over paying, and if he refused to accept money, she would put that everlasting "why" at him again. The water-colour paper and paint he could not forego. He could make a desire to have the moth coloured explain those, he thought.

Then he went to a furniture store and bought several articles, and forgetting his law against haste, he drove Betsy full speed to the river. He was rather heavily ladened as he went up the bank, and it was only one o'clock. There was an hour. He rolled away the log, raked together and removed the leaves to the ground. He tramped the earth level and spread a large cheap porch rug. On this he opened and placed a little folding table and chair. On the table he spread the pencils, paper, colour box, and brushes, and went to the river to fill the water cup. Then he sat on the log he had rolled to one side and waited. After two hours he arose and crept as close the house as he could through the woods, but he could not secure a glimpse of the Girl. He went back and waited an hour more, and then undid his work and removed it. When he came to the moth his face was very grim as he lifted the twig and helped the beautiful creature to climb on a limb. "You'll be ready to fly in a few hours," he said. "If I keep you in a box you will ruin your wings and be no suitable subject, and put you in a cyanide jar I will not. I am hurt too badly myself. I wonder if what Doc said was the right way! It's certainly a temptation."

Then he went home; and again Betsy veered at the hospital, and once more the Harvester explained to her that he did not want to see the doctor. That evening and the following forenoon were difficult, but the Harvester lived through them, and in the afternoon went back to the woods, spread his rug, and set up the table. Only one streak of luck brightened the gloom in his heart. A yellow emperor had emerged in the night, and now occupied the place of yesterday's luna. She never need know it was not the one he wanted, and it would make an excuse for the colour box.

He was watching intently and saw her coming a long way off. He noticed that she looked neither right nor left, but came straight as if walking a bridge. As she reached the place she glanced hastily around and then at him. The Harvester forgave her everything as he saw the look of relief with which she stepped upon the carpet. Then she turned to him.

"I won't have to ask 'why' this time," she said. "I know that you did it because I was baby enough to tell what a coward I am. I'm sure you can't afford it, and I know you shouldn't have done it, but oh, what a comfort! If you will promise never to do any such expensive, foolish, kind thing again, I'll say thank you this time. I couldn't come yesterday, because Aunt Molly was worse and Uncle Henry was at home all day."

"I supposed it was something like that," said the Harvester.

She advanced and handed him the roll of bills.

"I had a feeling you would be reckless," she said. "I saw it in your face, so I came back as soon as I could steal away, and sure enough, there lay your money and the books and everything. I hid them in the thicket, so they will be all right. I've almost prayed it wouldn't rain. I didn't dare carry them to the house. Please take the money. I haven't time to argue about it or strength, but of course I can't possibly use it unless I earn it. I'm so anxious to see the pencils and paper."

The Harvester thrust the money into his pocket. The Girl went to the table, opened and spread the paper, and took out the pencils.

"Is my subject in here?" she touched the colour box.

"No, the other."

"Is it alive? May I open it?"

"We will be very careful at first," said the Harvester. "It only left its case in the night and may fly. When the weather is so warm the wings develop rapidly. Perhaps if I remove the lid—"

He took off the cover, exposing a big moth, its lovely, pale yellow wings, flecked with heliotrope, outspread as it clung to a twig in the box. The Girl leaned forward.

"What is it?" she asked.

"One of the big night moths that emerge and fly a few hours in June."

"Is this what you want for your candlestick?"

"If I can't do better. There is one other I prefer, but it may not come at a time that you can get it right."

"What do you mean by 'right'?"

"So that you can copy it before it wants to fly."

"Why don't you chloroform and pin it until I am ready?"

"I am not in the business of killing and impaling exquisite creatures like that."

"Do you mean that if I can't draw it when it is just right you will let it go?"

"I do."

"Why?"

"I told you why."

"I know you said you were not in the business, but why wouldn't you take only one you really wanted to use?"

"I would be afraid," replied the Harvester.

"Afraid? You!"

"I must have a mighty good reason before I kill," said the man. "I cannot give life; I have no right to take it away. I will let my statement stand, I am afraid."

"Of what please?"

"An indefinable something that follows me and makes me suffer if I am wantonly cruel."

"Is there any particular pose in which you want this bird placed?"

"Allow me to present you to the yellow emperor, known in the books as eagles imperialis," he said. "I want him as he clings naturally and life size."

She took up a pencil.

"If you don't mind," said the Harvester, "would you draw on this other paper? I very much want the colour, also, and you can use it on this. I brought a box along, and I'll get you water. I had it all ready yesterday."

"Did you have this same moth?"

"No, I had another."

"Did you have the one you wanted most?"

"Yes—but it's no difference."

"And you let it go because I was not here?"

"No. It went on account of exquisite beauty. If kept in confinement it would struggle and break its wings. You see, that one was a delicate green, where this is yellow, plain pale blue green, with a lavender rib here, and long curled trailers edged with pale yellow, and eye spots rimmed with red and black."

As the Harvester talked he indicated the points of difference with a pencil he had picked up; now he laid it down and retreated beyond the limits of the rug.

"I see," said the Girl. "And this is colour?"

She touched the box.

"A few colours, rather," said the Harvester. "I selected enough to fill the box, with the help of the clerk who sold them to me. If they are not right, I have permission to return and exchange them for anything you want."

With eager fingers she opened the box, and bent over it a face filled with interest.

"Oh how I've always wanted this! I scarcely can wait to try it. I do hope I can have it for my very own. Was it quite expensive?"

"No. Very cheap!" said the Harvester. "The paper isn't worth mentioning. The little, empty tin box was only a few cents, and the paints differ according to colour. Some appear to be more than others. I was surprised that the outfit was so inexpensive."

A skeptical little smile wavered on the Girl's face as she drew her slender fingers across the trays of bright colour.

"If one dared accept your word, you really would be a comfort," she said, as she resolutely closed the box, pushed it away, and picked up a pencil.

"If you will take the trouble to inquire at the banks, post office, express office, hospital or of any druggist in Onabasha, you will find that my word is exactly as good as my money, and taken quite as readily."

"I didn't say I doubted you. I have no right to do that until I feel you deceive me. What I said was 'dared accept,' which means I must not, because I have no right. But you make one wonder what you would do if you were coaxed and asked for things and led by insinuations."

"I can tell you that," said the Harvester. "It would depend altogether on who wanted anything of me and what they asked. If you would undertake to coax and insinuate, you never would get it done, because I'd see what you needed and have it at hand before you had time."

The Girl looked at him wonderingly.

"Now don't spring your recurrent 'why' on me," said the Harvester. "I'll tell you 'why' some of these days. Just now answer me this question: Do you want me to remain here or leave until you finish? Which way would you be least afraid?"

"I am not at all afraid on the rug and with my work," she said. "If you want to hunt ginseng go by all means."

"I don't want to hunt anything," said the Harvester. "But if you are more comfortable with me away, I'll be glad to go. I'll leave the dog with you."

He gave a short whistle and Belshazzar came bounding to him. The Harvester stepped to the Girl's side, and dropping on one knee, he drew his hand across the rug close to her skirts.

"Right here, Belshazzar," he said. "Watch! You are on guard, Bel."

"Well of all names for a dog!" exclaimed the Girl. "Why did you select that?"

"My mother named my first dog Belshazzar, and taught me why; so each of the three I've owned since have been christened the same. It means 'to protect' and that is the office all of them perform; this one especially has filled it admirably. Once I failed him, but he never has gone back on me. You see he is not a particle afraid of me. Every step I take, he is at my heels."

"So was Bill Sikes' dog, if I remember."

The Harvester laughed.

"Bel," he said, "if you could speak you'd say that was an ugly one, wouldn't you?"

The dog sprang up and kissed the face of the man and rubbed a loving head against his breast.

"Thank you!" said the Harvester. "Now lie down and protect this woman as carefully as you ever watched in your life. And incidentally, Bel, tell her that she can't exterminate me more than once a day, and the performance is accomplished for the present. I refuse to be a willing sacrifice. 'So was Bill Sikes' dog!' What do you think of that, Bel?"

The Harvester arose and turned to go.

"What if this thing attempts to fly?" she asked.

"Your pardon," said the Harvester. "If the emperor moves, slide the lid over the box a few seconds, until he settles and clings quietly again, and then slowly draw it away. If you are careful not to jar the table heavily he will not go for hours yet."

Again he turned.

"If there is no danger, why do you leave the dog?"

"For company," said the Harvester. "I thought you would prefer an animal you are not afraid of to a man you are. But let me tell you there is no necessity for either. I know a woman who goes alone and unafraid through every foot of woods in this part of the country. She has climbed, crept, and waded, and she tells me she never saw but two venomous snakes this side of Michigan. Nothing ever dropped on her or sprang at her. She feels as secure in the woods as she does at home."

"Isn't she afraid of snakes?"

"She dislikes snakes, but she is not afraid or she would not risk encountering them daily."

"Do you ever find any?"

"Harmless little ones, often. That is, Bel does. He is always nosing for them, because he understands that I work in the earth. I think I have encountered three dangerous ones in my life. I will guarantee you will not find one in these woods. They are too open and too much cleared."

"Then why leave the dog?"

"I thought," said the Harvester patiently, "that your uncle might have turned in some of his cattle, or if pigs came here the dog could chase them away."

She looked at him with utter panic in her face.

"I am far more afraid of a cow than a snake!" she cried. "It is so much bigger!"

"How did you ever come into these woods alone far enough to find the ginseng?" asked the Harvester. "Answer me that!"

"I wore Uncle Henry's top boots and carried a rake, and I suffered tortures," she replied.

"But you hunted until you found what you wanted, and came again to keep watch on it?"

"I was driven—simply forced. There's no use to discuss it!"

"Well thank the Lord for one thing," said the Harvester. "You didn't appear half so terrified at the sight of me as you did at the mere mention of a cow. I have risen inestimably in my own self-respect. Belshazzar, you may pursue the elusive chipmunk. I am going to guard this woman myself, and please, kind fates, send a ferocious cow this way, in order that I may prove my valour."

The Girl's face flushed slightly, and she could not restrain a laugh. That was all the Harvester hoped for and more. He went beyond the edge of the rug and sat on the leaves under a tree. She bent over her work and only bird and insect notes and occasionally Belshazzar's excited bark broke the silence. The Harvester stretched on the ground, his eyes feasting on the Girl. Intensely he watched every movement. If a squirrel barked she gave a nervous start, so precipitate it seemed as if it must hurt. If a windfall came rattling down she appeared ready to fly in headlong terror in any direction. At last she dropped her pencil and looked at him helplessly.

"What is it?" he asked.

"The silence and these awful crashes when one doesn't know what is coming," she said.

"Will it bother you if I talk? Perhaps the sound of my voice will help?"

"I am accustomed to working when people talk, and it will be a comfort. I may be able to follow you, and that will prevent me from thinking. There are dreadful things in my mind when they are not driven out. Please talk! Tell me about the herbs you gathered this morning."

The Harvester gave the Girl one long look as she bent over her work. He was vividly conscious of the graceful curves of her little figure, the coil of dark, silky hair, softly waving around her temples and neck, and when her eyes turned in his direction he knew that it was only the white, drawn face that restrained him. He was almost forced to tell her how he loved and longed for her; about the home he had prepared; of a thousand personal interests. Instead, he took a firm grip and said casually, "Foxglove harvest is over. This plant has to be taken when the leaves are in second year growth and at bloom time. I have stripped my mullein beds of both leaves and flowers. I finished a week ago. Beyond lies a stretch of Parnassus grass that made me think of you, it was so white and delicate. I want you to see it. It will be lovely in a few weeks more."

"You never had seen me a week ago."

"Oh hadn't I?" said the Harvester. "Well maybe I dreamed about you then. I am a great dreamer. Once I had a dream that may interest you some day, after you've overcome your fear of me. Now this bed of which I was speaking is a picture in September. You must arrange to drive home with me and see it then."

"For what do you sell foxglove and mullein?"

"Foxglove for heart trouble, and mullein for catarrh. I get ten cents a pound for foxglove leaves and five for mullein and from seventy-five to a dollar for flowers of the latter, depending on how well I preserve the colour in drying them. They must be sealed in bottles and handled with extreme care."

"Then if I wasn't too childish to be out picking them, I could be earning seventy-five cents a pound for mullein blooms?"

"Yes," said the Harvester, "but until you learned the trick of stripping them rapidly you scarcely could gather what would weigh two pounds a day, when dried. Not to mention the fact that you would have to stand and work mostly in hot sunshine, because mullein likes open roads and fields and sunny hills. Now you can sit securely in the shade, and in two hours you can make me a pattern of that moth, for which I would pay a designer of the arts and crafts shop five dollars, so of course you shall have the same."

"Oh no!" she cried in swift panic. "You were charged too much! It isn't worth a dollar, even!"

"On the contrary the candlestick on which I shall use it will be invaluable when I finish it, and five is very little for the cream of my design. I paid just right. You can earn the same for all you can do. If you can embroider linen, they pay good prices for that, too and wood carving, metal work, or leather things. May I see how you are coming on?"

"Please do," she said.

The Harvester sprang up and looked over the Girl's shoulder. He could not suppress an exclamation of delight.

"Perfect!" he cried. "You can surpass their best drafting at the shop! Your fortune is made. Any time you want to go to Onabasha you can make enough to pay your board, dress you well, and save something every week. You must leave here as soon as you can manage it. When can you go?"

"I don't know," she said wearily. "I'd hate to tell you how full of aches I am. I could not work much just now, if I had the best opportunities in the world. I must grow stronger."

"You should not work at anything until you are well," he said. "It is a crime against nature to drive yourself. Why will you not allow—"

"Do you really think, with a little practice, I can draw designs that will sell?"

The Harvester picked up the sheet. The work was delicate and exact. He could see no way to improve it.

"You know it will sell," he said gently, "because you already have sold such work."

"But not for the prices you offer."

"The prices I name are going to be for *new, original designs*. I've got a thousand in my head, that old Mother Nature shows me in the woods and on the water every day."

"But those are yours; I can't take them."

"You must," said the Harvester. "I only see and recognize studies; I can't materialize them, and until they are drawn, no one can profit by them. In this partnership we revolutionize decorative art. There are actually birds besides fat robins and nondescript swallows. The crane and heron do not monopolize the water. Wild rose and golden-rod are not the only flowers. The other day I was gathering lobelia. The seeds are used in tonic preparations. It has an upright stem with flowers scattered along it. In itself it is not much, but close beside it always grows its cousin, tall bell-flower. As the name indicates, the flowers are bell shape and I can't begin to describe their grace, beauty, and delicate blue colour. They ring my strongest call to worship. My work keeps me in the woods so much I remain there for my religion also. Whenever I find these flowers I always pause for a little service of my own that begins by reciting these lines:

> *"'Neath cloistered boughs, each floral bell that swingeth*
> *And tolls its perfume on the passing air,*
> *Makes Sabbath in the fields, and ever ringeth*
> *A call to prayer."*

"Beautiful!" said the Girl.

"It's mighty convenient," explained the Harvester. "By my method, you see, you don't have to wait for your day and hour of worship. Anywhere the blue bell rings its call it is Sunday in the woods and in your heart. After I recite that, I pray my prayer."

"Go on!" said the Girl. "This is no place to stop."

"It is always one and the same prayer, and there are only two lines of it," said the Harvester. "It runs this way—Let me take your pencil and I will write it for you."

He bent over her shoulder, and traced these lines on a scrap of the wrapping paper:

> *"Almighty Evolver of the Universe:*
> *Help me to keep my soul and body clean,*
> *And at all times to do unto others as I would be done by.*
> *Amen."*

The Girl took the slip and sat studying it; then she raised her eyes to his face curiously, but with a tinge of awe in them.

"I can see you standing over a blue, bell-shaped flower reciting those exquisite lines and praying this wonderful prayer," she said. "Yesterday you allowed the moth you were willing to pay five dollars for a drawing of, to go, because you wouldn't risk breaking its wings. Why you are more like a woman!"

A red stream crimsoned the Harvester's face.

"Well heretofore I have been considered strictly masculine," he said. "To appreciate beauty or to try to be just commonly decent is not exclusively feminine. You must remember there are painters, poets, musicians, workers in art along almost any line you could mention, and no one calls them feminine, but there is one good thing if I am. You need no longer fear me. If you should see me, muck covered, grubbing in the earth or on a raft washing roots in the lake, you would not consider me like a woman."

"Would it be any discredit if I did? I think not. I merely meant that most men would not see or hear the blue bell at all—and as for the poem and prayer! If the woods make a man with such fibre in his soul, I must learn them if they half kill me."

"You harp on death. Try to forget the word."

"I have faced it for months, and seen it do its grinding worst very recently to the only thing on earth I loved or that loved me. I have no desire to forget! Tell me more about the plants."

"Forgive me," said the Harvester gently. "Just now I am collecting catnip for the infant and nervous people, hoarhound for colds and dyspepsia, boneset heads and flowers for the same purpose. There is a heavy head of white bloom with wonderful lacy leaves, called yarrow. I take the entire plant for a tonic and blessed thistle leaves and flowers for the same purpose."

"That must be what I need," interrupted the Girl. "Half the time I believe I have a little fever, but I couldn't have dyspepsia, because I never want anything to eat; perhaps the tonic would make me hungry."

"Promise me you will tell that to the doctor who comes to see your aunt, and take what he gives you."

"No doctor comes to see my aunt. She is merely playing lazy to get out of work. There is nothing the matter with her."

"Then why—"

"My uncle says that. Really, she could not stand and walk across a room alone. She is simply worn out."

"I shall report the case," said the Harvester instantly.

"You better not!" said the Girl. "There must be a mistake about you knowing my uncle. Tell me more of the flowers."

The Harvester drew a deep breath and continued:

"These I just have named I take at bloom time; next month come purple thorn apple, jimson weed, and hemlock."

"Isn't that poison?"

"Half the stuff I handle is."

"Aren't you afraid?"

"Terribly," said the Harvester in laughing voice. "But I want the money, the sick folk need the medicine, and I drink water."

The Girl laughed also.

"Look here!" said the Harvester. "Why not tell me just as closely as you can about your aunt, and let me fix something for her; or if you are afraid to trust me, let me have my friend of whom I spoke yesterday."

"Perhaps I am not so much afraid as I was," said the Girl. "I wish I could! How could I explain where I got it and I wonder if she would take it."

"Give it to her without any explanation," said the Harvester. "Tell her it will make her stronger and she must use it. Tell me exactly how she is, and I will fix up some harmless remedies that may help, and can do no harm."

"She simply has been neglected, overworked, and abused until she has lain down, turned her face to the wall, and given up hope. I think it is too late. I think the end will come soon. But I wish you would try. I'll gladly pay—"

"Don't!" said the Harvester. "Not for things that grow in the woods and that I prepare. Don't think of money every minute."

"I must," she said with forced restraint. "It is the price of life. Without it one suffers—horribly—as I know. What other plants do you gather?"

"Saffron," answered the Harvester. "A beautiful thing! You must see it. Tall, round stems, lacy, delicate leaves, big heads of bright yellow bloom, touched with colour so dark it appears black—one of the loveliest plants that grows. You should see my big bed of it in a week or two more. It makes a picture."

The words recalled him to the Girl. He turned to study her. He forgot his commission and chafed at conventions that prevented his doing what he saw was required so urgently. Fearing she would notice, he gazed away through the forest and tried to think, to plan.

"You are not making noise enough," she said.

So absorbed was the Harvester he scarcely heard her. In an attempt to obey he began to whistle softly. A tiny goldfinch in a nest of thistle down and plant fibre in the branching of a bush ten feet above him stuck her head over the brim and inquired, "P'tseet?" "Pt'see!" answer the Harvester. That began the duet. Before the question had been asked and answered a half dozen times a catbird intruded its voice and hearing a reply came through the bushes to investigate. A wren followed and became very saucy. From—one could not see where, came a vireo, and almost at the same time a chewink had something to say.

Instantly the Harvester answered. Then a blue jay came chattering to ascertain what all the fuss was about, and the Harvester carried on a conversation that called up the remainder of the feathered tribe. A brilliant cardinal came tearing through the thicket, his beady black eyes snapping, and demanded to know if any one were harming his mate, brooding under a wild grape leaf in a scrub elm on the river embankment. A brown thrush silently slipped like a snake between shrubs and trees, and catching the universal excitement, began to flirt his tail and utter a weird, whistling cry.

With one eye on the bird, and the other on the Girl sitting in amazed silence, the Harvester began working for effect. He lay quietly, but in turn he answered a dozen birds so accurately they thought their mates were calling, and closer and closer they came. An oriole in orange and black heard his challenge, and flew up the river bank, answering at steady intervals for quite a time before it was visible, and in resorting to the last notes he could think of a quail whistled "Bob White" and a shitepoke, skulking along the river bank, stopped and cried, "Cowk, cowk!"

At his limit of calls the Harvester changed his notes and whistled and cried bits of bird talk in tone with every mellow accent and inflection he could manage. Gradually the excitement subsided, the birds flew and tilted closer, turned their sleek heads, peered with bright eyes, and ventured on and on until the very bravest, the wren and the jay, were almost in touch. Then, tired of hunting, Belshazzar came racing and the little feathered people scattered in precipitate flight.

"How do you like that kind of a noise?" inquired the Harvester.

The Girl drew a deep breath.

"Of course you know that was the most exquisite sight I ever saw," she said. "I never shall forget it. I did not think there were that many different birds in the whole world. Of all the gaudy colours! And they came so close you could have reached out and touched them."

"Yes," said the Harvester calmly. "Birds are never afraid of me. At Medicine Woods, when I call them like that, many, most of them, in fact, eat from my hand. If you ever have looked at me enough to notice bulgy pockets, they are full of wheat. These birds are strangers, but I'll wager you that in a week I can make them take food from me. Of course, my own birds know me, because they are around every day. It is much easier to tame them in winter, when the snow has fallen and food is scarce, but it only takes a little while to win a bird's confidence at any season."

"Birds don't know what there is to be afraid of," she said.

"Your pardon," said the Harvester, "but I am familiar with them, and that is not correct. They have more to fear than human beings. No one is going to kill you merely to see if he can shoot straight enough to hit. Your life is not in danger because you have magnificent hair that some woman would like for an ornament. You will not be stricken out in a flash because there are a few bits of meat on your frame some one wants to eat. No one will set a seductive trap for you, and, if you are tempted to enter it, shut you from freedom and natural diet, in a cage so small you can't turn around without touching bars. You are in a secure and free position compared with the birds. I also have observed that they know guns, many forms of traps, and all of them decide by the mere manner of a man's passing through the woods whether he is a friend or an enemy. Birds know more than many people realize. They do not always correctly estimate gun range, they are foolishly venturesome at times when they want food, but they know many more things than most people give them credit for understanding. The greatest trouble with the birds is they are too willing to trust us and be friendly, so they are often deceived."

"That sounds as if you were right," said the Girl.

"I am of the woods, so I know I am," answered the Harvester.

"Will you look at this now?"

He examined the drawing closely.

"Where did you learn?" he inquired.

"My mother. She was educated to her finger tips. She drew, painted, played beautifully, sang well, and she had read almost all the best books. Besides what I learned at high school she taught me all I know. Her embroidery always brought higher prices than mine, try as I might. I never saw any one else make such a dainty, accurate little stitch as she could."

"If this is not perfect, I don't know how to criticise it. I can and will use it in my work. But I have one luna cocoon remaining and I would give ten dollars for such a drawing of the moth before it flies. It may open to-night or not for several days. If your aunt should be worse and you cannot come to-morrow and the moth emerges, is there any way in which I could send it to you?"

"What could I do with it?"

"I thought perhaps you could take a piece of paper and the pencils with you, and secure an outline in your room. It need not be worked up with all the detail in this. Merely a skeleton sketch would do. Could I leave it at the house or send it with some one?"

"No! Oh no!" she cried. "Leave it here. Put it in a box in the bushes where I hid the books. What are you going to do with these things?"

"Hide them in the thicket and scatter leaves over them."

"What if it rains?"

"I have thought of that. I brought a few yards of oilcloth to-day and they will be safe and dry if it pours."

"Good!" she said. "Then if the moth comes out you bring it, and if I am not here, put it under the cloth and I will run up some time in the afternoon. But if I were you, I would not spread the rug until you know if I can remain. I have to steal every minute I am away, and any day uncle takes a notion to stay at home I dare not come."

"Try to come to-morrow. I am going to bring some medicine for your aunt."

"Put it under the cloth if I am not here; but I will come if I can. I must go now; I have been away far too long."

The Harvester picked up one of the drug pamphlets, laid the drawing inside it, and placed it with his other books. Then he drew out his pocket book and laid a five-dollar bill on the table and began folding up the chair and putting away the things. The Girl looked at the money with eager eyes.

"Is that honestly what you would pay at the arts and crafts place?"

"It is the customary price for my patterns."

"And are you sure this is as good?"

"I can bring you some I have paid that for, and let you see for yourself that it is better."

"I wish you would!" she cried eagerly. "I need that money, and I would like to have it dearly, if I really have earned it, but I can't touch it if I have not."

"Won't you accept my word?"

"No. I will see the other drawings first, and if I think mine are as good, I will be glad to take the money to-morrow."

"What if you can't come?"

"Put them under the oilcloth. I watch all the time and I think Uncle Henry has trained even the boys so they don't play in the river on his land. I never see a soul here; the woods, house, and everything is desolate until he comes home and then it is like—" she paused.

"I'll say it for you," said the Harvester promptly. "Then it is like hell."

"At its worst," supplemented the Girl. Taking pencils and a sheet of paper she went swiftly through the woods. Before she left the shelter of the trees, the Harvester saw her busy her hands with the front of her dress, and he knew that she was concealing the drawing material. The colour box was left, and he said things as he put it with the chair and table, covered them with the rug and oilcloth, and heaped on a layer of leaves.

Then he drove to the city and Betsy turned at the hospital corner with no interference. He could face his friend that day. Despite all discouragements he felt reassured. He was progressing. Means of communication had been established. If she did not come, he could leave a note and tell her if the moth had not emerged and how sorry he was to have missed seeing her.

"Hello, lover!" cried Doctor Carey as the Harvester entered the office. "Are you married yet?"

"No. But I'm going to be," said the Harvester with confidence.

"Have you asked her?"

"No. We are getting acquainted. She is too close to trouble, too ill, and too worried over a sick relative for me to intrude myself; it would be brutal, but it's a temptation. Doc, is there any way to compel a man to provide medical care for his wife?"

"Can he afford it?"

"Amply. Anything! Worth thousands in land and nobody knows what in money. It's Henry Jameson."

"The meanest man I ever knew. If he has a wife it's a marvel she has survived this long. Won't he provide for her?"

"I suppose he thinks he has when she has a bed to lie on and a roof to cover her. He won't supply food she can eat and medicine. He says she is lazy."

"What do you think?"

"I quote Miss Jameson. She says her aunt is slowly dying from overwork and neglect."

"David, doesn't it seem pretty good, when you say 'Miss Jameson'?"

"Loveliest sound on earth, except the remainder of it."

"What's that?"

"Ruth!"

"Jove! That is a beautiful name. Ruth Langston. It will go well, won't it?"

"Music that the birds, insects, Singing Water, the trees, and the breeze can't ever equal. I'm holding on with all my might, but it's tough, Doc. She's in such a dreadful place and position, and she needs so much. She is sick. Can't you give me a prescription for each of them?"

"You just bet I can," said the doctor, "if you can engineer their taking them."

"I suppose you'd hold their noses and pour stuff down them."

"I would if necessary."

"Well, it is."

"All right—I'll fix something, and you see that they use it."

"I can try," said the Harvester.

"Try! Pah! You aren't half a man!"

"That's a half more than being a woman, anyway."

"She called you feminine, did she?" cried the doctor, dancing and laughing. "She ought to see you harvesting skunk cabbage and blue flag or when you are angry enough."

The doctor left the room and it was a half hour before he returned.

"Try that on them according to directions," he said, handing over a couple of bottles.

"Thank you!" said the Harvester. "I will!"

"That sounds manly enough."

"Oh pother! It's not that I'm not a man, or a laggard in love; but I'd like to know what you'd do to a girl dumb with grief over the recent loss of her mother, who was her only relative worth counting, sick from God knows what exposure and privation, and now a dying relative on her hands. What could you do?"

"I'd marry her and pick her out of it!"

"I wouldn't have her, if she'd leave a sick woman for me!"

"I wouldn't either. She's got to stick it out until her aunt grows better, and then I'll go out there and show you how to court a girl."

"I guess not! You keep the girl you did court, courted, and you'll have your hands full. How does that appear to you?"

The Harvester opened the pamphlet he carried and held up the drawing of the moth.

The doctor turned to the light.

"Good work!" he cried. "Did she do that?"

"She did. In a little over an hour."

"Fine! She should have a chance."

"She is going to. She is going to have all the opportunity that is coming to her."

"Good for you, David! Any time I can help!"

The Harvester replaced the sketch and went to the wagon; but he left Belshazzar in charge, and visited the largest dry goods store in Onabasha, where he held a conference with the floor walker. When he came out he carried a heaping load of boxes of every size and shape, with a label on each. He drove to Medicine Woods singing and whistling.

"She didn't want me to go, Belshazzar!" he chuckled to the dog. "She was more afraid of a cow than she was of me. I made some headway to-day, old boy. She doesn't seem to have a ray of an idea what I am there for, but she is going to trust me soon now; that is written in the books. Oh I hope she will be there to-morrow, and the luna will be out. Got half a notion to take the case and lay it in the warmest place I can find. But if it comes out and she isn't there, I'll be sorry. Better trust to luck."

The Harvester stabled Betsy, fed the stock, and visited with the birds. After supper he took his purchases and entered her room. He opened the drawers of the chest he had made, and selecting the labelled boxes he laid them in. But not a package did he open. Then he arose and radiated conceit of himself.

"I'll wager she will like those," he commented proudly, "because Kane promised me fairly that he would have the right things put up for a girl the size of the clerk I selected for him, and exactly what Ruth should have. That girl was slenderer and not quite so tall, but he said everything was made long on purpose. Now what else should I get?"

He turned to the dressing table and taking a notebook from his pocket made this list:

Rugs for bed and bath room.
Mattresses, pillows and bedding.
Dresses for all occasions.
All kinds of shoes and overshoes.

"There are gloves, too!" exclaimed the Harvester. "She has to have some, but how am I going to know what is right? Oh, but she needs shoes! High, low, slippers, everything! I wonder what that clerk wears. I don't believe shoes would be comfortable without being fitted, or at least the proper size. I wonder what kind of dresses she likes. I hope she's fond of white. A woman always appears loveliest in that. Maybe I'd better buy what I'm sure of and let her select the dresses. But I'd love to have this room crammed with girl-fixings when she comes. Doesn't seem as if she ever has had any little luxuries. I can't miss it on anything a woman uses. Let me think!"

Slowly he wrote again:

Parasols.
Fans.
Veils.
Hats.

"I never can get them! I think that will keep me busy for a few days," said the Harvester as he closed the door softly, and went to look at the pupae cases. Then he carved on the vine of the candlestick for her dressing table, with one arm around Belshazzar, re-read the story of John Muir's dog, went into the lake, and to bed. Just as he was becoming unconscious the beast lifted an inquiring head and gazed at the man.

"More 'fraid of cow," the Harvester was muttering in a sleepy chuckle.

Chapter 11

Demonstrated Courtship

When the Harvester saw the Girl coming toward the woods, he spread the rug, opened and placed the table and chair, laid out the colour box, and another containing the last luna.

"Did the green one come out?" she asked, touching the box lightly.

"It did!" said the Harvester proudly, as if he were responsible for the performance. "It is an omen! It means that I am to have my long-coveted pattern for my best candlestick. It also clearly indicates that the gods of luck are with me for the day, and I get my way about everything. There won't be the least use in your asking 'why' or interposing objections. This is my clean sweep. I shall be fearfully dictatorial and you must submit, because the fates have pointed out that they favour me to-day, and if you go contrary to their decrees you will have a bad time."

The Girl's smile was a little wan. She sank on a chair and picked up a pencil.

"Lay that down!" cried the Harvester. "You haven't had permission from the Dictator to begin drawing. You are to sit and rest a long time."

"Please may I speak?" asked the Girl.

The Harvester grew foolishly happy. Was she really going to play the game? Of course he had hoped, but it was a hope without any foundation.

"You may," he said soberly.

"I am afraid that if you don't allow me to draw the moth at once, I'll never get it done. I dislike to mention it on your good day, but Aunt Molly is very restless. I got a neighbour's little girl to watch her and call me if I'm wanted. It's quite certain that I must go soon, so if you would like the moth—"

"When luck is coming your way, never hurry it! You always upset the bowl if you grow greedy and crowd. If it is a gamble whether I get this moth, I'll take the chance; but I won't change my foreordained programme for this afternoon. First, you are to sit still ten minutes, shut your eyes, and rest. I can't sing, but I can whistle, and I'm going to entertain you so you won't feel alone. Ready now!"

The Girl leaned her elbows on the table, closed her eyes, and pressed her slender white hands over them.

"Please don't call the birds," she said. "I can't rest if you do. It was so exciting trying to see all of them and guess what they were saying."

"No," said the Harvester gently. "This ten minutes is for relaxation, you know. You ease every muscle, sink limply on your chair, lean on the table, let go all over, and don't think. Just listen to me. I assure you it's going to be perfectly lovely."

Watching intently he saw the strained muscles relaxing at his suggestion and caught the smile over the last words as he slid into a soft whistle. It was an easy, slow, old-fashioned tune, carrying along gently, with neither heights nor depths, just monotonous, sleepy, soothing notes, that went on and on with a little ripple of change at times, only to return to the theme, until at last the Girl lifted her head.

"It's away past ten minutes," she said, "but that was a real rest. Truly, I am better prepared for work."

"Broke the rule, too!" said the Harvester. "It was, for me to say when time was up. Can't you allow me to have my way for ten minutes?"

"I am so anxious to see and draw this moth," she answered. "And first of all you promised to bring the drawings you have been using."

"Now where does my programme come in?" inquired the Harvester. "You are spoiling everything, and I refuse to have my lucky day interfered with; therefore we will ignore the suggestion until we arrive at the place where it is proper. Next thing is refreshments."

He arose and coming over cleared the table. Then he spread on it a paper tray cloth with a gay border, and going into the thicket brought out a box and a big bucket containing a jug packed in ice. The Girl's eyes widened. She reached down, caught up a piece, and holding it to drip a second started to put it in her mouth.

"Drop that!" commanded the Harvester. "That's a very unhealthful proceeding. Wait a minute."

From one end of the box he produced a tin of wafers and from the other a plate. Then he dug into the ice and lifted several different varieties of chilled fruit. From the jug he poured a combination that he made of the juices of oranges, pineapples, and lemons. He set the glass, rapidly frosting in the heat, and the fruit before the Girl.

"Now!" he said.

For one instant she stared at the table. Then she looked at him and in the depths of her dark eyes was an appeal he never forgot.

"I made that drink myself, so it's all right," he assured her. "There's a pretty stiff touch of pineapple in it, and it cuts the cobwebs on a hot day. Please try it!"

"I can't!" cried the Girl with a half-sob. "Think of Aunt Molly!"

"Are you fond of her?"

"No. I never saw her until a few weeks ago. Since then I've seen nothing save her poor, tired back. She lies in a heap facing the wall. But if she could have things like these, she needn't suffer. And if my mother could have had them she would be living to-day. Oh Man, I can't touch this."

"I see," said the Harvester.

He reached over, picked up the glass, and poured its contents into the jug. He repacked the fruit and closed the wafer box. Then he made a trip to the thicket and came out putting something into his pocket.

"Come on!" he said. "We are going to the house."

She stared at him.

"I simply don't dare."

"Then I will go alone," said the Harvester, picking up the bucket and starting. The Girl followed him.

"Uncle Henry may come any minute," she urged.

"Well if he comes and acts unpleasantly, he will get what he richly deserves."

"And he will make me pay for it afterward."

"Oh no he won't!" said the Harvester, "because I'll look out for that. This is my lucky day. He isn't going to come."

When he reached the back door he opened it and stepped inside. Of all the barren places of crude, disheartening ugliness the Harvester ever had seen, that was the worst.

"I want a glass and a spoon," he said.

The Girl brought them.

"Where is she?"

"In the next room."

At the sound of their voices a small girl came to the kitchen door.

"How do you do?" inquired the Harvester. "Is Mrs. Jameson asleep?"

"I don't know," answered the child. "She just lies there."

The Harvester gave her the glass. "Please fill that with water," he said. Then he picked up the bucket and went into the front room. When the child came with the water he took a bottle from his pocket, filled the spoon, and handed it to her.

"Hold that steadily," he said.

Then he slid his strong hands under the light frame and turned the face of the faded little creature toward him.

"I am a Medicine Man, Mrs. Jameson," he said casually. "I heard you were sick and I came to see if a little of this stuff wouldn't brace you up. Open your lips."

He held out the spoon and the amazed woman swallowed the contents before she realized what she was doing. Then the Harvester ran a hand under her shoulders and lifting her gently he tossed her pillow with the other hand.

"You are a light little body, just like my mother," he commented. "Now I have something else sick people sometimes enjoy."

He held the fruit juice to her lips as he slightly raised her on the pillow. Her trembling fingers lifted and closed around the sparkling glass.

"Oh it's cool!" she gasped.

"It is," said the Harvester, "and sour! I think you can taste it. Try!"

She drank so greedily he drew away the glass and urged caution, but the shaking fingers clung to him and the wavering voice begged for more.

"In a minute," said the Harvester gently. But the fevered woman would not wait. She drank the cooling liquid until she could take no more. Then she watched him fill a small pitcher and pack it in a part of the ice and lay some fruit around it.

"Who, Ruth?" she panted.

"A Medicine Man who heard about you."

"What will Henry say?"

"He won't know," explained the Girl, smoothing the hot forehead. "I'll put it in the cupboard, and slip it to you while he is out of the room. It will make you strong and well."

"I don't want to be strong and well and suffer it all over again. I want to rest. Give me more of the cool drink. Give me all I want, then I'll go to sleep."

"It's wonderful," said the Girl. "That's more than I've heard her talk since I came. She is much stronger. Please let her have it."

The Harvester assented. He gave the child some of the fruit, and told her to sit beside the bed and hold the drink when it was asked for. She agreed to be very careful and watchful. Then he picked up the bucket, and followed by the Girl, returned to the woods.

"Now we have to begin all over again," he said, as she seated herself at the table. "Because of the walk in the heat, this time the programme is a little different."

He replaced the wafer box and opened it, filled the glass, and heaped the cold fruit.

"Your aunt is going to have a refreshing sleep now," he said, "and your mind can be free about her for an hour or two. I am very sure your mother would not want you deprived of anything because she missed it, so you are to enjoy this, if you care for it. At least try a sample."

The Girl lifted the glass to her lips with a trembling hand.

"I'm like Aunt Molly," she said; "I wish I could drink all I could swallow, and then lie down and go to sleep forever. I suppose this is what they have in Heaven."

"No, it's what they drink all over earth at present, but I have a conceit of my own brand. Some of it is too strong of one fruit or of the other, and all too sweet for health. This is compounded scientifically and it's just right. If you are not accustomed to cold drinks, go slowly."

"You can't scare me," said the Girl; "I'm going to drink all I want."

There was a note of excitement in the Harvester's laugh.

"You must have some, too!"

"After a while," he said. "I was thirsty when I made it, so I don't care for any more now. Try the fruit and those wafers. Of course they are not home made—they are the best I could do at a bakery. Take time enough to eat slowly. I'm going to tell you a tale while you lunch, and it's about a Medicine Man named David Langston. It's a very peculiar story, but it's quite true. This man lives in the woods east of Onabasha, accompanied by his dog, horse, cow, and chickens, and a forest full of birds, flowers, and matchless trees. He has lived there in this manner for six long years, and every spring he and his dog have a seance and agree whether he shall go on gathering medicinal herbs and trying his hand at making medicine or go to the city and live as other men. Always the dog chooses to remain in the woods.

"Then every spring, on the day the first bluebird comes, the dog also decides whether the man shall go on alone or find a mate and bring her home for company. Each year the dog regularly has decided that they live as always. This spring, for some unforeseen reason, he changed his mind, and compelled the man, according to his vow in the beginning, to go courting. The man was so very angry at the idea of having a woman in his home, interfering with his work, disturbing his arrangements, and perhaps wanting to spend more money than he could afford, that he struck the dog for making that decision; struck him for the very first time in his life—I believe you'd like those apricots. Please try one."

"Go on with the story," said the Girl, sipping delicately but constantly at the frosty glass.

The Harvester arose and refilled it. Then he dropped pieces of ice over the fruit.

"Where was I?" he inquired casually.

"Where you struck Belshazzar, and it's no wonder," answered the Girl.

Without taking time to ponder that, the Harvester continued:

"But that night the man had a wonderful, golden dream. A beautiful girl came to him, and she was so gracious and lovely that he was sufficiently punished for striking his dog, because he fell unalterably in love with her."

"Meaning you?" interrupted the Girl.

"Yes," said the Harvester, "meaning me. I—if you like—fell in love with the girl. She came so alluringly, and I was so close to her that I saw her better than I ever did any other girl, and I knew her for all time. When she went, my heart was gone."

"And you have lived without that important organ ever since?"

"Without even the ghost of it! She took it with her. Well, that dream was so real, that the next day I began building over my house, making furniture, and planting flowers for her; and every day, wherever I went, I watched for her."

"What nonsense!"

"I can't see it."

"You won't find a girl you dreamed about in a thousand years."

"Wrong!" cried the Harvester triumphantly. "Saw her in little less than three months, but she vanished and it took some time and difficult work before I located her again; but I've got her all solid now, and she doesn't escape."

"Is she a 'lovely and gracious lady'?"

"She is!" said the Harvester, with all his heart.

"Young and beautiful, of course!"

"Indeed yes!"

"Please fill this glass. I told you what I was going to do."

The Harvester refilled the glass and the Girl drained it.

"Now won't you set aside these things and allow me to go to work?" she asked. "My call may come any minute, and I'll never forgive myself if I waste time, and don't draw your moth pattern for you."

"It's against my principles to hurry, and besides, my story isn't finished."

"It is," said the Girl. "She is young and lovely, gentle and a lady, you have her 'all solid,' and she can't 'escape'; that's the end, of course. But if I were you, I wouldn't have her until I gave her a chance to get away, and saw whether she would if she could."

"Oh I am not a jailer," said the Harvester. "She shall be free if I cannot make her love me; but I can, and I will; I swear it."

"You are not truly in earnest?"

"I am in deadly earnest."

"Honestly, you dreamed about a girl, and found the very one?"

"Most certainly, I did."

"It sounds like the wildest romancing."

"It is the veriest reality."

"Well I hope you win her, and that she will be everything you desire."

"Thank you," said the Harvester. "It's written in the book of fate that I succeed. The very elements are with me. The South Wind carried a message to her for me. I am going to marry her, but you could make it much easier for me if you would."

"I! What could I do?" cried the Girl.

"You could cease being afraid of me. You could learn to trust me. You could try to like me, if you see anything likeable about me. That would encourage me so that I could tell you of my Dream Girl, and then you could show me how to win her. A woman always knows about those things better than a man. You could be the greatest help in all the world to me, if only you would."

"I couldn't possibly! I can't leave here. I have no proper clothing to appear before another girl. She would be shocked at my white face. That I could help you is the most improbable dream you have had."

"You must pardon me if I differ from you, and persist in thinking that you can be of invaluable assistance to me, if you will. But you can't influence my Dream Girl, if you fear and distrust me yourself. Promise me that you will help me that much, anyway."

"I'll do all I can. I only want to make you see that I am in no position to grant any favours, no matter how much I owe you or how I'd like to. Is the candlestick you are carving for her?"

"It is," said the Harvester. "I am making a pair of maple to stand on a dressing table I built for her. It is unusually beautiful wood, I think, and I hope she will be pleased with it."

"Please take these things away and let me begin. This is the only thing I can see that I can do for you, and the moth will want to fly before I have finished."

The Harvester cleared the table and placed the box, while the Girl spread the paper and began work eagerly.

"I wonder if I knew there were such exquisite things in all the world," she said. "I scarcely think I did. I am beginning to understand why you couldn't kill one. You could make a chair or a table, and so you feel free to destroy them; but it takes ages and Almighty wisdom to evolve a creature like this, so you don't dare. I think no one else would if they really knew. Please talk while I work."

"Is there a particular subject you want discussed?"

"Anything but her. If I think too strongly of her, I can't work so well."

"Your ginseng is almost dry," said the Harvester. "I think I can bring you the money in a few days."

"So soon!" she cried.

"It dries day and night in an even temperature, and faster than you would believe. There's going to be between seven and eight pounds of it, when I make up what it has shrunk. It will go under the head of the finest wild roots. I can get eight for it sure."

"Oh what good news!" cried the Girl. "This is my lucky day, too. And the little girl isn't coming, so Aunt Molly must be asleep. Everything goes right! If only Uncle Henry wouldn't come home!"

"Let me fill your glass," proffered the Harvester.

"Just half way, and set it where I can see it," said the Girl. She worked with swift strokes and there was a hint of colour in her face, as she looked at him. "I hope you won't think I'm greedy," she said, "but truly, that's the first thing I've had that I could taste in—I can't remember when."

"I'll bring a barrel to-morrow," offered the Harvester, "and a big piece of ice wrapped in coffee sacking."

"You mustn't think of such a thing! Ice is expensive and so are fruits."

"Ice costs me the time required to saw and pack it at my home. I almost live on the fruit I raise. I confess to a fondness for this drink. I have no other personal expenses, unless you count in books, and a very few clothes, such as I'm wearing; so I surely can afford all the fruit juice I want."

"For yourself, yes."

"Also for a couple of women or I am a mighty poor attempt at a man," said the Harvester. "This is my day, so you are not to talk, because it won't do any good. Things go my way."

"Please see what you think of this," she said.

The Harvester arose and bent over her.

"That will do finely," he answered. "You can stop. I don't require all those little details for carving, I just want a good outline. It is finished. See here!"

He drew some folded papers from his pocket and laid them before her.

"Those are what I have been working from," he said.

The Girl took them and studied each carefully.

"If those are worth five dollars to you," she said gently, "why then I needn't hesitate to take as much for mine. They are superior."

"I should say so," laughed the Harvester as he took up the drawing and laid down the money.

"If you would make it half that much I'd feel better about it," she said.

"How could I?" asked the Harvester. "Your fingers are well trained and extremely skilful. Because some one has not been paying you enough for your work is no reason why I should keep it up. From now on you must have what others get. As soon as you can arrange for work, I want to tell you about some designs I have studied out from different things, show you the plants and insects, and have you make some samples. I'll send them to proper places, and see what experts say about the ideas and drawing. Work in the woods is healthful, with proper precautions; it's easy compared with the exactions of being bound to sewing or embroidering in the confinement of a room; it's vividly interesting in the search for new subjects, changes of material, and differing harmonious combinations; it's truly artistic; and it brings the prices high grade stuff always does."

"Almost you give me hope," said the Girl. "Almost, Man—almost! Since mother died, I haven't thought or planned beyond paying for the medicine she took and the shelter she lies in. Oh I didn't mean to say that—!"

She buried her face in her hands. The Harvester suffered until he scarcely knew how to bear it.

"Please finish," he begged. "You hadn't planned beyond the debt, you were saying—"

The Girl lifted her tired, strained face.

"Give me a little more of that delicious drink," she said. "I am ravenous for it. It puts new life in me. This and what you say bring a far away, misty vision of a clean, bright, peaceful room somewhere, and work one could love and live on in comfort; enough to give a desire to finish life to its natural end. Oh Man, you make me hope in spite of myself!"

"'Praise God from whom all blessings flow,'" quoted the Harvester reverently. "Now try one of these peaches. It's juicy and cold. Get that room right in focus in your brain, and nurture the idea. Its walls shall be bright as sunshine, its floor creamy white, and it shall open into a little garden, where only yellow flowers grow, and the birds shall sing. The first ray of sun that peeps over the hills of morning shall fall through its windows across your bed, and you shall work only as you please, after you've had months of play and rest; and it's coming true the instant you can leave here. Dream of it, make up your mind to it, because it's coming. I have a little streak of second sight, and I see it on the way."

"You are talking wildly," said the Girl, "else you are a good genie trying to conjure a room for me."

"This room I am talking of is ready whenever you want to take possession," said the Harvester. "Accept it as a reality, because I tell you I know where it is, that it is waiting, and you can earn your way into it with no obligation to any one."

The Girl stretched out her right hand and slowly turned and opened and closed it. Then she glanced at the Harvester with a weary smile.

"From somewhere I feel a glimmering of the spirit, but Oh, dear Lord, the flesh is weak!" she said.

"That's where nourishing foods, appetizing drinks, plenty of pure, fresh air, and good water come in. Now we have talked enough for one day, and worked too much. The fruit and drink go with you. I will carry it to the house, and you can hide it in your room. I am going to put a bottle of tonic on top that the best surgeon in the state gave me for you. Try to eat something strengthening and then take a spoonful of this, and use all the fruit you want. I'll bring more to-morrow and put it here, with plenty of ice. Now suppose you let the moth go free," he suggested to avoid objections. "You must take my word for it, that it is perfectly harmless, lacking either sting or bite, and hold your hand before it, so that it will climb on your fingers. Then stand where a ray of sunshine falls and in a few minutes it will go out to live its life."

The Girl hesitated a second as she studied the clean-cut, interested face of the man; then she held out her hand, and he urged the moth to climb on her fingers. She stepped where a ray of strong light fell on the forest floor and held the moth in it. The brightness also touched her transparent hand and white face and the gleaming black hair. The Harvester choked down a rising surge of desire for her, and took a new grip on himself.

"Oh!" she cried breathlessly, as the clinging feet suddenly loosened and the luna slowly flew away among the trees. She turned on the Harvester. "You teach me wonders!" she cried. "You give life different meanings. You are not as other men."

"If that be true, it is because I am of the woods. The Almighty does not evolve all his wonders in animal, bird, and flower form; He keeps some to work out in the heart, if humanity only will go to His school, and allow Him to have dominion. Come now, you must go. I will come back and put away all the things and tomorrow I will bring your ginseng money. Any time you cannot come, if you want to tell me why, or if there is anything I can do for you, put a line under the oilcloth. I will carry the bucket."

"I am so afraid," she said.

"I will only go to the edge of the woods. You can see if there is any one at the house first. If not, you can send the child away, and then I will carry the bucket to the door for you, and it will furnish comfort for one night, at least."

They went to the cleared land and the Girl passed on alone. Soon she reappeared and the Harvester saw the child going down the road. He took up the bucket and set it inside the door.

"Is there anything I can do for you?"

"Nothing but go, before you make trouble."

"Will you hide that stuff and walk back as far as the woods with me? There is something more I want to say to you."

The Girl staggered under the heavy load, and the man turned his head and tried to pretend he did not see. Presently she came out to him, and they returned to the line of the woods. Just as they entered the shade there was a flash before them, and on a twig a few rods away a little gray bird alighted, while in precipitate pursuit came a flaming wonder of red, and in a burst of excited trills, broken whistles, and imploring gestures, perched beside her.

The Harvester hastily drew the Girl behind some bushes.

"Watch!" he whispered. "You are going to see a sight so lovely and so rare it is vouchsafed to few mortals ever to behold."

"What are they fighting about?" she whispered.

"You are witnessing a cardinal bird declare his love," breathed the Harvester.

"Do cardinals love different birds?"

"No. The female is gray, because if she is coloured the same as the trees and branches and her nest, she will have more chance to bring off her young in safety. He is blood red, because he is the bravest, gayest, most ardent lover of the whole woods," explained the Harvester.

The Girl leaned forward breathlessly watching and a slow surge of colour crept into her cheeks. The red bird twisted, whistled, rocked, tilted, and trilled, and the gray sat demurely watching him, as if only half convinced he really meant it. The gay lover began at the beginning and said it all over again with more impassioned gestures than before, and then he edged in touch and softly stroked her wing with his beak. She appeared startled, but did not fly. So again the fountain of half-whistled, half-trilled notes bubbled with the acme of pleading intonation and that time he leaned and softly kissed her as she reached her bill for the caress. Then she fled in headlong flight, while the streak of flame darted after her. The Girl caught her breath in a swift spasm of surprise and wonder. She turned to the Harvester.

"What was it you wanted to say to me?" she asked hurriedly.

The Harvester was not the man to miss the goods the gods provided. Truly this was his lucky day. Unhesitatingly he took the plunge.

"Precisely what he said to her. And if you observed closely, you noticed that she didn't ask him 'why.'"

Before she could open her lips, he was gone, his swift strides carrying him through the woods.

Chapter 12

"The Way of a Man
with a Maid"

The next day the Harvester lifted the oilcloth, and picking up a folded note he read—

"Aunt Molly found rest in the night. She was more comfortable than she had been since I have known her. Close the end she whispered to me to thank you if I ever saw you again. She will be buried to-morrow. Past that, I dare not think."

The Harvester sat on the log and studied the lines. She would not come that day or the next. After a long time he put the note in his pocket, wrote an answer telling her he had been there, and would come on the following day on the chance of her wanting anything he could do, and the next he would bring the ginseng money, so she must be sure to meet him.

Then he went back to the wagon, turned Betsy, and drove around the Jameson land watching closely. There were several vehicles in the barn lot, and a couple of men sitting under the trees of the door yard. Faded bedding hung on the line and women moved through the rooms, but he could not see the Girl. Slowly he drove on until he came to the first house, and there he stopped and went in. He saw the child of the previous day, and as she came forward her mother appeared in the doorway.

The Harvester explained who he was and that he was examining the woods in search of some almost extinct herbs he needed in his business. Then he told of having been at the adjoining farm the day before and mentioned the sick woman. He added that later she had died. He casually mentioned that a young woman there seemed pale and ill and wondered if the neighbours would see her through. He suggested that the place appeared as if the owner did not take much interest, and when the woman finished with Henry Jameson, he said how very important it seemed to him that some good, kind-hearted soul should go and mother the poor girl, and the woman thought she was the very person. Without knowing exactly how he did it, the Harvester left with her promise to remain with the Girl the coming two nights. The woman had her hands full of strange and delicious fruit without understanding why it had been given her, or why she had made those promises. She thought the Harvester a remarkably fine young man to take such interest in strangers and she told him he was welcome to anything he could find on her place that would help with his medicines.

The Harvester just happened to be coming from the woods as the woman freshly dressed left the house, so he took her in the wagon and drove back to the Jameson place, because he was going that way. Then he returned to Medicine Woods and worked with all his might.

First he polished floors, cleaned windows, and arranged the rooms as best he could inside the cabin; then he gave a finishing touch to everything outside. He could not have told why he did it, but he thought it was because there was hope that now the Girl would come to Onabasha. If he found opportunity to bring her to the city, he hoped that possibly he might drive home with her and show Medicine Woods, so everything must be in order. Then he worked with flying fingers in the dry-house, putting up her ginseng for market, and never was weight so liberal.

The next morning he drove early to Onabasha and came home with a loaded wagon, the contents of which he scattered through the cabin where it seemed most suitable, but the greater part of it was for her. He glanced at the bare floors and walls of the other rooms, and thought of trying to improve them, but he was afraid of not getting the right things.

"I don't know much about what is needed here," he said, "but I am perfectly safe in buying anything a girl ever used."

Then he returned to the city, explained the situation to the doctor, and selected the room he wanted in case the Girl could be persuaded to come to the hospital. After that he went to see the doctor's wife, and made arrangements for her to be ready for a guest, because there was a possibility he might want to call for help. He had another jug of fruit juice and all the delicacies he could think of, also a big cake of ice, when he reached the woods. There were only a few words for him.

"I will come to-morrow at two, if at all possible; if not, keep the money until I can."

There was nothing to do except to place his offering under the oilcloth and wait, but he simply was compelled to add a line to say he would be there, and to express the hope that she was comfortable as possible and thinking of the sunshine room. Then he returned to Medicine Woods to wait, and found that possible only by working to exhaustion. There were many things he could do, and one after another he finished them, until completely worn out; and then he slept the deep sleep of weariness.

At noon the next day he bathed, shaved, and dressed in fresh, clean clothing. He stopped in Onabasha for more fruit, and drove to the Jameson woods. He was waiting and watching the usual path the Girl followed, when her step sounded on the other side. The Harvester arose and turned. Her pallor was alarming. She stepped on the rug he had spread, and sank almost breathless to the chair.

"Why do you come a new way that fills you with fear?" asked the Harvester.

"It seems as if Uncle Henry is watching me every minute, and I didn't dare come where he could see. I must not remain a second. You must take these things away and go at once. He is dreadful."

"So am I," said the Harvester, "when affairs go too everlastingly wrong. I am not afraid of any man living. What are you planning to do?"

"I want to ask you, are you sure about the prices of my drawing and the ginseng?"

"Absolutely," said the Harvester. "As for the ginseng it went in fresh and early, best wild roots, and it brought eight a pound. There were eight pounds when I made up weight and here is your money."

He handed her a long envelope addressed to her.

"What is the amount?" she asked.

"Sixty-four dollars."

"I can't believe it."

"You have it in your fingers."

"You know that I would like to thank you properly, if I had words to express myself."

"Never mind that," said the Harvester. "Tell me what you are planning. Say that you will come to the hospital for the long, perfect rest now."

"It is absolutely impossible. Don't weary me by mentioning it. I cannot."

"Will you tell me what you intend doing?"

"I must," she said, "for it depends entirely on your word. I am going to get Uncle Henry's supper, and then go and remain the night with the neighbour who has been helping me. In the morning, when he leaves, she is coming with her wagon for my trunk, and she is going to drive with me to Onabasha and find me a cheap room and loan me a few things, until I can buy what I need. I am going to use fourteen dollars of this and my drawing money for what I am forced to buy, and pay fifty on my debt. Then I will send you my address and be ready for work."

She clutched the envelope and for the first time looked at him.

"Very well," said the Harvester. "I could take you to the wife of my best friend, the chief surgeon of the city hospital, and everything would be ease and rest until you are strong; she would love to have you."

The Girl dropped her hands wearily.

"Don't tire me with it!" she cried. "I am almost falling despite the stimulus of food and drink I can touch. I never can thank you properly for that. I won't be able to work hard enough to show you how much I appreciate what you have done for me. But you don't understand. A woman, even a poverty-poor woman, if she be delicately born and reared, cannot go to another woman on a man's whim, and when she lacks even the barest necessities. I don't refuse to meet your friends. I shall love to, when I can be so dressed that I will not shame you. Until that times comes, if you are the gentleman you appear to be, you will wait without urging me further."

"I must be a man, in order to be a gentleman," said the Harvester. "And it is because the man in me is in hot rebellion against more loneliness, pain, and suffering for you, that the conventions become chains I do not care how soon or how roughly I break. If only you could be induced to say the word, I tell you I could bring one of God's gentlest women to you."

"And probably she would come in a dainty gown, in her carriage or motor, and be disgusted, astonished, and secretly sorry for you. As for me, I do not require her pity. I will be glad to know the beautiful, refined, and gentle woman you are so certain of, but not until I am better dressed and more attractive in appearance than now. If you will give me your address, I will write you when I am ready for work."

Silently the Harvester wrote it. "Will you give me permission to take these things to your neighbour for you?" he asked. "They would serve until you can do better, and I have no earthly use for them."

She hesitated. Then she laughed shortly.

"What a travesty my efforts at pride are with you!" she cried. "I begin by trying to preserve some proper dignity, and end by confessing abject poverty. I yet have the ten you paid me the other day, but twenty-four dollars are not much to set up housekeeping on, and I would be more glad than I can say for these very things."

"Thank you," said the Harvester. "I will take them when I go. Is there anything else?"

"I think not."

"Will you have a drink?"

"Yes, if you have more with you. I believe it is really cooling my blood."

"Are you taking the medicine?"

"Yes," she said, "and I am stronger. Truly I am. I know I appear ghastly to you, but it's loss of sleep, and trying to lay away poor Aunt Molly decently, and—"

"And fear of Uncle Henry," added the Harvester.

"Yes," said the Girl. "That most of all! He thinks I am going to stay here and take her place. I can't tell him I am not, and how I am to hide from him when I am gone, I don't know. I am afraid of him."

"Has he any claim on you?"

"Shelter for the past three months."

"Are you of age?"

"I am almost twenty-four," she said.

"Then suppose you leave Uncle Henry to me," suggested the Harvester.

"Why?"

"Careful now! The red bird told you why!" said the man. "I will not urge it upon you now, but keep it steadily in the back of your head that there is a sunshine room all ready and waiting for you, and I am going to take you to it very soon. As things are, I think you might allow me to tell you—"

She was on her feet in instant panic. "I must go," she said. "Uncle Henry is dogging me to promise to remain, and I will not, and he is watching me. I must go—"

"Can you give me your word of honour that you will go to the neighbour woman to-night; that you feel perfectly safe?"

She hesitated. "Yes, I—I think so. Yes, if he doesn't find out and grow angry. Yes, I will be safe."

"How soon will you write me?"

"Just as soon as I am settled and rest a little."

"Do you mean several days?"

"Yes, several days."

"An eternity!" cried the Harvester with white lips. "I cannot let you go. Suppose you fall ill and fail to write me, and I do not know where you are, and there is no one to care for you."

"But can't you see that I don't know where I will be? If it will satisfy you, I will write you a line to-morrow night and tell you where I am, and you can come later."

"Is that a promise?" asked the Harvester.

"It is," said the Girl.

"Then I will take these things to your neighbour and wait until to-morrow night. You won't fail me?"

"I never in all my life saw a man so wild over designs," said the Girl, as she started toward the house.

"Don't forget that the design I'm craziest about is the same as the red bird's," the Harvester flung after her, but she hurried on and made no reply.

He folded the table and chair, rolled the rug, and shouldering them picked up the bucket and started down the river bank.

"David!"

Such a faint little call he never would have been sure he heard anything if Belshazzar had not stopped suddenly. The hair on the back of his neck arose and he turned with a growl in his throat. The Harvester dropped his load with a crash and ran in leaping bounds, but the dog was before him. Half way to the house, Ruth Jameson swayed in the grip of her uncle. One hand clutched his coat front in a spasmodic grasp, and with the other she covered her face.

The roar the Harvester sent up stayed the big, lifted fist, and the dog leaped for a throat hold, and compelled the man to defend himself. The Harvester never knew how he covered the space until he stood between them, and saw the Girl draw back and snatch together the front of her dress.

"He took it from me!" she panted. "Make him, oh make him give back my money!"

Then for a few seconds things happened too rapidly to record. Once the Harvester tossed a torn envelope exposing money to the Girl, and again a revolver, and then both men panting and dishevelled were on their feet.

"Count your money, Ruth?" said the Harvester in a voice of deadly quiet.

"It is all here," said she.

"Her money?" cried Henry Jameson. "My money! She has been stealing the price of my cattle from my pockets. I thought I was short several times lately."

"You are lying," said the Harvester deliberately. "It is her money. I just paid it to her. You were trying to take it from her, not the other way."

"Oh, she is in your pay?" leered the man.

"If you say an insulting word I think very probably I will finish you," said the Harvester. "I can, with my naked hands, and all your neighbours will say it is a a good job. You have felt my grip! I warn you!"

"How does my niece come to be taking money from you!"

"You have forfeited all right to know. Ruth, you cannot remain here. You must come with me. I will take you to Onabasha and find you a room."

A horrible laugh broke from the man.

"So that is the end of my saintly niece!" he said.

"Remember!" cried the Harvester advancing a step. "Ruth, will you go to the rest I suggested for you?"

"I cannot."

"Will you go to Doctor Carey's wife?"

"Impossible!"

"Will you marry me and go to the shelter of my home with me?"

Wild-eyed she stared at him.

"Why?"

"Because I love you, and want life made easier for you, above anything else on earth."

"But your Dream Girl!"

"YOU ARE THE DREAM GIRL! I thought the red bird told you for me! I didn't know it would be a shock. I believed I had made you understand."

By that time she was shaking with a nervous chill, and the sight unmanned the Harvester.

"Come with me!" he urged. "We will decide what you want to do on the way. Only come, I beg you."

"First it was marry, now it's decide later," broke in Henry Jameson, crazed with anger. "Move a step and I'll strike you down. I'd better than see you disgraced—"

The Harvester advanced and Jameson stepped back.

"Ruth," said the Harvester, "I know how impossible this seems. It is giving you no chance at all. I had intended, when I found you, to court you tenderly as girl ever was wooed before. Come with me, and I'll do it yet. The new home was built for you. The sunshine room is ready and waiting for you. There is pure air, fresh water, nothing but rest and comfort. I'll nurse you back to health and strength, and you shall be courted until you come to me of your own accord."

"Impossible!" cried the girl.

"Only if you make it so. If you will come now, we can be married in a few hours, and you can be safe in your own home. I realize now that this is unexpected and shocking to you, but if you will come with me and allow me to restore you to health and strength, and if, say, in a year, you are convinced that you do not love me, I will set you free. If you will come, I swear to you that you shall be my wife first, and my honoured guest afterward, until such time as you either tell me you love me or that you never can. Will you come on those terms, Ruth?"

"I cannot!"

"It will end fear, uncertainty, and work, until you are strong and well. It will give you home, rest, and love, that you will find is worth your consideration. I will keep my word; of that you may be sure."

"No," she cried. "No! But take back this money! Keep it until I tell you to whom to pay it."

She started toward him holding out the envelope.

Henry Jameson, with a dreadful oath, sprang for it, his contorted face a drawn snarl. The Harvester caught him in air and sent him reeling. He snatched the revolver from the Girl and put the money in his pocket.

"Ruth, I can't leave you here," he said. "Oh my Dream Girl! Are you afraid of me yet? Won't you trust me? Won't you come?"

"No."

"You are right about that, my lady; you will come back to the house, that's what you'll do," said Henry Jameson, starting toward her.

"No!" cried the Girl retreating. "Oh Heaven help me! What am I to do?"

"Ruth, you must come with me," said the Harvester. "I don't dare leave you here."

She stood between them and gave Henry Jameson one long, searching look. Then she turned to the Harvester.

"I am far less afraid of you. I will accept your offer," she said.

"Thank you!" said the Harvester. "I will keep my word and you shall have no regrets. Is there anything here you wish to take with you?"

"I want a little trunk of my mother's. It contains some things of hers."

"Will you show me where it is?"

She started toward the house; he followed, and Henry Jameson fell in line. The Harvester turned on him. "You remain where you are," he said. "I will take nothing but the trunk. I know what you are thinking, but you will not get your gun just now. I will return this revolver to-morrow."

"And the first thing I do with it will be to use it on you," said Henry Jameson.

"I'll report that threat to the police, so that they can see you properly hanged if you do," retorted the Harvester, as he followed the girl.

"Where is his gun?" he asked as he overtook her. When he reached the house he told her to watch the door. He went inside, broke the lock from the gun in the corner, found the trunk, and swinging it to his shoulder, passed Henry Jameson and went back through the woods. The Harvester set the trunk in the wagon, helped the Girl in, and returned for the load he had dropped at her call. Then he took the lines and started for Onabasha.

The Girl beside him was almost fainting. He stopped to give her a drink and tried to encourage her.

"Brace up the best you can, Ruth," he said. "You must go with me for a license; that is the law. Afterward, I'll make it just as easy for you as possible. I will do everything, and in a few hours you will be comfortable in your room. You brave girl! This must come out right! You have suffered more than your share. I will have peace for you the remainder of the way."

She lifted shaking hands and tried to arrange her hair and dress. As they neared the city she spoke.

"What will they ask me?"

"I don't know. But I am sure the law requires you to appear in person now. I can take you somewhere and find out first."

"That will take time. I want to reach my room. What would you think?"

"If you are of age, where you were born, if you are a native of this country, what your father and mother died of, how old they were, and such questions as that. I'll help you all I can. You know those things. don't you?"

"Yes. But I must tell you—"

"I don't want to be told anything," said the Harvester. "Save your strength. All I want to know is any way in which I can make this easier for you. Nothing else matters. I will tell you what I think; if you have any objections, make them. I will drive to the bank and get a draft for what you owe, and have that off your mind. Then we will get the license. After that I'll take you to the side door, slip you in the elevator and to the fitting room of a store where I know the manager, and you shall have some pretty clothing while I arrange for a minister, and I'll come for you with a carriage. That isn't the kind of wedding you or any other girl should have, but there are times when a man only can do his best. You will help me as much as you can, won't you?"

"Anything you choose. It doesn't matter—only be quick as possible."

"There are a few details to which I must attend," said the Harvester, "and the time will go faster trying on dresses than waiting alone. When you are properly clothed you will feel better. What did you say the amount you owe is?"

"You may get a draft for fifty dollars. I will pay the remainder when I earn it."

"Ruth, won't you give me the pleasure of taking you home free from the worry of that debt?"

"I am not going to 'worry.' I am going to work and pay it."

"Very well," said the Harvester. "This is the bank. We will stop here."

They went in and he handed her a slip of paper.

"Write the name and address on that?" he said.

As the slip was returned to him, without a glance he folded it and slid it under a wicket. "Write a draft for fifty dollars payable to that party, and send to that address, from Miss Ruth Jameson," he said.

Then he turned to her.

"That is over. See how easy it is! Now we will go to the court house. It is very close. Try not to think. Just move and speak."

"Hello, Langston!" said the clerk. "What can we do for you here?"

"Show this girl every consideration," whispered the Harvester, as he advanced. "I want a marriage license in your best time. I will answer first."

With the document in his possession, they went to the store he designated, where he found the Girl a chair in the fitting room, while he went to see the manager.

"I want one of your most sensible and accommodating clerks," said the Harvester, "and I would like a few words with her."

When she was presented he scrutinized her carefully and decided she would do.

"I have many thanks and something more substantial for a woman who will help me to carry through a slightly unusual project with sympathy and ability," he said, "and the manager has selected you. Are you willing?"

"If I can," said the clerk.

"She has put up your other orders," interposed the manager. "Were they satisfactory?"

"I don't know," said the Harvester. "They have not yet reached the one for whom they were intended. What I want you to do," he said to the clerk, "is to go to the fitting room and dress the girl you find there for her wedding. She had other plans, but death disarranged them, and she has only an hour in which to meet the event most girls love to linger over for months. She has been ill, and is worn with watching; but some time she may look back to her wedding day with joy, and if only you would help me to make the best of it for her, I would be, as I said, under more obligations than I can express."

"I will do anything," said the clerk.

"Very well," said the Harvester. "She has come from the country entirely unprepared. She is delicate and refined. Save her all the embarrassment you can. Dress her beautifully in white. Keep a memorandum slip of what you spend for my account."

"What is the limit?" asked the clerk.

"There is none," said the Harvester. "Put the prettiest things on her you have in the right sizes, and if you are a woman with a heart, be gentle!"

"Is she ready?" inquired the manager at the door an hour later.

"I am," said the Girl stepping through.

The astounded Harvester stood and stared, utterly oblivious of the curious people.

"Here, here, here!" suddenly he whistled it, in the red bird's most entreating tones.

The Girl laughed and the colour in her face deepened.

"Let us go," she said.

"But what about you?" asked the manager of the Harvester.

"Thunder!" cried the man aghast. "I was so busy getting everything else ready, I forgot all about myself. I can't stand before a minister beside her, can I?"

"Well I should say not," said the manager.

"Indeed yes," said the Girl. "I never saw you in any other clothing. You would be a stranger of whom I'd be afraid."

"That settles it!" said the Harvester calmly. "Thank all of you more than words can express. I will come in the first of the week and tell you how we get along."

Then they went to the carriage and started for the residence of a minister.

"Ruth, you are my Dream Girl to the tips of your eyelashes," said the Harvester. "I almost wish you were not. It wouldn't keep me thinking so much of the remainder of that dream. You are the loveliest sight I ever saw."

"Do I really appear well?" asked the Girl, hungry for appreciation.

"Indeed you do!" said the Harvester. "I never could have guessed that such a miracle could be wrought. And you don't seem so tired. Were they good to you?"

"Wonderfully! I did not know there was kindness like that in all the world for a stranger. I did not feel lost or embarrassed, except the first few seconds when I didn't know what to do. Oh I thank you for this! You were right. Whatever comes in life I always shall love to remember that I was daintily dressed and appeared as well as I could when I was married. But I must tell you I am not real. They did everything on earth to me, three of them working at a time. I feel an increase in self-respect in some way. David, I do appear better?"

When she said "David," the Harvester looked out of the window and gulped down his delight. He leaned toward her.

"Shut your eyes and imagine you see the red bird," he said. "In my soul, I am saying to you again and again just what he sang. You are wonderfully beautiful, Ruth, and more than wonderfully sweet. Will you answer me a question?"

"If I can."

"I love you with all my heart. Will you marry me?"

"I said I would."

"Then we are engaged, aren't we?"

"Yes."

"Please remove the glove from your left hand. I want to put on your ring. This will have to be a very short engagement, but no one save ourselves need know."

"David, that isn't necessary."

"I have it here, and believe me, Ruth, it will help in a few minutes; and all your life you will be glad. It is a precious symbol that has a meaning. This wedding won't be hurt by putting all the sacredness into it we can. Please, Ruth!"

"On one condition."

"What is it?"

"That you will accept and wear my mother's wedding ring in exchange," she said. "It is all I have."

"Ruth, do you really wish that?"

"I do."

"I am more pleased than I can tell you. May I have it now?"

She took off her glove and the Harvester held her hand closely a second, then lifted it to his lips, passionately kissed it and slipped on a ring, the setting a big, lustrous pearl.

"I looked at some others," he said, "but nothing got a second glance save this. They knew you were coming down the ages, and so they got the pearls ready. How beautiful it is on your hand! Put on the glove and wear that ring as if you had owned it for the long, happy year of betrothal every girl should have. You can start yours to-day, and if by this time next year I have not won you to my heart and arms, I'm no man and not worthy of you. Ruth, you will try just a little to love me, won't you?"

"I will try with all my heart," she said instantly.

"Thank you! I am perfectly happy with that. I never expected to marry you before a year, anyway. All the difference will be the blessed fact that instead of coming to see you somewhere else, I now can have you in my care, and court you every minute. You might as well make up your mind to capitulate soon. It's on the books that you do."

"If an instant ever comes when I realize that I love you, I will come straight and tell you; believe me, I will."

"Thank you!" said the Harvester. "This is going to be quite a proper wedding after all. Here is the place. It will be over soon and you on the home way. Lord, Ruth—!"

The Girl smiled at him as he opened the carriage door, helped her up the steps and rang the bell.

"Be brave now!" he whispered. "Don't lose your lovely colour. These people will be as kind as they were at the store."

The minister was gentle and wasted no time. His wife and daughter, who appeared for witnesses, kissed Ruth, and congratulated her. She and the Harvester stood, took the vows, exchanged rings, and returned to the carriage, a man and his wife by the laws of man.

"Drive to Seaton's cafe," the Harvester said.

"Oh David, let us go home!"

"This is so good I hate to stop it for something you may not like so well. I ordered lunch and if we don't eat it I will have to pay for it anyway. You wouldn't want me to be extravagant, would you?"

"No," said the Girl, "and besides, since you mention it, I believe I am hungry."

"Good!" cried the Harvester. "I hoped so! Ruth, you wouldn't allow me to hold your hand just until we reach the cafe? It might save me from bursting with joy."

"Yes," she said. "But I must take off my lovely gloves first. I want to keep them forever."

"I'd hate the glove being removed dreadfully," said the Harvester, his eyes dancing and snapping.

"I'm sorry I am so thin and shaky," said the Girl. "I will be steady and plump soon, won't I?"

"On your life you will," said the Harvester, taking the hand gently.

Now there are a number of things a man deeply in love can think of to do with a woman's white hand. He can stroke it, press it tenderly, and lay it against his lips and his heart. The Harvester lacked experience in these arts, and yet by some wonderful instinct all of these things occurred to him. There was real colour in the Girl's cheeks by the time he helped her into the cafe. They were guided to a small room, cool and restful, close a window, beside which grew a tree covered with talking leaves. A waiting attendant, who seemed perfectly adept, brought in steaming bouillon, fragrant tea, broiled chicken, properly cooked vegetables, a wonderful salad, and then delicious ices and cold fruit. The happy Harvester leaned back and watched the Girl daintily manage almost as much food as he wanted to see her eat.

When they had finished, "Now we are going home," he said. "Will you try to like it, Ruth?"

"Indeed I will," she promised. "As soon as I grow accustomed to the dreadful stillness, and learn what things will not bite me, I'll be better."

"I'll have to ask you to wait a minute," he said. "One thing I forgot. I must hire a man to take Betsy home."

"Aren't you going to drive her yourself?"

"No ma'am! We are going in a carriage or a motor," said the Harvester.

"Indeed we are not!" contradicted the Girl. "You have had this all your way so far. I am going home behind Betsy, with Belshazzar at my knee."

"But your dress! People will think I am crazy to put a lovely woman like you in a spring wagon."

"Let them!" said the Girl placidly. "Why should we bother about other people? I am going with Betsy and Belshazzar."

The Harvester had been thinking that he adored her, that it was impossible to love her more, but every minute was proving to him that he was capable of feeling so profound it startled him. To carry the Girl, his bride, through the valley and up the hill in the little spring wagon drawn by Betsy—that would have been his ideal way. But he had supposed that she would be afraid of soiling her dress, and embarrassed to ride in such a conveyance. Instead it was her choice. Yes, he could love her more. Hourly she was proving that.

"Come this way a few steps," he said. "Betsy is here."

The Girl laid her face against the nose of the faithful old animal, and stroked her head and neck. Then she held her skirts and the Harvester helped her into the wagon. She took the seat, and the dog went wild with joy.

"Come on, Bel," she softly commanded.

The dog hesitated, and looked at the Harvester for permission.

"You may come here and put your head on my knee," said the Girl.

"Belshazzar, you lucky dog, you are privileged to sit there and lay your head on the lady's lap," said the Harvester, and the dog quivered with joy.

Then the man picked up the lines, gave a backward glance to the bed of the wagon, high piled with large bundles, and turned Betsy toward Medicine Woods. Through the crowded streets and toward the country they drove, when a big red car passed, a man called to them, then reversed and slowly began backing beside the wagon. The Harvester stopped.

"That is my best friend, Doctor Carey, of the hospital, Ruth," he said hastily. "May I tell him, and will you shake hands with him?"

"Certainly!" said the Girl.

"Is it really you, David?" the doctor peered with gleaming eyes from under the car top.

"Really!" cried the Harvester, as man greets man with a full heart when he is sure of sympathy. "Come, give us your best send-off, Doc! We were married an hour ago. We are headed for Medicine Woods. Doctor Carey, this is Mrs. Langston."

"Mighty glad to know you!" cried the doctor, reaching a happy hand.

The Girl met it cordially, while she smiled on him.

"How did this happen?" demanded the doctor. "Why didn't you let us know? This is hardly fair of you, David. You might have let me and the Missus share with you."

"That is to be explained," said the Harvester. "It was decided on very suddenly, and rather sadly, on account of the death of Mrs. Jameson. I forced Ruth to marry me and come with me. I grow rather frightened when I think of it, but it was the only way I knew. She absolutely refused my other plans. You see before you a wild man carrying away a woman to his cave."

"Don't believe him, Doctor!" laughed the Girl. "If you know him, you will understand that to offer all he had was like him, when he saw my necessity. You will come to see us soon?"

"I'll come right now," said the doctor. "I'll bring my wife and arrive by the time you do."

"Oh no you won't!" said the Harvester. "Do you observe the bed of this wagon? This happened all 'unbeknownst' to us. We have to set up housekeeping after we reach home. We will notify you when we are ready for visitors. Just you subside and wait until you are sent for."

"Why David!" cried the astonished Girl.

"That's the law!" said the Harvester tersely. "Good-bye, Doc; we'll be ready for you in a day or two."

He leaned down and held out his hand. The grip that caught it said all any words could convey; and then Betsy started up the hill.

Chapter 13

When the Dream Came True

At first the road lay between fertile farms dotted with shocked wheat, covered with undulant seas of ripening oats, and forests of growing corn. The larks were trailing melody above the shorn and growing fields, the quail were ingathering beside the fences, and from the forests on graceful wings slipped the nighthawks and sailed and soared, dropping so low that the half moons formed by white spots on their spread wings showed plainly.

"Why is this country so different from the other side of the city?" asked the Girl.

"It is older," replied the Harvester, "and it lies higher. This was settled and well cultivated when that was a swamp. But as a farming proposition, the money is in the lowland like your uncle's. The crops raised there are enormous compared with the yield of these fields."

"I see," said she. "But this is much better to look at and the air is different. It lacks a soggy, depressing quality."

"I don't allow any air to surpass that of Medicine Woods," said the Harvester, "by especial arrangement with the powers that be."

Then they dipped into a little depression and arose to cross the railroad and then followed a longer valley that was ragged and unkempt compared with the road between cultivated fields. The Harvester was busy trying to plan what to do first, and how to do it most effectively, and working his brain to think if he had everything the Girl would require for her comfort; so he drove silently through the deepening shadows. She shuddered and awoke him suddenly. He glanced at her from the corner of his eye.

Her thoughts had gone on a journey, also, and the way had been rough, for her face wore a strained appearance. The hands lying bare in her lap were tightly gripped, so that the nails and knuckles appeared blue. The Harvester hastily cast around seeking for the cause of the transformation. A few minutes ago she had seemed at ease and comfortable, now she was close to open panic. Nothing had been said that would disturb her. With brain alert he searched for the reason. Then it began to come to him. The unaccustomed silence and depression of the country might have been the beginning. Coming from the city and crowds of people to the gloomy valley with a man almost a stranger, going she knew not where, to conditions she knew not what, with the experiences of the day vivid before her. The black valley road was not prepossessing, with its border of green pools, through which grew swamp bushes and straggling vines. The Harvester looked carefully at the road, and ceased to marvel at the Girl. But he disliked to let her know he understood, so he gave one last glance at those gripped hands and casually held out the lines.

"Will you take these just a second?" he asked. "Don't let them touch your dress. We must not lose of our load, because it's mostly things that will make you more comfortable."

He arose, and turning, pretended to see that everything was all right. Then he resumed his seat and drove on.

"I am a little ashamed of this stretch through here," he said apologetically. "I could have managed to have it cleared and in better shape long ago, but in a way it yields a snug profit, and so far I've preferred the money. The land is not mine, but I could grub out this growth entirely, instead of taking only what I need."

"Is there stuff here you use?" the Girl aroused herself to ask, and the Harvester saw the look of relief that crossed her face at the sound of his voice.

"Well I should say yes," he laughed. "Those bushes, numerous everywhere, with the hanging yellow-green balls, those, in bark and root, go into fever medicines. They are not so much used now, but sometimes I have a call, and when I do, I pass the beds on my—on our land, and come down here and get what is needed. That bush," he indicated with the whip, "blooms exquisitely in the spring. It is a relative of flowering dogwood, and the one of its many names I like best is silky cornel. Isn't that pretty?"

"Yes," she said, "it is beautiful."

"I've planted some for you in a hedge along the driveway so next spring you can gather all you want. I think you'll like the odour. The bark brings more than true dogwood. If I get a call from some house that uses it, I save mine and come down here. Around the edge are hop trees, and I realize something from them, and also the false and true bitter-sweet that run riot here. Both of them have pretty leaves, while the berries of the true hang all winter and the colour is gorgeous. I've set your hedge closely with them. When it has grown a few months it's going to furnish flowers in the spring, a million different, wonderful leaves and berries in the summer, many fruits the birds love in the fall, and bright berries, queer seed pods, and nuts all winter."

"You planted it for me?"

"Yes. I think it will be beautiful in a season or two; it isn't so bad now. I hope it will call myriads of birds to keep you company. When you cross this stretch of road hereafter, don't see fetid water and straggling bushes and vines; just say to yourself, this helps to fill orders!"

"I am perfectly tolerant of it now," she said. "You make everything different. I will come with you and help collect the roots and barks you want. Which bush did you say relieved the poor souls scorching with fever?"

The Harvester drew on the lines, Betsy swerved to the edge of the road, and he leaned and broke a branch.

"This one," he answered. "Buttonbush, because those balls resemble round buttons. Aren't they peculiar? See how waxy and gracefully cut and set the leaves are. Go on, Betsy, get us home before night. We appear our best early in the morning, when the sun tops Medicine Woods and begins to light us up, and in the evening, just when she drops behind Onabasha back there, and strikes us with a few level rays. Will you take the lines until I open this gate?"

She laid the twig in her lap on the white gloves and took the lines. As the gate swung wide, Betsy walked through and stopped at the usual place.

"Now my girl," said the Harvester, "cross yourself, lean back, and take your ease. This side that gate you are at home. From here on belongs to us."

"To you, you mean," said the Girl.

"To us, I mean," declared the Harvester. "Don't you know that the 'worldly goods bestowal' clause in a marriage ceremony is a partial reality. It doesn't give you 'all my worldly goods,' but it gives you one third. Which will you take, the hill, lake, marsh, or a part of all of them?"

"Oh, is there water?"

"Did I forget to mention that I was formerly sole owner and proprietor of the lake of Lost Loons, also a brook of Singing Water, and many cold springs. The lake covers about one third of our land, and my neighbours would allow me ditch outlet to the river, but they say I'm too lazy to take it."

"Lazy! Do they mean drain your lake into the river?"

"They do," said the Harvester, "and make the bed into a cornfield."

"But you wouldn't?"

She turned to him with confidence.

"I haven't so far, but of course, when you see it, if you would prefer it in a corn—Let's play a game! Turn your head in this direction," he indicated with the whip, "close your eyes, and open them when I say ready."

"All right!"

"Now!" said the Harvester.

"Oh," cried the Girl. "Stop! Please stop!"

They were at the foot of a small levee that ran to the bridge crossing Singing Water. On the left lay the valley through which the stream swept from its hurried rush down the hill, a marshy thicket of vines, shrubs, and bushes, the banks impassable with water growth. Everywhere flamed foxfire and cardinal flower, thousands of wild tiger lilies lifted gorgeous orange-red trumpets, beside pearl-white turtle head and moon daisies, while all the creek bank was a coral line with the first opening bloom of big pink mallows. Rank jewel flower poured gold from dainty cornucopias and lavender beard-tongue offered honey to a million bumbling bees; water smart-weed spread a glowing pink background, and twining amber dodder topped the marsh in lacy mist with its delicate white bloom. Straight before them a white-sanded road climbed to the bridge and up a gentle hill between the young hedge of small trees and bushes, where again flowers and bright colours rioted and led to the cabin yet invisible. On the right, the hill, crowned with gigantic forest trees, sloped to the lake; midway the building stood, and from it, among scattering trees all the way to the water's edge, were immense beds of vivid colour. Like a scarf of gold flung across the face of earth waved the misty saffron, and beside the road running down the hill, in a sunny, open space arose tree-like specimens of thrifty magenta pokeberry. Down the hill crept the masses of colour, changing from dry soil to water growth.

High around the blue-green surface of the lake waved lacy heads of wild rice, lower cat-tails, bulrushes, and marsh grasses; arrowhead lilies lifted spines of pearly bloom, while yellow water lilies and blue water hyacinths intermingled; here and there grew a pink stretch of water smartweed and the dangling gold of jewel flower. Over the water, bordering the edge, starry faces of white pond lilies floated. Blue flags waved graceful leaves, willows grew in clumps, and vines clambered everywhere.

Among the growth of the lake shore, duck, coot, and grebe voices commingled in the last chattering hastened splash of securing supper before bedtime; crying killdeers crossed the water, and overhead the nighthawks massed in circling companies. Betsy climbed the hill and at every step the Girl cried, "Slower! please go slower!" With wide eyes she stared around her.

"WHY DIDN'T YOU TELL ME IT WOULD BE LIKE THIS?" she demanded in awed tones.

"Have I had opportunity to describe much of anything?" asked the Harvester. "Besides, I was born and reared here, and while it has been a garden of bloom for the past six years only, it always has been a picture; but one forgets to say much about a sight seen every day and that requires the work this does."

"That white mist down there, what is it?" she marvelled.

"Pearls grown by the Almighty," answered the Harvester. "Flowers that I hope you will love. They are like you. Tall and slender, graceful, pearl white and pearl pure—those are the arrowhead Lilies."

"And the wonderful purplish-red there on the bank? Oh, I could kneel and pray before colour like that!'

"Pokeberry!" said the Harvester. "Roots bring five cents a pound. Good blood purifier."

"Man!" cried the Girl. "How can you? I'm not going to ask what another colour is. I'll just worship what I like in silence."

"Will you forgive me if I tell you what a woman whose judgment I respect says about that colour?"

"Perhaps!"

"She says, 'God proves that He loves it best of all the tints in His workshop by using it first and most sparingly.' Now are you going to punish me by keeping silent?"

"I couldn't if I tried." Just then they came upon the bridge crossing Singing Water, and there was a long view of its border, rippling bed, and marshy banks; while on the other hand the lake resembled a richly incrusted sapphire.

"Is the house close?"

"Just a few rods, at the turn of the drive."

"Please help me down. I want to remain here a while. I don't care what else there is to see. Nothing can equal this. I wish I could bring down a bed and sleep here. I'd like to have a table, and draw and paint. I understand now what you mean about the designs you mentioned. Why, there must be thousands! I can't go on. I never saw anything so appealing in all my life."

Now the Harvester's mother had designed that bridge and he had built it with much care. From bark-covered railings to solid oak floor and comfortable benches running along the sides it was intended to be a part of the landscape.

"I'll send Belshazzar to the cabin with the wagon," he said, "so you can see better."

"But you must not!" she cried. "I can't walk. I wouldn't soil these beautiful shoes for anything."

"Why don't you change them?" inquired the Harvester.

"I am afraid I forgot everything I had," said the Girl.

"There are shoes somewhere in this load. I thought of them in getting other things for you, but I had no idea as to size, and so I told that clerk to-day when she got your measure to put in every kind you'd need."

"You are horribly extravagant," she said. "But if you have them here, perhaps I could use one pair."

The Harvester mounted the wagon and hunted until he found a large box, and opening it on the bench he disclosed almost every variety of shoe, walking shoe and slipper, a girl ever owned, as well as sandals and high overshoes.

"For pity sake!" cried the Girl. "Cover that box! You frighten me. You'll never get them paid for. You must take them straight back."

"Never take anything back," said the Harvester. "'Be sure you are right, then go ahead,' is my motto. Now I know these are your correct size and that for differing occasions you will want just such shoes as other girls have, and here they are. Simple as life! I think these will serve because they are for street wear, yet they are white inside."

He produced a pair of canvas walking shoes and kneeling before her held out his hand.

When he had finished, he loaded the box on the wagon, gave the hitching strap to Belshazzar, and told him to lead Betsy to the cabin and hold her until he came. Then he turned to the Girl.

"Now," he said, "look as long as you choose. But remember that the law gives you part of this and your lover, which same am I, gives you the remainder, so you are privileged to come here at any hour as often as you please. If you miss anything this evening, you have all time to come in which to re-examine it."

"I'd like to live right here on this bridge," she said. "I wish it had a roof."

"Roof it to-morrow," offered the Harvester. "Simple matter of a few pillars already cut, joists joined, and some slab shingles left from the cabin. Anything else your ladyship can suggest?"

"That you be sensible."

"I was born that way," explained the Harvester, "and I've cultivated the faculty until I've developed real genius. Talking of sense, there never was a proper marriage in which the man didn't give the woman a present. You seem likely to be more appreciative of this bridge than anything else I have, so right here and now would be the appropriate place to offer you my wedding gift. I didn't have much time, but I couldn't have found anything more suitable if I'd taken a year."

He held out a small, white velvet case.

"Doesn't that look as if it were made for a bride?" he asked.

"It does," answered the Girl. "But I can't take it. You are not doing right. Marrying as we did, you never can believe that I love you; maybe it won't ever happen that I do. I have no right to accept gifts and expensive clothing from you. In the first place, if the love you ask never comes, there is no possible way in which

I can repay you. In the second, these things you are offering are not suitable for life and work in the woods. In the third, I think you are being extravagant, and I couldn't forgive myself if I allowed that."

"You divide your statements like a preacher, don't you?" asked the Harvester ingenuously. "Now sit thee here and gaze on the placid lake and quiet your troubled spirit, while I demolish your 'perfectly good' arguments. In the first place, you are now my wife, and you have a right to take anything I offer, if you care for it or can use it in any manner. In the second, you must recognize a difference in our positions. What seems nothing to you means all the world to me, and you are less than human if you deprive me of the joy of expressing feelings I am in honour bound to keep in my heart, by these little material offerings. In the third place, I inherited over six hundred acres of land and water, please observe the water—it is now in evidence on your left. All my life I have been taught to be frugal, economical, and to work. All I've earned either has gone back into land, into the bank, or into books, very plain food, and such clothing as you now see me wearing. Just the value of this place as it stands, with its big trees, its drug crops yielding all the year round, would be difficult to estimate; and I don't mind telling you that on the top of that hill there is a gold mine, and it's mine—ours since four o'clock."

"A gold mine!"

"Acres and acres of wild ginseng, seven years of age and ready to harvest. Do you remember what your few pounds brought?"

"Why it's worth thousands!"

"Exactly! For your peace of mind I might add that all I have done or got is paid for, except what I bought to-day, and I will write a check for that as soon as the bill is made out. My bank account never will feel it Truly, Ruth, I am not doing or going to do anything extravagant. I can't afford to give you diamond necklaces, yachts, and trips to Europe; but you can have the contents of this box and a motor boat on the lake, a horse and carriage, and a trip—say to New York perfectly well. Please take it."

"I wish you wouldn't ask me. I would be happier not to."

"Yes, but I do ask you," persisted the Harvester. "You are not the only one to be considered. I have some rights also, and I'm not so self-effacing that I won't insist upon them. From your standpoint I am almost a stranger. You have spent no time considering me in near relations; I realize that. You feel as if you were driven here for a refuge, and that is true. I said to Belshazzar one day that I must remember that you had no dream, and had spent no time loving me, and I do I know how this wedding seems to you, but it's going to mean something different and better soon, please God. I can see your side; now suppose you take a look at mine.

I did have a dream, it was my dream, and beyond the sum of any delight I ever conceived. On the strength of it I rebuilt my home and remodelled these premises. Then I saw you, and from that day I worked early and late. I lost you and I never stopped until I found you; and I would have courted and won you, but the fates intervened and here you are! So it's my delight to court and win you now. If you knew the difference between having a dream that stirred the least fibre of your being and facing the world in a demand for realization of it, and then finding what you coveted in the palm of your hand, as it were, you would know what is in my heart, and why expression of some kind is necessary to me just now, and why I'll explode if it is denied. It will lower the tension, if you will accept this as a matter of fact; as if you rather expected and liked it, if you can."

The Harvester set his finger on the spring.

"Don't!" she said. "I'll never have the courage if you do. Give it to me in the case, and let me open it. Despite your unanswerable arguments, I am quite sure that is the only way in which I can take it."

The Harvester gave her the box.

"My wedding gift!" she exclaimed, more to herself than to him. "Why should I be the buffet of all the unkind fates kept in store for a girl my whole life, and then suddenly be offered home, beautiful gifts, and wonderful loving kindness by a stranger?"

The Harvester ran his fingers through his crisp hair, pulled it into a peak, stepped to the seat and sitting on the railing, he lifted his elbows, tilted his head, and began a motley outpouring of half-spoken, half-whistled trills and imploring cries. There was enough similarity that the Girl instantly recognized the red bird. Out of breath the Harvester dropped to the seat beside her.

"And don't you keep forgetting it!" he cried. "Now open that box and put on the trinket; because I want to take you to the cabin when the sun falls level on the drive."

She opened the case, exposing a thread of gold that appeared too slender for the weight of an exquisite pendant, set with shimmering pearls.

"If you will look down there," the Harvester pointed over the railing to the arrowhead lilies touched with the fading light, "you will see that they are similar."

"They are!" cried the Girl. "How lovely! Which is more beautiful I do not know. And you won't like it if I say I must not."

She held the open case toward the Harvester.

"'Possession is nine points in the law,'" he quoted. "You have taken it already and it is in your hands; now make the gift perfect for me by putting it on and saying nothing more."

"My wedding gift!" repeated the Girl. Slowly she lifted the beautiful ornament and held it in the light. "I'm so glad you just force me to take it," she said. "Any half-normal girl would be delighted. I do accept it. And what's more, I am going to keep and wear it and my ring at suitable times all my life, in memory of what you have done to be kind to me on this awful day."

"Thank you!" said the Harvester. "That is a flash of the proper spirit. Allow me to put it on you."

"No!" said the Girl. "Not yet! After a while! I want to hold it in my hands, where I can see it!"

"Now there is one other thing," said the Harvester.

"If I had known for any length of time that this day was coming and bringing you, as most men know when a girl is to be given into their care, I could have made it different. As it is, I've done the best I knew. All your after life I hope you will believe this: Just that if you missed anything to-day that would have made it easier for you or more pleasant, the reason was because of my ignorance of women and the conventions, and lack of time. I want you to know and to feel that in my heart those vows I took were real. This is undoubtedly all the marrying I will ever want to do. I am old-fashioned in my ways, and deeply imbued with the spirit of the woods, and that means unending evolution along the same lines.

"To me you are my revered and beloved wife, my mate now; and I am sure nothing will make me feel any different. This is the day of my marriage to the only woman I ever have thought of wedding, and to me it is joy unspeakable. With other men such a day ends differently from the close of this with me. Because I have done and will continue to do the level best I know for you, this oration is the prologue to asking you for one gift to me from you, a wedding gift. I don't want it unless you can bestow it ungrudgingly, and truly want me to have it. If you can, I will have all from this day I hope for at the hands of fate. May I have the gift I ask of you, Ruth?"

She lifted startled eyes to his face.

"Tell me what it is?" she breathed.

"It may seem much to you," said the Harvester; "to me it appears only a gracious act, from a wonderful woman, if you will give me freely, one real kiss. I've never had one, save from a Dream Girl, Ruth, and you will have to make yours pretty good if it is anything like hers. You are woman enough to know that most men crush their brides in their arms and take a thousand. I'll put my hands behind me and never move a muscle, and I won't ask for more, if you will crown my wedding day with only one touch of your lips. Will you kiss me just once, Ruth?"

The Girl lifted a piteous face down which big tears suddenly rolled.

"Oh Man, you shame me!" she cried. "What kind of a heart have I that it fails to respond to such a plea? Have I been overworked and starved so long there is no feeling in me? I don't understand why I don't take you in my arms and kiss you a hundred times, but you see I don't. It doesn't seem as if I ever could."

"Never mind," said the Harvester gently. "It was only a fancy of mine, bred from my dream and unreasonable, perhaps. I am sorry I mentioned it. The sun is on the stoop now; I want you to enter your home in its light. Come!"

He half lifted her from the bench. "I am going to help you up the drive as I used to assist mother," he said, fighting to keep his voice natural. "Clasp your hands before you and draw your elbows to your sides. Now let me take one in each palm, and you will scoot up this drive as if you were on wheels."

"But I don't want to 'scoot'," she said unsteadily. "I must go slowly and not miss anything."

"On the contrary, you don't want to do any such thing—you should leave most of it for to-morrow."

"I had forgotten there would be any to-morrow. It seems as if the day would end it and set me adrift again."

"You are going to awake in the gold room with the sun shining on your face in the morning, and it's going to keep on all your life. Now if you've got a smile in your anatomy, bring it to the surface, for just beyond this tree lies happiness for you."

His voice was clear and steady now, his confidence something contagious. There was a lovely smile on her face as she looked at him, and stepped into the line of light crossing the driveway; and then she stopped and cried, "Oh lovely! Lovely! Lovely!" over and over. Then maybe the Harvester was not glad he had planned, worked unceasingly, and builded as well as he knew.

The cabin of large, peeled, golden oak logs, oiled to preserve them, nestled like a big mushroom on the side of the hill. Above and behind the building the trees arose in a green setting. The roof was stained to their shades. The wide veranda was enclosed in screening, over which wonderful vines climbed in places, and round it grew ferns and deep-wood plants. Inside hung big baskets of wild growth; there was a wide swinging seat, with a back rest, supported by heavy chains. There were chairs and a table of bent saplings and hickory withes. Two full stories the building arose, and the western sun warmed it almost to orange-yellow, while the graceful vines crept toward the roof.

The Girl looked at the rapidly rising hedge on each side of her, at the white floor of the drive, and long and long at the cabin.

"You did all this since February?" she asked.

"Even to transforming the landscape," answered the Harvester.

"Oh I wish it was not coming night!" she cried. "I don't want the dark to come, until you have told me the name of every tree and shrub of that wonderful hedge, and every plant and vine of the veranda; and oh I want to follow up the driveway and see that beautiful little creek—listen to it chuckle and laugh! Is it always glad like that? See the ferns and things that grow on the other side of it! Why there are big beds of them. And lilies of the valley by the acre! What is that yellow around the corner?"

"Never mind that now," said the Harvester, guiding her up the steps, along the gravelled walk to the screen that he opened, and over a flood of gold light she crossed the veranda, and entered the door.

"Now here it appears bare," said the Harvester, "because I didn't know what should go on the walls or what rugs to get or about the windows. The table, chairs, and couch I made myself with some help from a carpenter. They are solid black walnut and will age finely."

"They are beautiful," said the Girl, softly touching the shining table top with her fingers. "Please put the necklace on me now, I have to use my eyes and hands for other things."

She held out the box and the Harvester lifted the pendant and clasped the chain around her neck. She glanced at the lustrous pearls and then the fingers of one hand softly closed over them. She went through the long, wide living-room, examining the chairs and mantel, stopping to touch and exclaim over its array of half-finished candlesticks. At the door of his room she paused. "And this?" she questioned.

"Mine," said the Harvester, turning the knob. "I'll give you one peep to satisfy your curiosity, and show you the location of the bridge over which you came to me in my dream. All the remainder is yours. I reserve only this."

"Will the 'goblins git me' if I come here?"

"Not goblins, but a man alive; so heed your warning. After you have seen it, keep away."

The floor was cement, three of the walls heavy screening with mosquito wire inside, the roof slab shingled. On the inner wall was a bookcase, below it a desk, at one side a gun cabinet, at the other a bath in a small alcove beside a closet. The room contained two chairs like those of the veranda, and the bed was a low oak couch covered with a thick mattress of hemlock twigs, topped with sweet fern, on which the sun shone all day. On a chair at the foot were spread some white sheets, a blanket, and an oilcloth. The sun beat in, the wind drifted through, and one lying on the couch could see down the bright hill, and sweep the lake to the opposite bank without lifting the head. The Harvester drew the Girl to the bedside.

"Now straight in a line from here," he said, "across the lake to that big, scraggy oak, every clear night the moon builds a bridge of molten gold, and once you walked it, my girl, and came straight to me, alone and unafraid; and you were gracious and lovely beyond anything a man ever dreamed of before. I'll have that to think of to-night. Now come see the dining-room, kitchen, and hand-made sunshine."

He led her into what had been the front room of the old cabin, now a large, long dining-room having on each side wide windows with deep seats. The fire-place backwall was against that of the living-room, but here the mantel was bare. All the wood-work, chairs, the dining table, cupboards, and carving table were golden oak. Only a few rugs and furnishings and a woman's touch were required to make it an unusual and beautiful room. The kitchen was shining with a white hard-wood floor, white wood-work, and pale green walls. It was a light, airy, sanitary place, supplied with a pump, sink, hot and cold water faucets, refrigerator, and every modern convenience possible to the country.

Then the Harvester almost carried the Girl up the stairs and showed her three large sleeping rooms, empty and bare save for some packing cases.

"I didn't know about these, so I didn't do anything. When you find time to plan, tell me what you want, and I'll make—or buy it. They are good-sized, cool rooms. They all have closets and pipes from the furnace, so they will be comfort-able in winter. Now there is your place remaining. I'll leave you while I stable Betsy and feed the stock."

He guided her to the door opening from the living-room to the east.

"This is the sunshine spot," he said. "It is bathed in morning light, and sheltered by afternoon shade. Singing Water is across the drive there to talk to you always. It comes pelting down so fast it never freezes, so it makes music all winter, and the birds are so numerous you'll have to go to bed early for they'll wake you by dawn. I noticed this room was going to be full of sunshine when I built it, and I craved only brightness for you, so I coaxed all of it to stay that I could. Every stroke is the work of my hands, and all of the furniture. I hope you will like it. This is the room of which I've been telling you, Ruth. Go in and take possession, and I'll entreat God and all His ministering angels to send you sunshine and joy."

He opened the door, guided her inside, closed it, and went swiftly to his work.

The Girl stood and looked around her with amazed eyes. The floor was pale yellow wood, polished until it shone like a table top. The casings, table, chairs, dressing table, chest of drawers, and bed were solid curly maple. The doors were big polished slabs of it, each containing enough material to veneer all the furniture in the room. The walls were of plaster, tinted yellow, and the windows with yellow shades were curtained in dainty white. She could hear the Harvester carrying the load from the wagon to the front porch, the clamour of the barn yard; and as she went to the north window to see the view, a shining peacock strutted down the walk and went to the Harvester's hand for grain, while scores of snow-white doves circled over his head. She stepped on deep rugs of yellow goat skins, and, glancing at the windows on either side, she opened the door.

Outside it lay a porch with a railing, but no roof. On each post stood a box filled with yellow wood-flowers and trailing vines of pale green. A big tree rising through one corner of the floor supplied the cover. A gate opened to a walk leading to the driveway, and on either side lay a patch of sod, outlined by a deep hedge of bright gold. In it saffron, cone-flowers, black-eyed Susans, golden-rod, wild sunflowers, and jewel flower grew, and some of it, enough to form a yellow line, was already in bloom. Around the porch and down the walk were beds of yellow violets, pixie moss, and every tiny gold flower of the woods. The Girl leaned against the tree and looked around her and then staggered inside and dropped on the couch.

"What planning! What work!" she sobbed. "What taste! Why he's a poet! What wonderful beauty! He's an artist with earth for his canvas, and growing things for colours."

She lay there staring at the walls, the beautiful wood-work and furniture, the dressing table with its array of toilet articles, a low chair before it, and the thick rug for her feet. Over and over she looked at everything, and then closed her eyes and lay quietly, too weary and overwhelmed to think. By and by came tapping at the door, and she sprang up and crossing to the dressing table straightened her hair and composed her face.

"Ajax demands to see you," cried a gay voice.

The Girl stepped outside.

"Don't be frightened if he screams at you," warned the Harvester as she passed him. "He detests a stranger, and he always cries and sulks."

It was a question what was in the head of the bird as he saw the strange looking creature invading his domain, and he did scream, a wild, high, strident wail that delighted the Harvester inexpressibly, because it sent the Girl headlong into his arms.

"Oh, good gracious!" she cried. "Has such a beautiful bird got a noise in it like that? Why I've fed them in parks and I never heard one explode before."

Then how the Harvester laughed.

"But you see you are in the woods now, and this is not a park bird. It will be the test of your power to see how soon you can coax him to your hand."

"How do I work to win him?"

"I am afraid I can't tell you that," said the Harvester. "I had to invent a plan for myself. It required a long time and much petting, and my methods might not avail for you. It will interest you to study that out. But the member of the family it is positively essential that you win to a life and death allegiance is Belshazzar. If you can make him love you, he will protect you at every turn. He will go before you into the forest and all the crawling, creeping things will get out of his way. He will nose around the flowers you want to gather, and if he growls and the hair on the back of his neck rises, never forget that you must heed that warning. A few times I have not stopped for it, and I always have been sorry. So far as anything animate or uncertain footing is concerned, you are always perfectly safe if you obey him. About touching plants and flowers, you must confine yourself to those you are certain you know, until I can teach you. There are gorgeous and wonderfully attractive things here, but some of them are rank poison. You won't handle plants you don't know, until you learn, Ruth?"

"I will not," she promised instantly.

She went to the seat under the porch tree and leaning against the trunk she studied the hill, and the rippling course of Singing Water where it turned and curved before the cabin, and started across the vivid little marsh toward the lake. Then she looked at the Harvester. He seated himself on the low railing and smiled at her.

"You are very tired?" he asked.

"No," she said. "You are right about the air being better up here. It is stimulating instead of depressing."

"So far as pure air, location, and water are concerned," said the Harvester, "I consider this place ideal. The lake is large enough to cool the air and raise sufficient moisture to dampen it, and too small to make it really cold and disagreeable. The slope of the hill gives perfect drainage. The heaviest rains do not wet the earth for more than three hours. North, south, and west breezes sweep the cool air from the water to the cabin in summer. The same suns warm us here on the winter hillside. My violets, spring beauties, anemones, and dutchman's breeches here are always two weeks ahead of those in the woods. I am not afraid of your not liking the location or the air. As for the cabin, if you don't care for that, it's very simple. I'll transform it into a laboratory and dry-house, and build you whatever you want, within my means, over there on the hill just across Singing Water and facing the valley toward Onabasha. That's a perfect location. The thing that worries me is what you are going to do for company, especially while I am away."

"Don't trouble yourself about anything," she said. "Just say in your heart, 'she is going to be stronger than she ever has been in her life in this lovely place, and she has more right now than she ever had or hoped to have.' For one thing, I am going to study your books. I never have had time before. While we sewed or embroidered, mother talked by the hour of the great writers of the world, told me what they wrote, and how they expressed themselves, but I got to read very little for myself."

"Books are my company," said the Harvester.

"Do your friends come often?"

"Almost never! Doc and his wife come most, and if you look out some day and see a white-haired, bent old woman, with a face as sweet as dawn, coming up the bank of Singing Water, that will be my mother's friend, Granny Moreland, who joins us on the north over there. She is frank and brusque, so she says what she thinks with unmistakable distinctness, but her heart is big and tender and her philosophy keeps her sweet and kindly despite the ache of rheumatism and the weight of seventy years."

"I'd love to have her come," said the Girl. "Is that all?"

"Yes."

"Why?"

"Your favourite word," laughed the Harvester. "The reason lies with me, or rather with my mother. Some day I will tell you the whole story, and the cause. I think now I can encompass it in this. The place is an experiment. When medicinal herbs, roots, and barks became so scarce that some of the most important were almost extinct, it occurred to me that it would be a good idea to stop travelling miles and poaching on the woods of other people, and turn our land into an herb garden. For four years before mother went, and six since, I've worked with all my might, and results are beginning to take shape. While I've been at it, of course, my neighbours had an inkling of what was going on, and I've been called a fool, lazy, and a fanatic, because I did not fell the trees and plow for corn. You readily can see I'm a little short of corn ground out there," he waved toward the marsh and lake, "and up there," he indicated the steep hill and wood. "But somewhere on this land I've been able to find muck for mallows, water for flags and willows, shade for ferns, lilies, and ginseng, rocky, sunny spaces for mullein, and open, fertile beds for Bouncing Bet—just for examples. God never evolved a place better suited for an herb farm; from woods to water and all that goes between, it is perfect."

"And indescribably lovely," added the Girl.

"Yes, I think it is," said the Harvester. "But in the days when I didn't know how it was coming out, I was sensitive about it; so I kept quiet and worked, and allowed the other fellow to do the talking. After a while the ginseng bed grew a treasure worth guarding, and I didn't care for any one to know how much I had or where it was, as a matter of precaution. Ginseng and money are synonymous, and I was forced to be away some of the time."

"Would any one take it?"

"Certainly!" said the Harvester. "If they knew it was there, and what it is worth. Then, as I've told you, much of the stuff here must not be handled except by experts, and I didn't want people coming in my absence and taking risks. The remainder of my reason for living so alone is cowardice, pure and simple."

"Cowardice? You! Oh no!"

"Thank you!" said the Harvester. "But it is! Some day I'll tell you of a very solemn oath I've had to keep. It hasn't been easy. You wouldn't understand, at least not now. If the day ever comes when I think you will, I'll tell you. Just now I can express it by that one word. I didn't dare fail or I felt I would be lost as my father was before me. So I remained away from the city and its temptations and men of my age, and worked in the woods until I was tired enough to drop, read books that helped, tinkered with the carving, and sometimes I had an idea, and I went into that little building behind the dry-house, took out my different herbs, and tried my hand at compounding a new cure for some of the pains of humanity. It isn't bad work, Ruth. It keeps a fellow at a fairly decent level, and some good may come of it. Carey is trying several formulae for me, and if they work I'll carry them higher. If you want money, Girl, I know how to get it for you."

"Don't you want it?"

"Not one cent more than I've got," said the Harvester emphatically. "When any man accumulates more than he can earn with his own hands, he begins to enrich himself at the expense of the youth, the sweat, the blood, the joy of his fellow men. I can go to the city, take a look, and see what money does, as a rule, and it's another thing I'm afraid of. You will find me a dreadful coward on those two points. I don't want to know society and its ways. I see what it does to other men; it would be presumption to reckon myself stronger. So I live alone. As for money, I've watched the cross cuts and the quick and easy ways to accumulate it; but I've had something in me that held me to the slow, sure, clean work of my own hands, and it's yielded me enough for one, for two even, in a reasonable degree. So I've worked, read, compounded, and carved. If I couldn't wear myself down enough to sleep by any other method, I went into the lake, and swam across and back; and that is guaranteed to put any man to rest, clean and unashamed."

"Six years," said the Girl softly, as she studied him. "I think it has set a mark on you. I believe I can trace it. Your forehead, brow, and eyes bear the lines and the appearance of all experience, all comprehension, but your lips are those of a very young lad. I shouldn't be surprised if I had that kiss ready for you, and I really believe I can make it worth while."

"Oh good Lord!" cried the Harvester, turning a backward somersault over the railing and starting in big bounds up the drive toward the stable. He passed around it and into the woods at a rush and a few seconds later from somewhere on the top of the hill his strong, deep voice swept down, "Glory, glory hallelujah!"

He sang it through at the top of his lungs, that majestic old hymn, but there was no music at all, it was simply a roar. By and by he came soberly to the barn and paused to stroke Betsy's nose.

"Stop chewing grass and listen to me," he said. "She's here, Betsy! She's in our cabin. She's going to remain, you can stake your oats on that. She's going to be the loveliest and sweetest girl in all the world, and because you're a beast, I'll tell you something a man never could know. Down with your ear, you critter! She's going to kiss me, Betsy! This very night, before I lay me, her lips meet mine, and maybe you think that won't be glorious. I supposed it would be a year, anyway, but it's now! Ain't you glad you are an animal, Betsy, and can keep secrets for a fool man that can't?"

He walked down the driveway, and before the Girl had a chance to speak, he said, "I wonder if I had not better carry those things into your room, and arrange your bed for you."

"I can," she said.

"Oh no!" exclaimed the Harvester. "You can't lift the mattress and heavy covers. Hold the door and tell me how."

He laid a big bundle on the floor, opened it, and took out the shoes.

"Your shoe box is in the closet there."

"I didn't know what that door was, so I didn't open it."

"That is a part of my arrangements for you," said the Harvester. "Here is a closet with shelves for your covers and other things. They are bare because I didn't know just what should be put on them. This is the shoe box here in the corner; I'll put these in it now."

He knelt and in a row set the shoes in the curly maple box and closed it.

"There you are for all kinds of places and varieties of weather. This adjoining is your bathroom. I put in towels, soaps; brushes, and everything I could think of, and there is hot water ready for you—rain water, too."

The Girl followed and looked into a shining little bathroom, with its white porcelain tub and wash bowl, enamelled wood-work, dainty green walls, and white curtains and towels. She could see no accessory she knew of that was missing, and there were many things to which she never had been accustomed. The Harvester had gone back to the sunshine room, and was kneeling on the floor beside the bundle. He began opening boxes and handing her dresses.

"There are skirt, coat, and waist hangers on the hooks," he said. "I only got a few things to start on, because I didn't know what you would like. Instead of being so careful with that dress, why don't you take it off, and put on a common one? Then we will have something to eat, and go to the top of the hill and watch the moon bridge the lake."

While she hung the dresses and selected the one to wear, he placed the mattress, spread the padding and sheets, and encased the pillow. Then he bent and pressed the springs with his hands.

"I think you will find that soft and easy enough for health," he said. "All the personal belongings I had that clerk put up for you are in that chest of drawers there. I put the little boxes in the top and went down. You can empty and arrange them to-morrow. Just hunt out what you will need now. There should be every-thing a girl uses there somewhere. I told them to be very careful about that. If the things are not right or not to your taste, you can take them back as soon as you are rested, and they will exchange them for you. If there is anything I have missed that you can think of that you need to-night, tell me and I'll go and get it."

The Girl turned toward him.

"You couldn't be making sport of me," she said, "but Man! Can't you see that I don't know what to do with half you have here? I never saw such things closely before. I don't know what they are for. I don't know how to use them. My mother would have known, but I do not. You overwhelm me! Fifty times I've tried to tell you that a room of my very own, such a room as this will be when to-morrow's sun comes in, and these, and these, and these," she turned from the chest of boxes to the dressing table, bed, closet, and bath, "all these for me, and you know absolutely noth-ing about me—I get a big lump in my throat, and the words that do come all seem so meaningless, I am perfectly ashamed to say them. Oh Man, why do you do it?"

"I thought it was about time to spring another 'why' on me," said the Harvester. "Thank God, I am now in a position where I can tell you 'why'! I do it because you are the girl of my dream, my mate by every law of Heaven and earth. All men build as well as they know when the one woman of the universe lays her spell on them. I did all this for myself just as a kind of expression of what it would be in my heart to do if I could do what I'd like. Put on the easiest dress you can find and I will go and set out something to eat."

She stood with arms high piled with the prettiest dresses that could be selected hurriedly, the tears running down her white cheeks and smiled through them at him.

"There wouldn't be any of that liquid amber would there?" she asked.

"Quarts!" cried the Harvester. "I'll bring some. ... Does it really hit the spot, Ruth?" he questioned as he handed her the glass.

She heaped the dresses on the bed and took it.

"It really does. I am afraid I am using too much."

"I don't think it possibly can hurt you. To-morrow we will ask Doc. How soon will you be ready for lunch?"

"I don't want a bite."

"You will when you see and smell it," said the Harvester. "I am an expert cook. It's my chiefest accomplishment. You should taste the dishes I improvise. But there won't be much to-night, because I want you to see the moon rise over the lake."

He went away and the Girl removed her dress and spread it on the couch. Then she bathed her face and hands. When she saw the discoloured cloth, it proved that she had been painted, and made her very indignant. Yet she could not be altogether angry, for that flush of colour had saved the Harvester from being pitied by his friend. She stood a long time before the mirror, staring at her gaunt, colourless face; then she went to the dressing table and committed a crime. She found a box of cream and rubbed it on for a foundation. Then she opened some pink powder, and carefully dusted her cheeks.

"I am utterly ashamed," she said to the image in the mirror, "but he has done so much for me, he is so, so—I don't know a word big enough—that I can't bear him to see how ghastly I am, how little worth it. Perhaps the food, better air, and outdoor exercise will give me strength and colour soon. Until it does I'm afraid I'm going to help out all I can with this. It is wonderful how it changes one. I really appear like a girl instead of a bony old woman."

Then she looked over the dresses, selected a pretty white princesse, slipped it on, and went to the kitchen. But the Harvester would not have her there. He seated her at the dining table, beside the window overlooking the lake, lighted a pair of his home-made candles in his finest sticks, and placed before her bread, butter, cold meat, milk, and fruit, and together they ate their first meal in their home.

"If I had known," said the Harvester, "Granny Moreland is a famous cook. She is a Southern woman, and she can fry chicken and make some especial dishes to surpass any one I ever knew. She would have been so pleased to come over and get us an all-right supper."

"I'd much rather have this, and be by ourselves," said the Girl.

"Well, you can bank on it, I would," agreed the Harvester. "For instance, if any one were here, I might feel restrained about telling you that you are exactly the beautiful, flushed Dream Girl I have adored for months, and your dress most becoming. You are a picture to blind the eyes of a lonely bachelor, Ruth."

"Oh why did you say that?" wailed the Girl. "Now I've got to feel like a sneak or tell you—and I didn't want you to know."

"Don't you ever tell me or any one else anything you don't want to," said the Harvester roundly. "It's nobody's business!"

"But I must! I can't begin with deception. I was fool enough to think you wouldn't notice. Man, they painted me! I didn't know they were doing it, but when it all washed off, I looked so ghastly I almost frightened myself. I hunted through the boxes they put up for you and found some pink powder—"

"But don't all the daintiest women powder these days, and consider it indispensable? The clerk said so, and I've noticed it mentioned in the papers. I bought it for you to use."

"Yes, just powder, but Man, I put on a lot of cold cream first to stick the powder good and thick. Oh I wish I hadn't!"

"Well since you've told it, is your conscience perfectly at ease? No you don't! You sit where you are! You are lovely, and if you don't use enough powder to cover the paleness, until your colour returns, I'll hold you and put it on. I know you feel better when you appear so that every one must admire you."

"Yes, but I'm a fraud!"

"You are no such thing!" cried the Harvester hotly. "There hasn't a woman in ten thousand got any such rope of hair. I have been seeing the papers on the hair question, too. No one will believe it's real. If they think your hair is false, when it is natural, they won't be any more fooled when they think your colour is real, and it isn't. Very soon it will be and no one need ever know the difference. You go on and fix up your level best. To see yourself appearing well will make you ambitious to become so as soon as possible."

"Harvester-man," said the Girl, gazing at him with wet luminous eyes, "for the sake of other women, I could wish that all men had an oath to keep, and had been reared in the woods."

"Here is the place we adjourn to the moon," cried the Harvester. "I don't know of anything that can cure a sudden accession of swell head like gazing at the heavens. One finds his place among the atoms naturally and instantaneously with the eyes on the night sky. Should you have a wrap? You should! The mists from the lake are cool. I don't believe there is one among my orders. I forgot that. But upstairs with mother's clothing there are several shawls and shoulder capes. All of them were washed and carefully packed. Would you use one, Ruth?"

"Why not give it to me. Wouldn't she like me to wear her things better than to have them lying in moth balls?"

The Harvester looked at her and shook his head, marvelling.

"I can't tell how pleased she would be," he said.

"Where are her belongings?" asked the Girl. "I could use them to help furnish the house, and it wouldn't appear so strange to you."

The Harvester liked that.

"All the washed things are in those boxes upstairs; also some fine skins I've saved on the chance of wanting them. Her dishes are in the bottom of the china closet there; she was mighty proud of them. The furniture and carpets were so old and abused I burned them. I'll go bring a wrap."

He took the candle and climbed the stairs, soon returning with a little white wool shawl and a big pink coverlet.

"Got this for her Christmas one time," he said. "She'd never had a white one and she thought it was pretty."

He folded it around the Girl's shoulders and picked up the coverlet.

"You're never going to take that to the woods!" she cried.

"Why not?"

She took it in her hands to find a corner.

"Just as I thought! It's a genuine Peter Hartman! It's one of the things that money can't buy, or, rather, one that takes a mint of money to own. They are heirlooms. They are not manufactured any more. At the art store where I worked they'd give you fifty dollars for that. It is not faded or worn a particle. It would be lovely in my room; you mustn't take a treasure like that out of doors."

"Ruth, are you in earnest?" demanded the Harvester. "I believe there are six of them upstairs."

"Plutocrat!" cried the Girl. "What colours?"

"More of this pinkish red, blue, and pale green."

"Famous! May I have them to help furnish with to-morrow?"

"Certainly! Anything you can find, any way on earth you want it, only in my room. That is taboo, as I told you. What am I going to take to-night?"

"Isn't the rug you had in the woods in the wagon yet? Use that!"

"Of course! The very thing! Bel, proceed!"

"Are you going to leave the house like this?"

"Why not?"

"Suppose some one breaks in!"

"Nothing worth carrying away, except what you have on. No one to get in. There is a big swamp back of our woods, marsh in front, we're up here where we can see the drive and bridge. There is nothing possible from any direction. Never locked the cabin in my life, except your room, and that was because it was sacred, not that there was any danger. Clear the way, Bel!"

"Clear it of what?"

"Katydids, hoptoads, and other carnivorous animals."

"Now you are making fun of me! Clear it of what?"

"A coon that might go shuffling across, an opossum, or a snake going to the lake. Now are you frightened so that you will not go?"

"No. The path is broad and white and surely you and Bel can take care of me."

"If you will trust us we can."

"Well, I am trusting you."

"You are indeed," said the Harvester. "Now see if you think this is pretty."

He indicated the hill sloping toward the lake. The path wound among massive trees, between whose branches patches of moonlight filtered. Around the lake shore and climbing the hill were thickets of bushes. The water lay shining in the light, a gentle wind ruffled the surface in undulant waves, and on the opposite bank arose the line of big trees. Under a giant oak widely branching, on the top of the hill, the Harvester spread the rug and held one end of it against the tree trunk to protect the Girl's dress. Then he sat a little distance away and began to talk. He mingled some sense with a quantity of nonsense, and appreciated every hint of a laugh he heard. The day had been no amusing matter for a girl absolutely alone among strange people and scenes. Anything more foreign to her previous environment or expectations he could not imagine. So he talked to prevent her from thinking, and worked for a laugh as he laboured for bread.

"Now we must go," he said at last. "If there is the malaria I strongly suspect in your system, this night air is none too good for you. I only wanted you to see the lake the first night in your new home, and if it won't shock you, I brought you here because this is my holy of holies. Can you guess why I wanted you to come, Ruth?"

"If I wasn't so stupid with alternate burning and chills, and so deadened to every proper sensibility, I suppose I could," she answered, "but I'm not brilliant. I don't know, unless it is because you knew it would be the loveliest place I ever saw. Surely there is no other spot in the world quite so beautiful."

"Then would it seem strange to you," asked the Harvester going to the Girl and gently putting his arms around her, "would it seem strange to you, that a woman who once homed here and thought it the prettiest place on earth, chose to remain for her eternal sleep, rather than to rest in a distant city of stranger dead?"

He felt the Girl tremble against him.

"Where is she?"

"Very close," said the Harvester. "Under this oak. She used to say that she had a speaking acquaintance with every tree on our land, and of them all she loved this big one the best. She liked to come here in winter, and feel the sting of the wind sweeping across the lake, and in summer this was her place to read and to think. So when she slept the unwaking sleep, Ruth, I came here and made her bed with my own hands, and then carried her to it, covered her, and she sleeps well. I never have regretted her going. Life did not bring her joy. She was very tired. She used to say that after her soul had fled, if I would lay her here, perhaps the big roots would reach down and find her, and from her frail frame gather slight nourishment and then her body would live again in talking leaves that would shelter me in summer and whisper her love in winter. Of all Medicine Woods this is the dearest spot to me. Can you love it too, Ruth?"

"Oh I can!" cried the Girl; "I do now! Just to see the place and hear that is enough. I wish, oh to my soul I wish—"

"You wish what?" whispered the Harvester gently.

"I dare not! I was wild to think of it. I would be ungrateful to ask it."

"You would be ungracious if you didn't ask anything that would give me the joy of pleasing you. How long is it going to require for you to learn, Ruth, that to make up for some of the difficulties life has brought you would give me more happiness than anything else could? Tell me now."

"No!"

He gathered her closer.

"Ruth, there is no reason why you should be actively unkind to me. What is it you wish?"

She struggled from his arms and stood alone in white moonlight, staring across the lake, along the shore, deep into the perfumed forest, and then at the mound she now could distinguish under the giant tree. Suddenly she went to him and with both shaking hands gripped his arm.

"My mother!" she panted. "Oh she was a beautiful woman, delicately reared, and her heart was crushed and broken. By the inch she went to a dreadful end I could not avert or allay, and in poverty and grime I fought for a way to save her body from further horror, and it's all so dreadful I thought all feeling in me was dried and still, but I am not quite calloused yet. I suffer it over with every breath. It is never entirely out of my mind. Oh Man, if only you would lift her from the horrible place she lies, where briers run riot and cattle trample and the unmerciful sun beats! Oh if only you'd lift her from it, and bring her here! I believe it would take away some of the horror, the shame, and the heartache. I believe I could go to sleep without hearing the voice of her suffering, if I knew she was lying on this hill, under your beautiful tree, close the dear mother you love. Oh Man, would you—?"

The Harvester crushed the Girl in his arms and shuddering sobs shook his big frame, and choked his voice.

"Ruth, for God's sake, be quiet!" he cried. "Why I'd be glad to! I'll go anywhere you tell me, and bring her, and she shall rest where the lake murmurs, the trees shelter, the winds sing, and earth knows the sun only in long rays of gold light."

She stared at him with strained face.

"You—you wouldn't!" she breathed.

"Ruth, child," said the Harvester, "I tell you I'd be happy. Look at my side of this! I'm in search of bands to bind you to me and to this place. Could you tell me a stronger than to have the mother you idolized lie here for her long sleep? Why Girl, you can't know the deep and abiding joy it would give me to bring her. I'd feel I had you almost secure. Where is she, Ruth?"

"In that old unkept cemetery south of Onabasha, where it costs no money to lay away your loved ones."

"Close here! Why I'll go to-morrow! I supposed she was in the city."

She straightened and drew away from him.

"How could I? I had nothing. I could not have paid even her fare and brought her here in the cheapest box the decency of man would allow him to make if her doctor had not given me the money I owe. Now do you understand why I must earn and pay it myself? Save for him, it was charity or her delicate body to horrors. Money never can repay him."

"Ruth, the day you came to Onabasha was she with you?"

"In the express car," said the Girl.

"Where did you go when you left the train shed?"

"Straight to the baggage room, where Uncle Henry was waiting. Men brought and put her in his wagon, and he drove with me to the place and other men lowered her, and that was all."

"You poor Girl!" cried the Harvester. "This time to-morrow night she shall sleep in luxury under this oak, so help me God! Ruth, can you spare me? May I go at once? I can't rest, myself."

"You will?" cried the Girl. "You will?"

She was laughing in the moonlight. "Oh Man, I can't ever, ever tell you!"

"Don't try," said the Harvester. "Call it settled. I will start early in the morning. I know that little cemetery. The man whose land it is on can point me the spot. She is probably the last one laid there. Come now, Ruth. Go to the room I made for you, and sleep deeply and in peace. Will you try to rest?"

"Oh David!" she exulted. "Only think! Here where it's clean and cool; beside the lake, where leaves fall gently and I can come and sit close to her and bring flowers; and she never will be alone, for your dear mother is here. Oh David!"

"It is better. I can't thank you enough for thinking of it. Come now, let me help you."

He half carried her down the hill. Then he made the cabin a glamour of light by putting candles in the sticks he had carved and placing them everywhere.

"There is a lighting plant in the basement," he said, "but I had not expected to use it until winter, and I have no acetylene. Candles were our grandmothers' lights and they are the best anyway. Go bathe your face, Ruth, and wash away all trace of tears. Put on the pink powder, and in a few weeks you will have colour to outdo the wildest rose. You must be as gay as you can the remainder of this night."

"I will!" cried the Girl. "I will! Oh I didn't know a thing on earth could make me happy! I didn't know I really could be glad. Oh if the ice in my heart would melt, and the wall break down, and the girlhood I've never known would come yet! Oh David, if it would!"

"Before the Lord it shall!" vowed the Harvester. "It shall come with the fulness of joy right here in Medicine Woods. Think it! Believe it! Keep it before you! Work for it! Happiness is worth while! All of us have a right to it! It shall be yours and soon."

"I will try! I will!" promised the Girl. "I'll go right now and I'll put on the blessed pink powder so thickly you'll never know what is under it, and soon it won't be needed at all."

She was laughing as she left the room. The Harvester restlessly walked the floor a few minutes and then sat with a notebook and began entering stems.

When the Girl returned, he brought the pillow from her bed, folded the coverlet, and she lay on them in the big swing. He covered her with the white shawl, and while Singing Water sang its loudest, katydids exulted over the delightful act of their ancestor, and a million gauze-winged creatures of night hummed against the screen, in a voice soft and low he told her in a steady stream, as he swayed her back and forth, what each sound of the night was, and how and why it was made all the way from the rumbling buzz of the June bug to the screech of the owl and the splash of the bass in the lake. All of it, as it appealed to him, was the story of steady evolution, the natural processes of reproduction, the joy of life and its battles, and the conquest of the strong in nature. At his hands every sound was stripped of terror. The leaping bass was exulting in life, the screeching owl was telling its mate it had found a fat mouse for the children, the nighthawk was courting, the big bull frogs booming around the lake were serenading the moon. There was not a thing to fear or a voice left with an unsympathetic note in it. She was half asleep when at last he helped her to her room, set a pitcher of frosty, clinking drink on her table, locked her door and window screens inside, spread Belshazzar's blanket on her porch, and set his door wide open, that he might hear if she called, and then said good night and went back to his memorandum book.

"No bad beginning," he muttered softly, "no bad beginning, but I'd almost give my right hand if she hadn't forgotten—"

In her room the exhausted Girl slipped the pins from her hair and sank on the low chair before the dressing-table. She picked up the shining, silver backed brush and stared at the monogram, R. F. L., entwined on it.

"My soul!" she exclaimed. "WAS HE SO SURE AS THAT? Was there ever any other man like him?"

She dropped the brush and with tired hands pushed back the heavy braids. Then she arose and going to the chest of drawers began lifting lids to find a night robe. As she searched the boxes she found every dainty, pretty undergarment a girl ever used and at last the robes. She shook out a long white one, slipped into it, and walked to the bed. That stood as he had arranged it, white, clean, and dainty.

"Everything for me!" she said softly. "Everything for me! Shall there be nothing for him? Oh he makes it easy, easy!"

She stepped to the closet, picked down a lavender silk kimono and drawing it over her gown she gathered it around her and opening the bathroom door, she stepped into a little hall leading to the dining-room. As she entered the living-room the Harvester bent over his book. Her step was very close when he heard it and turned his head. In an instant she touched his shoulders. The Harvester dropped the pencil, and palm downward laid his hands on the table, his promise strong in his heart. The Girl slid a shaking palm under his chin, leaned his head against her breast, and dropped a sweet, tear-wet face on his. With all the strength of her frail arms she gripped him a second, and then gave the kiss, into which she tried to put all she could find no words to express.

Chapter 14

Snowy Wings

The Harvester sat at the table in deep thoughts until the lights in the Girl's room were darkened and everything was quiet. Then he locked the screens inside and went into the night. The moon flooded all the hillside, until coarse print could have been read with keen eyes in its light. A restlessness, born of exultation he could not allay or control, was on him. She had not forgotten! After this, the dream would be effaced by reality. It was the beginning. He scarcely had dared hope for so much. Surely it presaged the love with which she some day would come to him and crown his life. He walked softly up and down the drive, passing her windows, unable to think of sleep. Over and over he dwelt on the incidents of the day, so inevitably he came to his promise.

"Merciful Heaven!" he muttered. "How can such things happen? The poor, overworked, tired, suffering girl. It will give her some comfort. She will feel better. It has to be done. I believe I will do the worst part of it while she sleeps."

He went to the cabin, crept very close to one of her windows and listened intently. Surely no mortal awake could lie motionless so long. She must be sleeping. He patted Belshazzar, whispered, "Watch, boy, watch for your life!" and then crossed to the dry-house. Beside it he found a big roll of coffee sacks that he used in collecting roots, and going to the barn, he took a spade and mattock. Then he climbed the hill to the oak; in the white moonlight laid off his measurements and began work. His heart was very tender as he lifted the earth, and threw it into the tops of the big bags he had propped open.

"I'll line it with a couple of sheets and finish the edge with pond lilies and ferns," he planned, "and I'll drag this earth from sight, and cover it with brush until I need it."

Sometimes he paused in his work to rest a few minutes and then he stood and glanced around him. Several times he went down the hill and slipped close to a window, but he could not hear a sound. When his work was finished, he stood before the oak, scraping clinging earth from the mattock with which he had cut roots he had been compelled to remove. He was tired now and he thought he would go to his room and sleep until daybreak. As he turned the implement he remembered how through it he had found her, and now he was using it in her service. He smiled as he worked, and half listened to the steady roll of sound encompassing him. A cool breath swept from the lake and he wondered if it found her wet, hot cheek. A wild duck in the rushes below gave an alarm signal, and it ran in subdued voice, note by note, along the shore. The Harvester gripped the mattock and stood motionless. Wild things had taught him so many lessons he heeded their warnings instinctively. Perhaps it was a mink or muskrat approaching the rushes. Listening intently, he heard a stealthy step coming up the path behind him.

The Harvester waited. He soundlessly moved around the trunk of the big tree. An instant more the night prowler stopped squarely at the head of the open grave, and jumped back with an oath. He stood tense a second, then advanced, scratched a match and dropped it into the depths of the opening. That instant the Harvester recognized Henry Jameson, and with a spring landed between the man's shoulders and sent him, face down, headlong into the grave. He snatched one of the sacks of earth, and tipping it, gripped the bottom and emptied the contents on the head and shoulders of the prostrate man. Then he dropped on him and feeling across his back took an ugly, big revolver from a pocket. He swung to the surface and waited until Henry Jameson crawled from under the weight of earth and began to rise; then, at each attempt, he knocked him down. At last he caught the exhausted man by the collar and dragged him to the path, where he dropped him and stood gloating.

"So!" he said. "It's you! Coming to execute your threat, are you? What's the matter with my finishing you, loading your carcass with a few stones into this sack, and dropping you in the deepest part of the lake."

There was no reply.

"Ain't you a little hasty?" asked the Harvester. "Isn't it rather cold blooded to come sneaking when you thought I'd be asleep? Don't you think it would be low down to kill a man on his wedding day?"

Henry Jameson arose cautiously and faced the Harvester.

"Who have you killed?" he panted.

"No one," answered the Harvester. "This is for the victim of a member of your family, but I never dreamed I'd have the joy of planting any of you in it first, even temporarily. Did you rest well? What I should have done was to fill in, tread down, and leave you at the bottom."

Jameson retreated a few steps. The Harvester laughed and advanced the same distance.

"Now then," he said, "explain what you are doing on my premises, a few hours after your threat, and armed with another revolver before I could return the one I took from you this afternoon. You must grow them on bushes at your place, they seem so numerous. Speak up! What are you doing here?"

There was no answer.

"There are three things it might be," mused the Harvester. "You might think to harm me, but you're watched on that score and I don't believe you'd enjoy the result sure to follow. You might contemplate trying to steal Ruth's money again, but we'll pass that up. You might want to go through my woods to inform yourself as to what I have of value there. But, in all prob-ability, you are after me. Well, here I am. Go ahead! Do what you came to!"

The Harvester stepped toward the lake bank and Jameson, turning to watch him, exposed a face ghastly through its grime.

"Look here!" cried the Harvester, sickening. "We will end this right now. I was rather busy this afternoon, but I wasn't too hurried to take that little weapon of yours to the chief of police and tell him where and how I got it and what occurred. He was to return it to you to-morrow with his ultimatum. When I have added the history of to-night, reinforced by another gun, he will understand your intentions and know where you belong. You should be confined, but because your name is the same as the Girl's, and there is of your blood in her veins, I'll give you one more chance. I'll let you go this time, but I'll report you, and deliver this implement to be added to your collection at headquarters. And I tell you, and I'll tell them, that if ever I find you on my premises again, I'll finish you on sight. Is that clear?"

Jameson nodded.

"What I should do is to plump you squarely into confinement, as I could easily enough, but that's not my way. I am going to let you off, but you go know-ing the law. One thing more: Don't leave with any distorted ideas in your head. I saw Ruth the day she stepped from the cars in Onabasha and I loved her. I wanted to court and marry her, as any man would the girl he loves, but you spoiled that with your woman killing brutality. So I married her in Onabasha this afternoon. You can see the records at the county clerk's office and interview the minister who performed the ceremony, if you doubt me. Ruth is in her room, comfortable as I can make her, asleep and unafraid, thank God! This grave is for her mother. The Girl wants her lifted from the horrible place you put her, and laid where it is sheltered and pleasant. Now, I'll see you off my land. Hurry yourself!"

With the Harvester following, Henry Jameson went back over the path he had come, until he reached and mounted the horse he had ridden. As the Harvester watched him, Jameson turned in the saddle and spoke for the second time.

"What will you give me in cold cash to tell you who she is, and where her mother's people are?"

The Harvester leaped for the bridle and missed. Jameson bent over the horse and lashed it to a run. Half way to the oak the Harvester remembered the revolver, but being unaccustomed to weapons, he had forgotten it when he needed it most. He replaced the earth in the sack and dragged it away, then plunged into the lake, and afterward went to bed, where he slept soundly until dawn. First, he slipped into the living-room and wrote a note to the Girl. Then he fed Belshazzar and ate a hearty breakfast. He stationed the dog at her door, gave him the note, and went to the oak. There he arranged everything neatly and as he desired, and then hitching Betsy he quietly guided her down the drive and over the road to Onabasha. He went to an undertaking establishment, made all his arrangements, and then called up and talked with the minister who had performed the marriage ceremony the previous day.

The sun shining in her face awoke Ruth and she lay revelling in the light. "Maybe it will colour me faster than the powder," she thought. "How peculiar for him to say what he did! I always thought men detested it. But he is not like any one else." She lay looking around the beautiful room and wondering where the Harvester was. She could not hear him. Then, slowly and painfully, she dragged her aching limbs from the bed and went to the door. The dog was gone from the porch and she could not see the man at the stable. She selected a frock and putting it on opened the door. Belshazzar arose and offered this letter:

DEAR RUTH:

I have gone to keep my promise. You are locked in with Bel. Please obey me and do not step outside the door until four o'clock. Then put on a pretty white dress, and with the dog, come to the bridge to meet me. I hope you will not suffer and fret. Put away your clothing, arrange the rooms to keep busy, or better yet, lie in the swing and rest. There is food in the ice chest, pantry, and cellar. Forgive me for leaving you to day, but I thought you would feel easier to have this over. I am so glad to bring your mother here. I hope it will make you happy enough to meet us with a smile. Do not forget the pink box until the reality comes.

With love,
DAVID.

The Girl went to the kitchen and found food. She offered to share with Belshazzar, but she could see from his indifference he was not hungry. Then she returned to the room flooded with light, and filled with treasures, and tried to decide how she would arrange her clothing. She spent hours opening boxes and putting dainty, pretty garments in the drawers, hanging the dresses, and placing the toilet articles. Often she wearily dropped to the chairs and couches, or gazed from door and windows at the pictures they framed. "I wonder why he doesn't want me to go outside," she thought. "I wouldn't be afraid in the least, with Bel. I'd just love to go across to that wonderful little river of Singing Water and sit in the shade; but I won't open the door until four o'clock, just as he wrote."

When she thought of where he had gone, and why, the swift tears filled her eyes, but she forced them back and resolutely went to investigate the dining-room. Then for two hours she was a home builder, with a touch of that homing instinct found in the heart of every good woman. First, she looked where the Harvester had said the dishes were, and suddenly sat on the floor exulting. There was a quantity of old chipped and cracked white ware and some gorgeous baking powder prizes; but there were also big blue, green, and pink bowls, several large lustre plates, and a complete tea set without chip or blemish, two beautiful pitchers, and a number of willow pieces. She set the green bowl on the dining table, the blue on the living-room, and took the pink herself, while a beautiful yellow one she placed in the dining-room window seat.

"Oh, if I only dared fill them with those lovely flowers!" She stood in the window and gazed longingly toward the lake. "I know what colour I'd like to put in each of them," she said, "but I promised not to touch anything, and the ones I want most I never saw before, and I'm not to go out anyway. I can't see the sense in that, when I'm not at all afraid, but if he does this wonderful thing for me I must do what he asks. Oh mother, mother! Are you really coming to this beautiful place and to rest at last?"

She sank to the window seat and lay trembling, but she bravely restrained the tears. After a time she remembered the upstairs and went to see the coverlets. She found a half dozen beautiful ones, and smiled as she examined the stiffly conventionalized birds facing each other in the border designs, and in one corner of each blanket she read, woven in the cloth—

Peter and John
Hartman
Wooster
Ohio
1837

She took a blue and a green one, several fine skins from the fur box the Harvester had told her about, and went downstairs. It required all her strength to push the heavy tables before the fireplaces. She spread papers on them to stand on, and tacked a skin above each mantel. She set all of the candlesticks, except those she wanted to use, in the lower part of an empty bookcase. A pair of black walnut she placed on the living-room mantel, together with a big blue plate, a yellow one, and an old brass candlestick. She admired the effect very much. She spread the blue coverlet on the couch, and arranged the blue bowl and some books on the table. Here and there she hung a skin across a chair back, or spread it in a wide window seat. Having exhausted all her resources, she returned to the dining-room, spread a skin before the hearth and in each window seat, set a pink and green lustre plate on the mantel, and a pair of oak candlesticks, and arranged the lustre tea set on the side table. The pink coverlet she took for herself, and after resting a time she was surprised on going back to the rooms to see how homelike they appeared.

At three o'clock she dressed and at almost four unlocked the screen, called Belshazzar to her side, and slowly went down the drive to the bridge. She had used the pink powder, put on a beautiful white dress, carefully arranged her hair, and she wore the pearl ornament. Once her fingers strayed to the pendant and she said softly, "I think both he and mother would like me to wear it."

At the foot of the hill she stopped at a bench and sat in the shade waiting. Belshazzar stretched beside her, and gazed at her with questioning, friendly dog eyes. The Girl looked from Singing Water to the lake, and up the hill to make sure it was real. She tried to quiet her quivering muscles and nerves. He had asked her to meet him with a smile. How could she? He could not have understood what it meant when he made the request. There never would be any way to make him realize; indeed, why should he? The smile must be ready. He had loved his mother deeply, and yet he had said he did not grieve to lay her to rest. Earth had not been kind. Then why should she sorrow for her mother? Again life had been not only unkind, but bitterly cruel.

Belshazzar arose and watched down the drive. The Girl looked also. Through the gate and up the levee came a strange procession. First walked the Harvester alone, with bared head, and he carried an arm load of white lilies. A carriage containing a man and several women followed. Then came a white hearse with snowy plumes, and behind that another carriage filled with people, and Betsy followed drawing men in the spring wagon. The Girl arose and as she stepped to the drive she swayed uncertainly an instant.

"Gracious Heaven!" she gasped. "He is bringing her in white, and with flowers and song!"

Then she lifted her head, and with a smile on her lips she went to meet him. As she reached his side, he tenderly put an arm around her, and came on steadily.

"Courage Girl!" he whispered. "Be as brave as she was!"

Around the driveway and up the hill he half carried her, to a seat he had placed under the oak. Before her lay the white-lined grave, and the Harvester arranged his lilies around it. The teams stopped at the barn and men came up the hill bearing a white burden. Behind them followed the minister who yesterday had performed their marriage ceremony, and after him a choir of trained singers softly chanting:

"Blessed are the dead who die in the Lord,
For they shall cease from their labours."

"But David," panted the Girl, "It was mean and poor. That is not she!"

"Sush!" said the Harvester. "It is your mother. The location was high and dry, and it has been only a short time. We wrapped her in white silk, laid her on a soft cushion and pillow, and housed her securely. She can sleep well now, Ruth. Listen!"

Covered with white lilies, slowly the casket sank into earth. At its head stood the minister and as it began to disappear, the white doves, frightened by the strange conveyances at the stable, came circling above. The minister looked up. He lifted a clear tenor, and softly and purely he sang, while at a wave of his hand the choir joined him:

"Oh, come angel band! Oh, come, and around me stand!
Oh, bear me away on your snowy wings to my immortal home!"

He uttered a low benediction, and singing, the people turned and went downhill. The Harvester gathered the Girl in his arms and carried her to the lake. He laid her in his boat and taking the oars sent it along the bank in the shade, and through cool, green places.

"Now cry all you choose!" he said.

The overstrained Girl covered her face and sobbed wildly. After a time he began to talk to her gently, and before she realized it, she was listening.

"Death has been kinder to her than life, Ruth," he said. "She is lying as you saw her last, I think. We lifted her very tenderly, wrapped her carefully, and brought her gently as we could. Now they shall rest together, those little mothers of ours, to whom men were not kind; and in the long sleep we must forget, as they have forgotten, and forgive, as no doubt they have forgiven. Don't you want to take some lilies to them before we go to the cabin? Right there on your left are unusually large ones."

The Girl sat up, dried her eyes and gathered the white flowers. When the last vehicle crossed the bridge, the Harvester tied the boat and helped her up the hill.

The old oak stretched its wide arms above two little mounds, both moss covered and scattered with flowers. The Girl added her store and then went to the Harvester, and sank at his feet.

"Ruth, you shall not!" cried the man. "I simply will not have that. Come now, I will bring you back this evening."

He helped her to the veranda and laid her in the swing. He sat beside her while she rested, and then they went into the cabin for supper. Soon he had her telling what she had found, and he was making notes of what was yet required to transform the cabin into a home. The Harvester left it to her to decide whether he should roof the bridge the next day or make a trip for furnishings. She said he had better buy what they needed and then she could make the cabin homelike while he worked on the bridge.

Chapter 15

The Harvester Interprets Life

They went through the rooms together, and the Girl suggested the furnishings she thought necessary, while the Harvester wrote the list. The following morning he was eager to have her company, but she was very tired and begged to be allowed to wait in the swing, so again he drove away and left her with Belshazzar on guard. When he had gone, she went through the cabin arranging the furniture the best she could, then dressed and went to the swinging couch. It was so wide and heavy a light wind rocked it gently, and from it she faced the fern and lily carpeted hillside, the majesty of big trees of a thousand years, and heard the music of Singing Water as it sparkled diamond-like where the sun rays struck its flow. Across the drive and down the valley to the brilliant bit of marsh it hurried on its way to Loon Lake.

There were squirrels barking and racing in the big trees and over the ground. They crossed the sodded space of lawn and came to the top step for nuts, eating them from cunning paws. They were living life according to the laws of their nature. She knew that their sharp, startling bark was not to frighten her, but to warn straying intruders of other species of their kindred from a nest, because the Harvester had told her so. He had said their racing here and there in wild scramble was a game of tag and she found it most interesting to observe.

Birds of brilliant colour flashed everywhere, singing in wild joy, and tilted on the rising hedge before her, hunting berries and seeds. Their bubbling, spontaneous song was an instinctive outpouring of their joy over mating time, nests, young, much food, and running water. Their social, inquiring, short cry was to locate a mate, and call her to good feeding. The sharp wild scream of a note was when a hawk passed over, a weasel lurked in the thicket, or a black snake sunned on the bushes. She remembered these things, and lay listening intently, trying to interpret every sound as the Harvester did.

Birds of wide wing hung as if nailed to the sky, or wheeled and sailed in grandeur. They were searching the landscape below to locate a hare or snake in the waving grass or carrion in the fields. The wonderful exhibitions of wing power were their expression of exultation in life, just as the song sparrow threatened to rupture his throat as he swung on the hedge, and the red bird somewhere in the thicket whistled so forcefully it sounded as if the notes might hurt him.

On the lake bass splashed in a game with each other. Grebes chattered, because they were very social. Ducks dived and gobbled for roots and worms of the lake shore, and congratulated each other when they were lucky.

Killdeer cried for slaughter, in plaintive tones, as their white breasts gleamed silver-like across the sky. They insisted on the death of their ancient enemies, because the deer had trampled nests around the shore, roiled the water, spoiled the food hunting, and had been wholly unmindful of the laws of feathered folk from the beginning.

Behind the barn imperial cocks crowed challenges of defiance to each other and all the world, because they once had worn royal turbans on their heads, and ruled the forests, even the elephants and lions. Happy hens cackled when they deposited an egg, and wandered through their park singing the spring egg song unceasingly.

Upon the barn Ajax spread and exulted in glittering plumage, and screamed viciously. He was sending a wireless plea to the forests of Ceylon for a gray mate to come and share the ridge pole with him, and help him wage red war on the sickening love making of the white doves he hated.

Everything was beautiful, some of it was amusing, all instructive, and intensely interesting. The Girl wanted to know about the brown, yellow, and black butterflies sailing from flower to flower. She watched big black and gold bees come from the forest for pollen and listened to their monotonous bumbling. Her first humming bird poised in air, and sipped nectar before her astonished eyes. It was marvellous, but more wonderful to the Girl than anything she saw or heard was the fact that because of the Harvester's teachings she now could trace through all of it the ordained processes of the evolution of life. Everything was right in its way, all necessary to human welfare, and so there was nothing to fear, but marvels to learn and pictures to appreciate. She would have taken Belshazzar and gone out, but the Harvester had exacted a promise that she would not. The fact was, he could see that she was coming gradually to a sane and natural view of life and living things, and he did not want some sound or creature to frighten her, and spoil what he had accomplished. So she swayed in the swing and watched, and tried to interpret sights and sounds as he did.

Before an hour she realized that she was coming speedily into sympathy with the wild life around her; for, instead of shivering and shrinking at unaccustomed sounds, she was listening especially for them, and trying to arrive at a sane version. Instead of the senseless roar of commerce, manufacture, and life of a city, she was beginning to appreciate sounds that varied and carried the Song of Life in unceasing measure and absorbing meaning, while she was more than thankful for the fresh, pure air, and the blessed, God-given light. It seemed to the Girl that there was enough sunshine at Medicine Woods to furnish rays of gold for the whole world.

"Bel," she said to the dog standing beside her, "it's a shame to separate you from the Medicine Man and pen you here with me. It's a wonder you don't bite off my head and run away to find him. He's gone to bring more things to make life beautiful. I wanted to go with him, but oh Bel, there's something dreadfully wrong with me. I was afraid I'd fall on the streets and frighten and shame him. I'm so weak, I scarcely can walk straight across one of these big, cool rooms that he has built for me. He can make everything beautiful, Bel, a home, rooms, clothing, grounds, and life—above everything else he can make life beautiful. He's so splendid and wonderful, with his wide understanding and sane interpretation and God-like sympathy and patience. Why Belshazzar, he can do the greatest thing in all the world! He can make you forget that the grave annihilates your dear ones by hideous processes, and set you to thinking instead that they come back to you in whispering leaves and flower perfumes. If I didn't owe him so much that I ought to pay, if this wasn't so alluringly beautiful, I'd like to go to the oak and lie beside those dear women resting there, and give my tired body to furnish sap for strength and leaves for music. He can take its bitterest sting—from death, Bel—and that's the most wonderful thing—in life, Bel—"

Her voice became silent, her eyes closed; the dog stretched himself beside her on guard, and it was so the Harvester found them when he drove home from the city. He heaped his load in the dining-room, stabled Betsy, carried the things he had brought where he thought they belonged, and prepared food. When she awakened she came to him.

"How is it going, Girl?" asked the Harvester.

"I can't tell you how lovely it has been!"

"Do you really mean that your heart is warming a little to things here?"

"Indeed I do! I can't tell you what a morning I've had. There have been such myriad things to see and hear. Oh, Harvester, can you ever teach me what all of it means?"

"I can right now," said the Harvester promptly. "It means two things, so simple any little child can understand—the love of God and the evolution of life. I am not precisely clear as to what I mean when I say God. I don't know whether it is spirit, matter, or force; it is that big thing that brings forth worlds, establishes their orbits, and gives us heat, light, food, and water. To me, that is God and His love. Just that we are given birth, sheltered, provisioned, and endowed for our work. Evolution is the natural consequence of this. It is the plan steadily unfolding. If I were you, I wouldn't bother my head over these questions, they never have been scientifically explained to the beginning; I doubt if they ever will be, because they start with the origin of matter and that is too far beyond man for him to penetrate. Just enjoy to the depths of your soul—that's worship. Be thankful for everything—that's praising God as the birds praise him. And 'do unto others' that's all there is of love and religion combined in one fell swoop."

"You should go before the world and tell every one that!"

"No! It isn't my vocation," said the Harvester. "My work is to provide pain-killer. I don't believe, Ruth, that there is any one on the footstool who is doing a better job along that line. I am boastfully proud of it—just of sending in the packages that kill fever, refresh poor blood, and strengthen weak hearts; unadulterated, honest weight, fresh, and scrupulously clean. My neighbours have a different name for it; I call it a man's work."

"Every one who understands must," said the Girl. "I wish I could help at that. I feel as if it would do more to wipe out the pain I've suffered and seen her endure than anything else. Man, when I grow strong enough I want to help you. I believe that I am going to love it here."

"Don't ever suppress your feelings, Ruth!" hastily cried the Harvester. "It will be very bad for you. You will become wrought up, and 'het up,' as Granny Moreland says, and it will make you very ill. When we drive the fever from your blood, the ache from your bones, the poison of wrong conditions from your soul, and good, healthy, red corpuscles begin pumping through your little heart like a windmill, you can stake your life you're going to love it here. And the location and work are not all you're going to care for either, honey. Now just wait! That was not 'nominated in the bond.' I'm allowed to talk. I never agreed not to SAY things. What I promised was not to DO them. So as I said, honey, sit at this table, and eat the food I've cooked; and by that time the furniture van will be here, and the men will unload, and you shall reign on a throne and tell me where and how."

"Oh if I were only stronger, David!"

"You are!" said the Harvester. "You are much better than you were yesterday. You can talk, and that's all that's necessary. The rooms are ready for furniture. The men will carry it where you want it. A decorator is coming to hang the curtains.

By night we will be settled; you can lie in the swing while I read to you a story so wonderful that the wildest fairy tale you ever heard never touched it."

"What will it be, David?"

"Eat all the red raspberries and cream, bread and butter, and drink all the milk you can. There's blood, beefsteak, and bones in it. As I was saying, you have come here a stranger to a strange land. The first thing is for you to understand and love the woods. Before you can do that you should master the history of one tree; just the same as you must learn to know and love me before your childlike trust in all mankind returns again. Understand? Well, the fates knew you were on the way, coming trembling down the brink, Ruth, so they put it into the heart of a great man to write largely of a wonderful tree, especially for your benefit. After it had fallen he took it apart, split it in sections, and year by year spread out history for all the world to read. It made a classic story filled with unsurpassed wonders. It was a pine of a thousand years, close the age of our mother tree, Ruth, and when we have learned from Enos Mills how to wrest secrets from the hearts of centuries, we will climb the hill and measure our oak, and then I will estimate, and you will write, and we will make a record for our tree."

"Oh, I'd like that!"

"So would I," said the Harvester. "And a million other things I can think of that we can learn together. It won't require long for me to teach you all I know, and by that time your hand will be clasped in mine, and our 'hearts will beat as one,' and you will give me a kiss every night and morning, and a few during the day for interest, and we will go on in life together and learn songs, miracles, and wonders until the old oak calls us. Then we will ascend the hill gladly and lie down and offer up our bodies, and our children will lay flowers over our hearts, and gather the herbs and paint the pictures? Amen. I hear a van on the bridge. Just you go to your room and lie down until I get things unloaded and where they belong. Then you and the decorator can make us home-like, and to-morrow we will begin to live. Won't that be great, Ruth?"

"With you, yes, I think it will."

"That will do for this time," said the Harvester, as he opened the door to her room. "Lie and rest until I say ready."

As he went to meet the men, she could hear him singing lustily, "Praise God from whom all blessings flow."

"What a child he is!" she said. "And what a man!"

For an hour heavy feet sounded through the cabin carrying furniture to different rooms. Then with a floor brush in one hand, and a polishing cloth in the other, the Harvester tapped at her door and helped the Girl upstairs. He had divided the space into three large, square sleeping chambers. In each he had set up a white iron bed, a dressing table, and wash stand, and placed two straight-backed and one rocking chair, all white. The walls were tinted lightly with green added to the plaster. There was a mattress and a stack of bedding on each bed, and a large rug and several small ones on the floors. He led her to the rocking chair in the middle room, where she could see through the open doors of the other two.

"Now," said the Harvester, "I didn't know whether the room with two windows toward the lake and one on the marsh, or two facing the woods and one front, was the guest chamber. It seemed about an even throw whether a visitor would prefer woods or water, so I made them both guest chambers, and got things alike for them. Now if we are entertaining two, one can't feel more highly honoured than the other. Was that a scheme?"

"Fine!" said the Girl. "I don't see how it could be surpassed."

"'Be sure you are right, then go ahead,'" quoted the Harvester. "Now I'll make the beds and Mr. Rogers can hang the curtains. Is white correct for sleeping rooms? Won't that wash best and always be fresh?"

"It will," said the Girl. "White wash curtains are much the nicest."

"Make them short Mr. Rogers; keep them off the floor," advised the Harvester. "And simple—don't arrange any thing elaborate that will tire a woman to keep in order. Whack them off the right length and pin them to the poles."

"How about that, Mrs. Langston?" asked the decorator.

"I am quite sure that is the very best thing to do," said the Girl; and the curtains were hung while the mattress was placed.

"Now about this?" inquired the Harvester. "Do I put on sheets and fix these beds ready to use?"

"I would not," said the Girl. "I would spread the pad and the counterpane and lay the sheets and pillows in the closet until they are wanted. They can be sunned and the bed made delightfully fresh."

"Of course," said the Harvester.

When he had finished, he spread a cover on the dressing table and laid out white toilet articles and grouped a white wash set with green decorations on the stand. Then he brushed the floor, spread a big green rug in the middle and small ones before the bed, stand, and table, and coming out closed the door.

"Guest chamber with lake view is now ready for company," announced the Harvester. "Repeat the operation on the woods room, finished also. Why do some people make work of things and string them out eternally and fuss so much? Isn't this simple and easy, Ruth?"

"Yes, if you can afford it," said the Girl.

"Forbear!" cried the Harvester. "We have the goods, the dealer has my check. Excuse me ten minutes, until I furnish another room."

The laughing Girl could catch glimpses of him busy over beds and dresser, floor and rugs; then he came where she sat.

"Woods guest chamber ready," he said. "Now we come to the interior apartment, that from its view might be called the marsh room. Aside from being two windows short, it is exactly similar to the others. It occurred to me that, in order to make up for the loss of those windows, and also because I may be compelled to ask some obliging woman to occupy it in case your health is precarious at any time, and in view of the further fact that if any such woman could be found, and would kindly and willingly care for us, my gratitude would be inexpressible; on account of all these things, I got a shade the *best* furnishings for this room."

The Girl stared at him with blank face.

"You see," said the Harvester, "this is a question of ethics. Now what is a guest? A thing of a day! A person who disturbs your routine and interferes with important concerns. Why should any one be grateful for company? Why should time and money be lavished on visitors? They come. You overwork yourself. They go. You are glad of it. You return the visit, because it's the only way to have back at them; but why pamper them unnecessarily? Now a good housekeeper, that means more than words can express. Comfort, kindness, sanitary living, care in illness! Here's to the prospective housekeeper of Medicine Woods! Rogers, hang those ruffled embroidered curtains. Observe that whereas mere guest beds are plain white, this has a touch of brass. Where guest rugs are floor coverings, this is a work of art. Where guest brushes are celluloid, these are enamelled, and the dresser cover is hand embroidered. Let me also call your attention to the chairs touched with gold, cushioned for ease, and a decorated pitcher and bowl. Watch the bounce of these springs and the thickness of this mattress and pad, and notice that where guests, however welcome, get a down cover of sateen, the lady of the house has silkaline. Won't she prepare us a breakfast after a night in this room?"

"David, are you in earnest?" gasped the Girl.

"Don't these things prove it?" asked the Harvester. "No woman can enter my home, when my necessities are so great I have to hire her to come, and take the *worst* in the house. After my wife, she gets the best, every time. Whenever I need help, the woman who will come and serve me is what I'd call the real guest of the house. Friend? Where are your friends when trouble comes? It always brings a crowd on account of the excitement, and there is noise and racing; but if your soul is saved alive, it is by a steady, trained hand you pay to help you. Friends come and go, but a good housekeeper remains and is a business proposition—one that if conducted rightly for both parties and on a strictly common-sense basis, gives you living comfort. Now that we have disposed of the guests that go and the one that remains, we will proceed downward and arrange for ourselves."

"David, did you ever know any one who treated a housekeeper as you say you would?"

"No. And I never knew any one who raised medicinal stuff for a living, but I'm making a gilt-edged success of it, and I would of a housekeeper, too."

"It doesn't seem——"

"That's the bedrock of all the trouble on the earth," interrupted the Harvester. "We are a nation and a part of a world that spends our time on 'seeming.' Our whole outer crust is 'seeming.' When we get beneath the surface and strike the *being*, then we live as we are privileged by the Almighty. I don't think I give a tinker how anything *seems*. What concerns me is how it IS. It doesn't 'seem' possible to you to hire a woman to come into your home and take charge of its cleanliness and the food you eat—the very foundation of life—and treat her as an honoured guest, and give her the best comfort you have to offer. The cold room, the old covers, the bare floor, and the cast off furniture are for her. No wonder, as a rule, she gives what she gets. She dignifies her labour in the same ratio that you do. Wait until we need a housekeeper, and then gaze with awe on the one I will raise to your hand."

"I wonder——"

"Don't! It's wearing! Come tell me how to make our living-room less bare than it appears at present."

They went downstairs together, followed by the decorator, and began work on the room. The Girl was placed on a couch and made comfortable and then the Harvester looked around.

"That bundle there, Rogers, is the curtains we bought for this room. If you and my wife think they are not right, we will not hang them."

The decorator opened the package and took out curtains of tan-coloured goods with a border of blue and brown.

"Those are not expensive," said the Harvester, "but to me a window appears bare with only a shade, so I thought we'd try these, and when they become soiled we'll burn them and buy some fresh ones."

"Good idea!" laughed the Girl. "As a house decorator you surpass yourself as a Medicine Man."

"Fix these as you did those upstairs," ordered the Harvester. "We don't want any fol-de-rols. Put the bottom even with the sill and shear them off at the top."

"No, I am going to arrange these," said the decorator. "You go on with your part."

"All right!" agreed the Harvester. "First, I'll lay the big rug."

He cleared the floor, spread a large rug with a rich brown centre and a wide blue border. Smaller ones of similar design and colour were placed before each of the doors leading from the room.

"Now for the hearth," said the Harvester, "I got this tan goat skin. Doesn't that look fairly well?"

It certainly did; and the Girl and the decorator hastened to say so. The Harvester replaced the table and chairs, and then sat on the couch at the Girl's feet.

"I call this almost finished," he remarked. "All we need now is a bouquet and something on the walls, and that is serious business. What goes on them usually remains for a long time, and so it should be selected with care. Ruth, have you a picture of your mother?"

"None since she was my mother. I have some lovely girl photographs."

"Good!" cried the Harvester. "Exactly the thing! I have a picture of my mother when she was a pretty girl. We will select the best of yours and have them enlarged in those beautiful brown prints they make in these days, and we'll frame one for each side of the mantel. After that you can decorate the other walls as you see things you want. Fifteen minutes gone; we are ready to take up the line of march to the dining-room. Oh I forgot my pillows! Here are a half dozen tan, brown, and blue for this room. Ruth, you arrange them."

The Girl heaped four on the couch, stood one beside the hearth, and laid another in a big chair.

"Now I don't know what you will think of this," said the Harvester. "I found it in a magazine at the library. I copied this whole room. The plan was to have the floor, furniture, and casings of golden oak and the walls pale green. Then it said get yellow curtains bordered with green and a green rug with yellow figures, so I got them. I had green leather cushions made for the window seats, and these pillows go on them. Hang the saffron curtains, Rogers, and we will finish in good shape for dinner by six. By the way, Ruth, when will you select your dishes? It will take a big set to fill all these shelves and you shall have exactly what you want."

"I can use those you have very well."

"Oh no you can't!" cried the Harvester. "I may live and work in the woods, but I am not so benighted that I don't own and read the best books and magazines, and subscribe for a few papers. I patronize the library and see what is in the stores. My money will buy just as much as any man's, if I do wear khaki trousers. Kindly notice the word. Save in deference to your ladyship I probably would have said pants. You see how *elite* I can be if I try. And it not only extends to my wardrobe, to a 'yaller' and green dining-room, but it takes in the 'chany' as well.

I have looked up that, too. You want china, cut glass, silver cutlery, and linen. Ye! Ye! You needn't think I don't know anything but how to dig in the dirt. I have been studying this especially, and I know exactly what to get."

"Come here," said the Girl, making a place for him beside her. "Now let me tell you what I think. We are going to live in the woods, and our home is a log cabin—"

"With acetylene lights, a furnace, baths, and hot and cold water—" interpolated the Harvester.

The Girl and the decorator laughed.

"Anyway," said she, "if you are going to let me have what I would like, I'd prefer a set of tulip yellow dishes with the Dutch little figures on them. I don't know what they cost, but certainly they are not so expensive as cut glass and china."

"Is that earnest or is it because you think I am spending too much money?"

"It is what I want. Everything else is different; why should we have dishes like city folk? I'd dearly love to have the Dutch ones, and a white cloth with a yellow border, glass where it is necessary, and silver knives, forks, and spoons."

"That would be great, all right!" endorsed the decorator. "And you have got a priceless old lustre tea set there, and your willow ware is as fine as I ever saw. If I were you, I wouldn't buy a dish with what you have, except the yellow set."

"Great day!" ejaculated the Harvester. "Will you tell me why my great grandmother's old pink and green teapot is priceless?"

The Girl explained pink lustre. "That set in the shop I knew in Chicago would sell for from three to five hundred dollars. Truly it would! I've seen one little pink and green pitcher like yours bring nine dollars there. And you've not only got the full tea set, but water and dip pitchers, two bowls, and two bread plates. They are priceless, because the secret of making them is lost; they take on beauty with age, and they were your great-grandmother's."

The Harvester reached over and energetically shook hands.

"Ruth, I'm so glad you've got them!" he bubbled. "Now elucidate on my willow ware. What is it? Where is it? Why have I willow ware and am not informed. Who is responsible for this? Did my ancestors buy better than they knew, or worse? Is willow ware a crime for which I must hide my head, or is it further riches thrust upon me? I thought I had investigated the subject of proper dishes quite thoroughly; but I am very certain I saw no mention of lustre or willow. I thought, in my ignorance, that lustre was a dress, and willow a tree. Have I been deceived? Why is a blue plate or pitcher willow ware?"

"Bring that platter from the mantel," ordered the Girl, "and I will show you."

The Harvester obeyed and followed the finger that traced the design.

"That's a healthy willow tree!" he commented. "If Loon Lake couldn't go ahead of that it should be drained. And will you please tell me why this precious platter from which I have eaten much stewed chicken, fried ham, and in youthful days sopped the gravy—will you tell me why this relic of my ancestors is called a willow plate, when there are a majority of orange trees so extremely fruitful they have neglected to grow a leaf? Why is it not an orange plate? Look at that boat! And in plain sight of it, two pagodas, a summer house, a water-sweep, and a pair of corpulent swallows; you would have me believe that a couple are eloping in broad daylight."

"Perhaps it's night! And those birds are doves."

"Never!" cried the Harvester. "There is a total absence of shadows. There is no moon. Each orange tree is conveniently split in halves, so you can see to count the fruit accurately; the birds are in flight. Only a swallow or a stork can fly in decorations, either by day or by night. And for any sake look at that elopement! He goes ahead carrying a cane, she comes behind lugging the baggage, another man with a cane brings up the rear. They are not running away. They have been married ten years at least. In a proper elopement, they forget there are such things as jewels and they always carry each other. I've often looked up the statistics and it's the only authorized version. As I regard this treasure, I grow faint when I remember with what unnecessary force my father bore down when he carved the ham. I'll bet a cooky he split those orange trees. Now me—I'll never dare touch knife to it again. I'll always carve the meat on the broiler, and gently lift it to this platter with a fork. Or am I not to be allowed to dine from my ancestral treasure again?"

"Not in a green and yellow room," laughed the Girl. "I'll tell you what I think. If I had a tea table to match the living-room furniture, and it sat beside the hearth, and on it a chafing dish to cook in, and the willow ware to eat from, we could have little tea parties in there, when we aren't very hungry or to treat a visitor. It would help make that room 'homey,' and it's wonderful how they harmonize with the other things."

"How much willow ware have I got to 'bestow' on you?" inquired the Harvester. "Suppose you show me all of it. A guilty feeling arises in my breast, and I fear me I have committed high crimes!"

"Oh Man! You didn't break or lose any of those dishes, did you?"

"Show me!" insisted the Harvester.

The Girl arose and going to the cupboard he had designed for her china she opened it, and set before him a teapot, cream pitcher, two plates, a bowl, a pitcher, the meat platter, and a sugar bowl. "If there were all of the cups, saucers, and plates, I know where they would bring five hundred dollars," she said.

"Ruth, are you getting even with me for poking fun at them, or are you in earnest?" asked the Harvester.

"I mean every word of it."

"You really want a small, black walnut table made especially for those old dishes?"

"Not if you are too busy. I could use it with beautiful effect and much pleasure, and I can't tell you how proud I'd be of them."

The Harvester's face flushed. "Excuse me," he said rising. "I have now finished furnishing a house; I will go and take a peep at the engine." He went into the kitchen and hearing the rattle of dishes the Girl followed. She stepped in just in time to see him hastily slide something into his pocket. He picked up a half dozen old white plates and saucers and several cups and started toward the evaporator. He heard her coming.

"Look here, honey," he said turning, "you don't want to see the dry-house just now. I have terrific heat to do some rapid work. I won't be gone but a few minutes. You better boss the decorator.

"I'm afraid that wasn't very diplomatic," he muttered. "It savoured a little of being sent back. But if what she says is right, and she should know if they handle such stuff at that art store, she will feel considerably better not to see this."

He set his load at the door, drew an old blue saucer from his pocket and made a careful examination. He pulled some leaves from a bush and pushed a greasy cloth out of the saucer, wiped it the best he could, and held it to light.

"That is a crime!" he commented. "Saucer from your maternal ancestors' tea set used for a grease dish. I am afraid I'd better sink it in the lake. She'd feel worse to see it than never to know. Wish I could clean off the grease! I could do better if it was hot. I can set it on the engine."

The Harvester placed the saucer on the engine, entered the dry-house, and closed the door. In the stifling air he began pouring seed from beautiful, big willow plates to the old white ones.

"About the time I have ruined you," he said to a white plate, "some one will pop up and discover that the art of making you is lost and you are priceless, and I'll have been guilty of another blunder. Now there are the dishes mother got with baking powder. She thought they were grand. I know plenty well she prized them more than these blue ones or she wouldn't have saved them and used these for every day. There they set, all so carefully taken care of, and the Girl doesn't even look at them. Thank Heaven, there are the four remaining plates all right, anyway! Now I've got seed in some of the saucers; one is there; where on earth is the last one? And where, oh unkind fates! are the cups?"

He found more saucers and set them with the plates. As he passed the engine he noticed the saucer on it was bubbling grease, literally exuding it from the particles of clay.

"Hooray!" cried the Harvester. He took it up, but it was so hot he dropped it. With a deft sweep he caught it in air, and shoved it on a tray. Then he danced and blew on his burned hand. Snatching out his handkerchief he rubbed off all the grease, and imagined the saucer was brighter.

"If 'a little is good, more is better,'" quoted the Harvester.

Wadding the handkerchief he returned the saucer to the engine. Then he slipped out, dripping perspiration, glanced toward the cabin, and ran into the work room. The first object he saw was a willow cup half full of red paint, stuck and dried as if to remain forever. He took his knife and tried to whittle it off, but noticing that he was scratching the cup he filled it with turpentine, set it under a work bench, turned a tin pan over it, and covered it with shavings. A few steps farther brought one in sight, filled with carpet tacks. He searched everywhere, but could find no more, so he went to the laboratory. Beside his wash bowl at the door stood the last willow saucer. He had used it for years as a soap dish. He scraped the contents on the bench and filled the dish with water. Four cups held medicinal seeds and were in good condition. He lacked one, although he could not remember of ever having broken it. Gathering his collection, he returned to the dry-house to see how the saucer was coming on. Again it was bubbling, and he polished off the grease and set back the dish. It certainly was growing better. He carried his treasures into the work room, and went to the barn to feed. As he was leaving the stable he uttered a joyous exclamation and snatched from a window sill a willow cup, gummed and smeared with harness oil.

"The full set, by hokey!" marvelled the Harvester. "Say, Betsy, the only name for this is luck! Now if I only can clean them, I'll be ready to make her tea table, whatever that is. My I hope she will stay away until I get these in better shape!"

He filled the last cup with turpentine, set it with the other under the work bench, stacked the remaining pieces, polished the saucer he was baking, and went to bring a dish pan and towel. He drew some water from the pipes of the evaporator, put in the soap, and carried it to the work room. There he carefully washed and wiped all the pieces, save two cups and one saucer. He did not know how long it would require to bake the grease from that, but he was sure it was improving. He thought he could clean the paint cup, but he imagined the harness oil one would require baking also.

As he stood busily working over the dishes, with light step the Girl came to the door. She took one long look and understood. She turned and swiftly went back to the cabin, but her shoulders were shaking. Presently the Harvester came in and explained that after finishing in the dry-house he had gone to do the feeding. Then he suggested that before it grew dark they should go through the rooms and see how they appeared, and gather the flowers the Girl wanted. So together they decided everything was clean, comfortable, and harmonized.

Then they went to the hillside sloping to the lake. For the dining-room, the Girl wanted yellow water lilies, so the Harvester brought his old boat and gathered enough to fill the green bowl. For the living-room, she used wild ragged robins in the blue bowl, and on one end of the mantel set a pitcher of saffron and on the other arrowhead lilies. For her room, she selected big, blushy mallows that grew all along Singing Water and around the lake.

"Isn't that slightly peculiar?" questioned the Harvester.

"Take a peep," said the Girl, opening her door.

She had spread the pink coverlet on her couch, and when she set the big pink bowl filled with mallows on the table the effect was exquisite.

"I think perhaps that's a little Frenchy," she said, "and you may have to be educated to it; but salmon pink and buttercup yellow are colours I love in combination."

She closed the door and went to find something to eat, and then to the swing, where she liked to rest, look, and listen. The Harvester suggested reading to her, but she shook her head.

"Wait until winter," she said, "when the days are longer and cold, and the snow buries everything, and then read. Now tell me about my hedge and the things you have planted in it."

The Harvester went out and collected a bunch of twigs. He handed her a big, evenly proportioned leaf of ovate shape, and explained: "This is burning bush, so called because it has pink berries that hang from long, graceful stems all winter, and when fully open they expose a flame-red seed pod. It was for this colour on gray and white days that I planted it. In the woods I grow it in thickets. The root bark brings twenty cents a pound, at the very least. It is good fever medicine."

"Is it poison?"

"No. I didn't set anything acutely poisonous in your hedge. I wanted it to be a mass of bloom you were free to cut for the cabin all spring, an attraction to birds in summer, and bright with colour in winter. To draw the feathered tribe, I planted alder, wild cherry, and grape-vines. This is cherry. The bark is almost as beautiful as birch. I raise it for tonics and the birds love the cherries. This fern-like leaf is from mountain ash, and when it attains a few years' growth it will flame with colour all winter in big clusters of scarlet berries. That I grow in the woods is a picture in snow time, and the bark is one of my standard articles."

The Girl raised on her elbow and looked at the hedge.

"I see it," she said. "The berries are green now. I suppose they change colour as they ripen."

"Yes," said the Harvester. "And you must not confuse them with sumac. The leaves are somewhat similar, but the heads differ in colour and shape. The sumac and buckeye you must not touch, until we learn what they will do to you. To some they are slightly poisonous, to others not. I couldn't help putting in a few buckeyes on account of the big buds in early spring. You will like the colour if you are fond of pink and yellow in combination, and the red-brown nuts in grayish-yellow, prickly hulls, and the leaf clusters are beautiful, but you must use care. I put in witch hazel for variety, and I like its appearance; it's mighty good medicine, too; so is spice brush, and it has leaves that colour brightly, and red berries. These selections were all made for a purpose. Now here is wafer ash; it is for music as well as medicine. I have invoked all good fairies to come and dwell in this hedge, and so I had to provide an orchestra for their dances. This tree grows a hundred tiny castanets in a bunch, and when they ripen and become dry the wind shakes fine music from them. Yes, they are medicine; that is, the bark of the roots is. Almost without exception everything here has medicinal properties. The tulip poplar will bear you the loveliest flowers of all, and its root bark, taken in winter, makes a good fever remedy."

"How would it do to eat some of the leaves and see if they wouldn't take the feverishness from me?"

"It wouldn't do at all," said the Harvester. "We are well enough fixed to allow Doc to come now, and he is the one to allay the fever."

"Oh no!" she cried. "No! I don't want to see a doctor. I will be all right very soon. You said I was better."

"You are," said the Harvester. "Much better! We will have you strong and well soon. You should have come in time for a dose of sassafras. Your hedge is filled with that, because of its peculiar leaves and odour. I put in dogwood for the white display around the little green bloom, lots of alder for bloom and berries, haws for blossoms and fruit for the squirrels, wild crab apples for the exquisite bloom and perfume, button bush for the buttons, a few pokeberry plants for the colour, and I tried some mallows, but I doubt if it's wet enough for them. I set pecks of vine roots, that are coming nicely, and ferns along the front edge. Give it two years and that hedge will make a picture that will do your eyes good."

"Can you think of anything at all you forgot?"

"Yes indeed!" said the Harvester. "The woods are full of trees I have not used; some because I overlooked them, some I didn't want. A hedge like this, in perfection, is the work of years. Some species must be cut back, some encouraged, but soon it will be lovely, and its colour and fruit attract every bird of the heavens and butterflies and insects of all varieties. I set several common cherry trees for the robins and some blackberry and raspberry vines for the orioles. The bloom is pretty and the birds you'll have will be a treat to see and hear, if we keep away cats, don't fire guns, scatter food, and move quietly among them. With our water attractions added, there is nothing impossible in the way of making friends with feathered folk."

"There is one thing I don't understand," said the Girl. "You wouldn't risk breaking the wing of a moth by keeping it when you wanted a drawing very much; you don't seem to kill birds and animals that other people do. You almost worship a tree; now how can you take a knife and peel the bark to sell or dig up beautiful bushes by the root."

"Perhaps I've talked too much about the woods," said the Harvester gently. "I've longed inexpressibly for sympathetic company here, because I feel rooted for life, so I am more than anxious that you should care for it. I may have made you feel that my greatest interest is in the woods, and that I am not consistent when I call on my trees and plants to yield of their store for my purposes. Above everything else, the human proposition comes first, Ruth. I do love my trees, bushes, and flowers, because they keep me at the fountain of life, and teach me lessons no book ever hints at; but above everything come my fellow men. All I do is for them. My heart is filled with feeling for the things you see around you here, but it would be joy to me to uproot the most beautiful plant I have if by so doing I could save you pain. Other men have wives they love as well, little children they have fathered, big bodies useful to the world, that are sometimes crippled with disease. There is nothing I would not give to allay the pain of humanity. It is not inconsistent to offer any growing thing you soon can replace, to cure suffering. Get that idea out of your head! You said you could worship at the shrine of the pokeberry bed, you feel holier before the arrowhead lilies, your face takes on an appearance of reverence when you see pink mallow blooms. Which of them would you have hesitated a second in uprooting if you could have offered it to subdue fever or pain in the body of the little mother you loved?"

"Oh I see!" cried the Girl. "Like everything else you make this different. You worship all this beauty and grace, wrought by your hands, but you carry your treasure to the market place for the good of suffering humanity. Oh Man! I love the work you do!"

"Good!" cried the Harvester. "Good! And Ruth-girl, while you are about it, see if you can't combine the man and his occupation a little."

Chapter 16

Granny Moreland's Visit

The following morning the Girl was awakened by wheels on the gravel outside her window, and lifted her head to see Betsy passing with a load of lumber. Shortly afterward the sound of hammer and saw came to her, and she knew that Singing Water bridge was being roofed to provide shade for her. She dressed and went to the kitchen to find a dainty breakfast waiting, so she ate what she could, and then washed the dishes and swept. By that time she was so tired she dropped on a dining-room window seat, and lay looking toward the bridge. She could catch glimpses of the Harvester as he worked. She watched his deft ease in handling heavy timbers, and the assurance with which he builded. Sometimes he stood and with tilted head studied his work a minute, then swiftly proceeded. He placed three tree trunks on each side for pillars, laid joists across, formed his angle, and nailed boards as a foundation for shingling. Occasionally he glanced toward the cabin, and finally came swinging up the drive. He entered the kitchen softly, but when he saw the Girl in the window he sat at her feet.

"Oh but this is a morning, Ruth!" he said.

She looked at him closely. He radiated health and good cheer. His tanned cheeks were flushed red with exercise, and the hair on his temples was damp.

"You have been breaking the rules," he said. "It is the law that I am to do the work until you are well and strong again. Why did you tire yourself?"

"I am so perfectly useless! I see so many things that I would enjoy doing. Oh you can do everything else, make me well! Make me strong!"

"How can I, when you won't do as I tell you?"

"I will! Indeed I will!"

"Then no more attempts to stand over dishes and clean big floors. You mustn't overwork yourself at anything. The instant you feel in the least tired you must lie down and rest."

"But Man! I'm tired every minute, with a dead, dull ache, and I don't feel as if I ever would be rested again in all the world."

The Harvester took one of her hands, felt its fevered palm, fluttering wrist pulse, and noticed that the brilliant red of her lips had extended to spots on her cheeks. He formed his resolution.

"Can't work on that bridge any more until I drive in for some big nails," he said. "Do you mind being left alone for an hour?"

"Not at all, if Bel will stay with me. I'll lie in the swing."

"All right!" answered the Harvester. "I'll help you out and to get settled. Is there anything you want from town?"

"No, not a thing!"

"Oh but you are modest!" cried the Harvester. "I can sit here and name fifty things I want for you."

"Oh but you are extravagant!" imitated the Girl. "Please, please, Man, don't! Can't you see I have so much now I don't know what to do with it? Sometimes I almost forget the ache, just lying and looking at all the wonderful riches that have come to me so suddenly. I can't believe they won't vanish as they came. By the hour in the night I look at my lovely room, and I just fight my eyes to keep them from closing for fear they'll open in that stifling garret to the heat of day and work I have not strength to do. I know yet all this will prove to be a dream and a wilder one than yours."

The face of the Harvester was very anxious.

"Please to remember my dream came true," he said, "and much sooner than I had the least hope that it would. I'm wide awake or I couldn't be building bridges; and you are real, if I know flesh and blood when I touch it."

"If I were well, strong, and attractive, I could understand," she said. "Then I could work in the house, at the drawings, help with the herbs, and I'd feel as if I had some right to be here."

"All that is coming," said the Harvester. "Take a little more time. You can't expect to sin steadily against the laws of health for years, and recover in a day. You will be all right much sooner than you think possible."

"Oh I hope so!" said the Girl. "But sometimes I doubt it. How I could come here and put such a burden on a stranger, I can't see. I scarcely can remember what awful stress drove me. I had no courage. I should have finished in my garret as my mother did. I must have some of my father's coward blood in me. She never would have come. I never should!"

"If it didn't make any real difference to you, and meant all the world to me, I don't see why you shouldn't humour me. I can't begin to tell you how happy I am to have you here. I could shout and sing all day."

"It requires very little to make some people happy."

"You are not much, but you are going to be more soon," laughed the Harvester, as he gently picked up the Girl and carried her to the swing, where he covered her, kissed her hot hand, and whistled for Belshazzar. He pulled the table close and set a pitcher of iced fruit juice on it. Then he left her and she could hear the rattle of wheels as he crossed the bridge and drove away.

"Betsy, this is mighty serious business," said the Harvester. "The Girl is scorching or I don't know fever. I wonder—well, one thing is sure—she is bound to be better off in pure, cool air and with everything I can do to be kind, than in Henry Jameson's attic with everything he could do to be mean. Pleasant men those Jamesons! Wonder if the Girl's father was much like her Uncle Henry? I think not or her refined and lovely mother never would have married him. Come to think of it, that's no law, Betsy. I've seen beautiful and delicate women fall under some mysterious spell, and yoke their lives with rank degenerates. Whatever he was, they have paid the price. Maybe the wife deserved it, and bore it in silence because she knew she did, but it's bitter hard on Ruth. Girls should be taught to think at least one generation ahead when they marry. I wonder what Doc will say, Betsy? He will have to come and see for himself. I don't know how she will feel about that. I had hoped I could pull her through with care, food, and tonics, but I don't dare go any farther alone. Betsy, that's a thin, hot, little hand to hold a man's only chance for happiness."

"Well, bridegroom! I've been counting the days!" said Doctor Carey. "The Missus and I made it up this morning that we had waited as long as we would. We are coming to-night. David."

"It's all right, Doc," said the Harvester. "Don't you dare think anything is wrong or that I am not the proudest, happiest man in this world, because I appear anxious. I am not trying to conceal it from you. You know we both agreed at first that Ruth should be in the hospital, Doc. Well, she should! She is what would be a lovely woman if she were not full of the poison of wrong food and air, overwork, and social conditions that have warped her. She is all I dreamed of and more, but I've come for you. She is too sick for me. I hoped she would begin to gain strength at once on changed conditions. As yet I can't see any difference. She needs a doctor, but I hate for her to know it. Could you come out this afternoon, and pretend as if it were a visit? Bring Mrs. Carey and watch the Girl. If you need an examination, I think she will obey me. If you can avoid it, fix what she should have and send it back to me by a messenger. I don't like to leave her when she is so ill."

"I'll come at once, David."

"Then she will know that I came for you, and that will frighten her. You can do more good to wait until afternoon, and pretend you are making a social call.

I must go now. I'd have brought her in, but I have no proper conveyance yet. I'm promised something soon, perhaps it is ready now. Good-bye! Be sure to come!"

The Harvester drove to a livery barn and examined a little horse, a shining black creature that seemed gentle and spirited. He thought favourably of it. A few days before he had selected a smart carriage, and with this outfit tied behind the wagon he returned to Medicine Woods. He left the horse at the bridge, stabled Betsy, and then returned for the new conveyance, driving it to the hitching post. At the sound of unexpected wheels the Girl lifted her head and stared at the turnout.

"Come on!" cried the Harvester opening the screen. "We are going to the woods to initiate your carriage."

She went with little cries of surprised wonder.

"This is how you travel to Onabasha to do your shopping, to call on Mrs. Carey and the friends you will make, and visit the library. When I've tried out Mr. Horse enough to prove him reliable as guaranteed, he is yours, for your purposes only, and when you grow wonderfully well and strong, we'll sell him and buy you a real live horse and a stanhope, such as city ladies have; and there must be a saddle so that you can ride."

"Oh I'd love that!" cried the Girl. "I always wanted to ride! Where are we going?"

"To show you Medicine Woods," said the Harvester. "I've been waiting for this. You see there are several hundred acres of trees, thickets, shrubs, and herb beds up there, and if the wagon road that winds between them were stretched straight it would be many miles in length, so we have a cool, shaded, perfumed driveway all our own. Let me get you a drink before you start and the little shawl. It's chilly there compared with here. Now are you comfortable and ready?"

"Yes," said the Girl. "Hurry! I've just longed to go, but I didn't like to ask."

"I am sorry," said the Harvester. "Living here for years alone and never having had a sister, how am I going to know what a girl would like if you don't tell me? I knew it would be too tiresome for you to walk, and I was waiting to find a reliable horse and a suitable carriage."

"You won't scratch or spoil it up there?"

"I'll lower the top. It is not as wide as the wagon, so nothing will touch it."

"This is just so lovely, and such a wonderful treat, do you observe that I'm not saying a word about extravagance?" asked the Girl, as she leaned back in the carriage and inhaled the invigorating wood air.

The horse climbed the hill, and the Harvester guided him down long, dim roads through deep forest, while he explained what large thickets of bushes were, why he grew them, how he collected the roots or bark, for what each was used and its value. On and on they went, the way ahead always appearing as if it were too narrow to pass, yet proving amply wide when reached. Excited redbirds darted among the bushes, and the Harvester answered their cry. Blackbirds protested against the unusual intrusion of strange objects, and a brown thrush slipped from a late nest close the road wailing in anxiety.

One after another the Harvester introduced the Girl to the best trees, speculated on their age, previous history, and pointed out which brought large prices for lumber and which had medicinal bark and roots. On and on they slowly drove through the woods, past the big beds of cranesbill, violets, and lilies. He showed her where the mushrooms were most numerous, and for the first time told the story of how he had sold them and the violets from door to door in Onabasha in his search for her, and the amazed Girl sat staring at him. He told of Doctor Carey having seen her once, and inquired as they passed the bed if the yellow violets had revived. He stopped to search and found a few late ones, deep among the leaves.

"Oh if I only had known that!" cried the Girl, "I would have kept them forever."

"No need," said the Harvester. "Here and now I present you with the sole ownership of the entire white and yellow violet beds. Next spring you shall fill your room. Won't that be a treat?"

"One money never could buy!" cried the Girl.

"Seems to be my strong point," commented the Harvester. "The most I have to offer worth while is something you can't buy. There is a fine fairy platform. They can spare you one. I'll get it."

The Harvester broke from a tree a large fan-shaped fungus, the surface satin fine, the base mossy, and explained to the Girl that these were the ballrooms of the woods, the floors on which the little people dance in the moonlight at their great celebrations. Then he added a piece of woolly dog moss, and showed her how each separate spine was like a perfect little evergreen tree.

"That is where the fairies get their Christmas pines," he explained.

"Do you honestly believe in fairies?"

"Surely!" exclaimed the Harvester. "Who would tell me when the maples are dripping sap, and the mushrooms springing up, if the fairies didn't whisper in the night? Who paints the flower faces, colours the leaves, enamels the ripening fruit with bloom, and frosts the window pane to let me know that it is time to prepare for winter? Of course! They are my friends and everyday helpers. And the winds are good to me. They carry down news when tree bloom is out, when the pollen sifts gold from the bushes, and it's time to collect spring roots. The first bluebird always brings me a message. Sometimes he comes by the middle of February, again not until late March. Always on his day, Belshazzar decides my fate for a year. Six years we've played that game; now it is ended in blessed reality. In the woods and at my work I remain until I die, with a few outside tries at medicine making. I am putting up some compounds in which I really have faith. Of course they have got to await their time to be tested, but I believe in them. I have grown stuff so carefully, gathered it according to rules, washed it decently, and dried and mixed it with such scrupulous care. Night after night I've sat over the books until midnight and later, studying combinations; and day after day I've stood in the laboratory testing and trying, and two or three will prove effective, or I've a disappointment coming."

"You haven't wasted time! I'd much rather take medicines you make than any at the pharmacies. Several times I've thought I'd ask you if you wouldn't give me some of yours. The prescription Doctor Carey sent does no good. I've almost drunk it, and I am constantly tired, just the same. You make me something from these tonics and stimulants you've been telling me about. Surely you can help me!"

"I've got one combination that's going to save life, in my expectations. But Ruth, it never has been tried, and I couldn't experiment on the very light of my eyes with it. If I should give you something and you'd grow worse as a result—I am a strong man, my girl, but I couldn't endure that. I'd never dare. But dear, I am expecting Carey and his wife out any time; probably they will come to-day, it's so beautiful; and when they do, for my sake, won't you talk with him, tell him exactly what made you ill, and take what he gives you? He's a great man. He was recently President of the National Association of Surgeons. Long ago he abandoned general practice, but he will prescribe for you; all his art is at your command. It's quite an honour, Ruth. He performs all kinds of miracles, and saves life every day. He had not seen you, and what he gave me was only by guess. He may not think it is the right thing at all after he meets you."

"Then I am really ill?"

"No. You only have the germs of illness in your blood, and if you will help me that much we can eliminate them; and then it is you for housekeeper, with first assistant in me, the drawing tools, paint box, and all the woods for subjects. So, as I was going to tell you, Belshazzar and I have played our game for the last time. That decision was ultimate. Here I will work, live, and die. Here, please God, strong and happy, you shall live with me. Ruth, you have got to recover quickly. You will consult the doctor?"

"Yes, and I wish he would hurry," said the Girl. "He can't make me new too soon to suit me. If I had a strong body, oh Man, I just feel as if you could find a soul somewhere in it that would respond to all these wonders you have brought me among. Oh! make me well, and I'll try as woman never did before to bring you happiness to pay for it."

"Careful now," warned the Harvester. "There is to be no talk of obligations between you and me. Your presence here and your growing trust in me are all I ask at the hands of fate at present. Long ago I learned to 'labour and to wait.' By the way—here's my most difficult labour and my longest wait. This is the precious gingseng bed."

"How pretty!" exclaimed the Girl.

Covering acres of wood floor, among the big trees, stretched the lacy green carpet. On slender, upright stalks waved three large leaves, each made up of five stemmed, ovate little leaves, round at the base, sharply pointed at the tip. A cluster of from ten to twenty small green berries, that would turn red later, arose above. The Harvester lifted a plant to show the Girl that the Chinese name, Jin-chen, meaning man-like, originated because the divided root resembled legs. Away through the woods stretched the big bed, the growth waving lightly in the wind, the peculiar odour filling the air.

"I am going to wait to gather the crop until the seeds are ripe," said the Harvester, "then bury some as I dig a root. My father said that was the way of the Indians. It's a mighty good plan. The seeds are delicate, and difficult to gather and preserve properly. Instead of collecting and selling all of them to start rivals in the business, I shall replant my beds. I must find a half dozen assistants to harvest this crop in that way, and it will be difficult, because it will come when my neighbours are busy with corn."

"Maybe I can help you."

"Not with ginseng digging," laughed the Harvester. "That is not woman's work. You may sit in an especially attractive place and boss the job."

"Oh dear!" cried the Girl. "Oh dear! I want to get out and walk."

Gradually they had climbed the summit of the hill, descended on the other side, and followed the road through the woods until they reached the brier patches, fruit trees; and the garden of vegetables, with big beds of sage, rue, wormwood, hoarhound, and boneset. From there to the lake sloped the sunny fields of mullein and catnip, and the earth was molten gold with dandelion creeping everywhere.

"Too hot to-day," cautioned the Harvester. "Too rough walking. Wait until fall, and I have a treat there for you. Another flower I want you to love because I do."

"I will," said the Girl promptly. "I feel it in my heart."

"Well I am glad you feel something besides the ache of fever," said the Harvester. Then noticing her tired face he added: "Now this little horse had quite a trip from town, and the wheels cut deeply into this woods soil and make difficult pulling, so I wonder if I had not better put him in the stable and let him become acquainted with Betsy. I don't know what she will think. She has had sole possession for years. Maybe she will be jealous, perhaps she will be as delighted for company as her master. Ruth, if you could have heard what I said to Belshazzar when he decided I was to go courting this year, and seen what I did to him, and then take a look at me now—merciful powers, I hope the dog doesn't remember! If he does, no wonder he forms a new allegiance so easily. Have you observed that lately when I whistle, he starts, and then turns back to see if you want him? He thinks as much of you as he does of me right now."

"Oh no!" cried the Girl. "That couldn't be possible. You told me I must make friends with him, so I have given him food, and tried to win him."

"You sit in the carriage until I put away the horse, and then I'll help you to the cabin, and save you being alone while I work. Would you like that?"

"Yes."

She leaned her head against the carriage top the Harvester had raised to screen her, and watched him stable the horse. Evidently he was very fond of animals for he talked as if it were a child he was undressing and kept giving it extra strokes and pats as he led it away. Ajax disliked the newcomer instantly, noticed the carriage and the woman's dress, and screamed his ugliest. The Girl smiled. As the Harvester appeared she inquired, "Is Ajax now sending a wireless to Ceylon asking for a mate?"

The Harvester looked at her quizzically and saw a gleam of mischief in the usually dull dark eyes that delighted him.

"That is the customary supposition when he finds voice," he said. "But since this has become your home, you are bound to learn some of my secrets. One of them I try to guard is the fact that Ajax has a temper. No my dear, he is not always sending a wireless, I am sorry to say. I wish he was! As a matter of fact he is venting his displeasure at any difference in our conditions. He hates change. He learned that from me. I will enjoy seeing him come for favour a year from now, as I learned to come for it, even when I didn't get much, and the road lay west of Onabasha. Ajax, stop that! There's no use to object. You know you think that horse is nice company for you, and that two can feed you more than one. Don't be a hypocrite! Cease crying things you don't mean, and learn to love the people I do. Come on, old boy!"

The peacock came, but with feathers closely pressed and stepping daintily. As the bird advanced, the Harvester retreated, until he stood beside the Girl, and then he slipped some grain to her hand and she offered it. But Ajax would not be coaxed. He was too fat and well fed. He haughtily turned and marched away, screaming at intervals.

"Nasty temper!" commented the Harvester. "Never mind! He soon will become accustomed to you, and then he will love you as Belshazzar does. Feed the doves instead. They are friendly enough in all conscience. Do you notice that there is not a coloured feather among them? The squab that is hatched with one you may have for breakfast. Now let's go find something to eat, and I will finish the bridge so you can rest there to-night and watch the sun set on Singing Water."

So they went into the cabin and prepared food, and then the Harvester told the Girl to make herself so pretty that she would be a picture and come and talk to him while he finished the roof. She went to her room, found a pale lavender linen dress and put it on, dusted the pink powder thickly, and went where a wide bench made an inviting place in the shade. There she sat and watched her lightly expressed whim take shape.

"Soon as this is finished," said the Harvester, "I am going to begin on that tea table. I can make it in a little while, if you want it to match the other furniture."

"I do," said the Girl.

"Wonder if you could draw a plan showing how it should appear. I am a little shy on tea tables."

"I think I can."

The Harvester brought paper, pencil, and a shingle for a drawing pad.

"Now remember one thing," he said. "If you are in earnest about using those old blue dishes, this has got to be a big, healthy table. A little one will appear top heavy with them. It would be a good idea to set out what you want to use, arranged as you would like them, and let me take the top measurement that way."

"All right! I'll only indicate how its legs should be and we will find the size later. I could almost weep because that wonderful set is broken. If I had all of it I'd be so proud!"

The Girl bent over the drawing. The Harvester worked with his attention divided between her, the bridge, and the road. At last he saw the big red car creeping up the valley.

"Seems to be some one coming, Ruth! Guess it must be Doc. I'll go open the gate?"

"Yes," said the Girl. "I'm so glad. You won't forget to ask him to help me if he can?"

The Harvester wheeled hastily. "I won't forget!" he said, as he hurried to the gate. The car ran slowly, and the Girl could see him swing to the step and stand talking as they advanced. When they reached her they stopped and all of them came forward. She went to meet them. She shook hands with Mrs. Carey and then with the doctor.

"I am so glad you have come," she said.

"I hope you are not lonesome already," laughed the doctor.

"I don't think any one with brains to appreciate half of this ever could become lonely here," answered the Girl. "No, it isn't that."

"A-ha!" cried the doctor, turning to his wife. "You see that the beautiful young lady remembers me, and has been wishing I would come. I always said you didn't half appreciate me. What a place you are making, David! I'll run the car to the shade and join you."

For a long time they talked under the trees, then they went to see the new home and all its furnishings.

"Now this is what I call comfort," said the doctor. "David, build us a house exactly similar to this over there on the hill, and let us live out here also. I'd love it. Would you, Clara?"

"I don't know. I never lived in the country. One thing is sure: If I tried it, I'd prefer this to any other place I ever saw. David, won't you take me far enough up the hill that I can look from the top to the lake?"

"Certainly," said the Harvester. "Excuse us a little while, Ruth!"

As soon as they were gone the Girl turned to the doctor.

"Doctor Carey, David says you are great. Won't you exercise your art on me. I am not at all well, and oh! I'd so love to be strong and sound."

"Will you tell me," asked the doctor, "just enough to show me what caused the trouble?"

"Bad air and water, poor light and food at irregular times, overwork and deep sorrow; every wrong condition of life you could imagine, with not a ray of hope in the distance, until now. For the sake of the Harvester, I would be well again. Please, please try to cure me!"

So they talked until the doctor thought he knew all he desired, and then they went to see the gold flower garden.

"I call this simply superb," said he, taking a seat beneath the tree roof of her porch. "Young woman, I don't know what I'll do to you if you don't speedily grow strong here. This is the prettiest place I ever saw, and listen to the music of that bubbling, gurgling little creek!"

"Isn't he wonderful?" asked the Girl, looking up the hill, where the tall form of the Harvester could be seen moving around. "Just to see him, you would think him the essence of manly strength and force. And he is! So strong! Into the lake at all hours, at the dry-house, on the hill, grubbing roots, lifting big pillars to support a bridge roof, and with it all a fancy as delicate as any dreaming girl. Doctor, the fairies paint the flowers, colour the fruit, and frost the windows for him; and the winds carry pollen to tell him when his growing things are ready for the dry-house. I don't suppose I can tell you anything new about him; but isn't he a perpetual surprise? Never like any one else! And no matter how he startles me in the beginning, he always ends by convincing me, at least, that he is right."

"I never loved any other man as I do him," said the doctor. "I ushered him into the world when I was a young man just beginning to practise, and I've known him ever since. I know few men so scrupulously clean. Try to get well and make him happy, Mrs. Langston. He so deserves it."

"You may be sure I will," answered the Girl.

After the visitors had gone, the Harvester told her to place the old blue dishes as she would like to arrange them on her table, so he could get a correct idea of the size, and he left to put a few finishing strokes on the bridge cover. She went into the dining-room and opened the china closet. She knew from her peep in the work-room that there would be more pieces than she had seen before; but she did not think or hope that a full half dozen tea set and plates, bowl, platter, and pitcher would be waiting for her.

"Why Ruth, what made you tire yourself to come down? I intended to return in a few minutes."

"Oh Man!" cried the laughing Girl, as she clung pantingly to a bridge pillar for support, "I just had to come to tell you. There are fairies! Really truly ones! They have found the remainder of the willow dishes for me, and now there are so many it isn't going to be a table at all. It must be a little cupboard especially for them, in that space between the mantel and the bookcase. There should be a shining brass tea canister, and a wafer box like the arts people make, and I'll pour tea and tend the chafing dish and you can toast the bread with a long fork over the coals, and we will have suppers on the living-room table, and it will be such fun."

"Be seated!" cried the Harvester. "Ruth, that's the longest speech I ever heard you make, and it sounded, praise the Lord, like a girl. Did Doc say he would fix something for you?"

"Yes, such a lot of things! I am going to shut my eyes and open my mouth and swallow all of them. I'm going to be born again and forget all I ever knew before I came here, and soon I will be tagging you everywhere, begging you to suggest designs for my pencil, and I'll simply force life to come right for you."

The Harvester smiled.

"Sounds good!" he said. "But, Ruth, I'm a little dubious about force work. Life won't come right for me unless you learn to love me, and love is a stubborn, contrary bulldog element of our nature that won't be driven an inch. It wanders as the wind, and strikes us as it will. You'll arrive at what I hope for much sooner if you forget it and amuse yourself and be as happy as you can. Then, perhaps all unknown to you, a little spark of tenderness for me will light in your breast; and if it ever does we will buy a fanning mill and put it in operation, and we'll raise a flame or know why."

"And there won't be any force in that?"

"What you can't compel is the start. It's all right to push any growth after you have something to work on."

"That reminds me," said the Girl, "there is a question I want to ask you."

"Go ahead!" said the Harvester, glancing at her as he hewed a joist.

She turned away her face and sat looking across the lake for a long time.

"Is it a difficult question, Ruth?" inquired the Harvester to help her.

"Yes," said the Girl. "I don't know how to make you see."

"Take any kind of a plunge. I'm not usually dense."

"It is really quite simple after all. It's about a girl—a girl I knew very well in Chicago. She had a problem—and it worried her dreadfully, and I just wondered what you would think of it."

The Harvester shifted his position so that he could watch the side of the averted face.

"You'll have to tell me, before I can tell you," he suggested.

"She was a girl who never had anything from life but work and worry. Of course, that's the only kind I'd know! One day when the work was most difficult, and worry cut deepest, and she really thought she was losing her mind, a man came by and helped her. He lifted her out, and rescued all that was possible for a man to save to her in honour, and went his way. There wasn't anything more. Probably there never would be. His heart was great, and he stooped and pitied her gently and passed on. After a time another man came by, a good and noble man, and he offered her love so wonderful she hadn't brains to comprehend how or why it was."

The Girl's voice trailed off as if she were too weary to speak further, while she leaned her head against a pillar and gazed with dull eyes across the lake.

"And your question," suggested the Harvester at last.

She roused herself. "Oh, the question! Why this—if in time, and after she had tried and tried, love to equal his simply would not come would—would—she be wrong to PRETEND she cared, and do the very best she could, and hope for real love some day? Oh David, would she?"

The Harvester's face was whiter than the Girl's. He pounded the chisel into the joist savagely.

"Would she, David?"

"Let me understand you clearly," said the man in a dry, breathless voice. "Did she love this first man to whom she came under obligations?"

The Girl sat gazing across the lake and the tortured Harvester stared at her.

"I don't know," she said at last. "I don't know whether she knew what love was or ever could. She never before had known a man; her heart was as undeveloped and starved as her body. I don't think she realized love, but there was a SOME-THING. Every time she would feel most grateful and long for the love that was offered her, that 'something' would awake and hurt her almost beyond endurance. Yet she knew he never would come. She knew he did not care for her. I don't know that she felt she wanted him, but she was under such obligations to him that it seemed as if she must wait to see if he might not possibly come, and if he did she should be free."

"If he came, she preferred him?"

"There was a debt she had to pay—if he asked it. I don't know whether she preferred him. I do know she had no idea that he would come, but the POSSIBILITY was always before her. If he didn't come in time, would she be wrong in giving all she had to the man who loved her?"

The Harvester's laugh was short and sharp.

"She had nothing to give, Ruth! Talk about worm-wood, colocynth apples, and hemlock! What sort of husks would that be to offer a man who gave honest love? Lie to him! Pretend feeling she didn't experience. Endure him for the sake of what he offered her? Well I don't know how calmly any other man would take that proceeding, Ruth, but tell your friend for me, that if I offered a woman the deep, lasting, and only loving passion of my heart, and she gave back a lie and indifferent lips, I'd drop her into the deepest hole of my lake and take my punishment cheerfully."

"But if it would make him happy? He deserves every happiness, and he need never know!"

The Harvester's laugh raised to an angry roar.

"You simpleton!" he cried roughly. "Do you know so little of human passion in the heart that you think love can be a successful assumption? Good Lord, Ruth! Do you think a man is made of wood or stone, that a woman's lips in her first kiss wouldn't tell him the truth? Why Girl, you might as well try to spread your tired arms and fly across the lake as to attempt to pretend a love you do not feel. You never could!"

"I said a girl I knew!"

"'A Girl you knew,' then! Any woman! The idea is monstrous. Tell her so and forget it. You almost scared the life out of me for a minute, Ruth. I thought it was going to be you. But I remember your debt is to be paid with the first money you earn, and you can not have the slightest idea what love is, if you honestly ask if it can be simulated. No ma'am! It can't! Not possibly! Not ever! And when the day comes that its fires light your heart, you will come to me, and tell of a flood of delight that is tingling from the soles of your feet through every nerve and fibre of your body, and you will laugh with me at the time when you asked if it could be imitated successfully. No, ma'am! Now let me help you to the cabin, serve a good supper, and see you eat like a farmer."

All evening the Harvester was so gay he kept the Girl laughing and at last she asked him the cause.

"Relief, honey! Relief!" cried the man. "You had me paralyzed for a minute, Ruth. I thought you were trying to tell me that there was some one so possessing your heart that it failed every time you tried to think about caring for me. If you hadn't convinced me before you finished that love never has touched you, I'd be the saddest man in the world to-night, Ruth."

The Girl stared at him with wide eyes and silently turned away.

Then for a week they worked out life together in the woods. The Harvester was the housekeeper and the cook. He added to his store many delicious broths and stimulants he brought from the city. They drove every day through the cool woods, often rowed on the lake in the evenings, walked up the hill to the oak and scattered fresh flowers on the two mounds there, and sat beside them talking for a time. The Harvester kept up his work with the herbs, and the little closet for the blue dishes was finished. They celebrated installing them by having supper on the living-room table, with the teapot on one end, and the pitcher full of bellflowers on the other.

The Girl took everything prescribed for her, bathed, slept all she could, and worked for health with all the force of her frail being, and as the days went by it seemed to the Harvester her weight grew lighter, her hands hotter, and she drove herself to a gayety almost delirious. He thought he would have preferred a dull, stupid sleep of malaria. There was colour in plenty on her cheeks now, and sometimes he found her wrapped in the white shawl at noon on the warmest days Medicine Woods knew in early August; and on cool nights she wore the thinnest clothing and begged to be taken on the lake. The Careys came out every other evening and the doctor watched and worked, but he did not get the results he desired. His medicines were not effective.

"David," he said one evening, "I don't like the looks of this. Your wife has fever I can't break. It is eating the little store of vitality she has right out of her, and some of these days she is coming down with a crash. She should yield to the remedies I am giving her. She acts to me like a woman driven wild by trouble she is concealing. Do you know anything that worries her?"

"No," said the Harvester, "but I'll try to find out if it will help you in your work."

After they were gone he left the Girl lying in the swing guarded by the dog, and went across the marsh on the excuse that he was going to a bed of thorn apple at the foot of the hill. There he sat on a log and tried to think. With the mists of night rising around him, ghosts arose he fain would have escaped. "What will you give me in cold cash to tell you who she is, and who her people are?" Times untold in the past two weeks he had smothered, swallowed, and choked it down. That question she had wanted to ask—was it for a girl she had known, or was it for herself? Days of thought had deepened the first slight impression he so bravely had put aside, not into certainty, but a great fear that she had meant herself. If she did, what was he to do? Who was the man? There was a debt she had to pay if he asked it? What debt could a woman pay a man that did not involve money? Crouched on a log he suffered and twisted in agonizing thought. At last he arose and returned to the cabin. He carried a few frosty, blue-green leaves of velvet softness and unusual cutting, prickly thorn apples full of seeds, and some of the smoother, more yellowish-green leaves of the jimson weed, to give excuse for his absence.

"Don't touch them," he warned as he came to her. "They are poison and have disagreeable odour. But we are importing them for medicinal purposes. On the far side of the marsh, where the ground rises, there is a waste place just suited to them, and so long as they will seed and flourish with no care at all, I might as well have the price as the foreign people who raise them. They don't bring enough to make them worth cultivating, but when they grow alone and with no care, I can make money on the time required to clip the leaves and dry the seeds. I must go wash before I come close to you."

The next day he had business in the city, and again she lay in the swing and talked to the dog while the Harvester was gone. She was startled as Belshazzar arose with a gruff bark. She looked down the driveway, but no one was coming. Then she followed the dog's eyes and saw a queer, little old woman coming up the bank of Singing Water from the north. She remembered what the Harvester had said, and rising she opened the screen and went down the path. As the Girl advanced she noticed the scrupulous cleanliness of the calico dress and gingham apron, and the snowy hair framing a bronzed face with dancing dark eyes.

"Are you David's new wife?" asked Granny Moreland with laughing inflection.

"Yes," said the Girl. "Come in. He told me to expect you. I am so sorry he is away, but we can get acquainted without him. Let me help you."

"I don't know but that ought to be the other way about. You don't look very strong, child."

"I am not well," said the Girl, "but it's lovely here, and the air is so fine I am going to be better soon. Take this chair until you rest a little, and then you shall see our pretty home, and all the furniture and my dresses."

"Yes, I want to see things. My, but David has tried himself! I heard he was just tearin' up Jack over here, and I could get the sound of the hammerin', and one day he asked me to come and see about his beddin'. He had that Lizy Crofter to wash for him, but if I hadn't jest stood over her his blankets would have been ruined. She's no more respect for fine goods than a pig would have for cream pie. I hate to see woollens abused, as if they were human. My, but things is fancy here since what David planted is growin'! Did you ever live in the country before?"

"No."

"Where do you hail from?"

"Well not from the direction of hail," laughed the Girl. "I lived in Chicago, but we were—were not rich, and so I didn't know the luxury of the city; just the lonely, difficult part."

"Do you call Chicago lonely?"

"A thousand times more so than Medicine Woods. Here I know the trees will whisper to me, and the water laughs and sings all day, and the birds almost split their throats making music for me; but I can imagine no loneliness on earth that will begin to compare with being among the crowds and crowds of a large city and no one has a word or look for you. I miss the sea of faces and the roar of life; at first I was almost wild with the silence, but now I don't find it still any more; the Harvester is teaching me what each sound means and they seem to be countless."

"You think, then, you'll like it here?"

"I do, indeed! Any one would. Even more than the beautiful location, I love the interesting part of the Harvester's occupation. I really think that gathering material to make medicines that will allay pain is the very greatest of all the great work a man can do."

"Good!" cried Granny Moreland, her dark eyes snapping. "I've always said it! I've tried to encourage David in it. And he's just capital at puttin' some of his stuff in shape, and combinin' it in as good medicine as you ever took. This spring I was all crippled up with the rheumatiz until I wanted to holler every time I had to move, and sometimes it got so aggravatin' I'm not right sure but I done it. 'Long comes David and says, 'I can fix you somethin',' and bless you, if the boy didn't take the tucks out of me, until here I am, and tickled to pieces that I can get here. This time last year I didn't care if I lived or not. Now seems as if I'm caperish as a three weeks' lamb. I don't see how a man could do a bigger thing than to stir up life in you like that."

"I think this place makes an especial appeal to me, because, shortly before I came, I had to give up my mother. She was very ill and suffered horribly. Every time I see David going to his little laboratory on the hill to work a while I slip away and ask God to help him to fix something that will ease the pain of humanity as I should like to have seen her relieved."

"Why you poor child! No wonder you are lookin' so thin and peaked!"

"Oh I'll soon be over that," said the Girl. "I am much better than when I came. I'll be coming over to trade pie with you before long. David says you are my nearest neighbour, so we must be close friends."

"Well bless your big heart! Now who ever heard of a pretty young thing like you wantin' to be friends with a plain old country woman?"

"Why I think you are lovely!" cried the Girl. "And all of us are on the way to age, so we must remember that we will want kindness then more than at any other time. David says you knew his mother. Sometime won't you tell me all about her? You must very soon. The Harvester adored her, and Doctor Carey says she was the noblest woman he ever knew. It's a big contract to take her place. Maybe if you would tell me all you can remember I could profit by much of it."

Granny Moreland watched the Girl keenly.

"She wa'ant no ordinary woman, that's sure," she commented. "And she didn't make no common man out of her son, either. I've always contended she took the job too serious, and wore herself out at it, but she certainly done the work up prime. If she's above cloud leanin' over the ramparts lookin' down—though it gets me as to what foundation they use or where they get the stuff to build the ramparts—but if they is ramparts, and she's peekin' over them, she must take a lot of solid satisfaction in seeing that David is not only the man she fought and died to make him, but he's give her quite a margin to spread herself on. She 'lowed to make him a big man, but you got to know him close and plenty 'fore it strikes you jest what his size is. I've watched him pretty sharp, and tried to help what I could since Marthy went, and I'm frank to say I druther see David happy than to be happy myself. I've had my fling. The rest of the way I'm willin' to take what comes, with the best grace I can muster, and wear a smilin' face to betoken the joy I have had; but it cuts me sore to see the young sufferin'."

"Do you think David is unhappy?" asked the Girl eagerly.

"I don't see how he could be!" cried the old lady. "Of course he ain't! 'Pears as if he's got everythin' to make him the proudest, best satisfied of men. I'll own I was mighty anxious to see you. I know the kind o' woman it would take to make

David miserable, and it seems sometimes as if men—that is good men—are plumb, stone blind when it comes to pickin' a woman. They jest hitch up with everlastin' misery easy as dew rolling off a cabbage leaf. It's sech a blessed sight to see you, and hear your voice and know you're the woman anybody can see you be. Why I'm so happy when I set here and con-tem'-plate you, I want to cackle like a pullet announcin' her first egg. Ain't this porch the purtiest place?"

"Come see everything," invited the Girl, rising.

Granny Moreland followed with alacrity.

"Bare floors!" she cried. "Wouldn't that best you? I saw they was finished capital when I was over, but I 'lowed they'd be covered afore you come. Don't you like nice, flowery Brissels carpets, honey?"

"No I don't," said the Girl. "You see, when rugs are dusty they can be rolled, carried outside, and cleaned. The walls can be wiped, the floors polished, and that way a house is always fresh. I can keep this shining, germ proof, and truly clean with half the work and none of the danger of heavy carpets and curtains."

"I don't doubt but them is true words," said Granny Moreland earnestly. "Work must be easier and sooner done than it was in my day, or people jest couldn't have houses the size of this or the time to gad that women have now. From the looks of the streets of Onabasha, you wouldn't think a woman 'ud had a baby to tend, a dinner pot a-bilin', or a bakin' of bread sence the flood. And the country is jest as bad as the city. We're a apin' them to beat the monkeys at a show. I hardly got a neighbour that ain't got figgered Brissels carpet, a furnace, a windmill, a pianny, and her own horse and buggy. Several's got autermobiles, and the young folks are visitin' around a-ridin' the trolleys, goin' to college, and copyin' city ways. Amos Peters, next to us; goes bareheaded in the hay field, and wears gloves to pitch and plow in. I tell him he reminds me of these city women that only wears the lower half of a waist and no sleeves, and a yard of fine goods moppin' the floors. Well if that don't beat the nation! Ain't them Marthy's old blue dishes?"

"Let me show you!" The Girl opened the little cupboard and exhibited the willow ware. The eyes of the old woman began to sparkle.

"Foundation or no foundation, I do hope them ramparts is a go!" she cried. "If Marthy Langston is squintin' over them and she sees her old chany put in a fine cupboard, and her little shawl round as purty a girl as ever stepped, and knows her boy is gittin' what he deserves, good Lord, she'll be like to oust the Almighty, and set on the throne herself! 'Bout everythin' in life was a disappointment to her, 'cept David. Now if she could see this! Won't I rub it into the neighbours? And my boys' wives!"

"I don't understand," said the bewildered Girl.

"'Course you don't, honey," explained the visitor. "It's like this: I don't know anybody, man or woman, in these parts, that ain't rampagin' for CHANGE. They ain't one of them that would live in a log cabin, though they's not a house in twenty miles of here that fits its surroundin's and looks so homelike as this. They run up big, fancy brick and frame things, all turns and gables and gay as frosted picnic pie, and work and slave to git these very carpets you say ain't healthy, and the chairs you say you wouldn't give house room, an' they use their grandmother's chany for bakin', scraps, and grease dishes, and hide it if they's visitors. All of them strainin' after something they can't afford, and that ain't healthy when they git it, because somebody else is doin' the same thing. Mary Peters says she is afeared of her life in their new steam wagon, and she says Andy gits so narvous runnin' it, he jest keeps on a-jerkin' and drivin' all night, and she thinks he'll soon go to smash himself, if the machine doesn't beat him. But they are keepin' it up, because Graceston's is, and so it goes all over the country. Now I call it a slap right in the face to have a Chicagy woman come to the country to live and enjoy a log cabin, bare floors, and her man's grandmother's dishes. If there ain't Marthy's old blue coverlid also carefully spread on a splinter new sofy. Landy, I can't wait to get to my son John's! He's got a woman that would take two coppers off the collection plate while she was purtendin' to put on one, if she could, and then spend them for a brass pin or a string of glass beads. Won't her eyes bung when I tell her about this? She wanted my Peter Hartman kiver for her ironin' board. Show me the rest!"

"This is the dining-room," said the Girl, leading the way.

Granny Moreland stepped in and sent her keen eyes ranging over the floor, walls, and furnishings. She sank on a chair and said with a chuckle, "Now you go on and tell me all about it, honey. Jest what things are and why you fixed them, and how they are used."

The Girl did her best, and the old woman nodded in delighted approval.

"It's the purtiest thing I ever saw," she announced. "A minute ago, I'd 'a' said them blue walls back there, jest like October skies in Indian summer, and the brown rugs, like leaves in the woods, couldn't be beat; but this green and yaller is purtier yet. That blue room will keep the best lookin' part of fall on all winter, and with a roarin' wood fire, it'll be capital, and no mistake; but this here is spring, jest spring eternal, an' that's best of all. Looks like it was about time the leaves was bustin' and things pushin' up. It wouldn't surprise me a mite to see a flock of swallers come sailin' right through these winders. And here's a place big enough to lay down and rest a spell right handy to the kitchen, where a-body gits tiredest, without runnin' a half mile to find a bed, and in the mornin' you can look down to the 'still waters'; and in the afternoon, when the sun gits around here, you can pull that blind and 'lift your eyes to the hills,' like David of the Bible says. My, didn't he say the purtiest things! I never read nothin' could touch him!"

"Have you seen the Psalms arranged in verse as we would write it now?"

"You don't mean to tell me David's been put into real poetry?"

"Yes. Some Bibles have all the poetical books in our forms of verse."

"Well! Sometimes I git kind o' knocked out! As a rule I hold to old ways. I think they're the healthiest and the most faver'ble to the soul. But they's some changes come along, that's got sech hard common-sense to riccomend them, that I wonder the past generations didn't see sooner. Now take this! An hour ago I'd told you I'd read my father's Bible to the end of my days. But if they's a new one that's got David, Solomon, and Job in nateral form, I'll have one, and I'll git a joy I never expected out of life. I ain't got so much poetry in me, but it always riled me to read, '7. The law of the Lord is perfect, covertin' the soul. 8. The statutes of the Lord are right. 9. The fear of the Lord is clean.' And so it goes on, 'bout as much figgers as they is poetry. Always did worry me. So if they make Bibles 'cordin' to common sense, I'll have one to-morrow if I have to walk to Onabasha to get it. Lawsy me! if you ain't gathered up Marthy's old pink tea set, and give it a show, too! Did you do that to please David, or do you honestly think them is nice dishes?"

"I think they are beautiful," laughed the Girl, sinking to a chair. "I don't know that it did please him. He had been studying the subject, but something saved him from buying anything until I came. I'd have felt dreadfully if he had gotten what he wanted."

"What did he want, honey?" asked the old lady in an awestruck whisper.

"Egg-shell china and cut glass."

"And you wouldn't let him! Woman! What do you want?"

"A set of tulip-yellow dishes, with Dutch little figures on them. They are so quaint and they would harmonize perfectly with this room."

The old lady laughed gleefully.

"My! I wouldn't 'a' missed this for a dollar," she cried. "It jest does my soul good. More'n that, if you really like Marthy's dishes and are going to take care of them and use them right, I'll give you mine, too. I ain't never had a girl. I've always hoped she'd 'a' had some jedgment of her own, and not been eternally apin', if I had, but the Lord may 'a' saved me many a disappointment by sendin' all mine boys. Not that I'm layin' the babies on to the Lord at all—I jest got into the habit of sayin' that, 'cos everybody else does, but all mine, I had a purty good idy how I got them. If a girl of mine wouldn't 'a' had more sense, raised right with me, I'd 'a' been purty bad cut up over it. Of course, I can't be held responsible for the girls my boys married, but t'other day Emmeline—that's John's wife—John is the youngest, and I sort o' cling to him—Emmeline she says to me, 'Mother, can't I have this old pink and green teapot?' My heart warmed right up to the child, and I says, 'What do you want it for, Emmeline?' And she says, 'To draw the tea in.' Cracky Dinah! That fool woman meant to set my grandmother's weddin' present from her pa and ma, dishes same as Marthy Washington used, on the stove to bile the tea in. I jest snorted! 'No,' says I, 'you can't! 'Fore I die,' says I, 'I'll meet up with some woman that'll love dishes and know how to treat them.' I think jest about as much of David as I do my own boys, and I don't make no bones of the fact that he's a heap more of a man. I'd jest as soon my dishes went to his children as to John's. I'll give you every piece I got, if you'll take keer of them."

"Would it be right?" wavered the girl.

"Right! Why, I'm jest tellin' you the fool wimmen would bile tea in them, make grease sassers of them, and use them to dish up the bakin' on! Wouldn't you a heap rather see them go into a cupboard like David's ma's is in, where they'd be taken keer of, if they was yours? I guess you would!"

"Well if you feel that way, and really want us to have them, I know David will build another little cupboard on the other side of the fireplace to put yours in, and I can't tell you how I'd love and care for them."

"I'll jest do it!" said Granny Moreland. "I got about as many blue ones as Marthy had an' mine are purtier than hers. And my lustre is brighter, for I didn't use it so much. Is this the kitchen? Well if I ever saw sech a cool, white place to cook in before! Ain't David the beatenest hand to think up things? He got the start of that takin' keer of his ma all his life. He sort of learned what a woman uses, and how it's handiest. Not that other men don't know; it's jest that they are too mortal selfish and keerless to fix things. Well this is great! Now when you bile cabbage and the wash, always open your winders wide and let the steam out, so it won't spile your walls."

"I'll be very careful," promised the Girl. "Now come see my bathroom, closet and bedroom."

"Well as I live! Ain't this fine. I'll bet a purty that if I'd 'a' had a room and a trough like this to soak in when I was wore to a frazzle, I wouldn't 'a' got all twisted up with rheumatiz like I am. It jest looks restful to see. I never washed in a place like this in all my days. Must feel grand to be wet all over at once! Now everybody ought to have sech a room and use it at all hours, like David does the lake. Did you ever see his beat to go swimmin'? He's always in splashin'! Been at it all his life. I used to be skeered when he was a little tyke. He soaked so much 'peared like he'd wash all the substance out of him, but it only made him strong."

"Has he ever been ill?"

"Not that I know of, and I reckon I'd knowed it if he had. Well what a clothespress! I never saw so many dresses at once. Ain't they purty? Oh I wish I was young, and could have one like that yaller. And I'd like to have one like your lavender right now. My! You are lucky to have so many nice clothes. It's a good thing most girls haven't got them, or they'd stand primpin' all day tryin' to decide which one to put on. I don't see how you tell yourself."

"I wear the one that best hides how pale I am," answered the Girl. "I use the colours now. When I grow plump and rosy, I'll wear the white."

Granny Moreland dropped on the couch and assured herself that it was Martha's pink Peter Hartman. Then she examined the sunshine room.

"Well I got to go back to the start," she said at last. "This beats the dinin'-room. This is the purtiest thing I ever saw. Oh I do hope they ain't so run to white in Heaven as some folks seem to think! Used to be scandalized if a-body took any-thin' but a white flower to a funeral. Now they tell me that when Jedge Stilton's youngest girl come from New York to her pa's buryin' she fetched about a wash tub of blood-red roses. Put them all over him, too! Said he loved red roses livin' and so he was goin' to have them when he passed over. Now if they are lettin' up a little on white on earth, mebby some of the stylish ones will carry the fashion over yander. If Heaven is like this, I won't spend none of my time frettin' about the foundations. I'll jest forget there is any, even if we do always have to be so perticler to get them solid on earth. Talk of gold harps! Can't you almost hear them? And listen to the birds and that water! Say, you won't get lonesome here, will you?"

"Indeed no!" answered the Girl. "Wouldn't you like to lie on my beautiful couch that the Harvester made with his own hands, and I'll spread Mother Langs-ton's coverlet over you and let you look at all my pretty things while I slip away a few minutes to something I'd like to do?"

"I'd love to!" said the old woman. "I never had a chance at such fine things. David told me he was makin' your room all himself, and that he was goin' to fill it chuck full of everythin' a girl ever used, and I see he done it right an' proper. Away last March he told me he was buildin' for you, an' I hankered so to have a woman here again, even though I never s'posed she'd be sociable like you, that I egged him on jest all I could. I never would 'a' s'posed the boy could marry like this—all by himself."

The Girl went to the ice chest to bring some of the fruit juice, chilled berries, and to the pantry for bread and wafers to make a dainty little lunch that she placed on the veranda table; and then she and Granny Moreland talked, until the visitor said that she must go. The Girl went with her to the little bridge crossing Singing Water on the north. There the old lady took her hand.

"Honey," she said, "I'm goin' to tell you somethin'. I am so happy I can purt near fly. Last night I was comin' down the pike over there chasin' home a contrary old gander of mine, and I looked over on your land and I see David settin' on a log with his head between his hands a lookin' like grim death, if I ever see it. My heart plum stopped. Says I, 'She's a failure! She's a bustin' the boy's heart! I'll go straight over and tell her so.' I didn't dare bespeak him, but I was on nettles all night. I jest laid a-studyin' and a-studyin', and I says, 'Come mornin' I'll go straight and give her a curry-combin' that'll do her good.' And I started a-feelin' pretty grim, and here you came to meet me, and wiped it all out of my heart in a flash. It did look like the boy was grievin'; but I know now he was jest thinkin' up what to put together to take the ache out of some poor old carcass like mine. It never could have been about you. Like a half blind old fool I thought the boy was sufferin', and here he was only studyin'! Like as not he was thinkin' what to do next to show you how he loves you. What an old silly I was! I'll sleep like a log to-night to pay up for it. Good-bye, honey! You better go back and lay down a spell. You do look mortal tired."

The Girl said good-bye and staggering a few steps sank on a log and sat staring at the sky.

"Oh he was suffering, and about me!" she gasped. A chill began to shake her and feverish blood to race through her veins. "He does and gives everything; I do and give nothing! Oh why didn't I stay at Uncle Henry's until it ended? It wouldn't have been so bad as this. What will I do? Oh what will I do? Oh mother, mother! if I'd only had the courage you did."

She arose and staggered up the hill, passed the cabin and went to the oak. There she sank shivering to earth, and laid her face among the mosses. The frightened Harvester found her at almost dusk when he came from the city with the Dutch dishes, and helped a man launch a gay little motor boat for her on the lake.

"Why Ruth! Ruth-girl!" he exclaimed, kneeling beside her.

She lifted a strained, distorted face.

"Don't touch me! Don't come near me!" she cried. "It is not true that I am better. I am not! I am worse! I never will be better. And before I go I've got to tell you of the debt I owe; then you will hate me, and then I will be glad! Glad, I tell you! Glad! When you despise me? then I can go, and know that some day you will love a girl worthy of you. Oh I want you to hate me I am fit for nothing else."

She fell forward sobbing wildly and the Harvester tried in vain to quiet her. At last he said, "Well then tell me, Ruth. Remember I don't want to hear what you have to say. I will believe nothing against you, not even from your own lips, when you are feverish and excited as now, but if it will quiet you, tell me and have it over. See, I will sit here and listen, and when you have finished I'll pick you up and carry you to your room, and I am not sure but I will kiss you over and over. What is it you want to tell me, Ruth?"

She sat up panting and pushed back the heavy coils of hair.

"I've got to begin away at the beginning to make you see," she said. "The first thing I can remember is a small, such a small room, and mother sewing and sometimes a man I called father. He was like Henry Jameson made over tall and smooth, and more, oh, much more heartless! He was gone long at a time, and always we had most to eat, and went oftener to the parks, and were happiest with him away. When I was big enough to understand, mother told me that she had met him and cared for him when she was an inexperienced girl. She must have been very, very young, for she was only a girl as I first remember her, and oh! so lovely, but with the saddest face I ever saw. She said she had a good home and every luxury, and her parents adored her; but they knew life and men, and they would not allow him in their home, and so she left it with him, and he married her and tried to force them to accept him, and they would not. At first she bore it. Later she found him out, and appealed to them, but they were away or would not forgive, and she was a proud thing, and would not beg more after she had said she was wrong, and would they take her back.

"I grew up and we were girls together. We embroidered, and I drew, and sometimes we had little treats and good times, and my father did not come often, and we got along the best we could. Always it was worse on her, because she was not so strong as I, and her heart was secretly breaking for her mother, and she was afraid he would come back any hour. She was tortured that she could not educate me more than to put me through the high school. She wore herself out doing that, but she was wild for me to be reared and trained right. So every day she crouched over delicate laces and embroidery, and before and after school I carried it and got more, and in vacation we worked together. But living grew higher, and she became ill, and could not work, and I hadn't her skill, and the drawings didn't bring much, and I'd no tools—"

"Ruth, for mercy sake let me take you in my arms. If you've got to tell this to find peace, let me hold you while you do it."

"Never again," said the Girl. "You won't want to in a minute. You must hear this, because I can't bear it any longer, and it isn't fair to let you grieve and think me worth loving. Anyway, I couldn't earn what she did, and I was afraid, for a great city is heartless to the poor. One morning she fainted and couldn't get up. I can see the awful look in her eyes now. She knew what was coming. I didn't. I tried to be brave and to work. Oh it's no use to go on with that! It was just worse and worse. She was lovely and delicate, she was my mother, and I adored her. Oh Man! You won't judge harshly?"

"No!" cried the Harvester, "I won't judge at all, Ruth. I see now. Get it over if you must tell me."

"One day she had been dreadfully ill for a long time and there was no food or work or money, and the last scrap was pawned, and she simply would not let me notify the charities or tell me who or where her people were. She said she had sinned against them and broken their hearts, and probably they were dead, and I was desperate. I walked all day from house to house where I had delivered work, but it was no use; no one wanted anything I could do, and I went back frantic, and found her gnawing her fingers and gibbering in delirium. She did not know me, and for the first time she implored me for food.

"Then I locked the door and went on the street and I asked a woman. She laughed and said she'd report me and I'd be locked up for begging. Then I saw a man I passed sometimes. I thought he lived close. I went straight to him, and told him my mother was very ill, and asked him to help her. He told me to go to the proper authorities. I told him I didn't know who they were or where, and I had no money and she was a woman of refinement, and never would forgive me. I offered, if he would come to see her, get her some beef tea, and take care of her while she lived, that afterward—"

The Girl's frail form shook in a storm of sobs. At last she lifted her eyes to the Harvester's. "There must be a God, and somewhere at the last extremity He must come in. The man went with me, and he was a young doctor who had an office a few blocks away, and he knew what to do. He hadn't much himself, but for several weeks he divided and she was more comfortable and not hungry when she went. When it was over I dressed her the best I could in my graduation dress, and folded her hands, and kissed her good-bye, and told him I was ready to fulfill my offer; and oh Man!—He said he had forgotten!"

"God!" panted the Harvester.

"We couldn't bury her there. But I remembered my father had said he had a brother in the country, and once he had been to see us when I was very little, and the doctor telegraphed him, and he answered that his wife was sick, and if I was able to work I could come, and he would bury her, and give me a home. The doctor borrowed the money and bought the coffin you found her in. He couldn't do better or he would, for he learned to love her. He paid our fares and took us to the train. Before I started I went on my knees to him and worshipped him as the Almighty, and I am sure I told him that I always would be indebted to him, and any time he required I would pay. The rest you know."

"Have you heard from him, Ruth?"

"No."

"It WAS yourself the other day on the bridge?"

"Yes."

"Did he love you?"

"Not that I know of. No! Nobody but you would love a girl who appeared as I did then."

The Harvester strove to keep a set face, but his lips drew back from his teeth.

"Ruth, do you love him?"

"Love!" cried the Girl. "A pale, expressionless word! Adore would come closer! I tell you she was delirious with hunger, and he fed her. She was suffering horrors and he eased the pain. She was lifeless, and he kept her poor tired body from the dissecting table. I would have fulfilled my offer, and gone straight into the lake, but he spared me, Man! He spared me! Worship is a good word. I think I worship him. I tried to tell you. Before you got that license, I wanted you to know."

"I remember," said the Harvester. "But no man could have guessed that a girl with your face had agony like that in her heart, not even when he read deep trouble there."

"I should have told you then! I should have forced you to hear! I was wild with fear of Uncle Henry, and I had nowhere to go. Now you know! Go away, and the end will come soon."

The Harvester arose and walked a few steps toward the lake, where he paused stricken, but fighting for control. For him the light had gone out. There was nothing beyond. The one passion of his life must live on, satisfied with a touch from lips that loved another man. Broken sobbing came to him. He did not even have time to suffer. Stumblingly he turned and going to the Girl he picked her up, and sat on the bench holding her closely.

"Stop it, Ruth!" he said unsteadily. "Stop this! Why should you suffer so? I simply will not have it. I will save you against yourself and the world. You shall have all happiness yet; I swear it, my girl! You are all right. He was a noble man, and he spared you because he loved you, of course. I will make you well and rosy again, and then I will go and find him, and arrange everything for you. I have spared you, too, and if he doesn't want you to remain here with me, Mrs. Carey would be glad to have you until I can free you. Judges are human. It will be a simple matter. Hush, Ruth, listen to me! You shall be free! At once, if you say so! You shall have him! I will go and bring him here, and I will go away. Ruth, darling, stop crying and hear me. You will grow better, now that you have told me. It is this secret that has made you feverish and kept you ill. Ruth, you shall have happiness yet, if I have got to circle the globe and scale the walls of Heaven to find it for you."

She struggled from his arms and ran toward the lake. When the Harvester caught her, she screamed wildly, and struck him with her thin white hands. He lifted and carried her to the laboratory, where he gave her a few drops from a bottle and soon she became quiet. Then he took her to the sunshine room, laid her on the bed, locked the screens and her door, called Belshazzar to watch, and ran to the stable. A few minutes later with distended nostrils and indignant heart Betsy, under the flail of an unsparing lash, pounded down the hill toward Onabasha.

Chapter 17

Love Invades Science

The Harvester placed the key in the door and turned to Doctor Carey and the nurse.

"I drugged her into unconsciousness before I left, but she may have returned, at least partially. Miss Barnet, will you kindly see if she is ready for the doctor? You needn't be in the least afraid. She has no strength, even in delirium."

He opened the door, his head averted, and the nurse hurried into the room. The Girl on the bed was beginning to toss, moan, and mutter. Skilful hands straightened her, arranged the covers, and the doctor was called. In the living-room the Harvester paced in misery too deep for consecutive thought. As consciousness returned, the Girl grew wilder, and the nurse could not follow the doctor's directions and care for her. Then Doctor Carey called the Harvester. He went in and sitting beside the bed took the feverish, wildly beating hands in his strong, cool ones, and began stroking them and talking.

"Easy, honey," he murmured softly. "Lie quietly while I tell you. You mustn't tire yourself. You are wasting strength you need to fight the fever. I'll hold your hands tight, I'll stroke your head for you. Lie quietly, dear, and Doctor Carey and his head nurse are going to make you well in a little while. That's right! Let me do the moving; you lie and rest. Only rest and rest, until all the pain is gone, and the strong days come, and they are going to bring great joy, love, and peace, to my dear, dear girl. Even the moans take strength. Try just to lie quietly and rest. You can't hear Singing Water if you don't listen, Ruth."

"She doesn't realize that it is you or know what you say, David," said Doctor Carey gently.

"I understand," said the Harvester. "But if you will observe, you will see that she is quiet when I stroke her head and hands, and if you notice closely you will grant that she gets a word occasionally. If it is the right one, it helps. She knows my voice and touch, and she is less nervous and afraid with me. Watch a minute!"

The Harvester took both of the Girl's fluttering hands in one of his and with long, light strokes gently brushed them, and then her head, and face, and then her hands again, and in a low, monotonous, half sing-song voice he crooned, "Rest, Ruth, rest! It is night now. The moon is bridging Loon Lake, and the whip-poor-will is crying. Listen, dear, don't you hear him crying? Still, Girl, still! Just as quiet! Lie so quietly. The whip-poor-will is going to tell his mate he loves her, loves her so dearly. He is going to tell her, when you listen. That's a dear girl. Now he is beginning. He says, 'Come over the lake and listen to the song I'm singing to you, my mate, my mate, my dear, dear mate,' and the big night moths are flying; and the katydids are crying, positive and sure they are crying, a thing that's past denying. Hear them crying? And the ducks are cheeping, soft little murmurs while they're sleeping, sleeping. Resting, softly resting! Gently, Girl, gently! Down the hill comes Singing Water, laughing, laughing! Don't you hear it laughing? Listen to the big owl courting; it sees the coon out hunting, it hears the mink softly slipping, slipping, where the dews of night are dripping. And the little birds are sleeping, so still they are sleeping. Girls should be a-sleeping, like the birds a-sleeping, for to-morrow joy comes creeping, joy and life and love come creeping, creeping to my Girl. Gently, gently, that's a dear girl, gently! Tired hands rest easy, tired head lies still! That's the way to rest—"

On and on the even voice kept up the story. All over and around the lake, the length of Singing Water, the marsh folk found voices to tell of their lives, where it was a story of joy, rest, and love. Up the hill ranged the Harvester, through the forest where the squirrels slept, the owl hunted, the fire-flies flickered, the fairies squeezed flower leaves to make colour to paint the autumn foliage, and danced on toadstool platforms. Just so long as his voice murmured and his touch continued, so long the Girl lay quietly, and the medicines could act. But no other touch would serve, and no other voice would answer. If the harvester left the room five minutes to show the nurse how to light the fire, and where to find things, he returned to tossing, restless delirium.

"It's magic David," said Doctor Carey. "Magic!"

"It is love," said the Harvester. "Even crazed with fever, she recognizes its voice and touch. You've got your work cut out, Doc. Roll your sleeves and collect your wits. Set your heart on winning. There is one thing shall not happen. Get that straight in your mind, right now. And you too, Miss Barnet! There is nothing like fighting for a certainty. You may think the Girl is desperately ill, and she is, but make up your minds that you are here to fight for her life, and to save it. Save, do you understand? If she is to go, I don't need either of you. I can let her do that myself. You are here on a mission of life. Keep it before you! Life and health for this Girl is the prize you are going to win. Dig into it, and I'll pay the bills, and extra besides. If money is any incentive, I'll give you all I've got for life and health for the Girl. Are you doing all you know?"

"I certainly am, David."

"But when day comes you'll have to go back to the hospital and we may not know how to meet crises that will arise. What then? We should have a competent physician in the house until this fever breaks."

"I had thought of that, David. I will arrange to send one of the men from the hospital who will be able to watch symptoms and come for me when needed."

"Won't do!" said the Harvester calmly. "She has no strength for waiting. You are to come when you can, and remain as long as possible. The case is yours; your decisions go, but I will select your assistant. I know the man I want."

"Who is he, David?"

"I'll tell you when I learn whether I can get him. Now I want you to give the Girl the strongest sedative you dare, take off your coat, roll your sleeves, and see how well you can imitate my voice, and how much you have profited by listening to my song. In other words, before day calls, I want you to take my place so successfully that you deceive her, and give me time to make a trip to town. There are a few things that must be done, and I think I can work faster in the night. Will you?"

Doctor Carey bent over the bed. Gently he slipped a practised hand under the Harvester's and made the next stroke down the white arm. Gradually he took possession of the thin hands and his touch fell on the masses of dark hair. As the Harvester arose the doctor took the seat.

"You go on!" he ordered gruffly "I'll do better alone."

The Harvester stepped back. The doctor's touch was easy and the Girl lay quietly for an instant, then she moved restlessly.

"You must be still now," he said gently. "The moon is up, the lake is all white, and the birds are flying all around. Lie still or you'll make yourself worse. Stiller than that! If you don't you can't hear things courting. The ducks are quacking, the bull frogs are croaking, and everything. Lie still, still, I tell you!"

"Oh good Lord, Doc!" groaned the Harvester in desperation.

The Girl wrenched her hands free and her head rolled on the pillow.

"Harvester! Harvester!" she cried.

The doctor started to arise.

"Sit still!" commanded the Harvester. "Take her hands and go to work, idiot! Give her more sedative, and tell her I'm coming. That's the word, if she realizes enough to call for me."

The doctor possessed himself of the flying hands, and gently held and stroked them.

"The Harvester is coming," he said. "Wait just a minute, he's on the way. He is coming. I think I hear him. He will be here soon, very soon now. That's a good girl! Lie still for David. He won't like it if you toss and moan. Just as still, lie still so I can listen. I can't tell whether he is coming until you are quiet."

Then he said to the Harvester, "You see, I've got it now. I can manage her, but for pity sake, hurry man! Take the car! Jim is asleep on the back seat—Yes, yes, Girl! I'm listening for him. I think I hear him! I think he's coming!"

Here and there a word penetrated, and she lay more quietly, but not in the rest to which the Harvester had lulled her.

"Hurry man!" groaned the doctor in a whispered aside, and the Harvester ran to the car, awakened the driver and told him he had a clear road to Onabasha, to speed up.

"Where to?" asked the driver.

"Dickson, of the First National."

In a few minutes the car stopped before the residence and the Harvester made an attack on the front door. Presently the man came.

"Excuse me for routing you out at this time of night," said the Harvester, "but it's a case of necessity. I have an automobile here. I want you to go to the bank with me, and get me an address from your draft records. I know the rules, but I want the name of my wife's Chicago physician. She is delirious, and I must telephone him."

The cashier stepped out and closed the door.

"Nine chances out of ten it will be in the vault," he said.

"That leaves one that it won't," answered the Harvester. "Sometimes I've looked in when passing in the night, and I've noticed that the books are not always put away. I could see some on the rack to-night. I think it is there."

It was there, and the Harvester ordered the driver to hurry him to the telephone exchange, then take the cashier home and return and wait. He called the Chicago Information office.

"I want Dr. Frank Harmon, whose office address is 1509 Columbia Street. I don't know the 'phone number."

Then came a long wait, and after twenty minutes the blessed buzzing whisper, "Here's your party."

"Doctor Harmon?"

"Yes."

"You remember Ruth Jameson, the daughter of a recent patient of yours?"

"I do."

"Well my name is Langston. The Girl is in my home and care. She is very ill with fever, and she has much confidence in you. This is Onabasha, on the Grand Rapids and Indiana. You take the Pennsylvania at seven o'clock, telegraph ahead that you are coming so that they will make connection for you, change at twelve-twenty at Fort Wayne, and I will meet you here. You will find your ticket and a check waiting you at the Chicago depot. Arrange to remain a week at least. You will be paid all expenses and regular prices for your time. Will you come?"

"Yes."

"All right. Make no failure. Good-bye."

Then the Harvester left an order with the telephone company to run a wire to Medicine Woods the first thing in the morning, and drove to the depot to arrange for the ticket and check. In less than an hour he was holding the Girl's hands and crooning over her.

"Jerusalem!" said Doctor Carey, rising stiffly. "I'd rather undertake to cut off your head and put it back on than to tackle another job like that. She's quite delirious, but she has flashes, and at such times she knows whom she wants; the rest of the time it's a jumble and some of it is rather gruesome. She's seen dreadful illness, hunger, and there's a debt she's wild about. I told you something was back of this. You've got to find out and set her mind at ease."

"I know all about it," said the Harvester patiently between crooning sentences to the Girl. "But the crash came before I could convince her that it was all right and I could fix everything for her easily. If she only could understand me!"

"Did you find your man?"

"Yes. He will be here this afternoon."

"Quick work!"

"This takes quick work."

"Do you know anything about him?"

"Yes. He is a young fellow, just starting out. He is a fine, straight, manly man. I don't know how much he knows, but it will be enough to recognize your ability and standing, and to do what you tell him. I have perfect confidence in him. I want you to come back at one, and take my place until I go to meet him."

"I can bring him out."

"I have to see him myself. There are a few words to be said before he sees the Girl."

"David, what are you up to?"

"Being as honourable as I can. No man gets any too decent, but there is no law against doing as you would be done by, and being as straight as you know how. When I've talked to him, I'll know where I am and I'll have something to say to you."

"David, I'm afraid—"

"Then what do you suppose I am?" said the Harvester. "It's no use, Doc. Be still and take what comes! The manner in which you meet a crisis proves you a whining cur or a man. I have got lots of respect for a dog, as a dog; but I've none for a man as a dog. If you've gathered from the Girl's delirium that I've made a mistake, I hope you have confidence enough in me to believe I'll right it, and take my punishment without whining. Go away, you make her worse. Easy, Girl, the world is all right and every one is sleeping now, so you should be at rest. With the day the doctor will come, the good doctor you know and like, Ruth. You haven't forgotten your doctor, Ruth? The kind doctor who cared for you. He will make you well, Ruth; well and oh, so happy! Harmon, Harmon, Doctor Harmon is coming to you, Girl, and then you will be so happy!"

"Why you blame idiot!" cried Doctor Carey in a harsh whisper. "Have you lost all the sense you ever had? Stop that gibber! She wants to hear about the birds and Singing Water. Go on with that woods line of talk; she likes that away the best. This stuff is making her restless. See!"

"You mean you are," said the Harvester wearily. "Please leave us alone. I know the words that will bring comfort. You don't."

He began the story all over again, but now there ran through it a continual refrain. "Your doctor is coming, the good doctor you know. He will make you well and strong, and he will make life so lovely for you."

He was talking without pause or rest when Doctor Carey returned in the afternoon to take his place. He brought Mrs. Carey with him, and she tried a woman's powers of soothing another woman, and almost drove the Girl to fighting frenzy. So the doctor made another attempt, and the Harvester raced down the hill to the city. He went to the car shed as the train pulled in, and stood at one side while the people hurried through the gate. He was watching for a young man with a travelling bag and perhaps a physician's satchel, who would be looking for some one.

"I think I'll know him," muttered the Harvester grimly. "I think the masculine element in me will pop up strongly and instinctively at the sight of this man who will take my Dream Girl from me. Oh good God! Are You sure You ARE good?"

In his brown khaki trousers and shirt, his head bare, his bronze face limned with agony he made no attempt to conceal, the Harvester, with feet planted firmly, and tightly folded arms, his head tipped slightly to one side, braced himself as he sent his keen gray eyes searching the crowd. Far away he selected his man. He was young, strong, criminally handsome, clean and alert; there was discernible anxiety on his face, and it touched the Harvester's soul that he was coming just as swiftly as he could force his way. As he passed the gates the Harvester reached his side.

"Doctor Harmon, I think," he said.

"Yes."

"This way! If you have luggage, I will send for it later."

The Harvester hurried to the car.

"Take the shortest cut and cover space," he said to the driver. The car kept to the speed limit until toward the suburbs.

Doctor Harmon removed his hat, ran his fingers through dark waving hair and yielded his body to the swing of the car. Neither man attempted to talk. Once the Harvester leaned forward and told the driver to stop on the bridge, and then sat silently. As the car slowed down, they alighted.

"Drive on and tell Doc we are here, and will be up soon," said the Harvester. Then he turned to the stranger. "Doctor Harmon, there's little time for words. This is my place, and here I grow herbs for medicinal houses."

"I have heard of you, and heard your stuff recommended," said the doctor.

"Good!" exclaimed the Harvester. "That saves time. I stopped here to make a required explanation to you. The day you sent Ruth Jameson to Onabasha, I saw her leave the train and recognized in her my ideal woman. I lost her in the crowd and it took some time to locate her. I found her about a month ago. She was miserable. If you saw what her father did to her and her mother in Chicago, you should have seen what his brother was doing here. The end came one day in my presence, when I paid her for ginseng she had found to settle her debt to you. He robbed her by force. I took the money from him, and he threatened her. She was ill then from heat, overwork, wrong food—every misery you can imagine heaped upon the dreadful conditions in which she came. It had been my intention to court and marry her if I possibly could. That day she had nowhere to go; she was wild with fear; the fever that is scorching her now was in her veins then. I did an insane thing. I begged her to marry me at once and come here for rest and protection. I swore that if she would, she should not be my wife, but my honoured guest, until she learned to love me and released me from my vow. She tried to tell me something; I had no idea it was anything that would make any real difference, and I wouldn't listen. Last night, when the fever was beginning to do its worst, she told me of your entrance into her life and what it meant to her. Then I saw that I had made a mistake. You were her choice, the man she could love, not me, so I took the liberty of sending for you. I want you to cure her, court her, marry her, and make her happy. God knows she has had her share of suffering. You recognize her as a girl of refinement?"

"I do."

"You grant that in health she would be lovelier than most women, do you not?"

"She was more beautiful than most in sickness and distress."

"Good!" cried the Harvester. "She has been here two weeks. I give you my word, my promise to her has been kept faithfully. As soon as I can leave her to attend to it, she shall have her freedom. That will be easy. Will you marry her?"

The doctor hesitated.

"What is it?" asked the Harvester.

"Well to be frank," said Doctor Harmon, "it is money! I'm only getting a start. I borrowed funds for my schooling and what I used for her. She is in every way attractive enough to be desired by any man, but how am I to provide a home and support her and pay these debts? I'll try it, but I am afraid it will be taking her back to wrong conditions again."

"If you knew that she owned a comfortable cottage in the suburbs, where it is cool and clean, and had, say a hundred a month of her own for the coming three years, could you see your way?"

"That would make all the difference in the world. I thought seriously of writing her. I wanted to, but I concluded I'd better work as hard as I could for some practice first, and see if I could make a living for two, before I tried to start anything. I had no idea she would not be comfortably cared for at her uncle's."

"I see," said the Harvester. "If I had kept out, life would have come right for her."

"On the contrary," said the doctor, "it appears very probable that she would not be living."

"It is understood between us, then, that you will court and marry her so soon as she is strong enough?"

"It is understood," agreed the doctor.

"Will you honour me by taking my hand?" asked the Harvester. "I scarcely had hoped to find so much of a man. Now come to your room and get ready for the stiffest piece of work you ever attempted."

The Harvester led the way to the guest chamber over looking the lake, and installed its first occupant. Then he hurried to the Girl. The doctor was holding her head and one hand, his wife the other, and the nurse her feet. It took the Harvester ten strenuous minutes to make his touch and presence known and to work quiet. All over he began crooning his story of rest, joy, and love. He broke off with a few words to introduce Doctor Harmon to the Careys and the nurse, and then calmly continued while the other men stood and watched him.

"Seems rather cut out for it," commented Doctor Harmon.

"I never yet have seen him attempt anything that he didn't appear cut out for," answered Doctor Carey.

"Will she know me?" inquired the young man, approaching the bed.

When the Girl's eyes fell on him she grew rigid and lay staring at him. Suddenly with a wild cry she struggled to rise.

"You have come!" she cried. "Oh I knew you would come! I felt you would come! I cannot pay you now! Oh why didn't you come sooner?"

The young doctor leaned over and took one of the white hands from the Harvester, stroking it gently.

"Why you did pay, Ruth! How did you come to forget? Don't you remember the draft you sent me? I didn't come for money; I came to visit you, to nurse you, to do all I can to make you well. I am going to take care of you now so finely you'll be out on the lake and among the flowers soon. I've got some medicine that makes every one well. It's going to make you strong, and there's something else that's going to make you happy; and me, I'm going to be the proudest man alive."

He reached over and took possession of the other hand, stroking them softly, and the Girl lay tensely staring at him and gradually yielding to his touch and voice. The Harvester arose, and passing around the bed, he placed a chair for Doctor Harmon and motioning for Doctor Carey left the room. He went to the shore to his swimming pool, wearily dropped on the bench, and stared across the water.

"Well thank God it worked, anyway!" he muttered.

"What's that popinjay doing here?" thundered Doctor Carey. "Got some medicine that cures everybody. Going to make her well, is he? Make the cows, and the ducks, and the chickens, and the shitepokes well, and happy—no name for it! After this we are all going to be well and happy! You look it right now, David! What under Heaven have you done?"

"Left my wife with the man she loves, and to whom I release her, my dear friend," said the Harvester. "And it's so easy for me that you needn't give making it a little harder, any thought."

"David, forgive me!" cried Doctor Carey. "I don't understand this. I'm almost insane. Will you tell me what it means?"

"Means that I took advantage of the Girl's illness, utter loneliness, and fear, and forced her into marrying me for shelter and care, when she loved and wanted another man, who was preparing to come to her. He is her Chicago doctor, and fine in every fibre, as you can see. There is only one thing on earth for me to do, and that is to get out of their way, and I'll do it as soon as she is well; but I vow I won't leave her poor, tired body until she is, not even for him. I thought sure I could teach her to love me! Oh but this is bitter, Doc!"

"You are a consummate fool to bring him here!" cried Doctor Carey. "If she is too sick to realize the situation now, she will be different when she is normal again. Any sane girl that wouldn't love you, David, ain't fit for anything!"

"Yes, I'm a whale of a lover!" said the Harvester grimly. "Nice mess I've made of it. But there is no real harm done. Thank God, Harmon was not the only white man."

"David, what do you mean?"

"Is it between us, Doc?"

"Yes."

"For all time?"

"It is."

The Harvester told him. He ended, "Give the fellow his dues, Doc. He had her at his mercy, utterly alone and unprotected, in a big city. There was not a living soul to hold him to account. He added to his burdens, borrowed more money, and sent her here. He thought she was coming to the country where she would be safe and well cared for until he could support her. I did the remainder. Now I must undo it, that's all! But you have got to go in there and practise with him. You've got to show him every courtesy of the profession. You must go a little over the rules, and teach him all you can. You will have to stifle your feelings, and be as much of a man as it is in you to be, at your level best."

"I'm no good at stifling my feelings!"

"Then you'll have to learn," said the Harvester. "If you'd lived through my years of repression in the woods you'd do the fellow credit. As I see it, his side of this is nearly as fine as you make it. I tell you she was utterly stricken, alone, and beautiful. She sought his assistance. When the end came he thought only of her. Won't you give a young fellow in a place like Chicago some credit for that? Can't you get through you what it means?"

Doctor Carey stood frowning in deep thought, but the lines of his face gradually changed.

"I suppose I've got to stomach him," he said.

The nurse came down the gravel path.

"Mr. Langston, Doctor Harmon asked me to call you," she said.

The Harvester arose and went to the sunshine room.

"What does he want, Molly?" asked the doctor.

"Wants to turn over his job," chuckled the nurse. "He held it about seven minutes in peace, and then she began to fret and call for the Harvester. He just sweat blood to pacify her, but he couldn't make it. He tried to hold her, to make love to her, and goodness knows what, but she struggled and cried, 'David,' until he had to give it up and send me."

"Molly," said Doctor Carey, "we've known the Harvester a long time, and he is our friend, isn't he?"

"Of course!" said the nurse.

"We know this is the first woman he ever loved, probably ever will, as he is made. Now we don't like this stranger butting in here; we resent it, Molly. We are on the side of our friend, and we want him to win. I'll grant that this fellow is fine, and that he has done well, but what's the use in tearing up arrangements already made? And so suitable! Now Molly, you are my best nurse, and a good reliable aid in times like this. I gave you instructions an hour ago. I'll add this to them. YOU ARE ON THE HARVESTER'S SIDE. Do you understand? In this, and the days to come, you'll have a thousand chances to put in a lick with a sick woman. Put them in as I tell you."

"Yes, Doctor Carey."

"And Molly! You are something besides my best nurse. You're a smashing pretty girl, and your occupation should make you especially attractive to a young doctor. I'm sure this fellow is all right, so while you are doing your best with your patient for the Harvester, why not have a try for yourself with the doctor? It couldn't do any harm, and it might straighten out matters. Anyway, you think it over."

The nurse studied his face silently for a time, and then she began to laugh softly.

"He is up there doing his best with her," she said.

The doctor threw out his hands in a gesture of disdain, and the nurse laughed again; but her cheeks were pink and her eyes flashing as she returned to duty.

"Random shot, but it might hit something, you never can tell," commented the doctor.

The Harvester entered the Girl's room and stood still. She was fretting and raising her temperature rapidly. Before he reached the door his heart gave one great leap at the sound of her voice calling his name. He knew what to do, but he hesitated.

"She seems to have become accustomed to you, and at times does not remember me," said Doctor Harmon. "I think you had better take her again until she grows quiet."

The Harvester stepped to the bed and looked the doctor in the eye.

"I am afraid I left out one important feature in our little talk on the bridge," he said. "I neglected to tell you that in your fight for this woman's life and love you have a rival. I am he. She is my wife, and with the last fibre of my being I adore her. If you win, and she wants you to take her away, I will help you; but my heart goes with her forever. If by any chance it should occur that I have been mistaken or misinterpreted her delirium or that she has been deceived and finds she prefers me and Medicine Woods, to you and Chicago, when she has had opportunity to measure us man against man, you must understand that I claim her. So I say to you frankly, take her if you can, but don't imagine that I am passive. I'll help you if I know she wants you, but I fight you every inch of the way. Only it has got to be square and open. Do you understand?"

"You are certainly sufficiently clear."

"No man who is half a man sees the last chance of happiness go out of his life without putting up the stiffest battle he knows," said the Harvester grimly. "Ruth-girl, you are raising the fever again. You must be quiet."

With infinite tenderness he possessed himself of her hands and began stroking her hair, and in a low and soothing voice the story of the birds, flowers, lake, and woods went on. To keep it from growing monotonous the Harvester branched out and put in everything he knew. In the days that followed he held a position none could take from him. While the doctors fought the fever, he worked for rest and quiet, and soothed the tortured body as best he could, that the medicines might act.

But the fever was stubborn, and the remedies were slow; and long before the dreaded coming day the doctors and nurse were quietly saying to each other that when the crisis came the heart would fail. There was no vitality to sustain life. But they did not dare tell the Harvester. Day and night he sat beside the maple bed or stretched sleeping a few minutes on the couch while the Girl slept; and with faith never faltering and courage unequalled, he warned them to have their remedies and appliances ready.

"I don't say it's going to be easy," he said. "I just merely state that it must be done. And I'll also mention that, when the hour comes, the man who discovers that he could do something if he had digitalis, or a remedy he should have had ready and has forgotten, that man had better keep out of my sight. Make your preparations now. Talk the case over. Fill your hypodermics. Clean your air pumps. Get your hot-water bottles ready. Have system. Label your stuff large and set it conveniently. You see what is coming, be prepared!"

One day, while the Girl lay in a half-drugged, feverish sleep, the Harvester went for a swim. He dressed a little sooner than was expected and in crossing the living-room he heard Doctor Harmon say to Doctor Carey on the veranda, "What are we going to do with him when the end comes?"

The Harvester stepped to the door. "That won't be the question," he said grimly. "It will be what will *he* do with us?"

Then, with an almost imperceptible movement, he caught Doctor Harmon at the waist line, and lifted and dangled him as a baby, and then stood him on the floor. "Didn't hardly expect that much muscle, did you?" he inquired lightly. "And I'm not in what you could call condition, either. Instead of wasting any time on fool questions like that, you two go over your stuff and ask each other, have we got every last appliance known to physics and surgery? Have we got duplicates on hand in case we break delicate instruments like hypodermic syringes and that sort of thing? Engage yourselves with questions pertaining to life; that is your business. Instead of planning what you'll do in failure, bolster your souls against it. Granny Moreland beats you two put together in grip and courage."

The Harvester returned to his task, and the fight went on. At last the hour came when the temperature fell lower and lower. The feeble pulses flickered and grew indiscernible; a gray pallor hovered over the Girl, and a cold sweat stood on her temples.

"Now!" said the Harvester. "Exercise your calling! Fight like men or devils, but win you must."

They did work. They administered stimulants; applied heat to the chilled body; fans swept the room with vitalized air; hypodermics were used; and every last resort known to science was given a full test, and the weak heart throbbed slower and slower, and life ran out with each breath. The Harvester stood waiting with set jaws. He could detect no change for the better. At last he picked up a chilled hand and could discover no pulse, and the gray nails and the dark tips told a story of arrested circulation. He laid down the hand and faced the men.

"This is what you'd call the crisis, Doc?" he asked gently.

"Yes."

"Are you stemming it? Are you stemming it? Are you sure she is holding her own?"

Doctor Carey looked at him silently

"Have you done all you can do?" asked the Harvester.

"Yes."

"You believe her going out?"

"Yes."

The Harvester turned to Doctor Harmon. "Do you concur in that?"

"Yes."

Then to the nurse, "And you?"

"Yes."

"Then," said the Harvester, "all of you are useless. Get out of here. I don't want your atmosphere. If you can believe only in death, leave us! She is my wife, and if this is the end she belongs to me, and I will do as I choose with her. All of you go!"

The Harvester stepped to the bathroom door and called Granny Moreland. "Granny," he said, "science has turned tail, and left me in extremity. Fill your hot-water bottles and come in here with your heart big with hope and help me save my Dream Girl. She is breathing Granny; we've got to make her keep it up, that's all—just keep her breathing."

He returned to the sunshine room, placed a small table beside the bed, and on it a glass of water, spoon, and a hypodermic syringe. When Granny Moreland came he said: "Now you begin on her feet and rub with long, sweeping, upward strokes to drive the blood to her heart."

Around the Girl he piled hot-water bottles and breathlessly hung over her, rubbing her hands. He wiped the perspiration from her forehead, and then dropped by her bed and for a second laid his face on her cold palm.

"If I am wrong, Heaven forgive me," he prayed. "And you, oh, my darling Dream Girl, forgive me, but I am forced to try—God helping me! Amen."

He arose, took a small bottle from his pocket, filled the spoon with water, and measured into it three drops of liquid as yellow as gold. Then he held the spoon to the blue lips, and with his fingers worked apart the set teeth, and poured the medicine down her throat. Then they rubbed and muttered snatches of prayer for fifteen minutes when the Harvester administered another three drops. It might have been fancy, but it seemed to him her jaws were not so stiff. Faster flew his hands and he sent Granny Moreland to refill the hot bottles. When he gave the Girl the third dose he injected some of the liquid over her heart and of the glycerine the doctors had left, in the extremities. He released more air and began rubbing again.

The second hour started in the same way, and ended with slowly relaxing muscles and faint tinges of colour in the white cheeks. The feet were not so cold, and when the Harvester held the spoon he knew that the Girl made an effort to swallow, and he could see her eyelids tremble. Thereupon he pointed these signs to Granny, and implored her to rub and pray, and pray and rub, while he worked until the perspiration rolled down his gray face. At the end of the second hour he began decreasing the doses and shortening the time, and again he commenced in a low rumble his song of life and health, to encourage the Girl as consciousness returned.

Occasionally Doctor Carey opened the door slightly and peeped in to see if he were wanted, but he received no invitation to enter. The last time he left with the impression that the Harvester was raving, while he worked over a lifeless body. He had the Girl warmly covered and bent over her face and hands. At her feet crouched Granny Moreland, rubbing, still rubbing, beneath the covers, while in a steady stream the Harvester was pouring out his song. If he had listened an instant longer he would have recognized that the tone and the words had changed. Now it was, "Gently, breathe gently, Girl! Slowly, steadily, easily! Deeper, a little deeper, Ruth! Brave Girl, never another so wonderful! That's my Dream Girl coming from the shadows, coming to life's sunshine, coming to hope, coming to love! Deeper, just a little deeper! Smoothly and evenly! You are making it, Girl! You are making it! By all that is holy and glorious! Stick to it, Ruth, hold tight to me! I'll help you, dear! You are coming, coming back to life and love. Don't worry yourself trying too hard, if only you can send every breath as deeply as the last one, you can make it. You brave girl! You wonderful Dream Girl! Ah, Ruth, the name of this is victory!"

An hour before Doctor Carey had said to Doctor Harmon and the nurse, as he softly closed the door: "It is over and the Harvester is raving. We'll give him a little more time and see if he won't realize it himself. That will be easier for him than for us to try to tell him."

Now he opened the door, stared a second, and coming to the opposite side of the bed, he leaned over the Girl. Then he felt her feet. They were warm and slightly damp. A surprised look crept over his face. He gently reached for a hand that the Harvester yielded to him. It was warm, the blue tips becoming rosy, the wrist pulse discernible. Then he bent closer, touched her face, and saw the tremulous eyelids. He turned back the cover, and held his ear over her heart. When he straightened, "As God lives, she's got a chance, David!" he exulted in an awed whisper.

The Harvester lifted a graven face, down which the sweat of agony rolled, and his lips parted in a twitching smile. "Then this is where love beats the doctors, Carey!" he said.

"It is where love has ventured what science dares not. Love didn't do all of this. In the name of the Almighty, what did you give her, David?"

"Life!" cried the Harvester. "Life! Come on, Ruth, come on! Out of the valley come to me! You are well now, Girl! It's all over! The last trace of fever is gone, the last of the dull ache. Can you swallow just two more drops of bottled sunshine, Ruth?"

The flickering lids slowly opened, and the big black eyes looked straight into the Harvester's. He met them steadily, smiling encouragement.

"Hang on to each breath, dear heart!" he urged. "The fever is gone. The pain is over! Long life and the love you crave are for you. You've only to keep breathing a few more hours and the battle is yours. Glorious Girl! Noble! You are doing finely! Ruth, do you know me?"

Her lips moved.

"Don't try to speak," said the Harvester. "Don't waste breath on a word. Save the good oxygen to strengthen your tired body. But if you do know me, maybe you could smile, Ruth!"

She could just smile, and that was all. Feeble, flickering, transient, but as it crossed the living face the Harvester lifted her hands and kissed them over and over, back, palm, and finger tips.

"Now just one more drop, honey, and then a long rest. Will you try it again for me?"

She assented, and the Harvester took the bottle from his pocket, poured the drop, and held the spoon to willing lips. The big eyes were on him with a question. Then they fell to the spoon. The Harvester understood.

"Yes, it's mine! It's got sixty years of wonderful life in it, every one of them full of love and happiness for my dear Dream Girl. Can you take it, Ruth?"

Her lips parted, the wine of life passed between. She smiled faintly, and her eyelids dropped shut, but presently they opened again.

"David!"

"My Dream Girl!"

"Harvester?"

"Yes!"

"Medicine Man?"

"Don't, Ruth! Save every breath to help your heart."

"Life?"

"Life it is, Girl!" exulted the Harvester. "Long life! Love! Home! The man you love! Every happiness that ever came to a girl! Nothing shall be denied you! Nothing shall be lacking! It's all in your hands now, Ruth. We've all done everything we can; you must do the remainder. It's your work to send every breath as deeply as you can. Doc, release another tank of air. Are her feet warm, Granny? Let the nurse take your place now. And, honey, go to sleep! I'll keep watch for you. I'll measure each breath you draw. If they shorten or weaken, I'll wake you for more medicine. You can trust me! Always you can trust me, Ruth."

The Girl smiled and fell into a light, even slumber. Granny Moreland stumbled to the couch and rolled on it sobbing with nervous exhaustion. Doctor Carey called the nurse to take her place. Then he came to the Harvester's side and whispered, "Let me, David!"

The Harvester looked up with his queer grin, but he made no motion to arise.

"Won't you trust me, David? I'll watch as if it were my own wife."

"I wouldn't trust any man on earth, for the coming three hours," replied the Harvester. "If I keep this up that long, she is safe. Go and rest until I call you."

He again bent over the Girl, one hand on her left wrist, the other over her heart, his eyes on her lips, watching the depth and strength of her every breath. Regularly he administered the medicine he was giving her. Sometimes she took it half asleep; again she gave him a smile that to the Harvester was the supreme thing of earth or Heaven. Toward the end of the long vigil, in exhaustion he slipped to the floor, and laid his head on the side of the bed, and for a second his hand relaxed and he fell asleep. The Girl awakened as his touch loosened and looking down she saw his huddled body. A second later the Harvester awoke with a guilty start to find her fingers twisted in the shock of hair on the top of his head.

"Poor stranded Girl," he muttered. "She's clinging to me for life, and you can stake all you are worth she's going to get it!"

Then he gently relaxed her grip, gave her the last dose he felt necessary, yielded his place to Doctor Carey and staggered up the hill. As the sun peeped over Medicine Woods he stretched himself between the two mounds under the oak, and for a few minutes his body was rent with the awful, torn sobbing of a strong man. Belshazzar nosed the twisting figure and whined pitifully. A chattering little marsh wren tilted on a bush and scolded. A blue jay perched above and tried to decide whether there was cause for an alarm signal. A snake coming from the water to hunt birds ran close to him, and changing its course, went weaving away among the mosses. Gradually the pent forces spent themselves, and for hours the Harvester lay in the deep sleep of exhaustion, and stretched beside him, Belshazzar guarded with anxious dog eyes.

Chapter 18

The Better Man

In the middle of the afternoon the Harvester arose and went into the lake, ate a hearty dinner, and then took up his watch again. For two days and nights he kept his place, until he had the Girl out of danger, and where careful nursing was all that was required to insure life and health. As he sat beside her the last day, his physical endurance strained to the breaking point, she laid her hand over his, and looked long and steadily into his eyes.

"There are so many things I want to know," she said.

The Harvester's firm fingers closed over hers. "Ruth, have you ever been sorry that you trusted me?"

"Never!" said the Girl instantly.

"Then suppose you keep it up," said he. "Whatever it is that you want to know, don't use an iota of strength to talk or to think about it now. Just say to yourself, he loves me well enough to do what is right, and I know that he will. All you have to do is to be patient until you grow stronger than you ever have been in your life, and then you shall have exactly what you want, Ruth. Sleep like a baby for a week or two. Then, slowly and gradually, we will build up such a constitution for you that you shall ride, drive, row, swim, dance, play, and have all that your girlhood has missed in fun and frolic, and all that your womanhood craves in love and companionship. Happiness has come at last, Ruth. Take it from me. Everything you crave is yours. The love you want, the home, and the life. As soon as you are strong enough, you shall know all about it. Your business is to drink stimulants and sleep now, dear."

"So tired of this bed!"

"It won't be long until you can lie on the couch and the veranda swing again."

"Glory!" said the Girl. "David, I must have been full of fever for a long time. I can't remember everything."

"Don't try, I tell you. Life is coming out right for you; that's all you need know now."

"And for you, David?"

"Whenever things are right for you, they are for me, Ruth."

"Don't you ever think of yourself?"

"Not when I am close you."

"Ah! Then I shall have to grow strong very soon and think of you."

The Harvester's smile was pathetic. He was unspeakably tired again.

"Never mind me!" he said. "Only get well."

"David, was there a little horse?"

"There certainly was and is," said the Harvester. "You had not named him yet, but in a few days I can lead him to the window."

"Was there something said about a boat?"

"Two of them."

"Two?"

"Yes. A row boat for you, and a launch that will take you all over the lake with only the exertion of steering on your part."

"David, I want my pendant and ring. I am so tired of lying here, I want to play with them."

"Where do you keep them, Ruth?"

"In the willow teapot. I thought no one would look there."

The Harvester laughed and brought the little boxes. He had to open them, but the Girl put on the ring and asked him if he would not help her with the pendant. He slipped the thread around her neck and clasped it. With a sigh of satisfaction she took the ornament in one hand and closed her eyes. He thought she was falling asleep, but presently she looked at him.

"You won't allow them to take it from me?"

"Indeed no! There is no reason on earth why you should not have that thread around your neck if you want it."

"I am going to sleep now. I want two things. May I have them?"

"You may," said the Harvester promptly, "provided they are not to eat."

"No," said the Girl. "I've suffered and made others trouble. I won't bother you by asking for anything more than is brought me. This is different. You are completely worn out. Your face frightens me, David, and white hairs that were not there a few days ago have come along your temples. I can see them."

"You gave me a mighty serious scare, Ruth."

"I know," said the Girl. "Forgive me. I didn't mean to. I want you to leave me to Doctor Harmon and the nurse and go sleep a week. Then I will be ready for the swing, and to hear some more about the trees and birds."

"I can keep it up if you really need me, but if you don't I am sleepy. So, if you feel safe, I think I will go."

"Oh I am safe enough," said the Girl. "It isn't that. I'm so lonely. I've made up my mind not to grieve for mother, but I miss her so now. I feel so friendless."

"But, honey," said the Harvester, "you mustn't do that! Don't you see how all of us love you? Here is Granny shutting up her house and living here, just to be with you. The nurse will do anything you say. Here is the man you know best, and think so much of, staying in the cabin, and so happy to give you all his time, and anything else you will have, dear. And the Careys come every day, and will do their best to comfort you, and always I am here for you to fall back on."

"Yes, I'm falling right now," said the Girl. "I almost wish I had the fever again. No one has touched me for days. I feel as if every one was afraid of me."

The Harvester was puzzled.

"Well, Ruth, I'm doing the best I know," he said. "What is it you want?"

"Nothing!" answered the Girl with slightly dejected inflection. "Say good-bye to me, and go sleep your week. I'll be very good, and then you shall take me a drive up the hill when you awaken. Won't that be fine?"

"Say good-bye to me!" She felt a "little lonely!" They all acted as if they were "afraid" of her. The Harvester indulged in a flashing mental review and arrived at a decision. He knelt beside the bed, took both slender, cool hands and covered them with kisses. Then he slid a hand under the pillow and raised the tired head.

"If I am to say good-bye, I have to do it in my own way, Ruth," he said.

Thereupon he began at the tumbled mass of hair and kissed from her forehead to her lips, kisses warm and tender.

"Now you go to sleep, and grow strong enough by the time I come back to tell me whom you love," he said, and went from the room without waiting for any reply.

With short intervals for food and dips in the lake the Harvester very nearly slept the week. When he finally felt himself again, he bathed, shaved, dressed freshly, and went to see the Girl. He had to touch her to be sure she was real. She was extremely weak and tremulous, but her face and hands were fuller, her colour was good, she was ravenously hungry. Doctor Harmon said she was a little tryant, and the nurse that she was plain cross. The first thing the Harvester noticed was that the dull blue look in the depth of the dark eyes was gone. They were clear, dusky wells, with shining lights at the bottom.

"Well I never would have believed it!" he cried. "Doctor Harmon, you are a great physician! You have made her all over new, and in a few more days she will be on the veranda. This is great!"

"Do I appear so much better to you, Harvester?" asked the Girl.

"Has no one thought to show you," cried the Harvester. "Here, let me!"

He stepped to her dressing table, picked up a mirror, and held it before her so that she could see herself.

"Seems to me I am dreadfully white and thin yet!"

"If you had seen what I saw ten days ago, my Girl, you would think you appear like a pink, rosy angel now, or a wonderful dream."

"Truly, do I in the least resemble a dream, David?"

"You are a dream. The loveliest one a man ever had. With three months of right care and exercise you'll be the beautiful woman nature intended. I'm so proud of you. You are being so brave! Just lie there in patience a few more days, and out you come again to life; and life that will thrill your being with joy."

"All right," said the Girl, "I will. David are you attending to your herbs?"

"Not for a few weeks."

"You are very much behind?"

"No. Nothing important. I don't make enough to count on what is ready now. I can soon gather jimson leaves and seed to fill orders, the hemlock is about right to take the fruit, the mustard is yet in pod, and the saffron and wormseed can be attended later. I can catch up in two days."

"What about—about the big bed on the hill?"

The Harvester experienced an inward thrill of delight. She was so impressed with the value of the ginseng she would not mention it, even before the man she loved— no more than that—"adored"— "worshipped!" He smiled at her in understanding.

"I'll have to take a peep at that and report," he said.

"Are you rested now?"

"Indeed yes!"

"You are dreadfully thin."

"I always am. I'll pick up a little when I get back to work."

"David, I want you to go to work now."

"Can you spare me?"

"Haven't we done well these last few days?"

"I can't tell you how well."

"Then please go gather everything you need to fill orders except the big bed, and by that time maybe you could take another week off, and I could go to the hill top and on the lake. I'm so anxious to put my feet on the earth. They feel so dead."

"Are your feet well rubbed to draw down the circulation?"

"They are rubbed shiny and almost skinned, David. No one ever had better care, of that I am sure. Go gather what you should have."

"All right," said the Harvester.

He arose and as he started to leave the room he took one last look at the Girl to see if he could detect anything he could suggest for her comfort, and read a message in her eyes. Instantly there was an answering flash in his.

"I'll be back in a minute," he said. "I just noticed discorea villosa has the finest rattle boxes formed. I've been waiting to show you. And the hop tree has its castanets all green and gold. In a few more weeks it will begin to play for you. I'll bring you some."

Soon he returned with the queer seed formations, and as he bent above her, with his back to Doctor Harmon, he whispered, "What is it?"

Her lips barely formed the one word, "Hurry!"

The Harvester straightened.

"All comfortable, Ruth?" he asked casually.

"Yes."

"You understand, of course, that there is not the slightest necessity for my going to work if you really want me for anything, even if it's nothing more than to have me within calling distance, in case you SHOULD want something. The whole lot I can gather now won't amount to twenty dollars. It's merely a matter of pride with me to have what is called for. I'd much rather remain, if you can use me in any way at all."

"Twenty dollars is considerable, when expenses are as heavy as now. And it's worth more than any money to you not to fail when orders come. I have learned that, and David, I don't want you to either. You must fill all demands as usual. I wouldn't forgive myself this winter if you should be forced to send orders only partly filled because I fell ill and hindered you. Please go and gather all you possibly will need of everything you take at this season, only remember!"

"There is no danger of my forgetting. If you are going to send me away to work, you will allow me to kiss your hand before I go, fair lady?"

He did it fervently.

"One word with you, Harmon," he said as he left the room.

Doctor Harmon arose and followed him to the gold garden, and together they stood beside the molten hedge of sunflowers, coneflowers, elecampane, and jewel flower.

"I merely want to mention that this is your inning," said the Harvester. "Find out if you are essential to the Girl's happiness as soon as you can, and the day she tells me so, I will file her petition and take a trip to the city to study some little chemical quirks that bother me. That's all."

The Harvester went to the dry-house for bags and clipping shears, and the doctor returned to the sunshine room.

"Ruth," he said, "do you know that the Harvester is the squarest man I ever met?"

"Is he?" asked the Girl.

"He is! He certainly is!"

"You must remember that I have little acquaintance with men," said she. "You are the first one I ever knew, and the only one except him."

"Well I try to be square," said Doctor Harmon, "but that is where Langston has me beaten a mile. I have to try. He doesn't. He was born that way."

The Girl began to laugh.

"His environment is so different," she said. "Perhaps if he were in a big city, he would have to try also."

"Won't do!" said the doctor. "He chose his location. So did I. He is a stronger physical man than I ever was or ever will be. The struggle that bound him to the woods and to research, that made him the master of forces that give back life, when a man like Carey says it is the end, proves him a master. The tumult in his soul must have been like a cyclone in his forest, when he turned his back on the world and stuck to the woods. Carey told me about it. Some day you must hear. It's a story a woman ought to know in order to arrive at proper values. You never will understand the man until you know that he is clean where most of us are blackened with ugly sins we have no right on God's footstool to commit and not so much reason as he. Every man should be as he is, but very few are. Carey says Langston's mother was a wonderful element in the formation of his character; but all mothers are anxious, and none of them can build with no foundation and no soul timber. She had material for a man to her hand, or she couldn't have made one."

"I see what you mean."

"So far as any inexperienced girl ever sees," said the doctor. "Some day if you live to fifty you will know, but you can't comprehend it now."

"If you think I lived all my life in Chicago's poverty spots and don't know unbridled human nature!"

"I found you and your mother unusually innocent women. You may understand some things. I hope you do. It will help you to decide who is the real man among the men who come into your life. There are some men, Ruth, who are fit to mate with a woman, and to perpetuate themselves and their mental and moral forces in children, who will be like them, and there are others who are not. It is these 'others' who are responsible for the sin of the world, the sickness and suffering. Any time you are sure you have a chance at a moral man, square and honest, in control of his brain and body, if you are a wise woman, Ruth, stick to him as the limpet to the rock."

"You mean stick to the Harvester?"

"If you are a wise woman!"

"When was a woman ever wise?"

"A few have been. They are the only care-free, really happy ones of the world, the only wives without a big, poison, blue-bottle fly in their ointment."

"I detest flies!" said the Girl.

"So do I," said the doctor. "For this reason I say to you choose the ointment that never had one in it. Take the man who is 'master of his fate, captain of his soul.' Stick to the Harvester! He is infinitely the better man!"

"Well have you seen anything to indicate that I wasn't sticking?" asked the Girl.

"No. And for your sake I hope I never will."

She laughed softly.

"You do love him, Ruth?"

"As I did my mother, yes. There is not a trace in my heart of the thing he calls love."

"You have been stunted, warped, and the fountains of life never have opened. It will come with right conditions of living."

"Do you think so?"

"I know so. At least there is no one else you love, Ruth?"

"No one except you."

"And do you feel about me just as you do him?"

"No! It is different. What I owe him is for myself. What I owe you is for my mother. You saw! You know! You understand what you did for her, and what it meant to me. The Harvester must be the finest man on earth, but when I try to think of either God or Heaven, your face intervenes."

"That's all right, Ruth, I'm so glad you told me," said Doctor Harmon. "I can make it all perfectly clear to you. You just go on and worship me all you please. It's bound to make a cleaner, better man of me. What you feel for me will hold me to a higher moral level all my life than I ever have known before; but never forget that you are not going to live in Heaven. You will be here at least sixty years yet, so when you come to think of selecting a partner for the relations of the world, you stick to the finest man on earth; see?"

"I do!" said the Girl. "I saw you kiss Molly a week ago. She is lovely, and I hope you will be perfectly happy. It won't interfere with my worshipping you; not the least in the world. Go ahead and be joyful!"

The doctor sprang to his feet in crimson confusion. The Girl lay and laughed at him.

"Don't!" she cried. "It's all right! It takes a weight off my soul as heavy as a mountain. I do adore you, as I said. But every hour since I left Chicago a big, black cloud has hung over me. I didn't feel free. I didn't feel absolved. I felt that my obligations to you were so heavy that when I had settled the last of the money debt I was in honour bound—"

"Don't, Ruth! Forget those dreadful times, as I told you then! Think only of a happy future!"

"Let me finish," said the Girl. "Let me get this out of my system with the other poison. From the day I came here, I've whispered in my heart, 'I am not free!' But if you love another woman! If you are going to take her to your heart and to your lips, why that is my release. Oh Man, speak the words! Tell me I am free indeed!"

"Ruth, be quiet, for mercy sake! You'll raise a temperature, and the Harvester will pitch me into the lake. You are free, child, of course! You always have been. I understood the awful pressure that was on you with the very first glimpse I had of your mother. Who was she, Ruth?"

"She never would tell me."

"She thought you would appeal to her people?"

"She knew I would! I couldn't have helped it."

"Would you like to know?"

"I never want to. It is too late. I infinitely prefer to remain in ignorance. Talk of something else."

"Let me read a wonderful book I found on the Harvester's shelves."

"Anything there will contain wonders, because he only buys what appeals to him, and it takes a great book to do that. I am going to learn. He will teach me, and when I come within comprehending distance of him, then we are going on together."

"What an attractive place this is!"

"Isn't it? I only have seen enough to understand the plan. I scarcely can wait to set my feet on earth and go into detail. Granny Moreland says that when spring comes over the hill, and brings up the flowers in the big woods, she'd rather walk through them than to read Revelation. She says it gives her an idea of Heaven she can come closer realizing and it seems more stable. You know she worries about the foundations. She can't understand what supports Heaven. But up there in Medicine Woods the old dear gets so close her God that some day she is going to realize that her idea of Heaven there is quite as near right as marble streets and gold pillars and vastly more probable. The day I reach that hill top again, Heaven begins for me. Do you know the wonderful thing the Harvester did up there?"

"Under the oak?"

"Yes."

"Carey told me. It was marvellous."

"Not such a marvel as another the doctor couldn't have known. The Harvester made passing out so natural, so easy, so a part of elemental forces, that I almost have forgotten her tortured body. When I think of her now, it is to wonder if next summer I can distinguish her whisper among the leaves. Before you go, I'll take you up there and tell you what he says, and show you what he means, and you will feel it also."

"What if I shouldn't go?"

"What do you mean?"

"Doctor Carey has offered me a splendid position in his hospital. There would be work all day, instead of waiting all day in the hope of working an hour. There would be a living in it for two from the word go. There would be better air, longer life, more to be got out of it, and if I can make good, Carey's work to take up as he grows old."

"Take it! Take it quickly!" cried the Girl. "Don't wait a minute! You might wear out your heart in Chicago for twenty years or forever, and not have an opportunity to do one half so much good. Take it at once!"

"I was waiting to learn what you and Langston would say."

"He will say take it."

"Then I will be too happy for words. Ruth, you have not only paid the debt, but you have brought me the greatest joy a man ever had. And there is no need to wait the ages I thought I must. He can tell in a year if I can do the work, and I know I can now; so it's all settled, if Langston agrees."

"He will," said the Girl. "Let me tell him!"

"I wish you would," said the doctor. "I don't know just how to go at it."

Then for two days the Harvester and Belshazzar gathered herbs and spread them on the drying trays. On the afternoon of the third, close three, the doctor came to the door.

"Langston," he said, "we have a call for you. We can't keep Ruth quiet much longer. She is tired. We want to change her bed completely. She won't allow either of us to lift her. She says we hurt her. Will you come and try it?"

"You'll have to give me time to dip and rub off and get into clean clothing," he said. "I've been keeping away, because I was working on time, and I smell to strangulation of stramonium and saffron."

"Can't give you ten seconds," said the doctor. "Our temper is getting brittle. We are cross as the proverbial fever patient. If you don't come at once we will imagine you don't want to, and refuse to be moved at all."

"Coming!" cried the Harvester, as he plunged his hands in the wash bowl and soused his face. A second later he appeared on the porch.

"Ruth," he said, "I am steeped in the odours of the dry-house. Can't you wait until I bathe and dress?"

"No, I can't," said a fretful voice. "I can't endure this bed another minute."

"Then let Doctor Harmon lift you. He is so fresh and clean."

The Harvester glanced enviously at the shaven face and white trousers and shirt of the doctor.

"I just hate fresh, clean men. I want to smell herbs. I want to put my feet in the dirt and my hands in the water."

The Harvester came at a rush. He brought a big easy chair from the living-room, straightened the cover, and bent above the Girl. He picked her up lightly, gently, and easing her to his body settled in the chair. She laid her face on his shoulder, and heaved a deep sigh of content.

"Be careful with my back, Man," she said. "I think my spine is almost worn through."

"Poor girl," said the Harvester. "That bed should be softer."

"It should not!" contradicted the Girl. "It should be much harder. I'm tired of soft beds. I want to lie on the earth, with my head on a root; and I wish it would rain dirt on me. I am bathed threadbare. I want to be all streaky."

"I understand," said the Harvester. "Harmon, bring me a pad and pencil a minute, I must write an order for some things I want. Will you call up town and have them sent out immediately?"

On the pad he wrote: "Telephone Carey to get the highest grade curled-hair mattress, a new pad, and pillow, and bring them flying in the car. Call Granny and the girl and empty the room. Clean, air, and fumigate it thoroughly. Arrange the furniture differently, and help me into the living room with Ruth." He handed the pad to the doctor.

"Please attend to that," he said, and to the Girl: "Now we go on a journey. Doc, you and Molly take the corners of the rug we are on and slide us into the other room until you get this aired and freshened."

In the living-room the Girl took one long look at the surroundings and suddenly relaxed. She cuddled against the Harvester and lifting a tremulous white hand, drew it across his unshaven cheek.

"Feels so good," she said. "I'm sick and tired of immaculate men."

The Harvester laughed, tucked her feet in the cover and held her tenderly. The Girl lay with her cheek against the rough khaki, palpitant with the excitement of being moved.

"Isn't it great?" she panted.

He caught the hand that had touched his cheek in a tender grip, and laughed a deep rumble of exultation that came from the depths of his heart.

"There's no name for it, honey," he said. "But don't try to talk until you have a long rest. Changing positions after you have lain so long may be making unusual work for your heart. Am I hurting your back?"

"No," said the Girl. "This is the first time I have been comfortable in ages. Am I tiring you?"

"Yes," laughed the Harvester. "You are almost as heavy as a large sack of leaves, but not quite equal to a bridge pillar or a log. Be sure to think of that, and worry considerably. You are in danger of straining my muscles to the last degree, my heart included."

"Where is your heart?" whispered the Girl.

"Right under your cheek," answered the Harvester. "But for Heaven's sake, don't intimate that you are taking any interest in it, or it will go to pounding until your head will bounce. It's one member of my body that I can't control where you are concerned."

"I thought you didn't like me any more."

"Careful!" warned the Harvester. "You are yet too close Heaven to fib like that, Ruth. What have I done to indicate that I don't love you more than ever?"

"Stayed away nearly every minute for three awful days, and wouldn't come without being dragged; and now you're wishing they would hurry and fix that bed, so you can put me down and go back to your rank old herbs again."

"Well of all the black prevarications! I went when you sent me, and came when you called. I'd willingly give up my hope of what Granny calls 'salvation' to hold you as I am for an hour, and you know it."

"It's going to be much longer than that," said the Girl nestling to him. "I asked for you because you never hurt me, and they always do. I knew you were so strong that my weight now wouldn't be a load for one of your hands, and I am not going back to that bed until I am so tired that I will be glad to lie down."

For a long time she was so silent the Harvester thought her going to sleep; and having learned that for him joy was probably transient, he deliberately got all he could. He closely held the hand she had not withdrawn, and often lifted it to his lips. Sometimes he stroked the heavy braid, gently ran his hands across the tired shoulders, or eased her into a different position. There was not a doubt in his mind

700

of one thing. He was having a royal, good time, and he was thankful for the work he had set his assistants that kept them out of the room. They seemed in no hurry, and from scuffling, laughing, and a steady stream of talk, they were entertained at least. At last the Girl roused.

"There is something I want to ask you," she said. "I promised Doctor Harmon I would."

Instantly the heart of the Harvester gave a leap that jarred the head resting on it.

"You don't like him?" questioned the Girl.

"I do!" declared the Harvester. "I like him immensely. There is not a fine, manly good-looking feature about him that I have missed. I don't fail to do him justice on every point."

"I'm so glad! Then you will want him to remain."

"Here?" asked the Harvester with a light, hot breath.

"In Onabasha! Doctor Carey has offered him the place of chief assistant at the hospital. There is a good salary and the chance of taking up the doctor's work as he grows older. It means plenty to do at once, healthful atmosphere, congenial society—everything to a young man. He only had a call once in a while in Chicago, often among people who received more than they paid, like me, and he was very lonely. I think it would be great for him."

"And for you, Ruth?"

"It doesn't make the least difference to me; but for his sake, because I think so much of him, I would like to see him have the place."

"You still think so much of him, Ruth?"

"More, if possible," said the Girl. "Added to all I owed him before, he has come here and worked for days to save me, and it wasn't his fault that it took a bigger man. Nothing alters the fact that he did all he could, most graciously and gladly."

"What do you mean, Ruth?" stammered the Harvester.

"Oh they have worn themselves out!" cried the Girl impatiently. "First, Granny Moreland told me every least little detail of how I went out, and you resurrected me. I knew what she said was true, because she worked with you. Then Doctor Carey told me, and Mrs. Carey, and Doctor Harmon, and Molly, and even Granny's little assistant has left the kitchen to tell me that I owe my life to you, and all of them might as well have saved breath. I knew all the time that if ever I came out of this, and had a chance to be like other women, it would be your work, and I'm glad it is. I'd hate to be under obligations to some people I know; but I feel honoured to be indebted to you."

"I'm mighty sorry they worried you. I had no idea—"

"They didn't 'worry,' me! I am just telling you that I knew it all the time; that's all!"

"Forget that!" said the Harvester. "Come back to our subject. What was it you wanted, dear?"

"To know if you have any objections to Doctor Harmon remaining in Onabasha?"

"Certainly not! It will be a fine thing for him."

"Will it make any difference to you in any way?"

"Ruth, that's probing too deep," said the Harvester.

"I don't see why!"

"I'm glad of it!"

"Why?"

"I'd least rather show my littleness to you than to any one else on earth."

"Then you have some feeling about it?"

"Perhaps a trifle. I'll get over it. Give me a little time to adjust myself. Doctor Harmon shall have the place, of course. Don't worry about that!"

"He will be so happy!"

"And you, Ruth?"

"I'll be happy too!"

"Then it's all right," said the Harvester.

He laid down her hand, drew the cover over it, and slightly shifted her position to rest her. The door opened, and Doctor Harmon announced that the room was ready. It was shining and fresh. The bed was now turned with its head to the north, so that from it one could see the big trees in Medicine Woods, the sweep of the hillside, the sparkle of mallow-bordered Singing Water, the driveway and the gold flower garden. Everything was so changed that the room had quite a different appearance. The instant he laid her on it the Girl said, "This bed is not mine."

"Yes it is," said the Harvester. "You see, we were a little excited sometimes, and we spilled a few quarts of perfectly good medicine on your mattress. It was hopelessly smelly and ruined; so I am going to cremate it and this is your splinter new one and a fresh pad and pillow. Now you try them and see if they are not much harder and more comfortable."

"This is just perfect!" she sighed, as she sank into the bed.

The Harvester bent over her to straighten the cover, when suddenly she reached both arms around his neck, and gripped him with all her strength.

"Thank you!" she said.

"May I hold you to-morrow?" whispered the Harvester, emboldened by this.

"Please do," said the Girl.

The Harvester, with dog to heel, went to the oak to think.

"Belshazzar, kommen Sie!" said the man, dropping on the seat and holding out his hand. The dog laid his muzzle in the firm grip.

"Bel," said the Harvester, "I am all at sea. One day I think maybe I have a little chance, the next—none at all. I had an hour of solid comfort to-day, now I'm in the sweat box again. It's a little selfish streak in me, Bel, that hates to see Harmon go into the hospital and take my place with the Careys. They are my best and only friends. He is young, social, handsome, and will be ever present. In three months he will become so popular that I might as well be off the earth. I wish I didn't think it, but I'm so small that I do. And then there is my Dream Girl, Bel. The girl you found for me, old fellow. There never was another like her, and she has my heart for all time. And he has hers. That hospital plan is the best thing in the world for her. It will keep her where Carey can have an eye on her, where the air is better, where she can have company without the city crush, where she is close the country, and a good living is assured. Bel, it's the nicest arrangement you ever saw for every one we know, except us."

The Harvester laughed shortly. "Bel," he said, "tell me! If a man lived a hundred years, could he have the heartache all the way? Seems like I've had it almost that long now. In fact, I've had it such ages I'd be lonesome without it. This is some more of my very own medicine, so I shouldn't make a wry face over taking it. I knew what would happen when I sent for him, and I didn't hesitate. I must not now.

"Only I got to stop one thing, Bel. I told him I would play square, and I have. But here it ends. After this, I must step back and be big brother. Lots of fun in this brother business, Bel. But maybe I am cut out for it. Anyway it's written! But if it is, how did she come to allow me such privileges as I took to-day? That wasn't professional by any means. It was just the stiffest love-making I knew how to do, Bel, and she didn't object by the quiver of an eyelash. God knows I was watching closely enough for any sign that I was distasteful. And I might have been well enough. Rough, herb-stained old clothes, unshaven, everything to offend a dainty girl. She said I might hold her again to-morrow. And, Bel, what the nation did she hug me like that for, if she's going to marry him? Boy, I see my way clear to an hour more. While I'm at it, just to surprise myself, I believe I'll take it like other men. I think I'll go on a little bender, and make what probably will be the last day a plumb good one. Something worth remembering is better than nothing at all, Bel! He hasn't told me that he has won. She didn't SAY she was going to marry him, and she did say he hurt her, and she wanted me. Bel, how about the grimness of it, if she should marry him and then discover that he hurts her, and she wants me. Lord God Almighty, if you have any mercy at all, never put me up against that," prayed the Harvester, "for my heart is water where she is concerned."

The Harvester arose, and going to the lake, he cut an arm load of big, pink mallows, covered each mound with fresh flowers, whistled to the dog, and went to his work. Many things had accumulated, and he cleaned the barn, carried herbs from the dry-house to the store-room, and put everything into shape. Close noon the next day he went to Onabasha, and was gone three hours. He came back barbered in the latest style, and carrying a big bundle. When the hour for arranging the bed came, he was yet in his room, but he sent word he would be there in a second.

As he crossed the living-room he pulled a chair to the veranda and placed a footstool before it. Then he stepped into the sunshine room. A quizzical expression crossed the face of Doctor Harmon as he closed the book he was reading aloud to the Girl and arose. Wholly unembarrassed the Harvester smiled.

"Have I got this rigging anywhere near right?" he inquired.

"David, what have you done?" gasped the amazed Girl.

"I didn't feel anywhere near up to the 'mark of my high calling' yesterday," quoted the Harvester. "I don't know how I appear, but I'm clean as shaving, soap, and hot water will make me, and my clothing will not smell offensively. Now come out of that bed for a happy hour. Where is that big coverlet? You are going on the veranda to-day."

"You look just like every one else," complained Doctor Harmon.

"You look perfectly lovely," declared the Girl.

"The swale sends you this invitation to come and see star-shine at the foot of mullein hill," said the Harvester, offering a bouquet. It was a loose bunch of long-stemmed, delicate flowers, each an inch across, and having five pearl-white petals lightly striped with pale green. Five long gold anthers arose, and at their base gold stamens and a green pistil. The leaves were heart-shaped and frosty, whitish-green, resembling felt. The Harvester bent to offer them.

"Have some Grass of Parnassus, my dear," he said.

The Girl waved them away. "Go stand over there by the door and slowly turn around. I want to see you."

The Harvester obeyed. He was freshly and carefully shaven. His hair was closely cropped at the base of the head, long, heavy, and slightly waving on top. He wore a white silk shirt, with a rolling collar and tie, white trousers, belt, hose, and shoes, and his hands were manicured with care.

"Have I made a mess of it, or do I appear anything like other men?" he asked, eagerly.

The Girl lifted her eyes to Doctor Harmon and smiled.

"Do you observe anything messy?" she inquired.

"You needn't fish for compliments quite so obviously," he answered. "I'll pay them without being asked. I do not. He is quite correct, and infinitely better looking than the average. Distinguished is a proper word for the gentleman in my opinion. But why, in Heaven's name, have we never had the pleasure of seeing you thus before?"

"Look here, Doc," said the Harvester, "do you mean that you enjoy looking at me merely because I am dressed this way?"

"I do indeed," said the doctor. "It is good to see you with the garb of work laid aside, and the stamp of cleanliness and ease upon you."

"By gum, that is rubbing it in a little too rough!" cried the Harvester. "I bathe oftener than you do. My clothing is always clean when I start out. Of course, in my work I come hourly in contact with muck, water, and herb juices."

"It's understood that is unavoidable," said Doctor Harmon.

"And if cleanliness is made an issue, I'd rather roll in any of it than put my finger tips into the daily work of a surgeon," added the Harvester, and the Girl giggled.

"That's enough Medicine Man!" she said. "You did not make a 'mess' of it, or anything else you ever attempted. As for appearing like other men, thank Heaven, you do not. You look just a whole world bigger and better and finer. Come, carry me out quickly. I am wild to go. Please put my lovely flowers in water, Molly, only give me a few to hold."

The Harvester arranged the pink coverlet, picked up the Girl, and carried her to the living-room.

"We will rest here a little," he said, "and then, if you feel equal to it, we will try the veranda. Are you easy now?"

She nestled her face against the soft shirt and smiled at him. She lifted her hand, laid it on his smooth cheek and then the crisp hair.

"Oh Man!" she cried. "Thank God you didn't give me up, too! I want life! I want LIFE!"

The Harvester tightened his grip just a trifle. "Then I thank God, too," he said. "Can you tell me how you are, dear? Is there any difference?"

"Yes," she answered. "I grow tired lying so long, but there isn't the ghost of an ache in my bones. I can just feel pure, delicious blood running in my veins. My hands and feet are always warm, and my head cool."

The Harvester's face drew very close. "How about your heart, honey?" he whispered. "Anything new there?"

"Yes, I am all over new inside and out. I want to shout, run, sing, and swim. Oh I'd give anything to have you carry me down and dip me in the lake right now."

"Soon, Girl! That will come soon," prophesied the Harvester.

"I scarcely can wait. And you did say a saddle, didn't you? Won't it be great to come galloping up the levee, when the leaves are red and the frost is in the air. Oh am I going fast enough?"

"Much faster than I expected," said the Harvester. "You are surprising all of us, me most of any. Ruth, you almost make me hope that you regard this as home. Honey, you are thinking a little of me these days?"

The hand that had fallen from his hair lay on his shoulder. Now it slid around his neck, and gripped him with all its strength.

"Heaps and heaps!" she said. "All I get a chance to, for being bothered and fussed over, and everlastingly read mushy stuff that's intended for some one else. Please take me to the veranda now; I want to tell you something."

His head swam, but the Harvester set his feet firmly, arose, and carried his Dream Girl back to outdoor life. When he reached the chair, she begged him to go a few steps farther to the bench on the lake shore.

"I am afraid," said the man.

"It's so warm. There can't be any difference in the air. Just a minute."

The Harvester pushed open the screen, went to the bench, and seating himself, drew the cover closely around her.

"Don't speak a word for a long time," he said. "Just rest. If I tire you too much and spoil everything, I will be desperate."

He clasped her to him, laid his cheek against her hair, and his lips on her forehead. He held her hand and kissed it over and over, and again he watched and could find no resentment. The cool, pungent breeze swept from the lake, and the voices of wild life chattered at their feet. Sometimes the water folks splashed, while a big black and gold butterfly mistook the Girl's dark hair for a perching place and settled on it, slowly opening its wonderful wings.

"Lie quietly, Girl," whispered the Harvester. "You are wearing a living jewel, an ornament above price, on your hair. Maybe you can see it when it goes. There!"

"Oh I did!" she cried. "How I love it here! Before long may I lie in the dining-room window a while so I can see the water. I like the hill, but I love the lake more."

"Now if you just would love me," said the Harvester, "you would have all Medicine Woods in your heart."

"Don't hurry me so!" said the Girl. "You gave me a year; and it's only a few weeks, and I've not been myself, and I'm not now. I mustn't make any mistake, and all I know for sure is that I want you most, and I can rest best with you, and I miss you every minute you are gone. I think that should satisfy you."

"That would be enough for any reasonable man," said the Harvester angrily. "Forgive me, Ruth, I have been cruel. I forgot how frail and weak you are. It is having Harmon here that makes me unnatural. It almost drives me to frenzy to know that he may take you from me."

"Then send him away!"

"SEND HIM AWAY?"

"Yes, send him away! I am tired to death of his poetry, and seeing him spoon around. Send both of them away quickly!"

The Harvester gulped, blinked, and surreptitiously felt for her pulse.

"Oh, I've not developed fever again," she said. "I'm all right. But it must be a fearful expense to have both of them here by the week, and I'm so tired of them, Granny says she can take care of me just as well, and the girl who helps her can cook. No one but you shall lift me, if I don't get my nose out until I can walk alone. Both of them are perfectly useless, and I'd much rather you'd send them away."

"There, there! Of course!" said the Harvester soothingly. "I'll do it as soon as I possibly dare. You don't understand, honey. You are yet delicate beyond measure, internally. The fever burned so long. Every morsel you eat is measured and cooked in sterilized vessels, and I'd be scared of my life to have the girl undertake it."

"Why she is doing it straight along now! She and Granny! Molly isn't out of Doctor Harmon's sight long enough to cook anything. Granny says there is 'a lot of buncombe about what they do, and she is going to tell them so right to their teeth some of these days, if they badger her much more,' and I wish she would, and you, too."

The Harvester gathered the Girl to him in one crushing bear hug.

"For the love of Heaven, Ruth, you drive me crazy! Answer me just one question. When you told me that you 'adored and worshipped' Doctor Harmon, did you mean it, or was that the delirium of fever?"

"I don't know WHAT I told you! If I said I 'adored' him, it was the truth. I did! I do! I always will! So do I adore the Almighty, but that's no sign I want him to read poetry to me, and be around all the time when I am wild for a minute with you. I can worship Doctor Harmon in Chicago or Onabasha quite as well. Fire him! If you don't, I will!"

"Good Lord!" cried the Harvester, helpless until the Girl had to cling to him to prevent rolling from his nerveless arms. "Ruth, Ruth, will you feel my pulse?"

"No, I won't! But you are going to drop me. Take me straight back to my beautiful new bed, and send them away."

"A minute! Give me a minute!" gasped the Harvester. "I couldn't lift a baby just now. Ruth, dear, I thought you *loved* the man."

"What made you think so?"

"You did!"

"I didn't either! I never said I loved him. I said I was under obligations to him; but they are as well repaid as they ever can be. I said I adored him, and I tell you I do! Give him what we owe him, both of us, in money, and send them away. If you'd seen as much of them as I have, you'd be tired of them, too. Please, please, David!"

"Yes," said the Harvester, arising in a sudden tide of effulgent joy. "Yes, Girl, just as quickly as I can with decency. I—I'll send them on the lake, and I'll take care of you."

"You won't read poetry to me?"

"I will not."

"You won't moon at me?"

"No!"

"Then hurry! But have them take your boat. I am going to have the first ride in mine."

"Indeed you are, and soon, too!" said the Harvester, marching up the hill as if he were leading hosts to battle.

He laid the Girl on the bed and covered her, and called Granny Moreland to sit beside her a few minutes. He went into the gold garden and proposed that the doctor and the nurse go rowing until supper time, and they went with alacrity. When they started he returned to the Girl and, sitting beside her, he told Granny to take a nap. Then he began to talk softly all about wild music, and how it was made, and what the different odours sweeping down the hill were, and when the red leaves would come, and the nuts rattle down, and the frost fairies enamel the windows, and soon she was sound asleep. Granny came back, and the Harvester walked around the lake shore to be alone a while and think quietly, for he was almost too dazed and bewildered for full realization.

As he softly followed the foot path he heard voices, and looking down, he saw the boat lying in the shade and beneath a big tree on the bank sat the doctor and the nurse. His arm was around her, and her head was on his shoulder; and she said very distinctly, "How long will it be until we can go without offending him?"

Chapter 19

A Vertical Spine

By middle September the last trace of illness had been removed from the premises, and it was rapidly disappearing from the face and form of the Girl. She was showing a beautiful roundness, there was lovely colour on her cheeks and lips, and in her dark eyes sparkled a touch of mischief. Rigidly she followed the rules laid down for diet and exercise, and as strength flowed through her body, and no trace of pain tormented her, she began revelling in new and delightful sensations. She loved to pull her boat as she willed, drive over the wood road, study the books, cook the new dishes, rearrange furniture, and go with the Harvester everywhere.

But that was greatly the management of the man. He was so afraid that something might happen to undo all the wonders accomplished in the Girl, and again whiten her face with pain, that he scarcely allowed her out of his sight. He remained in the cabin, helping when she worked, and then drove with her and a big blanket to the woods, arranged her chair and table, found some attractive subject, and while the wind ravelled her hair and flushed her cheeks, her fingers drew designs. At noon they went to the cabin to lunch, and the Girl took a nap, while the Harvester spread his morning's reaping on the shelves to dry. They returned to the woods until five o'clock; then home again and the Girl dressed and prepared supper, while the Harvester spread his stores and fed the stock. Then he put on white clothing for the evening. The Girl rested while he washed the dishes, and they explored the lake in the little motor boat, or drove to the city for supplies, or to see their friends.

"Are you even with your usual work at this time of the year?" she asked as they sat at breakfast.

"I am," said the Harvester. "The only things that have been crowded out are the candlesticks. They will have to remain on the shelf until the herbs and roots are all in, and the long winter evenings come. Then I'll use the luna pattern and finish yours first of all."

"What are you going to do to-day?"

"Start on a regular fall campaign. Some of it for the sake of having it, and some because there is good money in it. Will you come?"

"Indeed yes. May I help, or shall I take my drawing along?"

"Bring your drawing. Next fall you may help, but as yet you are too close suffering for me to see you do anything that might be even a slight risk. I can't endure it."

"Baby!" she jeered.

"Christen me anything you please," laughed the Harvester. "I'm short on names anyway."

He went to harness Betsy, and the Girl washed the dishes, straightened the rooms, and collected her drawing material. Then she walked up the hill, wearing a shirt and short skirt of khaki, stout shoes, and a straw hat that shaded her face. She climbed into the wagon, laid the drawing box on the seat, and caught the lines as the Harvester flung them to her. He went swinging ahead, Belshazzar to heel, the Girl driving after. The white pigeons circled above, and every day Ajax allowed his curiosity to overcome his temper, and followed a little farther.

"Whoa, Betsy!" The Girl tugged at the lines; but Betsy took the bit between her teeth, and plodded after the Harvester. She pulled with all her might, but her strength was not nearly sufficient to stop the stubborn animal.

"Whoa, David!" cried the Girl.

"What is it?" the Harvester turned.

"Won't you please wait until I can take off my hat? I love to ride bareheaded through the woods, and Betsy won't stop until you do, no matter how hard I pull."

"Betsy, you're no lady!" said the Harvester. "Why don't you stop when you're told?"

"I shan't waste any more strength on her," said the Girl. "Hereafter I shall say, 'Gee, David,' 'Haw, David,' 'Whoa, David,' and then she will do exactly as you."

The Harvester stopped half way up the hill, and beside a large, shaded bed spread the rug, and set up the little table and chair for the Girl.

"Want a plant to draw?" he asked. "This is very important to us. It has a string of names as long as a princess, but I call it goldenseal, because the roots are yellow. The chemists ask for hydrastis. That sounds formidable, but it's a cousin of buttercups. The woods of Ohio and Indiana produce the finest that ever grew, but it is so nearly extinct now that the trade can be supplied by cultivation only. I suspect I'm responsible for its disappearance around here. I used to get a dollar fifty a pound, and most of my clothes and books when a boy I owe to it. Now I get two for my finest grade; that accounts for the size of these beds."

"It's pretty!" said the Girl, studying a plant averaging a foot in height. On a slender, round, purplish stem arose one big, rough leaf, heavily veined, and having from five to nine lobes. Opposite was a similar leaf, but very small, and a head of scarlet berries resembling a big raspberry in shape. The Harvester shook the black woods soil from the yellow roots, and held up the plant.

"You won't enjoy the odour," he said.

"Well I like the leaves. I know I can use them some way. They are so unusual. What wonderful colour in the roots!"

"One of its names is Indian paint," explained the Harvester. "Probably it furnished the squaws of these woods with colouring matter. Now let's see what we can get out of it. You draw the plant and I'll dig the roots."

For a time the Girl bent over her work and the Harvester was busy. Belshazzar ranged the woods chasing chipmunks. The birds came asking questions. When the drawing was completed, other subjects were found at every turn, and the Girl talked almost constantly, her face alive with interest. The May-apple beds lay close, and she drew from them. She learned the uses and prices of the plant, and also made drawings of cohosh, moonseed and bloodroot. That was so wonderful in its root colour, the Harvester filled the little cup with water and she began to paint. Intensely absorbed she bent above the big, notched, silvery leaves and the blood-red roots, testing and trying to match them exactly. Every few minutes the Harvester leaned over her shoulder to see how she was progressing and to offer suggestions. When she finished she picked up a trailing vine of moonseed.

"You have this on the porch," she said. "I think it is lovely. There is no end to the beautiful combinations of leaves, and these are such pretty little grape-like clusters; but if you touch them the slightest you soil the wonderful surface."

"And that makes the fairies very sad," said the Harvester. "They love that vine best of any, because they paint its fruit with the most care. 'Bloom' the scientists call it. You see it on cultivated plums, grapes, and apples, but never in any such perfection as on moonseed and black haws in the woods. You should be able to design a number of pretty things from the cohosh leaves and berries, too. You scarcely can get a start this fall, but early in the spring you can begin, and follow the season. If your work comes out well this winter, I'll send some of it to the big publishing houses, and you can make book and magazine covers and decorations, if you would like."

"'If I would like!' How modest! You know perfectly well that if I could make a design that would be accepted, and used on a book or magazine, I would almost fly. Oh do you suppose I could?"

"I don't 'suppose' anything about it, I know," said the Harvester. "It is not possible that the public can be any more tired of wild roses, golden-rod, and swallows than the poor art editors who accept them because they can't help themselves. Dangle something fresh and new under their noses and see them snap. The next time I go to Onabasha I'll get you some popular magazines, and you can compare what is being used with what you see here, and judge for yourself how glad they would be for a change. And potteries, arts and crafts shops, and wall paper factories, they'd be crazy for the designs I could furnish them. As for money, there's more in it than the herbs, if I only could draw."

"I can do that," said the Girl. "Trail the vine and give me an idea how to scale it. I'll just make studies now, and this winter I'll conventionalize them and work them into patterns. Won't that be fun?"

"That's more than fun, Ruth," said the Harvester solemnly. "That is creation. That touches the provinces of the Almighty. That is taking His unknown wonders and making them into pleasure and benefit for thousands, not to mention filling your face with awe divine, and lighting your eyes with interest and ambition. That is life, Ruth. You are beginning to live right now."

"I see," said the Girl. "I understand! I am!"

"You get your subjects now. When the harvest is over I'll show you what I have in my head, and before Christmas the fun will begin."

"What next?"

"Sketch a sarsaparilla plant and this yam vine. It grows on your veranda too—the rattle box, you remember. The leaves and seeding arrangements are wonderful. You can do any number of things with them, and all will be new."

He called her attention to and brought her samples of ginger leaves, Indian hemp, queen-of-the-meadow, cone-flower, burdock, baneberry, and Indian turnip, as he harvested them in turn. When they came to the large beds of orange pleurisy root the Girl cried out with pleasure.

"We will take its prosaic features first," said the Harvester. "It is good medicine and worth handling. Forget that! The Bird Woman calls it butterfly flower. That's better. Now try to analyze a single bloom of this gaudy mass, and you will see why there's poetry coming."

He knelt beside the Girl, separating the blooms and pointing out their marvellous colour and construction. She leaned against his shoulder, and watched with breathless interest. As his bare head brought its mop of damp wind-rumpled hair close, she ran her fingers through it, and with her handkerchief wiped his forehead.

"Sometimes I almost wish you'd get sick," she said irrelevantly.

"In the name of common sense, why?" demanded the Harvester.

"Oh it must be born in the heart of a woman to want to mother something," answered the Girl. "I feel sometimes as if I would like to take care of you, as if you were a little fellow. David, I know why your mother fought to make you the man she desired. You must have been charming when small. I can shut my eyes and just see the boy you were, and I should have loved you as she did."

"How about the man I am?" inquired the Harvester promptly. "Any leanings toward him yet, Ruth?"

"It's getting worser and worser every day and hour," said the Girl. "I don't understand it at all. I wouldn't try to live without you. I don't want you to leave my sight. Everything you do is the way I would have it. Nothing you ever say shocks or offends me. I'd love to render you any personal service. I want to take you in my arms and hug you tight half a dozen times a day as a reward for the kind and lovely things you do for me."

A dull red flamed up the neck and over the face of the Harvester. One arm lifted to the chair back, the other dropped across the table so that the Girl was almost encircled.

"For the love of mercy, Ruth, why haven't I had a hint of this before?" he cried.

"You said you'd hate me. You said you'd drop me into the deepest part of the lake if I deceived you; and if I have to tell the truth, why, that is all of it. I think it is nonsense about some wonderful feeling that is going to take possession of your heart when you love any one. I love you so much I'd gladly suffer to save you pain or sorrow. But there are no thrills; it's just steady, sober, common sense that I should love you, and I do. Why can't you be satisfied with what I can give, David?"

"Because it's husks and ashes," said the Harvester grimly. "You drive me to desperation, Ruth. I am almost wild for your love, but what you offer me is plain, straight affection, nothing more. There isn't a trace of the feeling that should exist between man and wife in it. Some men might be satisfied to be your husband, and be regarded as a father or brother. I am not. The red bird didn't want a sister, Ruth, he was asking for a mate. So am I. That's as plain as I know how to put it. There is some way to awaken you into a living, loving woman, and, please God, I'll find it yet, but I'm slow about it; there's no question of that. Never you mind! Don't worry! Some of these days I have faith to believe it will sweep you as a tide sweeps the shore, and then I hope God will be good enough to let me be where you will land in my arms."

The Girl sat looking at him between narrowed lids. Suddenly she took his head between her hands, drew his face to hers and deliberately kissed him. Then she drew away and searched his eyes.

"There!" she challenged. "What is the matter with that?"

The Harvester's colour slowly faded to a sickly white.

"Ruth, you try me almost beyond human endurance," he said. "'What's the matter with that?'" He arose, stepped back, folded his arms, and stared at her. "'What's the matter with that?'" he repeated. "Never was I so sorely tempted in all my life as I am now to lie to you, and say there is nothing, and take you in my arms and try to awaken you to what I mean by love. But suppose I do—and fail! Then comes the agony of slow endurance for me, and the possibility that any day you may meet the man who can arouse in you the feelings I cannot. That would mean my oath broken, and my heart as well; while soon you would dislike me beyond tolerance, even. I dare not risk it! The matter is, that was the loving caress of a ten-year-old girl to a big brother she admired. That's all! Not much, but a mighty big defect when it is offered a strong man as fuel on which to feed consuming passion."

"Consuming passion," repeated the Girl. "David you never lie, and you never exaggerate. Do you honestly mean that there is something—oh, there is! I can see it! You are really suffering, and if I come to you, and try my best to comfort you, you'll only call it baby affection that you don't want. David, what am I going to do?"

"You are going to the cabin," said the Harvester, "and cook us a big supper. I am dreadfully hungry. I'll be along presently. Don't worry, Ruth, you are all right! That kiss was lovely. Tell me that you are not angry with me."

Her eyes were wet as she smiled at him.

"If there is a bigger brute than a man anywhere on the footstool, I should like to meet it," said the Harvester, "and see what it appears like. Go along, honey; I'll be there as soon as I load."

He drove to the dry-house, washed and spread his reaping on the big trays, fed the stock, dressed in the white clothing and entered the kitchen. That the Girl had been crying was obvious, but he overlooked it, helped with the work, and then they took a boat ride. When they returned he proposed that she should select her favourite likeness of her mother, and the next time he went to the city he would take it with his, and order the enlargements he had planned. To save carrying a lighted lamp into the closet he brought her little trunk to the living-room, where she opened it and hunted the pictures. There were several, and all of them were of a young, elegantly dressed woman of great beauty. The Harvester studied them long.

"Who was she, Ruth?" he asked at last.

"I don't know, and I have no desire to learn."

"Can you explain how the girl here represented came to marry a brother of Henry Jameson?"

"Yes. I was past twelve when my father came the last time, and I remember him distinctly. If Uncle Henry were properly clothed, he is not a bad man in appearance, unless he is very angry. He can use proper language, if he chooses. My father was the best in him, refined and intensified. He was much taller, very good looking, and he dressed and spoke well. They were born and grew to manhood in the East, and came out here at the same time. Where Uncle Henry is a trickster and a trader in stock, my father went a step higher, and tricked and traded in men—and women! Mother told me this much once. He saw her somewhere and admired her. He learned who she was, went to her father's law office and pretended he was representing some great business in the West, until he was welcomed as a promising client. He hung around and when she came in one day her father was forced to introduce them. The remainder is the same world-old story—a good looking, glib-tongued man, plying every art known to an expert, on an innocent girl."

"Is he dead, Ruth?"

"We thought so. We hoped so."

"Your mother did not feel that her people might be suffering for her as she was for them?"

"Not after she appealed to them twice and received no reply."

"Perhaps they tried to find her. Maybe she has a father or mother who is longing for word from her now. Are you very sure you are right in not wanting to know?"

"She never gave me a hint from which I could tell who or where they were. In so gentle a woman as my mother that only could mean she did not want them to know of her. Neither do I. This is the photograph I prefer; please use it."

"I'll put back the trunk in the morning, when I can see better," said the Harvester.

The Girl closed it, and soon went to bed. But there was no sleep for the man. He went into the night, and for hours he paced the driveway in racking thought. Then he sat on the step and looked at Belshazzar before him.

"Life's growing easier every minute, Bel," said the Harvester. "Here's my Dream Girl, lovely as the most golden instant of that wonderful dream, offering me—offering me, Bel—in my present pass, the lips and the love of my little sister who never was born. And I've hurt Ruth's feelings, and sent her to bed with a heartache, trying to make her see that it won't do. It won't, Bel! If I can't have genuine love, I don't want anything. I told her so as plainly as I could find words, and set her crying, and made her unhappy to end a wonderful day. But in some way she has got to learn that propinquity, tolerance, approval, affection, even—is not love. I can't take the risk, after all these years of waiting for the real thing. If I did, and love never came, I would end—well, I know how I would end—and that would spoil her life. I simply have got to brace up, Bel, and keep on trying. She thinks it is nonsense about thrills, and some wonderful feeling that takes possession of you. Lord, Bel! There isn't much nonsense about the thing that rages in my brain, heart, soul, and body. It strikes me as the gravest reality that ever overtook a man.

"She is growing wonderfully attached to me. 'Couldn't live without me,' Bel, that is what she said. Maybe it would be a scheme to bring Granny here to stay with her, and take a few months in some city this winter on those chemical points that trouble me. There is an old saying about 'absence making the heart grow fonder.' Maybe separation is the thing to work the trick. I've tried about everything else I know.

"But I'm in too much of a hurry! What a fool a man is! A few weeks ago, Bel, I said to myself that if Harmon were away and had no part in her life I'd be the happiest man alive. Happiest man alive! Bel, take a look at me now! Happy! Well, why shouldn't I be happy? She is here. She is growing in strength and beauty every hour. She cares more for me day by day. From an outside viewpoint it seems as if I had almost all a man could ask in reason. But when was a strong man in the grip of love ever reasonable? I think the Almighty took a pretty grave responsibility when He made men as He did. If I had been He, and understood the forces I was handling, I would have been too big a coward to do it. There is nothing for me, Bel, but to move on doing my level best; and if she doesn't awaken soon, I will try the absent treatment. As sure as you are the most faithful dog a man ever owned, Bel, I'll try the absent treatment."

The Harvester arose and entered the cabin, stepping softly, for it was dark in the Girl's room, and he could not hear a sound there. He turned up the lights in the living-room. As he did so the first thing he saw was the little trunk. He looked at it intently, then picked up a book. Every page he turned he glanced again at the trunk. At last he laid down the book and sat staring, his brain working rapidly. He ended by carrying the trunk to his room. He darkened the living-room, lighted his own, drew the rain screens, and piece by piece carefully examined the contents. There were the pictures, but the name of the photographer had been removed. There was not a word that would help in identification. He emptied it to the bottom, and as he picked up the last piece his fingers struck in a peculiar way that did not give the impression of touching a solid surface. He felt over it carefully, and when he examined with a candle he plainly could see where the cloth lining had been cut and lifted.

For a long time he knelt staring at it, then he deliberately inserted his knife blade and raised it. The cloth had been glued to a heavy sheet of pasteboard the exact size of the trunk bottom. Beneath it lay half a dozen yellow letters, and face down two tissue-wrapped photographs. The Harvester examined them first. They were of a man close forty, having a strong, aggressive face, on which pride and dominant will power were prominently indicated. The other was a reproduction of a dainty and delicate woman, with exquisitely tender and gentle features. Long the Harvester studied them. The names of the photographer and the city were missing. There was nothing except the faces. He could detect traces of the man in the poise of the Girl and the carriage of her head, and suggestions of the woman in the refined sweetness of her expression. Each picture represented wealth in dress and taste in pose. Finally he laid them together on the table, picked up one of the letters, and read it. Then he read all of them.

Before he finished, tears were running down his cheeks, and his resolution was formed. These were the appeals of an adoring mother, crazed with fear for the safety of an only child, who unfortunately had fallen under the influence of a man the mother dreaded and feared, because of her knowledge of life and men of his character. They were one long, impassioned plea for the daughter not to trust a stranger, not to believe that vows of passion could be true when all else in life was false, not to trust her untried judgment of men and the world against the experience of her parents. But whether the tears that stained those sheets had fallen from the eyes of the suffering mother or the starved and deserted daughter, there was no way for the Harvester to know. One thing was clear: It was not possible for him to rest until he knew if that woman yet lived and bore such suffering. But every trace of address had been torn away, and there was nothing to indicate where or in what circumstances these letters had been written.

A long time the Harvester sat in deep thought. Then he returned all the letters save one. This with the pictures he made into a packet that he locked in his desk. The trunk he replaced and then went to bed. Early the next morning he drove to Onabasha and posted the parcel. The address it bore was that of the largest detective agency in the country. Then he bought an interesting book, a box of fruit, and hurried back to the Girl. He found her on the veranda, Belshazzar stretched close with one eye shut and the other on his charge, whose cheeks were flushed with lovely colour as she bent over her drawing material. The Harvester went to her with a rush, and slipping his fingers under her chin, tilted back her head against him.

"Got a kiss for me, honey?" he inquired.

"No sir," answered the Girl emphatically. "I gave you a perfectly lovely one yesterday, and you said it was not right. I am going to try just once more, and if you say again that it won't do, I'm going back to Chicago or to my dear Uncle Henry, I haven't decided which."

Her lips were smiling, but her eyes were full of tears.

"Why thank you, Ruth! I think that is wonderful," said the Harvester. "I'll risk the next one. In the meantime, excuse me if I give you a demonstration of the real thing, just to furnish you an idea of how it should be."

The Harvester delivered the sample, and went striding to the marsh. The dazed Girl sat staring at her work, trying to realize what had happened; for that was the first time the Harvester had kissed her on the lips, and it was the material expression a strong man gives the woman he loves when his heart is surging at high tide. The Girl sat motionless, gazing at her study.

In the marsh she knew the Harvester was reaping queen-of-the-meadow, and around the high borders, elecampane and burdock. She could hear his voice in snatches of song or cheery whistle; notes that she divined were intended to keep her from worrying. Intermingled with them came the dog's bark of defiance as he digged for an escaping chipmunk, his note of pleading when he wanted a root cut with the mattock, his cry of discovery when he thought he had found something the Harvester would like, or his yelp of warning when he scented danger. The Girl looked down the drive to the lake and across at the hedge. Everywhere she saw glowing colour, with intermittent blue sky and green leaves, all of it a complete picture, from which nothing could be spared. She turned slowly and looked toward the marsh, trying to hear the words of the song above the ripple of Singing Water, and to see the form of the man. Slowly she lifted her handkerchief and pressed it against her lips, as she whispered in an awed voice,

"My gracious Heaven, is *that* the kind of a kiss he is expecting me to give *him*? Why, I couldn't—not to save my life."

She placed her brushes in water, set the colour box on the paper, and went to the kitchen to prepare the noon lunch. As she worked the soft colour deepened in her cheeks, a new light glowed in her eyes, and she hummed over the tune that floated across the marsh. She was very busy when the Harvester came, but he spoke casually of his morning's work, ate heartily, and ordered her to take a nap while he washed roots and filled the trays, and then they went to the woods together for the afternoon.

In the evening they came home to the cabin and finished the day's work. As the night was chilly, the Harvester heaped some bark in the living-room fireplace, and lay on the rug before it, while the Girl sat in an easy chair and watched him as he talked. He was telling her about some wonderful combinations he was going to compound for different ailments and he laughingly asked her if she wanted to be a millionaire's wife and live in a palace.

"Of course I could if I wanted to!" she suggested.

"You could!" cried the Harvester. "All that is necessary is to combine a few proper drugs in one great remedy and float it. That is easy! The people will do the remainder."

"You talk as if you believe that," marvelled the Girl.

"Want it proven?" challenged the Harvester.

"No!" she cried in swift alarm. "What do we want with more than we have? What is there necessary to happiness that is not ours now? Maybe it is true that the 'love of money is the root of all evil.' Don't you ever get a lot just to find out. You said the night I came here that you didn't want more than you had and now I don't. I won't have it! It might bring restlessness and discontent. I've seen it make other people unhappy and separate them. I don't want money, I want work. You make your remedies and offer them to suffering humanity for just a living profit, and I'll keep house and draw designs. I am perfectly happy, free, and unspeakably content. I never dreamed that it was possible for me to be so glad, and so filled with the joy of life. There is only one thing on earth I want. If I only could—"

"Could what, Ruth?"

"Could get that kiss right—"

The Harvester laughed.

"Forget it, I tell you!" he commanded. "Just so long as you worry and fret, so long I've got to wait. If you quit thinking about it, all 'unbeknownst' to yourself you'll awake some morning with it on your lips. I can see traces of it growing stronger every day. Very soon now it's going to materialize, and then get out of my way, for I'll be a whirling, irresponsible lunatic, with the wild joy of it. Oh I've got faith in that kiss of yours, Ruth! It's on the way. The fates have booked it. There isn't a reason on earth why I should be served so scurvy a trick as to miss it, and I never will believe that I shall—"

"David," interrupted the Girl, "go on talking and don't move a muscle, just reach over presently and fix the fire or something, and then turn naturally and look at the window beside your door."

"Shall miss it," said the Harvester steadily. "That would be too unmerciful. What do you see, Ruth?"

"A face. If I am not greatly mistaken, it is my Uncle Henry and he appears like a perfect fiend. Oh David, I am afraid!"

"Be quiet and don't look," said the Harvester.

He turned and tossed a piece of bark on the fire. Then he reached for the poker, pushed it down and stirred the coals. He arose as he worked.

"Rise slowly and quietly and go to your room. Stay there until I call you."

With the Girl out of the way, the Harvester pottered over the fire, and when the flame leaped he lifted a stick of wood, hesitated as if it were too small, and laying it down, started to bring a larger one. In the dining-room he caught a small stick from the wood box, softly stepped from the door, and ran around the house. But he awakened Belshazzar on the kitchen floor, and the dog barked and ran after him. By the time the Harvester reached the corner of his room the man leaped upon a horse and went racing down the drive. The Harvester flung the stick of wood, but missed the man and hit the horse. The dog sprang past the Harvester and vanished. There was the sound and flash of a revolver, and the rattle of the bridge as the horse crossed it. The dog came back unharmed. The Harvester ran to the telephone, called the Onabasha police, and asked them to send a mounted man to meet the intruder before he could reach a cross road; but they were too slow and missed him. However, the Girl was certain she had recognized her uncle, and was extremely nervous; but the Harvester only laughed and told her it was a trip made out of curiosity. Her uncle wanted to see if he could learn if she were well and happy, and he finally convinced her that this was the case, although he was not very sanguine himself.

For the next three days the Harvester worked in the woods and he kept the Girl with him every minute. By the end of that time he really had persuaded himself that it was merely curiosity. So through the cooling fall days they worked together. They were very happy. Before her wondering eyes the Harvester hung queer branches, burs, nuts, berries, and trailing vines with curious seed pods. There were masses of brilliant flowers, most of them strange to the Girl, many to the great average of humanity. While she sat bending over them, beside her the Harvester delved in the black earth of the woods, or the clay and sand of the open hillside, or the muck of the lake shore, and lifted large bagfuls of roots that he later drenched on the floating raft on the lake, and when they had drained he dried them. Some of them he did not wet, but scraped and wiped clean and dry. Often after she was sleeping, and long before she awoke in the morning, he was at work carry-ing heaped trays from the evaporator to the store-room, and tying the roots, leaves, bark, and seeds into packages.

While he gathered trillium roots the Girl made drawings of the plant and learned its commercial value. She drew lady's slipper and Solomon's seal, and learned their uses and prices; and carefully traced wild ginger leaves while nibbling the aromatic root. It was difficult to keep from protesting when the work carried them around the lake shore and to the pokeberry beds, for the colour of these she loved. It required careful explanation as to the value of the roots and seeds as blood purifier, and the argument that in a few more days the frost would level the bed, to induce her to consent to its harvesting. But when the case was properly presented, she put aside her drawing and stained her slender fingers gathering the seeds, and loved the work.

The sun was golden on the lake, the birds of the upland were clustering over reeds and rushes, for the sake of plentiful seed and convenient water. Many of them sang fitfully, the notes of almost all of them were melodious, and the day was a long, happy dream. There was but little left to gather until ginseng time. For that the Harvester had engaged several boys to help him, for the task of digging the roots, washing and drying them, burying part of the seeds and preparing the remainder for market seemed endless for one man to attempt. After a full day the Harvester lay before the fire, and his head was so close the Girl's knee that her fingers were in reach of his hair. Every time he mended the fire he moved a little, until he could feel the touch of her garments against him. Then he began to plan for the winter; how they would store food for the long, cold days, how much fuel would be required, when they would go to the city for their winter clothing, what they would read, and how they would work together at the drawings.

"I am almost too anxious to wait longer to get back to my carving," he said. "Whoever would have thought this spring that fall would come and find the birds talking of going, the caterpillars spinning winter quarters, the animals holing up, me getting ready for the cold, and your candlesticks not finished. Winter is when you really need them. Then there is solid cheer in numbers of candles and a roaring wood fire. The furnace is going to be a good thing to keep the floors and the bathroom warm, but an open fire of dry, crackling wood is the only rational source of heat in a home. You must watch for the fairy dances on the backwall, Ruth, and learn to trace goblin faces in the coals. Sometimes there is a panorama of temples and trees, and you will find exquisite colour in the smoke. Dry maple makes a lovely lavender, soft and fine as a floating veil, and damp elm makes a blue, and hickory red and yellow. I almost can tell which wood is burning after the bark is gone, by the smoke and flame colour. When the little red fire fairies come out and dance on the backwall it is fun to figure what they are celebrating. By the way, Ruth, I have been a lamb for days. I hope you have observed! But I would sleep a little sounder to-night if you only could give me a hint whether that kiss is coming on at all."

He tipped back his head to see her face, and it was glorious in the red firelight; the big eyes never appeared so deep and dark. The tilted head struck her hand, and her fingers ran through his hair.

"You said to forget it," she reminded him, "and then it would come sooner."

"Which same translated means that it is not here yet. Well, I didn't expect it, so I am not disappointed; but begorry, I do wish it would materialize by Christmas.

I think I will work for that. Wouldn't it make a day worth while, though? By the way, what do you want for Christmas, Ruth?"

"A doll," she answered.

The Harvester laughed. He tipped his head again to see her face and suddenly grew quiet, for it was very serious.

"I am quite in earnest," she said. "I think the big dolls in the stores are beautiful, and I never owned only a teeny little one. All my life I've wanted a big doll as badly as I ever longed for anything that was not absolutely necessary to keep me alive. In fact, a doll is essential to a happy childhood. The mother instinct is so ingrained in a girl that if she doesn't have dolls to love, even as a baby, she is deprived of a part of her natural rights. It's a pitiful thing to have been the little girl in the picture who stands outside the window and gazes with longing soul at the doll she is anxious to own and can't ever have. Harvester, I was always that little girl. I am quite in earnest. I want a big, beautiful doll more than anything else."

As she talked the Girl's fingers were idly threading the Harvester's hair. His head lightly touched her knee, and she shifted her position to afford him a comfortable resting place. With a thrill of delight that shook him, the man laid his head in her lap and looked into the fire, his face glowing as a happy boy's.

"You shall have the loveliest doll that money can buy, Ruth," he promised. "What else do you want?"

"A roasted goose, plum pudding, and all those horrid indigestible things that Christmas stories always tell about; and popcorn balls, and candy, and everything I've always wanted and never had, and a long beautiful day with you. That's all!"

"Ruth, I'm so happy I almost wish I could go to Heaven right now before anything occurs to spoil this," said the Harvester.

The wheels of a car rattled across the bridge. He whirled to his knees, and put his arms around the Girl.

"Ruth," he said huskily. "I'll wager a thousand dollars I know what is coming. Hug me tight, quick! and give me the best kiss you can—any old kind of a one, so you touch my lips with yours before I've got to open that door and let in trouble."

The Girl threw her arms around his neck and with the imprint of her lips warm on his the Harvester crossed the room, and his heart dropped from the heights with a thud. He stepped out, closing the door behind him, and crossing the veranda, passed down the walk. He recognized the car as belonging to a garage in Onabasha, and in it sat two men, one of whom spoke.

"Are you David Langston?"

"Yes," said the Harvester.

"Did you send a couple of photographs to a New York detective agency a few days ago with inquiries concerning some parties you wanted located?"

"I did," said the Harvester. "But I was not expecting any such immediate returns."

"Your questions touched on a case that long has been in the hands of the agency, and they telegraphed the parties. The following day the people had a letter, giving them the information they required, from another source."

"That is where Uncle Henry showed his fine Spencerian hand," commented the Harvester. "It always will be a great satisfaction that I got my fist in first."

"Is Miss Jameson here?"

"No," said the Harvester. "My wife is at home. Her surname was Ruth Jameson, but we have been married since June. Did you wish to speak with Mrs. Langston?"

"I came for that purpose. My name is Kennedy. I am the law partner and the closest friend of the young lady's grandfather. News of her location has prostrated her grandmother so that he could not leave her, and I was sent to bring the young woman."

"Oh!" said the Harvester. "Well you will have to interview her about that. One word first. She does not know that I sent those pictures and made that inquiry. One other word. She is just recovering from a case of fever, induced by wrong conditions of life before I met her. She is not so strong as she appears. Understand you are not to be abrupt. Go very gently! Her feelings and health must be guarded with extreme care."

The Harvester opened the door, and as she saw the stranger, the Girl's eyes widened, and she arose and stood waiting.

"Ruth," said the Harvester, "this is a man who has been making quite a search for you, and at last he has you located."

The Harvester went to the Girl's side, and put a reinforcing arm around her.

"Perhaps he brings you some news that will make life most interesting and very lovely for you. Will you shake hands with Mr. Kennedy?"

The Girl suddenly straightened to unusual height.

"I will hear why he has been making 'quite a search for me,' and on whose authority he has me 'located,' first," she said.

A diabolical grin crossed the face of the Harvester, and he took heart.

"Then please be seated, Mr. Kennedy," he said, "and we will talk over the matter. As I understand, you are a representative of my wife's people."

The Girl stared at the Harvester.

"Take your chair, Ruth, and meet this as a matter of course," he advised casually. "You always have known that some day it must come. You couldn't look in the face of those photographs of your mother in her youth and not realize that somewhere hearts were aching and breaking, and brains were busy in a search for her."

The Girl stood rigid.

"I want it distinctly understood," she said, "that I have no use on earth for my mother's people. They come too late. I absolutely refuse to see or to hold any communication with them."

"But young lady, that is very arbitrary!" cried Mr. Kennedy. "You don't understand! They are a couple of old people, and they are slowly dying of broken hearts!"

"Not so badly broken or they wouldn't die slowly," commented the Girl grimly. "The heart that was really broken was my mother's. The torture of a starved, overworked body and hopeless brain was hers. There was nothing slow about her death, for she went out with only half a life spent, and much of that in acute agony, because of their negligence. David, you often have said that this is my home. I choose to take you at your word. Will you kindly tell this man that he is not welcome in this house, and I wish him to leave it at once?"

The Harvester stepped back, and his face grew very white.

"I can't, Ruth," he said gently.

"Why not?"

"Because I brought him here."

"You brought him here! You! David, are you crazy? You!"

"It is through me that he came."

The Girl caught the mantel for support.

"Then I stand alone again," she said. "Harvester, I had thought you were on my side."

"I am at your feet," said the man in a broken voice. "Ruth dear, will you let me explain?"

"There is only one explanation, and with what you have done for me fresh in my mind, I can't put it into words."

"Ruth, hear me!"

"I must! You force me! But before you speak understand this: Not now, or through all eternity, do I forgive the inexcusable neglect that drove my mother to what I witnessed and was helpless to avert."

"My dear! My dear!" said the Harvester, "I had hoped the woods had done a more perfect work in your heart. Your mother is lying in state now, Girl, safe from further suffering of any kind; and if I read aright, her tired face and shrivelled frame were eloquent of forgiveness. Ruth dear, if she so loved them that her heart was broken and she died for them, think what they are suffering! Have some mercy on them."

"Get this very clear, David," said the Girl. "She died of hunger for food. Her heart was not so broken that she couldn't have lived a lifetime, and got much comfort out of it, if her body had not lacked sustenance. Oh I was so happy a minute ago. David, why did you do this thing?"

The Harvester picked up the Girl, placed her in a chair, and knelt beside her with his arms around her.

"Because of the *pain in the world*, Ruth," he said simply. "Your mother is sleeping sweetly in the long sleep that knows neither anger nor resentment; and so I was forced to think of a gentle-faced, little old mother whose heart is daily one long ache, whose eyes are dim with tears, and a proud, broken old man who spends his time trying to comfort her, when his life is as desolate as hers."

"How do you know so wonderfully much about their aches and broken hearts?"

"Because I have seen their faces when they were happy, Ruth, and so I know what suffering would do to them. There were pictures of them and letters in the bottom of that old trunk. I searched it the other night and found them; and by what life has done to your mother and to you, I can judge what it is now bringing them. Never can you be truly happy, Ruth, until you have forgiven them, and done what you can to comfort the remainder of their lives. I did it because of the pain in the world, my girl."

"What about my pain?"

"The only way on earth to cure it is through forgiveness. That, and that only, will ease it all away, and leave you happy and free for life and love. So long as you let this rancour eat in your heart, Ruth, you are not, and never can be, normal. You must forgive them, dear, hear what they have to say, and give them the comfort of seeing what they can discover of her in you. Then your heart will be at rest at last, your soul free, you can take your rightful place in life, and the love you crave will awaken in your heart. Ruth, dear you are the acme of gentleness and justice. Be just and gentle now! Give them their chance! My heart aches, and always will ache for the pain you have known, but nursing and brooding over it will not cure it. It is going to take a heroic operation to cut it out, and I chose to be the surgeon. You have said that I once saved your body from pain Ruth, trust me now to free your soul."

"What do you want?"

"I want you to speak kindly to this man, who through my act has come here, and allow him to tell you why he came. Then I want you to do the kind and womanly thing your duty suggests that you should."

"David, I don t understand you!"

"That is no difference," said the Harvester. "The point is, do you TRUST me?"

The Girl hesitated. "Of course I do," she said at last.

"Then hear what your grandfather's friend has come to say for him, and forget yourself in doing to others as you would have them—really, Ruth, that is all of religion or of life worth while. Go on, Mr. Kennedy."

The Harvester drew up a chair, seated himself beside the Girl, and taking one of her hands, he held it closely and waited.

"I was sent here by my law partner and my closest friend, Mr. Alexander Herron, of Philadelphia," said the stranger. "Both he and Mrs. Herron were bitterly opposed to your mother's marriage, because they knew life and human nature, and there never is but one end to men such as she married."

"You may omit that," said the Girl coldly. "Simply state why you are here."

"In response to an inquiry from your husband concerning the originals of some photographs he sent to a detective agency in New York. They have had the case for years, and recognizing the pictures as a clue, they telegraphed Mr. Herron. The prospect of news after years of fruitless searching so prostrated Mrs. Herron that he dared not leave her, and he sent me."

"Kindly tell me this," said the Girl. "Where were my mother's father and mother for the four years immediately following her marriage?"

"They went to Europe to avoid the humiliation of meeting their friends. There, in Italy, Mrs. Herron developed a fever, and it was several years before she could be brought home. She retired from society, and has been confined to her room ever since. When they could return, a search was instituted at once for their daughter, but they never have been able to find a trace. They have hunted through every eastern city they thought might contain her."

"And overlooked a little insignificant place like Chicago, of course."

"I myself conducted a personal search there, and visited the home of every Jameson in the directory or who had mail at the office or of whom I could get a clue of any sort."

"I don't suppose two women in a little garret room would be in the directory, and there never was any mail."

"Did your mother ever appeal to her parents?"

"She did," said the Girl. "She admitted that she had been wrong, asked their forgiveness, and begged to go home. That was in the second year of her marriage, and she was in Cleveland. Afterward she went to Chicago, from there she wrote again."

"Her father and mother were in Italy fighting for the mother's life, two years after that. It is very easy to become lost in a large city. Criminals do it every day and are never found, even with the best detectives on their trail. I am very sorry about this. My friends will be broken-hearted. At any time they would have been more than delighted to have had their daughter return. A letter on the day following the message from the agency brought news that she was dead, and now their only hope for any small happiness at the close of years of suffering lies with you. I was sent to plead with you to return with me at once and make them a visit. Of course, their home is yours. You are their only heir, and they would be very happy if you were free, and would remain permanently with them."

"How do they know I will not be like the father they so detested?"

"They had sufficient cause to dislike him. They have every reason to love and welcome you. They are consumed with anxiety. Will you come?"

"No. This is for me to decide. I do not care for them or their property. Always they have failed me when my distress was unspeakable. Now there is only one thing I ask of life, more than my husband has given me, and if that lay in his power I would have it. You may go back and tell them that I am perfectly happy. I have everything I need. They can give me nothing I want, not even their love. Perhaps, sometime, I will go to see them for a few days, if David will go with me."

"Young woman, do you realize that you are issuing a death sentence?" asked the lawyer gently.

"It is a just one."

"I do not believe your husband agrees with you. I know I do not. Mrs. Herron is a tiny old lady, with a feeble spark of vitality left; and with all her strength she is clinging to life, and pleading with it to give her word of her only child before she goes out unsatisfied. She knows that her daughter is gone, and now her hopes are fastened on you. If for only a few days, you certainly must go with me."

"I will not!"

The lawyer turned to the Harvester.

"She will be ready to start with you to-morrow morning, on the first train north," said the Harvester. "We will meet you at the station at eight."

"I—I am afraid I forgot to tell my driver to wait."

"You mean your instructions were not to let the Girl out of your sight," said the Harvester. "Very well! We have comfortable rooms. I will show you to one. Please come this way."

The Harvester led the guest to the lake room and arranged for the night. Then he went to the telephone and sent a message to an address he had been furnished, asking for an immediate reply. It went to Philadelphia and contained a description of the lawyer, and asked if he had been sent by Mr. Herron to escort his grand-daughter to his home. When the Harvester returned to the living-room the Girl, white and defiant, waited before the fire. He knelt beside her and put his arms around her, but she repulsed him; so he sat on the rug and looked at her.

"No wonder you felt sure you knew what that was!" she cried bitterly.

"Ruth, if you will allow me to lift the bottom of that old trunk, and if you will read any one of the half dozen letters I read, you will forgive me, and begin making preparations to go."

"It's a wonder you don't hold them before me and force me to read them," she said.

"Don't say anything you will be sorry for after you are gone, dear."

"I'm not going!"

"Oh yes you are!"

"Why?"

"Because it is right that you should, and right is inexorable. Also, because I very much wish you to; you will do it for me."

"Why do you want me to go?"

"I have three strong reasons: First, as I told you, it is the only thing that will cleanse your heart of bitterness and leave it free for the tenanting of a great and holy love. Next, I think they honestly made every effort to find your mother, and are now growing old in despair you can lighten, and you owe it to them and yourself to do it. Lastly, for my sake. I've tried everything I know, Ruth, and I can't make you love me, or bring you to a realizing sense of it if you do. So before I saw that chest I had planned to harvest my big crop, and try with all my heart while I did it, and if love hadn't come then, I meant to get some one to stay with you, and I was going away to give you a free perspective for a time. I meant to plead that I needed a few weeks with a famous chemist I know to prepare me better for my work. My real motive was to leave you, and let you see if absence could do anything for me in your heart. You've been very nearly the creature of my hands for months, my girl; whatever any one else may do, you're bound to miss me mightily, and I figured that with me away, perhaps you could solve the problem alone I seem to fail in helping you with. This is only a slight change of plans. You are going in my stead. I will harvest the ginseng and cure it, and then, if you are not at home, and the loneliness grows unbearable, I will take the chemistry course, until you decide when you will come, if ever."

"'If ever?'"

"Yes," said the Harvester. "I am growing accustomed to facing big propositions— I will not dodge this. The faces of the three of your people I have seen prove

728

refinement. Their clothing indicates wealth. These long, lonely years mean that they will shower you with every outpouring of loving, hungry hearts. They will keep you if they can, my dear. I do not blame them. The life I propose for you is one of work, mostly for others, and the reward, in great part, consists of the joy in the soul of the creator of things that help in the world. I realize that you will find wealth, luxury, and lavish love. I know that I may lose you forever, and if it is right and best for you, I hope I will. I know exactly what I am risking, but I yet say, go."

"I don't see how you can, and love me as you prove you do."

"That is a little streak of the inevitableness of nature that the forest has ground into my soul. I'd rather cut off my right hand than take yours with it, in the parting that will come in the morning; but you are going, and I am sending you. So long as I am shaped like a human being, it is in me to dignify the possession of a vertical spine by acting as nearly like a man as I know how. I insist that you are my wife, because it crucifies me to think otherwise. I tell you to-night, Ruth, you are not and never have been. You are free as air. You married me without any love for me in your heart, and you pretended none. It was all my doing. If I find that I was wrong, I will free you without a thought of results to me. I am a secondary proposition. I thought then that you were alone and helpless, and before the Almighty, I did the best I could. But I know now that you are entitled to the love of relatives, wealth, and high social position, no doubt. If I allowed the passion in my heart to triumph over the reason of my brain, and worked on your feelings and tied you to the woods, without knowing but that you might greatly prefer that other life you do not know, but to which you are entitled, I would go out and sink myself in Loon Lake."

"David, I love you. I do not want to go. Please, please let me remain with you."

"Not if you could say that realizing what it means, and give me the kiss right now I would stake my soul to win! Not by any bribe you can think of or any allurement you can offer. It is right that you go to those suffering old people. It is right you know what you are refusing for me, before you renounce it. It is right you take the position to which you are entitled, until you understand thoroughly whether this suits you better. When you know that life as well as this, the people you will meet as intimately as me, then you can decide for all time, and I can look you in the face with honest, unwavering eye; and if by any chance your heart is in the woods, and you prefer me and the cabin to what they have to offer—to all eternity your place here is vacant, Ruth. My love is waiting for you; and if you come under those conditions, I never can have any regret. A clear conscience is worth restraining passion a few months to gain, and besides, I always have got the fact to face that when you say 'I love,' and when I say 'I love,' it means two entirely different things. When you realize that the love of man for woman, and woman for man, is a thing that floods the heart, brain, soul, and body with a wonderful and all-pervading ecstasy, and if I happen to be the man who makes you realize it, then come tell me, and we will show God and His holy angels what earth means by the Heaven inspired word, 'radiance.'"

"David, there never will be any other man like you."

"The exigencies of life must develop many a finer and better."

"You still refuse me? You yet believe I do not love you?"

"Not with the love I ask, my girl. But if I did not believe it was germinating in your heart, and that it would come pouring over me in a torrent some glad day, I doubt if I could allow you to go, Ruth! I am like any other man in selfishness and in the passions of the body."

"Selfishness! You haven't an idea what it means," said the Girl. "And what you call love—there I haven't. But I know how to appreciate you, and you may be positively sure that it will be only a few days until I will come back to you."

"But I don't want you until you can bring the love I crave. I am sending you to remain until that time, Ruth."

"But it may be months, Man!"

"Then stay months."

"But it may be—"

"It may be never! Then remain forever. That will be proof positive that your happiness does not lie in my hands."

"Why should I not consider you as you do me?"

"Because I love you, and you do not love me."

"You are cruel to yourself and to me. You talk about the pain in the world. What about the pain in my heart right now? And if I know you in the least, one degree more would make you cry aloud for mercy. Oh David, are we of no consideration at all?"

The muscles of the Harvester's face twisted an instant.

"This is where we lop off the small branches to grow perfect fruit later. This is where we do evil that good may result. This is where we suffer to-night in order we may appreciate fully the joy of love's dawning. If I am causing you pain, forgive me, dear heart. I would give my life to prevent it, but I am powerless. It is right! We cannot avoid doing it, if we ever would be happy."

He picked up the Girl, and held her crushed in his arms a long time. Then he set her inside her door and said, "Lay out what you want to take and I will help you pack, so that you can get some sleep. We must be ready early in the morning."

When the clothing to be worn was selected, the new trunk packed, and all arrangements made, the Girl sat in his arms before the fire as he had held her when she was ill, and then he sent her to bed and went to the lake shore to fight it out alone. Only God and the stars and the faithful Belshazzar saw the agony of a strong man in his extremity.

Near dawn he heard the tinkle of the bell and went to receive his message and order a car for morning. Then he returned to the merciful darkness of night, and paced the driveway until light came peeping over the tree tops. He prepared breakfast and an hour later put the Girl on the train, and stood watching it until the last rift of smoke curled above the spires of the city.

Chapter 20

The Man in the Background

Then the Harvester returned to Medicine Woods to fight his battle alone. At first the pain seemed unendurable, but work always had been his panacea, it was his salvation now. He went through the cabin, folding bedding and storing it in closets, rolling rugs sprinkled with powdered alum, packing cushions, and taking window seats from the light.

"Our sleeping room and the kitchen will serve for us, Bel," he said. "We will put all these other things away carefully, so they will be as good as new when the Girl comes home."

The evening of the second day he was called to the telephone.

"There is a telegram for you," said a voice. "A message from Philadelphia. It reads: 'Arrived safely. Thank you for making me come. Dear old people. Will write soon. With love, Ruth.'

"Have you got it?"

"No," lied the Harvester, grinning rapturously. "Repeat it again slowly, and give me time after each sentence to write it. Now! Go on!"

He carried the message to the back steps and sat reading it again and again.

"I supposed I'd have to wait at least four days," he said to Ajax as the bird circled before him. "This is from the Girl, old man, and she is not forgetting us to begin with, anyway. She is there all safe, she sees that they need her, they are lovable old people, she is going to write us all about it soon, and she loves us all she knows how to love any one. That should be enough to keep us sane and sensible until her letter comes. There is no use to borrow trouble, so we will say everything in the world is right with us, and be as happy as we can on that until we find something we cannot avoid worrying over. In the meantime, we will have faith to believe that we have suffered our share, and the end will be happy for all of us. I am mighty glad the Girl has a home, and the right kind of people to care for her. Now, when she comes back to me, I needn't feel that she was forced, whether she wanted to or not, because she had nowhere to go. This will let me out with a clean conscience, and that is the only thing on earth that allows a man to live in peace with himself. Now I'll go finish everything else, and then I'll begin the ginseng harvest."

So the Harvester hitched Betsy and with Belshazzar at his feet he drove through the woods to the sarsaparilla beds. He noticed the beautiful lobed leaves, at which the rabbits had been nibbling, and the heads of lustrous purple-black berries as he began digging the roots that he sold for stimulants.

"I might have needed a dose of you now myself," the Harvester addressed a heap of uprooted plants, "if the electric wires hadn't brought me a better. Great invention that! Never before realized it fully! I thought to-day would be black as night, but that message changes the complexion of affairs mightily. So I'll dig you for people who really are in need of something to brace them up."

After the sarsaparilla was on the trays, he attacked the beds of Indian hemp, with its long graceful pods, and took his usual supply. Then he worked diligently on the warm hillside over the dandelion. When these were finished he brought half a dozen young men from the city and drilled them on handling ginseng. He was warm, dirty, and tired when he came from the beds the evening of the fourth day. He finished his work at the barn, prepared and ate his supper, slipped into clean clothing, and walked to the country road where it crossed the lane. There he opened his mail box. The letter he expected with the Philadelphia postmark was inside. He carried it to the bridge, and sitting in her favourite place, with the lake breeze threading his hair, opened his first letter from the Girl.

"My dear Friend, Lover, Husband," it began.

The Harvester turned the sheets face down across his knee, laid his hand on them, and stared meditatively at the lake. "'Friend,'" he commented. "Well, that's all right! I am her friend, as well as I know how to be. 'Lover.' I come in there, full force. I did my level best on that score, though I can't boast myself a howling success; a man can't do more than he knows, and if I had been familiar with all the wiles of expert, professional love makers, they wouldn't have availed me in the Girl's condition. I had a mighty peculiar case to handle in her, and not a particle of training. But if she says 'Lover,' I must have made some kind of a showing on the job. 'Husband.'" A slow flush crept up the brawny neck and tinged the bronzed face. "That's a good word," said the Harvester, "and it must mean a wonderful thing—to some men. 'Who bides his time.' Well, I'm 'biding,' and if my time ever comes to be my Dream Girl's husband, I'll wager all I'm worth on one thing. I'll study the job from every point of the compass, and I'll see what showing I can make on being the kind of a husband that a woman clings to and loves at eighty."

Taking a deep breath the Harvester lifted the letter, and laying one hand on Belshazzar's head, he proceeded—"I might as well admit in the beginning that I cried most of the way here. Some of it was because I was nervous and dreaded the people I would meet, and more on account of what I felt toward them, but most of it was because I did not want to leave you. I have been spoiled dreadfully! You have taught me so to depend on you—and for once I feel that I really can claim to have been an apt pupil—that it was like having the heart torn out of me to come. I want you to know this, because it will teach you that I have a little bit of appreciation of how good you are to me, and to all the world as well. I am glad that I almost cried myself sick over leaving you. I wish now I just had stood up in the car, and roared like a burned baby.

"But all the tears I shed in fear of grandfather and grandmother were wasted. They are a couple of dear old people, and it would have been a crime to allow them to suffer more than they must of necessity. It all seems so different when they talk; and when I see the home, luxuries, and friends my mother had, it appears utterly incomprehensible that she dared leave them for a stranger. Probably the reason she did was because she was grandfather's daughter. He is gentle and tender some of the time, but when anything irritates him, and something does every few minutes, he breaks loose, and such another explosion you never heard. It does not mean a thing, and it seems to lower his tension enough to keep him from bursting with palpitation of the heart or something, but it is a strain for others. At first it frightened me dreadfully. Grandmother is so tiny and frail, so white in her big bed, and when he is the very worst, and she only smiles at him, why I know he does not mean it at all. But, David, I hope you never will get an idea that this would be a pleasant way for you to act, because it would not, and I never would have the courage to offer you the love I have come to find if you slammed a cane and yelled, 'demnation,' at me. Grandmother says she does not mind at all, but I wonder if she did not acquire the habit of lying in bed because it is easier to endure in a prostrate position.

"The house is so big I get lost, and I do not know yet which are servants and which friends; and there is a steady stream of seamstresses and milliners making things for me. Grandmother and father both think I will be quite passable in appearance when I am what they call 'modishly dressed.' I think grandmother will forget herself some day and leave her bed before she knows it, in her eagerness to see how something appears. I could not begin to tell you about all the lovely things to wear, for every occasion under the sun, and they say these are only temporary, until some can be made especially for me.

"They divide the time in sections, and there is an hour to drive, I am to have a horse and ride later, and a time to shop, so long to visit grandmother, and set hours to sleep, dress, to be fitted, taken to see things, music lessons, and a dancing teacher. I think a longer day will have to be provided.

"I do not care anything about dancing. I know what would make me dance nicely enough for anything, but I am going to try the music, and see if I can learn just a few little songs and some old melodies for evening, when the work is done, the fire burns low, and you are resting on the rug. There is enough room for a piano between your door and the south wall and that corner seems vacant anyway. You would like it, David, I know, if I could play and sing just enough to put you to sleep nicely. It is in the back of my head that I will try to do every single thing, just as they want me to, and that will make them happy, but never forget that the instant I feel in my soul that your kiss is right on my lips, I am coming to you by lightning express; and I told them so the first thing, and that I only came because you made me.

"They did not raise an objection, but I am not so dull that I cannot see they are trying to bind me to them from the very first with chains too strong to break. We had just one little clash. Grandfather was mightily pleased over what you told Mr. Kennedy about my never having been your wife, and that I was really free. There seems to be a man, the son of his partner, whom grandfather dearly loves, and he wants me to be friends with his friend. One can see at once what he is planning, because he said he was going to introduce me as Miss Jameson. I told him that would be creating a false impression, because I was a married woman; but he only laughed at me and went straight to doing it.

"Of course, I know why, but he is so terribly set I cannot stop him, so I shall have to tell people myself that I am a staid, old married lady. After all, I suppose I might as well let him go, if it pleases him. I shall know how to protect myself and any one else, from any mistakes concerning me; and in my heart I know what I know, and what I cannot make you believe, but I will some day.

"I suspect you're harvesting the ginseng now. The roar and rush of the city seem strange, as if I never had heard it before, and I feel so crowded. I scarcely can sleep at night for the clamour of the cars, cabs, and throbbing life. Grandfather will not hear a word, and he just sputters and says 'demnation' when I try to tell him about you; but grandmother will listen, and I talk to her of you and Medicine Woods by the hour. She says she thinks you must be a wonderfully nice person. I haven't dared tell her yet the thing that will win her. She is so little and frail, and she has heart trouble so badly; but some day I shall tell her all about Chicago that I can, and then of Uncle Henry, and then about you and the oak, and that will make her love you as I do. There are so many things to do; they have sent for me three times. I shall tell them they must put you on the schedule, and give me so much time to write or I will upset the whole programme.

"I think you will like to know that Mr. Kennedy told grandfather all you said to him about my illness, for almost as soon as I came he brought a very wonderful man to my room, and he asked many questions and I told him all about it, and what I had been doing. He made out a list of things to eat and exercises. I am being taken care of just as you did, so I will go on growing well and strong. The trouble is they are too good to me. I would just love to shuffle my feet in dead leaves, and lie on the grass this morning. I never got my swim in the lake. I will have to save that until next summer. He also told grandfather what you said about Uncle Henry, and I think he was pleased that you tried to find him as soon as you knew. He let me see the letter Uncle Henry wrote, and it was a vile thing—just such as he would write. It asked how much he would be willing to pay for information concerning his heir. I told grandfather all about it, and I saw the answer he wrote. I told him some things to say, and one of them was that the honesty of a man without a price prevented the necessity of anything being paid to find me. The other was that you located my people yourself, and at once sent me to them against my wishes. I was determined he should know that. So Uncle Henry missed his revenge on you. He evidently thought he not only would hurt you by breaking up your home and separating us, but also he would get a reward for his work. He wrote some untrue things about you, and I wish he hadn't, for grandfather can think of enough himself. But I will soon change that. Please, please take good care of all my things, my flowers and vines, and most of all tell Belshazzar to protect you with his life. And you be very good to my dear, dear lover. I will write again soon, Ruth."

When the Harvester had studied the letter until he could repeat it backward, he went to the cabin and answered it. Then he sent subscriptions for two of Philadelphia's big dailies, and harvested ginseng from dawn until black darkness. Never was such a crop grown in America. The beds had been made in the original home of the plant, so that it throve under perfectly natural conditions in the forest, but here and there branches had been thinned above, and nature helped by science below. This resulted in thick, pulpy roots of astonishing size and weight. As the Harvester lifted them he bent the tops and buried part of the seed for another crop. For weeks he worked over the bed. Then the last load went down the hill to the dry-house and the helpers were paid. Next the fall work was finished. Fuel and food were stored for winter, while the cold crept from the lake, swept down the hill and surrounded the cabin.

The Harvester finished long days in the dry-house and store-room, and after supper he sat by the fire reading over the Girl's letters, carving on her candlesticks, or in the work room, bending above the boards he was shaving and polishing for a gift he had planned for her Christmas. The Careys had him in their home for Thanksgiving. He told them all about sending the Girl away himself, read them some of her letters, and they talked with perfect confidence of how soon she would come home. The Harvester tried to think confidently, but as the days went by the letters became fewer, always with the excuse that there was no time to write, but with loving assurance that she was thinking of him and would do better soon.

However they came often enough that he had something new to tell his friends so that they did not suspect that waiting was a trial to him. A few days after Thanksgiving the gift that he had planned was finished. It was a big, burl-maple box, designed after the hope chests that he saw advertised in magazines. The wood was rare, cut in heavy slabs, polished inside and out, dove-tailed corners with ornate brass bindings, hinges and lock, and hand-carved feet. On the inside of the lid cut on a brass plate was the inscription, "Ruth Langston, Christmas of Nineteen Hundred and Ten. David."

Then he began packing the chest. He put in the finished candlesticks and a box of candleberry dips he had made of delightfully spiced wax, coloured pale green. He ordered the doll weeks before from the largest store in Onabasha, and the dealer brought on several that he might make a selection. He chose a large baby doll almost life size, and sent it to the dress-making department to be completely and exquisitely clothed. Long before the day he was picking kernels to glaze from nuts, drying corn to pop, and planning candies to be made of maple sugar. When he figured it was time to start the box, he worked carefully, filling spaces with chestnut and hazel burs, and finishing the tops of boxes with gaudy red and yellow leaves he had kept in their original brightness by packing them in sand. He put in scarlet berries of mountain ash and long twining sprays of yellow and red bitter-sweet berries, for her room. Then he carefully covered the chest with cloth, packed it in an outside box, and sent it to the Girl by express. As he came from the train shed, where he had helped with loading, he met Henry Jameson. Instantly the long arm of the Harvester shot out, and in a grip that could not be broken he caught the man by the back of the neck and proceeded to dangle him. As he did so he roared with laughter.

"Dear Uncle Henry!" he cried. "How did you feel when you got your letter from Philadelphia? Wasn't it a crime that an honest man, which same refers to me, beat you? Didn't you gnash your teeth when you learned that instead of separating me from my wife I had found her people and sent her to them myself? Didn't it rend your soul to miss your little revenge and fail to get the good, fat reward you confidently expected? Ho! Ho! Thus are lofty souls downcast. I pity you, Henry Jameson, but not so much that I won't break your back if you meddle in my affairs again, and I am taking this opportunity to tell you so. Here you go out of my life, for if you appear in it once more I will finish you like a copperhead. Understand?"

With a last shake the Harvester dropped him, and went into the express office, where several men had watched the proceedings.

"Been dipping in your affairs, has he?" asked the expressman.

"Trying it," laughed the Harvester.

"Well he is just moving to Idaho, and you probably won't be bothered with him any more."

"Good news!" said the Harvester. He felt much relieved as he went back to Betsy and drove to Medicine Woods.

The Careys had invited him, but he chose to spend Christmas alone. He had finished breakfast when the telephone bell rang, and the expressman told him there was a package for him from Philadelphia. The Harvester mounted Betsy and rode to the city at once. The package was so very small he slipped it into his pocket, and went to the doctor's to say Merry Christmas! To Mrs. Carey he gave a pretty lavender silk dress, and to the doctor a new watch chain. Then he went to the hospital, where he left with Molly a set of china dishes from the Girl, and a fur-lined great coat, his gift to Doctor Harmon. He rode home and stabled Betsy, giving her an extra quart of oats, and going into the house he sat by the kitchen fire and opened the package.

In a nest of cotton lay a tissue-wrapped velvet box, and inside that, in a leather pocket case, an ivory miniature of the Girl by an artist who knew how to reproduce life. It was an exquisite picture, and a face of wonderful beauty. He looked at it for a long time, and then called Belshazzar and carried it out to show Ajax. Then he put it into his breast pocket squarely over his heart, but he wore the case shiny the first day taking it out. Before noon he went to the mail box and found a long letter from the Girl, full of life, health, happiness, and with steady assurances of love for him, but there was no mention made of coming home.

She seemed engrossed in the music lessons, riding, dancing, pretty clothing, splendid balls, receptions, and parties of all kinds. The Harvester answered it with his heart full of love for her, and then waited. It was a long week before the reply came, and then it was short on account of so many things that must be done, but she insisted that she was well, happy, and having a fine time. After that the letters became less frequent and shorter. At times there would be stretches of almost two weeks with not a line, and then only short notes to explain that she was too busy to write.

Through the dreary, cold days of January and February the Harvester invented work in the store-room, in the workshop, at the candlesticks, sat long over great books, and spent hours in the little laboratory preparing and compounding drugs.

In the evenings he carved and read. First of all he scanned the society columns of the papers he was taking, and almost every day he found the name of Miss Ruth Jameson, often a paragraph describing her dress and her beauty of face and charm of manner; and constantly the name of Mr. Herbert Kennedy appeared as her escort. At first the Harvester ignored this, and said to himself that he was glad she could have enjoyable times and congenial friends, and he was. But as the letters became fewer, paper paragraphs more frequent, and approaching spring worked its old insanity in the blood, gradually an ache crept into his heart again, and there were days when he could not work it out.

Every letter she wrote he answered just as warmly as he felt that he dared, but when they were so long coming and his heart was overflowing, he picked up a pen one night and wrote what he felt. He told her all about the ice-bound lake, the lonely crows in the big woods, the sap suckers' cry, and the gay cardinals' whistle. He told her about the cocoons dangling on bushes or rocking on twigs that he was cutting for her. He warned her that spring was coming, and soon she would begin to miss wonders for her pencil. Then he told her about the silent cabin, the empty rooms, and a lonely man. He begged her not to forget the kiss she had gone to find for him. He poured out his heart unrestrainedly, and then folded the letter, sealed and addressed it to her, in care of the fire fairies, and pitched it into the ashes of the living-room fire place. But expression made him feel better.

There was another longer wait for the next letter, but he had written her so many in the meantime that a little heap of them had accumulated as he passed through the living-room on his way to bed. He had supposed she would be gone until after Christmas when she left, but he never had thought of harvesting sassafras and opening the sugar camp alone. In those days his face appeared weary, and white hairs came again on his temples. Carey met him on the street and told him that he was going to the National Convention of Surgeons at New York in March, and wanted him to go along and present his new medicine for consideration.

"All right," said the Harvester instantly, "I will go."

He went and interviewed Mrs. Carey, and then visited the doctor's tailor, and a shoe store, and bought everything required to put him in condition for travelling in good style, and for the banquet he would be asked to attend. Then he got Mrs. Carey to coach him on spoons and forks, and declared he was ready. When the doctor saw that the Harvester really would go, he sat down and wrote the president of the association, telling him in brief outline of Medicine Woods and the man who had achieved a wonderful work there, and of the compounding of the new remedy.

As he expected, return mail brought an invitation for the Harvester to address the association and describe his work and methods and present his medicine. The doctor went out in the car over sloppy roads with that letter, and located the Harvester in the sugar camp. He explained the situation and to his surprise found his man intensely interested. He asked many questions as to the length of time, and amount of detail required in a proper paper, and the doctor told him.

"But if you want to make a clean sweep, David," he said, "write your paper simply, and practise until it comes easy before you speak."

That night the Harvester left work long enough to get a notebook, and by the light of the camp fire, and in company with the owls and coons, he wrote his outline. One division described his geographical location, another traced his ancestry and education in wood lore. One was a tribute to the mother who moulded his character and ground into him stability for his work. The remainder described his methods in growing drugs, drying and packing them, and the end was a presentation for their examination of the remedy that had given life where a great surgeon had conceded death. Then he began amplification.

When the sugar making was over the Harvester commenced his regular spring work, but his mind was so busy over his paper that he did not have much time to realize just how badly his heart was beginning to ache. Neither did he consign so many letters to the fire fairies, for now he was writing of the best way to dry hydrastis and preserve ginseng seed. The day before time to start he drove to Onabasha to try on his clothing and have Mrs. Carey see if he had been right in his selections.

While he was gone, Granny Moreland, wearing a clean calico dress and carrying a juicy apple pie, came to the stretch of flooded marsh land, and finding the path under water, followed the road and crossing a field reached the levee and came to the bridge of Singing Water where it entered the lake. She rested a few minutes there, and then went to the cabin shining between bare branches. She opened the front door, entered, and stood staring around her.

"Why things is all tore up here," she said. "Now ain't that sensible of David to put everything away and save it nice and careful until his woman gets back. Seems as if she's good and plenty long coming; seems as if her folks needs her mighty bad, or she's having a better time than the boy is or something."

She set the pie on the table, went through the cabin and up the hill a little distance, calling the Harvester. When she passed the barn she missed Betsy and the wagon, and then she knew he was in town. She returned to the living-room and sat looking at the pie as she rested.

"I'd best put you on the kitchen table," she mused. "Likely he will see you there first and eat you while you are fresh. I'd hate mortal bad for him to overlook you, and let you get stale, after all the care I've took with your crust, and all the sugar, cinnamon, and butter that's under your lid. You're a mighty nice pie, and you ort to be et hot. Now why under the sun is all them clean letters pitched in the fireplace?"

Granny knelt and selecting one, she blew off the ashes, wiped it with her apron and read: "To Ruth, in care of the fire fairies."

"What the Sam Hill is the idiot writin' his woman like that for?" cried Granny, bristling instantly. "And why is he puttin' pages and pages of good reading like this must have in it in care of the fire fairies? Too much alone, I guess! He's going wrong in his head. Nobody at themselves would do sech a fool trick as this. I believe I had better do something. Of course I had! These is writ to Ruth; she ort to have them. Wish't I knowed how she gets her mail, I'd send her some. Mebby three! I'd send a fat and a lean, and a middlin' so's that she'd have a sample of all the kinds they is. It's no way to write letters and pitch them in the ashes. It means the poor boy is honin' to say things he dassent and so he's writin' them out and never sendin' them at all. What's the little huzzy gone so long for, anyway? I'll fix her!"

Granny selected three letters, blew away the ashes, and tucked the envelopes inside her dress.

"If I only knowed how to get at her," she muttered. She stared at the pie. "I guess you got to go back," she said, "and be et by me. Like as not I'll stall myself, for I got one a-ready. But if David has got these fool things counted and misses any, and then finds that pie here, he'll s'picion me. Yes, I got to take you back, and hurry my stumps at that."

Granny arose with the pie, cast a lingering and covetous glance at the fireplace, stooped and took another letter, and then started down the drive. Just as she reached the bridge she looked ahead and saw the Harvester coming up the levee. Instantly she shot the pie over the railing and with a groan watched it strike the water and disappear.

"Lord of love!" she gasped, sinking to the seat, "that was one of grandmother's willer plates that I promised Ruth. 'Tain't likely I'll ever see hide ner hair of it again. But they wa'ant no place to put it, and I dassent let him know I'd been up to the cabin. Mebby I can fetch a boy some day and hire him to dive for it. How long can a plate be in water and not get spiled anyway? Now what'll I do? My head's all in a whirl! I'll bet my bosom is a sticking out with his letters 'til he'll notice and take them from me."

She gripped her hands across her chest and sat staring at the Harvester as he stopped on the bridge, and seeing her attitude and distressed face, he sprang from the wagon.

"Why Granny, are you sick?" he cried anxiously.

"Yes!" gasped Granny Moreland. "Yes, David, I am! I'm a miserable woman. I never was in sech a shape in all my days."

"Let me help you to the cabin, and I'll see what I can do for you," offered the Harvester.

"No. This is jest out of your reach," said the old lady. "I want—I want to see Doctor Carey bad."

"Are you strong enough to ride in or shall I bring him?"

"I can go! I can go as well as not, David, if you'll take me."

"Let me run Betsy to the barn and get the Girl's phaeton. The wagon is too rough for you. Are the pains in your chest dreadful?"

"I don't know how to describe them," said Granny with perfect truth.

The Harvester leaped into the wagon and caught up the lines. As he disappeared around the curve of the driveway Granny snatched the letters from her dress front and thrust them deep into one of her stockings.

"Now, drat you!" she cried. "Stick out all you please. Nobody will see you there."

In a few minutes the Harvester helped her into the carriage and drove rapidly toward the city.

"You needn't strain your critter," said Granny. "It's not so bad as that, David."

"Is your chest any better?"

"A sight better," said Granny. "Shakin' up a little 'pears to do me good."

"You never should have tried to walk. Suppose I hadn't been here. And you came the long way, too! I'll have a telephone run to your house so you can call me after this."

Granny sat very straight suddenly.

"My! wouldn't that get away with some of my foxy neighbours," she said. "Me to have a 'phone like they do, an' be conversin' at all hours of the day with my son's folks and everybody. I'd be tickled to pieces, David."

"Then I'll never dare do it," said the Harvester, "because I can't keep house without you."

"Where's your own woman?" promptly inquired Granny.

"She can't leave her people. Her grandmother is sick."

"Grandmother your foot!" cried the old woman. "I've been hearing that song and dance from the neighbours, but you got to fool younger people than me on it, David. When did any grandmother ever part a pair of youngsters jest married, for months at a clip? I'd like to cast my eyes on that grandmother. She's a new breed! I was as good a mother as 'twas in my skin to be, and I'd like to see a child of mine do it for me; and as for my grandchildren, it hustles some of them to re-cog-nize me passing on the big road, 'specially if it's Peter's girl with a town beau."

The Harvester laughed. The old lady leaned toward him with a mist in her eyes and a quaver in her voice, and asked softly, "Got ary friend that could help you, David?"

The man looked straight ahead in silence.

"Bamfoozle all the rest of them as much as you please, lad, but I stand to you in the place of your ma, and so I ast you plainly—got ary friend that could help?"

"I can think of no way in which any one possibly could help me, dear," said the Harvester gently. "It is a matter I can't explain, but I know of nothing that any one could do."

"You mean you're tight-mouthed! You *could* tell me just like you would your ma, if she was up and comin'; but you can't quite put me in her place, and spit it out plain. Now mebby I can help you! Is it her fault or yourn?"

"Mine! Mine entirely!"

"Hum! What a fool question! I might a knowed it! I never saw a lovinger, sweeter girl in these parts. I jest worship the ground she treads on; and you, lad you hain't had a heart in your body sence first you saw her face. If I had the stren'th, I'd haul you out of this keeridge and I'd hammer you meller, David Langston. What in the name of sense have you gone and done to the purty, lovin' child?"

The Harvester's face flushed, but a line around his mouth whitened.

"Loosen up!" commanded Granny. "I got some rights in this case that mebby you don't remember. You asked me to help you get ready for her, and I done what you wanted. You invited me to visit her, and I jest loved her sweet, purty ways. You wanted me to shet up my house and come over for weeks to help take keer of her, and I done it gladly, for her pain and your sufferin' cut me as if 'twas my livin' flesh and blood; so you can't shet me out now. I'm in with you and her to the end. What a blame fool thing have you gone and done to drive away for mouths a girl that fair worshipped you?"

"That's exactly the trouble, Granny," said the Harvester. "She didn't! She merely respected and was grateful to me, and she loved me as a friend; but I never was any nearer her husband than I am yours."

"I've always knowed they was a screw loose somewhere," commented Granny. "And so you've sent her off to her worldly folks in a big, wicked city to get weaned away from you complete?"

"I sent her to let her see if absence would teach her anything. I had months with her here, and I lay awake at nights thinking up new plans to win her.

743

I worked for her love as I never worked for bread, but I couldn't make it. So I let her go to see if separation would teach her anything."

"Mercy me! Why you crazy critter! The child did love you! She loved you 'nough an' plenty! She loved you faithful and true! You was jest the light of her eyes. I don't see how a girl could think more of a man. What in the name of sense are you expecting months of separation to teach her, but to forget you, and mebby turn her to some one else?"

"I hoped it would teach her what I call love, means," explained the Harvester.

"Why you dratted popinjay! If ever in all my born days I wanted to take a man and jest lit'rally mop up the airth with him, it's right here and now. 'Absence teach her what you call love.' Idiot! That's your job!"

"But, Granny, I couldn't!"

"Wouldn't, you mean, no doubt! I hain't no manner of a notion in my head but that child, depending on you, and grateful as she was, and tender and loving, and all sech as that I hain't a doubt but she come to you plain and told you she loved you with all her heart. What more could you ast?"

"That she understand what love means before I can accept what she offers."

"You puddin' head! You blunderbuss!" cried Granny. "Understand what you mean by love. If you're going to bar a woman from being a wife 'til she knows what you mean by love, you'll stop about nine tenths of the weddings in the world, and t'other tenth will be women that no decent-minded man would jine with."

"Granny, are you sure?"

"Well livin' through it, and up'ard of seventy years with other women, ort to teach me something. The Girl offered you all any man needs to ast or git. Her foundations was laid in faith and trust. Her affections was caught by every loving, tender, thoughtful thing you did for her; and everybody knows you did a-plenty, David. I never see sech a master hand at courtin' as you be. You had her lovin' you all any good woman knows how to love a man. All you needed to a-done was to take her in your arms, and make her your wife, and she'd 'a' waked up to what you meant by love."

"But suppose she never awakened?"

"Aw, bosh! S'pose water won't wet! S'pose fire won't burn! S'pose the sun won't shine! That's the law of nature, man! If you think I hain't got no sense at all I jest dare you to ask Doctor Carey. 'Twouldn't take him long to comb the kinks out of you."

"I don't think you have left any, Granny," said the Harvester. "I see what you mean, and in all probability you are right, but I can't send for the Girl."

"Name o' goodness why?"

"Because I sent her away against her will, and now she is remaining so long that there is every probability she prefers the life she is living and the friends she has made there, to Medicine Woods and to me. The only thing I can do now is to await her decision."

"Oh, good Lord!" groaned Granny. "You make me sick enough to kill. Touch up your nag and hustle me to Doc. You can't get me there quick enough to suit me."

At the hospital she faced Doctor Carey. "I think likely some of my innards has got to be cut out and mended," she said. "I'll jest take a few minutes of your time to examination me, and see what you can do."

In the private office she held the letters toward the doctor. "They hain't no manner of sickness ailin' me, Doc. The boy out there is in deep water, and I knowed how much you thought of him, and I hoped you'd give me a lift. I went over to his place this mornin' to take him a pie, and I found his settin' room fireplace heapin' with letters he'd writ to Ruth about things his heart was jest so bustin' full of it eased him to write them down, and then he hadn't the horse sense and trust in her jedgment to send them on to her. I picked two fats, a lean, and a middlin' for samples, and I thought I'd send them some way, and I struck for home with them an' he ketched me plumb on the bridge. I had to throw my pie overboard, willer plate and all, and as God is my witness, I was so flustered the boy had good reason to think I was sick a-plenty; and soon as he noticed it, I thought of you spang off, and I knowed you'd know her whereabouts, and I made him fetch me to you. On the way I jest dragged it from him that he'd sent her away his fool self, because she didn't sense what he meant by love, and she wa'ant beholden to him same degree and manner he was to her. Great day, Doc! Did you ever hear a piece of foolishness to come up with that? I told him to ast you! I told him you'd tell him that no clean, sweet-minded girl ever had known nor ever would know what love means to a man 'til he marries her and teaches her. Ain't it so, Doc?"

"It certainly is."

"Then will you grind it into him, clean to the marrer, and will you send these letters on to Ruthie?"

"Most certainly I will," said the doctor emphatically. Granny opened the door and walked out.

"I'm so relieved, David," she said. "He thinks they won't be no manner o' need to knife me. Likely he can fix up a few pills and send them out by mail so's that I'll be as good as new again. Now we must get right out of here and not take valuable time. What do I owe you, Doc?"

"Not a cent," said Doctor Carey. "Thank you very much for coming to me. You'll soon be all right again."

"I was some worried. Much obliged I am sure. Come on!"

"One minute," said the doctor. "David, I am making up a list of friends to whom I am going to send programmes of the medical meeting, and I thought your wife might like to see you among the speakers, and your subject. What is her address?"

A slow red flushed the Harvester's cheeks. He opened his lips and hesitated. At last he said, "I think perhaps her people prefer that she receive mail under her maiden name while with them. Miss Ruth Jameson, care of Alexander Herron, 5770 Chestnut Street, Philadelphia, will reach her."

The doctor wrote the address, as if it were the most usual thing in the world, and asked the Harvester if he was ready to make the trip east.

"I think we had best start to-night," he said. "We want a day to grow accustomed to our clothes and new surroundings before we run up squarely against serious business."

"I will be ready," promised the Harvester.

He took Granny home, set his house in order, installed the man he was leaving in charge, touched a match to the heap in the fireplace, and donning the new travelling suit, he went to Doctor Carey's.

Mrs. Carey added a few touches, warned him to remember about the forks and spoons, and not to forget to shave often, and saw them off. At the station Carey said to him, "You know, David, we can change at Wayne and go through Buffalo, or we can take the Pittsburg and go and come through Philadelphia."

"I am contemplating a trip to Philadelphia," said the Harvester, "but I believe I will not be ready for, say a month yet. I have a theory and it dies hard. If it does not work out the coming month, I will go, perhaps, but not now. Let us see how many kinds of a fool I make of myself in New York before I attempt the Quakers."

Almost to the city, the doctor smiled at the Harvester.

"David, where did you get your infernal assurance?" he asked.

"In the woods," answered the Harvester placidly. "In doing clean work. With my fingers in the muck, and life literally teeming and boiling in sound and action, around, above, and beneath me, a right estimate of my place and province in life comes naturally in daily handling stores on which humanity depends, I go even deeper than you surgeons and physicians. You are powerless unless I reinforce your work with drugs on which you can rely. I do clean, honest work. I know its proper place and value to the world. That is why I called what I have to say, 'The Man in the Background.' There is no reason why I should shiver and shrink at meeting and explaining my work to my fellows. Every man has his vocation, and some of you in the limelight would cut a sorry figure if the man in the background should fail you at the critical moment. Don't worry about me, Doc. I am all serene. You won't find I possess either nerves or fear. 'Be sure you are right, and then go ahead,' is my law."

"Well I'll be confounded!" said the doctor.

In a large hall, peopled with thousands of medical men, the name of the Harvester was called the following day and his subject was announced. He arose in his place and began to talk.

"Take the platform," came in a roar from a hundred throats.

The Harvester hesitated.

"You must, David," whispered Carey.

The Harvester made his way forward and was guided through a side door, and a second later calmly walked down the big stage to the front, and stood at ease looking over his audience, as if to gauge its size and the pitch to which he should raise his voice. His lean frame loomed every inch of his six feet, his broad shoulders were square, his clean shaven face alert and afire. He wore a spring suit of light gray of good quality and cut, and he was perfect as to details.

"This scarcely seems compatible with my subject," he remarked casually. "I certainly appear very much in the foreground just at present, but perhaps that is quite as well. It may be time that I assert myself. I doubt if there is a man among you who has not handled my products more or less; you may enjoy learning where and how they are prepared, and understanding the manner in which my work merges with yours. I think perhaps the first thing is to paint you as good a word picture as I can of my geographical location."

Then the Harvester named latitude and longitude and degrees of temperature. He described the lake, the marsh, the wooded hill, the swale, and open sunny fields. He spoke of water, soil, shade, and geographical conditions. "Here I was born," he said, "on land owned by my father and grandfather before me, and previous to them, by the Indians. My male ancestors, so far as I can trace them, were men of the woods, hunters, trappers, herb gatherers. My mother was from the country, educated for a teacher. She had the most inexorable will power of any woman I ever have known. From my father I inherited my love for muck on my boots, resin in my nostrils, the long trail, the camp fire, forest sounds and silences in my soul. From my mother I learned to read good books, to study subjects that puzzled me, to tell the truth, to keep my soul and body clean, and to pursue with courage the thing to which I set my hand.

"There was not money enough to educate me as she would; together we learned to find it in the forest. In early days we sold ferns and wild flowers to city people, harvested the sap of the maples in spring, and the nut crop of the fall. Later, as we wanted more, we trapped for skins, and collected herbs for the drug stores. This opened to me a field I was peculiarly fitted to enter. I knew woodcraft instinctively, I had the location of every herb, root, bark, and seed that will endure my climate; I had the determination to stick to my job, the right books to assist me, and my mother's invincible will power to uphold me where I wavered.

"As I look into your faces, men, I am struck with the astounding thought that some woman bore the cold sweat and pain of labour to give life to each of you. I hope few of you prolonged that agony as I did. It was in the heart of my mother to make me physically clean, and to that end she sent me daily into the lake, so long as it was not ice covered, and put me at exercises intended to bring full strength to every sinew and fibre of my body. It was in her heart to make me morally clean, so she took me to nature and drilled me in its forces and its methods of reproducing life according to the law. Her work was good to a point that all men will recognize. From there on, for a few years, she held me, not because I was man enough to stand, but because she was woman enough to support me. Without her no doubt I would have broken the oath I took; with her I won the victory and reached years of manhood and self-control as she would have had me. The struggle wore her out at half a lifetime, but as a tribute to her memory I cannot face a body of men having your opportunities without telling you that what was possible to her and to me is possible to all mothers and men. If she is above and hears me perhaps it will recompense some of her shortened years if she knows I am pleading with you, as men having the greatest influence of any living, to tell and to teach the young that a clean life is possible to them. The next time any of you are called upon to address a body of men tell them to learn for themselves and to teach their sons, and to hold them at the critical hour, even by sweat and blood, to a clean life; for in this way only can feeble-minded homes, almshouses, and the scarlet woman be abolished. In this way only can men arise to full physical and mental force, and become the fathers of a race to whom the struggle for clean manhood will not be the battle it is with us.

"By the distorted faces, by the misshapen bodies, by marks of degeneracy, recognizable to your practised eyes everywhere on the streets, by the agony of the mother who bore you, and later wept over you, I conjure you men to live up to your high and holy privilege, and tell all men that they can be clean, if they will. This in memory of the mother who shortened her days to make me a moral man. And if any among you is the craven to plead immorality as a safeguard to health, I ask, what about the health of the women you sacrifice to shield your precious bodies, and I offer my own as the best possible refutation of that cowardly lie.

748

I never have been ill a moment in all my life, and strength never has failed me for work to which I set my hand.

"The rapidly decreasing supply of drugs and the adulterated importations early taught me that the day was coming when it would be an absolute necessity to raise our home supplies. So, while yet in my teens, I began collecting from the fields and woods for miles around such medicinal stuff as grew in my father's fields, marsh, and woods, and planting more wherever I found anything growing naturally in its prime. I merely enlarged nature's beds and preserved their natural condition. As the plants spread and the harvest increased, I built a dry-house on scientific principles, a large store-room, and later a laboratory in which I have been learning to prepare some of my crude material for the market, combining ideas of my own in remedies, and at last producing one your president just has indicated that I come to submit to you as a final resort in certain conditions.

"My operations now have spread to close six hundred acres of almost solid medicinal growth, including a little lake, around the shores of which flourish a quadruple setting of water-loving herbs."

Occasionally he shifted his position or easily walked across the platform and faced his audience from a different direction. His voice was strong, deep, and rang clearly and earnestly. His audience sat on the front edge of their chairs, and listened to something new, with mouths half agape. A few times Carey turned from the speaker to face the audience. He agonized in his heart that it was a closed session, and that his wife was not there to hear, and that the Girl was missing it.

By the bent backs and flying fingers of the reporters at their table in front he could see that to-morrow the world would read the Harvester's speech; and if it were true that the little mother had shortened her days to produce him, she had done earth a service for which many generations would call her blessed. For the doctor could look ahead, and he knew that this man would not escape. The call for him and his unimpeachable truth would come from everywhere, and his utterances would carry as far as newspapers and magazines were circulated. The good he would do would be past estimation.

The Harvester continued. He was describing the most delicate and difficult of herbs to secure. He was telling how they could be raised, prepared, kept, and compounded. He was discussing diseases that did not readily yield to treatment, pointing out what drugs were customarily employed and offering, if any of them had such cases, and would send to him, to forward samples of unadulterated stuff sufficient for a test comparison with what they were using. He was walking serenely and surely into the heart of every man before him.

Just at the point where it was the psychological time to close, he stopped and stood a long instant facing them, and then he asked softly, "Did any man among you ever see the woman to whom he had given a strong man's first passion of love, slowly dying before him?"

One breathless instant he waited and then continued, "Gentlemen, I recently saw this in my own case. For days it was coming, so at night I shut myself in my laboratory, and from the very essence of the purest of my self-compounded drugs I distilled a stimulant into which I put a touch of heart remedy, a brace for weakening nerves, a vitalization of sluggish blood. As I worked, I thought in that thought which embodied the essence of prayer, and when my day and my hour came, and a man who has been the president of your honourable body, and is known to all of you, said it was death, I took this combination that I now present to you, and with the help of the Almighty and a woman above the price of rubies, I kept breath in the girl I love, and to-day she is at full tide of womanhood. As a thank offering, the formula is yours. Test it as you will. Use it if you find it good. Gentlemen, I thank you!"

Carey sank in his chair and watched the Harvester cross the stage. As he disappeared the tumult began, and it lasted until the president arose and brought him back to make another bow, and then they rioted until they wore themselves out. In an immaculate dress suit the Harvester sat that night on the right of the gray-haired president and responded to the toast, "The Harvester of the Woods." Then the reporters carried him away to be photographed, and to show him the gay sights of New York.

In the train the next day, steadily speeding west, he said to Doctor Carey: "I feel as the old woman of Mother Goose who said, 'Lawk-a-mercy on us, can this be really I?'"

"You just bet it is!" cried the doctor. "And you have cut out work for yourself in good shape."

"What do you mean?"

"I mean that this is a beginning. You will be called upon to speak again and again."

"The point is, do you honestly think I helped any?"

"You did inestimable good. It only can help men to hear plain truth that is personal experience. As for that dope of yours, it will come closer raising the dead than anything I ever saw. Next case I see slipping, after I've done my best, I'm going to try it out for myself."

"All right! 'Phone me and I'll bring some fresh and help you."

At Buffalo the doctor left the car and bought a paper. As he had expected the portrait and speech of the Harvester were featured. The reporters had been gracious. They had done all that was just to a great event, and allowed themselves some latitude. He immediately mailed the paper to the Girl, and at Cleveland bought another for himself. When he showed it to the Harvester, as he glanced at it he observed, "Do I appear like that?" Then he went on talking with a man he had met who interested him.

Chapter 21

The Coming of the Bluebird

The Harvester stopped at the mail box on his way home and among the mass of matter it contained was something from the Girl. It was a scrap as long as his least finger and three times as wide, and by the postmark it had lain four days in the box. On opening it, he found only her card with a line written across it, but the man went up the hill and into the cabin as if a cyclone were driving him, for he read, "Has your bluebird come?"

He threw his travelling bag on the floor, ran to the telephone, and called the station. "Take this message," he said. "Mrs. David Langston, care of Alexander Herron, 5770 Chestnut Street, Philadelphia. Found note after four days' absence. Bluebird long past due. The fairies have told it that my fate hereafter lies in your hands.

"As always. David."

The Harvester turned from the instrument and bent to embrace Belshazzar, leaping in ecstasy beside him.

"Understand that, Bel?" he asked. "I don't know but it means something. Maybe it doesn't—not a thing! And again, there is a chance—only the merest possibility—that it does. We'll risk it, Bel, and to begin on I have nailed it as hard as I knew how. Next, we will clean the house—until it shines, and then we will fill the cupboard, and if anything does happen we won't be caught napping. Yes, boy, we will take the chance! We can't be any worse disappointed than we have been before and survived it. Come along!"

He picked up the bag and arranged its contents, carefully brushed and folded on his shelves and in his closet. Then he removed the travelling suit, donned the old brown clothes and went to the barn to see that his creatures had been cared for properly. Early the next morning he awoke and after feeding and breakfasting instead of going to harvest spice brush and alder he stretched a line and hung the bedding from room after room to air and sun. He swept, dusted, and washed windows, made beds, and lastly polished the floors throughout the cabin. He set everything in order, and as a finishing touch, filled vases, pitchers, and bowls with the bloom of red bud and silky willow catkins. He searched the south bank, but there was not a violet, even in the most exposed places. By night he was tired and a little of the keen edge of his ardour was dulled. The next day he worked scrubbing the porches, straightening the lawn and hedges, even sweeping the driveway to the bridge clear of wind-whirled leaves and straw. He scouted around the dry-house and laboratory, and spent several extra hours on the barn so that when evening came everything was in perfect order. Then he dressed, ate his supper and drove to the city.

He stopped at the mail box, but there was nothing from the Girl. The Harvester did not know whether he was sorry or glad. A letter might have said the same thing. Nothing meant a delightful possibility, and between the two he preferred the latter. He whistled and sang as he drove to Onabasha, and Belshazzar looked at him with mystified eyes, for this was not the master he had known of late. He did not recognize the dress or the manner, but his dog heart was sympathetic to the man's every mood, and he remembered times when a drive down the levee always had been like this, for to-night the Harvester's tongue was loosened and he talked in the old way.

"Just four words, Bel," he said. "And, as I remarked before, they may mean the most wonderful thing on earth, and possibly nothing at all. But it is in the heart of man to hope, Bel, and so we are going to live royally for a week or two, just on hope, old boy. If anything should happen, we are ready, rooms shining, beds fresh, fireplaces filled and waiting a match, ice chest cool, and when we get back it will be stored. Also a secret, Bel; we are going to a florist and a fruit store. While we are at it, we will do the thing right; but we will stay away from Doc, until we are sure of something. He means well, but we don't like to be pitied, do we, Bel? Our friends don't manage their eyes and voices very well these days. Never mind! Our time will come yet. The bluebird will not fail us, but never before has it been so late."

On his return he filled the pantry shelves with packages, stored the ice chest, and set a basket of delicious fruit on the dining table. Two boxes remained. He opened the larger one and took from it an arm load of white lilies that he carried up the hill and divided between the mounds under the oak. Then he uncovered his head, and standing at the foot of them he looked among the boughs of the big tree and listened intently. After a time a soft, warm wind, catkin-scented, crept from the lake, and began a murmur among the clusters of brown leaves clinging to the branches.

"Mother," said the Harvester, "were you with me? Did I do it right? Did I tell them what you would have had me say for the boys? Are you glad now you held me to the narrow way? Do you want me to go before men if I am asked, as Doc says I will be, and tell them that the only way to abolish pain is for them to begin at the foundation by living clean lives? I don't know if I did any good, but they listened to me. Anyway, I did the best I knew. But that isn't strange; you ground it into me to do that every day, until it is almost an instinct. Mother, dear, can you tell me about the bluebird? Is that softest little rustle of all your voice? And does it say 'hope'? I think so, and I thank you for the word."

The man's eyes dropped to earth.

"And you other mother," he said, "have you any message for me? Up where you are can you sweep the world with understanding eyes and tell me why my bluebird does not come? Does it know that this year your child and not chance must settle my fate? Can you look across space and see if she is even thinking of me? But I know that! She had to be thinking of me when she wrote that line. Rather can you tell me—will she come? Do you think I am man enough to be trusted with her future, if she does? One thing I promise you: if such joy ever comes to me, I will know how to meet it gently, thankfully, tenderly, please God. Good night, little women. I hope you are sleeping well—"

He turned and went down the hill, entered the cabin and took from the other box a mass of Parma violets. He put these in the pink bowl and placed it on the table beside the Girl's bed. He stood for a time, and then began pulling single flowers from the bowl and dropping them over the pillow and snowy spread.

"God, how I love her!" he whispered softly.

At last he went out and closed the door. He was tired and soon fell asleep with the night breeze stirring his hair, and the glamour of moonlight flooding the lake touched his face. Clearly it etched the strong, manly features, the fine brow and chin, and painted in unusual tenderness the soft lines around the mouth. The little owl wavered its love story, a few frogs were piping, and the Harvester lay breathing the perfumed spring air deeply and evenly. Near midnight Belshazzar awakened him by arising from the bedside and walking to the door.

"What is it, Bel?" inquired the Harvester.

The dog whined softly. The man turned his head toward the lake. A ray of red light touched the opposite embankment and came wavering across the surface. The Harvester sat up. Two big, flaming eyes were creeping up the levee.

"That," said the Harvester, "might be Doc coming for me to help him try out my bottled sunshine, or it might be my bluebird."

He tossed back the cover, swung his feet to the floor, setting each in a slipper beside the bed, and arose, dressing as he started for the door. As he opened the screen and stepped on the veranda a passenger car from the city stopped, and the Harvester went down the walk to meet it. His heart turned over when he saw a woman's hand on the door.

"Permit me," he said, taking the handle and bringing it back with a sweep. A tall form arose, bent forward, and descended to the step. The full flare of moonlight fell on the glowing face of the Girl.

"Harvester, is it you?" she asked.

"Yes," gasped the man.

Two hands came fluttering out, and he just had presence of mind to step in range so that they rested on his shoulders.

"Has the bluebird come?"

"Not yet!"

"Then I am not too late?"

"Never too late to come to me, Ruth."

"I am welcome?"

"I have no words to tell you how welcome."

She swayed forward and the Harvester tried to reach her lips, but they brushed his cheek and touched his ear.

"I have brought one more kiss I want to try," she whispered.

The Harvester crushed her in his arms until he frightened himself for fear he had hurt her, and murmured an ecstasy of indistinct love words to her. Presently her feet touched the ground and she drew away from him.

"Harvester," she whispered, "I couldn't wait any longer; indeed I could not: and I couldn't leave grandfather and grandmother, and I didn't know what in the world to do, so I just brought them along. Are they welcome?"

"Aside from you, I would rather have them than any people on earth," said the Harvester.

There were two sounds in the car; one was an approving murmur, and the other an undeniable snort. The Harvester felt the reassuring pressure of the Girl's hand.

"Please, Ruth," he said, "go turn on the light so that I can see to help grandmother."

A foot stamped before the front seat. "Madam Herron, if you please!" cried an acrid voice.

"'Madam Herron,'" said the Harvester gently, as he set a foot on the step, reached in and bodily picked up a little old lady and started up the walk with her in his arms.

"Careful there, sir!" roared a voice after him.

The Harvester could feel the quake of the laughing woman and he smiled broadly as he entered the cabin, and placed her in a large chair before the fire. Then he wheeled and ran back to the car, reaching it as the man was making an effort to descend. It could be seen that he had been tall, before time and sorrow had bent him, and keen eyes gleamed below shaggy white brows from under his hat brim. He had a white moustache, and his hair was snowy.

"Allow me," said the Harvester reaching a hand.

"If you touch me I will cane you," said Mr. Alexander Herron.

There was nothing to do but step back. The cane, wheel, and a long coat skirt interfering, the old man fell headlong, and only quick hands saved him a severe jolt and bruises. He stood glaring in the moonlight while his hat was restored.

"If you run your car to the curve you can back toward the south and turn easily," said the Harvester to the driver. As the automobile passed them he offered his arm. "May I show you to the fire? These spring nights are chilly."

"'Chilly!' Demnition cold is what they are! I'm frozen to the bone! This will be the end of us both! Dragging people of our age around at this hour of night. Of all the accursed stubbornness!"

"There are three low steps," said the Harvester, "now a straight stretch of walk, now two steps; there you are on the level. Here is an easy chair. It would be better to leave on your coat, until I light the fire."

He knelt and scratched a match, and almost instantly a flame sprang from the heap of dry kindling, and began to wrap around the big logs.

"How pretty!" exclaimed a soft voice.

"Kind of a hunting lodge in the wilds, is it?" growled a rough one. "Marcella, you will take your death here!"

"I'm sure I feel no exposure. Really, Alexander, if I had passed away every time you have prophesied that I would in the past twenty years you'd have the largest private cemetery in existence. If you would not be so pessimistic I could quite enjoy the trip. It's so long since I've ridden in the cars."

"Of all the abandoned places! And for you to be here, after your years in bed!"

"But I'm not nearly so tired as I am at home, Alexander, truly."

"Let me help you, grandfather," offered the Girl.

She went to him and took his hat and stick.

"Leave me my cane," he cried. "Any instant that beast may attack some of us."

The Girl laughed merrily.

"Why grandfather!" she chided, "Bel is the finest dog you ever knew, he is my best friend here. By the hour he has protected me, and he is gentle as a kitten. He's crazy over my coming home."

She knelt on the floor, put her arms around the dog's neck, and the delighted brute quivered with the joy of her caress and the sound of her loved voice.

"Ruthie!" cautioned the gentle lady.

"Put that cur out of doors, where animals belong," roared the old man, lifting his stick.

"Careful!" warned the grave voice of the Harvester.

"I thought you said he was gentle as a kitten!"

"Grandfather, I said that," cried the Girl.

"Well wasn't it the truth?"

"You can see how he loves me. Didn't I ever tell you that Bel made the first friendly overture I ever received in this part of the country? He's watched me by the day, even while I slept."

"Then what's all this infernal fuss about?"

"Try striking him if you want to find out," explained the Harvester gently. "You see, Belshazzar and I are accustomed to living here alone and very quietly. He is excited over the Girl's return, because she is his friend, and he has not forgotten her. Then this is the first time in his life he ever heard an irritable voice from a visitor or saw a cane, and it angers him. He is perfectly safe to guard a baby, if he is gently treated, but he is a sure throat hold to a stranger who bespeaks him roughly or attempts to strike. He would be of no use as a guard to valuable property while I sleep if he were otherwise. Bel, come here! Lie still."

The dog sank to the floor beside the Harvester, but his sharp eyes followed the Girl, and the hair arose on his neck at every rasping note of the old man's voice.

"I wouldn't give such a creature house room for a minute," insisted the guest.

"Wait until you see him work and become acquainted with him, and you will change that verdict," prophesied the Harvester.

"I never was known to change an opinion. Never, sir! Never!" cried the testy voice.

"How unfortunate!" remarked the Harvester suavely.

"Explain yourself! Explain yourself, sir!"

"There never has been, there never will be, a man on this earth," said the Harvester, "wholly free from mistakes. Are you warm now?" He turned to the little lady, cutting off a reply with his question.

"Nice and warm and quite sleepy," she said.

"What may I bring you for a light lunch before you go to bed?"

"Oh, could I have a bite of something?"

"If only I am fortunate enough to have anything you will care for. What about a bowl of hot milk and a slice of toast?"

"Why I think that would be just the thing!"

"Excuse me," said the Harvester rising.

He went to the kitchen and they could hear him moving around.

"I wish the big brute would take his beast along," growled Mr. Alexander Herron.

"Come, Bel," ordered the Girl. "Let's go to the kitchen."

The dog instantly arose and followed her.

"What can I do to help?" she asked as they reached the door.

"Remain where you won't dazzle my eyes," said the Harvester, "until I help the gentle lady and the gentle man to bed."

Presently he came with a white cloth, two spoons, and a plate of bread. He spread the cloth on the table, laid the spoons on it, and opening the little cupboard, took out a long toasting fork, and sticking it into a slice of bread, he held it over the coals. When it grew golden brown he lifted the table beside the chair, and brought a bowl of scalded milk.

"Marcella, that stuff will be too smoky for you! Your stomach will rebel at it."

"Grandfather, there will not be a suspicion of odour," said the Girl. "I have had it that way often."

"Then no wonder you came from this place looking like a picked crane, if that is a sample of what you were fed on!"

The face of the Harvester grew redder than the heat of the fire necessitated, but at the ringing laugh of the Girl he set his teeth and went on toasting bread. Grandmother crumbled some in the milk and picking up the spoon tested the combination. She was very hungry, and it was good. She began eating with relish.

"Alexander, you will be the loser if you don't have some of this," she said. "It's just delicious!"

"Maybe smoked spoon victuals are proper for invalid women," he retorted, "but they are mighty thin diet for a hardy man."

"What about a couple of eggs and some beef extract?" suggested the cook.

"Sounds more sensible by a long shot."

"Ruth, you make this toast," said the Harvester and disappeared.

Presently he placed before his guest a couple of eggs poached in milk, a steaming bowl of beef juice, and a plate of toast. For one instant the Harvester thought this was going into the fire, the next a slice was picked up and smelled testily. The Girl sat on her grandfather's chair arm, and breaking a morsel of toast dipped it into the broth and tasted it.

"Oh but that is good!" she cried. "Why haven't I some also? Am I supposed to have no 'tummy'?"

"Your turn next," said the Harvester, as he again gave her the fork and went to the kitchen.

When he returned and served the Girl he found her grandfather eating heartily.

"Why I think this is fun," said the gentle lady. "I haven't had such a fine time in ages. I love the heat of the flame on my body and things taste so good. I could go to sleep without any narcotic, right now."

Close her knee the Harvester knelt on the hearth with his toasting fork. She leaned forward and ran her fingers through his hair.

"You're a braw laddie," she said. "Now I see why Ruthie *would* come."

The Harvester took the frail hand and kissed it. "Thank you!" he returned.

"Mush!" exploded the grizzled man in the rear.

When no one wanted more food the Harvester stacked and carried away the dishes, swept the hearth, and replaced the toaster.

"Ruth and I often lunched this way last fall," he said. "We liked it for a change."

"Alexander, have you noticed?" asked the little woman as she lifted wet eyes to a beautiful portrait of her daughter beside the chimney.

"D'ye think I'm blind? Saw it as I entered the door. Poor taste! Very! Brown may match the rug and wood-work, but it's a wretched colour for a young girl in her gay time. Should be pink and white with a gold frame."

"That would be beautiful," agreed the Harvester. "We must have one that way. This is not an expensive picture. It is only an enlargement from an old photograph."

"We have a number of very handsome likenesses. Which one can you spare Ruth, Marcella?"

"The one she likes best," said the lady promptly.

"And the other is your mother, no doubt. What a girlish, beautiful face!"

"Wonderfully fine!" growled a gruff old voice tinctured with tears, and the Harvester began to see light.

The old man arose. "Ruthie, help your grandmother to bed," he said. "And you, sir, have the goodness to walk a few steps with me."

The Harvester sprang up and brought Mr. Herron his coat and hat and held the door. The Girl brushed past him.

"To the oak," she whispered.

They went into the night, and without a word the Harvester took his guest's arm and guided him up the hill. When they reached the two mounds the moon shining between the branches touched the lily faces with with holy whiteness.

"She sleeps there," said the Harvester, indicating the place.

Then he turned and went down the path a little distance and waited until he feared the night air would chill the broken old man.

"You can see better to-morrow," he said as he touched the shaking figure and assisted it to arise.

"Your work?" Mr. Alexander Herron touched the lilies with his walking stick.

The Harvester assented.

"Do you mind if I carry one to Marcella?"

The Harvester trembled as he stooped to select the largest and whitest, and with sudden illumination, he fully understood. He helped the tottering old man to the cabin, where he sat silently before the fireplace softly touching the lily face with his lips.

"I have put grandmother in my bed, tucked her in warmly, and she says it is soft and fine," laughed the Girl, coming to them. "Now you go before she falls asleep, and I hope you will rest well."

She bent and kissed him.

The Harvester held the door.

"Can I be of any service?" he inquired.

"No, I'm no helpless child."

"Then to my best wishes for sound sleep the remainder of the night, I will add this," said the Harvester—"You may rest in peace concerning your dear girl. I sympathize with your anxiety. Good night!"

Alexander Herron threw out his hands in protest.

"I wouldn't mind admitting that you are a gentleman in a month or two," he said, "but it's a demnation humiliation to have it literally wrung from me to-night!"

He banged the door in the face of the amazed Harvester, who turned to the Girl as she leaned against the mantel. He stood absorbing the glowing picture of beauty and health that she made. She had removed her travelling dress and shoes, and was draped in a fleecy white wool kimono and wearing night slippers. Her hair hung in two big braids as it had during her illness. She was his sick girl again in costume, but radiant health glowed on her lovely face. The Harvester touched a match to a few candles and turned out the acetylene lights. Then he stood before her.

"Now, bluebird," he said gently. "Ruth, you always know where to find me, if you will look at your feet. I thought I loved you all in my power when you went, but absence has taught its lessons. One is that I can grow to love you more every day I live, and the other that I probably trifled with the highest gift you had to offer, when I sent you away. I may have been right; Granny and Doc think I was wrong. You know the answer. You said there was another kiss for me. Ruth, is it the same or a different one?"

"It is different. Quite, quite different!"

"And when?" The Harvester stretched out longing arms. The Girl stepped back.

"I don't know," she said. "I had it when I started, but I lost it on the way."

The Harvester staggered under the disappointment.

"Ruth, this has gone far enough that you wouldn't play with me, merely for the sake of seeing me suffer, would you?"

"No!" cried the Girl. "No! I mean it! I knew just what I wanted to say when I started; but we had to take grandmother out of bed. She wouldn't allow me to leave her, and I wouldn't stay away from you any longer. She fainted when we put her on the car and grandfather went wild. He almost killed the porters, and he raved at me. He said my mother had ruined their lives, and now I would be their death. I got so frightened I had a nervous chill and I'm so afraid she will grow worse—"

"You poor child!" shuddered the Harvester. "I see! I understand! What you need is quiet and a good rest."

He placed her in a big easy chair and sitting on the hearth rug he leaned against her knee and said, "Now tell me, unless you are so tired that you should go to bed."

"I couldn't possibly sleep until I have told you," said the Girl.

"If you're merciful, cut it short!" implored the Harvester.

"I think it begins," she said slowly, "when I went because you sent me and I didn't want to go. Of course, as soon as I saw grandfather and grandmother, heard them talk, and understood what their lives had been, and what might have been, why there was only one thing to do, as I could see it, and that was to compensate their agony the best I could. I think I have, David. I really think I have made them almost happy. But I told them all any one could tell about you in the start, and from the first grandmother would have been on your side; but you see how grandfather is, and he was absolutely determined that I should live with them, in their home, all their lives. He thought the best way to accomplish that would be to separate me from you and marry me to the son of his partner.

"There are rooms packed with the lovely things they bought me, David, and everything was as I wrote you. Some of the people who came were wonderful, so gracious and beautiful, I loved almost all of them. They took me places where there were pictures, plays, and lovely parties, and I studied hard to learn some music, to dance, ride and all the things they wanted me to do, and to read good books, and to learn to meet people with graciousness to equal theirs, and all of it. Every day I grew stronger and met more people, and there were different places to go, and always, when anything was to be done, up popped Mr. Herbert Kennedy and said and did exactly the right thing, and he could be extremely nice, David."

"I haven't a doubt!" said the Harvester, laying hold of her kimono.

"And he popped up so much that at last I saw he was either pretending or else he really was growing very fond of me, so one day when we were alone I told him all about you, to make him see that he must not. He laughed at me, and said exactly what you did, that I didn't love you at all, that it was gratitude, that it was the affection of a child. He talked for hours about how grandfather and grand-mother had suffered, how it was my duty to live with them and give you up, even if I cared greatly for you; but he said what I felt was not love at all. Then he tried to tell me what he thought love was, and I could see very clearly that if it was like that, I didn't love you, but I came a whole world closer it than loving him, and I told him so. He laughed again and said I was mistaken, and that he was going to teach me what real love was, and then I could not be driven back to you. After that, everybody and everything just pushed me toward him with both hands, except one person. She was a young married woman and I met her at the very first. She was the only real friend I ever had, and at last, the latter part of February, when things were the very worst, I told her. I told her every single thing. She was on your side. She said you were twice the man Herbert Kennedy was, and as soon as I found I could talk to her about you, I began going there and staying as long as I could, just to talk and to play with her baby.

"Her husband was a splendid young fellow, and I grew very fond of him. I knew she had told him, because he suddenly began talking to me in the kind-est way, and everything he said seemed to be what I most wanted to hear. I got along fairly well until hints of spring began to come, and then I would wonder about my hedge, and my gold garden, and if the ice was off the lake, and about my boat and horse, and I wanted my room, and oh, David, most of all I wanted you! Just you! Not because you could give me anything to compare in richness with what they could, not because this home was the best I'd ever known except theirs, not for any reason at all only just that I wanted to see your face, hear your voice, and have you pick me up and take me in your arms when I was tired. That was when I almost quit writing. I couldn't say what I wanted to, and I wouldn't write trivial things, so I went on day after day just groping."

"And you killed me alive," said the Harvester.

"I was afraid of that, but I couldn't write. I just couldn't! It was ten days ago that I thought of the bluebird's coming this year and what it would mean to you, and *that* killed me, Man! It just hurt my heart until it ached, to know that you were out here alone; and that night I couldn't sleep, because I was thinking of you, and it came to me that if I had your lips then I could give you a much, much better kiss than the last, and when it was light I wrote that line.

"Nearly a week later I got your answer early in the morning, and it almost drove me wild. I took it and went for the day with May, and I told her. She took me upstairs, and we talked it over, and before I left she made me promise that I would write you and explain how I felt, and ask you what you thought. She wanted you to come there and see if you couldn't make them at least respect you. I know I was crying, and she was bathing the baby. She went to bring something she had forgotten, and she gave him to me to hold, just his little naked body. He stood on my lap and mauled my face, and pulled my hair, and hugged me with his stout little arms and kissed me big, soft, wet kisses, and something sprang to life in my heart that never before had been there. I just cried all over him and held him fast, and I couldn't give him up when she came back. I saw why I'd wanted a big doll all my life, right then; and oh, dear! the doll you sent was beautiful, but, David, did you ever hold a little, living child in your arms like that?"

"I never did," said the Harvester huskily.

He looked at her face and saw the tears rolling, but he could say no more, so he leaned his head against her knee, and finding one of her hands he drew it to his lips.

"It is wonderful," said the Girl softly. "It awakens something in your heart that makes it all soft and tender, and you feel an awful responsibility, too. Grandmother had them telephone at last, and May helped me bathe my face and fix my hat. When we went to the carriage Mr. Kennedy was there to take me home. We went past grandmother's florist to get her some violets—David, she is sleeping under yours, with just a few touching her lips. Oh it was lovely of you to get them; your fairies must have told you! She has them every day, and one of the objections she made to coming here was that she couldn't do without them in winter, and she found some on her pillow the very first thing. David, you are wonderful! And grandfather with his lily! I know where he found that! I knew instantly. Ah, there are fairies who tell you, because you deserve to know."

The Girl bent and slipping her arm around his neck hugged him tight an instant, and then she continued unsteadily: "While he was in the shop—Harvester, this is like your wildest dream, but it's truest truth—a boy came down the walk crying papers, and as I live, he called your name. I knew it had to be you because he said, 'First drug farm in America! Wonderful medicine contributed to the cause of science! David Langston honoured by National Medical Association!' I just stood in the carriage and screamed, 'Boy! Boy!' until the coachman thought I had lost my senses. He whistled and got me the paper. I was shaking so I asked him how to find anything you wanted quickly, and he pointed the column where events are listed; and when I found the third page there was your face so splendidly reproduced, and you seemed so fine and noble to me I forgot about the dress suit and the badge in your buttonhole, or to wonder when or how or why it could have happened. I just sat there shouting in my soul, 'David! David! Medicine Man! Harvester Man!' again and again."

"I don't know what I said to Mr. Kennedy or how I got to my room. I scanned it by the column, at last I got to paragraphs, and finally I read all the sentences. David, I kissed that newspaper face a hundred times, and if you could have had those, Man, I think you would have said they were right. David, there is nothing to cry over!"

"I'm not!" said the Harvester, wiping the splashes from her hand. "But, Ruth, forget what I said about being brief. I didn't realize what was coming. I should have said, if you've any mercy at all, go slowly! This is the greatest thing that ever happened or ever will happen to me. See that you don't leave out one word of it."

"I told you I had to tell you first," said the Girl.

"I understand now," said the Harvester, his head against her knee while he pressed her hand to his lips. "I see! Your coming couldn't be perfect without knowing this first. Go on, dear heart, and slowly! You owe me every word."

"When I had it all absorbed, I carried the paper to the library and said, 'Grandfather, such a wonderful thing has happened. A man has had a new idea, and he has done a unique work that the whole world is going to recognize. He has stood before men and made a speech that few, oh so few, could make honestly, and he has advocated right living, oh so nobly, and he has given a wonderful gift to science without price, because through it he first saved the life he loved best. Isn't that marvellous, grandfather?' And he said, 'Very marvellous, Ruth. Won't you sit down and read to me about it?' And I said, 'I can't, dear grandfather, because I have been away from grandmother all day, and she is fretting for me, and to-night is a great ball, and she has spent millions on my dress, I think, and there is an especial reason why I must go, and so I have to see her now; but I want to show you the man's face, and then you can read the story.'

"You see, I knew if I started to read it he would stop me; but if I left him alone with it he would be so curious he would finish. So I turned your name under and held the paper and said, 'What do you think of that face, grandfather? Study it carefully,' and, Man, only guess what he said! He said, 'I think it is the face of one of nature's noblemen.' I just kissed him time and again and then I said, 'So it is grandfather, so it is; for it is the face of the man who twice saved my life, and lifted my mother from almost a pauper grave and laid her to rest in state, and the man who found you, and sent me to you when I was determined not to come.' And I just stood and kissed that paper before him and cried, again and again, 'He is one of nature's noblemen, and he is my husband, my dear, dear husband and to-morrow I am going home to him.' Then I laid the paper on his lap and ran away. I went to grandmother and did everything she wanted, then I dressed for the ball. I went to say good-bye to her and show my dress and grandfather was there, and he followed me out and said, 'Ruth, you didn't mean it?' I said, 'Did you read the paper, grandfather?' and he said 'Yes'; and I said, 'Then I should think you would know I mean it, and glory in my wonderful luck. Think of a man like that, grandfather!'

"I went to the ball, and I danced and had a lovely time with every one, because I knew it was going to be the very last, and to-morrow I must start to you.

"On the way home I told Mr. Kennedy what paper to get and to read it. I said good-bye to him, and I really think he cared, but I was too happy to be very sorry. When I reached my room there was a packet for me and, Man, like David of old, you are a wonderful poet! Oh Harvester! why didn't you send them to me instead of the cold, hard things you wrote?"

"What do you mean, Ruth?"

"Those letters! Those wonderful outpourings of love and passion and poetry and song and broken-heartedness. Oh Man, how could you write such things and throw them in the fire? Granny Moreland found them when she came to bring you a pie, and she carried them to Doctor Carey, and he sent them to me, and, David, they finished me. Everything came in a heap. I would have come without them, but never, never with quite the understanding, for as I read them the deeps opened up, and the flood broke, and there did a warm tide go through all my being, like you said it would; and now, David, I know what you mean by love. I called the maids and they packed my trunk and grandmother's, and I had grandfather's valet pack his, and go and secure berths and tickets, and learn about trains, and I got everything ready, even to the ambulance and doctor; but I waited until morning to tell them. I knew they would not let me come alone, so I brought them along. David, what in the world are we going to do with them?"

The Harvester drew a deep breath and looked at the flushed face of the Girl.

"With no time to mature a plan, I would say that we are going to love them, care for them, gradually teach them our work, and interest them in our plans here;

and so soon as they become reconciled we will build them such a house as they want on the hill facing us, just across Singing Water, and there they may have every luxury they can provide for themselves, or we can offer, and the pleasure of your presence, and both of them can grow strong and happy. I'll have grandmother on her feet in ten days, and the edge off grandfather's tongue in three. That bluster of his is to drown tears, Ruth; I saw it to-night. And when they pass over we will carry them up and lay them beside her under the oak, and we can take the house we build for them, if you like it better, and use this for a store-room."

"Never!" said the Girl. "Never! My sunshine room and gold garden so long as I live. Never again will I leave them. If this cabin grows too small, we will build all over the hillside; but my room and garden and this and the dining-room and your den there must remain as they are now."

The Harvester arose and drew the davenport before the fireplace, and heaped pillows. "You are so tired you are trembling, and your voice is quivering," he said. He lifted the Girl, laid her down and arranged the coverlet.

"Go to sleep!" he ordered gently. "You have made me so wildly happy that I could run and shout like a madman. Try to rest, and maybe the fairies who aid me will put my kiss back on your lips. I am going to the hill top to tell mother and my God."

He knelt and gathered her in his arms a second, then called Belshazzar to guard, and went into the sweet spring night, to jubilate with that wild surge of passion that sweeps the heart of a strong man when he is most nearly primal. He climbed the hill at a rush, and standing beneath the oak on the summit, he faced the lake, and stretching his arms widely, he waved them, merely to satisfy the demand for action. When urgency for expression came upon him, he laughed a deep rumble of exultation.

The night wind swept the lake and lifted his hair, the odour of spring was intoxicating in his nostrils, small creatures of earth stirred around him, here and there a bird, restless in the delirium of mating fever, lifted its head and piped a few notes on the moon-whitened air. The frogs sang uninterruptedly at the water's edge. The Harvester stood rejoicing. Beating on his brain came a rush of love words uttered in the Girl's dear voice. "I wanted you! Just you! He is my husband! My dear, dear husband! To-morrow I am going home! Now, David, I know what you mean by love!" The Harvester laughed again and sounds around him ceased for a second, then swelled in fuller volume than before. He added his voice. "Thank God! Oh, thank God!" he cried. "And may the Author of the Universe, the spirits of the little mothers who loved us, and all the good fairies who guide us, unite to bring unbounded joy to my Dream Girl and to guard her safely."

The cocks of Medicine Woods began their second salute to dawn. At this sound and with the mention of her name, the Harvester turned down the hill, and striding forcefully approached the cabin. As he passed the Girl's room he stepped softly, smiling as he wondered if its unexpected occupants were resting. He followed Singing Water, and stood looking at the hillside, studying the exact location most suitable for a home for the old people he was so delighted to welcome. That they would remain he never doubted. His faith in the call of the wild had been verified in the Girl; it would reach them also. The hill top would bind them. Their love for the Girl would compel them. They would be company for her and a new interest in life.

"Couldn't be better, not possibly!" commented the delighted Harvester.

He followed the path down Singing Water until he reached the bridge where it turned into the marsh. There he paused, looking straight ahead.

"Wonder if I would frighten her?" he mused. "I believe I'll risk it."

He walked on rapidly, vaulted the fence enclosing his land, crossed the road, and unlatched the gate. As he did so, the door opened, and Granny Moreland stood on the sill, waiting with keen eyes.

"Well I don't need neither specs nor noonday sun to see that you're steppin' like the blue ribbon colt at the County Fair, and lookin' like you owned Kingdom Come," she said. "What's up, David?"

"You are right, dear," said the Harvester. "I have entered my kingdom. The Girl has come and crowned me with her love. She had decided to return, but the letters you sent made her happier about it. I wanted you to know."

Granny leaned against the casing, and began to sob unrestrainedly.

The Harvester supported her tenderly.

"Why don't do that, dear. Don't cry," he begged. "The Girl is home for always, Granny, and I'm so happy I am out to-night trying to keep from losing my mind with joy. She will come to you to-morrow, I know."

Granny tremulously dried her eyes.

"What an old sap-head I am!" she commented. "I stole your letters from your fireplace, pitched a willer plate into the lake—you got to fish that out, come day, David—fooled you into that trip to Doc Carey to get him to mail them to Ruth, and never turned a hair. But after I got home I commenced thinkin' 'twas a pretty ticklish job to stick your nose into other people's business, an' every hour it got worse, until I ain't had a fairly decent sleep since. If you hadn't come soon, boy, I'd 'a' been sick a-bed. Oh, David! Are you sure she's over there, and loves you to suit you now?"

"Yes dear, I am absolutely certain," said the Harvester. "She was so determined to come that she brought the invalid grandmother she couldn't leave and her grandfather. They arrived at midnight. We are all going to live together now."

"Well bless my stars! Fetched you a family! David, I do hope to all that's peaceful I hain't put my foot in it. The moon is the deceivingest thing on earth I know, but does her family 'pear to be an a-gre'-able family, by its light?"

The Harvester's laugh boomed a half mile down the road.

"Finest people on earth, next to you, dear. I'm mighty glad to have them. I'm going to build them a house on my best location, and we are all going to be happy from now on. Go to bed! This night air may chill you. I can't sleep. I wanted you to know first—so I came over. In mother's stead, will you kiss me, and wish me happiness, dear friend?"

Granny Moreland laid an eager, withered hand on each shoulder, and bent to the radiant young face.

"God bless you, lad, and grant you as great happiness as life ort to fetch every clean, honest man," she prayed fervently, with closed eyes and her lined old face turned skyward. "And, O God, bless Ruth, and help her as You never helped mortal woman before to know her own mind without 'variableness, neither shadow of turnin'.'"

The Harvester was on Singing Water bridge before he gave way. There he laughed as never before in his life. Finally he controlled himself and started toward the cabin; but he was chuckling as he passed the driveway, and walked down the broad cement floor leading to his bathing pool, where the moonlight bridged the lake, and fell as a benediction all around him.

He stood a long time, when he recognized the familiar crash of a breaking backlog falling together, and heard the customary leap of the frightened dog. He walked to his door and listened intently, but there was no sound; so he decided the Girl had not been awakened. In the midst of a whitening sheet of gold the Harvester dropped to his stoop and leaned his head against the broad casing. He broke a twig from a hawthorn bush beside him, and sat twisting it in his fingers as he stared down the line of the gold bridge. Never had it seemed so material, so like a path that might be trodden by mortal feet and lead them straight to Heaven. As on the hill top, night again surrounded him and the Harvester's soul drank deep wild draughts of a new joy. Sleep was out of the question. He was too intensely alive to know that he ever again could be weary. He sat there in the moonlight, and with unbridled heart gloried in the joy that had come to him.

He turned his face from the bridge as he heard the click of Belshazzar's nails on the floor of the bathing pool. Then his heart and breath stopped an instant. Beside the dog walked the Girl, one hand on his head the other holding the flowing white robe around her and grasping one of the Harvester's lilies. His first thought was sheer amazement that she was not afraid, for it was evident now that the backlog had awakened her, and she had taken the dog and gone to her mother.

Then she had followed the path leading down the hill, around the cabin, and into the sheet of moonlight gilding the shore. She stood there gazing over the lake, oblivious to all things save the entrancing allurement of a perfect spring night beside undulant water. Screened from her with bushes and trees the Harvester scarcely breathed lest he startle her. Then his head swam, and his still heart leaped wildly. She was coming toward him. On her left lay the path to the hill top. A few steps farther she could turn to the right and follow the driveway to the front of the cabin. He leaned forward watching in an agony of suspense. Her beautiful face was transfigured with joy, aflame with love, radiant with smiles, and her tall figure fleecy white, rimmed in gold. Up the shining path of light she steadily advanced toward his door. Then the Harvester understood, and from his exultant heart burst the wordless petition:

"LORD GOD ALMIGHTY, HELP ME TO BE A MAN!"

With outstretched arms he arose to meet her.

"My Dream Girl!" he cried hoarsely. "My Dream Girl!"

"Coming, Harvester!" she answered in tones of joy, as she dropped the white flower and lifted her hands to draw his face toward her.

"Is that the kiss you wanted?" she questioned.

"Yes, Ruth," breathed the Harvester.

"Then I am ready to be your wife," she said. "May I share all the remainder of life's joys and sorrows with you?"

The Harvester gathered her in his arms and carried her to the bench on the lake shore. He wrapped the white robe around her and clasped her tenderly as behooved a lover, yet with arms that she knew could have crushed her had they willed. The minutes slipped away, and still he held her to his heart, the reality far surpassing his dream; for he knew that he was awake, and he realized this as the supreme hour that comes to the strongman who knows his love requited.

When the first banner of red light arose above Medicine Woods and Singing Water the cocks on the hillside announced the dawn. As the gold faded to gray, a burst of bubbling notes swelled from a branch almost over their heads where stood a bark-enclosed little house.

"Ruth, do you hear that?" asked the Harvester softly.

"Yes," she answered, "and I see it. A wonderful bird, with Heaven's deepest blue on its back and a breast like a russet autumn leaf, came straight up the lake from the south, and before it touched the limb that song seemed to gush from its throat."

"And for that reason, the greatest nature lover who ever lived says that it 'deserves preeminence.' It always settles from its long voyage through the air in an ecstasy of melody. Do you know what it is, Ruth?"

The Girl laid a hand on his cheek and turned his eyes from the bird to her face as she answered, "Yes, Harvester-man, I know. It is your first bluebird—but it is far too late, and Belshazzar has lost high office. I have usurped both their positions. You remain in the woods and reap their harvest, you enter the laboratory and make wonderful, life-giving medicines, you face the world and tell men of the high and holy life they may live if they will, and then—always and forever, you come back to Medicine Woods and to me, Harvester."